SKIN
IN
DARKNESS

SKIN
IN
DARKNESS

Maxim Jakubowski

ibooks

DISTRIBUTED BY PUBLISHERS GROUP WEST

A Publication of ibooks, inc.

Distributed by Publishers Group West
1700 Fourth Street, Berkeley, CA 94710
www.pgw.com

ibooks, inc.
24 West 25th Street
New York, NY 10010

ISBN: 1-59687-359-0
First ibooks, inc. printing December 2005
10 9 8 7 6 5 4 3 2 1

Cover design: M. Postawa

Printed in the U.S.A.

Contents

Introduction

I had, for some years, been toiling in the galleys of erotic writing, fantasising, obsessing, transmuting memories of real people, fictional characters and mirror images of myself into a maelstrom of sexual acts, tenderness, sweet depravities and warped emotions. It was my secret life. In my more mundane day-to-day existence, I was better known as Mr Crime, an editor and publisher of crime and mystery fiction, owner of a notorious book shop, reviewer and film festival consultant when it came to matters hardboiled and roaming the streets of noir.

After completing a whole cycle of short stories and collected them in a book, I thought I had reached a dead end in my quest to exorcise the past, and my thoughts naturally turned to what the next book project would be.

I had vague notions of a tortuous love story set in Paris in the late 1940s and early 1950s, a period in time seldom written about in English, the years of American jazz musicians discovering Europe and its charms, expatriates, existentialism, the heyday of the Left Bank as a Promised Land. It felt like a seductive background for a tale of bruised souls and lost hopes. I was also contemplating a return to my first love: science fiction and a tale of impossible love and time travel; Isaac Asimov's THE END OF ETERNITY but with more pathos and yearning. I still have those notions and might actually surprise you all by actually writing those books one day. But neither concept felt ready yet. Sometimes ideas have to mature inside until the day the mental pregnancy suddenly comes to term and there is nothing to stop you any longer putting the words down and spinning the tale as a form of relief and release.

I knew what my problem as an author was, and has always been: I am not a writer of ideas. I have never as a person or a word dabbler had any ambition to convey a message or change the world. I just like to tell stories, create characters that feel real, and examine the interface between emotions, how people react to events, how one thing leads to another. After all, isn't that what life is like for most of us: small things, minor epiphanies, the business of living?

Of course, I had done some crime writing also, but I had no truck about whodunits or the crossword puzzle nature of crime and subsequent investigation. As much as I admired the sheer ingenuity and constructive wit of locked room mysteries and police procedural plots, what attracted me more about the genre were its zones of darkness, its insights into the ink night of the soul and the thin line between living a life of good or transgressing and inhabiting a world of evil. My influences were Jim Thompson, David Goodis, James M. Cain and Cornell Woolrich (three of whom I had actually been instrumental in publishing and reviving), but as I reflected on this I also came to realise that they were also men, writers of their time and, as intemporal that their writing was, it also reflected the years they lived in and missed out on all the further complications of life in the 1990s: rock music, drug culture, sexual permissiveness, women's empowerment, etc . . . And few of the powerful noir contemporary writers practising their craft there and then also displayed the same sense of despair and obsession as the pulp paperback writers of the 1950s who affected me deep inside (with the exception maybe of James Ellroy, but then he lives in a mad world all of his own, encased like amber in an era he has made his own forever).

I had come in for criticism when sexuality reared its seemingly ugly head too often for the likes of some in my science fiction or crime stories, although for me it just came naturally. Characters are people; people have a sex life, ipso ergo. A particular critic had taken umbrage at one of my most-reprinted stories 'Rite of Seduction' and confused the in-your-face sexuality of the piece for violence and accused me of turning crime writing into the literary equivalent of a snuff movie. Which surprised me. The sad characters in the story fucked abundantly, yes, but there was no actual description of violence. But sex and violence are awkward partners on the page. I admit (and there are still episodes in some of the novels you are about to read that do disturb me sometimes) but this Pavlovian reaction had set my grey cells on a tortuous journey. And I took the conscious decision to try writing a crime novel, with violence and with sex. I'd just see what happened. At first, the plot was thin: a couple on the run from the Southern tip of the USA to the far North. From Miami to Seattle, as I had spent time in both cities. In my mind, I saw the book as a road movie, an obligatory homage of sorts to all the films I enjoyed and envied (I had curated a season of such films for London's National Film Theatre under the title 'Love On The Run'). It was my turn to enjoy the form.

This was early in 1996. Little did I know then where the journey would take me.

There was Jake, in Miami and in need of a woman, a body, human contact. Anne arrived, physically inspired by a young woman I had known all to briefly before she moved out of my life, but very quickly she changed as a character into another ghostly incarnation of the blonde femme fatale who had inhabited all the short stories from my previous book. I soon realised I couldn't escape her, the ghost hadn't been exorcised. It was to be a crime novel, so I needed villains. Why skimp? I created them as sheer evil incarnate, and to demonstrate to the reader I should not after all be taken too seriously, I actually called one Mr Evil and gave the others somewhat cliched names. Maybe this was fear on my part that people would come to believe in them and the dreadful violence they were capable of? To jump start the plot, I required a detonator, a McGuffin. Drugs and diamonds it became. So there I was: two not so innocent but normal people and the forces of evil, shake once and open the lid. There was music I listened to as I wrote the book and it seeped between the lines and formed a natural soundtrack which only I could hear of course, there were feelings I had experienced that I generously donated to some of my characters, there were fears, there was even an old science fiction plot I was still fond of, there was an element of irony, call it my post-modernist death wish if you will, there was love and along the way much unhappiness. The book wrote it itself, an improvisation on themes by others which I just colored in through the prism of my own personality, obsessions and memories.

By the time I'd completed IT'S YOU THAT I WANT TO KISS, it wasn't any longer the book I thought I was writing. It was harsh, it was violent, it was damn sexy, it didn't seem to fit in anywhere in the canon of crime and mystery fiction and maybe was too plot heavy for an erotic book. I was in two minds about it, but it found its readers, in English and other languages. Beyond the fucking, the pain and the wild chases, what sticks out in my mind and what works for me in the novel is the sheer sense of abysmal tenderness some of the characters feel for each other, and the longing for another life and for roads not taken. Guilty, m'Lord.

There was a rock group from Seattle called The Walkabouts, whose music hit me square in the guts and which I listened to a lot while writing KISS. Some of their songs get a mention in the book. When they were next playing in London, I smuggled a copy of the book to them, and some time later on another tour, they kindly asked me to open their major London concert.

There I was, in front of a 500+ theatre audience, standing with my book in hand, a mere writer in lieu of a support band, a writer who can't even play a musical instrument. The lights came on, and I began reading about Jake wanting a fuck on that fateful Miami night. To my surprise, no one protested at my presence and my obscene words. A curious if liberating experience; so thank you, Chris and Carla and The Walkabouts.

I was on a roll and having completed my road movie, I now felt I now had to fulfil another homage and write a straight hardboiled tale of lust and crime. Again, I could visualise the opening: a dark rainy street and another soundtrack by all my favourite bands. So I switched on the computer and began typing. And all of a sudden I was back in that fictional world I knew so well: an adulterous couple whose affair evoked pain and desire in equal parts, a superfluous husband, transgression. It began in London but soon moved to Paris and then yet again to America. As ever, the cold-hearted heroine felt oh so familiar, but I also introduced Cornelia, strip tease artiste and hit woman extraordinaire, a character I gently fell in love with and who reappears in the final novel and might do so again in future novels maybe. Lust to the nth degree, betrayal, loss, the feeling that words cannot fully express and another romp through idenikit hotel rooms where sheets tangle with naked bodies.

OK; I confess: hotel rooms are for me synonymous of sex, private worlds where anything can happen and minds and flesh mingle to disarming but revealing effect. Halfway through writing BECAUSE SHE THOUGHT SHE LOVED ME, I became aware of this singular leitmotif of sex in hotel rooms and, once conscious of it, played along with this idiosyncratic obsession of mine. To the extent of which, by the time the novel reached its bloody conclusion, I knew I still had things to say, further tales of men and women whose embraces in these anonymous rooms had to be charted and dissected.

It had to be a trilogy, then. Or maybe even a quartet if you took into consideration that fact that LIFE IN THE WORLD OF WOMEN (the initial short story collection in which some of the themes and characters of the novels first made an appearance, albeit under different names or variations) had come before, like a stepping stone to the trilogy.

ON TENDERNESS EXPRESS thus was seen from the outset as the conclusion to this involuntary series, a third novel that would conclude once and for all all the sound and fury of all the curious characters my imagination and life had dangerously conjured up into a fictional reality. To make it harder for myself, I also decided to make it a-a private eye novel (because it's the format that every crime writer worth his or her salt must conquer one day) and b-a book written in the first person (if only to defuse all the reviewers and readers who have over the years confused me with my male characters to sometimes amusing effect; after all every one knows Maxim Jakubowski is a 5 ft 9 writer with greying hair and glasses and not a private detective!).

Cornelia returned, deadly as ever, so did episodes from previous books and stories, all to close the loop on 4 years of my writing life once and for all. Again, there are men caught in the web of desire, women as predators and betrayers, much activity between the sheets, on the floors and bathtubs of hotel rooms. There is emotional pain of the worst kind, for the first time even in the three books some glimmer of hope, there are cities I have taken to my heart, there are lingering and I think yearning descriptions of the sublime beauty of the bodies and eyes of women because I feel there are no better things for a writer like me to write about. Some will call my pages pornographic and you will not find me objecting. There is a romance

about the best kind of pornography, that which celebrates bodies, lust and life. Sometimes love is close to death, life is close to death but that's a philosophical consideration I will leave to critics. So call me a romantic pornographer, if you will. I'll carry that cross with pride.

So enjoy this accidental trilogy of novels about love in hotel rooms, these crime books with no puzzles or worthwhile police investigations, these erotic books that have more than just sex scenes or sexual hydraulics. These are first and foremost stories about people, imperfect men and women seeking happiness, and if their words and tortured bodies on the page move you, then I will feel I have accomplished a worthy task.

—Maxim Jakubowski
April 2001

Because She Thought
She Loved Me

For my mother, Brenda Rothberg
For Robin Cook
For all those who are no longer here
This book about tenderness and death

"We were perfect when we started,
I've been wondering where we've gone."

'A Murder of One'
Counting Crows

PART ONE

DYING THE DEATH THAT EVERYONE DOES

1.

A Woman, A Man, A Bed

The wind was howling like an apprentice banshee outside the hotel windows. The Bloomsbury pavements were wet. It was dark and cold, a Dashiell Hammett kind of night. Completely wrong weather for the season.

'Are you sure you still want to do this?' Caitleen asked me.

The warmest place would be between the sheets.

'Yes,' I told her. 'I haven't come this far to just stand and shiver.'

'Undress me then,' Caitleen said.

The drive through the rain had felt endless, trying to find a hotel room for the night, parking on double yellow lines and frantically inquiring about vacancies from bored-looking duty clerks or managers, hoping all the while that back in the dulling cocoon of the car she would not change her mind.

Again.

As she had, once already back in July, fearful of taking that final, decisive step that would have seen us become lovers. Her hesitation at the final hurdle had thrown me into despair.

But tonight, squeezed into the corner of a small unfashionable Clapham bar, she had suddenly said 'Yes, I will.'

At first, I hadn't quite understood. My mind raced back to our aimless, low-key conversation. What was she referring to? My eyes must have betrayed my puzzlement.

'I will sleep with you,' Caitleen had said.

'Really?' was all I could gracelessly say.

I had taken her hand in mine.

'Tonight. Find a place,' she added quickly.

'Now?'

'Yes. I've told him I had to go to Birmingham for my job and wouldn't be back until tomorrow. It's safe.'

I had quickly asked for the bill and we'd made for the darkness and the centre of town.

Where sinful beds were available if you had the will and the cash.

*

I'm a master of fantasies. For a scene like this I would have imagined a wonderfully emotional, magic soundtrack. Not massed violins, more of a sensuous, sad electric guitar solo, slide, steel or even dobro. With echoes of country. But I'd had no time to mentally prepare. This was all too unexpected. Silence would have to do. The sound of real life special occasions.

I moved closer to Caitleen.

Her coat was wet and heavy, but she had dried her hair with a thin towel from the hotel room's bathroom on arrival.

'Allow me.'

I helped her out of it and draped it over the back of the only chair in the room.

'Put the light out,' she asked me.

'No,' I said. 'I want to see all of you.'

'Must you?'

'Yes, I insist,' I added.

I unbuttoned her black leather waistcoat and felt her warm breath on my cheek. Kissed her throat with all the resources of tenderness that I could summon from within the fear that rose inside me on a wave of apprehensiveness and greedy desire.

She raised her arms upwards and straightened them as I pulled the flimsy white top over her face and long tousled hair. She kicked her shoes off. I did likewise.

I kissed her again, my tongue tracing the soft contour of her lips, systematically licking away the final remnants of her lipstick, felt the jagged resistance of her teeth as I probed further. My hands tightened around her waist, pulling her towards me. Our mouths stayed joined together. Humidities mingling in another escalation of our intimacy.

So many questions assailed my mind but I tried to blank them out.

The wind kept on roaring outside, shaking the window panes with every new savage gust. Was this to be a hurricane night? A once in a lifetime London twister of a storm?

Our lips separated as we gasped for air. I got down on my knees and helped her out of her jeans, her long unending legs emerging from the material as it rolled down from waist to thighs to white-socked feet.

Caitleen was now in her underwear.

I avidly drank in every scent rising from her unclad body.

I rose to my feet, gazing in awe at the whiteness of her flesh, the flimsy black bra and briefs that concealed so little.

'You're beautiful,' I told her.

She loosened my trouser belt.

We kissed again.

The room around us lost its focus and the force field of our desire grew stronger with every continuing moment of physical contact.

As my hands wandered over the wondrous acres of her unveiled skin, I relished the silken softness, familiarised myself with the outer texture of her body, mapped the topography of delicate curves, the gentle swell of her small breasts, the blinding heat that rushed through the thin material as my fingers lingered over the mound of her sex.

The indiscreet camera inside my brain recorded every detail. A beauty spot. A small scar. An imperfection. The way her eyes peered at me with curiosity and, dare I say it, love? The subtle grain of her epidermis. The cabalistic distribution of darker moles along the map of her body. I knew already that these stretched-out moments would have to last me a lifetime.

'Your shirt,' she asked.

I undid the buttons and allowed her to pull it off and away from me. She avidly buried her fingers through the streaky maze of my chest hair, as if it were a totally new experience, relishing the novelty of another man's particularities.

My own hands cupped her breasts, slipping with no resistance between them and the material of her bra. Getting drunk on the warmth of her softness; a nail grazed a nipple, and I felt it harden, lowered my lips towards it.

She moaned.

Disengaged from my tentative embrace and took a couple of steps back towards the bed that dominated the barely-furnished hotel room. Sat down on it.

'Fuck me now,' Caitleen asked.

Standing there, I shed the rest of my clothes, facing her, our assorted attire in a small crumpled pile on the brown shag carpet. She brushed her hand against my growing cock. I knelt down and indicated she should raise herself slightly as I pulled her knickers down, revealing the flattened darker curls surrounding the warm territory of her cunt. Her pungent, released odour wafted towards me, and I immediately became drunk on it. I looked Caitleen in the eyes. She nodded in approval. I lowered my lips towards her.

'Oh, Jesus Christ!' she said.

So began the slow, slow story of how I die.

*

We made love with lingering compassion. Copulated, fucked, shagged, screwed wildly with lingering compassion well into the night and all the way through to a grey morning. Every new first time is like a rebirth, something so desperately unique it marks you forever. It was no different for us than it was for no doubt a hundred or so other couples doing the dirty that same night among the thousand and more regulation-shaped rooms of the Bloomsbury area and its countless hotels.

Caitleen.

When pleasure threatened to overtake her, she would invariably clench her teeth and mutter 'Christ, oh God!' under her breath. I soon began to measure the intensity of our lovemaking by the punctuation of her quietly blasphemous vocal interruptions. And her long drawn-out sighs as we moved in and out of each other. Of pleasure. Of guilt.

I don't think I slept at all that night.

She did. In patches. Exhausted by our frenetic gymnastics, overcome by the sexual frenzy of it all. Not much. But enough for me to lie by her side on the bed and admire with wonder the way her chest rose in her sleep and her skin silently irradiated desire, in these drawn-out minutes of leisure unbelieving the sheer beauty of her features in repose, the line of her cheekbones, the hypnotic tangle of her hair, the curve of her shoulder, all the things that made her so dear to me. Quickly, she would somehow sense that I was there, watching her in the penumbra, and her eyes would open, aware of my persistent gaze, and her lips would invite me back towards her.

An invisible request I could not disobey.

I would taste her again and soon my fingers were wandering wildly across her skin, awakening points of lust among the softness and the sweat. One touch was often enough, bringing the fire to life again as if it had never even been dimmed, and we would devour each other again, pushing ourselves to the limit, trying every geographical and anatomical position in search of greater degrees of mutual combustion. And by trial and error we somehow did everything right. There were no limits, no shame to anything we did.

Everything seemed natural. Innocently self-evident. This was how to make love: how our bodies fitted together by wonderful design.

From that first night together on, I knew we were made for each other and that my life would never be the same again.

Whatever happened.

The way she would take me deep inside her mouth, her throat and tongue joyfully cleaning away in one gulp all our joint secretions.

How she would shift to invite even deeper penetration, the shallowness of her breath welcoming just the right amount of violence and pain.

Her long fingers, her tongue exploring the deep valley where my desire was most acute, moving with excruciating slowness across the ridge of my swollen balls down to the odorous depths of my darkness.

Her lack of shame or inhibitions had my heart in instant meltdown.

Between the sex, we spoke.

Of experiences past, people, partners, things and such. But we knew that the conversation meant nothing and was just a pretext to fill the time between the fucking, while our bodies, or rather mine, accumulated enough energy to make the act possible again. At times, the thirst in the sparkle of her eyes was enough to harden me within an instant, as she looked down at the soft cock nestling between my spread thighs with gentle irony and hunger.

Bathed together, the tepid soapy water overflowing onto the tiled floor of the narrow hotel bathroom, my wet fingers teasing her nipples into pink hardness and she moaned 'Not again.'

'Yes, again,' I said, raising myself from the tub and carrying her dripping from the bath, accumulating a trail of water stains across the hotel room carpet, spreading the ample form of her white body out on the bed, opening her legs at their appetising widest and digging my face into her soaking crotch. Let my mouth and tongue do the talking inside her damp warmth.

'Christ, oh God!' she said, in predictable response.

Then, quickly:

'Enough! I want you inside me. Now.'

The serious talking, wives, husbands, life, would have to wait for tomorrow or another damn day.

We fumbled our way toward ecstasy.

*

I walked over to the windows and pulled the heavy curtain aside. 'Breakfast?' I enquired.

'You bet!' Caitleen said. 'I'm famished.'

'I'm not surprised,' I chuckled.

'Do you think they have room service?' she asked, turning in bed toward the nearby telephone, one breast slipping out from between the white sheets, seeking a possible menu among the various hotel brochures and the Gideon Bible in the bedside drawer.

'I'm sure they do.'

She found the laminated plastic sheet and examined it.

'I want the whole lot. Eggs, bacon, sausages, tomato and mush-rooms,' Caitleen said, with a glint of mischief in her eyes, both her breasts now peering daintily above the crumpled material of the bed sheets. 'And lots of toast,' she added, throwing the menu towards me.

'No kippers?'

'No. There are limits to my turpitude,' she said.

'Thank goodness,' I remarked, walking back towards the bed. 'I would have to call the whole thing off if you'd been a kipper person, you know?'

'You bastard.'

She aimed the remote at the television. A weatherman was going on at inordinate length about the freaky weather.

It was August in London. The town was full of tourists humping shopping bags and brandishing cameras. It was a Tuesday. How come I remember that so well? We had become lovers at last, and it was unforgettable.

Foolishly, I thought it could only get better.

There were good moments to come, of course, but on the whole it did get worse. Much worse.

'And cereals. And lots of milk,' Caitleen asked, as I ordered breakfast over the phone, her cheeks still flushed from our earlier excesses, her mouth only inches away from my dangling cock as I stood by the bed, vainly attempting to hold my stomach in and cut a somewhat more elegant posture.

'It'll be about a quarter of an hour,' I told her, putting the receiver down.

'Whatever shall we do in the meantime?' she said, her fingers extending towards my tired genitals.

'I know you'll think of something,' I smiled.

'I'm quite sure I will,' Caitleen said.

I drew nearer to the bed.

'When is he expecting you back?' I asked, part of my brain already back in the real world.

'Who cares?' she said brusquely.

As she brushed teasingly against my cock, a sudden urge overtook me.

'Gotta pee,' I told her, moving away from the bed.

She threw the covers and the sheets aside, stepped regally from the bed, her tall frame invading my horizon. She did look truly wonderful, quite naked as she was. A natural. The object of my affection. I lingered over the spectacle of her small breasts and their gentle upward tilt, the wide, strong hips and their captivating centre of gravity, her still damp pubic hair, its million curls parting to reveal the dark red engorged lips through which I had ventured all night in search of unaccountable pleasure.

'I want to watch,' she said.

'What? You're mad.'

'I'll even hold it. Please,' she pleaded.

'You're really crazy,' I said. 'I love you.'

And I realised this was the very first time I had said the fateful words 'I love you' to Caitleen. All night, even in the indescribable throes of passion, a part of me had held back, not wanting to say the words, even as I thrust relentlessly into her and sought to consume her in the rage of my passion. I knew it was too early. Not yet. Not quite yet. And now it had just slipped out. So naturally.

She followed me into the bathroom. We hadn't emptied the bath water a few hours before. She dipped a finger in it.

'It's cold,' she remarked.

Then turned towards me, impishly waiting for me to urinate.

Sensing my hesitancy, she said:

'You can watch me afterwards, if you want.'

*

I felt like a right pervert, transfixed by the quiet arc of water spurting out through the slightly wrinkled lower lips of her cunt. She kept on smiling at me, in a knowing sluttish and childish way, enjoying the sight of my embarrassment, sneakily observing the spectacle of my unavoidable excitement as my cock began to harden in response to the spectacle of such daring intimacy.

'Do you like it?' she asked me.

'I do.' I could not lie. My body would only betray me.

The trickle came to a slow end.

'Lick me clean,' she demanded.

I knelt down on the floor, my face entering the daring territory between her open thighs. Witnessed a last drip.

I obeyed.

'I've always wanted a man to do that to me,' Caitleen said, with a sigh of satisfaction.

My tongue retreated from her half-gaping lips.

'Is there anything else you've always wanted but never could have?' I asked her. Thinking all the time of her damn husband.

'To be fucked in the arse,' she calmly said.

'You've never?'

'No. He's much too conservative for that,' she said, reading my thoughts. 'Have you ever done it?' she enquired.

'Not very often,' I admitted.

'What was it like?'

'A bit awkward,' I revealed.

'Practice could make perfect,' Caitleen said, rising from the toilet seat where she had unceremoniously been squatting.

'I suppose so,' I said, unsure whether this was a signal.

We didn't experiment that day. More common pleasures of the flesh were enough for us, and we had to interrupt another hectic bout of lovemaking when room service finally knocked at the door. We'd almost forgotten.

Check-out was at noon.

I suggested we stay another night.

'No, Joe, I can't,' Caitleen said. 'Two nights, he'd become suspicious. I don't want to take that risk. I've never been away for work more than a day before. It would feel wrong, all of a sudden.'

I meekly agreed.

'We can still have lunch,' she proposed.

'That would be great.'

As we left the hotel and melted among the crowds of holiday makers milling around Russell Square, we each nervously looked in both directions for possible familiar faces in the vicinity. But we were quite anonymous. Sin might have been etched deeply under the skin of our bodies, but we looked quite normal on the outside.

We walked past the British Museum, uneasy. Wanting to maybe hold hands, but not able to. Feeling conspicuous in public together. Our conversation was rare and strained. We drifted into Soho and decided to eat Indian at Dean Street's Red Fort. We requested a table at the back, where no one outside could see through the street window of the restaurant.

Eating together. My mistress and me. Her lover and her.

'It was good,' I said.

'Yes,' Caitleen said.

'Really good . . . The sex, I mean,' I added pedantically.

'I know,' she nodded, perusing the menu.

'I felt so close to you, I . . . It wasn't just the sex, you see . . .' I mumbled.

'I understand,' said Caitleen.

'I wanted to say that . . .'

'Don't, Joe. Don't say anything that you might regret, please. Not now.' She was going to add something to the still-born conversation, but the turbaned waiter approached the table to see if we were ready to order. We were.

Most of the meal continued in relative silence. A group of Japanese businessmen occupied the table to our left, while a trio of advertising executives drank heavily on our right, arguing the respective pros and cons of the government's ban on alcopops and the direct consequences for some of their respective accounts. It was impossible not to eavesdrop on them. Another good reason for neither of us to be particularly communicative or loquacious.

We were slowly sipping our coffees.

'What now?' Caitleen asked.

'What do you mean?' I queried.

'I told them at the office I'd be away all day on research business. My train home is not for another few hours.'

'Drink?'

'Yeah . . . Where? The pubs are closed and I don't think I could stand another hotel bar.'

'The Groucho's down the road. I'm a member.'

'Great. I've always wanted to go there.'

*

'I want to see you again,' I told Caitleen.

'Of course,' she said. She had just returned from the basement toilets where she had readjusted the bright lipstick on her beestung lips. 'Did you think I want things to stop? I want more, Joe, like you.'

'Good.'

'Next time, it'd be nice to do something normal,' Caitleen remarked.

'What do you mean by something normal?' I asked, not quite sure what she meant.

'Like seeing a movie, for instance. We can't spend all our time in bed.'

'Perish the thought.'

'I know,' she smiled at last; the first time, I reflected, since we had left the Bloomsbury hotel.

So, the following week, we caught an American indie production in a small screening room off the Tottenham Court Road, meeting up in the cinema's foyer shortly after she had left her office around six. The film was full of shattering, loud explosions, gun battles and breathless chases down unending blacktop highways and Technicolour landscapes. But neither of us could concentrate on the action, painfully aware of the other's presence and intoxicating warmth nearby, fingers surreptitiously grazing knees and thighs in the surrounding darkness. We almost ran out of the movie house as the credits unrolled on the screen. We didn't even speak. I had the keys to my office and within a minute of locking the door behind us we were tearing at each other's clothes and embracing frantically on the thick-carpeted floor. Caitleen insisted on keeping her stockings and garter belt on as I eagerly raised her rump and entered her from behind with little in the way of foreplay. She was already soaking and my erection buried itself inside her like a well oiled drill. We fucked. The sound of our breath and deep sighs the only sound in the otherwise empty managerial office in which I usually processed mountains of paperwork in quiet contemplation. As I pushed still harder into her, Caitleen turned her head towards me, a bemused look on her face as she watched me labouring. What could she be thinking? I wondered, the rhythm of my thrusts assured and repetitive, shaking her body, spasms rippling all the way down from her cunt to her gently hanging breasts as she willingly accepted the metronomic movement I was imposing on her, riding the waves of pleasure, indulgent in the lust that kept us in its thrall.

I was about to come inside her.

I literally felt like screaming and as the release surged onward from the hollow of my stomach, through my innards to the tip of my warmly-embedded cock, I suddenly corkscrewed a finger into her other aperture, as its small crevice dilated slightly with every successive forward thrust of my penis below.

Caitleen shouted 'Jesus, Jeezuuuus!' but I knew it wasn't pain.

We came together and collapsed, still intimately entwined, onto the rough fabric of the industrial-issue carpeting, hastily trying to catch our breath as the room seemed to spin madly around us, as if the whole planet was out of control. It wasn't; but we were.

'Wow,' Caitleen said. 'That sure was intense.'

I silently nodded my agreement. My throat was parched and speech felt beyond me right now.

We finally disentangled.

'Shit!' she remarked. 'I've left a stain on the floor. I think my period's begun. I'm sorry, Joe, I wasn't expecting us to get it together tonight, somehow...'

'It's okay,' I answered. 'No one is going to notice or put two and two together. The stain will fade away eventually.'

There were only soft drinks in the small office fridge. I seldom entertained there. Cuddled together with our backs to the heavy oak desk, we drank slowly, lost in thought. The minutes remorselessly ticked away to the time of her last train to the suburbs.

She separated from me and rose from the floor. She began to dress. With every successive garment she slipped on, the harder my desire for her became. Never had a reverse striptease appeared so indelibly alluring to me, and a fully-dressed young woman looked so sexily naked.

'I don't want you to go,' I pleaded. Unconvincingly.

'I must,' she answered.

'Stay longer,' I asked Caitleen. 'You can get a cab back later. I'll pay.'

'No, Joe. It wouldn't work. He'd realise something was up. He knows the train timetables. Might actually be waiting at the station for me. There's no way I could explain it.'

Caitleen returned to her husband, after we arranged another meet five days later. I caught a cab back home. Another late night entertaining clients, I explained to my wife. I don't think she believed me. But she remained silent, curiously uninquisitive. I had reached the point when I didn't care. Only Caitleen mattered.

Another evening, another fuck.

I couldn't use my office premises. Something or other going on, one of my partners in the practice, someone who worked on the necessary legitimate side of the company, having a drinks party, I think. And my office was just too close to the seldom used boardroom for our frenzied and lustful activities of the flesh to go unnoticed.

Soho Square. A wooden bench. A stolen public kiss. More frustration.

'I just can't stand this any more.'

'Do you wish to break it off?'

'No, that's not what I mean. At all.'

'So? Tell me.'

'I want all of you. I just don't want to have to share you with him all the time. To know in my mind that he can still touch you at night in all the places that I did after you return to his bed...'

'To our bed. He is my husband.'

'He doesn't deserve you.'

It was September. The storms were but a distant memory. The weather was again oppressively warm and humid. The sky was still pale blue past nine at night. Caitleen wore a thin T-shirt and no bra. The muted curves of her breasts pressed gently against the thin material.

'Come away with me. We'll go to the South of France, to New York, I don't know, Prague, they say it's nice there. Anywhere . . .'

'I can't Joe, I can't . . .' She was almost in tears. Imagine my own state.

Pale pocked moon rising above London. Our hands gripped tight.

'What can we do?' I asked Caitleen, almost rhetorically, not even expecting an answer from this no-exit emotional road we were stumbling along, reinventing the gestures of passion and the meaning of despair as we advanced blindly.

'He won't let me go quietly,' she said. 'No way.'

'I think my wife will,' I said. 'There'll be a bloody fight. But I'll manage. Somehow or other. I'd go through with it. What about you?' I asked her.

She avoided my eyes, turned her head away and gazed at the small pavilion that formed the centre of the square.

'Then there's no alternative,' Caitleen softly said.

The warmth of her body was like a pool in the advancing darkness of night.

'He'll have to die,' she added.

'Yes,' I heard myself saying. Sealing my fate.

2.

Night Town, Night People

As night fell like a cloak of forgiveness across the silences of London, all the creatures of darkness would come out and play and Zeusmark would sit back and contemplate his domain. And we would meet, as arranged, for one of our irregular update and new ventures meetings, this time around in a quiet Clerkenwell private-members-only bar, full of shadows and discretion.

This was the man I worked for.

A long story.

He looked much like any ordinary middle-aged suburban chartered accountant, and he could switch an affable sort of corporate charm on at will when the occasion required. But he was also very clever, in his innocuous way. I'd heard on the money grapevine that he had actually begun his career many years before as a minor magazine reporter, restricted to the dead-end of the business patch which few other ambitious journos aspired to. He had accidentally come across some electronic scam in City corridors which had put him in contact with a group of powerful South London villains looking to diversify their activities away from mere prostitution, drugs and pornography. He had eagerly advanced the cause of new technology and how the vice trade could take advantage of it. Sex on the Internet. Lucrative and safe.

Zeusmark had recognised the opportunity of a lifetime and had never looked back.

Very soon, he had given up the writing racket and his operation was up and running. The villains provided the muscle and the spe-

cialised know-how, and took their hefty back-end percentage of the
profits, but it was all Zeusmark's baby and it minted a fortune.

I should know.

Even though he often looked like one, in his boring dark brown
pinstriped suits and paisley ties, Zeusmark was no accountant.

I was.

I called myself a consultant by then. But I was the one he re-
cruited from the backwaters of my auditor's desk, who looked after
his books, organised the necessary laundering routes through banking channels to make his income respectable to the outside world,
suggested variations, additions, strategies, ensured he maximised his
revenues to the hilt.

You've got to earn a living one way or the other. I'm no angel, I
know, but at least this way I was removed from the more unsavoury
aspects of his life and business. My forte was tax evasion, the legal
way, navigating through all the loopholes and offshore havens and
dodgy investment schemes. That was how Zeusmark had found me
in the first place. I'd somehow gained a decent reputation as a re-
sourceful foe of the tax man. He was quite open about how the
money was made. I entered into the association with open eyes. I'd
done well out of it. Financially. And I wouldn't have met Caitleen
otherwise.

I stumbled in to the penumbra of the shady club where Zeusmark held fort.

Mark the Roadie, a tall, gregarious guy who had once been on
the road with the Hollies and the Searchers, casually frisked me. I
knew it wasn't for concealed weapons, this wasn't that sort of operation, but for possible listening devices. Which would have been
more likely. Adjudging me clean, he pointed me in the direction of
a booth at the back of the room.

'Hello, Joseph,' Zeusmark greeted me.

Because of holidays and a series of unavoidable overseas trips,
we hadn't seen each other in a couple of months. His hair was thinning at an alarming rate, and his growing paunch had made notice-
able progress. I hated that name. He knew it. This was his unsubtle
way of defining our relationship. My parents, in a fit of left-wing
fervour, had called me after Stalin. Everyone but Zeusmark called
me Joe.

'Hi.'

'Nice to see you again. It's been some time.'

'It has.' I sat down facing him.

'Have a drink. Markie?' he called out to his henchman.

'A Seven-Up,' I replied. I don't drink alcohol. Not principle, just taste.

'Ah, Joseph,' Zeusmark said. 'You never change, do you?

'Why should I?' I ingenuously asked him. He always enjoyed preliminary banter before getting on to the evening's agenda.

He slowly sipped his beer. Mark brought my soft drink can.

I pulled the files from my briefcase and laid them out across the table. Zeusmark brushed them aside.

'Business can wait,' he said.

'As you wish.'

'You know my wife, don't you?' he asked me.

He knew I did. A chill went through me as I feared the worse.

'Sure.'

'So we can talk, hey?' he inquired.

. I nodded silently. My brain was travelling in overdrive through every possible permutation of where Caitleen and I might have gone wrong. We'd taken so many precautions. Concocted all the plausible alibis in the world. My thoughts zigzagged in a jumble as I struggled to recall where in hell the damn slip-up might have occurred. How could he know? Had someone seen us together? Had I left a mark on her body, had he smelled what was left of me on her, had she moaned my name in her sleep as he lay awake next to her? I could imagine his anger: his wife and his accountant, how humiliating it would appear to him. How he would engineer his revenge. My imagination slipped into yet a higher gear. Fortunately it was too dark in here for him to notice how all colour had drained from my features. Shot? Tortured? Knife in my gut, strangled with my own intestines, castrated and left in a quarry with my bloodied and severed genitals stuffed down my throat as a warning to allcomers who might even dare think of meddling with Zeusmark? Caitleen? Punished severely no doubt, given as a plaything to his henchmen, gang-raped, forced to work on his damn videos or to perform every conceivable perversion on his live-on-the-Internet, pay-by-credit-card-as-you-watch connection sites? Which I had helped him set up while desperately trying to ignore their likely contents. The pornography of my imagination was rampant.

If he had confronted me right there and then, I know I would have said yes, admitted everything. Betrayed us. Gutless.

His voice snapped me out of my gloom-laden reverie.

'You know I keep her away from the details of the business. I just would be satisfied with a nice, quiet home-life, want to see her happy,' Zeusmark said. 'I've told her, time and time again there is no need for her to work. We don't need the money. I could afford anything she wanted. But she enjoys the independence her job provides her. I understand that. I was just hoping one day she might change her mind. I love her so much, Joseph. I'd do anything for her.'

'I know,' I said, still trying to anticipate what would come next in his soliloquy of domesticity.

'She just doesn't want us to have children, you see. I don't understand, really,' he added. 'I'm scared, Joseph.'

'Why?' I asked, relief already flooding across me as the conversation took this strange and unexpected turn.

'She's been acting so remote lately. I know she's always been somewhat aloof, a bit of a loner, but it's different. You notice things like that after eight years together. Did I ever tell you we met at university? She was a year ahead of me. She was reading English, while I was doing History. Anyway, she somehow no longer talks to me unless I deliberately start a conversation. As if she's not completely there. Lost in dreams that will not allow me in. Feels as if I'm slowly losing her.'

You are.

To me.

'Something has happened,' he added, 'I don't know what, but Joseph, I fear she might be seeing someone else.'

'Really?' I said, disingenuously.

'I need your help,' he said.

'How?'

'Mark and the other guys my partners could provide me with are wrong. You're in a different class. You'd know how to be discreet,' he said. 'I'm asking you this as a friend, not as a business thing, you understand.'

'You mean you want me to investigate her, see if anything is happening? I dotted the i's.

'Absolutely,' Zeusmark confirmed.

'It's not my sort of job.'

'That's why you're right for it,' he insisted. 'I don't wish to rent some private dick or other. This is not a commercial transaction. If the news is bad, I'd rather it reached me through the mouth of someone I know. And trust.'

I put my drink down, looked him in the eyes and reassured him.

'I'll do what I can. No promises, though. You know it's not quite banking or telegraphic transfers territory.'

'I know you will, Joseph,' he said, rearranging the files in one tidy pile in front of him, and opening the Grand Cayman account ledger. 'On to business, then.'

'Yes,' I agreed.

Things never quite happen the way you expect, do they?

I had embarked on a slow boat. I was unsure about the destination. But I had already paid for the journey, and there was now no turning back.

*

'It's crazy,' Caitleen said. 'Sheer undiluted lunacy.'

We had met again as conspirators, taking extreme precautions, as we had seen people do in the movies. Switching cabs, answering phone calls on the prearranged fourth ring, weaving both credible and preposterous excuses and all that silly melodramatic jazz.

A landscape of twisted lies surrounded us, tainting everything we touched.

And neither of us liked it.

A client owed me some favours, and had allowed me to borrow his London flat for the afternoon.

Caitleen began crying.

'Please,' I implored her. 'Don't . . .'

God, I was scared of losing her right then and now, as she sobbed quietly.

'We can just run away,' I said. 'Please . . .'

'You know it wouldn't work,' she said, between tears. 'He wouldn't let us go. He wouldn't let me go. He's taken me for granted all these years, and he's not about to change. I know him too well, he would hurt badly and it would just bring out the worst in him. Wherever we went, he would follow, arrange for his acolytes to find us. We can't escape. Oh, Joe . . .'

'Yes?' I asked hopefully, wiping her left cheek with my fingers.

'We have to get rid of him. As we agreed.'

'How?'

'We'll find a way, you'll see. We have to be patient. Think. Plan.'

Her lips approached me and we kissed.

Her taste was electric as her hot breath moved inside me like a strong peppermint-flavoured Gulf Stream of unchecked desire and reached every extremity of my body with its velvet caress. My fingers moved to her tangled hair, pulling her face still closer towards me as we tumbled clumsily on to the small, single bed.

'I just don't care any more,' I told her, short of breath from our kissing, as we tore each other's clothes off. 'I'll kill him. For you. I'm tired of this whole stupid charade he's making us endure. I'm no more a spy on our love than I am a killer. But so be it.'

'Yes,' Caitleen gasped, helping me pull my still partly buttoned-up shirt over my head. 'Yes, yes, yes.'

We made love as if there was to be no tomorrow. For the first time, we even inflicted violence on each other as the longing and the despair got the better of us. And the anger. She asked me about all the terrible things men asked to be done to the women on Zeus-mark's on-line sex site. I explained the tariffs he had devised, and how the instant credit card transactions filled his coffers, paid for the bed she slept in and the roof above and the clothes and the lifestyle. How the subscribers could type out their special requests at their computer keyboards anywhere on the planet, and their demands would be acted upon in a matter of minutes at the other end of the word, in a makeshift studio in London's Docklands or in Amster-dam's Red Light district. Caitleen wanted to know it all, not just the vibrators in both orifices, the coke bottles, the whips, the bondage and erotic asphyxiation, the fisting, the violations of all sorts which were committed if the money was right. And if the invisible sub-scriber had no imagination, there was also a convenient menu which suggested more extreme practices, should he so desire and be able to afford the steep-rising prices in the escalation of depravity in his Internet live services.

'Where does he find all these women?' she asked.

'I don't think he does,' I said. 'His associates provide the fresh meat. I once heard one of them boast of how easy it was. All these young kids who arrive without a penny at King's Cross or St Pancras ready for the bright lights of the big city are quickly charmed into a life of vice, probably quickly hooked on drugs. Soon, they have little choice. It's either the on-line sex or plying their trade on the streets or sharp withdrawal symptoms, or beatings or worse. At least in the studio it's just an assortment of regular hard-cocked studs and the duty cameraman, not unknown punters of dubious cleanliness. Maybe, in a way, it makes it all impersonal, remote-controlled. It's also safe for the guy at the other end of the computer, who gets his rocks off with no risk of infection or being brought to the attention of the law. Rape by proxy. A nice little earner,' I remarked as her hands on my rump pulled me deeper into her.

'The bastard,' Caitleen said. I moved inside her, riding the waves of her shallow breathing. Her nails furiously raked my back, probably drawing blood, but I was beyond care, forever lost in the deep dark lake of her pleading eyes, as she urged me to keep on thrusting against her inner walls and actually hurt her, mark her in some dreadful irreversible way.

Maybe she imagined we were performing for the Zeusmark coffers, in a hastily converted, white-walled attic just a stone's throw from Canary Wharf, and that it was actually her husband adjusting the lens behind the purring camera as we raced through the rituals of love for the benefit of some sex-starved, deranged nerd, sitting at his terminal in a small condominium in Bellevue, on the other side of Lake Washington near Seattle.

I WANT HER TO SUCK HIM OFF, the client ordered.

Twenty dollars were deducted from his credit.

She could sense my orgasm approaching as my body tensed and the rhythm of our union intensified, and backed suddenly away from me, disengaging quickly from my penis, swiftly pushing me back on the narrow bed and crouching towards my splendid erection, which she swallowed in one hungry gulp, her tongue teasing my inflamed tip until I could hold out no longer and exploded inside her mouth. A radiant smile of pleasure spreading across her face, she retreated, now squatting obscenely on the bed cover, her vaginal opening still heavily dilated from my earlier intrusion, and looked toward me with a definite look of mischief.

I WANT HIM TO DRINK HIS OWN COME FROM HER MOUTH, Bellevue requested.

Fifty dollars. Press Alt key if you agree with charge.

She moved the come inside her mouth in a circular motion, from cheek to cheek, spreading its load around, careful not to swallow my milky secretion. Our lips met and for the first time in my life I tasted my ejaculate. By now, the sticky liquid had been augmented by an equal quantity of Caitleen's saliva. Her mouth adhered to mine, her agile tongue invading me, stirring the load inside closer to the back of my throat as I gasped for breath.

NOW HE MUST SPIT THE STUFF BACK INTO HER CUNT, Bellevue requested, a gentleman of perverse imagination.

An extra seventy dollars is required. Credit rating verification is positive. Press Alt key now.

We separated as she eased herself onto her back, opening her legs wide, spreading her engorged lips further apart with her fingers in a figure of offering. I lowered myself down on her, opened my lips slowly, aimed and watched as our combined secretions pearled back into her shining, nacreous insides.

Caitleen smiled sweetly, pleased by our unholy gesture of communion.

STRONGER STUFF, NOW I WANT ANOTHER GUY TO FUCK HER, ENDING UP WITH A JUICY DOUBLE PENETRATION.

Bellevue was anything but predictable: this was one of the more popular choices on the live on-line menu. The reason why there's always another stud on duty at the studio. But not today. There's only Zeusmark handling the camera, and Caitleen and Joe performing. Caitleen wondered briefly whether the two men in her life might wish to take on the challenge.

One hundred dollars. Press Alt key.

Transaction accepted.

Zeusmark fixed the camera on the tripod and moved towards the bed and the two naked sex artists.

MODEM ERROR. TYPE R11. CHECK PORT CONNECTION.

Caitleen closed her eyes, I pulled the cover back over our sweating bodies. It was Saturday, a Golders Green afternoon. Outside the borrowed flat, Jewish kids in their best attire and newly-shined shoes were dutifully following their dark-clothed parents and relatives back from the synagogue, towards the saloon cars which had been parked out of harm's way.

I checked my watch. We could afford another couple of hours, while our lies and respective alibis held out.

I moved closer to her.

*

Why was I having this mad affair with Caitleen?

So, she was younger. So, to me, she was damn fucking beautiful. And the vision of her body alone turned me into another crazy, and her eyes gazing down on me made nonsense of my sanity. Yes, all that and more.

Or had my cock finally gone independent and taken control of my weakened mental functions?

Not far off.

But, really, I think death made me do it.

Or at any rate that's what psychology by numbers suggested.

I had reached that stage of life where night, for me, seemed to be encroaching on everything that surrounded me. After the sports columns, my next port of call in the morning newspapers had invariably become the obituary pages, where I would discover how many more people I had known, come across even casually, or read, had kicked the bucket.

I missed them all. Those who had been younger as well as those who had been older. There was no right time to die. Of course.

It was all accumulating, somewhere inside me.

The crematorium waiting rooms where conversation was scarce. The hollow eulogies, the uncontrollable choking in our collective throats as another coffin inched its way towards the flames. The cheerless parties that followed. The long, silent drives back to town from the suburban cemeteries where like in the camps the smoke from the chimney would not bother the residents. It was those of us who were left behind by their passing who really suffered, I felt. All a litany of grief and a sure sign I was not getting any younger.

Among the disappeared.

Some women I had slept with.

Others I had got drunk with.

Friends. Would-be lovers.

And even worse was the inner knowledge that so many more I had known were also dead, somewhere out there in this too-big world and I couldn't even say which, having long since lost contact with them through the vagaries of life.

Christel, a German girl who seemed so old and desirable to my fifteen-year-old soul, the first in my spreading parade of unrequited loves.

Lois Elizabeth, who came from Greenwich, my intoxicating first blonde, for whom I had clumsily slit my wrists in my late teens in a confused scream for more attention.

Catherine, who broke my heart when she slept with another. All I remembered of her now was the prosaic fact that she was rather short.

Where were they all now? Absence, ignorance was as bad as death, I reckoned.

They were all now people of the night, passed onto darkness, ghosts roaming the world I still lived in, crisscrossing the busy map of dreams and forgetfulness. And even those who might still be alive, would I still recognise them, if they passed me on the street or sat a table or two away in a bar or a restaurant?

Were they the reason I had collided with Caitleen with such irresistible, bone-crunching impact?

Her youth, her sad eyes? Maybe. Though everyone I knew always said she appeared older than she was, burdened by the weight of her natural melancholy, the inherent quietness of her soul.

With these all too familiar images and idle thoughts of death swirling wildly around my mind, I watched Caitleen briskly move away towards her South East region train and another parade of suburbs as she travelled back to the marital bed. Another night of many apart. It was a West End full moon, restless crowds milling aimlessly between Leicester Square and the Charing Cross Road, women in skimpy, revealing attire and too much make-up, rushing from disco doors to the Underground while others queued for their turn on the dance-floor, under the questioning stare of burly bouncers. Fire-eaters performed to naive, admiring crowds of easy-to-please young-sters, the muffled sounds of the nearby summer fun fair drowning the sound of individual conversations until it all blurred into a hope-less cacophony of sound, movement and colours. In darker corners, dossers were taking their stations for the night under the arches of the Newport Terrace development, where they could shelter from unlikely rain, huddled in their filthy sleeping bags with cheap booze and lighter fuel. Tourists queued for cabs and increasing layers of traffic disgorged in belching streams from the underground car parks as the metaphorical strokes of midnight approached and the territory of night lengthened.

I elbowed my way through the crowds. I could still smell Caitleen all over me, inside my mouth, her delicate fragrance between my fingers, her absent touch still teasing the tip of my cock, the imprint of her intimacy delicately tattooed forever on the back projection of my mind.

The corridor leading to the subterranean, cavernous parking lot smelled of urine. As did the rickety lift.

I pressed. Level 3C.

The lift moved downwards.

The repulsive smell almost had me gagging.

Already I missed the clean fresh air of the night and the rush of the night people and their protective cocoon.

How could I kill Zeusmark and get away with it?

3.

More Songs About Sex and the Weather

She moved, a ballet of white skin in motion against the rough, hair-strewn backdrop of my fading tan—what still remained of a few days on a South Miami beach prior to a conference on international tax avoidance and financial safe havens a couple of months back.

My fingers were digging deep into her wetness as she adjusted her position to increase the pressure of my intrusion against her pubic bone. Under her breath, Caitleen mumbled a series of gentle obscenities to urge my violation further, stoking up her lust as my carefully trimmed nails now raked across the running secretions pouring like a flood from her inner walls. She twisted her whole body again, impaling herself on my hand in one savage thrust.

'Yes!' she shouted out loud. 'Yes, yes, yes!'

I watched how the pleasure now coursing through her changed her whole features. There was a triumphant smile running from the corner of her mouth to her sharp, prominent cheekbones, trailing hot pink colours across her face, her dark eyes now deep, cruel pools of selfish passion. The metamorphosis from shy, almost demure Irish lass to raging Amazon was almost complete, and she was so damn splendid as she rode the waves of her orgasm like a crazed queen of the elements, squeezing every drop of joy out of her cunt and my buried fingers, ruthlessly taking what she deserved, using me as a sheer object in her implacable pursuit.

My wrist was beginning to cramp, immobilised by the weight of her body, my fingers jammed inside her, deluged by the warmth of her juices, fearful of any sudden further movement lest I hurt her, scratch her.

'Yes!' she said again.

Her desire fulfilled.

For now.

It was another anonymous hotel room. A grey day. We had both concocted elaborate, complicated, hopefully foolproof alibis for our respective absences. The carpet was frayed, the curtains on the windows hung shapelessly and there were framed prints of cats all around the walls. The drabness of the decor only made us more desperate, as we searched for solutions.

'You'll have to do it,' Caitleen told me. 'I've known him so long, that I know I would flinch at the last moment, and make a mess of the whole thing.'

'I know,' I said to her. 'I don't mind doing it on my own.'

'Thanks.'

'But how?' I asked.

Killing a man. Easier said than done.

Books and the movies make it look too easy. Gun, knife, poison, car crash. Piece of cake.

First of all, Zeusmark always seemed to have some acolyte in tow whenever I met him. Markie or another well-trained thug. Either as protection or a sign that his shady partners liked to keep an eye on him at all time. Poison and strangling were out, impracticable, we decided. Tampering with his car was also a no-no; neither of us had even an idea where to start loosening a screw in the engine or the braking apparatus. And there was no guarantee such a crash would be fatal. Even with a weapon, I would be no match for a bodyguard, and even if I could somehow sneakily do the dastardly deed with the main man, how would I deal with the attendant gorilla? And then the choice of instrument entered the equation: a gun seemed fine, but it can be noisy—a silencer would help, we supposed. Mind you, we didn't have a clue where to obtain a gun. All our obvious contacts were already friends of Zeusmark, which was bound to raise suspicion. Too many questions might be asked. A knife on the other hand was quiet, a sharp kitchen implement that could be purchased in any supermarket, but it would prove messy, there was bound to be a struggle, and Zeusmark was a big man. It could all so easily go wrong. An explosion of some sort? Forget about it, we were only two London lovers, not terrorists, and the only bomb we knew was the itch in our pants that propelled us so strongly towards each other.

So: the weapon? The time and place? The problem of the second guy?

That was only the beginning of our dilemma.

Even if we managed to kill her husband, how would we get away with it afterwards?

There was the police after all. Caitleen would be an obvious suspect as his nearest and dearest and likely beneficiary of the money, not that cash was in any way one of our foremost preoccupations. So would I be, as one of his legitimate business contacts. There would be forensics, a likely lack of verifiable alibis. If we succeeded and were then seen together again, they would find the motivation handed to them on a platter.

Then there were his partners. If the police didn't come after us, we knew they would.

It was bloody scary once we began analysing the whole scam in the bright, logical light of day.

Caitleen raised herself, allowing me to pull my fingers from her volcanic warmth. I affectionately brought them to my nose, to smell her.

She smiled.

'Nice?' she asked.

'Wonderful,' I said, drunkenly bathing in the shocking fragrance of her intimacy.

She changed her position on the bed. In our unseemly haste for lust and instant gratification we hadn't even bothered pulling the covers off.

'Your turn,' Caitleen said, bending towards me, taking my half tumescent cock into her hands and lowering her scarlet lips to it. I lay down on my back and passively allowed her full access to my crotch, my eyes sinking into the swirling maelstrom of her abundant curls, a forest enveloping my rising penis as the heat of her mouth surrounded its tip and then swallowed it whole, forcing me to hold my breath back as the pleasure rose so fast inside me in response to her careful ministrations. Her tongue roamed up and down the stiffness of my stem, teasing the sensitive glans at regular intervals, while outside her long, wandering fingers gently scratched and cupped my balls and travelled a lingering and treacherous slow road to the opening of my anus. I knew that when she reached its aperture, I would no longer be able to hold on and would come like a geyser against the back of her throat. She kept on teasing my cock with her roaming tongue and her fingers still moved agonisingly closer. She knew it too.

'I don't know,' Caitleen said later as we relaxed momentarily, finally between the sheets, already counting down the minutes we had left for today. 'There seems to be no way that is safe, or even likely to work.'

'There is,' I said. I'd been thinking.

Somehow, while we had been making love earlier, I had briefly been distracted. There had been a strong gust of wind outside, and I had felt the draught that entered the room casually swim along the raised curve of my bare backside as I frantically tangled with Caitleen on the bed. It had incongruously made me conjure the ridiculousness of the image of the two of us fucking crazily and what we would look like to some fly on the wall. Or to some private detective engaged to discover our adultery. Caught in flagrante. I've always been told my mind works in devious ways.

'What?' she asked me.

'It's a long shot, but . . .' I ventured, 'it might just work.'

'Tell me,' she said, pouring herself another glass of white wine from the bottle we'd brought along. Neither of us smoked.

'We agree that doing it in public is too risky?'

'Yes.'

'So, it has to be inside?'

'Yes,' she agreed again.

'And where is he most likely to be, without a sidekick?'

She didn't ponder long.

'At home?'

'Absolutely,' I said.

'So?' she questioned.

My mind was in a whirl, as all the complicated pieces of the emerging idea gradually fell into place. Like a game of chess, as soon as one element slotted in I conjured the possible objections and countermanded them. Quickly, it all became clear to me. A devious, cunning plan. Straight out of a Gold Medal pulp paperback. Yes. This could be the way we freed ourselves from Zeusmark's shadow.

'It's not going to be easy,' I told her, cuddling up to her between the starched sheets of the hotel bed. 'Are you sure you want to go through with it?' I asked.

'If we don't,' Caitleen said, 'there's no point in us staying to-gether. Every time we meet, we're already taking awful risks. He already suspects something. We have no choice, Joe.'

'It's because he suspects something is up that it will work. And the fact he's actually asked me to help.'

And, improvising part of the way, still perfecting the details of the plan, I explained how we would kill her husband.

Caitleen listened quietly. Nodded regularly. Then suggested some changes to the scheme, further improvisations.

It all came together clearly in our muddled, frightened minds.

And, if luck was on our side, we would get away with it.

There were still many ifs-and-buts to factor in, and Caitleen's necessary participation in the scheme we had pieced together might entail some pretty awkward situations and risks, but in our shared madness we thought we had found a way to salvation.

*

'Two.'

'Two hundred?'

'No,' the bookseller smiled smugly. 'Two thousand dollars.'

'Oh,' Cornelia said, biting her lip slightly in surprise.

'I know it's a lot of money . . .'

'It is,' Cornelia interjected.

'But it's not often one comes across a copy in such impeccable condition, you know. Look at that dust-jacket. Not a tear or smudge. And no trace of yellowing. It's really what I would confidently term a book in perfect condition, genuinely as new. I would certainly catalogue it as such.'

'May I?'

The balding dealer handed Cornelia the rare book.

The much sought-after Doubleday edition of JG Ballard's *The Atrocity Exhibition*, most copies of which had been pulped pre-publication, due to the repressive political climate at the time.

She allowed her fingers to linger slowly over the plastic protective jacket, before carefully opening the volume to the title page. Even though the book was now several decades old, she thought she could smell the fresh odour of paper and ink, as if it were straight from the printers, that wonderful, characteristic smell of new books.

She had already read the book, of course. In the Research expanded large-format new edition. And owned the Jonathan Cape genuine British first. But this was such a rarity that Cornelia knew the moment she touched the book that she had to own it.

The dealer could see the lust in her eyes as she weighed the book in her hands and knew he had a sale; the glamorous young woman was hooked. But she had never purchased anything so expensive from the gallery before. An early John Irving first in almost fine, either *Setting Free the Bears* or *The Water Method Man*, he couldn't quite recall, and she had forked out three hundred bucks for a signed first of Crumley's *The Last Good Kiss*, but this was in another league for her.

Cornelia Irish intrigued him. Not that many women were such keen collectors of modern firsts. They usually preferred older stuff, Americana, leather bindings, saw it all as part of a grand design, a bit like decorating an apartment. But this dazzling redhead was different. She had until now mostly been purchasing from dealer's catalogues and her want-list had been referred to him by a friendly dealer out in Texas who knew he owned the Irving.

She gingerly handed the book back to him and stood there, pensive. He watched her closely in silence, observing the way her long straight hair fell to her shoulders, the alluring curve of her chest under the skin-tight X-Girl white T-shirt. She was visibly wearing no bra. Her nipples had even seemed to harden as she had briefly handled the book. The book dealer sighed. She was much too young for him. Unattainable.

She finally spoke.

'I haven't got access to that sort of money right now,' she told him. 'How long can you hold the book for me, Mr Hopley? I want it. Very much. I'll find the cash. Definitely.'

'Well,' he said. 'You're becoming a regular customer of the gallery's. I suppose I could hold it for up to ten days.'

'Make it two weeks, to be on the safe side. I have to make a number of calls, to get the money, but I'm confident I can. I won't let you down,' she said.

'I'll trust you, Miss Irish. I will,' Hopley said.

A few extra days made no difference to him. If she didn't raise the cash, there would still be time enough to list the item in the next mail-order catalogue. Since the film of *Crash,* the rank of Ballard collectors had grown even larger.

'Thank you,' she told him, her eyes lingering on the volume as he took it for safekeeping to the gallery's back room. 'I'll be back in under two weeks. I promise.'

Cornelia swept out of the dimly-lit gallery onto 52nd Street and faded into the Saturday crowds. She still didn't know how she was going to afford the book, but already felt gloriously happy at the prospect of owning it and adding it to her collection. She crossed Madison and reached the uptown Victoria's Secret. After all, it was only money. She sashayed into the lingerie shop in fine mood, knew she would treat herself to a few hundred dollars' worth of wonderfully silky, flowing underwear to celebrate. As for the cash she thought the book was going to cost her, she'd get the two thousand, no problem. A new model of bra caught her attention; she selected her size and went to the changing booth.

'Been shopping again?' the burly Russian bouncer at the club asked her as she settled at the familiar bar a few hours later.

'Yeah, Yevgeni, shopping and fucking, that's me!' Cornelia said.

'Isn't it your day off?' he remarked.

'Hmm,' she agreed. 'Just popped by to see if Clarence is in. Need to talk.' The barman shifted the usual glass of gin and orange towards her. 'Thanks,' she said.

'Yes, Clarence is in. Shall I call him?' Yevgeni suggested.

'No need,' Cornelia said, sliding off the stool and shuffling away past the stage where a short dark-haired girl who only did weekends was shaking her booty to the sound of Led Zeppelin. 'I'll surprise him.'

She reached the door labelled 'Manager' and knocked.

'Come in,' the voice inside said.

She pushed the door open.

Clarence was a barrel-shaped black guy who always wore a Panama hat, even indoors. Many of the dancers even speculated that he wore it to bed, or even to screw.

'Hi, how's my favourite upper-class stripper?' Clarence said, recognising her.

'Fine, as usual, Clarence,' Cornelia answered and settled herself on the couch that faced his paper-laden desk.

'This ain't one of your working days, is it? What can I do you for?' Clarence asked.

'I need a favour, Clarence,' Cornelia said, shifting restlessly on the leather couch which stuck uncomfortably to her jeans.

'How much?' Clarence asked, sadly accustomed to his girls always being short and requiring advances on their wages. He was a family man himself, just didn't want to know what they spent their cash on, drugs, pimps, flashy clothes, who cared? Cornelia, however, had always seemed different, ever since she had one day a couple of years ago walked off the street asking for a dancing job, to make ends meet while she completed her doctoral dissertation. That in itself made her unusual. At first, he hadn't believed her, but he had witnessed her filling pages and pages in her spidery handwriting between sets, as she completed her thesis (on the old 42nd Street and Times Square Burlesque days, no less). A genuine student being practical for once. Then she had obtained her diploma and left. But within a couple of months, she had returned to the club and the dancing. Things were boring out there, she had told him. This was as good a way as others to earn a living, she explained. Strange lady. But he had a weak spot for her. She was bright. And a good dancer, and pretty in an unspoilt way. She also had principles. Stuck to her strip act, and refused to do lap dances or private sessions, never turned tricks. For her, it appeared, this was a job, and she did it as a consummate professional.

Cornelia lowered her eyes.

'A lot.' She had never been short of cash before, Clarence remembered.

'How much, I said?' he repeated.

'Two thousand,' she blurted out, embarrassed.

'That is a lot,' he remarked.

'I know,' she agreed.

'I never ask why,' Clarence said. 'But this time, I will. What for?'

'A book.'

'No book is worth that much money,' Clarence protested.

'This one is,' Cornelia calmly answered.

'You must be kidding. At those prices, I wouldn't even dare read a book if it cost that much.'

'I don't intend to read it, Clarence. I already have. I just want to have it.'

'Whatever,' he sighed. 'A few hundred I could do, Cornelia, you know that. But there are house rules. I only manage the joint. I don't own it. There are people I report to. They wouldn't like it if I advanced you that much cash. I'm sorry, I can't,' he concluded.

'I see,' she said.

'Maybe you should bend your rules a bit, Cornelia. The men all like you. You're different from all the other girls. You could tout after your set for some lap or table dancing, maybe even some private sessions,' he suggested. 'With your class, you could raise the cash in just a couple of weeks, I'm sure. The word would spread quickly, they'd soon be rushing in from all parts for some extra time with you.'

'No, Clarence. No way. I display my body when I dance, but I won't have them jerking off over me in some dark backstage corner. I have no desire to cater to their cheap fantasies and frig myself under a lukewarm shower while they watch. I enjoy dancing; I happen to do it in the nude but I won't go further down that path. I spread my legs apart enough as it is. Sorry.'

'I understand,' he said.

'Surely you know some way to raise quick money, Clarence. Not involving sex, I mean. In your job, you must have some idea, contacts. I'll find a way, I know. But with your help, it could happen faster. Come on? Point me in the right direction, please?'

He shuffled some of the mountains of paper on his desk as he pondered. She watched him quietly.

'There are ways,' he finally said.

'How?' she asked.

She was undeniably bright, he thought, in no way a bimbette. Yes, she could conceivably fit the bill. And the initial commission for the introduction would certainly be welcome.

'Give me your telephone number.' He handed her a scrap of paper and a ballpoint pen.

She scribbled it down and passed it back to him.

'You'll be getting a call within a day or two, Cornelia. But, please, I don't wish to know what happens thereafter. Whatever you decide as a result, this conversation never took place, understood?'

'Fine with me,' she said. 'But, Clarence, no sex?'

'No sex,' he confirmed.

*

The phone call came quickly. She was trying on her brand-new Victoria's Secret silk underwear, parading proudly in front of her bedroom mirror, sketching possible new erotic dance steps for her act in her newly-acquired skimpy attire.

'Hello, Cornelia here.'

'Clarence said you would be waiting for my call,' the voice said. There was a faint hint of an Eastern European accent.

Cornelia calmly sat down.

'Yes, I was,' she answered.

She slipped the brassiere off, holding the phone in her other hand while she did so. Her nipples were tingling. She could feel a strange sense of excitement running across the surface of her bare flesh. Like the prelude to sex. Which she always found the most exciting part. The act itself always left her hungry, disappointed. Men were just too damn clumsy.

'I'm told you're willing to do certain . . . illegal things for cash?'

'Yes,' Cornelia said.

'I'm assured you can be discreet?'

'I can be.'

'Reliable?'

His dark voice literally caressed her.

'Yes.'

Cornelia allowed a finger to graze across her right nipple. She had never seen it grow so hard. Its sensitivity was incredible. She was turned on as seldom before. This was amazing, she thought. The sense of danger? Her whole body sang as she anticipated the crux of the transaction. She now sensed this was not going to a drug deal as she had earlier expected. Not that she wouldn't have been willing to become involved in one. She only held contempt for people who took drugs. They had no self control.

No, this was going to be different.

There was a prolonged silence at the other end of the telephone line as the unknown man presumably thought hard about the matter at hand.

'If you say no, we won't hold it against you. That will just be the end of our contact and you will forget all about it.'

Cornelia did not react.

The man understood her silence.

'You will be given a target and you will eliminate it. That's the deal in a nutshell. We will provide the necessary information and the means to do so. You will ask no questions. You will be well-paid. All our transactions will take place over the telephone. We will never meet. If you fail, you take the fall and we can provide no assistance...'

'I understand,' Cornelia said, interrupting him. 'I will,' she hastened to say.

She swallowed hard, her breath still beating an exhilarating light fandango. She could see the stain spreading at the front of the new underpants. She had come, just like that, a gushing nova of a climax, wildly aroused by the situation. Shit, this was better than dancing.

'Fine,' the man concluded. 'I shall contact you tomorrow with the details of your first job and we shall agree terms. Be there when I ring.'

He hung up.

'I will,' Cornelia said into the empty phone, her whole body still shaking with the shock of her uncommon orgasm and the enormity of what she had agreed to do for the unknown party at the other end.

Cold sweat now coated the upper part of her body. She shifted in her seat, acutely aware of the stickiness still spreading slowly between her legs. Finally, she stood up shakily, and headed straight for the bathroom where she adjusted the heat controls on the shower and plunged in to clean away the magnificence of her coming.

*

We agreed on our plan.

Next time around with Zeusmark, I would set matters in motion. Once this happened, there would be no turning back.

There wasn't long to wait.

I was summoned by him to meet up in a small West End drinking club he was a founder member of. Probably owned the joint, but had omitted to tell me, to avoid further taxation. I knew I wasn't the only accountant he was using. There was a small glitch in the transfer system to the Panama accounts. He needed me to sort it out. Local partners had encountered some minor difficulties and I had to arrange new proxy signatures for the accounts. Not traceable to him, as usual.

It was early morning. There were freshly baked croissants on the table and a piping hot mug of coffee. I helped myself and presented him the necessary documents, and the flow chart which I was proposing for the Panama laundering operation.

'That seems fine,' Zeusmark said. 'Your customary high standard of work. I'm pleased.' He signed the papers where the pencilled crosses required him to do so. He seldom questioned my advice when it came to financial matters.

'Thanks, Mr Zeusmark,' I replied, diffidently, seeing him somehow from a different perspective now that Caitleen and I had decided to kill him. It made him look smaller.

He watched me close the files and replace them inside my black leather briefcase, then asked:

'What we discussed last time . . . Any progress?'

'Slow, very slow,' I replied.

'But some news?'

I answered hesitantly. Putting the hook in.

Here we go.

'Well, I'm still not sure, you see. She's very careful, that is if she is actually involved with someone else. I don't think it's anyone at her office, anyway. I've made a useful contact there, and everything appears normal on that front. Just goes to the pub every Friday lunch hour with the other women in the editorial department, none of the men ever join them. Girls only.'

'So?'

'She does have a lot of early evening meetings, which my inside person can't account for. This week, I'm proposing to follow her myself when she leaves the building. Better to keep it discreet, at this stage, not involve any one else.'

'Good idea,' Zeusmark said.

I coughed to clear my throat.

'Tell me?'

'Yes?'

'If I do catch her with another guy, what would you do?'

'I'd go ballistic, that's what. I've trusted her all this time. I just can't imagine, don't want to imagine it. It's disgusting, just the idea of another man fucking my wife. On the one hand, I don't want to know, but on the other if it is happening, I can't allow it to continue.'

I pressed on.

'What would you do to the guy who's fucking her?'

'I'd kill him, of course. Probably with my own bare hands,' he added. 'I wouldn't wish to give any hired hand the damn pleasure. And if it's someone I know, I'd make it last ages, make the bastard suffer as he's never hurt before, believe me, I would.'

My stomach tightened.

'What about her? Caitleen?'

'I don't know,' he sighed. 'I really don't know. I do love her so badly. I suppose I'd probably beat her at first—it would be difficult to resist the initial rage—and then ask her for forgiveness, because it's after all my fault I haven't looked after her well enough. Not her fault. I would hope she would have the compassion to also forgive me as I try to live with the memory for the rest of my life, watching her every time in bed and knowing she gave herself freely to another man.'

'I see.' I shifted uneasily on my feet at the spectacle of his distress.

'Why do you ask?' he questioned me. 'What's it looking like?'

'Too early to say,' I said. 'But I think I'm getting closer.'

'At least, provide me with a hint,' Zeusmark begged.

'Not yet,' I said. 'It might just prove to be a false lead. I need another week or two to solidify my suspicions.'

'Do it, Joseph. Do it.'

4.

She Knows, She Knows

The plan was crazy. She knew it. I knew it too.

Something inside us screamed out wildly, pointing out the inadequacies, the heavy reliance on coincidence, the easy assumptions about human nature and the reaction of others we were banking on. But longing and despair provide the voluntary blind with a new, distorted view of things, and you ignore the danger signs and recklessly switch your speed into higher gear and boogie down that road to nowhere with wild abandon.

We should have known it wouldn't work, or at any rate not exactly the way we had planned, but neither of us could any longer bear the thought of separation, furtive sex and life on the never-never instalment plan, where happiness was only granted at the discretion of others, and just a word or a phone call could prove sufficient to break our fragile hearts in an instant.

Desperate thoughts; dangerous measures.

Markie the Roadie was going to be the instrument.

We both quite liked the guy. One of the less unlikeable associates of Zeusmark's. In effect just a minder during day hours. Neither of us believed that he was used by her husband for more than his powers of persuasion. His towering bulk was there to intimidate, to act as a warning against potential acts of anger from visitors unprepared for Zeusmark's customary ruthlessness. Markie always had a wry smile on his face as he stooped along, fetching drinks and cups of coffee and completing minor errands across South London at his boss' behest. A bit of a pussy really, although I was confident he could hold his own in a fight with the worst of thugs. I had once seen him briefly in action in a pub brawl, as he quickly silenced a bunch of drunken Queen's Park Rangers soccer fans who were threatening to draw us into a loud, arcane dispute that was quickly turning to violence. A well-aimed punch from Markie and a drawn-out stare was all that was needed to quieten the fighting velleities of the football supporters. And a discreet glimpse of the automatic in the holster under his armpit.

All Markie loved was to spend time at the bar, telling you all his great stories of life in the rock and roll fast lane during the good old days. Some of them were even quite funny.

Beyond the fifth or six pint of each late-night encounter, he invariably returned to his favourite souvenir, his pride and joy. The tale of how his penis had followed in the immediate footsteps of Jimmy Page's of Led Zeppelin, fucking the same groupie who had just a few hours earlier serviced the guitarist. How Markie was proud of the feat! He couldn't recall her name or even what she looked like, when I asked him, but still gloated at the thought that his cock had travelled the same orifice.

'Jimmy Page, man,' he drunkenly blurted out. 'Do you realise, Jimmy Page ...'

'Yeah, Markie.'

'And then me, man.'

And went on to tell you about this other chick who'd had Jimi Hendrix but refused him the same favour, after all he was just the drum roadie, 'but at least she gave me a blow job, to let her go backstage at the gig, man. I think it was in Brussels, or maybe it was Hamburg.'

'You do like your women, don't you, Markie?'

We were drinking at the Spice of Life by Cambridge Circus, where he'd brought me some files Zeusmark wanted checked.

'Yeah, they were scrubbers, but they were fun, man.' His eyes waxed nostalgic as he recalled his riotous past.

'Listen, Markie,' I said, conspiratorially lowering my voice. 'Can I tell you something in confidence?'

'Sure, man. What?' he inquired.

I looked around us at the sparse mid-afternoon crowd milling around the pub. No familiar faces. Anonymous incorporated.

'The boss, Zeusmark, you've met his wife, haven't you?'

'Yeah,' Markie answered. 'Mrs Caitleen. A damn foxy lady. Those long legs of hers, they could drive a man to sin, hey man?'

'They sure could,' I told him, and for once I was even telling the truth. Just thinking of Caitleen's legs could give me a raging hard-on, regardless of where I might be. Bewitched, that's what I was.

'He's a very lucky man, that woman's got class to spare, I tell you,' Markie continued.

'I agree,' I said.

He downed his pint, and nodded to the publican for another. My glass was still almost full.

'So, what about her?' he asked.

'Well . . . it's a bit delicate . . .' I deliberately hesitated.

'Come on, tell me,' he said, louder. Not a patient man.

'You know I see her sometimes, she occasionally has to sign some of the legal documents for the boss. She's a signatory for some of the offshore companies, for tax reasons. A bit complicated.'

'Yeah?' Markie said, already losing much of his interest, his eyes wandering around the pub, following a young woman sporting a bare midriff.

'Well, we talk. Of this and that. Small things really but, you know, last week, somehow the conversation moved curiously from movies and the weather to men, must have been discussing some actor in a film and . . .' I took a sip from my glass, interrupting my unsteady elaboration.

'So?' Markie asked.

'We began discussing what women really like about men. Distinctive features, attitudes, body shapes, all that . . . Sure was difficult to start discussing men's bums with the boss' wife, but she was the one who'd got us on to the subject. Turns out she likes tall men.'

'Makes sense,' Markie remarked. 'She's quite tall herself is Caitleen, for a woman.'

'Yes,' I agreed. Smiled at Markie in a knowing way. I could see he was now most interested in what I was going to say. Our calculations were going right, so far. 'She likes you, you know.'

'Yeah?' His eyes widened.

'Yes.'

'Oh man! Caitleen?'

'She made it quite clear to me. It was in fact her who suggested I let you know. She never has the opportunity to be alone with you, the boss is always around.'

'Yeah, I know,' Markie sighed. 'Damn, I'd sell my soul to the devil for a woman like her,' he admitted. I could literally see his grey cells churn in dizzying motion behind his eye balls as he attempted to digest the newly-provided information.

He quickly downed the fresh pint in one long gulp. My glass was still almost full.

'I have her private line at her job,' I said. 'Do you want it?'

Markie didn't give the matter too much thought.

'Gimme.'

I wrote down Caitleen's telephone number on a piece of paper torn from the corner of that day's *Independent*.

'Thanks, man,' Markie said. 'This stays strictly between the two of us.'

'Of course,' I remarked. Then: 'Do you plan to do something about it?'

'It's fucking dangerous,' he said. 'But you know me, rich pussy like that is worth all the risks in the world. And you're sure she suggested you approach me, man?'

'Sure, Markie,' I replied, 'you don't think I'd invent something like this?'

The beatific smile on his face said, 'Of course not.'

*

We'd burned our bridges. Caitleen had managed to free herself for a couple of hours later that day, without evoking further suspicion, and we had met up. She was having her period and we couldn't make love. It hadn't stopped us in the past, but we were being more cautious now.

'Christ, I want you so bad,' she said. There were dark lines under her eyes. She hadn't been sleeping well since we had agreed on our course of action. Neither had I. We hadn't compared nightmares. She was wearing a clinging white cotton top and the leather waistcoat Zeusmark had bought her for her recent birthday when he had insisted they do an inane musical on Shaftesbury Avenue followed by dinner in the hubbub of Brown's on St Martin's Lane. I had spent that same evening in my apartment, wrought by pain and jealousy that I could not be with her on her birthday. Her 30th.

'Me too.' I could feel the velvet softness of her breasts through the thin material and my lust was gently rampant.

She sighed. 'It's almost over,' she said, referring to her bothersome menstrual flow. 'Just another day, or two.'

'Good,' I said.

The sexual frustration was getting at us.

She lowered her hand below the belt of my trousers.

'Do you want me to?' she asked.

'No,' I replied, turning down her offer of fellatio. 'It's too much one-way,' I said.

'I don't mind,' Caitleen protested.

'No,' I insisted, kissing her gently on the cheek.

She straightened her posture on the sofa. 'Do you think he will phone?' she asked me.

'Absolutely,' I said. 'Markie took the bait, hook, line and sinker. I'd say tomorrow. He won't wait any longer.'

'I'm scared,' Caitleen said.

'So am I.'

But she was the one who would be taking the biggest risk in the next instalment of our ill-conceived conspiracy. While I could only be a distant, powerless bystander.

This is what we had concocted: Caitleen would respond positively to Markie's approach, they would arrange a discreet meeting at which she would tearfully complain to him about how deeply unhappy she was with Zeusmark and how attracted she felt to him. We knew the response of his cock would be more powerful than that of his brains. After much hesitation, she would promise to sleep with him, but invoke fear of her husband and possible retribution if they were discovered. This is where our jigsaw of a plan forked into two possibilities. Markie would be so touched by Caitleen's plight that he would agree to dispose of Zeusmark. If this happened, Caitleen and I could then flee abroad for a period, following a tip-off to the police which would put Markie away. Anything but foolproof: we weren't really sure if Markie was a potential killer, even under the influence of his gonads, and if he did follow the path we had assigned to him, he would not reveal Caitleen's influence to the crime investigation. We thought not. We hoped not. The other, dicier alternative was that Markie would want his pound of flesh before agreeing to further action and would insist on bedding Caitleen first. Should this arise, she would reluctantly agree and we would arrange an assignment at the right time and place and I would leak the details to Zeusmark. All hell would obviously break loose, but Caitleen would ensure Markie left his gun out of the bedroom, where I could get my hands on it. And use it. On both men, if need be, in the fracas of the pantomime in flagrante scene. We hadn't rationally thought beyond this.

'I just don't want him to touch you,' I had told Caitleen when she had engineered this part of the scheme.

'He won't,' she had reassured me. 'At the worst, I'll have to get down to my underwear before Zeusmark barges in to make it look credible. I'll see that Markie is well and duly stripped already for the requisite realism.'

'I still don't like the idea of the two of you in that room together,' I added.

'If the first option doesn't work, it's all we have left. I'll have to go through with it, Joe. There is no other alternative.'

'I suppose so.'

'We'll just have to time everything damn carefully, like clockwork. The time Markie and I arrive at the rented flat. When you tell Zeusmark about it. How long it will take him to get here. It can be done,' she said.

It would be done, but we all knew the best-laid plans of mice and adulterers obey a different set of rules altogether.

*

Zeusmark had earmarked a week for business at his Amsterdam studios, and Caitleen had to keep Markie on the boil, despite his insistence on this being a perfect occasion for them to meet up, while her husband was away. They had spoken several times on the phone already and she had led him on sufficiently to have whetted his sexual appetite, but it was still too early to raise the tricky subject of a dead spouse. This would have to await for his return. We also agreed that we could not take any further risks at this stage of the game and did not see each other. I yearned for her in unimaginable ways, had never thought her absence would hurt me so much. I busied myself with work, beginning the necessary preparations and paperwork for the days after.

Whichever scenario unfolded, we would need access to ready cash, probably new credit cards. I engineered all the necessary legal documents to leave the house we'd paid off to my wife, and painfully drafted my letter to her announcing my departure and that fact that I was leaving her financially secure. I didn't think it would come as too much of a surprise. I had been painfully distant for some time now, and our relationship had gradually cooled to a state of quiet indifference over the passing years as we manoeuvred separate paths through life. I don't think she'd ever forgiven me for settling down as an accountant. I'd once had artistic ambitions. We'd never had children. Which helped. All this took time, and occupied my mind.

Zeusmark finally returned.

He rang. He'd set up another two live studios to which all his worldwide computer subscribers could dictate their sexual fantasies down the line, and the women at the Dutch end would perform obediently, however extreme or bizarre the suggestion, which the camera would then digitally process and forward to the masturbating corners of the globe, while the clock ticked on and the ever-rising tariff of computer sex transferred the cash through a maze of credit card accounts until the monies were safely out of reach and in his porn empire's possession.

He explained triumphantly how his European associates had re-cruited a bunch of new women, mostly German and Hungarian, who could cater to the most extreme requirements. 'Ah, but it's still safe sex, isn't it, Joseph?' The Middle-East market was becoming so much more demanding, and its customers imaginative, he remarked.

'A bit of a steep increase in the immediate overhead, I suppose,' he told me, 'but I'm sure it will be a good investment. Probably real-ise a tenfold return in the long run.'

I allowed him to babble on. He finally got to the point.

'Joseph, let's meet next Tuesday. I want to move some of the Jersey assets to the Caymans. As you suggested last year. I think it's time to do it, the funds will sit safer there. I'd also like to hear of any developments in the other matter.'

Tuesday it was, then.

I arranged the weekly rental of the small Mayfair flat we had agreed on. Did it in Zeusmark's name, and with his money. It would help muddy any later investigation. The letting agency was quite familiar with these short-term rentals. It could all be discreetly trans-acted over the telephone. Yes, the key would be left with the care-taker. Mrs Zeusmark would pick it up when required.

Caitleen was still at her office.

'He's back.'

'I know, he brought me back the usual perfume from Schipol duty-free.'

'It's Tuesday.'

'Fine. What time are you seeing him?'

'Three p.m.'

'I'll try and get Markie to the Mayfair place for five.'

'OK.'

'Five, Joe, for God's sake, don't be late.'

'I won't,' I said. 'Anyway, it might not come to that. After your sad tale of sorrows, Markie might agree to go ahead with it and we won't have to go through the whole contrived farce.'

'And if he does, I'll call you on the mobile to cancel the Shepherd Market visit, as we agreed.'

We'd rehearsed the careful timing of the events several times: the come-on to Markie, the request, the time they would reach the flat, when I would advise Zeusmark that his wife was up to no good, the time it would take for him to reach the Mayfair area from South London, how long she would have to hold Markie's advances at bay.

Clockwork. Just like movie heists. Where everything can still go wrong, with a vengeance.

She would call me the next day if Markie couldn't make the Tuesday.

She didn't.

All set, then.

*

I kept on looking nervously at my watch. An expensive Tag Heuer sports model I'd acquired on the cheap in Hong Kong. The cellophane in my jacket pocket had remained forcefully silent all afternoon. By now, I knew, Caitleen and Markie had been talking for a couple of hours and would be soon leaving for the flat. Zeusmark spoke.

'What's the matter, Joseph? You look uncomfortable. I hope it's not those oysters we had for lunch? My digestive system is a bit on the slow side: if you're suffering now, it's bound to hit me soon. Think it's the oysters?'

'No,' I said. 'I don't think so.' Glanced again at the time.

'Good, I hate having an upset stomach. You lose all dignity when you have the runs. Smells awfully bad, too,' he chuckled.

I looked up from the deskful of legal documents.

'Where's Markie?' I asked him.

'Had to take the day off. Some family thing, he said,' Zeusmark answered.

'I see.'

My throat felt all dry now.

'Are you sure you're OK?' he inquired.

'Yes. But it's ... awkward, Mr Zeusmark,' I said tentatively. 'It's just that you're not going to like what I have to tell you.'

'Shit,' he said. 'Not Caitleen?'

'Yes.'

'I was dreading this. Tell me. You have to.'

'I found out. You were right. She is seeing another guy.'

'Who?'

'It's Markie.'

The colour drained away from his face and a look of incredulity and pain engulfed him.

'I can't believe it,' he said, a tear welling up in the corner of one eye. 'Do you have proof of this?'

'I'm afraid so.'

'So?'

'They're together now. A block of flats in Shepherd Market in Mayfair.'

He picked up his mobile phone from the desk and dialled Caitleen's office. They confirmed she had taken the afternoon off. Zeusmark regained his composure and rose from his chair.

'Now, you say?'

'I'm afraid so.'

'You know the address?'

'Yes.'

His jaw tightened and his his features took on a steely, angry determination as he moved for the door.

'Come on, Joseph, take me there. We'll take your car,' he said, noticing my red BMW parked right outside the dingy club where we conducted our business. 'You drive.'

The traffic was light and very soon we were crossing the river over Vauxhall Bridge. He hadn't said a word since we had driven off. But I could feel his rage rise as we neared the flat.

He finally snapped out of his silence as we were briefly held up by a red light at the junction between Pall Mall and Lower Regent Street.

'Joseph?'

'Yes?'

'I know this is not the sort of business you usually get involved in. But whatever you see, whatever happens over there must remain a secret forever. No one else must know. Swear.'

I agreed and roared off as the green light flashed on.

We parked on a double yellow line near the Curzon, which was the nearest we could get with the car. Zeusmark hurried on, while I struggled to keep up with him. I had told him I had made arrangements with the caretaker for the door to the love nest to stay unlocked. Caitleen and I had planned this. Having the front door kicked in would bring unnecessary attention to the proceedings. And for her to demand that Markie leave his gun on the telephone table by the door before she allowed him to enter the bedroom. Not an unreasonable demand for her peace of mind if he wanted to screw her.

'Stay here,' Zeusmark ordered as we reached the second floor landing, and he gingerly approached the flat's thick wooden door. His hand softly alighted on the door knob and turned. It gave and he pushed the door quietly open. He entered, the bulky horizon of his back obscuring the inside of the apartment from me as he tiptoed forward, getting his bearings. I ignored his request and followed him in.

Initially, there was silence, just the sound of our heavy breathing as we had run up the stairs, too impatient to wait for the lift. Muted voices reached us from the room at the end of the hallway.

The bedroom, I knew.

As Zeusmark walked towards the door, I saw him move a hand to his coat pocket and experienced a flash of panic. I hadn't expected him to be armed. My nerve ends tingled with awful dread at the prospect of him angrily wishing to take his revenge on Caitleen. And realised I'd forgotten to check the telephone table for Markie's gun. I frantically looked back towards the front door, adrenalin flooding my system as I noticed the dark shape of the weapon where it should have been all along.

With the tip of his black suede brogue, Zeusmark pushed the door open and we both gasped in disbelief.

Caitleen was on her knees in front of the bed, quite naked, her clothing carefully draped over the blue bed cover. The heavy brocade curtains of the bedroom were drawn but the light of day still filtered through. Markie stood facing her, head held back, eyes closed, his trousers and underpants unceremoniously rolled down to his ankles, sporting a dark, monstrous erection.

Which she was taking into her mouth, sucking methodically on his cock until her cheeks bulged and still only half of his length breached her lips' frontiers.

It was like taking a boxer's punch straight in my gut. The pain inside me was immediate.

No doubt Zeusmark was experiencing a similar feeling. Did it hurt him as much, I wondered?

Seeing this woman we shared in this humiliating posture.

Then it all happened so quickly.

Zeusmark roared like a wounded beast. I don't even know whether he called out Caitleen's or Markie's name, reeling as I was from the shock.

Caitleen's eyes darted round as she almost spat Markie's penis out of her mouth and gazed at the two of us, eyes round with fear.

Zeusmark rushed forward like an animal.

Markie jumped with surprise. I thought for a moment as he bent over quickly that he was ashamed of being caught with his jeans down and was desperately attempting to pull them up to cover his manhood, but he was in fact reaching for his left boot and pulled out a sharp knife.

He straightened up just as Zeusmark launched his bulk at him.

And impaled himself on the extended blade of the knife Markie was holding ahead of him in an instinctive bid for protection.

Caitleen screamed, still on her knees on the floor.

I rushed back into the hallway and grabbed the gun.

Markie just stood there, arm extended, Zeusmark's bulk surrounding him, as Caitleen's husband quivered frantically and the blade inside him kept on churning away at his innards. Everything was happening in slow motion.

There were gurgling, unintelligible sounds coming from Zeusmark's mouth. Blood also. Markie took one step backwards, pulling the knife from Zeusmark's stomach. His blade-wielding arm was soaked in his boss' blood and dark red drops pearled down to the floor, splashing his still half-erect cock in their fall. No longer supported by his henchman, Zeusmark sank slowly to the floor, clutching his gut, a look of utter serenity now spreading across his whitening features.

Caitleen was crying.

Zeusmark's eyes closed, as his body spread itself over the floor at Markie's leather-booted feet.

Markie looked around at me, total incomprehension on his face. His eyes wildly asked me, 'Why?'

I didn't know what to say.

To either of them.

Slowly, it appears, some pieces began to fit in Markie's brain and the look on his face changed as he guessed he had been set up.

'It was you. Wasn't it? Who set this up?' he haltingly asked me.

Caitleen had now risen from the floor. A speck of blood bloomed like a small rose near her right nipple.

She carefully watched the two of us as we grappled with our indecision.

Markie briefly looked away from me and gazed down at his cock.

'Shoot him! Shoot him now!' Caitleen shouted at me.

I levelled the gun and pulled the trigger. I'd never shot one before. The recoil gave my shoulder a sharp shock. Markie fell to the ground.

*

'He wanted sex straight away, Joe. I was playing for time, playing hard to get without getting him angry. First, he had me strip. He didn't even touch me, I swear. Then, he wanted a blow-job. I just couldn't delay him any longer, you understand.'

'I know,' I sadly said, as she dressed.

The two bodies lay at our feet in the Mayfair flat.

'It could have been worse, Joe. At least you got here before it did,' Caitleen insisted.

Worse? Just two dead men on our hands. And the image of Caitleen and Markie joined so obscenely, carved deeply in the permanent screen of my mind.

'At least we can be together now,' I said.

'I know, I know,' Caitleen said.

5.

Words Unsaid

'What now?' I asked Caitleen. She had dressed, freshened up and looked radiant again, as if nothing untoward had happened. Late afternoon in Central London. The rental flat smelled of sex, blood and fear. Or maybe that was our imagination.

As clumsily as we had planned for Zeusmark's elimination, this was not what we had anticipated. The two bodies on the floor appeared to be impossibly growing in bulk with every passing minute as both of us silently pondered their unwelcome presence and the consequences of the bloody scene that now confronted us.

'You were going to say?'

'Nothing,' she said.

A heavy silence surrounded us. I watched Caitleen sitting on a chair, thinking. She was wearing one of my favourite dresses, a swirling thin confection of multi-coloured whirlpools that went down all the way to her ankles, with a wide slit on each side that ran up to mid-thigh, where you could catch a fleeting glimpse of the stocking top and the metal clip of the suspender-belt strap. Her seduction outfit.

Markie and her.

I tried to banish the memory from my mind. But it was anything but easy.

'We could just leave the bodies here. Think of where we might have left fingerprints and dust them off,' she suggested. 'After all, you did rent the place in his name. They'll think it's just some gang reckoning, something to do with his business. We wouldn't be implicated, would we?'

'It wouldn't work,' I pointed out to her. 'The caretaker saw you pick up the keys. He knows a Mrs Zeusmark was supposed to get them. That's the arrangement I'd made with the agency.'

'Shit! You're right.'

She crossed her legs, and a flash of white skin peered above the darker line of her stocking top. My heart jumped the proverbial beat. Just the effect she had on me. Even at the wrong time and in the wrong place.

'I love you, Caitleen,' I told her. 'This whole mess doesn't change anything about it. Not a damn thing.'

'Me too, Joe,' she responded, that usual gut-wrenching look of helplessness flooding her eyes as she looked over at me.

I melted inside.

'So there's no other alternative, is there?' she said.

'No,' I agreed with her. 'We have to get rid of the bodies.'

We'd seen all the movies. It would be tough and dirty but it seemed there was no other way out of the predicament. I pulled the heavy curtains an inch or two apart and peered outside onto Shepherd Market.

'It should be dark in an hour or so,' I said.

Caitleen rose, moved closer and kissed me gently, seeking tenderness and reassurance. The warmth of her body infected me immediately and I pulled her tighter against me, my lips hunting for her desire, furiously battling the earlier images still polluting my thoughts. I had to have her, to know her again. It had become a matter of dire urgency.

She sensed it too, as our embrace grew stronger and our bodies responded with the same madness that always dominated our lust for each other.

'Not here,' Caitleen mumbled quickly, indicating the bodies on the floor as our hands went a-roving indiscriminately.

'Yes,' I acquiesced. 'I agree.'

We separated and hustled out of the room, into the narrow hallway with its framed prints of English village fairs and barking hounds, saw the door to the kitchen and rushed through.

We made love wildly on the stripped-pine kitchen table. Caitleen bent forward with her breasts mashing against the wood as I savagely entered her from behind, her knickers just stretched aside enough to ease my entry, still wearing her fuck-me stockings and encouraging every one of my forward thrusts with verbal obscenities and cries of lust.

I assaulted her inner walls with undisguised fury, digging my manhood through every successive fold of delicate mucous flesh with sheer anger in a bid to make her totally mine again, eagerly watching the to and fro of my cock flowing past her puffy lips and the alternate contraction and dilation of her arsehole as I proceeded. I couldn't contain the intensity of the lust very long.

I was hard again barely minutes after coming like a torrent inside her. Caitleen straightened up, my come dripping down across her thighs, and pushed the table away towards the wall to clear space on the tiled floor, pulled me back, skilfully handled my cock and, spread out on her back, limbs akimbo, her wet cunt gaping, guided me back inside her, her pelvis convulsively seizing forward to meet my advance.

We screwed on, waiting for the darkness to set, prisoners of an X-rated James M. Cain movie, while in the other room rigor mortis no doubt set in. We were excited, spurred on by the feel, the acid proximity of death, by the fact we had now achieved the freedom we had sought so badly. Don't let anyone ever tell you that desperation is not the best friend of lust.

Finally, our physical endurance and soreness inevitably brought the fleshy carnival to an end, and we tiredly gathered together the strewn pieces of clothing we had spread across the kitchen, and dressed again. Caitleen's stockings were generously laddered and my shirt was missing a button. The love bites and scratches from our disorderly coupling, however, were hidden from sight.

The smell in the room where the bodies were was now stronger. We carefully rolled them out to the hallway. Fortunately, there wasn't much blood on the carpet. Just isolated spots, manageable stains which Caitleen attempted to reduce to the size of faded islands, to mere colour variations in the fabric of the shag pile carpet, with the help of assorted powders and chemicals stored in the flat's well-equipped toilet cupboard.

We agreed on our scenario. We'd carry each man down to the car, which I would move nearer to the block of flats' main entrance. The caretaker didn't work nights, that I knew. Should we alight on anyone on the stairs, we'd just laugh of our companion's drunken state and hope this would pass muster. The same in the street. We would do this one at a time. Couldn't run the risk of a seemingly unconscious person in the back seat attracting attention in the parked car as we were in the process of bringing the second body down from the flat. In between the conveying of the respective bodies, we would lock the flat. Zeusmark would be first. He was the heaviest. Caitleen took the wallet from his inside jacket pocket and searched the garment for other possible identification. Left the coins and assorted keys. We had decided that we would dispose of them in different places, hoping to make it more difficult for the likely investigation to make an immediate connection between them. Everything made sense to us in an absurd sort of way, running as we now were on automatic pilot.

'I'd slip a towel around his stomach, stuff something there or We'll get blood stains all over us,' I pointed out, as we readied for the first journey of disposal across London.

*

Cornelia had written everything down as she had been instructed, carefully memorised the modus operandi and then torn up the sheet of paper into a dozen pieces and flushed them down the toilet, observing the scraps drowning in the whirlpool motion of the water.

She had settled on her student garb for today. White jeans, a black halter top with cutaway sleeves and her old leather sandals. A perfect picture of innocence, she thought mischievously. She lived in a small condo close to Varick Street in the Village and blended in with the passing crowds as she hit the sunny sidewalk.

She walked across 6th Avenue and took the E line in the uptown direction near 14th Street. The pungent summer smells of the subway assaulted her as she waited for the incoming roar of the train, standing between two old black women trailing shopping bags stretched to bursting point.

Cornelia exited the subway system one stop beyond 42nd Street, quickly found her bearings again and walked over to Seventh Avenue and the partly derelict stretch full of shuttered burlesque theatres, sex shops and dubiously-lit delicatessens. Tourists from the nearby row of hotels paraded up and down on both sides of the street, middle-aged men in carefully casual attire and cameras, youngsters with backpacks and well-worn trainers, Japanese in thick groups seeking comfort in numbers.

She quickly spotted the place. A drab marquee advertising 'The Masquerade Sex Emporium'. Flickering neon lights in the window promised NUDE, LIVE DANCERS and 25 cents BOOTHS and other dubious delights. Cornelia smiled. Compared to this, the clubs where she danced were the upper, respectable end of the market. She jaywalked across the empty avenue. A Pakistani attendant gave her the once-over as she entered the sex shop.

Cornelia flashed her teeth at him and asked for the gay booths.

The man looked at her with disapproval.

'Richard sent me,' she added, and the frown disappeared from his face and he pointed to the back and the darker recesses of the joint.

A few men were hanging around, who all blushed when they saw her approach the section where they had been browsing the back covers of the video boxes displaying images of impossibly hung, buffed hunks, and quietly eying each other with undisguised interest. They carefully looked away as she marched past them and found a free compartment in the network of booths surrounding the central boxed-in area of the male peepshow.

Cornelia pushed the bolt down behind her and settled into the hard plastic chair that faced the opening rectangle in the thin wall. She foraged in her handbag and found she was clean out of quarters. She pulled out a dollar bill and fed it to the slot in the partition. As the apparatus swallowed the bill, the mechanism operated and the window to the peepshow opened, a lighted electronic display near the money mouth beginning to count down from 240, as the time she had bought ticked off.

Cornelia looked up. Under the cruel harsh lighting, two young men danced with slow abandon to a scratchy 60s disco tune. Both were nude. Slim. Oiled all over. Great, tight butts, she noticed. She could see the faces of staring men at the other raised windows, and watched their faces with fascination as the windows went up and down around the dance floor with ballet-like precision. She imagined most of them were masturbating. Casually realised she'd never actually witnessed a man masturbate. Must be interesting, she reckoned. The display flashed 167. Then, within an instant, the count was already down to 152.

She rapped on the glass partition to catch the attention of one of the nude dancers. He moved nearer, his half-tumescent, uncircumcised cock flopping right in front of her eyes, every pulsing vein on display an inch or so away from her. Without looking down at her, he began to caress himself, smoothing the oil he was coated in up and down his growing stem. Behind him, Cornelia noticed the other dancer approach a window at the opposite end, lower his hand to disable the window's descent mechanism, and grab a couple of bills. Probably tens, she guessed and observed him lower his pelvis and insert his member through the opening. Cornelia gulped. This sure was the other side of life . . .

The count was down to 78 on the lighted display. She scraped her nails against the partition. Her dancer finally acknowledged her and assuming hers was going to be the customary request and exchange of money, neutralised and opened the rectangular window that separated them. His hand approached the opening.

'Yeah?' he asked.

'Richard sent me. Something for me to pick up,' Cornelia said.

The nude dancer stepped back slightly, visibly surprised by the sound of a woman's voice.

He retreated quickly to the back of the dance area and picked up a large brown envelope which had been concealed by the clothing he had shed. Still not saying a word, he passed it over to Cornelia. She took hold of it. His cock was definitely smaller now, she noticed.

'Go. Now,' he nervously ordered her.

Cornelia promptly stuffed the envelope in her bag and left the store, leaving the gay sex workers to their rather interesting life.

*

The hit was a middle-aged Latino businessman. The file she was given provided no explanation as to what he might have done wrong. Some things she was not supposed to know. But everything else was there: where he lived, where he worked, his telephone, fax, office and e-mail coordinates, his tastes in women—she was certainly the right type, they had made certain of that—food and clothes, his likely itinerary for the next two weeks, where he shopped, where he liked to entertain. A man's whole life seemingly distilled into a three-page dossier. 'Does not customarily carry weapons' she noted with some comfort.

The final page was succinct: '5000 dollars on execution. Straight to your bank account'.

If they could find out so much about a man, they must know where she banked.

In addition to the dossier, there was also a gun in the envelope, a dainty small calibre of East German manufacture, the sort of thing a woman could conceivably carry as protection in her handbag. The registration numbers had been carefully filed away and a label attached to the gun reminded her to dispose of the weapon after the job.

All very professional, Cornelia considered.

She took a last bite of the hard, juicy apple she had taken from the fridge, collected her thoughts and sat herself down by the telephone. Dialled carefully. This was not the time to get a wrong number.

'Hola,' the deeply-accented voice at the other end of the line said.

'Mr Vargas?'

'Yes? Who is this?'

'I hope I'm not disturbing you?' She peered at the notes she had studiously been taking while going through his dossier. 'My name is Holly. Holly De la Tour. I'm a friend of Michael Perkins at the Dark Matters Company. He suggested I might call you for some advice.'

'Certainly, Miss De la Tour.'

'Holly, call me Holly,' Cornelia insisted.

She breathlessly explained to Vargas the vague nature of the assistance she required. The dossier had indicated that Perkins and his company were a discreet front for a highly-specialised escort service the businessman occasionally used. Vargas calmly took the bait. He asked her to describe herself. Cornelia didn't even have to lie.

They agreed to meet the following evening in the bar of the Royalton Hotel on 44th Street. Cornelia was obliged to phone Clarence and excuse herself from dancing that evening. He was far from pleased.

'It's because of that other one-off job you put my way,' she explained to him.

'I see,' he said. That was enough for him.

Cornelia sat back and considered.

Ah! What does the girl about town wear for an assassination?

Within minutes half the contents of her wardrobe were laid out over her futon and the bedroom rug as she sought the right outfit for the job at hand. Something seductive? Yes, that was her way in. Something colourful? No, it would draw too much attention to itself. So: discretion combined with sexiness. 'Hmmm...' she murmured to herself. She could manage that. And smiled.

As long as you had the right attitude, this could be great fun.

By the next day, Cornelia had made her mind up.

Her power suit. A warm, pinstriped grey trouser suit, with a high waistline that emphasised her long, elegant legs. And her tallest set of heels. The ones that forced her to walk along with her breasts aggressively thrust forward to maintain the right equilibrium. And under the jacket, she decided not even to wear a blouse or a shirt or a bra. The two buttons would barely keep the folds of the soft material together, revealing the deepness of her cleavage and the appetising curves of her breasts. Very alluring.

And her new Victoria's Secret silk underwear. Of course. If you've bought them, flaunt them, she smiled quietly.

A long, warm bubble bath followed, singing along, no doubt out of tune, to a Leonard Cohen song of woe and wonder. She rose, dripping, and admired her wet, glistening body in the full-length mirror. This was flesh that could drive men crazy, she knew, content with the knowledge of the power she could wield over men, as only a dancer could be.

She dried herself and sprayed talcum powder across her acres of pale skin.

Followed by a gentle dab of Calvin Klein's Obsession. She loved the name of the perfume as much as its fragrance.

She moved to the apartment's main room where she had carefully draped her designated uniform across the couch, and slipped into it like a second skin. Cornelia was ready.

*

'Very elegant,' Vargas agreed as he hailed a bartender to order the dry Martini Cornelia had requested.

A slim man, in a dark blue blazer with gold buttons and studiously washed-out jeans, with a crease like a razor blade. Silver hair slicked back. An annoying trimmed moustache. He rose to admire her. Very tight jeans. Which he filled in a very inviting way. A nice bulge, Cornelia noticed. She allowed him to indulge in the necessary small talk. He inquired about her price for the night. Cornelia didn't have a clue what the going tariff was and acted all coy, indicating that she did not wish to discuss money beforehand. This was fine by him. She could see how he was hypnotised by the gap in her jacket, which gaped every time she moved her arm to fetch her glass on the bar. Nice guy, a bit oily though, she thought as he waited for her to finish her drink.

'I have booked a room upstairs, Miss De la Tour,' Vargas said.

'How convenient,' Cornelia smiled.

'Shall we?'

'Why not?' she agreed.

The old tuxedoed bartender who had been serving them had been rushed off his feet, and had barely even looked at her. There were a lot of other classy, expensive women in the Plaza bar. He was unlikely to remember her, she knew. This was all too easy.

As the pencil-thin Latino businessman led the way to the hotel elevators, and Cornelia's gaze was transfixed by his narrow backside, she realised it had been a long time since she'd had a man. And wasn't this the best way? A one-off, just a pleasant bit of fun with no emotional commitment or later come-back. Consider it a parting gift. He wouldn't even have to pay her; that would have been quite unfair after all when he was part of the price coming her way. Yes, Mr Vargas, I will partake, Cornelia decided.

She could always kill him in the morning.

Pity about missing breakfast, though. But an order for two and room service delivery was taking just a bit too much of a risk.

As the elevator doors closed, Cornelia extended one hand and patted Vargas' tightly-jeaned backside.

'Holly!' he exclaimed, a wicked grin of expectation spreading across his thick lips. 'That's quite bold of you, but I like it.'

'Oh, I'm just an impulsive kind of girl,' Cornelia said.

The room beckoned.

*

The car slithered its way through the sparse night traffic as we approached the North Circular junction at the Crooked Billet. We had decided to dispose of her husband's body by the small pond I remembered from my childhood, on the outskirts of Epping Forest. I don't know why I chose the place. It suddenly came to me as I was scrambling for resting places. Maybe it was symbolically closing the circle on the life I now knew I was leaving behind. Some subconscious form of resolution. Markie was destined for the river, later, by the flood barriers, we had agreed. For the last half-hour, as I carefully manoeuvred my way out of the town centre, driving with utmost care and courtesy to avoid attention, Caitleen hadn't whispered a single word. She sat beside me, hands between her clasped knees, lost in contemplation, oblivious of the outside lights drifting by in balletic motion. The presence of Zeusmark's inert body on the back seat grew heavier and heavier on my mind as the time went by.

What could she be thinking of? Of the times when she had been happy with him? There must have been some. Of the way he would touch her and cause her to emote whether she wished to or not? As a man, I knew he had. Frequently. Before me. Of the first time she had known him, touched him, kissed him, made love with him? No, it wasn't Caitleen who was thinking of all this, it was me, I knew.

And the dark scarlet of her lips devouring Markie's prominent cock.

'What are you thinking of?' I asked her.

'Nothing,' she answered.

'Really?'

'Yes,' Caitleen said. 'My mind is a complete blank. That's the way I want it to be right now, Joe.'

And I thought I knew why.

It was me who had made demands, who had sought her exclusivity. My jealousy, my possessiveness. Who had pushed her too far. Convincing her the plan we had devised was the only available solution to my longing. Pushed her into the sheer obscenity of Markie's seduction. To free her, I had become her pimp. And the jealousy was now spreading like a rotten apple from the very core of my stomach, eating away at my sanity.

Disposing of bodies, I could cope with. It was something mechanical, instinctive. But the feeling inside I knew would never fade.

No more cars around. A deeper form of darkness. The ill-lit facade of Whipps Cross Hospital. The forest. Skeletal trees peering out of the night. A pocked half-moon above us as I parked, lights switched off. The pond was barely fifty yards from the road.

'I'll take him,' I told her. 'You can stay in the car.'

'Are you sure?'

'Yes. I'll manage. Don't worry.'

I felt like asking her whether she had any last words for him, this man she had spent the last ten years with. But I tactfully remained silent as I pulled his heavy frame from the back of my car.

My back hurt as I part-carried, part-dragged him along the ground. I would have to remember to disguise the track in the sparse grass on my way back to the car. Make things less obvious. I was soon out of breath. At last I reached the edge of the rather shallow water and rolled Zeusmark into it. The body floated briefly on the surface and then slowly sank. You could vaguely see its thick outline as it settled at the bottom of the pond. I knew it would eventually be found. I wasn't even trying to hide it. In those sort of circumstances, your thought processes abandon all apparent logic. I was sure that, once discovered, even with the lack of documents, he would promptly be identified. He was after all a reasonably prominent businessman, even if only a minority of his acquaintances were aware of the criminal side of his affairs.

He was dead. That was all that mattered right now.

I walked back to the car.

Caitleen sat crying.

'Are you alright?'

She looked up at me and asked 'He's gone?'

'Yes.'

'I'll be fine,' she said. 'Let's do the other one.'

The drive back to Mayfair was another silent epic. Markie was where we had left him. The journey down the stairs, supporting his lanky frame, went like clockwork. I'd locked the rental flat and placed the key under the caretaker's door. It was one of those no-questions-asked places. The car. The road again.

Mist was rising from the Thames as morning neared.

Markie sank faster.

PART TWO

DYING IN THE SHADOW
OF THE SHADOWS

6.

I Was a Letter with the Seal Unbroken

It was now autumn and the Seine dragged its way between the Paris banks with sluggish apathy. The rain fell down, curtaining the city in a grey, dirty shroud. A Derek Raymond sort of afternoon. We were seeking shelter from the weather and Caitleen suggested we take refuge in a small club on the Left Bank and have a coffee, a drink, anything to get away from the drizzle. I agreed.

We'd been here three months or so already.

A few hours on Eurostar, then disgorged with the tourists and backpackers into the cavernous hall of the Gare du Nord. Queuing in the bowels of the station for a cab and the ride across town, under the Louvre portals, across the river and, finally, a small St Germain des Prés hotel I had booked by phone from London the day before. Carrying two suitcases with all the belongings we had managed to squeeze in. What was left of our life. The beginning of a new one, we hoped. Away from our earlier married incarnations, far from the bodies we had consigned to water. But the nightmares had followed us and we fought to banish them.

Later, we had managed to rent a small apartment in the rue St Denis, a stone's throw from my beloved Left Bank. The contract was for three months. Expensive. Starting again, we soon realised, wasn't cheap. I didn't know how long the money I'd managed to transfer over would last at this rate. Not as long as I had hoped, at any rate. Caitleen didn't like to cook. Vegetable soup was her forte, but didn't afford much in the way of variety. So we ate out most evenings. One of the joys of Paris. There were so many basics we had to acquire. The place was sparsely furnished and the bed provided was on that

uncomfortable borderline between antique and just damn old. Caitleen soon decreed it definitely had to go.

The replacement we chose cost almost a thousand pounds, once
mattress, headrest, clean sheets, covers and other trimmings were
thrown in. Well, a bed was the one thing we weren't going to skimp
on, were we, in our heightened state of carnal excitement at being
able to fuck at all hours of the day and not worry about trains back
to suburbia or tell-tale signs of lust tattooed across the guilty panorama of our bodies?

And flowers. Caitleen needed fresh flowers in every corner of the
small flat. Said that she needed cheering up so badly. How could I
say no?

And being semi-illegal, we had to pay full price for medicine.
And her pills. No way did she even want to run the risk of getting
pregnant. And we hated to practice safe sex.

Between the lovemaking marathons, the unending walks separating our embraces punctuated by bar stops, the movies, the books
we piled up by the bed, you could almost hear our financial clock
ticking away in overdrive.

Does anyone live happily ever after?

Once they've disposed of the big bad wolf.

I was beginning to worry.

But it was wet that day and the rain was sneakily making its way
through to my bones. My knee hurt; not a touch of arthritis at my
age, I hoped. Any bar light was welcome.

There was the sound of jazz coming from the cellar and a narrow
stairway leading down.

'Looks nice,' Caitleen said, rolling up her umbrella. 'Great music.
Love it, just great. Reminds me a bit of my university days.'

'Hmm . . .' I mumbled. 'I'd never been a great jazz fan. I'd grown
up with the beat of rock 'n' roll and mournful country tunes. This
was an area of life together where Caitleen and I had agreed to dis-
agree.

We circled our way down into the place's bowels and emerged
into a high-ceilinged patio-like enclosure. A stark stone floor dance
area with a gaudily-lit bar on one side, and a currently empty band-
stand on the other. A half-dozen or so guys were crowded around a
few tables, with a couple of women and their male companions
perched on stalls at the bar, where a lugubrious stick of a man wearing a dusty black beret stood tending drinks. He looked up at us as
we entered.

'C'est un club privé,' he said, with a strong Brit accent tempering his French tone.

'Can we join?' I asked, in English.

A smile lit up his gaunt face.

'Dear boy, you should have said,' he beamed. 'Consider yourself enrolled. What's your poison?'

Caitleen settled for her customary gin and orange. I surprised the bartender with my request for a diabolo grenadine, a sickeningly sweet concoction I'd grown a taste for long ago on family holidays to Brittany.

'We've draught Guinness. Like back home in dear old Blighty,' he insisted.

'No. Thanks. I'm not a beer man.'

'Gin and orange for the lady and French kid's stomach rot for you,' he said, reaching for the bottle of Gordon's behind him.

This was how we met Brownie.

He had great stories and the subterranean club soon became a home away from home for both of us, fascinated by the ebullient character of the man and the womb-like comfort of this Left Bank cellar in which he presided with inimitable warmth and cheery gusto.

It was called Brownie's Bar, but he didn't own the place. Just looked after it. He was the perfect front man, with his fruity British upper-class tones and ebullient personality and ever-courteous manners with all women present. Caitleen adored him. The real owners were bad people, he said. Weren't the men in the shadows always the bad ones, I reckoned.

'You're better off not knowing them,' Brownie would say conspiratorially, and then point out that he had come across much worse villains over the years, and regale us with his well-worn stories of smuggling stolen cars across the Franco-Spanish border, or acting as a straight man for dubious companies run by Kray Brothers acolytes in 1960s London, pulling yellowing photographs from a battered wallet depicting him as a dapper, slightly louche approximation of a City gent when younger.

'I was the black sheep of the family.' He talked with great relish about his colourful past, contrasting his public school and National Service upper-class shenanigans with the rough years he had had to spend picking vines in the Italian countryside or digging graves in the Dordogne. And then there were the women. He seemed to have been married five times, he wasn't even sure of the number, the stories varied according to the day of the week. But still, the women flocked to him, as we saw in the bar. Brownie was like a walking skeleton of a man, quite often wracked by a deep, tubercular cough, but the young women flocked to his bar, hoping to be asked for an after-hours drink following official closing time. And he kindly obliged. The younger, the better. Even Caitleen found him wonderful, swept away as they all were by his old-world courtesy and endearments.

'Dear boy,' he would say to me, 'I don't even know how many children I've fathered. And who cares, as long as they're all happy somewhere, I suppose.'

We were soon regulars at the bar, seeking solace from our troubled memories in its smoky cocoon of familiarity. Caitleen soon knew every jazz tune on the jukebox and its corresponding number. Duke Ellington, Miles Davis, John Coltrane, Keith Jarrett, Gato Barbieri. Brownie always wanted her to play Louis Armstrong, but she wasn't that much into Dixie.

'The band podium over there not used any more, is it?' I asked Brownie one evening as we sipped our drinks at the bar, Caitleen gently tipsy on the stall next to me, humming a familiar tune.

'No,' he said evasively. 'The only music here's from the jukebox. Musicians come too expensive these days.'

I knew he wasn't telling the truth. I'd noticed occasional changes on the podium. A few broken drumsticks that had not always been there, an instrument case left lying around which would no longer be there the next day, the piano in a slightly different position. Curious.

We never went to Brownie's on Sunday. That was the day the place was closed, we had been warned as soon as we had become regulars at the drinking hole. I hadn't given the matter much thought.

Then, one weekend, Caitleen and I were walking back from a movie we'd caught at Beaubourg and she impatiently asked me for a nightcap.

'It's just a short detour to Brownie's,' she pointed out.

'It's Sunday,' I reminded her. 'It will be closed.'

'Oh, yes,' Caitleen said. But then she suggested 'Let's check, anyway. Maybe this week they've made an exception.'

'Why should they?' I pointed out. 'He needs a day off, you know. Can't tend bar all the time.'

'Oh, come on, let's go and see.'

It was closed.

But through the front door, we could dimly see the lights were on further down in the cellar. And there was music. Which wasn't jazz. Sounded real, too. Not the sharp, echoing tones of the familiar jukebox.

CLUB PRIVÉ, said the piece of cardboard hanging on the other side of the glass pane of the door.

We looked at each other with surprise.

Tried the door.

Well locked.

Intrigued, Caitleen rapped on the door until someone downstairs heard and a thick-set man with close-cropped hair moved up the stairs. He saw us and pointed silently at the sign.

I shouted that we were members.

He shook his head negatively and walked back downstairs, leaving us quite puzzled.

Disappointed, we returned to the flat.

*

'No, Joe, not today, my period's still going on,' Caitleen said, as my arm moved in her direction, in a bid for warmth.

She was lying. Caitleen was a maniac for tidiness and I'd noticed the evening before how she had put away the box of tampons at the back of the drawer where she always kept it, indicating that her time of month had passed by.

I said nothing.

Felt there was no point in doing so.

Everything seemed to be working out fine. Nobody knew we were in Paris. I read the British papers with religious attention and hadn't found a single word about the mess we had left behind. We were together. What more could we ask? Maybe a bit more tenderness and quiet satisfaction between our times in bed, Caitleen losing some of her damn aloofness, more communication. We had thrown ourselves into this relationship so quickly, so frantically, and now that it had been thrust upon us, I knew we were still feeling our way. As if it wasn't quite real. The silences were lengthening, awkwardly. The eating out, the countless movies, the long quiet walks were expanding to fill our time together, so that no embarrassing gaps remained when we might be left questioning our course of action, ourselves as a newly-minted couple.

I felt uneasy.

And I didn't wish to understand why.

Caitleen was leafing through *Pariscope*, searching for today's movie.

'There's nothing on,' she complained. 'We've seen them all.'

'Surely not,' I said. 'There must be something. Some good American indie, or a foreign classic we've never caught before.'

'I don't like your thrillers,' Caitleen said.

'It doesn't have to be one ... Listen, maybe we can hire a car, drive to the countryside, or the coast for a day or two. A change of horizon?'

'I don't feel like it,' Caitleen answered. 'I'd rather stay in Paris. I want to go to Brownie's tonight. I want to ask him what's going on on Sunday nights. I'm intrigued.'

'So am I.'

She shifted in her chair, and set the magazine back down on the kitchen table.

'Where shall we eat beforehand?' she asked.

'A good couscous in Montmartre?' I suggested.

'Yes, that will be good.'

She rose. 'I'm going to take a shower.'

I looked at my watch. Mid-afternoon. The best time of day for the water pressure in our block of flats.

'Do you want me to join you?' I asked, hopefully.

'No, Joe. Not today.'

*

'Dear boy, do you really want to know?' Brownie asked, after I had quizzed him about the case of the Sunday night mystery.

'I think I do,' I said, Caitleen was at the jukebox. I could almost guess her initial choices for the evening before the coins even moved into the slot. 'Mood Indigo', 'A Love Supreme'. The sadder she became living with me, the more mournful the music. Like a mirror to that part of her soul I couldn't seem to reach these days.

'It's rather sordid,' he warned me, flashing his trademark almost-toothless smile.

'Tell me more, Brownie,' I said, leaning closer to the bar. 'I'm intrigued, to say the least.' Though truthfully, I half-expected to know already what the dreaded revelations would be. I'd worked for Zeusmark long enough to be familiar with the nooks and crannies of clandestinity, sex and money.

And I was partly right.

Very sordid.

'So?' Caitleen asked. Brownie was now serving another bunch of Monday night suited regulars. Her coins in the music machine had run out and the jukebox's random selection process invariably displayed bad taste when it came to free tunes.

'Sex.'

'What do you mean?' she queried. She was already on her second drink. We hadn't eaten anything yet, and her eyes had a glazed fluidity about them.

'Sex shows. With music. And other trimmings. Strictly for the private membership,' I informed her, glossing over some of Brownie's more colourful descriptions of the regular week-end frolics.

'Really?'

Her husband had always kept the more salacious details of his activities from Caitleen, although I reckoned there were some things she had guessed. I'd always believed there's a sort of peculiar, recognisable scent to sex and that it navigates from person to person with unnerving facility, clearly unable to avoid detection if your nose had ever become remotely familiar with its fragrance.

With Zeusmark, the sex came with cameras.

At Brownie's they had more class, according to the chummy old Etonian rogue, and live music added that extra touch of spice to the proceedings.

Nothing new under the sun of Eros.

'Tell him to let us in,' Caitleen begged.

Brownie listened to our request and promised he would talk to the people involved.

'But don't say you haven't been warned,' he told us, with an air of reproach. 'These are dangerous waters you're dipping your toes in. There are certain unwritten rules you will have to obey.'

'Danger is us,' Caitleen chirped merrily, well on her way to being drunk.

*

The pianist lazily moved his fingers over the keyboard and the tinkling rhythm of a tune took form.

The cellar bar was pitch black, flickering streams of light smoking away from a single lit candle on each table. Brownie had been true to his word. None of the crowd present were familiar to us. The British bartender had excused himself for the evening. From the low buzz of the conversations as we had been sitting awaiting the show, a single bottle of white wine on each table, we guessed most of the people here tonight were French. Interested glances in our direction. All couples. Formally dressed. It was the first time since London I had had to wear a suit and tie. Almost felt like an accountant again, ready for meetings with bank officials or Companies House clerks. Caitleen wore her favourite short black dress, emphasising the delicate pallor of her skin, with a shiny set of leather high heels that helped her tower over me.

The Italian appeared. We had once been introduced to him by Brownie. Hair slicked back, thin pencil moustache, wiry frame. He had no name, was just called the Italian. He wore an elegant tuxedo with a red rose attached to his lapel. He paraded theatrically around the wagon train of the tables surrounding the dance floor. Spotlights came to life in each corner of the cellar as he completed his circle of introduction.

The drummer began, bass pedal to the fore, to weave a gentle beat.

The lanky master of ceremonies swivelled his way between the tables, shooting meaningful smiles at all and sundry as he moved. All eyes were on him, as if they were waiting for a predetermined signal to begin some barbaric festivities. The music ebbed.

'From now on . . . silence,' the Italian whispered. Clearly instructions for the audience. The music rose as the saxophone player completed the trio and added his sharp tones to the developing melody the piano and drums had until now been sketching.

Caitleen put her hand on my knee and squeezed.

From nowhere, like a cartoon magician, the Italian conjured a top hat, and presented it to the couple at the table he was now passing.

Their hands dipped into the hollow of the upturned hat and they picked a folded square of paper. The tuxedoed conjuror moved on to the next table where he repeated the operation, and then another. I noticed none of the couples yet unfolding the pieces of paper they had picked. The Italian continued his journey between the spectators. Our turn came. I picked a square. Caitleen's grip on my knee tightened. He moved on and soon every table had helped itself from the hat. The musicians playing on the slightly elevated platform meandered sensually through a jazzy, lazy tune. You could feel the tension in the air, a palpable sense of excitement racing through all our hearts.

Our designated conductor threw the top hat aside and clapped his hands together.

Around us, the spectators began to slowly unfold their respective squares of paper. I did likewise, Caitleen's eye following the movements of my fingers as I did so. The piece of paper was blank. I looked around at the others. Waited.

At the table nearest to us on the right, a woman rose, and became the focus of attention. Her companion remained seated, his face turning ash-white as she raised one arm high and waved her piece of paper upwards for all to see a thick red circle defacing it.

She must have been in her mid-thirties, conservatively dressed in a pastel two-piece tailleur, a string of thick pearls around her neck. Her dark hair was tightly bunched up in a matronly chignon, highlighting her long neck. She moved away from the table.

The music shimmered.

Tonight's chosen.

The corner spotlights dimmed until there was only one left on, bathing the woman now standing in the geographical centre of the club.

She stood proudly, moving a hand to her head and removing the plastic clip that had kept her long hair under control and released her mane, which unfolded, almost in slow motion, until it reached just above her waist, wave upon wave of lustrous dark current flowing against the muted colour of her clothing.

Two strongly built men emerged from the seated audience and placed themselves on either side of the woman. She extended her arms towards the men and they helped her undress. She unbuttoned, unclipped, unzipped and detached herself from her outer skin and soon emerged fully nude, her voluptuous body spreading its curves in all directions now that it was no longer fettered by her clothes. There was something wonderfully old-fashioned about her full, ample contours. She wasn't particularly tall but the flesh flowed in long streams of pink under the light, her breasts plump and upright, dark aureolae highlighting their comfortable bulk. She moved her legs slightly apart. Her shaved pudenda caught the light, the mouth of her bare sex gently open, revealing two gold rings pierced through both her inner lips.

Next to me, Caitleen caught her breath.

As did other members of the audience.

Caitleen's hand moved away from my knee and I glanced back at her, noticing how it was now buried between the material of her skirt at crotch level, underneath the table in an even greater pool of darkness.

The two burly men shed their shirts, revealing shiny, buffed torsos. Each had a single nipple pierced.

The Italian peered out of the shadows, and feathered by the moonlight of the lone spotlight handed each man a thin metal chain, and disappeared again. The men attached them at the extremity of each to their nipple ring, then knelt by the woman and fixed the chains' other ends to her labial attachments. The men then retreated sideways, gradually straightening up, pulling on the two chains connecting them to the woman's genitals, their careful movements exerting delicate traction on the unstretching line and opening her sex and its pink innards to the view of all and sundry. The woman remained this way, splayed wide open, for an eternity, both men unmoving at her side. The saxophone had moved from the jazzy beat to an ululating, Arab-like melody.

'Jesus,' Caitleen whispered in my ear, 'I'm all wet.'

'Are you?'

'Oh yes.' she said.

Finally, the music slowed to a sigh and the woman turned round, the men accompanying her movement in unison and, bare backside to the audience, she got down on all fours, offering us now a grand view of both her winking, visibly moist apertures.

Out of the corner of my eye, I noticed the Italian pointing to another of the candle-lit tables, and the man seated there rose promptly, followed by his female companion. The man, pony tailed and bearded, wore tight leather trousers as did the sluttish-looking blonde bursting out of a narrow white halter top and sporting an exaggerated, impossible cleavage. The man placed himself behind the kneeling, naked woman whose sex lips were still held apart by the chains, and the blonde he was with unzipped him, extracting a thick, pink member which she proceeded to swiftly suck on with hungry gusto until he quickly became quite hard in her mouth and she retreated, as the pony tailed man placed his erect cock at the entrance of the offered woman's puckered sphincter and entered her with one swift, violent thrust. The blonde moved round the kneeling woman being buggered, also got down on her knees and proceeded to kiss the woman her mate was fucking on the lips, her tongue visibly darting deep inside the offered mouth, her spare hands kneading the dark-haired woman's breasts and twisting her hard nipples with unconcealed greed.

The audience remained uncannily silent, and the music adopted the beat of the man's movements in and out of the woman's bowels, his motions steady and exaggerated to enable the spectators to catch every detail of the violation.

Tremors rushed through the mistreated body of the woman being fucked in the arse so unceremoniously, as pleasure got the better of her and the man digging inside her shuddered briefly and came with a muffled, throaty roar. His blonde companion (Wife? Mistress? Whore rented for the evening?) detached herself from the dark-haired woman, slithered out of her own leather trousers under which she wore nothing, and placed her own hirsute cunt against the woman's mouth, silently instructing her to pleasure her. Soon the man withdraw from the arse and the blonde, her leather trousers trailing from one ankle, positioned herself behind the sacrificial woman and obscenely sucked the come out of the still-kneeling woman's rear orifice before spitting it out again all over her capacious rear.

The couple straightened their clothing and faded back into the audience as the master of ceremonies designated another table. A corpulent bald man emerged, but his wife shook her head and declined to join him. He instructed the two men with the nipple rings and connecting chains to turn the dark-haired woman over and place her on her back, legs raised up and pulled wide apart, and proceeded to fuck her in the missionary position. Another couple followed; this time, the woman chose to eat the still-dripping sex of the well-fucked woman on display while the man positioned himself and plunged his lengthy cock down her mouth and seemingly all the way down her throat. Two more men also chose to be serviced this way, while their women contented themselves with extended caresses of the soft, prone body on offer.

The procession continued. A litany of mouths, fingers, fiery cocks, hot cunts using the spreadeagled body of the chosen dark-haired woman and her dilated, puffed apertures. Eventually, the Italian pointed to our table. I shook my head, declining the offer to take my turn in the festivities, but Caitleen turned to me and mischievously said 'Go on, have a go, Joe, I don't mind.'

'No, Caitleen, I don't . . .'

'Please,' she insisted. 'I want to see her suck your cock. I really do. I want to see you with another woman.'

I reckoned it was the least of the evils and walked to the main area, unzipped and allowed the woman to fellate me. I came very quickly, all the time avoiding the eyes in the audience, and Caitleen's. The woman was an expert, her tongue quickly identifying with unerring certainty every sensitive spot and dancing like a snake around my erection until I felt the unstoppable hot stream running from my loins through my stem and exploded.

Two men followed me as I retreated to the table where Caitleen had finished the wine while I performed. They carried the dark-haired woman to one corner, detached her from the nipple rings and proceeded to athletically take her simultaneously, one of them, settled on a chair, impaling her arsehole on his raised cock while the other positioned himself in front of them and entered her gaping sex folds. Caitleen later told me that, towards the end of the act, they had actually both managed to penetrate her vagina in unison, but my mind was no longer concentrating on the events unfolding on that Paris Sunday night.

Finally, everyone seemed to have taken their turn. The music slowed and stopped. The spotlights faded to dark and, under cover of the new-found darkness, the ravaged woman disappeared from centre stage.

It was a bit like the end of a movie after the credits have duly rolled. Brief conversations emerged as the audience gradually rose, coats and macs were sought and the club emptied. Still, no one had talked to each other amongst the spectating crowd.

It felt cold outside. Winter was nearing and a savage wind buffeted the Left Bank as we crossed the Seine to return to our flat.

*

'So?'

'So what?' Caitleen quizzed me ingenuously.

'Why did you want me to get involved?' I asked her.

'It felt right. It felt good.'

'It turned you on, didn't it?'

'Yes,' she replied, moving closer to me to loosen my tie and expertly unbutton my shirt. She had already got down to her silky black underwear. I could see the damp patch spreading across the deep crease of her genital valley. 'Let's fuck. Now,' she ordered me, with a determined, hungry tone in her voice.

I was ready, too.

I didn't wish to remind her of the fact that this was the first time we would be making love since I had caught her lying about her period a few weeks back.

It was good, strong, breathless in the way early clandestine days had been back in London. Before Zeusmark.

I told her so.

'I love you, Caitleen. That was so good, you know.'

'Yes, it was,' she agreed, disengaging herself from me to stretch her limbs, my seed spilling abundantly from her, irrigating the bed cover we hadn't pulled away in in our haste to embrace.

'Put it down to experience,' I said. 'Now you know what happens at Brownie's on Sundays.'

'I'd like to see more,' Caitleen said softly.

'You're kidding,' I said.

'It's interesting. Really.'

'And what if you had picked the square of paper with the red mark?'

'Interesting is what I said,' she giggled, and made a grab for my cock.

7.

When Carla Sang

There was this Seattle rock group she liked. Not grunge, more kind of Country and sweetly melodic in a mournful sort of way. Couldn't even recall their name. She had taped a few tunes off the radio and all she knew was that the woman who sang in the band was called Carla.

When the mood suited, Cornelia would use one of their tunes in her set. For the middle part. The slow one, where she unveiled her assets. Like all striptease artistes, it was a three-step number. Full costume and hints of plenty during the first song ending up in skimpy, alluring undies; shedding these final bastions at the end of the second tune to stand proudly with the thinnest of g-strings and, finally, the athletic scherzo to the beat of a bouncy dance tune in which she paraded in all her nude glory.

It was a boring tradition. The occasional dancer would sometimes change the routine. A particularly brazen girl who'd worked here a few months ago, called Lisa, would come on nude from the onset which delighted the punters, but the novelty palled quickly and her last five minutes garnered few tips, as the customers grew drearily familiar with her contours and mechanical bump-and-grind routine.

One day, Cornelia thought, she might experiment. Do her set the wrong way round. Beginning naked and ending up dressed. Might prove amusing.

She stood by the greased metal pole at the centre of the stage, her skin wet with sweat—the heating was too high again—clad in her matching black silk underwear, the pair with short pearl-ended tassels she had bought on a week-end trip to Vegas in one of those awfully vulgar shops in the Caesar's Palace mock-Roman mall.

There was a pizzicato of strings and Carla's strong, emotive voice surged above the melody.

It always gave Cornelia the shivers.

She set in motion.

There was a sparse audience out there. It was always that way in the afternoon. But that's how Cornelia liked it. She seldom performed evenings or week-ends. Too noisy. Couldn't concentrate on her thoughts. Missing out on the big spenders no longer bothered her, now that she had found another way of raising cash.

There was a young kid clutching a beer in the first row, his eyes fixed on her as she moved to the rhythm. He looked so young. Must have flashed a forged ID to get in, no doubt. Clean-cut, probably still only shaved once a week or less. On furlough from an Ivy League college. He kept on staring at her with puppy dog eyes, lost in admiration. Cornelia remembered the frat boys who would ask her out at high school. Smiled.

The young man must have thought she had smiled at him and his face went all radiant. How touching, Cornelia felt. Her hands busy behind her back unhooking the flimsy bra, she moved nearer to his end of the stage and deliberately smiled back. The bra fell away and her freed breasts fell forward; she jiggled them softly just a few inches from the boy's nose and he went all red in the face, quite unready for her attention.

She stayed there a few seconds, almost inviting him to touch her, to let his fingers graze over the softness of her breasts. Carla's voice soared above the strident, heartbreaking guitar solo.

The boy shyly extended his hand and dropped a ten dollar bill on the edge of the wooden stage.

Cornelia retreated. Pressed her bare breasts against the central pole, threw her body back while holding on to the pole with her hands, sketching the opening part of a back somersault and, catching up with the flow of the music, resumed her routine.

*

'Mr Hopley is away on vacation,' the deputy manager at the uptown gallery told Cornelia as she inquired.

'I see,' she said. Once again, she was in her student-like uniform of T-shirt and jeans, not your typical moneyed customer in his evaluation. 'I'm one of his book clients,' she added as the pasty-faced red-haired man looked her over.

'That would be why I'm not familiar with you,' he said. 'I mostly look after the old prints part of the business. Ms?'

'Miss Irish. The last time I was here, Mr Hopley told me that he was in the process of cataloguing the Lloyd Currey collection he'd purchased at auction during the summer. Said the catalogue wouldn't be ready until next month, but I could have an advance peek at the listings?'

The gallery apparatchik paused for a moment's thought, then relented.

'I'm sure it will be fine, Miss Irish, if Mr Hopley has suggested it.'

He deferentially escorted her to an office at the back where she sunk into the plush leather upholstery and was offered a cup of herbal tea. The deputy manager went searching for Hopley's hand-written valuations of the items in the collection, which one of the part-time secretaries they employed was about to type up and print as a mail-order catalogue for the collectors on their list.

Cornelia pulled her glasses case from her backpack. She wore contact lenses on stage and most of the rest of the time, but preferred her square, tinted John Lennon-like square spectacles for reading.

'Make yourself comfortable,' the old prints expert said, handing her a sheaf of papers. 'Do you want a piece of paper, a pen, to make notes?'

'No,' Cornelia answered. 'This should do fine.' She waved her small notebook and the silver Parker she carried everywhere and had written the first draft of her thesis with.

He departed into the bowels of the gallery, leaving her with the lists, as she inhaled with sensual pleasure the pungent smell of the hot tea.

A first read-through uncovered untold treasures that made her tingle all over. A mint hardback copy of *The Man From Sonora* she had seldom come across in catalogues before, but then she didn't collect westerns. Several early non-criminous Woolrich titles, still with dust jackets. A complete run of pre-WW2 *Black Mask* maga-zines, a William Burroughs *Naked Lunch* in the Paris Olympia edition, first issue, signed, in dust jacket, a keenly-priced first of Clancy's *The Hunt For Red October*, but Cornelia hated techno-thrillers, so that would have defeated the object, a good selection of Faulkner, F Scott Fitzgerald and Hemingway firsts inscribed to a well-known critic. Some wonderful stuff, but Cornelia had sworn from her early days as a book collector on that she would never purchase more than one expensive book from a dealer's catalogue at a time. Otherwise, she knew, it became a vice, sheer greed. Moderation, young lady, she would mutter to herself as her eyes raced from desirable book to coveted novels, biographies and travel narratives.

But the one line that truly caught her attention, the book that said 'buy me, you must have me' at first sight was a copy of Malcolm Lowry's *Under The Volcano*, inscribed by the author to his mentor Conrad Aiken. Not only was this one of Cornelia's favourite books, one that spoke to her heart and senses, but her Penguin Modern Classics paperback was falling apart and she had been meaning to replace it for quite some time already, only to discover from book-stores she had visited that it was between printings.

Yes, this was the one.

And a snip at 3,500 bucks.

Ouch!

Cornelia rose from the sinking folds of the leather couch and peered through the door to catch the attention of the gallery staff. The lanky old prints expert soon came to her.

'A marvellous choice,' she told him.

'Oh yes, Mr Hopley is very particular about his acquisitions. Only goes for quality material,' he said.

'Indeed,' Cornelia replied. 'And I fear there is one item I am definitely most keen to acquire.' She handed the sheaf of lists back to him. 'Number 94.'

He leafed through the pages. Peered.

'Very nice,' he answered. 'Not cheap.'

'I realise, but that's the one for me.'

'I see.'

'I would be most obliged if you could set the item aside for me. I shall come with the money in a week or thereabouts,' Cornelia said. Adding 'Mr Hopley usually agrees the modus operandi.'

He escorted her out, presuming rich parents and watching with undisguised delight the way her rear wiggled from side to side in her tight jeans. A very tasty young lady . . .

Sashaying down 52nd Street, Cornelia reflected that she should have asked to see the book, touch it briefly, smell its unique odour, but it was too late now. She was already tingling nicely at the prospect of owning it. And as she was already in this part of town, she would visit Victoria's Secret for an added treat. Dark, maroony red lace matching bra and pants. She had spotted them in the window on her way over. She so hoped they had her size in store.

*

'Hello?'

The same voice.

'This is Cornelia. I'm ready for another job. You hinted there would usually be something available?'

'Indeed, Cornelia,' he said. 'Congratulations on your last. Cool, calm, clean and collected. As you know we have high standards, and I'm pleased to say you seem to be quite professional.'

'I'll take that as a compliment.'

'You should, young lady, you should.'

He paused for a moment at the invisible end of the phone.

'Give us a couple of hours to decide on the assignment and we shall phone you with the dossier pick-up details. Will you be at the same number?'

'Yes. It's my day off work. I was planning to see a movie at the Angelika, but not before the midnight screening. The queues earlier are much too bothersome. I'll be waiting for your call.'

'Speak to you.'

Cornelia moved to the kitchen and unhurriedly completed her domestic chores, took her dirty washing down to the big machine in the apartment block's basement. Read a few pages from the book again, nightmarish vistas of drunken horror on the edge of a Mexican mountain. Emptied her bulging cupboard and with undue ceremony laid out all her dancing outfits across the bed and settled on which she would wear at the club this coming week. The others she would drop off next morning at the Chinese dry-cleaners.

The call came.

'Hello, Cornelia?'

'Yes. It's me. Hello again.'

'Tomorrow morning. Eleven and a half. First floor at the Astor Place Barnes and Noble. Hang around the magazine racks and We'll get the stuff to you.'

'You don't know what I look like,' Cornelia protested.

'We do. Of course we do, dear Cornelia. We'd be negligent not to, wouldn't we?'

'I suppose so.' She was lying on the bed, stomach down, wearing only her earlier T-shirt, uncovered rear regally exposed to the faint breeze moving through the room.

'How much is the book costing you this time?'

'You know?'

'Of course we do, Cornelia,' he said quietly.

'Three and a half thousand,' she whispered.

'We'll pay you four thousand. That way, you'll have a bit left over. Like a bonus.'

'That would be nice,' Cornelia said.

'Done,' he said and promptly hung up on her, cutting her possible new questions short.

*

She was idly leafing through the pages of a glossy fashion magazine when the little black kid came up to her. The bookshop cafeteria was still mostly empty at this time of morning.

'Miss Cornelia?' he asked her.

She had noticed him earlier polishing shoes outside.

'Yes.'

'This is for you.'

He handed her a yellow Tower Records plastic bag, its top carefully sealed by a parade of staples. Looked up at her with saucer eyes, hoping for a tip. She knew he had probably already been paid but hunted for a couple of dollar bills in her pocket, which he enthusiastically grabbed before rushing to the stairs and running down past the mural of famous writers.

There was an attractive designer bikini pictured in the magazine she was still holding in her other hand. Would suit her strip routine well, Cornelia reckoned. She jotted down the manufacturer's name. They had a store close by in the Village. This would be her next port of call, she decided, as money was presently no object.

*

The woman was sipping a cocktail at this bar off Wall Street. It was a plush and fashionable establishment, where leather seats gleamed under the dim, discreet lights as if recently polished and wooden ceiling beams crisscrossed the room from wall to wall.

A few conservatively-suited stockbrokers or foreign exchange dealers populating the bar nursed half-empty martini glasses, either juggling cell phones or calculators. Happy hour was still forty minutes away.

The immaculately starched bartender polished glasses in readiness for the later rush when the banks and insurance companies would disgorge their salarymen, on their one-stop before the New Jersey or Connecticut trains home.

The seat next to her was empty.

Cornelia took possession.

She was, again, wearing her power suit. Couldn't think of what else to wear. This time, though, she had slipped on a white silk shirt underneath it for decorum. She would have to think of another outfit next time, she knew, didn't want this to become a uniform. How the proper angel of death should dress for the ceremony.

The barman came over.

'What will you have, ma'am?' he asked her.

'Gin and orange,' Cornelia requested.

'Very British, ma'am.'

'Indeed.'

The woman next to her was sipping from her cocktail glass, lost in thought.

Cornelia's drink came.

She turned slightly to the other woman.

'Cheers!' she said.

The woman glanced at her, smiled and nodded back.

'Unusual for two lone women to be sitting drinking here, isn't it?' Cornelia said, for her opening gambit.

'I suppose so,' the woman reluctantly said.

'I was thirsty, walking around outside. Thought the place looked nice, discreet, not the sort of place where men would bother you if you wanted your privacy.'

'You're right,' the older woman responded. 'Men here are too busy thinking of more ways of making money.'

'That sort of place?'

'Quite.' The woman looked up at Cornelia. 'Hi,' she said. 'My name's Fox.'

She was wearing a free-flowing dress, which looked as if it were cut from expensive strands of silk. Carefully made-up. Strong cheek-bones. Everything about her shouted high society.

'I'm Holly,' Cornelia said. Why complicate things? It had worked before.

'What do you do?' she was asked.

'I'm a dancer. Exotic. Well, a stripper,' she was surprised to hear herself saying. She hadn't intended do. It was just that talking with a woman, it felt different. There would be no reason for lying.

'Really?' Fox queried.

'Yes. It's not bad, it's a good living. Nobody forces me to. I'm independent.'

'You don't look like one,' the older woman pointed out.

'Well, there's no point in being a cliché,' Cornelia said truthfully. 'When I'm on stage, I dress a certain way. Or undress. Life outside is different. I can just be me. My other life's a secret. Look at them,' she pointed to some of the men in the bar, all in identical dark-coloured suits, white shirts and sober ties. 'Isn't that their stage uniform?'

'You're right, Holly. Fuck 'em,' Fox responded approvingly. 'Let's have another drink. On me,' she offered.

'Why not?' Cornelia agreed.

Happy hour came. Happy hour went.

'A damn bastard, that's what he was,' Fox said, downing another glass. Cornelia nodded approvingly as the older woman spoiled her with her woes. With a listening ear at her disposal, she had been regaling Cornelia with the story of the fateful holiday her husband, a wealthy socialite banker, and she had taken at an exotic Caribbean resort.

'I know I always flirt outrageously with good-looking men, and we were by the pool, and this rather attractive younger guy was sunning himself, with his rather mousy wife at his side. The children were all playing together in the water, so it was only natural that we should talk to each other. We all had dinner that evening, got on well.

'The following day, we agreed to go to the beach together. Here, Gregory—that was his name—and I kept on schmoozing when he stood up and asked if we wanted to surf. No way I would, but my husband agreed to join him. Would you believe it, they slept together that night while I agreed to babysit both families' kids? Gregory was gay, and was taking a holiday with his ex-wife for the sake of the children.'

'Incredible,' commented Cornelia, fascinated.

'I knew my husband always shot envious glances at other men. But then so did I,' Fox continued, 'I'd always been interested in all forms of sexuality, but I would never have believed I would lose my husband to another man. If it had been a woman, I would have screamed, fought and pleaded with him. But what do you think I feel like, him leaving me like this for a guy?'

'Awful, I suppose,' Cornelia said, taking the other woman's hand in hers in a gesture of sympathy.

Fox, who had been close to crying, looked down at their hands then up again at Cornelia's face, almost pleading.

Cornelia pulled her hand back, but Fox wouldn't let her go.

Their eyes met.

'You're so . . . soft,' Fox said.

Cornelia felt a familiar buzz circumnavigate her stomach. Fox moved a finger inside Cornelia's extended palm.

Both their glasses were now empty.

They kept on looking deep into each other's eyes in utter silence, as the final commuter suits faded in the background. As always, the bartender ignored them, the very soul of discretion.

'So . . . you don't think he'll come back?' Cornelia finally asked.

'No way. He knows I'm going to sue him for half of the business, the house, the cars, any spare cash that he hasn't nailed down, the whole farrago. I'll get my own back, you just see.' The venom was almost spilling from her lips and Cornelia began to guess where her job had originated.

Cornelia wondered one short moment.

Of the best way to dispose of Fox. The best place.

Fox's fingers still lingered.

Cornelia lowered her eyes, all bashful.

'Let's go somewhere else,' Fox suggested quietly.

'Why not?' Cornelia answered, looking up again and holding the older woman's questioning gaze. 'It is getting rather stuffy here,' she pointed out. 'God, how I'd love to be able to take a shower right now.'

Fox smiled at her.

'We can get a cab. I live in this brownstone near Gramercy Park. We could be there in less than ten minutes. You could freshen up there, and then we can have some cool drinks at our leisure.'

'That sounds nice,' Cornelia agreed.

The cab driver was from Haiti and insisted on keeping his radio on, tuned to a blurred pirate Caribbean station, playing loud music as he waltzed across the gridlocked streets. Fox had moved close to Cornelia on the back seat and was now touching her knee. Cornelia shivered slightly.

'Are you OK?' Fox inquired.

'Yes, I'm fine.'

'You don't mind? You do look so beautiful, you know. I've never been with a woman before. Just something I feel I have to try at least once.'

'Neither have I,' Cornelia answered truthfully. 'But it would be nice, I reckon. With you.' She cuddled up to Fox. Both women were blushing, surprised by the brazen turn of events neither of them had planned.

'Oh, Holly,' Fox sighed. 'Tell me . . .' she hesitated.

'Yes?'

The yellow cab roared across Park Avenue South, dodging delivery vans.

'Would you dance for me?'

'Of course, Fox.'

'In the nude?'

'Absolutely. It's the best, the only way to dance,' Cornelia added.

'That'll be really great,' Fox said. 'Do you know, I've never been to a striptease show.'

'It will be a very private one, just for you,' Cornelia said, slipping her hand under Fox's lacy blouse.

*

The musky scent of another woman's cunt.

It was certainly something new for Cornelia and she wallowed in the novelty of the experience. Often imagining she was in fact a man and was right now actually making love to herself, tongue slithering deep between labial folds and sucking inner juices with undisguised delight, analysing the taste and the texture as she went along, feeling the excitement rise and propagate through the soft body of flesh she was patiently exploring. Is this how she, Cornelia, tasted? Smelled? Felt to the touch?

The two women reversed their positions and Cornelia compared how the teeth of another woman gently stretching, nibbling, pulling on her clitoris, differed from the lips of a man, the degree of added caress and knowledge that coloured every iota of movement. Fox probed with velvet delicacy, while her hands roamed across the surface of Cornelia's breasts, kneading her, twisting her elongated nipples almost to the point of pain, not like a man would, not like her last lover: that heartbreaking Harvard professor who had so badly betrayed her would have manipulated the tenderness of her breasts a different way. A married man. Of course. Weren't all the best ones? Cornelia moaned. Fox sighed. Their limbs kept on intertwining with ease and lithe flexibility.

'This is good, so good,' Fox muttered, her mouth chewing on Cornelia's puffed inner lips.

'Yes,' Cornelia whispered, stretching with total abandon, utterly spreadeagled in a crucified position of total availability, complete obscenity as the other woman worked assiduously on her genitals with an expertise borne of intimate knowledge of the private parts of a woman.

Cornelia adjusted her position, intimating to the other woman they should pleasure each other simultaneously. She slid over the creased sheets, disturbing their geography of lust into even further contortions.

But there was something detached about the situation, as she thought of the tongues of men and how much more daring they would be. She elevated her backside slightly, thrusting her cunt hard at the older woman's face, intimating that she should now move further to her even more private intimacy, between the crack separating her arse cheeks. 'Rim me, rim me hard,' she felt like asking her. The Harvard man would have done so without hesitation. Some men, her last man, had all the daring. She couldn't help but see herself as a fly on the wall, an insect voyeur calmly watching this tangle of limbs and sopping juices as Fox continued her assault of the fortress of the dancer's tuned body.

Tremors navigated between them as varying degrees of pleasure laid foundation to their lust.

Eros occupied the room with ease as the two women drank from each other and swam in the seas of joy.

Time vanished, New York hours blending into each other.

Fox and Cornelia had exhausted themselves and were both on their backs, spent, tired, all topics of casual conversation exhausted. Both somewhat taken back with the ease with which their encounter had developed.

'First time?' Fox asked Cornelia.

'Yes, of course,' she replied with a wry smile.

In truth, in the clubs, she had seen the naked bodies of many other women, young and older, short and tall, pale and tanned, but she had never craved for the other fruit, really.

Call it pleasure. Or pity, she reckoned.

'Me too, I swear.' Fox said and began giggling nervously. 'I'd always wondered, though.'

'Curiosity satisfied?' Cornelia queried.

'I think so,' Fox said. 'God,' she added, 'I am shit tired. What about you?'

'Sure. I have to work tomorrow.'

'Listen. Why don't you sleep over? There's no point you rushing off. We can be civilised. No more funny business. It would be nice to have someone to cuddle up to.'

'Sure,' Cornelia agreed.

'And we can have a nice breakfast together in the morning?'

'Maybe,' Cornelia said. She stretched her arms. Rose from the bed, the other woman's eyes spying every inch of her body as she moved sensually aside. 'I'll get some water from the bathroom, shall I? My mouth always gets dry when I sleep. What about you?'

'Me also,' said Fox, yawning already.

Cornelia had left her small handbag in the bathroom when she had earlier undressed to dance for Fox. She closed the door, turned the tap on and took out the small bottle of pills. She crushed four of them into a fine powder which she added to the large mug of water she had prepared and returned to the bed, where Fox had slipped between the straightened, starched sheets.

'There we are, drink. I've added some aspirin, it'll help us sleep. Always works well with me.'

'How kind you are, Holly. You really are.'

Fox took the porcelain mug from her.

In the morning, she was dead. Cornelia had been told it would look like a heart attack.

She was pleased it had been so painless.

And that she had been able to give the woman a last flash of pleasure beforehand.

Cornelia dressed and let herself out of the two-storey brown-stone. On the way out she spotted a side room with a dozen or so bookshelves and couldn't help her curiosity. Anyway, there was no risk. The husband wasn't likely to return at this early hour from his new lover. And Fox had mentioned the fact she no longer had domestic help.

In truth, the library was disappointing. Too many bestsellers and *New York Times* top twenty discounted titles, still with their 25% off stickers attached. There was a book club edition of the Lowry book, but Cornelia wasn't a thief.

There was something stuffy about the proximity of death and she needed the fresh air.

She briskly walked up twenty blocks to Mom's Bagel on the corner of 45th Street and Fifth Avenue and treated herself to a bumper garlic bagel with Nova Scotia lox and frumptious cream cheese.

8.

In the Heart of the Longing

I suppose it's like being caught up in a road accident. You see the car heading for you, you watch the headlights flashing madly nearer, but you can't do anything about it at all. Events unfold in terrible slow motion and, countless moments before the impact, you just know it's bound to happen. The adrenalin hasn't even begun its journey through your bloodstream all the way to the tip end of your nerves. You're serene. Waiting for the moment with quiet resignation. It's all so inevitable. Natural, somehow.

That's the way things were with Caitleen.

One part of me, the impartial observer, could see the break coming. Read the many signals punctuating our road. It was loud and clear as hell. In the words we said to each other, in those we didn't say. The way we touched. The flashes of fury that consumed our fucking, as if a savage physicality was a buoy we could latch on to in our search for salvation.

And the other part, the one that loved Caitleen with all the mournfulness my heart harboured, ignored the signals. Or denied them. Could not accept the fact of us not lasting as a couple. Hoping against hope and all that.

I should have been more realistic.

But what could I have done?

I still ask myself that now.

Later.

I'm not into astrology. It wasn't written in the stars or in other sanctimonious new-age baloney. It was just life that interfered. The way it does. Getting two men killed, pimping the woman I worshipped (I just could not erase that searing vision of her lips on Markie), leaving messes behind and the life of others in a state of ruin and neglect was not the proper way for Caitleen and Joe to begin the happily-ever-after charade.

Too late.

There was no way we could change the past. The story would have to go on to its rightful, designated conclusion.

December in Paris, skies the colour of slate, as the cold insidiously entered our bones as the darker seasons took over, limiting the sun to only special occasions. We were standing on one of the bridges over the Seine, watching the barges make their way past the Ile de la Cité, the gothic mass of Notre Dame dominating the horizon of the river.

Caitleen was wearing a heavy coat we'd bought the week before at the Samaritaine. Our London *garde-robe* was now inadequate and we were thinking of possible warmer climes.

'Spain? One of the Balearic Islands? Just for the winter,' I had suggested.

'Why?' Caitleen had asked.

'It'll be warmer, and cheaper also. Nice weather will keep our spirits up,' I said. Caitleen looked at me, dubious.

'We'll just be bored stiff. There's no culture. Little for us to do. The Caribbean or Florida, I'd understand . . .'

'I don't think we can afford to go that far,' I indicated.

'We can't seem to afford Paris, can we?'

'Not really,' I admitted.

Our funds were melting away. There was a possibility of getting some more funds transferred from London, but then that would be it. No more where that came from. I did have access to some of Zeusmark's offshore accounts, but was afraid this would attract unwanted attention.

'We'll have to begin looking for jobs,' Caitleen suggested.

'Won't be easy,' I said.

'I know,' she agreed. 'My French isn't that good.'

'I've a few contacts, from the times before I began working for him,' I told her. 'I could make a few phone calls tomorrow. Offer some sort of consulting service for expatriates. Help them with their financial investments, show them how to avoid double taxation and protect their assets.'

'Maybe you should,' Caitleen said. 'And I'll ask Brownie if he can help me find something.'

'Are you sure?' I queried. 'I can't see you as topless waitress or cleaning floors in a bar. What could he know?'

'Who knows?' Caitleen said. 'Let's go early next Sunday and try and catch him before the show at the club.'

'We can see him any other day,' I pointed out. 'I'm not too keen on us being involved in their games again,' I said.

'Why?' Caitleen asked, a hint of irritation in her manner.

'It's . . . not right. We get our kicks in other ways, don't we?'

'Do we?' she queried.

'You know what I mean, Caitleen. There's something unhealthy, twisted, about that Sunday scene.'

'It's just sex. A ritual,' she pointed out.

'And sex is private, something that happens between the two of us. We don't need company, other participants, people we don't even know and would be quite unlikely to socialise with if we came across them anywhere else, anywhere normal.' I could hear the tone of my voice rising.

'Fine, fine, Joe, don't get so heated up,' Caitleen smiled, and that disarming, kindly parting of her lips and the amused grin spreading across her features had me melting inside like butter again. 'Anyway,' she added, 'if they want us to get involved, we can just do it together, can't we? We'll give them lessons,' she laughed gently.

But I knew she was serious.

'You'll soon have us fucking for the delight of voyeurs in porno booths,' I said.

'Pays well, I gather.' She laid on the irony.

I wondered how much she had known about Zeusmark's activities.

'You're crazy,' I said, taking her gloved hand in mine.

'I know,' she said and gripped me.

A *bateau-mouche* full of shivering tourists passed slowly under the bridge, waves rippling on either side of the sleek hull.

*

I was already sleeping badly during those Paris nights. Strange dreams, couldn't really call them nightmares. Like a litany of repetition, odd stories and images invaded my mind when I least expected them. Dreams of other women I didn't even know.

Of wild nights of overbearing excess in small wooden-furnitured hotel rooms.

Didn't make sense.

Of waiting for hours on end in the luggage hall of Newark airport for the appearance of a dark-haired woman with a hat.

A story unfurled through my sleeping hours, night after night, Caitleen purring softly beside me, meandering endlessly on to some kind of warped conclusion. Which never came. I awoke, ever on the brink of revelation. At six in the morning or thereabouts, that quiet, desolate time when night is over but day isn't yet in control and the heart is at sea, far from familiar land, abandoned, quite alone in your own mental wilderness.

Why did I always wake up so early, with a head full of questions and too many uncertainties?

*

But when Caitleen had decided on something, I knew there was little chance of my changing her mind. A powerful streak of childish obstinacy riddled her character. I had come across it before. Then it had delighted me, involving me in the special endearments of love, the laughter, the joy of unpredictability, the silly surprises, the games, the conspiracy of intimacy.

We reached Brownie's bar much earlier than usual on the Sunday evening. Again, he had decided to pass, but we were let in with no further questions. A few couples sipped drinks quietly, already at their tables. The woman who had displayed herself so wantonly a few weeks before was there, with her husband. She greeted us amiably as we looked for a table. We nodded silently in acknowledgment.

'Ah, the young British couple. You look so sweet,' she exclaimed.

Her husband remained silent. Somehow, we didn't think it was his idea to attend these weekly ceremonials.

Without being asked, they moved to our table, bringing their bottle and glasses with them. The musicians were trailing in, unpacking their instruments.

'I see you decided to come back to our gathering,' the woman said. 'Good. Most newcomers don't.'

'I wasn't sure if . . .' I began to say.

'No need for explanations,' the woman cut me off peremptorily. 'The main thing is that you're here, *non*?'

Caitleen nodded, evidently fascinated by her.

I could see the husband peering intensely at her, undressing her as he looked up and down her body with unfeigned interest.

The crowds grew. The tables filled.

This week, there was no master of ceremonies, but all here seemed to know the unwritten rules. Once the club was full and the music began, the lights dimmed without any signal being given and the woman at our table, that last time's sacrificial body, rose. She had pulled a bunch of small, carefully folded sheets of white paper from her Dolce and Gabbana handbag and scattered them inside a deep earthenware ashtray and began her passage from table to table, where people took their pick. Halfway through her journey around the room, she alighted at our table and Caitleen beat me to it, her long arm hastily reaching for the papers on offer.

My heart skipped a beat as I watched her unfold the note, imagining the red circle or square or whatever shape my fate would be taking.

The piece of paper was blank.

Maybe it was a faint trace of disappointment I read on Caitleen's features, but I know I breathed easily again.

The woman completed her circle.

The beat of the music had reached a crescendo.

All the papers had been taken. She returned to our table and set the empty ashtray down.

The music quietened.

At the far end of the club's cavernous ersatz ballroom, a tall man rose, waving his paper and its red symbol for all to see.

Some of the crowd clapped hands as he made his way to the centre of the floor, to the improvised stage. He was a handsome, grey-haired man with slicked-back hair that petered out just short of a pony tail, expensively dressed in a three-piece anthracite suit. The lights dimmed, as the gentle applause died away and a hush of expectancy settled over the audience.

Two women emerged from the surrounding darkness, his handmaidens in waiting, and as the grey-haired man stood, legs and arms wide apart in the beam of the spotlight, in a parody of a crucifixion, they proceeded to systematically undress him, one item of clothing at a time, in teasing slow motion.

'This will be good,' the woman at our table whispered in confidence to Caitleen and me, as we watched with increasing fascination, second-guessing what might happen next, and she filled our glasses with more wine. Lambs to the sacrifice.

The women on either side of him now retreated and the man stood nude, his lean, smooth, athletic body utterly displayed. He was quite hairless, chest and legs shaven to shining effect in the pool of radiant light. Even his crotch had been depilated and his dangling, pink cock appeared abnormally long due to the lack of pubic hair to disguise where it took root in the skin. Unless it was the beginning of arousal. I could feel the heat of Caitleen's body next to me rise, her perspiration steadily making its way through her pores, as the man came into focus. He was uncircumcised, sported thin, golden metal rings in his nipples, and the tip of his cock was pierced, a thick steel stud peering from the top of his glans as it disappeared into the loose foreskin.

One of the women who had helped undress him, middle-aged, her voluptuous curves released from the straitjacket of her conservative garments, returned, now down to matching white silk underwear, garter belt and black stockings. She circled the silent, immobile, naked man a few times, admiring the hardness of his muscles, the taut stretched line of his gleaming skin. The other woman who had helped earlier, still in her elegant Armani tailleur, brought a chair to the central area, and, after turning him around, had the man bend over it, with his jutting rear in full view of the audience.

'Yes,' our female companion hissed. I looked around at her, beyond Caitleen. The woman's hands were greedily manipulating the growing length of her own husband's cock, which she had pulled out of his trousers. Caitleen's eyes were fully on the events unfolding on the improvised stage.

The ceremony began.

From the darkness beyond the circle of light they now inhabited, the women brought out all the necessary implements.

The grey-haired man was first gagged with a red plastic ball, which they stuffed inside his mouth and held there by a contraption of thin leather straps that tightened around the back of his head.

The whips followed.

A whole arsenal of various-shaped ones, thick, long, serpent-like thin, interrupted by leather knots spaced at regular intervals down the length, sharp as knives, bisected ends like a snake's tongue, circus parade whips, animal whips, thongs and such. Enough to make my own flesh shiver as I watched in frozen awe from the dark comfort of the audience, hearing only Caitleen's short breath at my side, the music just an echo in a distant background as the proceedings accelerated.

The two women took it in turns. Using every one of the whips at their disposal. The lashes beat down, first on the man's back, later on his buttocks, with metronomic precision and regularity. Not a sound ever passed from his lips, even when the leather began biting into his flesh, crisscrossing his whiteness with sharp weals, cutting it, drawing thin streaks of blood, repeatedly biting into the opened wounds as the women wielded their lashes of torture with knowing pleasure, moving from one body area to another, cultivating the pain, caressing every damn sensitive area of the man's flesh with the lingering tips of their stings before punishing him again with added energy. Every time they would make contact with the back of his thighs, I could see him flinch, feel the vibration, the tremor moving through his body. Below the darker crack of his arse, below the puffed redness of his beaten cheeks, I could see his long cock dangle, seemingly hanging from the chocolate sack of his balls, which the whips would, from time to time, caress with tantalising calculation before making sharp contact. I winced.

Finally, the two women tired. Others were rising from the tables. Picking up the bunch of whips they had been using, the older woman in the suspenders savagely drove the thick wooden pommel of one of the thongs into the man's rear as she departed, leaving him there, still bent over the chair, unceremoniously stuffed up the backside like a chicken.

There were only women attending to him this evening.

Each in turn moved front-stage.

With her own brand of torture.

I sat there, quite desensitised by the developing events, dreading the time when the women at our table would be summoned to participate.

Caitleen was on her third or fourth glass of wine by now, past the point of no return. It never took her much to reach that zone of gentle mirth and irresponsibility where she lightly said anything that came into her head or moved beyond the boundaries I was trying to erect around our stumbling relationship.

A splendid blonde in a very short and tight black leather skirt sat the grey-haired man on the chair, straddled him so that his cock emerged from between her thighs and proceeded to light a candle she had borrowed from the bar and drip the melting wax at close range on the tip of the man's penis, watching it grow to full erection as she did so. I gritted my teeth. The red wax fell in droplets on him, like thick globules of blood, cooling down over the surface of his member until his whole tip was coated with a second, matt bloody skin. Which the pert blonde proceeded to manipulate until she brought the silent man to a powerful orgasm, his come bubbling through under the solidified wax coating, drifting down to the woman's open thighs and onto the floor.

The next torturer, a small redhead with rimmed glasses which made her look like a schoolteacher gone wrong, concentrated on his nipple rings, twisting them into every conceivable position, with her fingers, with her sharp teeth, away from his body, extending his skin into unknown shapes and variations. Drawing blood again, whether from her sly bites or the tears her unrelenting pull on his metal attachments had created.

They displayed a wonderful perverted imagination, these women at Brownie's club, as they dispensed punishment on the man's willing body. Soon, not one part, no square inch of skin had been spared as they took full advantage of the offering he provided. Lips, eyelids, cheeks, ears, tongue, chest, genitals, legs, toes, all had to bear the brunt of their deliberate torture.

A thick-set brunette reluctantly abandoned him after maliciously teasing his cock and cock stud for what had seemed like ages without ever allowing him to come again, denying him the release he sought so badly.

'That leaves us,' the French woman at our table said to Caitleen as she stood, indicating to Caitleen she should follow.

I looked at her as she rose, despair and resignation taking firm hold of my senses, and our eyes locked. There were a million things unsaid. Which would remain that way.

As they made their way to the improvised stage, I could see the older woman whisper quickly into Caitleen's ear. She nodded in approval.

The man was slumped across the chair, exhausted, totally spent, all energy dissipated.

They reached the heart of the spotlight. The woman with Caitleen roughly kicked the grey-haired man off the chair and to the ground. She stood tall by his reclining form, bent her knees, buried her hands inside her dress and slipped her knickers off. Caitleen hesitatingly followed suit, shooting a panicked glance at the audience as she did so. She was wearing her short black dress and we could all almost see all the way up her as she struggled to grip the tight elastic holding her undies up.

With a triumphant smile, the other woman positioned himself above the prone man, pulled her skirt up all the way to her waist, once again revealing her naked cunt and its prominent jewellery. And began to pee on him. I watched with sick fascination as the liquid trickled out between her shaven lips and surged in an unbroken arc over the man's face. With a look of pleasure, he opened his mouth to catch the warm flow of her urine. The stream from her body quickly came to a halt, sputtered and faded.

She looked to Caitleen, took her hand and installed her in a similar position above the now-wet body of the grey-haired man, whispered once more in her ear and retreated behind Caitleen, where she pulled the bottom of the short black dress upwards, rolling its folds as she went along until Caitleen's bottom half was fully revealed. The dark curls surrounding her cunt were shiny with perspiration.

She shifted slightly on her legs, parted them a few inches, and I was hypnotised by the spectacle of her gash widening imperceptibly as the flow of her pee gushed through the lips like a raging torrent, splashing down onto the man's hair, head and face.

It seemed to go on forever.

My face was flushed, my throat in the grip of dry agony. Even secretly wishing it might be me on that floor, imbibing the juice of her insides.

And on, and on, as every man and woman in the audience feasted on the sight of my lover's nether lips disgorging all the earlier wine she had stored inside her seemingly for this very moment, spied her wonderful intimacy, shared willingly with these strangers what had once been only mine.

A faint smile coloured Caitleen's features as the stream from her finally dried up and the man lay there in a spreading pool, drenched, aching, in sweet agony as the acid of the women's urine seeped into his still-open wounds.

The spotlight died and the stage reverted to darkness, just as the musicians stopped on cue, as if everything had been rehearsed earlier in the most minute of details.

The man at my table turned to me and uttered, I think, his first words.

'Congratulations,' he said. 'That's quite a young lady you have there, sir. I think she will go far.'

'Thanks,' I somehow heard myself saying, for lack of a better response.

*

We ended the evening with drinks at Josiane and Franck's place, off the rue de Rivoli, a plush, lived-in apartment, with a maze of corridors and Persian carpets adorning the walls. After the evening's performance, and all back at our table, the conversation had drifted aimlessly and, I think, neither Caitleen or I wished to be left alone with each other right then. Avoiding painful truths.

They were in textiles, well-off, had no children and tried to explain to us how they had initially become involved in the club. Spoke good, cultured English. Bored, fearful of the emotional involvements outside affairs might bring, they had been looking for thrills, a way to broaden their sexual horizons. Wasn't this the perfect way? The rules dictated no rules whatsoever, you indulged, you pleasured or were pleasured, never any way of planning the events, you just went with the flow. Didn't the sheer unpredictability of matters carnal give it such a wonderful thrill, they asked us?

We pretended to agree.

They wanted to know more about us. It appeared we were not your typical club couple.

We had long before agreed on our doctored story. It had elements of truth. An affair, fleeing from a rich and powerful husband, trying to keep away from the limelight. Enjoying Paris but finding it all rather expensive.

Josiane and Franck took pity on us. Felt they had adopted us. He asked me to come to his office in Aubervilliers, in the Paris suburbs, the next day. Was interested in my having a look at his financial structure. His local accountants and finance advisors had little expertise in the offshore funds I had hinted of. He would explain to me the intricacies of the French tax regime. Felt confident an outside eye might perceive some genuine opportunities. I quickly agreed: a new set of eyes always brought a new perspective to things, didn't it? Maybe we could so some business after all, he said. And was sure we could come to some form of arrangement as far as compensation went. We fixed an appointment.

'And you, Caitleen?' Josiane inquired. 'You lovely girl, can we do something for you?'

Caitleen explained how her lack of language skills didn't help.

'And I have no wish to put on an apron and serve tea at the W. H. Smith Salon de Thé round the corner,' she added petulantly.

'I understand,' Josiane said. 'I had something else in mind. A friend of ours, not from the club, a banker who's done the family some past favours, has a substantial investment in a classy art gallery on the Rive Gauche. He was telling me just the other day that he was seeking someone who presents well to work there, to greet the important Japanese and American customers. And all the French girls with good English he's employed there so far have proven too aggressive, think that being polite to foreign visitors is below them. Wouldn't pay much in the way of basic, but there would be a commission on sales.'

Caitleen agreed this could be of interest and Josiane promised to call her acquaintance the next day.

By the time they drove us back to our rue St Denis flat, we had become the best of friends and our material future appeared a touch brighter. Neither and Caitleen or I, tired, emotionally sucked dry by the evening, wished to discuss the rest. The French couple were a godsend and my initial suspicions were ill-founded: they didn't appear to want anything from us. Just the pleasure of our company and our complicity.

Within a week, our financial worries had been banished away. Caitleen was already in place at the art gallery on the rue Monsieur Le Prince and I was on a handsome retainer to dig out the many loopholes in local tax legislation to enable Franck's company to shelter some of its profits in out-of-reach and utterly legal places.

This honeymoon lasted three weeks, as our confidence returned, and I could freely watch the smile on Caitleen's face broaden on a daily basis, as she added to her wardrobe with gay abandon. And French clothes suited her so well. She loved the art gallery, meeting the collectors, some of the artists and their agents, and closing the sales was a cinch, she claimed, relishing her new duties. I must come and see the current exhibition they had on. Bizarre but deeply fascinating, she said. Maybe in a week, I had promised, still busy setting up Franck's basic new investment structure.

Brownie's club was closed for a few weeks for refurbishment, so we had to find new watering places for our evenings. Memories of the sexual excesses faded slightly.

Josiane and Franck invited us out for a meal at a fashionable restaurant near the Faubourg St Honoré, which had just been given its second Michelin star.

'The club reopens next week,' Franck pointed out as we sipped at our coffees. 'A special evening is being arranged for Thursday, for a change. There's bound to be a lot of us; a grand celebration. The owners want us to celebrate with a difference so there's a theme.'

'Yes?' Caitleen asked.

'Leather,' he said. 'Very English, no? It will make you feel very much at home, I think. English clubs go big on leather, don't they?'

'I'm afraid,' I interjected, 'that we don't have much in the way of leather clothing, have we, Caitleen?'

'No matter,' Josiane said, taking Caitleen's hand and winking gently at her. 'Those who do not wish to wear leather can come without.'

'What do you mean?' I asked.

'Totally nude. It's always the agreed alternative for theme evenings. And I do think Caitleen would look quite splendid, don't you think?'

Franck nodded. Caitleen lowered her eyes.

'So you wander in stackers, in from the street?' I asked.

'No, of course not. Don't be ridiculous, Joe,' Josiane said. 'You wear a coat. Take it off inside.'

'I don't know,' I replied.

'But let it be a surprise,' Franck said, slapping his credit card on the table to pay the substantial bill. 'Please, don't tell us what you are planning to to wear. And let it be an evening to remember.' He raised his glass of cognac in a toast to the following Thursday.

*

'I don't want us to go.'

'Why, Joe?'

'I just don't, that's all.'

'That sounds very childish. Give me an explanation. Be rational.'

'You want me to be rational? What if you get the red circle, what am I going to feel seeing you in the centre, prey to all their perversions?'

'It's not just you, you know. Haven't you thought of what I might feel?'

'Sure. And it's not right.'

'Anyway, there's only a chance in, say, a hundred of being chosen.'

'That's too much of a risk.'

'But Joe, doesn't it give you a thrill? That you or I might have to go on to that stage and perform? Sure gives me a buzz, you know.'

'No. It doesn't give me a buzz, just makes me sick at the prospect, Caitleen, and I'm amazed you're so fascinated by this disgusting circus at the club.'

'Anyway, you said it at dinner, we don't have leather gear.'

'Yes, and I can see your eyes sparkle at the sheer thought of the alternative.'

'Well, you do have a leather jacket, I suppose.'

'Oh, come on, Caitleen . . .'

'Come to think of it, I've always thought leather is rather pervy, goes with bikers and tattoos and chicks with Goth hairstyles and Doc Martens shoes. Not me, I fear.'

'So, it's agreed, we don't go?'

'I don't know, Joe, let me think. I'm too sleepy to argue about it now. Let's just go to bed.'

Caitleen disappeared into the narrow bathroom to wash her teeth.

We didn't discuss it again.

I was working late at the Aubervilliers offices. Franck had given me a key. Examining some of the company's records was easier done after working hours when the secretaries and junior management staff were no longer around to raise awkward questions about my presence or function.

It was already eight o'clock and I realised I still had at least a couple of hours work on the dossiers, so I rang Caitleen at the flat.

The phone rang and rang. We had no answering machine. It then dawned on me what evening it was and a deep pit dug itself in the core of my stomach.

It took me ten minutes before I could hail a cab. Another half an hour to reach the Grands Boulevards and our small flat. Caitleen was still not home. I pulled my old black leather jacket from the hanger and rushed out onto the street. The road to the Left Bank was all one-way, so a cab was out. I began running.

The bouncer at the door recognised me, frowned slightly at my conventional attire. I had slipped the leather jacket on over my day suit. He let me through. I could hear the strains of the music rising from the basement, hypnotic, tinkling melodies on the edge of sensuality. I slowed my pace as I walked down the stairs.

The club was packed.

The unholy pallor of Caitleen's unveiled body was like a magnet at the centre of the pool of light. She had been laid out on the floor, where a small rug had been placed to cushion her body from the coldness of the stone. Her eyes were closed. Her legs splayed apart, her whole crotch wet, matted with the spent emissions of I knew not how many men. On either side of her an escort of nude men, four here, three there, were masturbating over her quiet body, their cascading ejaculations falling down on her like a rain of love.

There was a faint smile on her face as the come splashed down all over her skin, reaching face, chest, stomach, and thighs, and I watched in dread as her arms moved and her hands smeared the stuff even further afield, massaging it deeply into the softness of her breasts. A line of men awaited in the semi-darkness by the stage area, next in line for the show, already stroking their cocks aloft in readiness.

I was sick there and then at the floor of the stairs.

No one took any notice of me. The spectacle had their undivided attention.

I ran back up the stairs.

9.

Forgiveness Song

By morning, Caitleen had not returned to the rue Saint Denis. I have been known to cry. This was one of those nights. I assumed she must have returned to Josiane and Franck's place for a shower and a clean-up. I waited patiently for her return, all of my senses in constant uproar, my whole soul at sea without a compass, struggling for my sanity, confusingly thinking of the way I could still rebuild our life together, the words I should say, the words I should have said, the words I would say.

Words. The foundation still holding up the fragile edifice of my sanity, sheltering the still-burning intensity of the love I carried inside me for Caitleen. The capricious, the whore, the woman I still loved with all the energy of despair. I had once thought I had reached the pits of pain when I used to evoke her in the arms of Zeusmark. This was much worse.

Mid-morning came and I hesitated for a long time before calling the gallery.

She was there. Answered the phone in her chirpy accented French.

'Caitleen?'

'Oh, it's you. I was told you were seen at the club yesterday night.'

'Yes. I was. Briefly. Arrived late, I think.'

'Listen, Joe. I'm not going to apologise. I went there with my eyes wide open.'

'Of course.'

'I had to try. Do it once. You know how it is, you'd always wonder how it might have been had you not tried. Isn't that what we said before we first agreed to sleep together? Remember, Joe?'

'That was a long time ago, Caitleen. A lot has happened to us since as a result.'

'Well, I've tried. I know. And some of it was good. Maybe now I'm aware of my true nature . . . Listen, there's a client who's just walked in. I'll be home later, normal time, OK?'

She put the phone down.

Throughout the afternoon, I found it difficult to concentrate on my work and the files full of facts and figures scattered untidily across the kitchen table which I had to use as a desk.

A peck on the cheek when she returned home after six. She hung her coat up on the peg on the back of the front door. I'd never seen the grey dress she was wearing before.

'I had to borrow it from Josiane. Doesn't fit me well, too loose under the arms,' Caitleen said, making for the bedroom to change into her jeans and a T-shirt.

'I guess you didn't wear leather after all, to begin with?'

'No. You guessed right.'

The chill of the Paris winter had entered the apartment with her and was seeping under my skin.

I watched her change. Secretly searching for traces of yesterday on her body. There were none. Just her pale nakedness.

'Couldn't catch a cab to go to the club,' she said. 'Had to walk there. A very odd feeling, journeying along the Paris streets with nothing on underneath my coat. Felt rather self-conscious; but also madly excited. Sexually.'

'Must we talk about it?' I asked, not yet ready for sordid details or explanations.

But she was intent on discussing yesterday.

'Yes, we do,' she answered. 'We do indeed, Joe.'

'If that's what you want.'

'I said it earlier, I'm not going to apologise to you for what I did. I was hoping, though, you would come, be there, be with me, involved.'

'What, to provide you with moral support while others fucked you as if you were no more than an inflatable doll?'

'That's not the way it is, Joe.'

'That's what I saw. Or at least what I could stand seeing, Caitleen.'

'No, you're wrong. Very wrong.'

'Tell me, then. I see you're aching to do so. Put me right on what happened.'

'I was assuming my sexuality, Joe. We talked about it later with Franck and Josiane. It helped me understand. You see, with us two, sex is good, sometimes it's even really great, Joe, it was in those early days in London, maybe because of the fear of being discovered. There was a joy in the clandestinity. Something forbidden. Yes, it was great then.'

'You mean it no longer is?'

'We've grown accustomed to each other, Joe. When I was married, I didn't realise life could be more. Then I met you and saw how much I was missing. Fucking with you added a wonderful, new, emotional dimension to the sex. That's why I fell in love with you and soon couldn't do without. At the cost we know. Now I have you, but there is still this nagging feeling lurking inside that there is something more out there. That's what it's about, Joe. I do love you still, but I want to experience more, experience it all.'

'Caitleen's philosophy.'

'You don't have be sarcastic. It's an exciting new road and I want us to go down it together.'

'Even if it means I have to watch you being fucked by other men?'

'Yes, Joe, and one day, I even want to watch you make love to other women too. I want to offer you to another, Josiane maybe, I think you would like her. I want to wet your cock inside my mouth and see it rise and position you at her gates, and caress your balls as you enter her and thrust with that wonderful energy of yours. And I want you to be there by my side and give me to other men and caress my breasts as they pleasure me. Don't you see, it's not one-sided, we can explore these new horizons together.'

'You're crazy, Caitleen.'

'No, I'm not. I'm just becoming awake, like a flower, Joe, I've only begun to bloom. We must crave for new experiences. It will make us stronger, keep us together, you see.'

My mind was reeling. Everything inside in me was in a state of rebellion against what Caitleen sought.

If I closed my eyes, she would have sounded like just another new-age philosopher spouting crackpot nonsense, but my eyes were open and it was Caitleen there, a Caitleen I didn't recognise.

'Together, Joe. Indulge me, I want us to try everything and . . . '

'What else is still left?' I interrupted her, my voice raised in anger. 'Do you wish to see me flogged, hammer nails through my cock, brand me? Maybe that would be fun. Is that what you want?'

'Please, listen, try to understand.' Her hand moved to my cheek. I brushed it aside.

'What else, Caitleen? What else do you want us to go through, tell me!' I shouted at her. The pain inside was speaking.

She sat down on the corner of our bed.

'Much more than you can imagine, Joe,' she answered calmly.

'Surprise me.'

'I want us to do it all. To give you to others, to share you, to . . .'

I snapped. Could no longer take all this. From her, of all people.

'Enough, Caitleen, I just don't want to hear any more. Please. I didn't come to bloody Paris to share you, or to be shared. You're making me feel sick again. I need some air. I'll be back later.'

I slammed the door behind me, seeking refuge in the cold arms of night.

I walked for over an hour, trying to calm myself down, down the rue St Denis to the Chatelet, crossing the river through gusts of freezing wind and downing coffees in busy bars off the Place Saint Michel to warm myself and then back up Sébastopol.

Caitleen was no longer in. I checked her wardrobe and all her favourite clothes had gone.

*

The dreams.

A large room with a king-size bed. Photographs on the wall, of airport luggage arrival areas. I recognise Newark, although I've only passed through there once, some years ago. The sheets are whiter than white, luminous, shine with the brightness of fire. Events unfold slowly, like a slow-motion silent film. Caitleen is there, quite nude and resplendent, more beautiful than ever, flashing the broad smile I'd loved so much in London when we first met and touched. Tenderness radiates all over from her lithe body, every part of her is alive. The tender, pale pink tips of her breasts beckon my lips, the intricate hieroglyphic patterns of the curls of her pubic hair beckon my eyes, the familiar mole at the onset of her cleavage resonates like a beacon. Her hand moves towards me as she solicits my presence on the bed.

I wallow in the starchy texture of the sheets as Caitleen tongues me from top to bottom, inveigling herself into the space between my toes, moving up my legs, coating my cock and balls with the sweetness of her saliva, licks under the acrid hollow of my arms, nibbles excruciatingly on my ear lobe before guiding her wet tool inside its waxy hollow.

I close my eyes to allow the pleasure to take over. As I do so, I feel a subtle change in the sensation crawling across my body and open my eyes. It is no longer Caitleen touching me, but a man. I don't recognise his face. Bland, reasonably good-looking, younger. His hands and mouth explore me with professional ease, like a masseur at work. I turn my head round to see where Caitleen is. And find her.

At the foot of the bed, greedily swallowing the dark cock of the man whose mouth freely roams over me. She works her thick scarlet lips up and down his cock with manic energy, taking him all the way to his dangling, hairless balls, and I imagine briefly his head beating against the further recess of her throat as her cheeks swell and she gasps for breath. He comes inside Caitleen's mouth and a spasm courses through his body as he gently bites my shoulder and his hand tightens around my own cock. Which, I see with horror, is quickly becoming erect under his expert touch.

My mind is detached from my body as my eyes glance at the nearby window. Where are we? It's sunny outside. California? Santa Monica maybe, and the warm beach lies beyond?

Caitleen soaks up, wipes the man's dripping come from her lips with her tongue as she detaches herself from him. She bends again and holds the still-pulsing penis, still spewing intermittently its hot, white seed, looks at me invitingly and, in my dream state, I can lip-read what she is saying: 'this is my gift to you, you are my gift to him'. I raise myself and approach my trembling lips closer to the stranger's penis and Caitleen delicately inserts its length inside my mouth, smiling as she does so, partaking in this unholy communion.

It is a dream, I struggle to remind myself and I awake, in sweat, alone in our Paris bed, distressed. I thrash around for another hour or so before I manage to fall asleep again.

And the narrative resumes almost where it had previously ended.

We are still all three entwined among the white sheets. I am on my back. The other man is vigorously fellating me, while behind his supple body, Caitleen is inserting her hand deep into his rear, stimulating his prostate to alarming effect as his cock surges from between his legs like a long dagger of hard flesh.

We change positions. Caitleen is our ring mistress.

She instructs us. Determines our placings, our couplings.

Goes down on all fours on the bed, thrusting her heart-shaped rear at me with her wonderful lack of modesty. I obey and I breach her in one swift movement, balancing the forward weight of my body on my knees to accentuate the penetration. Behind me, the other man readies himself, I can smell his breath, the pungent odour of his perspiration. He seizes my arse cheeks, pulls them apart, widens his target and still lubricated from our earlier combined secretions, enters me with one savage thrust that tears me apart and pushes me deeper into Caitleen's innards as his momentum increases and my own fucking of Caitleen borrows his rhythm, so that she might soon feel that both of us are copulating with her at the same time.

The dream becomes an obscene loop that fucks on forever, like a peepshow out of control.

Caitleen roars aloud as she orgasms. Even though the film we are participating in is silent, I hear her in my mind. A lusty, vulgar shriek of intense satisfaction, an animal yell rising deep inside her, rocketing towards the surface of her skin, electrifying every nerve-ending in a volcano of an explosion.

Suspended between layers of sleep, I sigh deeply, praying for the dream to end, for an end to the pain.

Morning finally comes. Premature. Cold.

And I would awake again in the solitary bed, with every image of the dream still etched deeply on the back screen of my brain. There were variations. The airport. The colours of the sheets. Sometimes it would be another unknown woman, rather than a man, joining our carnal thrashings, dark-haired, tanned, slim. Once or twice, I guessed the city outside the window was New York. But every time, I would be used and have to watch impassively as the smile spread over Caitleen's face while others pleasured her in ways I could not.

Dreams of America.

*

Cornelia had changed clubs. Some new owners had bought the place, all part of the frantic shuffle and realignments of properties caused by the impending Disneyfication of the Times Square area, as many old-timers decided to cash in on their investments and leases. The new management weren't comfortable about her loose working hours and the fact that she preferred to sit out more lucrative days and times.

And the fact that one of their factotums appeared over-keen to get into her knickers and felt offended that a mere stripper might play hard to get. She was willing to get used to innuendo and the occasional pinched bottom, but she could see in the guy's eyes that one day he wouldn't take no for an answer any longer and that a bad surprise might lie in waiting for her one evening after the late shift. Cornelia regretted that she'd always had to dispose of the weapons she had been provided with for the jobs. She would have felt safer with one now, she reckoned. But then that had been the point. 'Stripper slays pimp, questions asked about weapon' headlines would prove unwelcome for her erstwhile employers.

She took a break. Spring in the city, picnics in the Park, window shopping, catching up on the books she had accumulated but not yet read, movies galore, followed by a weekend sailing off Cape Cod, but the money she had left over from the last extra-curricular job soon ran out.

The time soon came to dust off her dancing gear and do the rounds. She knew it was still what she was best at.

She had been auditioning for over a week. Most places were happy to offer a slot, but balked when she set her usual conditions: no lap dancing, table numbers, funny business or week-end nights. Well, a girl still needed some principles, didn't she?

Options were running out.

Soon the only options left would be the more disreputable venues, fleapit category or thereabouts. The danger zone; the lowest rung on the ladder of the sex trade. A prospect she didn't relish, but then neither did she wish to update her resumé and apply to academic institutions and return to the fold. She'd written a few anecdotal articles about the sex trade for a publisher of erotic magazines, under pseudonym, but they paid badly and late, and that wouldn't bring much to the kitchen table. And the next rent bill was soon due.

She was glumly considering her limited options when the phone rang.

'Hello?'

'Good afternoon, sweet, Cornelia.'

'Oh, it's you. I was sort of hoping it might be, you know?'

'Strapped for cash, hey?'

'Indeed. By the way, you've never given me a name to call you by. Feels odd not to be able to.'

'Names are unimportant, Cornelia. Just call me Mr X.'

'That's not a name, that's a code.'

'It will do for now ... Listen, my dear Cornelia, we understand you are in a bit of a predicament.'

'You said it, you know everything, don't you?'

'We also know that you're too proud to ask for help.'

'You're right, Mr X. It's a flaw in my character. My way of retaining my total independence from what they call society, I suppose.'

'I understand,' he said. 'Let me make you an offer.'

'I don't think I'd want to ... eliminate, kill, whatever you call it ... full-time, you see. It would be unhealthy, I fear. I'd always seen it as a practical way of getting the extra cash for special occasions.'

'Books?'

'Exactly. I reckon you think my values are pretty odd, but they are worth killing for, as far as I am concerned. Food, clothes, it's different. It's life. I can make sacrifices, compromise ... ' her thoughts were getting all muddled up as she attempted to explain her curious rationale to him.

'No, Cornelia,' he interrupted her rambling monologue. 'We wouldn't you to work for us full-time. There's not enough work, anyway. The more irregular your pattern of hits, the less risks are involved for all of us.'

'So?'

'So, basically, we want you to remain available to us whenever the right assignment comes up. We like you. There is elegance in the way you function. We wouldn't wish to lose your positive frame of mind. You need a job. It's good for your cover.'

'And the cash,' Cornelia added.

'Absolutely. I take it you intended to remain in the same line of work?'

'Yes. I enjoy dancing.'

'We can arrange matters. We have a controlling interest in a small, clean, well-run club on 57th Street, between 7th and Broadway, the Vegas Lounge.'

'I know it. Tried for a job there just yesterday.'

'I'm aware of that.'

'They said they had no need for extra dancers,' Cornelia said.

'The people in charge didn't know it was you, dear Cornelia. A job there is yours. On your terms, as usual.'

'Gee, what can I say?'

'You can start on Monday, the afternoon shift, the one you prefer. Be there. The management know you'll be coming. The necessary paperwork will be ready. More or less the same basic wages as your last place, okay?'

'Great,' she said, with much relief.

'We shall remain in touch.'

He hung up.

Cornelia was already buzzing at the prospect of dancing again.

Decided there and then that she would have to devise a new routine for herself. For which a new selection of music would be required. She rose from the sofa and began picking through her CD collection, mentally sequencing new combinations. Yes. That song was classy, that one slow and sensual, another a tad mournful but just right for the gyrations with the g-string. She already felt childishly excited.

She now had a full weekend ahead of her. Why was spring in Manhattan so enticing now, so earthy, so sexy, she wondered?

After she had completed the tapes, she knew she would treat herself. Indulge. But what? Her funds were too low for clothes or shoes. She hunted through her wallet, counted the sparse green bills.

Sex? Yes, sex was always free.

That's what she would treat herself to.

*

He was browsing through the crime and mystery racks at the back of the Strand's cavern-like ground floor. Cornelia had spotted him earlier when she had brushed against him as they both looked through the half-price hardback review copies section. He must have been in his mid-thirties, wore black Farrah slacks and a black Wranglers cotton shirt, with his grey jacket hanging from his shoulders as he examined the books on offer. His hair was turning grey and he needed a shave. His light brown loafers were badly scuffed and didn't go well with the rest of his clothes. She liked the fact that he didn't appear to worry too much about his appearance. Different from so many others, she felt. Maybe he wouldn't be as boring. Might even be fun.

He was stretching for a volume on an upper shelf, among the L's.

Cornelia approached him.

'They have steps in the next aisle,' she said.

'That'll be alright, thanks,' he said. 'I have it.' He pulled the dusty book from the shelf. Opened its pages, still ignoring her. He had an accent she couldn't quite place.

He had left two books on the floor.

Cornelia knelt to see the titles.

Out of the corner of his eyes, he must have caught sight of her movement.

'Those are mine,' he pointed out, turning towards her.

'Oh,' Cornelia feigned surprise, and then, deciphering the spine of one of the books, disappointment.

'Isn't that the new John Irving?' she asked.

'Yes,' he said, looking up at her. 'Just a collection of stories and essays.'

'I love his books,' Cornelia gushed truthfully.

'I know,' the man said.

'He's so . . . unique,' Cornelia continued. 'What's your favourite of his?'

The man thought briefly before answering.

'*Garp*,' he told her.

'Yes, it's great, but I have a soft spot for *The Cider House Rules*, you know. Parts of it still can make me cry. I can identify so much with some of the characters.'

'I understand,' the man said but then fell silent, visibly struggling as to the means of moving the conversation along before it foundered on the rocks of literary criticism.

Cornelia handed him the books he had left on the floor. Examined the other as she did so, but did not recognise it.

'Haven't heard of this one,' she queried.

'Saw a review in the *Voice* or somewhere,' the man said, taking the books back from her. 'It's the story of a French student who fell into a sadomasochistic relationship. Supposed to be autobiographical.'

'Sounds rather sexy,' Cornelia smiled at him.

'I gather,' he said, blushing slightly. At that moment, Cornelia knew he would be the one.

She extended her hand. 'My name is Cornelia.'

He reciprocated. 'Gregory.'

'Where are you from?'

'Sydney, in Australia.'

'Ah, I knew it wasn't a British accent,' she said.

'It was once,' he said. 'I was born there but moved to Australia some time ago. Better work prospects.'

They were blocking the entrance to the narrow aisle, and an older woman in earth-mother hippy garb indicated her displeasure. They moved aside.

He was still hesitant. Visibly not used to pretty young women making the first step.

'What are you doing in New York?' Cornelia asked.

'I'm here for six months. Covering for one of our correspondents here who was having a child and chose to return home to have it. Health costs are cheaper. A news agency,' he explained.

'Interesting,' Cornelia commented.

'What about you?' he asked her. They were now moving slowly together towards the cashiers and the Broadway exit.

'Still a student, I'm afraid, although getting a bit long in the teeth,' Cornelia lied. 'Working on my masters. I have another year to go,' she explained. Well, it was only a white lie.

He paid for his books by credit card. Cornelia hadn't picked any up during her journey through the bookshop. They passed the security panels and both retrieved their bags from the guard on duty.

Gregory finally risked it.

'Are you doing anything? If you weren't, I was sort of wondering, maybe I could offer you a drink?'

'That would be nice,' Cornelia agreed. 'I'd love to have a drink.'

'Good,' he said, stuffing the two books he had purchased into his tote bag. 'There are some nice bars south of Houston, what do you think?'

'Sounds good,' she said and followed him down Broadway, past the cheap fashion shops and trainer emporiums through the tourist crowds.

It was nice to be able to talk about books, Cornelia reckoned. One of the drawbacks of working day after day in a strip club environment was its distinct lack of conversation. The customers were out and the other dancers didn't have much in the way of verbal gambits. She almost felt like rambling down a university campus again. With an older man.

It was easy to find books in common with this guy, as they began comparing endless experiences and discoveries.

'Call me Greg,' he insisted after the first two rounds of drinks. 'Only my mother and the people at the office call me Gregory.'

'Greg. Greg.' Cornelia slowly enunciated. 'Yes, that sounds fine,' she laughed.

'You're still in no rush?' he inquired. Outside, night was falling on SoHo. Cornelia felt good.

'No, not at all,' she told him.

'Maybe we could eat together, or you'd like to see a movie? Or we could go to a club, listen to some jazz? There's a good cajun band playing at that place around the block, I'm told,' Greg suggested.

At last a guy with manners, Cornelia thought, maybe that was the British part of him. She decided to put him out of his misery. Already over the last half an hour, she had noticed him on several occasions pondering whether to make contact with her hand across the table.

'That all sounds nice, very nice, Greg. Maybe another time.'

Disappointment spread across his face.

'But,' she continued, 'a nice quiet drink would suit me best. I only live five minutes away. Why don't we go to my place? I've some cold wine in the fridge . . . and I could show you my books.'

He eagerly called the waiter over and asked for the check.

Yes, Cornelia felt, it would be nice to wake in the morning with a warm, live body still cuddling up to her. Her feet always got so cold at night and there was no better cure than a man.

10.

The Shadow of her Absence

'Yes,' Franck said, as I eagerly listened at my end of the line. 'She is staying with us, so there is no need for you to worry, Joe.'

'Will she speak to me?' I asked him.

'No. She said she needed a few weeks apart from you. To reflect. To think.'

'I see.'

'It was difficult for us too, Joe, when we began this exploration of our sexuality. It's rare for both partners to begin the journey on the same wavelength, you know. And you're both so much younger. And in a foreign land. I'm sure it will work out. With time, Caitleen will figure things out and you'll come together again with a full and total acceptance of what you want to be. Believe me,' he assured me.

'I've got this nagging feeling swirling around me telling me that I might never accept it all, Franck,' I said.

'Patience, Joe, Patience. And keep an open mind.'

'I shall try.'

'Do.'

I plunged back into the financial paperwork and its myriad complexities, hoping it would take my mind off my errant Caitleen. But all those obscene images kept on returning, never letting go. Nights were worst, seeking her warmth in the bed next to me and embracing emptiness, and then imagining her again and again in the arms of others, inventing my own pornographic film which I projected onto some kind of wide vision mental screen in which penis after penis, cut, uncut, long, thick, in all shades of pink and brown, veins throbbing, wet and slippery, would enter her cunt in slow motion, forward, out, forward, out, until it would just turn me mad. But it didn't stop there. I could close my eyes and cut off the images of Caitleen being defiled by stangers but the sound stayed on and all I could hear were all the things shad once said to me in the throes of desire as well as things she had not yet said. 'Jeezzus, Jeezus, oh Christ, it's good, it's so good; and on and on. Hell became a movie. And I was the director.

Two weeks went by without Caitleen even contacting me.

I knew from Josiane and Franck that she was still staying in their guest room at the Paris apartment. I would deliberately phone them on Sunday evenings, but there never was an answer, so I knew they must all be at Brownie's. I stayed away. Feared the pain.

I had to go down to Montpellier for a week to look after the books in another company of Franck's, where the accounting system had to be rejigged to fall in line with the banking arrangements I had set in place with the head office in Aubervilliers.

I wandered the southern town's streets, indifferent to the smells of the nearby sea and the delicate spices suspended in the air, wandering like a ghost every night before collapsing on my hotel bed and crying in the privacy of the comforting darkness.

I missed Caitleen so badly. Wanted her back.

I was ready to forgive.

To forget.

If this had to be the way too keep her, I would join in, I decided, become a reluctant libertine. Eventually, I knew, Caitleen would tire of the excesses and be the same again, and would welcome the harbour of tenderness I knew I would represent when the time was right.

Franck was right: I had to remain patient.

Understanding was another thing altogether, though.

But on my first day back in Paris, my insecurity just exploded inside of me and I walked across the bridge and made my way to the Odéon area, avoiding the Boulevards by cutting across the rue Gît-le-Coeur past the kebab joints and remainder bookshops, emerging on the main thoroughfare by the Metro station and the clock which always seemed to be running five minutes faster than my watch. I crossed. Already rehearsing all the right words in my mind.

Past the chemist, the imitation Irish pub, the cheap Japanese restaurant and the small tourist hotels, and I began climbing the rue Monsieur le Prince.

The art gallery was at the Luxembourg end of the street, on the right hand side, sandwiched between a *bandes dessinées* store and a Thai restaurant. I was slightly breathless after the climb.

As I pushed the glass door open, I instantly forgot every word I had been storing away for the argument to come and knew that I would give in to any demand or condition Caitleen might put forward. Putty in her hands. A slave meekly obedient to his mistress' demands and harsh orders.

The white walls of the gallery were a jumble of images. Which I totally ignored. At the back of the L-shaped area, past the hanging art and all the way down the heavily-varnished brown parquet floor, was an information desk where I thought Caitleen might be lurking, away from the sharp glare of the ceiling lights. There was no one sitting there as I approached, the occupant of the canvas director's chair having momentarily moved away to the back office. A cigarette butt with a red lipstick ring smoked away in a big glass ashtray, among piles of catalogues, thick phone books and scattered paperwork.

Caitleen didn't smoke.

There were noises coming from the office.

'Il y a quelqu' un?' I shouted.

'Tout de suite, tout de suite,' a female voice rang out.

A tall, dark-haired woman in a black leather suit walked out. Her voluptuous shape stretched the costume in all the right places. Thin sculpted eyebrows, long lashes and Jagger-like lips. She looked me up and down.

'Oui, Monsieur?'

I reverted to English.

'I'm looking for Caitleen,' I answered.

'She is away,' I was told.

'When do you expect her back?' I inquired.

'I don't know. She's working for a client of ours,' the woman said. 'And who are you?'

'My name is Joe. Caitleen is ... a friend. I work for Monsieur Franck. I understand he has connections with the gallery.'

She smiled broadly.

'Ah, Joe. *Oui*, we know who you are. And it's true, Franck is a friend.'

'Good.'

'I am Chloe,' she said, extending her hand in greeting. She had expensive rings on almost every finger.

'Hello, Chloe,' I acknowledged. 'Nice to meet you.'

'Chloe Délices,' she added. 'It means Chloe Delicious, you know. But the lovely Caitleen must have told you about me, *non*?'

She sat herself down in the chair behind the desk, offering me a premium view of her spectacular cleavage.

'No, I'm afraid Caitleen hasn't. She doesn't talk much about her work, you see. Well, the fact is I haven't seen her for a bit.'

'Ah,' she nodded understandingly.

'So,' I continued, 'you don't know when she is expected back? Later this afternoon, maybe?'

'I don't think so, Joe,' Chloe said. 'I gather the work might take a few weeks.'

'Really?'

'Yes, we have this wonderful American artist, Staton Kearn, under contract. He's promised us an exhibition for next spring. He's in France for some time, said he was tired of painting New York girls. Wanted new faces. On his first day over, he walked into the gallery, and loved the way Caitleen looked. So we agreed he could have her on loan, and she was happy to be used as a model. We're so excited, he's such a vibrant talent. Caitleen was thrilled. I know from experience how much a woman loves to be a muse.'

The familiar knot of pain was tightening in my stomach as she spoke.

'Anyway,' Chloe went on, 'while the current exhibition is running, I wanted to be present in the gallery, so there wasn't much for Caitleen to do. All the photographs have already sold following the opening *vernissage*. I was allowed to keep my favourite, though.'

I must have appeared puzzled.

Chloe Délices rose from behind the desk.

'I see you were too busy worrying about your Caitleen to look at the exhibition, weren't you?' she said.

'Yes,' I answered as she came up to me and took my arm. Her smell was musky, green, fruity, a sensual cocktail that quickly laid siege to my senses.

'Let me be your guide. Let me see these amazing pictures for the first time through your eyes, dear Joe.'

She escorted me through the images on display. It was an exhibition of black-and-white photographs titled Porn Art, in which Chloe herself was at the centre of every single shot. The photographer had a Turkish name. He was vaguely familiar to me, I must have seen him mentioned in magazines before, maybe even on the cover of a book of nudes I had browsed through, but none of his previous glamour photography had been anywhere as extreme as this.

The pictures had been blown up to large size and were aligned along both walls of the gallery, sleek, shiny prints mounted on panels and protected by glass.

They must have been shot over a period of a few years as Chloe's appearance often changed. In some she sported short, page-boy like hair, unveiling a dark beauty spot at the top of her right cheek, which was hidden from sight in other photographs where her hair had grown long again. Sometimes her hair was swept back, luxuriant like the mane of a lion, in other images it was held tight, giving her the studious appearance of a school teacher, while the parting varied and moved along her scalp. But always, the dark lipstick that delineated the appetising contours of her full lips and those captivating eyes that looked at me now as I made my way between the art Chloe had become. This unholy celebration of her.

The clothes were different in every photograph, whenever she wore any that is, ranging from shimmering, transparent lingerie to shiny rubber gear, sleek leather belts and braces, high-heeled studded fuck-me shoes and boots, prim and demure polka-dot dresses and a dazzling array of stockings and garter belts high-lighting her genital area and her regal moon-shaped arse in all their brazen glory. The focus was always on her cunt and rear, the angle of the shot often magnifying their size to dizzying effect so that they dominated each photograph and you couldn't take your eye away from the giant whiteness of her intimacy.

In most photos, Chloe was on her own. Only a handful saw her in the company of others. An old man here with his arm draped around her shoulders as she reclined on a table with a massive black dildo sticking out of her arse. A shaven-headed black guy, his dark dome carefully placed below her magnificent breasts as she sat on a high stool in some club; a young dyke half Chloe's size holding her hand in a country lane while she raised one leg to reveal another implement emerging from her rear. A young man, in a park, as she lay back in his lap, both of them against a tree, her summer dress raised to her waist revealing a phallic-shaped piece of wood inserted deep into her vagina.

Somehow, the photographs of Chloe on display rode that thin line between overt pornography and wanton exhibitionism. Even though she was seen to be penetrated in almost every image, there were no men's cocks to do the deed, no flesh inside flesh. Only objects, things, thus sanitising the obscenity of the intrusions.

The majority of the penetrations were anal, and whenever her rear entrance was free of implements, it still dominated the image, dilated, stretched, puckered, frowning darkly from the repeated invasions: smooth metal dildos planted deep inside her, a pencil, a lipstick tube, the neck of a coke bottle, monstrous two-headed parodies of male members, pale and bumpy, black turd-like plastic cocks, the pommel of a whip, small white ben-wah balls, carrot-like objects; and in the most outrageous of all the images, another bottle whose top barely emerged from her wildly distended orifice, revealing its square trunk deeply embedded in her innards, as Chloe kneeled on all fours in garden full of dark trees, a lacy dress pulled short of her resplendent buttocks, head looking back at the camera, mouth open in a picture of fear and pleasure combined, her long hair falling down over her shoulders, where the strap of her dress had slipped slightly. How the squat bottle (a milk bottle?) had been pushed so deep inside her without tearing her apart I could not imagine, a living testimony to the magic elasticity—and training—of her sphincter muscles, no doubt.

'Yes,' Chloe said, watching my reaction. 'That is one of my favourites. Amazing, *non*?'

'You bet,' was all I could find to say. 'Looks painful.'

'Yes,' she answered. 'Took us a long time to get right. But that look on my face, it's so innocent, isn't it?'

'I don't know I would call it that,' I reacted.

'The image exists because we purged it of all that might weigh it down, and all that remains are precious forms, chiselled contours and inspired compositions,' Chloe said, reading from the catalogue she was holding. 'These images celebrate womanly beauty as never before. I offered the photographer's lens, and the man behind it, all the brazenness of a free woman, don't you think?'

'Well, you've got guts,' I told her.

'Since the exhibition opened,' Chloe said, 'I've had all these hardcore film-makers getting in touch with me, offering me parts in their production. They just don't understand, do they? Can I offer you a coffee, Joe? We have a machine in the office at the back.'

'Sure,' I accepted. As we walked back down the gallery floor again, I asked her:

'Staton Kearn, what sort of work does he do?'

'You've never come across his art?' she was surprised.

'No.'

'He's sensational,' she said. 'I'll show you some of his books, we have them on the shelves, I think.'

Staton Kearn's art was bizarre and I took an immediate dislike to him and it. His forte was the meticulous photographic reconstruction of bondage and S/M scenes from cheap, clandestine 1950s comic strips and illustrations. His fetishistic obsessions came through strongly in the meticulous care with which every corset and stocking seam was lovingly emphasised amongst the clutter of Heath Robinson contraptions of suburban would-be torture chambers. The models had all been groomed carefully, hair and lipstick, to recall women of forty years back, although their body shapes often belied this. Many of the women he used were Betty Page look-alikes, but without the grace.

'His masters are John Willie and Irving Klaw,' Chloe indicated as I raced through the pages.

'What's the new project? The one he wants Caitleen to help out with?' I asked her.

'Something completely new. He wants to go beyond bondage,' she said. 'There's too much of it around. It's difficult to innovate. He's done it all, you see, the ropes, the helpless women, the fighting women in black stockings, the whips. He said he wanted to find a new form of eroticism. The event horizon of sex, without all the old apparatus and cliches, Staton said the other day.'

'And what does that mean when it's at home?' I queried.

'Somewhere around, I know,' Chloe said, searching through the mess on the reception desk, 'there's some of the tests he did with Caitleen.'

'Show me,' I demanded, much too fast, much too eager.

'Here we are,' she held up a couple of Polaroids.

It was just Caitleen's face.

Bare.

Natural.

The way I would always want to remember her.

Her dark eyes staring straight at the lens. Her mouth half-open. Both heartbreakingly innocent and mischievously knowing. Sad and happy. Severe and questioning.

Right there and then, I missed her. Awfully.

'His idea,' Chloe interrupted my reverie, 'is to just have images of faces. Naked. Unadorned. Out of context. Isolated from their bodies. Those would be the main photographs in the exhibition. Where the spectator would have to guess the emotions, the feelings, the sensations by the expression in the woman's eyes. Then, separately, there would be an identical number of smaller pictures, maybe even Polaroids, of the bodies, and looking at these you would have to guess which face matched which body, according to the body scene, where all sorts of things might be happening: breasts being touched, tortured with pins, whipped, or just caressed by anonymous hands,

male and female, where her genitals might be splayed open, penetrated with objects, fucked, licked, pierced. Isn't it a great artistic
concept? From just the look in the model's eyes you would have to
know in which image hot wax was being dripped over her skin, or
warm come, or pegs being attached to her breasts. So exciting.'

Nothing surprised me any longer.

'And Staton just loved Caitleen's face, said it was so expressive.
Like a blank canvas. Even mentioned she could model every photograph in the collection. A one-woman show, just like mine,' she
continued.

I had seen and heard enough.

'You don't think I could keep one of these?' I asked Chloe, as I
handed her back the two Polaroids.

'I don't think so, Joe. The gallery might need them, and they're
only tests, anyway. Staton might not approve. But you could always
ask him, he's working at an atelier we recommended. Has hired it
for another couple of weeks.' She hunted for the address and gave
it to me. Mentioned, though, that Staton was back in New York for
a couple of days, right now, to complete some unfinished business.
Would be back by the end of the week.

*

'I'm afraid she's moved out, Joe,' Josiane said. I had rushed her
to their flat straight from the gallery, foolishly taking a cab, wasting
too much time crawling at a snail's pace between the Left Bank and
the Champs Elysées, caught up in the midday traffic. It would have
been faster by the metro.

'When?'

'Just a few days ago.'

'Why?'

'Said she didn't want to impose on us any longer. She had been
invited to stay with this American artist she had met through the
gallery.'

'Staton Kearn?'

'I don't know,' Josiane said unconvincingly. 'She didn't say what
his name was. I'm sorry, Joe.'

'Are you?'

'I'm sure Caitleen will contact you again when the time is right,'
Josiane said.

I quickly backtracked to the Latin Quarter. The studio Kearn had
hired was in Montparnasse, coincidentally above a small art cinema
Caitleen and I had often visited. There was no answer at the door
and no sound beyond. I bribed the concierge to let me in to have a

look around. Explained I was an art journalist and hoped to get an idea what Staton Kearn was working on next. For a scoop. He accepted my explanation and took the cash.

The large, mostly empty area was quite bare. Rolls of canvas and paper sheets in all colours stood against one wall, past and future backdrops to the studio's activities. A few threadbare carpets littered the wooden floor. There was little evidence of anything that might have happened here recently. I nosed around. Abandoned canvases, some abstract, others of *natures mortes*, washed out flowers and vases and glass bowls against muddy backgrounds.

I searched through a waste basket in one corner of the brightly-lit atelier with its glass roof and pools of silence, and found what I had been looking for. Rejected Polaroids, some crumpled beyond recognition, others still viewable. All images of Caitleen. Serene. Laughing. Frowning. Smiling. Worried. Vacant. Childish. Pensive.

Every one was like an arrow aimed at my heart and invariably hitting the bulls-eye.

In some of the remaining photographs, isolated body parts.

A bare pale shoulder. A knee. A navel. A breast. Hers, I recognised it from a beauty spot. Acres of skin, like a desert landscape.

I pocketed all the Polaroids.

Another note got me the address where Kearn was staying in Paris. A small hotel near the Place de la République.

Which became my next port of call.

No. Monsieur Kearn was not in. Yes, he was in Paris. Had only gone out an hour or so before. Did I wish to leave a message? No, they didn't know whether a lady was staying with him. That would be privileged information. Could they be of further assistance?

I found myself a dark porch across the road from the hotel, positioned myself there in the shadows and waited.

Her absence weighed on me like a knife twisting in my gut, but still my love rushed out in her direction like a sailing ship without a rudder, hankering for land, a Flying Dutchman of the soul seeking his salvation. I had found her once; I knew I could not bear to lose her again. We had unwittingly stumbled onto the madness that is sex and drowned ourselves voluntarily in it, and now the undertow was barking at us like a mad, illogical beast, and in our fear, it had separated us, as we both now floated like seaweed, carried by the tides into conflicting directions, on different levels of the madness.

Night came.

I lurked, like a crazy stalker, I thought.

My stomach felt like a deep hole.

I abandoned my vantage point and rushed to a corner all-hours épicerie where I picked up a couple of bars of chocolate and a bottle of mineral water.

Non, monsieur, he has not returned. Are you sure you do not wish to leave a message?

I rejoined my observation post where I could spy on all the comings and goings at the hotel.

Daydreamed for what felt like hours on end, rehashing the past, my life before Caitleen, my life with Caitleen, attempting to find a compass to guide me through my ever-increasing confusion and desolation, to decipher all the small tell-tale signs that had littered the bumpy journey. Recalling the good times, the epiphanies, the colours of flesh and sweat, the beds we had fucked in, her eyes, her smiles, her touch.

It must have been around midnight—I was no longer even checking on my watch—when a cab drew up outside the hotel and a stocky middle-aged man stepped out, followed by Caitleen. The first thing that occurred to me was that she was wearing the same blouse and dress she had worn on that long-gone day in London when she had agreed to sleep with me for the first time. I was too far away to see the expression on their faces, but as the cab sped away and they walked into the hotel, I did notice the man patting her affectionately on the backside. And the fact that she didn't object to his familiarity.

They disappeared into the light of the hotel's lobby.

I remained where I was standing, shivering now. Maybe it was the cold approaching or the knowledge that I was losing her for the third time. First, the pantomime with Markie, then on that disgusting stage at Brownie's club and now this.

I waited. Closely observing the hotel windows.

The light came on behind a window on the second floor.

Stayed on another ten minutes, then was switched off.

I could spy nothing behind the drawn curtains, not even a fleeting shadow of Kearn or Caitleen.

The lights never came back on all night, as I patiently stood guard in the street outside.

My thoughts were utterly obscene as I imagined their lovemaking in every perverse, sick detail, torturing myself as I did so, picturing every twist and turn of slithering limbs and appendages in the moist refuge of crumpled bedsheets. I was the fly on the wall seeking unheard-of pain in every image I feverishly dredged up in my most fertile of imaginations.

It was my night in the concentric circles of hell.

By morning, I was a mess, trying to keep my eyes open, my throat dry and a bitter, acrid taste filling my mouth. The surrounding streets slowly came to life. A dustmen's lorry noisily cruising by, its scruffy attendants emptying the voluminous plastic bins along the street, women and kids walking to the nearby *boulangerie* and returning laden with fresh sticks of bread. Coffee smells poured from windows.

I kept on waiting. Secretly hoping that Kearn might leave Caitleen back at the hotel while he went out on some errand. I would then barge in. Speak to her, plead. Something. I wasn't even thinking straight by then.

But, around nine-thirty, a cab drew up outside the hotel and Kearn and Caitleen emerged together, dragging three suitcases along with them which the cab driver helped them place in the car boot, after which they drove off.

For a moment, I quickly thought of finding another taxi and becoming part of a bad 'follow that cab' movie, but there were none cruising around anyway, so that was that. When you're helpless, you're truly helpless. So I was left stranded as morning unfolded in that small road off the Place de la République, far away from everything and feeling a right fool.

I found out later that day they had left for Roissy-Charles De Gaulle where they had caught a flight to New York.

Newark, to be more precise. Just like in the dreams.

PART THREE

DEATH THE DARK LOVER
GOING DOWN ON HIM

11.

Manhattan Love Song: Giving the Words to Sorrow

The chattering crowds swirled noisily across the illuminated geography of Times Square, the neon lights and advertising hoardings shining with riotous, brash energy as night settled in for the count all across the island of Manhattan. The diners were mostly full and harried waitresses were swept off their feet as the orders from the floor accumulated. Traffic roared down Broadway. A Cornell Woolrich kind of night.

I had landed here on Caitleen's trail a few days before. Just one lone suitcase with a basic complement of clothes and barely four hundred and fifty dollars after the exchange commission in my wallet. When they had asked me at JFK immigration the reason for my visit, I had answered it was a holiday. It would have been too difficult to explain the line of work I was now in.

Tracking down the ghost of my love.

With a handful of smudgy Polaroids in my pocket, hope and a resolute sense of purpose. And little in the way of clues. Well, Philip Marlowe and his detecting ilk usually had less to go on.

I had found a cheap room, rented by the week, in a hotel off 42nd and Broadway which hookers and transvestites used for their business. It was quiet during the day but at night it was like a ghostly procession of johns, anonymous identikit grey-suited businessmen and under-age college kids meekly walking up and down the ill-lit stairs or crowding the lift and looking elsewhere whenever your eyes caught theirs. But it was cheap and central so it didn't bother me.

On the plane coming over to the land of the free and the brave,

I had tried to organise myself and had jotted down pages of notes, plans, alternatives. I knew it would be a rush against time to find Kearn or Caitleen in this teeming city. I'd remembered from the books Chloe had handed me at the gallery that Staton Kearn lived and worked in New York, so it had to be my first natural port of call.

The end-of-millennium detective would have to be computerised, I reckoned, so I quickly found a cyber-café where I could log on to the Internet. And sip strong coffee to keep my energy going. As I well knew from my earlier work with Zeusmark, sex and crime were always in the vanguard when it came to new technology. After barely half an hour of using the search machines available, I had located Kearn's web site. The perfect entrepreneur, he previewed some of his work on the site, together with his diary, and sold personally-signed prints of his photographs and books. I browsed what was on show, but there were as yet no images of Caitleen in evidence and the last diary entry had been entered prior to his Parisian trip by his web master.

I e-mailed him, using my previous cover as an art journalist—it had worked once, so why not use this perfectly good front?—requesting an interview to discuss his new direction; I hinted that I knew some of it from discussions with people back in France. Hopefully, this would tickle his interest. I arranged an electronic mail-box c/o the café. And waited.

I spent a few days cruising New York's more dubious clubs and pseudo-bohemian joints. Something inside me told me that Caitleen would similarly sniff them out. I was trying to put myself inside her, to think what she thought, to guess at her newfound fascinations.

I got the appointment, and the address of his New York studio where he wished to conduct the meeting. Just what I had hoped.

*

'I'm told by reliable sources that you came across a woman in Paris who might be the subject for your next project?'

'That's incredible. How did you find out about that?'

'It's my job.'

'Very few people knew.'

'So is it true?'

'Yes, it is. A truly wonderful young British woman ...'

His voice tailed off.

'And?' I quizzed him further.

'Very beautiful, but strange. Would never talk about her past. Could never get any information out of her about why she was in Paris, what she had done before. Cultured, though.'

'Did she have a name?'

'Of course, but I don't think she would approve my telling you.'

'Come on . . . It just gives me a better feel of things. I'll keep it strictly off the record. Will definitely change it when I write the piece.'

'Caitleen.'

'I see. So how is the new project developing, Mr Kearn?'

'It's not.'

'How come?'

'She's gone. She was going to be the perfect model for these new images I had been dreaming of. We'd done some test shots back in Paris and I decided that if we returned to New York, we could get the whole project done here fairly quickly. She agreed to come.'

'What happened?'

'She just disappeared a few days ago. Without a word of warning. We hadn't quarrelled, or had a disagreement. Just like that, walked out one morning while I was out buying some more film stock. Took her suitcase and clothes along. Didn't steal anything, but left no note, not a hint of explanation. I was just devastated, I can tell you.'

'There was no prior indication?'

'No, not at all. Don't think I've haven't reflected about it for hours since. Not a clue. I tell you, I was heartbroken. Truth is I was beginning to fall in love with her. You know how it is with artists, you always mistake models for potential muses. I could have sworn she was going to be it. Maybe she could read the signs, I dunno, and she ran as soon as she sensed my feelings switching from professional to personal. There are women like that, you know, who run as soon as you talk about love.'

'I know,' I said.

'So I'm no longer sure whether I'm going to stick to this particular project. Without Caitleen, it's not going to be the same. The tests we'd done were just incredible. Anybody else would make it all feel second-rate.'

'Could I see some of the test shots?' I asked.

'Let me explain first what I had in mind, then you'll understand better what a change of direction this project would have been.'

The way he presented the series of photographs he had been hoping to assemble made them sound more interesting than Chloe's second-hand Paris account. A simple thread of logic almost turned them into things of beauty, into art.

'Mind you,' he added, genuinely forlorn by Caitleen's disappearing act, just another middle-aged man sulking for a lost dream,

'I might have guessed early on she had some form of personality defect. When we discussed the photos, she would come up with the weirdest suggestions for the body shots. She did to seem to cultivate a strange fascination for the extreme shores of sexual activity. Like a morbid curiosity that just demanded to be fed. It was fascinating in a worrying sort of way, because she was so young and outwardly could look so pure and damn innocent. Then, shortly after we'd come back to New York and I was planning to do an initial series of head shots in the studio I have upstairs, she went out and had her hair changed. Completely. I almost didn't recognise her when she returned. Not only had she trimmed those wonderful dark blonde curls, but she had dyed her hair jet black. Quite a shock.'

My stomach dropped.

'She said,' Kearn continued, 'that she wanted to feel different, like the second incarnation of Kim Novak in *Vertigo*. Then, the next day, she was gone. Caitleen . . . a strange girl. I will miss her though.'

I tried to get the bogus interview to a perfunctory end.

'So it's back to stockings and bondage scenes now, is it?' I asked him.

'I don't think so,' he replied pensively, 'I'm still going to try and do those photographs I initially had in mind. In a way, Caitleen did give me an idea I could utilise: I'll hire some New York girls I've worked with before. Reliable ones. And I'll have them change their hair and colour to Caitleen's. So she will still be in the photographs, as a ghost, I suppose.'

'That's fascinating,' I concluded.

I rose to depart.

'Didn't you want to see some of the test shots I did of her?' he asked.

'Of course.'

It was Caitleen, but it was also Kim Novak in the Hitchcock movie all over again. The dark, tightly pulled-back hair, gave her a slightly Hispanic hint and the ghostly pallor of her skin was even more accentuated by her new colouring.

'I might begin looking for her,' I told him.

'It's something I had thought of, too,' Staton Kearn said. 'But life has to go on. You can't allow a woman to take it all over.'

'How sensible.'

'I'd sniff around private sex clubs, some of those shady downtown places. She was always asking me questions about that scene. As I said, there was some warped fascination at play there.'

'I'll remember that.'

*

It felt like a dead end.

She no longer even looked the same now and New York was a city where sex was always in the air, on every corner, on every skyscraper floor and dimly-lit bar. No wonder Caitleen had gravitated here. You sniffed the air here and it was everywhere, like a thousand possibilities opening up, from cut-price blow jobs on the Bowery to clandestine afternoons of illicit sex in the small bedrooms of the Algonquin Hotel. Where could I even begin to pick up her elusive trail?

I could waste a lifetime trooping across Manhattan in search of her, checking out strip shows, porno booths, lap and table dancing joints, cruising the dark corridors of the Port Transit Authority or Penn Central and still not get a whiff of her. And then I knew she didn't equate sex and money, so those would be dead ends anyway. It was the thrills Caitleen was after. Those raw, unique sensations neither Zeusmark nor I could provide her with.

Arriving in New York, I had been quietly determined, planning to be methodical and systematic in the search for her. But at the first possible fork along the road, Caitleen abandoning Staton Kearn so quickly, I been had derailed and I was off the tracks again. Stranded.

When we had been together, we had sometimes talked of America, of coming to New York and, later, many other places. But New York always came first. She had never been. I tried to recall the small things we had discussed, to remember her words, what we might have planned in our then-wild dreams, searching for clues to her current whereabouts, but then I recognised the fact that all the dreams, all the talking had been mine and she had listened quietly to all the promises of great sex in tall buildings, walks down to the Village and the farmer's market in Union Square, summer mornings in Central Park reading the hundred Sunday newspapers supplements. New York had been a magic wand I had waved at her like a pied piper. It had always been my idea, I realised.

And now we were both here, but apart. She with dark hair, nigh unrecognisable and me just being me. It felt much like a book coming to an end, where every future line was already written and all we could do now was mechanically go through the motions, play our parts as dutiful puppets, mouth our given dialogue, follow the allotted path of the fiction we were entangled in.

*

Cornelia woke and immediately became conscious of the alien body sleeping beside her in the bed.

Greg. She remembered.

She looked at him.

She liked the fact he had a hairy chest. So many men were too smooth there. Made them look like clothes store mannequins. The thin dark curls moved up all the way to the top of his shoulders. Nice.

He groaned lightly in his sleep, moved, made contact with her. He opened his eyes. Met hers.

'Morning . . . Cornelia,' he mumbled.

Even better, he remembered her name.

'Good morning, Gregory,' she answered.

He smiled gently at her, rubbed his eyes and straightened himself out, raising his back against the pillow his head had been buried in. The sheet was pulled down to Cornelia's waist, her breasts were free. Greg kept on gazing at them in quiet fascination and adoration. He looked up. Their eyes met.

'I suppose this where you ask me to leave and indicate I've outstayed my welcome?' he said.

'Not at all,' Cornelia answered. 'I'm not that sort of girl. I thought we could actually have breakfast together.'

'That would certainly be pleasant,' he said.

'But before . . .'

'Yes?'

'You could kiss me again.'

'I see I was forgetting my manners,' he said, leaning over towards her. His lips were dry but hers were as fragrant and soft as yesterday night.

'You know, what I like,' she said, after they had finally parted for breath, 'is making love first thing in the morning. It feels just like indulging in luxury.'

'Before breakfast?' he asked, with a touch of irony.

'Of course, sex is always better on an empty stomach,' Cornelia said, pulling the bed cover to her side, unveiling his nakedness.

They kissed again.

And more.

*

'Will you call me?'

'Of course I will. Promise.'

It was already mid-morning. They had showered together in the narrow curtained-off area of Cornelia's bathroom. But had then succumbed again to desire. And had to shower again. Separately this time, to avoid further temptation. Greg had rang his agency warning of his lateness.

'When?'

'This evening, I swear.'

He was dressing hurriedly as she sprawled in a white robe on the unmade bed, watching him with a quizzical smile on her face.

'What are you doing this afternoon?' he asked. She had told him she would be out and not to bother phoning until early evening.

'Things to do,' Cornelia said.

He slipped his jacket on and made for the door. She rose to give him a final peck on the cheek.

'By the way . . .'

'Yes?' she inquired.

'You seem to have some great books over there, Cornelia. I must come back, if only to read them.'

'They're my pride and joy,' she shouted out after him as he ran down the stairs. She closed the door, feeling light as air, and shedding the robe fell down on the bed with a great feeling of liberation. Yes, this had been nice. Really nice. She lazily stretched her limbs akimbo, then set the alarm for two in the afternoon. Neither of them had caught much sleep the night before and she was due at her new club for the three o'clock shift. She would need all her energy for her first turn on stage. They would expect her to put on a good show. Cornelia closed her eyes, and sailed off to sleep without even bothering to pull the bed cover over.

*

'So, you're Cornelia,' the guy in charge of the afternoon shift said, looking her up and down.

'Yes, that's me,' she replied.

'You certainly come highly recommended.'

'That's very flattering.'

'I understand you've danced around here before, so you'll know all the basic rules. We like things nicely raunchy, but you have to know where to draw the line. This is uptown, not a Times Square burlesque, understand?'

'Sure,' she answered. 'I assume you've been told all I do is dance on stage. No private shows, shower cubicles or other fancy business. I made it quite clear when I was offered the job.'

'Yes, I was told,' he answered. 'But you'll miss out on a lot of good tips and commission. When the clients here like a girl, they're not mean when it comes to extras.'

'I'm not in it for the money,' Cornelia said.

'That's your problem, lady. Some of us are,' he said.

'In that case,' she added, 'I'll take care of the problem myself, if you don't mind.'

'Fine. Your choice. I must say, you don't look the type. For a stripper, I mean, no offence.'

'None taken.'

'Most of your kind would arrive for their first gig in a flashier outfit,' he said, pointing to her jeans and short-sleeved white T-shirt.

'I don't like to bring attention to myself,' Cornelia explained. 'Offstage, I wear what I feel is comfortable.'

He looked at the large canvas Barnes and Noble tote bag she was carrying.

'I presume you've got decent stage gear in there?' he queried.

'Yes,' Cornelia agreed. 'And my tapes and make-up.'

'Good. I'll show you to the dressing room. The other girls will show you where everything is. You're on in half an hour. There are four of you doing the afternoon shift. You'll have to do four turns on stage. Maybe an extra one if the girls on later arrive late.'

'Fine. That's no problem.'

The stage was smaller than the one she had previously been used to, she noticed, as she positioned herself centrally in the darkness. The guy at the bar operated the sound system and was looking her way, awaiting her signal to switch the music on.

She peered into the room. Not too bad an audience for the time of day. She had watched the previous dancer's set. Hadn't been impressed. She knew she could put on a better show. Demonstrate that she had class to spare, even for a second-rate club like this.

She gave the barman a nod and the beat took over.

The stage lights came on and Cornelia shone like a beacon in the spotlight. She had embroidered sparkling pieces of coloured glass into the translucent fabric of the Victoria's Secret underwear she had carefully selected, and their reflection mirrored across the room like a small moving strobe light. She liked the effect. Worked even better under the yellow-green lights than she had envisaged.

She began her gyrating.

Some of the men craned forward on their barstools. Probably regulars, intrigued by the appearance of a dancer they hadn't come across before.

As she danced, she spun her body around a few revolutions, to enable all the spectators to take it all in, her tall frame, her round poetic buttocks, the suppleness of her waists as she undulated in rhythm with the loud music spilling out from the speakers at either end of the stage.

The first song hadn't yet reached its opening chorus when the first extended arm emerged from the room's darkness into the light, waving a greenback. She moved nearer and allowed the man to tuck the bill under the elastic of the lone scarlet garter she sported at mid-height across her right thigh. Her improvised money-belt. His fingers brushed her skin. Cornelia felt good already. Retreated back into the centre of the spotlight, where she belonged. Her own world. Of movement and familiar, evocative sounds.

There was faint applause at the end of the first piece of music. She had not yet shed any piece of clothing. Sweat was already running down her body as she settled into position, legs wide apart, arms held high above her head, for the second, slower piece in her repertoire.

She snapped apart the velcro strips holding her bra on and, following a rapid ballerina-like spin, released her small, pert breasts from their embrace. As she sensually dragged her hands across the top of her body, Cornelia could feel that her nipples were painfully erect. Still bearing the trace of Gregory's mouth and tongue, no doubt. The sensitivity of her body seemed magnified by her memories of the night before as her thoughts kept on returning to the concerto of flesh she had enjoyed with the journalist. She turned her back on the audience and her hands began a slow, teasing caress of her shoulders before moving lower, in the parody of a man's embrace. Only her buttocks now moved, shimmered to the sound of the guitar solo that snaked its way through the darkness of the club. Cornelia closed her eyes and completed the middle part of her set like a blind woman in a sea of fog, with only her body responding to the pulsing, languorous beat of the song, her thoughts elsewhere in a bed of sweetly entwined limbs.

The finale was upon her almost too soon. She was buzzing all over as she seldom had before. She realised this was the first time she had danced on stage so soon after a night of good sex. It was like entering another dimension. Much ahead of schedule, she slithered swiftly out of her knickers and then with no further delay her g-string, revealing her whole nudity in one full swoop. She wanted to be naked. Her whole body cried out for it. She continued dancing as in a trance, her hands roaming restlessly across the dampness of her skin. She opened her legs and allowed a finger to brush imperceptibly across her pubic thatch, feeling the dampness rising, swelling between her cunt lips and soaking curls as she squatted briefly for another revealing *entrechat*. She swivelled round and positioned herself on all fours, grinding her arse to give the men out there a complete view of her intimacy. She blushed, realising how unusually open her lips must be, how much her secretions must be showing in the strong glare of the light. So what the hell, she concluded as she rose to her feet again for some more bump and grind, that's what they were paying for. The fact she was getting a strong sexual kick out of it today was her own bonus.

She circled the brass pole in what was for her a final improvised bout of obscenity, feeling the hardness of the metal press firmly against her pubic bone as she ground herself against it, still thinking of how Greg had thrust so well into her depths just a few hours earlier. The music came to a halt as she was still moving, having lost her synchronisation in the sexual tumult of the moment. Cornelia quickly shifted her stance, gave the audience a quick bow, gathered her abandoned pieces of clothing and rushed off the stage. Some of the men were still clapping out there as she slammed the dressing-room door behind her, out of breath and utterly confused. She had never been so turned on, she knew. Hoped she hadn't made too much of a spectacle of herself. That she wouldn't lose the job on the very first day.

'That was great, lady.' The manager's head peered round the corner of the door. 'Damn sexy. If you were trying to impress me with your debut, you succeeded. Just great!'

Cornelia sat facing the make-up mirror, still naked and dripping with sweat, watching the deep pink orgasmic flush drain slowly from her cheeks, neck and upper chest.

Shit, she realised with horror, feeling the volcanic warmth still seeping from in between her legs, she had never actually come on stage before! This was wild, and maybe dangerous, she thought.

She adjusted the shower to cold and stood under the cooling jets of water until the frenzy had left her body and she had regained her composure. After drying herself, she took the colourful silk kimono from her tote bag and slipped it on before seating herself in a remote corner of the dressing-room to read a book while awaiting her next turn on stage. Ironically, it was a book about strippers doing the rounds of shitty working men's clubs in the wilderness forests of British Columbia in Canada, where the godforsaken women moved relentlessly between highways and dancehalls. Maybe she would too write a book about the dancing life one day.

Her next three dances reverted to normality as she concentrated on the job at hand with attention to detail and a measured dose of sexuality. Earlier must remain an exception, she had sensibly decided.

*

'Hi!'

'What are you doing here?' Cornelia asked him. Greg was sitting by the door to her apartment, reading a newspaper.

'Left work early. Tried to phone you, but forgot you were not going to be in. Wanted to see you again. Do you mind?'

Cornelia inserted the key into the front door lock.

'No, not at all.'

He followed her inside.

'I've been thinking of you all day, Cornelia,' he said. 'Just couldn't get you out of my mind. Couldn't focus on my work. Not that there was anything much happening. Just lots of press releases and uninteresting pieces from foreign agencies we couldn't use for our bulletins.'

'It's nice to see you, Greg. I'm happy you came. Really.'

'You look tired?'

'I am tired. Didn't sleep much yesterday. As you well know,' she chuckled.

They kissed, feeling the familiar fire moving between their bodies. It felt so natural. As if they had been kissing for years.

Cornelia disengaged herself. She remembered she hadn't cleaned up following her final dance of the afternoon. Had been in too much of a hurry to return home. Had somehow been hoping that Greg might be there.

'I need to take a shower, Greg. Do you mind?'

'No, not at all.'

'Alone,' she said, noticing the gentle smile spreading across his face. 'I really need to wash. I've done so much walking today, have to clean up to be presentable for you, hey?'

'That's absolutely fine,' Greg said. 'I'll wait. Afterwards we could go out, have a sushi together, maybe?'

'Yes,' Cornelia agreed.

She returned twenty minutes later to the room to find a sullen Gregory and her tote bag emptied all across the sofa: towels, make-up, tapes, purse, notebook and the soaking pieces of flimsy underwear that could scarcely be mistaken for what they were not. He looked accusingly at her.

'What's all this?' he asked. 'I wasn't trying to be inquisitive, just saw it was a book bag and was wondering, was just curious what you might have bought or were reading.'

'It's ... it's ...' Cornelia couldn't conjure up a believable lie fast enough.

'It's underwear, Cornelia, and it smells of you, so strong. What are you doing, walking around town with this sort of underwear in your bag? I shudder to think.'

She was still fishing for plausible explanations, but she knew that nothing she could invent would convince him. She had to tell him the truth. Or part of it, at any rate.

'Listen, Greg, it's not what it really seems. Being a student, you need money to make ends meet. I don't enjoy being poor. I want to be able to buy the books I want, to live in a decent apartment, get nice clothes.'

'So?'

'I strip.'

'You're a stripper?'

'Not always. Sometimes,' she said. Then, 'But I'm not a hooker, Greg, I swear. All I do is strip, nothing else. No one-on-one shows, no funny business.' She repeated her mantra.

He appeared unconvinced, but they still went out to her favourite Japanese restaurant, on the corner of 13th Street and Americas. The conversation was heavier on silences than words as they ate, lost in private thoughts. She pleaded with him to come back to her place after the meal and Greg relented.

They made love, but it didn't have the fervour of the previous night, the same frenzied sense of discovery, and they both fell asleep shortly after.

By morning, Greg had gone.

He had left her a scribbled note explaining how he couldn't live with the knowledge of what she did and the fact that he wouldn't accept sharing her with eyes of others. And how sorry he was.

Damn you, Cornelia cried softly as she crumpled the too-brief letter, I'm sorry too . . .

12.

Reconsider Me

'Hello, this is Cornelia.'

'Hello, dear Cornelia, what brings you around?' the man at the other end of the telephone said. 'I hadn't heard of another rare book catching your fancy.'

'You're right, there is no book,' she told him.

'So why are you phoning?'

'I need an assignment.'

'Isn't your new dancing gig working out? I was told you were pretty good. My colleagues weren't disappointed.'

'No, it's fine. I just thought taking another job on might clear my mind. Clear some annoying distractions away. Something personal,' she added.

'I see,' he said pensively.

'It's not the money,' she assured him. 'I just need something that could keep me fully occupied, so to speak. A challenge, maybe?'

'I understand, Cornelia,' he said.

'If you haven't anything to give me, it'll be fine, too. I just thought I would ask,' Cornelia continued.

'That's fine, Cornelia, no need to explain. You know the routine. Give us day or two and we shall back in contact with you. I can't make any promises right now, but there is a possibility. Bye.'

Cornelia had for some time been mentally attempting to put a face on the man's voice. She knew they would never meet, but suspected he had seen her, watched her dancing at the club, walking down the streets, somewhere. She could sense it in the tone of his voice. The gentle demonstration of affection tempered by cold professionalism. The unflappable tone, the relaxed certitude of his own power. But every image she managed to conjure refused to stay long enough in her brain before fading away into another amorphous, unseizable portrait.

Her call was returned as early as the following day, catching her at the bathroom sink washing her smalls.

There was a job. In California. Her absence from the club would present no problem; everything had been arranged. She would find her flight ticket and an advance on expenses later that evening at the United Airlines counter at La Guardia. She would hire a car at LAX and make for the coast where a room was already reserved for her under the name of Holly Callahan in a small inn in Marina del Rey.

Her instructions would be passed on to her locally. Just a word of warning: the target was elusive, slippery, dangerous. She was to tread with particular care and take all the time she needed to complete the assignment. There was no need to rush. Her job at the club was secure. It would be there for her whenever she returned. Anyway, the deep-voiced man said, almost flirting with her, she would enjoy the West Coast sun and sand. It would take her mind off New York things, wouldn't it?

She looked at her watch. She barely had three hours to pack and get ready before making her way to the airport.

Consider it a holiday in the sun, Cornelia reckoned.

Just what the doctor ordered for a broken heart, maybe.

The assignment took just over five weeks to complete and turned out more difficult than she had expected. And unavoidably messy. The target was a wealthy Santa Monica masseur. As she researched him, Cornelia quickly guessed why his name had been placed on the contract. Most week-ends he would breeze off to Las Vegas in his Lamborghini where he would invariably lose inordinate amounts of money he no longer had. She guessed the gambling debts had mounted and passed the critical stage, and the creditors, having given up on the prospect of ever recovering the monies again, now required their pound of flesh as fair compensation. It helped her if she guessed at the motivation behind the hit. Provided her with a sense of purpose.

However, using her feminine wiles was out of the question this time around: the masseur was openly gay, and likely to be impervious to her natural charms. She would have to make contact a different way.

His professional services didn't come cheap, but then that was what the expenses she had been provided for were there for. He was good, she had to admit; firm, male hands pummelling her skin into soft submission, banishing the tension and raising a most pleasant tingle from the bottom of her stomach upwards all the way through her system to the tip of her fingers, the edges of her cunt and across the whole landscape of her easily-aroused skin.

'If I'm not mistaken,' the masseur said, as he worked on her, 'this is the body of a dancer.'

'You're right,' Cornelia answered.

He continued the massage, rubbing the aromatic oil deep into her shoulders, as his thumbs put exquisite pressure on the bone.

'Where do you work?' he asked.

'In New York. I'm just over here resting,' she told him, enjoying every single second of exhilarating sensation.

He never worked alone with a client, though. Always had an assistant or two on hand to help him with towels, creams and oils, all impossibly pneumatic siliconed bimbos from the same California beach-blonde production mould, hovering around the massage table, spilling out of their tight white nurse-like uniforms. The male visitors probably appreciated the view. But Cornelia needed quality time with him, without the interference of others.

She studied the dossier on him her employers had supplied with much care, searching for the gap that might allow her entry into his graces. She tailed him to Vegas, observed him at the tables, picking up hustlers for a night's entertainment. Didn't appear to have a regular boyfriend. Played the field. Cruised the Venice Beach front on Sundays looking for fresh meat. Which he always found. She continued visiting him. He made her body feel good.

'Jorge?'

'Yes, Miss Holly?'

'I was wondering . . . you know . . . you see a lot of beautiful people, you have connections I haven't. I'm still new to the West Coast. I'm looking for some work.'

'What sort of work?' he enquired as he continued the vigorous massage.

'I'm game for anything. Sex, you know. But I'd want good money, you know . . . And it would have to be discreet, if you see what I mean. A private party or something like that. With people one could rely on, trust. Somebody you might know, perhaps?'

He remained silent for a few more minutes while he went about his work, toning her nude and now fully-tanned body.

Finally, he made up his mind and waved the blonde assistant away so that they might talk in privacy.

'There is something, Holly. Could be interesting. You're different, you have a real touch of class. You're quite beautiful but you also radiate intelligence. A wonderful combination. Women here, they're so . . . interchangeable.' He indicated the door through which the bimbo had disappeared at his command. 'Girls like that do everything on automatic pilot, smile, fuck, act, whatever. She'd have the same expression on her face whether she was being fucked in the arse or sipping vodka or watching TV. So boring.'

'What did you have in mind, Jorge?' Cornelia rolled over onto her back, dropping the white towel aside and lying there with her legs slightly parted in a blatant indication of willingness.

'I have customers. Very wealthy people. They like to collect private films. Often, they will pen a short scenario for me, and I shoot it. For their consumption only. Very discreet. There are no other copies of the movie. The negatives are destroyed. Top quality pornography for collectors.'

'Interesting,' Cornelia said. 'Years ago, famous writers would pen erotic stories for rich collectors. I suppose this is the modern version.'

'Exactly,' Jorge said. 'You're so perceptive, Holly. In a way you could even call it art.'

'How much would it pay? For me?' she asked, confirming her interest.

He quoted a handsome sum.

She nodded her acceptance.

He smiled broadly.

She knew the hook was in.

'Crime of passion on amateur gay porn shoot'—she could see the headlines already. She knew the given scenario would involve at least one other man, and it was well-known most porn studs were homosexual. Jorge probably had a whole stable of willing bodies at his beck and call. She was, however, wondering where she might fit in.

Arrangements were made for the following Sunday at Jorge's Spanish stucco villa half a mile away from the shore between Santa Monica and Venice Beach. She would be given the script then, he said.

'Anything goes?' he enquired as she dressed to leave.

'Anything goes,' Cornelia winked back at him. If it was a snuff movie he had in mind, it would certainly have a different outcome, she knew.

She made arrangements to check out of her inn on the Saturday, just a general precaution, and returned her rental car to the airport, where she also booked herself a reservation on the Sunday night red-eye to New York and left her luggage in a locker. She returned to the coast on the airport shuttle, crowded between a group of Italian tourists, and found herself a bed and breakfast for the night.

They were ready for her at Jorge's place when she arrived shortly after breakfast. She had noticed a mountain bike in the drive which would make for a perfect drive-away vehicle. No one would notice her as she made her way to the airport later. Sunday here was exercise day and she would just be one more would-be sportswoman cycling in the sun. The final details were all fitting into place.

Jorge had set up the 16mm camera on a tripod at the back of the house, in the open air, near the pool.

There were two guys, young hungry hustlers, flexing their muscles by the water, helping each other spread oily tanning lotion over their lean bodies. They were already in the buff, dark uncut cocks dangling rampant, thick and impossibly long even in repose.

Jorge greeted her.

He took her to one side and explained the scenario he wished to film.

There were only so many combinations possible for one woman and two men, and they had all been written in to the script and more. Cornelia swallowed hard as Jorge unctuously explained how the double penetrations could be assisted with the right amount of lubrication and that she shouldn't worry, he had seen it done before. Then, in an attempt to reassure her further, he added he would join the celebrations later. Sure, he was into men, and would gladly avail himself of those present, but Holly was so special, he'd like to have a taste of her too, as the opportunity presented itself. One woman and three men. Yet more possible combinations.

'Shall we begin?' he said, taking her shoulder bag, and sitting down on the white marble surface of the pool's perimeter, began unbuttoning the white silk blouse she had on. The two other men walked over to join them and, without a word of introduction, helped her out of the rest of her clothing.

Cornelia was unprepared for the festivities to begin so early. Her instant nudity made concealing the weapon still in her bag somewhat academic. She would have to play along until the right opportunity arose. One of the young men was already nibbling on a nipple, almost drawing blood with his sharp, hungry teeth while the other had already slipped two long-nailed fingers inside her vagina, investigating her warmth and wetness. Jorge had quickly moved behind the camera. Damn, Cornelia thought, this wasn't happening the way she had innocently planned.

It took almost an hour before she could make it to the bag to retrieve the small revolver awaiting her there, using a necessary trip to the bathroom as a pretext. By now, she was truly angry with herself, with the men, feeling dirty, bruised and scratched. God, how she hated giving blow jobs . . . She genuinely needed to wash all the filth away from her body, out of herself. But she couldn't leave any evidence around for forensics and would have to wait till the airport to clean up properly. This made Cornelia even angrier. The rush of adrenaline calmed her down and she twisted the silencer on to the weapon.

It didn't take her long. None of the three men momentarily resting from their exertions were prepared for her return as she stood by them, still gloriously nude in the high heel shoes she had been asked to wear for the damn party, legs apart and, without a word, assumed a firing position. Jorge, who was nearest, got his in the right eye and crumpled down silently to the ground. She unloaded the rest of the ammunition into the two bug-eyed hustlers, distributing the bullets into their chests, gut and crotch.

They slumped wordlessly, one of them still desperately clutching his stomach in instinctual defence as his cock began peeing blood. A bullet must have hit him right in the bladder.

It only took Cornelia ten minutes to arrange the scene realistically, clean her prints from the gun with one of the towels they had earlier used to bind her with while they had brutally invaded her, and dress again. She pulled the film cartridge from the camera and dumped it into her bag. She would arrange to destroy it later, burn it somewhere remote, certainly had no intention of ever viewing it.

She slept all the way back to New York.

By the time her plane landed, she felt so raw inside she decided she needed another holiday and rented a small house in the Hamptons for a week which she spent reading, sleeping and greedily sipping ice-cream, systematically testing all the flavours Hägen Dasz had on offer. She could afford it.

*

Cornelia returned to her gig at the club. It was as if she'd never left, and the tan she had acquired in Santa Monica suited the quiet pallor of her body in subtle ways. Her tips increased considerably.

A complete set of the Dennis MacMillan editions of Fredric Brown's short stories came up for sale and she acquired the books by completing a job in Brooklyn, eliminating a young Russian immigrant who looked like the British actor Tim Roth and couldn't even speak proper English. She left him, sound asleep, in a car in a locked garage after connecting the exhaust and its emissions to the sealed car. Looked like a suicide. She was glad she didn't have to use a gun this time; California hadn't been a very pleasant experience. One hit at at a time was enough for the nerves.

Apart from her books and pretty clothes and lingerie, Cornelia's needs were quite modest and the cash in her bank account was now accumulating nicely. Soon, it would be the New Year, the coming of the millennium. One more job, she decided, and she'd leave America for Europe. Paris or London or both. She'd always wanted to go. A pilgrimage to the sources of culture.

There would always be a job for a good striptease artist, even there, she knew. In the meantime, life and its comforting routines would go on: the club, dancing, good Japanese meals, her books. She knew she couldn't complain: others had worse lives.

*

Almost six months had gone by since I'd reached New York and began my investigation into the whereabouts of Caitleen. I had by now drawn a complete blank. She had disappeared into thin air since Staton Kearn had last seen her. I was no longer even sure what she now looked like. All I had were a few photos which went back to London days, Caitleen as I once loved her. For all I knew, her hair was now a different colour, another shape, she might have a ring through her nose, God knows what. I suddenly realised how little I really knew her that she could have changed so much.

I was now technically an illegal immigrant. My tourist visa had long expired. I had managed to get some work to make ends meet, paid for in cash, doing the books for a few rock joints down in the Village and advising a few tyro groups I had met there, whose management was on the cheap side and needed someone like me to decipher the book-length boilerplate contracts inflicted on them by music publishers and record companies. Being an accountant with flexible ethics had its advantages.

I had remained in touch with Kearn, who seemed as forlorn over her as I was, but he had now decamped to San Francisco, where the sex scene was hotter. We'd speak over the phone from time to time, but he hadn't come across any information about Caitleen on the West Coast, despite all his connections in the twilight world. He asked me to join him over there, said there was so much good material for me to write about, but I stayed put. Something inside me still insisted that Caitleen was somewhere in Manhattan and all I needed was a bit of luck and I would come across her when I least expected it.

But what would I then say, apart from begging her to come back? That all was forgiven? That even though the inner scars were permanent, I could find it in my heart to forget and forgive her? I knew it would all sound pretty unconvincing. But I had no other options.

Some of the money I earned went on a small network of informants I had assembled on the fringes of the sex world, who kept a watch for Caitleen in all the seedy places I feared might catch her attention. The fast-disappearing drop-a-coin, watch-and-touch parlours around the Times Square area falling prey to the demolition contractors who were Disneyfying the historical centre of the city, the fading burlesque shows, the strip joints, even the couple or so clandestine studios where porno shoots took place away from the Californian sun, the S/M dungeons, the swing establishments. But we drew a blank everywhere.

Invisible Caitleen.

Her body a tenuous ghost in the market of flesh.

I met a woman. Her name was Cree. She was from New Zealand. She had fallen hard for a Turkish-American guy during a holiday in the Greek Islands. She thought it might have been more than a summer romance and had flown to New York some months later to join him, only to discover he already had a woman here and no longer wished to see her. It was another four weeks before her flight back to Auckland and she couldn't afford to change the fixed-price air ticket. At least he had let her use his apartment in Queens while he stayed elsewhere, so she had somewhere to live while she explored Manhattan where she knew no one else.

We connected, in a bar or somewhere. She was available, lonely, longing radiated from her like a wonderful form of energy. She told me her story, how she had become stranded. Her words touched me. After all, like her, I was shipwrecked in New York too. We both had been abandoned by others, crossed deep seas and vast distances to land here.

We fucked.

Brutally.

And she accepted all the anger that was in me.

Asking no questions about my rage as I mounted her, spread out on all fours on the floor of my dingy hotel room, watching as my rigid, bursting cock entered her flesh, stretching her puffy brown sex lips in its vengeful wake, then dug itself deep inside her arse, widening her sphincter muscles to an obscene width as I forced myself through, aiming at her heart in my simmering fury. With my free hand I held the belt of my trousers which I had earlier tightened around her slim throat, holding her head back as if in a leash in a painful upright position as I repeatedly thrust into her.

I must have been hurting her, but she said nothing and offered me the magic of her body in a glorious act of sacrifice.

She stayed the night, after which we both lay exhausted and spent from our sexual exertions in a landscape of crumpled sheets and unanswered questions.

The next morning, we made love again, more tenderly. Cree accepted my silences, understood that my roughness and despair were an attempt to exorcise the ghostly presences of my past. My giving her pleasure was enough for her. She knew certain things took time.

Cree had ten days left in New York. We spent most of them together.

Listening to jazz and rough-at-the-edges rock groups in the myriad small clubs that were scattered across the Village and the Bowery while sipping endless cups of coffee, walking miles hand-in-hand talking about nothing in particular, getting accustomed to our bodies and the way they repeatedly fitted together and reacted to each other in the comfort of darkness.

So, it reminded me of other times, but there was no anguish this time around, no deep pit in my stomach, full of fear and knots.

Peace was returning to my mind.

But there was still that nagging feeling about matters unresolved with Caitleen. Which I had not told Cree anything about. I needed closure. Something that would help me draw a line under the whole thing. Somehow.

'It's been nice, Joe. Really nice,' Cree said. Her flight was on the next day. She had moved her case of clothes to my hotel room, had abandoned the apartment in Queens.

'Yes, it has,' I replied.

'I have to go back, you know.'

'I realise that.'

'We're having this big family reunion at the end of the year. 2,000 and all that. They're coming from all over the place, England, Czechoslovakia, Australia. It's going to be crazy.'

'And you have to be there.'

'Yes, I have to. Have you made any plans for New Year's Eve?'

'Still a bit early. Almost six months to go. No, I don't know what I'll be doing.'

'If you want, I could come back to New York in the New Year, Joe. Would you want that?'

'Are you sure you'd want that, Cree? I'm not an easy bugger. You know how moody I am.'

'I would like to Joe, really. I could save up between now and then. I'm sure my father would lend me a bit of a money. I'm sure I could get a job here. I'm a good legal editor.'

'I'd love it, Cree. Yes,' I replied.

She fell into my arms and began crying. She did so often when she was happy, even when we made love. She didn't know the meaning of a cold heart.

'Five and a half months, Joe. It's going to feel so long.'

'It's nothing, Cree. We'll keep in touch, write, phone. I'll get myself a computer and we can send each other daily lovebytes.'

'And you'll be my e-male,' she laughed.

That last afternoon together, I insisted she walk everywhere with me with no underwear on under her short flimsy dress.

'You're crazy, Joe. I'll feel so self-conscious.'

'But it'll turn you on, won't it?' I knew her quirks by now.

'You bet. I'll be so wet it'll be pouring down between my thighs.'

'Good.'

It turned out to be a memorable day, but there was an innocent joy in its lustful excess as we counted the hours to the Grey Line bus that would take her to the airport, punctuating the wait with sweet, frenzied, imaginative love.

But those sorts of nights never last forever. And the morning came.

Neither of us enjoyed partings.

As the packed bus disappeared through the traffic across Times Square to pick up another passenger at a tourist hotel, I suddenly realised that New Zealand was literally on the other side of the world.

Did I have a knack for choosing the wrong women? or the wrong time in their lives?

13.

The Lives we Never Had

Time was like a slow, slow river as I counted the days to Cree's return from her antipodes, exchanging both platitudes and pornography over the net. Why did the Internet always have sexual connotations for me?

It was mid-September. I was waiting for a train at Penn Station. Some financial paperwork that had to be picked up in Washington DC. I was killing time browsing through the newsstand and spotted a postcard with a Paul Klee reproduction. Echoes of Caitleen again, pursuing me. Her favourite painter. The second anniversary of our first time together was just a few days away, evoking balmy sensations of my fingers slipping through her curls and the oh-so-tender softness of her uncovered, shivering breasts. I instinctively bought the card. Wrote 'I miss you still' on the back, and then lacking an address as usual buried it inside my jacket pocket, into oblivion again, until the next absurd celebration of her continuing absence.

Suddenly.

Realised.

That despite the time, the pain and sweet Cree, missing her was an understatement.

Every day and every night.

Still.

The station's tannoy system announced a fifteen minute delay of the incoming train. I had to sign for the documents a junior clerk was couriering over. Copyright registration papers, duplicates issued by the Library of Congress for a set of songs for one of my groups. I backtracked to to the newsstand, searching for a magazine to occupy the delay, but none caught my attention. Moved over to the book racks.

At first, it was the cover illustration that I noticed. A photographic close-up of a woman's leg (thigh?), the constricted flesh bursting through the fishnet patterns of a stocking. An image that struck a responsive chord inside my dormant libido.

The Man Who Didn't Understand Women by Katherine Blackheath.

I seldom read women's fiction, but the back cover blurb intrigued me. Something about a man and a woman, London, anonymous hotel rooms, three months of forbidden passion.

Standing in the centre of the station's main concourse, I began reading.

I finished the book at two the following morning. I'd cancelled a routine business meeting at one of the clubs earlier.

It was all there.

Our story.

Without the killings of course. But all the rest of our sad story was there, of the time when Caitleen and I had been a fragile couple.

With some subtle changes: did I really never smile? I was no longer a financial consultant, but an insurance investigator. Our week-end away no longer took place in Eastbourne but in Brighton. There was no mention of her husband, but I now had two children ... Wholesale chunks of conversations we had had, in our usual bed, in bed, were accurately evoked. The letters I had written her. She even described the sounds I would make when I came, the words I would say, those she would herself whisper. The rituals of undressing and kissing. And the woman in the book was also called Caitleen.

I can't say I was shocked. Surprised, maybe. It was strange to see myself in print like that. Or at any rate a character whom I could recognise as me. Possibly angry that she should steal our story in this way.

Towards the end of the novel, after the two lovers had badly betrayed each other, they both travelled a lot, enjoying rather sordid adventures. Mine, I didn't mind. Hers, I winced at the thought she might have actually fucked all these other men, it was so realistic. I even recognised Kearn. His was a somewhat utilitarian romp between the sheets, with a final mercy fuck as a thank-you note. Difficult to know where the fiction and the reality took divergent paths. She wrote well, Caitleen or was it Katherine did. I could sense the emotions, the feelings oozing from the pages as the narrative developed.

But nowhere was there an explanation for her actions, her disappearing act, all the obvious preparations she would have had to undertake to escape my pursuit, deny her very existence. And neither was there a reason why the character in her novel did what she did to me, to him, the somewhat passive, seemingly spineless male protagonist.

Because she thought she loved him, she wrote somewhere in the book.

Which made the whole affair no easier to understand.

The novel ended with a melodramatic shoot-out straight out of a hardboiled noir movie, in which most of the characters, including the two of us, perished. Gave things a sense of finality, but felt all wrong, though.

I was tired. It was dark outside. I was puzzled. I was hungry.

But I had found her, the trail had warmed up again: The Curious Case of Katherine Blackheath.

The next morning I contacted the publicity department of the book's publishers in an attempt to obtain information about the author of the novel. They promised something in the mail. All I received was a flimsy press release, which clumsily summarised the plot and promised oodles of promotions and reviews. About Caitleen, all it revealed was that she was British and lived in New York.

Donning my journalistic persona, I tried to get more specific details through a junior in the publicity department, but there was nothing of substance to be had. The manuscript had been bought from a local literary agent, and the author had been unwilling to provide any further biographical details, let alone a photograph.

My hotel on West 44th Street was undergoing renovation and cheaply-imported Polish builders tramped up and down the corridors, peppering the lift and lobby with thin, white dust. The television set in my room wasn't working. I called out for a Chinese meal. By the time the food arrived it was lukewarm and underspiced. By now, I had jotted down on a pad my course of action. The art of detecting is to be methodical, organised and, most of all, patient. Even though I was not a patient person. But I had made contact with Caitleen again and the fire was burning bright in my heart again. My e-mails to Cree became more infrequent.

I had it all figured out.

Call the New York agent. Arrange for an appointment. Have some bogus business cards printed up to present some sort of front. I had over the past months collected an assortment of glossy British magazines in my room, had noted some of the bylines I would be borrowing for the occasion. I was confident few, if any, of the journalists involved would be known here. Small risk involved, really. Visit the *New York Times* cuttings library to assemble American reviews of the book which might possibly provide some information about the author's whereabouts, in the likely absence of interviews. Determine how regulated British residents were. Was she here on a visitor's visa or did she have a green card? More likely technically illegal like me. Government offices were a weak link where the right amount of money spread around might earn me some valuable information.

That would do to begin with.

If, as I expected, this failed, the second angle of attack would involve more shady methods to trace financial records at the publishers or the literary agency. This was problematic, though.

The biggest risk might involve breaking into her agent's offices to check their records.

Not something I was looking forward to.

But if it came to that, I knew I would. I could sense it in the air. Caitleen was in Manhattan. Probably no more than a mile or two away. I had to find her. I would find her.

*

I finally managed a meeting with her agent, a perky preppy twerp who wore regulation red braces and an insincere smile. No, Ms Blackheath is quite adamant that she wishes to retain her privacy. All their transactions were by phone or mail. Had a nice voice, though.

'Did you know we've a Hollywood option for the book? Not one of the majors, I'll concede, but a production house with a very good track record. They're hoping to line Gwyneth Paltrow up. Personally, I'd have gone for Anne Heche, you know, but she's a hard sell for romantic stories now, of course. See, Mr Edwards, if it were up to me, I'd love her to consent to an interview. It would help sales. The absent author lark has its drawbacks, you see.'

He relented slightly, assuring me he would contact her and strongly recommend she agree to seeing me. Absolutely loved the magazine I was pretending to write for. Really. But that's all he could do. He did have this other client, an ex-classical musician who was now a dominatrix and lived in Alphabet City and penned very erotic books indeed. Great angle. Wouldn't a feature on her be great? She wouldn't mind being photographed in the nude, you see. He would get in touch, one way or the other when Katherine Blackheath responded to my request. No, he didn't know how long it would take.

I attempted to squeeze some more information out of him. Background stuff for my piece. How had he come to represent her? In fact she had initially contacted another agent who had since departed the agency and he had only just taken over her clients. Had never actually met her. Loved the book. So funny. I noted the previous agent's name. She'd moved to Los Angeles to become a reader for a film company.

In her novel, Caitleen's character had decamped to California and become involved in the making of hardcore porno films. Jotting things down on automatic pilot in the agent's office, with its panoramic views of downtown Manhattan, I suddenly recalled with acute precision the feel of Caitleen's lips, in London rooms, caressing the dangling sack of my balls, teasing my rigid stem, before tenderly devouring me whole.

'I don't think I can really tell you more,' her agent said, rising from his padded chair. On the way out, I smiled broadly at one of the young women at a nearby desk. Asked her if she was his assistant. No, just an intern. I smiled again. English accents were popular here. A possible future, useful contact?

*

'I know it's you, Joe,' the letter said. 'Masquerading as Mark Edwards doesn't fool me for one moment. I don't know how you've come so far, so close. But do not try and find me any more, I implore you, if you have any decency left in your body. Don't you realise how you're pursuing a lost cause? Let me be.' She didn't even sign it, but I recognised her handwriting.

'Who the fuck cares about decency? What the hell does it have to do with us? I must see you, Caitleen, or Katherine as you call yourself now. PLEASE,' I answered, sending the letter care of the agency.

At night in my hotel room, I read her few lines a thousand times over. Smelled the paper, desperately attempting to retrieve even a trace of her scent. Those years ago, I had mentally catalogued every one of her fragrances, from the bittersweet smell of her breath on awakening in strange, sordid hotel rooms, which she always tried to obliterate with mints, to the pungent aroma of her under-arm perspiration following our energetic sexual exertions, to the unique perfumes of her inner secretions which I would greedily suck from her as she spread herself open for me.

'I still love you madly,' I wrote her with a distinct lack of originality. 'And whatever I have done wrong, I beg for your forgiveness. I must see you. At least, let's talk. It kills me that I don't know the answers.'

*

'No. I swore it was all over, Joe and nothing you could say or write could make me change my mind now.

Stop stalking me. It doesn't suit you. At all.

It will soon be the year 2,000. Can't you understand once and for all that I have rejected you and call an end to this whole sorry episode?

Get yourself a new life. I have.

Do not write again. I will not answer any more.'

She signed the letter Katherine Blackheath this time. The new her. It was addressed to Joe. Not even to Dear Joe.

How definitive she could be in her vindictiveness.

And no, I didn't understand women.

Her harsh words both pained and angered me. I resolved that we would meet again before the bloody year 2,000. Just wait and see.

*

I arranged to see Stevie for drinks. She was the young woman with the kindly, responsive smile at Caitleen's literary agency. Exploring one further avenue.

In the meantime, I had given out almost five hundred dollars among various contacts I'd been given at the immigration offices to track Katherine Blackheath down. None of them asked questions. They took the money and made vague promises.

It was just a question of waiting, I reckoned.

As our first date ended, Stevie allowed me to kiss her briefly, as we reached the door to the flat she shared with two other ex-Benington graduates in a Lexington Street brownstone.

I'd laid on the charm like a real hypocrite, never even hinting at the true reason behind my attentions. How easy it was becoming to live a lie.

We'd be eating out the following night.

Stevie's freckles made her look even younger than she was.

I was no longer answering Cree's frantic e-mails and cancelled my Internet subscription, putting me out of reach of her. It was too much of a distraction now.

Within days, Stevie and I were sleeping together. The first night was good; I didn't even to have to pretend she was another to maintain my erection. We went to the Hamptons for the weekend. I hired a car.

Stevie was a sweet kid but it annoyed me that she talked too much. But then maybe I was too quiet and it balanced out in the order of things.

But London nights were, so quickly, back at the forefront of my mind again, as I wished Stevie's fingers might move a little further, a bit harder, differently, as we made love between crispy white sheets and she caught her breath in spasms as she lay under the weight of my body. I closed my eyes to banish the ghost creeping between us. It didn't help. She was too close now.

*

There was only a month and a half left to the millennium. All the newspapers and TV news (the hotel had finally put my set right) and chat shows were already rambling on interminably about the parties and celebrations worldwide on New Year's Eve. Times Square would be a killer.

I had six weeks left to locate her.

It would be strange seeing her again, I knew. I knew there was no point in rehearsing a speech or something, I'd forget it in her incredible presence anyway. I'd have to overcome her initial anger, of course.

She wasn't here on a Green Card. I had managed to determine that. Expensively.

Next Sunday, I was intending to ask Stevie an important favour.

*

'No, not there,' Stevie screamed out as we fucked.

'I'm sorry,' I told her. 'I don't know what came over me,' I pleaded, but I knew she didn't believe me.

But I was sorry. She was just the wrong person at the wrong time. I was too tough because she was not the woman my whole body screamed for in an act of madness. I didn't like hurting people. But Stevie was just a means to an end.

She'd agreed to look up the Katherine Blackheath file for me some time the following week, when she would get an opportunity to get into the agent's office during the course of a lunch break. Probably Wednesday as he'd booked for lunch at the Metropole Hotel for a meeting with some Bertelsmann top brass.

*

Stevie provided me with an address. On McDougall Street. In the Village. I must have passed the building on countless occasions.

Stevie had also told me it would be better if we didn't see each other any more. She guessed she had been badly used.

It was a small three-storey building. There was an ansaphone by the front door; there were no names on two of the bells. I tried all of them. None answered. This was in the morning. Same again in the afternoon. Maybe Caitleen worked somewhere during the day. The book couldn't have made that much money. I returned in the evening and the building was still empty. I lurked outside until three in the morning. Couldn't stand it any longer. Felt like a fool. Major calibre schmuck. Freezing my balls off. I gave up for the day and returned to the uptown hotel.

Resolved to visit McDougall Street again at the week-end.

*

They were already spreading decorations throughout the island in preparation for the festivities. Twinkling coloured lightbulbs adorned the bare branches of the trees around Union Square. I was the one who was anything but cheerful.

I'd finally made contact with the other two occupants of her building in the Village. They knew very little of her. Very quiet. Discreet. Kept to herself. Couldn't even describe her in terms I could recognise. She hadn't been seen around much for a few weeks now. The merchant banker who rented the top floor thought he remembered her catching a yellow cab, holding a suitcase, just a week before, although he wasn't sure of the exact day. Maybe a trip to the West Coast because of the film rights to her novel, I wondered?

I tried her bell every two days.

Surely she would be back for Christmas?

*

She missed Thanksgiving in New York.

Well, she wasn't a Yank, was she?

*

Caitleen was back in town a few days later.

But I managed to miss her.

She knew I'd been lurking around, asking questions, spying on her patch, though.

There was a large manila envelope with my name hastily scrawled on it, sellotaped to the bell.

'How dare you follow me the way that you do,' Caitleen said. 'Just go away. I can't stand it any longer, Joe.

If you don't cease this ridiculous, hopeless obsession of yours, I will have to do something drastic about it, believe me.

Accept it: we are no more. Nothing can ever change that fact. You are an intelligent man, Joe, I know that. Can't you understand once and for all that I have rejected you. Full stop.'

It was signed C.

The longest letter I had been blessed with so far.

She had vacated the apartment the same morning. I promptly contacted the letting agent whose sign was already on display and arranged to visit the premises, maybe hoping in vain she had left something, papers that might provide me with a clue to where she had decamped to.

The place was so empty, even the furniture left behind had an insubstantial feel. Wooden floorboards, polished to a high sheen. A desk. Bare cupboards. A bath tub, beginning to rust in places. An old stove. Kitchen utensils. A leaking washing machine. The small, cozy bedroom.

This was the bed in which she had slept.

Alone, I thought. There were no indications of anyone else. The neighbours I had questioned didn't recall any regular visitors.

'No, I think the place is a bit too small for me,' I told the hopeful realtor.

I was back to square one. Just didn't have a clue where to go now, what avenue to pursue next in my search. But still ready to do anything to make contact, touch her again, even for only a minute. Begging for small mercies.

And needing her was eating me up like a cancer.

*

If this had been a book or a movie, this valiant amateur detective would have been working the phones tracking down the cab she would have had to take to carry her belongings away from the Mc-Dougall Street apartment. By now I would have had another address and the chase would be on again. Frantic, faster than before, leading to some explosive climax, with an appropriate pounding soundtrack and slow-mo thrills.

But I stood at my hotel window in a deep blue funk, observing the movements of the whores and their orbiting, hesitant johns on the streets below.

I knew there was something wrong with me. But nothing I could do would change the sickness. It was already an intimate part of me. I couldn't choose between the good and the bad.

I wanted the sun and the moon. Nothing less.

And, in my mindless search for the impossible, I had badly hurt people who didn't deserve any of the pain: Markie, even Zeusmark, Cree, Stevie.

Thoughts of death assailed me as the countdown to the next century accelerated. The crash barriers were being set up around the whole area in preparation for the festivities a few days down the road. Music reached me, broken-up, interrupted melodies flying by my high window as the rehearsals began on Times Square. Streams of workmen with orange hard hats converged on Broadway like flies to honey, their resolute patterns merging with the stop-and-go dance of the sex workers on the dark grey granite-like crowded pavement.

I walked back from the open window. The room's central heating was fighting a losing battle with the cold rushing in from the outside. I didn't care.

By the bed, there was the last photo I had left of Caitleen. I'd had to give all the others out in my search for information about her. It wasn't even a very good one. A black-and-white passport photograph in which she sketched the bare trace of a smile, her eyes deep pools of remote darkness echoing the flash of light in the Goodge Street tube station photo booth where it had been taken.

The telephone rang. Nobody ever rang me here. Must be the reception desk calling by mistake or making a wrong connection.

'Hello?'

There was silence at the other end of the line. Just the faint hint of someone breathing.

'Hello?' I asked again, ready to put the phone down, in no mood to be disturbed.

'Joe.'

Plaintive. Soft. Caitleen.

'Yes?'

'It's me.'

'I know.'

How had she found me? Maybe she was a better detective than I was.

'I'll keep this short, because I know how painful it is for the both of us,' she said. 'You must stop looking for me, Joe. I have another life now and it's important to me that you no longer try and invade it.'

'I . . .' I tried to interject.

'Not a word, Joe. You're stalking me and I just won't have it. You have no right and if there was a decent bone in your body, you would stop. I'm asking you one last time, will you call an end to your sad attempts to contact me. I need your word. Now,' she insisted.

'Caitleen, I can't . . . I just can't . . . I still want you, need you . . .'

'You don't, Joe, Don't be pathetic. What you lust after is just an idea of me, not what I really am.'

'I can't give you my word, Caitleen,' I said. 'And even if I did, I know I would break it one day. I'd . . .'

'You leave me no choice then, Joe,' Caitleen angrily said. And put the phone down on me.

A lone firework shot across the night sky outside. Dancing its meagre way to the end of time.

I closed my eyes.

Only sounds.

And smells.

14.

Too Many Things I Know About Love and Death

She danced.
Oh, how Cornelia danced.
Bumps and grinds in harmony with REM's 'The Wake-Up Bomb'.

It was the late afternoon shift and the audience was sparse. The suits hadn't yet left their offices, by which time they would have just an hour to spare before catching their commuter trains to New Jersey or Connecticut comforts, time enough to down enough alcoholic energy before they had to confront their home life again. Time enough to ogle flesh that was firmer and warmer than the merchandise back in the old homestead.

As she moved, she surveyed the seated spectacle. A few identikit Japanese tourists in assorted grey colours, a bunch of sniggering nerds pretending to each other that sex was not the reason they were here, oh yeah, a couple of serious drinkers who paid little attention to her gyrations on the stage, an under-age teenager who should not be there, nursing a beer, hypnotised by her nudity, some regulars.

She knew already those who would tip well and those who would feign embarrassment when the song ended and she moved towards them to solicit the obligatory donation, the crumpled dirty green dollar bills she would slip under the red garter on her left thigh, before she would move on to the final song in her set and take the G-string off. Which was, of course, the only thing that interested them.

Lefty the Kleptomaniac visited the joint every week on the same day. He always gave her a ten-dollar bill. A generous soul, or else a profound connoisseur of genital anatomy. He had acquired his so-briquet because he invariably pocketed as many as he could manage of the complimentary match books the club scattered across the tables and the bar. No problem, they just charged him a few bucks more for his drinks.

'Hi, Lefty,' Cornelia said as the music momentarily ended and she bent down towards him. He obliged with a ten. Never said a word. She moved on to the other punters and, as half expected, only reaped a meagre harvest of cash.

It made no difference. The rules of the game were that you had to show pussy. Even when the bastards were mean tippers.

She winked at Ade the film freak, the big, bulky barman and bouncer, and he pressed the the the start button on the CD player to trigger the final song in her sequence.

He was okay; spent all his free time at the movies. Never missed a single new release. Always wanted to know your opinion, if you had seen any of them and whether you shared his wide-eyed verdicts. His own views were not very critical, but he just loved the conversation. Read all the magazines.

He had once told her she looked like Nicole Kidman.

She didn't see it, personally, but if it made him happy it was just fine with her. If the drinkers appreciated the way her body moved, the uncommonly creamy pallor of her skin and the way her sex lips widened moistly apart when she did her act-closing back stand to reveal the pinkness of her insides. It was just dandy with Cornelia.

It was just a job, after all.

Unlike the scherzo-andante-scherzo of a symphony, the punctuation of a good strip act is quick-quick-slow; movement in the final part should be limited, not too frantic. To allow the spectators a good view of her intimate geography. That's what they paid for.

Her music began and she straightened up.

Sarah McLachlan's 'Fumbling Towards Ecstasy'.

A long time ago, Cornelia had learned never to look the men in the eyes as she danced on stage. This way she could retain her power over them. Pretend she was manipulating them. Imagine she was maybe on her own up there bathing in the strong light.

She just loved dancing so.

As a child she would spend hours twirling in front of her bedroom mirror until she felt dizzy. Later, as a teenager, she would do so naked, feeling the excitement rise slowly through her body until her face was flushed with forbidden pleasure, admiring the flat planes and smooth curves of her grown-up anatomy.

She closed her eyes as the music surged.

A quarter turn. Slow. Kicked off the until-now obligatory red high-heeled shoes. Someone in the audience whooped and yelled in anticipation. Cornelia smiled. She knew she was tall enough without heels.

Her legs were undeniably her best feature.

Her fingers moved under the G-string's elastic and she pulled quickly until the velcro fastener snapped as planned. As the flimsy piece of material floated to the floor of the stage, she shyly placed her hands in front of her, denying the voyeurs facing her the sight of what they really wanted.

This morning she had severely trimmed her pubes, and was more naked than usual. Club rules. Which she didn't appreciate. She liked the way her public hair curled and curled when left to grow naturally. Loved to play with the curls. But the more hirsute you were, the less there was for the punters to see. Rules of the house.

As her hands moved away from her groin, Cornelia essayed a mock ballet step and raised her right leg to a brief but impossible angle, revealing her cunt in all its splendour. The men were now quiet silent, as the seductive music filled the air in the low-ceilinged room. She tip-toed, she jigged, she quivered, she danced with all the slowness of a princess royal and the bearing of a wild amazon, her long body sliding across the small stage, followed by her accompanying shroud of blinding light. Her movements allied themselves with the sensuous arab-like drone of the song's melody as the waves carried her in their multi-voiced embrace.

Lost in her own world, oh how Cornelia danced.

She glided over to a stool and lowered herself onto it, the small of her back supporting the weight of her whole body, leaning back and gently forcing her legs wide, scissoring her legs open and closed and open again, every time feeling the conjugated stares of all the men present on her unveiled, helplessly wet delta.

She moved off the stool. Turned towards it, bent over, placing her breasts on the seat, and slowly began to widen further the angle between her legs.

A few dollar bills fluttered onto the stage.

From the Japanese contingent.

You could always count on them to cough up the readies in the presence of beauty.

The angle of revelation increased; the men peered freely at the soft pinkness of her inner corridor and the star-like conic depression of her anus. Nothing was private. Everything was for sale.

Cornelia, utterly spread open and on full display, was lost in her thoughts.

The final harmonies of the song intruded on her consciousness and she quickly resumed her routine, a shimmer here, another set of splits there, the backward flap for the whole gynaecological vista, another bump and grind and a quick bow as the record ended. She picked up the dollar bills and moved off the stage. The Japanese were still heartily applauding and jabbering between themselves.

She was now in the changing room, her robe still half-open when Ade the film freak put his head around the doorway.

'One of them is offering fifty for a lap dance,' he told her.

'You know I don't do private dances, Ade,' Cornelia answered distractedly.

'I know,' he answered, with a sigh. 'You could make a fortune, you know, you get more requests than a lot of the other girls.'

Cornelia knew that. She may not be as obviously sexy as the other strippers at the club, but there was something about the way she surrendered to the dance that made men hard in the places that ruled their reason or the lack of it.

'It's still no, Ade.'

He left.

Some whores don't kiss; Cornelia just wouldn't do lap dances.

She was taking a shower, scrubbing herself thoroughly, washing away all the abundant sweat with rose-flavoured soap and jets of lukewarm water. Angie, who started off the evening shift, shuffled into the next, narrow shower cubicle.

'Hi, Cornie,' she said. 'I just don't believe you turning down all that easy cash.'

'I don't need it, Angie,' Cornelia answered, switching the water off on her side of the glass partition.

'Everybody needs money,' the other stripper pointed out.

'It's just a means to an end,' Cornelia said, wrapping a towel around her midriff.

'What?' Angie said. 'I just don't understand you. This lap dance lark is a cinch. Rub against them long enough for them to come in their trousers. It's painless. Safe. Clean. In the old Times Square days we had to supplement the cash in the peepshows, where the bastards could cop a feel for just another dollar, slipping their dirty fingers inside you, scratching your tits or worse. I really hated all that, you know . . .'

But Cornelia, who had heard it all before, was already back in the dressing room, slipping into her white Calvin Klein jeans and short-sleeved black T-shirt. Her customary New York uniform. A bit cold for winter, but she wore her long black leather trenchcoat above when she ventured outside. She might be a stripper, she knew, but she didn't have to dress like one.

*

'And it's a first edition, not the later hardback reprint they brought out following the movie?'

'Definitely,' the manager of the antiquarian bookshop assured her.

'Great,' Cornelia said.

'O'Brien signed it shortly before his death. There aren't many around, you know,' he said.

'I really love that book,' Cornelia said. 'How much?'

'Two thousand dollars.'

'That's quite a lot for a modern first,' she remarked.

'It doesn't come up that often. In perfect condition. Signed.'

'I realise,' Cornelia answered. 'When will you have it?'

'In a week or so,' the salesman said. 'Our West Coast store only acquired it a few days ago. Part of a large collection bought from the estate of some Hollywood honcho.'

'I see.'

'When I saw the book on their inventory, I knew I should drop you a line. It was on your want list.'

'It was. I have the Watermark Press reprint, of course, but this is a great upgrade,' Cornelia said.

'We'll put it aside for you. To inspect. As you're such a good customer, there will as usual be no need for a deposit.'

'That's very kind of you, Mr Hopley.'

A couple of thousand bucks, she pondered as she walked down 52nd Street back towards Fifth. She didn't wish to dip into her savings. Forty lap dances? More, in truth: the club would probably take a hefty commission. But she didn't have to demean herself that way, she knew. The book would be evermore tainted if she obtained the cash that way. No problem.

There was a telephone in the foyer of the Ziegfeld, her favourite Manhattan movie house, with its splendid candelabraladen foyer and deep, comfortable seats.

She inserted a handful of quarters and dialled.

The call was picked up on the sixth ring.

'Cornelia,' she stated.

'Nice to hear from you,' a basso profundo voice on the other end said. It wasn't her usual contact.

'Any jobs going?' she enquired.

'I'm sure we can find something suitable for you, Cornelia,' she was told. He sounded a bit terse.

'I'm game.'

'Aren't you always?' the man said. 'You freelancers, all you charming dilettantes. What is it this time? A new couture evening dress, jewellery, an overseas vacation?'

'A book,' Cornelia truthfully said.

'Charming,' he said approvingly. Amateurs like her were the best people to use. Nobody would suspect them. This woman was a real find. Six jobs already, and she had never disappointed. Reliable. Discreet. Calmly efficient. He sort of wondered what she looked like.

'Same place as last time?' Cornelia asked.

'Yes,' he confirmed.' Any time from noon tomorrow.'

'How much?'

'Standard. Two and a half.'

'Good,' she nodded as she spoke. 'I'm on.'

'We're on,' the man said and hung up.

Cornelia treated herself to the movie as she was already at the theatre. It turned out to be a mediocre summer big-budget catastrophe epic. It would give her something to talk about with Big Ade. Crowds were already milling around the Hilton by the time she walked by down 6th, a sultry summer night. One day she would leave this town. She was running out of space at her expensively-rented apartment and had no place left on the walls to fix extra bookshelves. Yes, that trip to Europe was getting closer.

The following day was a Saturday and Cornelia never worked week-ends at the club, even though the pay was better. The people there just didn't understand her needs, she reckoned. If she stayed in New York any longer, she might soon have to find another dance floor to parade her wares on. Mick the Knot, who either owned the place or more likely fronted for the real proprietors, was becoming too insistent on her being more accommodating with her liberal schedule, and looked her up and down too often with a far-from-hidden agenda on his mind. She didn't wish to stay there long enough to find out how he had acquired his nickname. Not a matter she wished to bring up with her her other contacts. She liked to keep the dancing and the killing parts of her life strictly segregated. Made good business sense.

She slipped on her running gear, checked her Walkman batteries still had enough juice, selected a few tapes and jogged for an hour up Canal to 2nd and St Mark's Place and then to Union Square and back, stopping en route for a glass of freshly pressed vegetable juice at a market stall on Astor Place. Dancers had to keep in shape. She cleaned up and dressed. Nike track suit trousers and a light brown halter top that left her midriff bare. She wondered whether she should have her navel pierced. No. Too many of the girls in the clubs did that already. It was nifty, but she thought it looked somewhat vulgar. Something else, maybe?

She took the subway uptown to Lexington and 82nd. The Good Times sex emporium was on the same block as the subway's exit. She walked in quite brazenly. Some of the Indian male clerks raised their eyebrows but she walked straight down to the gay section in the basement. They ignored her, she wasn't going to give any furtive male customer upstairs closely examining the explicit images on the hardcore video tape boxes the creeps. Just a woman who wanted to get her rocks off, they guessed. Some did. The row of private cabins was on the basement's right-hand side. She counted, and entered the seventh cabin. The light outside switched from green to red as Cornelia lowered the latch on the door and the cabin darkened.

They probably had monitors at the register upstairs, so she inserted a ten dollar bill, face upwards as required, into the gaping mouth of the machine, underneath the screen. The gay porn menu flashed on. Cornelia pushed a number at random. Two studs with flat-top haircuts and improbably buffed biceps and rippling pecs were fellating each other, splayed into a difficult physical configuration so that the camera didn't miss any detail. She flicked on to the next movie. Another California-standard prototype hunk here vigorously thrust about, buggering furiously another's backside in daunting close-up. All the men in these films were monstrously hung, Cornelia reflected; she'd never come across normal men so well endowed. She smiled quietly. Placed her hand under the hard plastic chair in which she was sitting, face to the screen. As expected, the package was sellotaped to the underneath of the chair. She pulled it loose and slipped it into her Gotham Book Mart Edward Gorey tote bag and left the cabin.

There was still over eight dollars worth of sodomy counting down in the top right corner of the screen.

Back at her apartment, she opened the thick padded envelope. Standard: the gun, a photograph and two pages of typed data. Her clandestine employers were always very thorough. Made the job so much easier. She studied the material she had been provided with.

Yes, tonight would be as good a time as ever, she reckoned. Why delay matters? She studied the information closely. Concealed the package and its contents in a safe place behind one of the book-shelves and went searching for a public telephone somewhere down in the Village. The second one she came upon on Greenwich Avenue was free and there was no one hanging around it. She inserted the coin. The number rang.

A male British-sounding voice answered.

'Hello?'

She mentioned his name.

'Yes. Speaking. Can I help you?'

'I'm calling on behalf of Mrs Caitleen Zeusmark,' Cornelia said.

'Caitleen? Oh, God. How is she? Where is she? Please?'

'I don't really wish to speak on the telephone, mister. Can we meet?'

'Yes. Of course, yes, we can. Meet,' he said, obviously shaken by her call.

'Tonight?'

'Yes, Tonight is fine. Absolutely. What time?'

'Say ten pm,' she suggested.

'No problem,' he answered. 'Where?' he asked her.

'Do you know the Angelika Theatre, corner of Mercer and Hous-ton, in the Village?' Cornelia suggested.

'Of course, the British guy said. 'I've been there quite often.'

'There's a very large lobby, upstairs, with a bar.'

'Yes.'

'We meet there,' she said.

'How will I ... ?' he enquired.

'I know what you look like. I'll find you,' Cornelia told him. 'OK?'

'Fine, but ...'

'We can talk tonight. See you.' She hung up on him.

*

She waited until ten-thirty. By now the lobby was full. People exiting the early evening performance and crowds queuing for the late-night showings on all five screens. Cornelia wore grey. The most forgettable of all colours. He was standing in a corner, looking ner-vous, worried about her lateness. But not likely to leave, she knew.

She walked over to the middle-aged guy she had recognised from the photograph. Dark lines surrounded his eyes. He was wear-ing a lightweight cream-coloured cotton suit and a black silk shirt, open at the neck. Dark brown thick-heeled loafers clashed with his clothes.

'Hello,' Cornelia said.

'It's you?'

'Yes.'

'Who are you? Where is Caitleen?'

'Later,' she humoured him gently. 'We have all the time in the world to talk,' she added, to put him at ease.

'I suppose so,' the English guy said.

'Come,' Cornelia suggested, touching his arm. 'Let's go somewhere else. I didn't realise it would be so crowded here.'

'Fine,' he agreed.

'Let's walk,' she suggested.

They meandered towards Lafayette, down the Bowery, towards Alphabet City. There were fewer and fewer other passers-by as they moved on at a leisurely pace. Every time he tried to start a conversation, she suggested they wait until later. He complied reluctantly, visibly impatient for news of the errant Caitleen. Their story would have been interesting, Cornelia knew, but she was aware it was better not to know too much. It was just a job.

Finally, they reached a pool of darkness near the crumbling porch of a derelict-looking building.

'Here,' she said.

He stopped in his tracks and faced Cornelia.

'Here?'

'Yes,' she confirmed.

He looked at her questioningly.

'Caitleen's sent me. I have a very special message from her.'

'Tell me,' the man said impatiently, a look of hope spreading across his features.

Cornelia quietly pulled the gun from her Gucci handbag.

His eyes froze. But he didn't run. As if he knew he wouldn't stand a chance.

'So this is it?' he asked.

'Yes,' Cornelia said. 'Caitleen wants you dead.'

She clicked the safety catch off.

'I suppose it doesn't really surprise me,' the English guy said with resignation.

Cornelia's gun was equipped with a silencer.

She shot him twice in the heart, and as he slumped mournfully to the ground, she finished him off with a third bullet above his eyes. His body disappeared in the shadows of the deserted street as Cornelia swiftly walked away without a backward glance.

When she reached Houston again, she hailed a yellow cab and had herself dropped off near the Javits Centre. From here she walked to the edge of the water and disposed of the gun. All according to plan. She caught another cab home near Gramercy Park. By the time she unlocked her front door it was barely midnight.

On Sunday, she rested. The millennium celebrations at the club in a few days would no doubt be loud and rowdy and she would need all her energy.

She packed some bagels from the corner deli and, wearing her heavy trenchcoat and a thick woollen scarf, found herself an empty bench in Washington Square and spent the afternoon reading. A paperback. Her first edition of the same book was too valuable to actually read.

She knew the two thousand five hundred dollars for the elimination job would follow promptly, reaching her PO box on Monday or Tuesday in used denominations. It was nice: even after paying the antiquarian dealers' exorbitant price, she would still have an extra five hundred. She decided she would treat herself to something special this time. Money was there to be spent, not worried about.

Her shift at the strip club didn't begin until five in the afternoon on Mondays. It was always a quiet day with few punters, and even worse tippers. Men's generosity was wiped out following the weekend. Still, it meant she could dance quietly, enjoy the way her lithe body moved around the floor and the stage lights shimmered against her unveiled skin.

She thought again of piercing her navel.

No.

Maybe some sort of piece of jewellery there. Like an Indian belly-dancer. Not really her style, she felt.

She left the apartment an hour earlier than usual. Strolled along the busy Village streets, zigzagging her way towards the club in no particular hurry, checking out the windows and the fashions. In Christopher Street, a sign caught her attention. She walked into the cluttered store.

'I want a tattoo,' she resolutely told the square-bearded biker-like attendant.

'Easy, lady,' he said. 'That's what we do. Where?'

'Somewhere rather private,' Cornelia said, holding his stare.

'No problem. It's a house specialty. We've seen all sorts,' he added.

He waved her through to the back of the store and indicated a black leather dentist's chair.

Cornelia smiled.

'So, lady, where do you want it. Your butt, your tit, above your pussy?' he asked her.

'Pussy,' Cornelia said, although she really hated the word. It was so vulgar. Cunt, she didn't mind. It was right. Appropriate.

He pulled a large scroll of paper from a nearby table and handed it over to her.

'A rose is our most popular request. But we can do names, birds, leaves, any sort of decoration. Take your pick.'

Cornelia looked down at the selection of gaudy illustrations.

The parlour even had skulls, bones and daggers.

'Yes,' she said. 'I see there is one.'

She pointed to the image of a gun.

The large tattooist raised his bushy eyebrows.

'Are you sure? We've only ever done that one on arms. And men at that.'

'That's the one I really want,' Cornelia indicated.

He sighed.

'One hundred bucks,' he said.

'Fine,' Cornelia said, slipping out of her jeans and knickers and moving towards the dark chair.

'It's your hard-earned money,' the big man said, no doubt thinking to himself that students these days did the weirdest things.

'You said it,' Cornelia confirmed, as she opened her legs wide.

'I'll need to trim you a bit more, lady,' the tattoo artist said.

'Go ahead,' Cornelia said. The large man turned to his counter to pick up a small electric razor.

Yes, Cornelia thought, it would be nice. A gun and a cunt. Sig Sauer and sex. Love and death.

It's You That I Want to Kiss

A book for Dolly
for the years, the wait and the doubts.

"Sometimes we come to learn
by mistake that the love
you once made can't be undone."
–Sheryl Crow, *The Book*

1.

Requite My Love

All he really wanted was a fuck.

Not even a good fuck. Any one would do. The earth didn't have to move. It need not be the fuck of the century. The fuck of the day would do. A small one, a nice one. Just the feel of a woman's skin, soft and welcoming, next to him. The touch of a body, the perfume of alien flesh. That wasn't asking for much, was it?

It had been seven months since London. A long time. And the women of Miami sashayed madly around everywhere he went. Supple, tanned, sensual, sexual. Vibrant and alive. At night, it almost drove him mad. With longing, with lust.

Soon the rainy season would come.

He knew it was illogical, but he had to do something about it before the first major storm. Make contact. Meet someone.

Sitting at a table on the terrace of the Baja Café, he watched the girls pass by, the women trooping up and down Collins Avenue. Imagining all too often the shape of their bodies under the thin summer dresses, the curve of their heavy breasts, the possible colour of their hidden skin. Occasionally one would glance briefly back at him, frown or smile, but invariably walk on.

He knew he was out of practice with this man-woman thing. It had been years since he'd had to take the first step, and he had no confidence any more. Once or twice, in restaurants or at the beach, he'd thought of trying, responding like an automaton to the pleasing sparkle in some woman's eye, or to the enticing sight of a black bra strap slipping across a shoulder, but he'd frozen, done nothing. Hunting for sex, he concluded, wasn't like riding a bicycle; you did forget.

It was a perfect night. The sounds of music from the open windows of the bars and nearby clubs mingled in the air, blending pungent salsa rhythms and the heavy bass of anonymous rock beats. The sky over the ocean was turning dark blue as evening crept nearer, and the waves lapped the shore with metronomic precision. A few cruise boats blended with the flat horizon. Faraway lay Cuba. Jacob sipped the last drop of his espresso, enjoying the almost syrupy texture of the sugar that had settled at the bottom of the small cup. He always swamped his coffee with too much sugar. The check was already settled. He rose and walked the half dozen blocks back to his hotel. There was a buzz in the air, he could feel it. The daylight denizens of Miami Beach were fading into the background while the more exotic, colourful, electric night creatures were slowly beginning to emerge from their magical lairs.

Following an energetic shower, and quickly dousing an involuntary erection, he blow-dried his hair and began shaving, peering myopically at his features in the cabinet's spotted mirror, as the blade brushed the white foam and hard bristles away from his skin. He turned his head sideways to check that he had trimmed both sideburns to the same length. Flecked with grey. He looked into his own eyes, noting the ever-deepening darkness spreading below them, sighed.

'Just one fuck,' he mumbled aloud. 'That's all I want today.'

A knock at the door interrupted his thoughts. Just the bellboy returning his laundry. Tonight he would wear the short-sleeved black silk shirt. It was something he felt comfortable wearing. He dried himself. Slipped the newly-cleaned shirt on. The material felt good against his skin. Black cotton socks. Black Calvin Klein jeans. He moved toward the door.

The world outside was beckoning. An unreal world.

*

Teddy Caliban called for Anne to come out of the bathroom.

'What are you doing in there all this time, for God's sake?' he shouted in her direction.

She finally emerged. She had dressed again.

She wore the short white dress, tight against her compact body, her bare, pale shoulders obscured by the long auburn hair flowing down in wondrous waves. The material was so thin he could see the whiter shape of her knickers outlined underneath. White against white. She wore no bra and her nipples pressed against the fabric.

Teddy was sprawled out on the sofa, a cigarette dangling from his lips, ash dropping carelessly over his washed-out slacks, his hair-less torso still shiny with sweat.

'Who the hell said you could get dressed? I didn't say we'd fin-ished, did I?' he said.

She stood at the bathroom door, motionless, puzzled.

'I thought . . .' she began.

'No one asked you to think, babe,' he interrupted.

She looked at him. Fortunately he didn't appear angry, merely annoyed. She'd been warned he could be awkward, violent. She had to tread carefully. 'Come over here,' he beckoned.

Barefoot, she moved toward the sofa.

He straightened up and emptied the sachet of white powder over the glass surface of the coffee table. With his gold American Express card, he separated the small mound into parallel lines, then licked the card clean.

'There. Enjoy,' he said.

'Thanks.'

Caliban burst out in raucous laughter.

'She says, "Thanks". You English bitches kill me. Ha . . . she says, "Thanks". Sells her pussy for the stuff and still remembers to be polite. So, what are you waiting for? Put your damn nose into the trough,' he ordered.

She got down on her knees by the low table. The dress was too tight around her thighs and she had to hitch it up. She lowered her head and began sniffing up the cocaine. As the first hit impacted with her brain cells, she distractedly noticed Teddy Caliban rising from the sofa and, in the periphery of her field of vision, positioning himself behind her. She continued inhaling the magic powder. It felt good. Christ, it was so powerful. Seemed to turn her whole head to mush, instantly. Clearing the confusion. Obliterating the past. Puri-fying her. A nervous shudder jolted through her whole body as the high moved to yet another level. There was still a line left on the glass. The last one was often the best. She held her breath and forced herself to wait at least a few more seconds.

As she waited, Caliban pulled the skirt up to her waist and, twist-ing the knickers aside, brutally inserted a finger—or was it two?—into her. Penetrating deep inside her, his signet ring scratched her still-engorged lips. As he cleverly moved within her, she could feel the wetness return and the familiar electricity stretch through her limbs.

'Jesus,' she whispered and greedily inhaled the last of the co-caine. The warmth drowned her.

Her head dropped to the coffee table as her body went limp, her rump still being explored by Caliban's rough fingers. This seemed to go on for ever. Finally, the man extracted his fingers from her sex and viciously slapped her bare rump.

'Nice ass,' he remarked.

He made his way back to the sofa.

Anne thought she recognised a familiar tune waft in to the apartment from the street outside, beyond the open window and the balcony.

He pulled her face up from the table, which he calmly kicked away, and positioned himself in front of her face. He pulled his trouser zipper down.

'Get to it,' he instructed.

This was the part she liked least. She hated to swallow. Tasted so acid. Made her want to retch.

She pulled his cock out from the slacks. He wore no underpants. Took it in her mouth. He was already hard. She couldn't really feel much; the cocaine had by now dulled her senses. Later, what she remembered most was somehow recognising the taste of her own cunt on his rod. He hadn't cleaned himself since his earlier probing and digging inside her.

To her relief, Teddy Caliban didn't make her swallow. When he came, he pulled out his cock and spurted all over her face.

Back in the bathroom, she cleaned the mess away and applied a new coat of lipstick.

'Yes, no questions asked,' she told him later, as they sipped cool drinks together in the room—lemonade for him, vodka and cola for her—both fully dressed again, as if nothing had happened between them earlier. 'I can do with the cash. Just let me know what I have to do; I'll do it.'

'There could be very substantial sums involved,' he said.

'But there's no danger, is there?' Anne asked.

'Not really,' Caliban said.

'Apart from the fact it's quite illegal, you mean,' she said, with a chuckle.

Teddy Caliban opened his eyes wide and gazed at the red-haired young woman.

'You limeys, I'll never understand your sense of humour,' and poured himself another drink, pondering if he could get it up again. There was something about the bitch, he reflected. That deceptive coolness, those lips, those small tits, those eyes. Yes, he'd really like to do her real harm one day. Maybe after the deal. He'd see how much she would really enjoy it. Yes, he was getting hard just thinking about it. She didn't notice the bulge forming in his jeans. He was pressed for time, anyway.

'I'll call you in a week or so, when it's all set up, okay?'

'Sure, honey; you call and I'll come running,' Anne said.

She was coming down from the high but there was a quiet sense of satisfaction settling over her. She'd made the connection. The big time was only a few miles away, now. The fuck-you money she'd been after, ever since she'd landed in America. No longer any need for all the grubby sex, the groping, the humiliation.

She set her glass down, rose and even gave Caliban a peck on the cheek. He escorted her to the door.

The elevator was glass-lined. She looked at herself. Christ, she looked tired, used. Her gaze moved down her body. Her knickers were in her handbag. She'd had to take them off. After being so diligently fingered by the guy, they'd been soaking in juices and she had no wish to troop down Miami Beach smelling of cunt. However, she could see that the outline of her public hair was clearly visible through the thin white dress. Shit, I'll get myself raped. I'll have to find a cab. Always difficult now, when the offices were closing and so many people were making it back to the city or to the mainland.

Maybe one day I should shave down there. Problem is, it grows back so fast, they say. And you get rashes. Bloody Florida, just too hot to wear normal clothes . . .

Still, things were looking up, Anne decided. Her escort days were coming to an end. After a thorough clean-up, she might go out dancing. On her own. The way she liked it. Yes.

*

Night clouds danced over the Caribbean.

The green and pink neon lights of Miami Beach emerged in all their gaudy splendour.

A storm brewed faraway above the Everglades. The bridges and causeways from Coral Gables filled with one-way traffic.

Jacob followed the crowds, aimless, just like throwing a coin in the air and waging your next step on how it would fall. Past the clear cut lines of the Fontainebleau Hotel, a right turn by the giant Convention Centre and into the fragrant, crazy Art Deco District avenues. Humidity was high. He stopped for a soft drink at a busy cafe. He had to stand at the bar, all the outside tables were full, mostly with seemingly under-age Latino schoolgirls giggling wildly and sporting clinging half tops, belly buttons, many pierced, on display. Not his cup of tea. Shiny, lovingly-polished open sports cars paraded up and down the main drag with boom-boxes drowning the sound of the revved-up engines and raucous male banter leapfrogging between the competing vehicles.

Why was everyone so fucking happy—or drunk?—Jacob wondered. It was a state of mind he found difficult to understand. He didn't drink. Hadn't since his distant student days. Maybe he was afraid of losing control, or something. Repressed stuff and all that. To hell with it, leave that to psychiatrists, he decided. He walked on. Nearing the tip of the beach, lights dimming already. But still the stream of the night crowds surrounding him, carrying him along to some unknown destination.

Jacob floated along, catching the smell of pungent cigar smoke here, his eyes lingering on the angle between a woman's knee and leg there, spying a strand of dark hair out of alignment, a copper bracelet on a slender wrist, the flash of white teeth between a pair of lips moving toward him and then passing away into instant oblivion.

The multitude thinned and he found himself on a noisy side street. The Kool Club had once been a church, but it had fallen into disrepair and been deconsecrated before some local entrepreneur bought it on the cheap and reopened it as a night dive. It had already had it's hour of glory, but that was a few years back. In Miami Beach, night spots never stayed in fashion very long, there was always a new one emerging somewhere, where the music was louder, the drugs better or the DJ hipper.

Two of the electric letters were out and the sign above the joint's entrance read 'The Ko 1 C ub'. Jacob smiled quietly. He'd read about the place a few weeks back in the local paper. Some English rock singer had been mugged in the car park at the back by a transvestite hooker, hustling for cash to have the operation.

The entrance fee was only ten bucks, and that included the first drink.

He followed a group of Dutch tourists in; the two women were blonde and shapely, but their escorts looked rather rough and ready. Pity, Jacob had always liked Dutch women. The way they spoke English with that gut-disturbing accent. Anyway, he should have stayed in Europe if that's what he wanted.

It was crowded inside. It took him a good quarter of an hour to get used to the sound level, as he circled the ground floor to get the lay of the land. The glittering electric-lit bar was where the altar must have been. Some stained-glass windows remained, with images of saints and angels in bucolic repose, but most had been replaced by more sacrilegious images of unclad south sea islanders, palm trees and sand galore. Cool indeed! There was a gallery upstairs for those who only wished to spectate, or preferred a relative state of darkness for other nocturnal activities.

Jacob made his way to the crowded bar and submitted his drink coupon to one of the frilly-shirted bartenders. The juice was severely watered down. He hadn't expected anything else.

Anne was on the dance floor. Swaying gently with the ebb and flow of the beat. At times almost immobile, standing like a tree, her eyes closed, her head turning in a circular motion on the pivot of her neck, the long hair barely brushing against her shoulders, faint tremors moving down her legs to the wooden floor, oblivious to the throng of bodies enveloping her. As the music rose, her head and shoulders moved again, the upper part of her body swivelling with languor as her hips remained motionless. Other dancers, more manic, moved against her, past her but all were repulsed as she stood her ground, trance-like, feet slightly apart, just rooted there and surrounded by the criss-cross currents of the heavy rock music.

Jacob caught sight of her.

The way she danced, the way she moved, reminded him of an old documentary on a rock festival where a beautiful blonde had danced topless in a field of mud, every inch of her unveiled skin communing with the sounds, her whole soul wedded to the moment, totally oblivious to the world outside and the voyeuristic gaze of the bearded hippies shimmying clumsily next to her and the unforgiving gaze of the camera. Yes, that's what this woman reminded him of. A similar sense of savage freedom.

He kept on watching, hypnotised by her fragile beauty. Asked the barman for another drink. Which cost him another ten bucks.

As the record ended, the young woman kept on swaying imperceptibly to silent music, her eyes still closed tight. When the disc jockey segued into another dance tune, the rhythm of her body remained the same, a primeval shimmer, like branches carried sideways and back by a gentle summer wind. Jacob gazed on. She wasn't very tall. What, five foot four or five at the most? She seemed to be wearing a white body stocking and a long, frilly, colourful cotton skirt and flat white sandals. Whenever the spotlight revolving across the dance floor hit her, he saw dark reddish reflections in her hair. A redhead? She wore it long, it reached down halfway down her back. He moved nearer to the crowd of dancers to see her better.

As a couple clumsily jitterbugging their way across the floor bumped into her, she opened her eyes and displayed her irritation, frowning, lips curling up. She stepped aside, nearer to the edge of the dance area, closer to the observing Jacob, and again began her hypnotic sway, but her concentration had lapsed and she could not recapture the initial private grace of her movements. She convulsed more mechanically now as a faster track played and began waving her arms as her whole body embraced the song and, for the watching Jacob, she somehow no longer stood out so sharply from all the other gesticulating dancers. He sipped his drink, articulating his thoughts.

'Oh, why not?' he said to himself, as he walked down the step on to the wooden floor.

Cut a short swathe between waltzing couples and found himself face to face with the young woman. Her forehead was shiny with sweat as her entire body tried to keep time with the accelerating music.

'May I?' Jacob shouted over the din. Inviting himself to join her.

She looked at him briefly.

Barely acknowledged him and nodded her head negatively.

And continued with her increasingly frenzied dancing, while around them the bopping customers closed in on them in a mad St Vitus's throng, cutting off his retreat.

Jacob just stood there. Not quite knowing what to do next.

Looking at her right now, he could feel something like a knot tightening low in his stomach. Hell, he knew that feeling all too well. Not again. Not again. The last time, it had been Lynda. I don't need the grief, he thought. But his stomach was telling him things. Maybe that's where his bloody heart took refuge when it wanted to communicate important things.

She looked up at him again and opened her mouth wide. He couldn't hear what she said as the loud track reached its climax.

He indicated his lack of understanding.

This time, she shouted louder and he heard her: 'Fuck off.'

There was no answer to that, he reckoned. Nor was there any harm in trying, he supposed.

Right then the music stopped.

Seeing him still there, facing her like a jerk, Anne said: 'Just leave me alone. I'd rather be on my own.'

The silence continued. Maybe the DJ was taking a pee, or perhaps it was like the interval in cinemas when you were expected to go and buy popcorn.

The sound of her words circled around his brain.

She had an English accent.

She's English.

He had to find the right things to say.

Quickly, before another record came on and he lost her.

'You're British, I see,' Jacob blurted out.

How boring. How British.

The faint trace of a smile appeared on Anne's lips.

'So it seems,' she answered.

'And you want to dance alone.'

'Yes, I do.'

'Why?'

'Because it's the best way to dance.'

'Is it really?'

'Because dancing is something very private.'

'I know,' Jacob said. 'I'm a pretty poor dancer myself. It's safer when I dance alone in front of a mirror.'

'So why did you want to join me?' Anne asked.

'Dunno. You looked good.'

'Good?'

'Pretty, I suppose.'

'Pretty? It's a long time since someone has called me that. I reckon only a Brit would call me pretty.'

'Well, calling you beautiful is a bit too obvious.'

'And you're not the obvious type, I suppose?'

Jacob was searching for the right answer when the music roared back on. It would be *Satisfaction*. Damn. He just couldn't dance properly to the fast pieces. He shouted over the noise:

'Would you?'

'No,' Anne screamed back. 'I don't feel like dancing any longer. I'm too hot and sticky from my earlier exertions.'

'A drink, then?' he quickly suggested.

She hesitated briefly.

Finally: 'Okay.'

Following the lull in the music, the bar had become too crowded to approach. She agreed to try one of the terraces on Collins Avenue. The nearest was the one where Jacob had noticed the group of navel-pierced schoolgirls. They had now departed. Past their curfews, no doubt.

'Vodka and cola . . . No, hold on, no, I'll have a gin and orange.'

'Like back home, hey?'

'Yes,' Anne said.

The waiter had his thinning hair slicked back and you could smell the oil from miles away.

The drinks came.

'Tell me all about yourself,' Jacob said.

'There's nothing to tell,' she answered. 'I'm not a very interesting person, you know.'

'You have a name?'

'Anne.'

'Anne what?'

'God, you are getting personal . . . Anne Ryan. From London. Finchley in north London, in fact.'

'Irish background?'

'Yes. My parents. But I was born in England. Only ever been to Ireland on holiday. No family left there.'

'I'm Jacob.'

'Hello, Jacob. You Jewish?'

'Yes. Only been to a synagogue once, though.'

'What, to be circumcised?'

'Now that's personal.'

She chuckled. Like arrows piercing his heart.

'I've always liked Jewish men,' Anne said.

'Have there been many?'

'You're being personal again,' she smiled. 'Try another question, though.'

'The obvious one: what are you doing in Miami? How long have you been here?'

'Must be just over half a year . . .'

'Me too. Doing what?'

'Odd jobs, you know. A bit of modelling, but really I'm not tall enough, I just get the young mum and screaming kid sessions for mail-order sensible wear catalogues. The most regular gig, though, this will amuse you, is for this illustrator who does the cover paintings for romance novels; you know, the ones where the heroine is in a deep clinch with some macho bare-chested hunk.'

'Really?'

'Yeah. We simulate a passionate embrace, pause for a whole series of photographs. Later, he paints from the photo, adds the exotic background. I always get the Regency outfits. Have to wear a bra with uplift, to show sufficient cleavage. And the male models are always gay or dumb . . . My luck.'

'I'll have to look out on the bookstands,' said Jacob.

'I'm not recognisable. Fortunately.'

'You can make a living out of it?'

'Not really. I also do some escort work. They like my accent here, I could do more, but I'm choosy.'

'What sort of escort work?' he asked.

'Do you really want to know?' Anne queried.

'Probably not.'

'Don't disapprove, a girl has to make a living.'

'If you say so. So why did you come here?'

'That's one question I'd rather leave unanswered, Jacob.'

It was the first time she'd said his name. It felt warm, unusual, frightening also. A first, faint indication of intimacy. He'd ordered coffees.

'Make mine a cappuccino,' she'd said.

He continued to gently probe into her past and background, but she was not forthcoming. She was also seemingly quite incurious about him. Which suited him well. A perfect status quo. Still, he could feel there was a core of something hidden inside her and it was nagging at him already. She would talk about her parents, her childhood, but no hint would emerge of why and how she had left London and was tramping around Miami.

It was already three in the morning; they'd been talking for ages, making the coffees last an eternity. The Florida moon peered between darker clouds and there was a slight chill in the air. He noticed goose pimples on her bare arms, spreading across her chest, mingling with the hundred or so light brown freckles scattered like gunshot over the onset of her breasts. Her nipples were outlined, sharply erect, under the opaque white body stocking.

'You're cold,' he remarked. 'I haven't even got a jacket to offer you.'

'No need,' Anne answered. 'I'll have to be going, anyway.'

Say something. Keep her here. Something funny, something witty, anything.

He swallowed once, twice.

This woman touched him in all the right places. Or maybe they happened to be all the wrong places?

The knot in his stomach was pulsing again.

'Anne?'

'Yes?' she enquired, looking straight into his eyes.

'Anne?' he repeated.

'Yes,' she said again, patiently.

'Sleep with me tonight.'

'But it's only a first date,' she smiled gently.

'I know,' was his only response.

There was a long silence.

Then:

'Okay, Jacob, I will.'

It was his turn to be speechless.

'But,' she continued. 'I make no promises about anything, about any future. I'll sleep with you because I think it would be fun. And you have to promise me you will not ask any more questions afterwards. We'll just see how it goes. One step at a time. Okay? Promise. Please'

'I do,' he obeyed.

'Good,' Anne said, rising from the chair. 'Let's make it to your place; my room's a dump; where are you staying?'

He mentioned the hotel. The Governor.

She nodded approvingly.

'It'll be good, I swear,' Jacob added.

'I hope so,' Anne said.

The clouds broke and the heavens began pouring down on the peninsula just as they reached the hotel's front steps.

2.

Women In Their Beds

Teddy Caliban had never liked Shakespeare.

Maybe because he lacked a sense of humour. Or the right education. He'd never been one for school glory. He'd come up through the streets. He had the smarts. Was proud of the fact.

And, right now, two of the only three all-night cable channels featured Shakespeare, an old black-and-white movie here and a pompous *Masterpiece Theatre* drama full of thees and thous there. The third available channel was showing some documentary in Spanish on methods of land irrigation in the Third World.

How in hell was he supposed to stay awake?

He walked over to the bar and poured himself another glass of bourbon. Didn't bother about ice. He wondered where the English bitch might be at this moment, what she was doing? Sleeping, probably. He must have tired her out. There was something about her that bugged him. Badly. She hadn't been such a good screw anyway. Too passive. Biding her time. Selling her services with a distinct lack of enthusiasm. Indifferent, in the way so many women would lend men their bodies for profit. Even though, when he'd fingered her as she took her payment in kind, he'd felt how really wet she was inside. But still she showed no sign of passion. Refused to. One day, he'd make her come. Whether she liked it or not. Very soon, yes. Teddy Caliban had plans for her.

He switched the TV set off and began his wait.

The call came half an hour later. He listened to the phone ring five times, without picking it up. It stopped. He looked at the time on his Tag Heuer. He had three minutes. The Compaq laptop was already by the telephone. He connected the small computer to the phone's wall socket. Switched the laptop on. The computer booted up. The second phone call came through as arranged, and the modem inside the computer buzzed and then whined in recognition. A further minute went by as the security scans checked the integrity of the connection. The screen lit up and a succession of meaningless numbers appeared.

There was a click as the connection was broken off.

Caliban inserted a diskette into the laptop's thin mouth. Clicked the in-built mouse twice. The message became clear.

The meeting was scheduled for the Avventura Mall car park at 3:30am.

Jesus, he barely had an hour to get there! The mall was all the way up Collins, a massive white concrete bunker, far beyond the plush strip of expensive hotels, after the cluster of cheap tourist motels which had sprung up by the beach, where property costs were still lower.

He seized his cotton jacket and slammed the door behind him as he took the elevator straight down to the apartment block's underground car park.

The white Alfa's engine started up like a dream.

The drive up Collins towards North Beach was an effortless cruise. There was no traffic.

Teddy Caliban had always thought of himself as a pretty cool customer. Few things phased him. If and when trouble came, he could deal with matters calmly. Panic was a stranger. But, threading his way towards the appointment, he could feel the butterflies in his gut. This could be the big one. The deal he'd been working for all these past months. The Venezuelans had agreed to work with him and he wasn't going to disappoint them.

He switched the car radio on to an AOR station and punctuated the beat of the all-too-familiar songs on the brim of the steering wheel with his heavily-ringed fingers.

Almost there.

The sports car sleekly took a sharpish left turn where the main road separated and Collins continued, on the right, toward the Everglades. In the darkness, still a mile away, partly hidden by clumps of trees, he could already see the roof of the sprawling shopping centre.

'Yeah,' Teddy Caliban said to himself. 'Yeah, yeah, yeah.'

Let the good times roll.

*

Jacob slowly let his fingers roam through Anne's long, unfurling hair. He closed his eyes. It felt like silk, somehow even softer than soft. She stood quietly, silhouetted between the door that led to the bedroom, silent, expectant or submissive? as he ventured on his first exploration of her. He was in no hurry. Had all the time in the world. Certainly didn't wish to rush things. She was here. Willing. Able. Bloody beautiful. Young. Fascinating. Paradoxically English. He smiled inwardly, was this what he had come all the way to Miami Beach for?

He lowered his mouth to her ear.

Whispered.

'Yes, it'll be good,' he told her. 'Even the first time. I know we are still strangers and uneasy with each other, tentative, but we'll do it right, do it nice. Then, the second time will be even better as we become more familiar. Learn all the right spots, the ever so special touches, the contours of feelings.'

'Yes,' Anne said.

'And the third time will be just great,' he added, almost losing his breath, dizzy with anticipation.

'Please,' she said.

His fingers combed through the young woman's red hair, enjoying the yielding way her strands parted as he pursued a wandering, aimless path through her exquisite jungle, evoking exotic cobwebs of lust.

He opened his eyes. The room was still in darkness. A soft breeze blew across them from the open windows.

'Shall I switch the light on?' he asked, his fingers still embedded in her hair.

'No, not yet, I like it like this,' Anne answered.

Once again, Jacob closed his eyes, trying to capture this first moment with her in the butterfly net of his memory. Knowing he would never forget it. Would never wish to. The gentle smell of the young woman. 'Tell me, can I smell apricot all over you?' 'Yes, it's the shampoo I use; do you like it?' 'Yes, I do.' Anne turned her head up slightly, sniffed in his direction. 'And you smell of Old Spice. Your aftershave?' 'No. Deodorant spray. I don't use aftershave.' The dazzling softness of her hair travelled from the tip of his fingers all the way through his body, irrigating his heart, his stomach, his cock with shimmering currents of gentle pleasure. He held her hair in the cup of his hand, sculpting its pliant mass into waves, unending flowing patterns.

Lynda had permed hair and he used to love twirling and uncurling it, pulling mischievously on its thousand tiny whirlpools. No. This was Miami. This was now.

He redirected his memories.

The way he had walked up the stairs behind Anne when they had reached the hotel. The lift was not operational this late at night. How he had gleefully enjoyed the sight of the fabric of her thin dress stretched against her backside as she climbed the steps. The sway, the waltzing movement her hips impressed on the material. Oh, how the voyeur in him, the sensual epicure loved to watch women walk and move, guessing erotically at the shape of the concealed bodies beneath their clothes, the curvature of an arse, the line of a leg that stretched endlessly on, the weight of a breast, the fragility of a neck. He couldn't help himself. Anne's hourglass figure outlined in the penumbra of the staircase had given him a first fleeting hard-on.

'Undress me,' she asked.

He reluctantly pulled his hand away from her head.

She turned round to face him.

Jacob knelt down. Pushed his face against her crotch and kissed her through the material of the skirt. He put his hands up and felt for the elastic keeping the skirt in place around her slender waist. Found it and hitched a couple of fingers inside and ever so slowly pulled her skirt down. When the multicoloured garment reached her feet, he let go and the unfurled material sprawled out in a circle on the marble floor of the otherwise empty room.

Anne raised one foot and then the other and stepped out of the skirt.

She stood motionless sheathed in the white body stocking that adhered like a second skin to her compact body. Like a doll, a crazy image of perfection.

Jacob took hold of one ankle and she lifted her foot up a few inches. He slid the white sandal from her small foot. Then they repeated the operation with the other foot.

He brought one foot toward his lips and licked the shiny scarlet coating of her toe nail, his mouth continuing downward over the skin and all the way to her ankle, where the slithering wet tonguing turned into a kiss. Still on his knees, he straightened up, his face once again at crotch level. He moved his lips towards her genital area, kissed the shiny, tasteless texture of the opaque body stocking, buried his face against her, into her, until the warmth from her sex reached him through the final layer of clothing, extended his tongue into the central crease, pushing as hard as he could against the material until their respective humidities met halfway and imperceptibly began to blend.

'Oh,' Anne moaned.

Through the broken wall of the body stocking, Jacob avidly sucked at her, tasting the young woman for the first time.

'Yes,' she said, encouraging his indirect incursion.

As his mouth sucked in her early juices through the now wet material, he raised both his hands behind her back and cupped her arse cheeks forward, forcing her whole body harder against him.

Her skin was warm.

Finally, he pulled his mouth away from her crotch, and rose to his feet.

He was a full head taller than her.

He tugged sideways on the body stocking's thin shoulder straps.

'Put your hands up,' Jacob ordered her.

She did. Extricating her arms from the straps, now dangling against her sides.

He looked down at her dark green eyes.

She looked back.

Expressionless.

'Now, I undress you at last,' he said.

'Yes,' she answered calmly.

He pulled the elastic material all the way down to her feet, kneeling as he did so, his eyes zooming down the length of her pale body, admiring how the thin nylon peeled away from the gentle hills of her breasts to reveal sharp pale brown nipples, then the intricately-carved mini crevice of her navel and, joy, the flattened curls of her pubic thatch, as red as her hair, and, final panorama, the dizzy expanse of her long shapely thighs and legs, ending with the fragile angle between her slender ankles and her bare feet.

He stood up.

Anne was nude.

In front of him.

Silent.

She drew her tongue over her lips, wetting their dryness.

He feasted on the spectacle of her body.

Around them, the darkness deepened.

'Your turn,' she said. 'I want you to undress.'

He began to unbutton his shirt, disappointed she did not wish to undress him herself. It would have added one more thrill to the occasion.

'I want to see your cock,' Anne said.

After the shirt, he took off his socks before pulling down his trousers. There was no more ridiculous spectacle than a trouserless man wearing socks, he'd always felt.

At last, he stood there naked. In all his imperfection. Tanned but overweight.

Anne extended a hand forward and took his penis in her hand.

'It'll do nicely,' she remarked.

'Thanks.'

'Let's fuck, then,' she said.

As they moved toward the bedroom, Jacob fleetingly caressed her left breast. She stopped momentarily. Took a deep breath. He pulled his hand away.

'Touch me there again,' Anne said.

'I don't know how to put it, but I haven't got protection, condoms,' Jacob told her as they neared the hotel bed.

'It's okay,' she said. 'I'll trust you if you trust me.'

'I will,' he agreed.

'Anyway, it's always better without. Stronger sensations, you know,' Anne told him.

'Wouldn't dare contradict you,' he answered.

They kissed.

*

'This is Evil,' the Man From Caracas said, pointing out his acolyte to Teddy Caliban.

He was big, looked mean in the extreme, shaven-head, scarred features, standing there like a monument.

'Is that a first name or a family name?' Caliban asked, in a feeble attempt to alleviate the tension.

'Just call me Evil,' the large hood said in a deep voice.

'You see, Caliban,' said the Man From Caracas, buried in the plush upholstery of the stretch limo, 'We've never worked with you before and I need reassurance. Until the deal is done and everybody is happy, Evil will keep you company.'

'But . . .' Caliban began to protest.

'No buts,' the Man said. 'Just think of him as security. Like a bodyguard, eh?'

Evil, obediently standing outside the car's open door, just kept on smiling.

The moon was hidden behind the concrete mass of the shopping mall and the trees surrounding the car park moved quietly in the night breeze.

'Yeah, insurance, like,' Caliban approved.

'Exactly.'

Caliban nodded.

'So, let's go over the procedures once again.'

Caliban straightened up and ran through the operation.

'She's English. Looks quite wholesome. Has never done anything like this before. No one will suspect her. At all.'

'She'll use her own credit cards for the plane ticket and the hotel booking?'

'Yes, I've checked with her. Visa. I'll advance the cash to cover it. It's Okay with her.'

'Good,' the Man From Caracas said. 'And she makes all the bookings herself. No one must know you're involved, connect you to her. Must look just like a normal tourist on a weekend away.'

'Yes,' Caliban said.

'We make the contact once she has reached the hotel. She waits. As long as it takes. You will make that quite clear to her. There must be no variation to the plan. And when she returns to Miami, you wait until Evil gives you the word before meeting up with her again to pick up the stuff. We'll have someone shadowing her. Just in case. He'll let us know if the coast is clear.'

'It looks foolproof.'

'Nothing is ever foolproof,' the Man From Caracas insisted, annoyed.

'I understand,' Caliban said.

'I sure hope you do,' the Man added. Then, as an afterthought: 'The woman worries me, though. You said she's been whoring. How can I know she can be trusted?'

'She doesn't do it full time. I don't think she even does it for the money. It's a good agency she uses. They only supply the best women. Nothing cheap. Very select. Classy. I think she's in it more for the kicks than cash, though.'

'That worries me, you see,' the Man said. Listening to the conversation, Evil shifted on his feet and nodded approval.

'I want to see what she looks like,' the Man suddenly said.

'Now? I thought the idea was she should not have any contact . . .' Caliban protested.

'I didn't say she had to see me in person,' the Man From Caracas said, handing his portable phone to Caliban. 'Phone her. Arrange to have breakfast with her. Somewhere public, somewhere we can watch.'

Caliban dialled Anne's number.

Silence settled uneasily between the three men.

He listened to the phone ringing. On and on.

He finally returned the phone to the other man.

'There's no answer,' he said.

'Whoring, eh?' the Man said, looking at his watch. 'Must enjoy the overtime . . . Doesn't matter. Next time you see her, point her out to Evil here. He'll check her out.'

'Fine,' Teddy Caliban agreed.

'Anyway, she's your choice,' the Man said. 'And it's your ass on the line if anything goes wrong.'

'Nothing will go wrong, I assure you.'

'Evil enjoys putting things right when things go wrong, don't you, Evil?' he questioned his big acolyte.

'I do,' the big thug laconically replied.

The man put a hand on Teddy Caliban's knee and continued.

'He's very good at hurting people, you see. In his way, he's an artist in pain. Always finds a perfect way of harming people, where it hurts both the flesh and the soul. Don't you?'

Evil nodded.

'Listen. Let this be a warning. I'll tell you a story. Back home, my organisation uses accountancy students from a very good school to help out with the books. I don't trust professionals, they're too easily corrupted. There was this young couple, a brother and sister. What was their name again, Evil?' he asked.

'Cris and Edwina,' he replied.

'Yes, that's right. Well, Edwina was rather pretty and many of us fancied her. But business is business and you never mix business with pleasure. A pity. Looked real good in her summer dresses. Showed a lot of skin. Dark brown, tanned. She looked after the real estate portfolios. The investments. Her brother was four or five years younger, eighteen or nineteen, and she'd lobbied hard for us to give him a job in the accounts department. We never did find out whether it was her idea or his to fiddle around with the books and divert funds in their own direction. Because they weren't very good at it. We employ good people. Their pitiful scheme barely lasted a month. Not even that much money. Petty greed. But we had to punish them, see, set an example. In our business, fear is a potent currency and what happened to them would become a deterrent for years to come to anyone else whose imagination might wander down the path of wrongdoing. It could have been a bullet in the back of a head and down a jungle ravine, but it pissed me off, you know. If she'd wanted more money, she only had to ask, show me some more flesh, you see, I would have been quite understanding. I liked the girl. So, once we found out she and her brother were screwing us, what should I do? Evil knew, didn't you?'

'Yes,' Evil said.

'We had them come to the finance office after hours on some pretext. It's on the top floor of one of the city's tallest buildings. No one else around; very quiet. There was Evil, me and a couple of other guys she'd been gently cock-teasing along. Reckoned they might as well get their kicks off, too. Once the door was locked, I told them we knew. She was terrified. Peed in her pants right there. Her brother went as pale as a sheet. Seeing that she'd soiled herself and the stain was spreading fast across her dress, I told her she might as well strip. She did. And yes, it was a great body, really was. 'All yours, Evil,' I said. An artist I tell you. He had her bend over, on her knees on the floor and got her younger brother to also strip. With a knife to the kid's throat, Evil forced him to fuck her in the ass. He wasn't very hard at first. In the circumstance, you sort of understand. She began screaming as he desperately tried to penetrate her. So Evil lubricated them both with chilli sauce. He comes prepared for all occasions. Worked a miracle. Cris was soon at it like a dog, stiff and breathless while the panting Edwina kept on screaming, in fear and pain, her insides literally on fire I guess. Finally, Evil got the boy to pull out and ordered the girl to suck him clean. You could see her heart wasn't in it, tears pouring down her cheeks and all that, so after gagging the brother's mouth he transferred the knife to her throat and forced her to bite into the cock trapped inside her mouth until it was completely severed. It took a long time. Teeth aren't as sharp as you think, skin and gristle are much, much tougher.'

Teddy Caliban gulped his saliva down as he listened to the horror tale of retribution.

'Yes,' the Man From Caracas continued, 'a very long time. The other guys were holding Cris up to prevent him from collapsing. She was choking on it by the time her teeth completed the job, moaning like an infant and shuddering in place like an epileptic. As Evil pulled her face away from the brother's groin, the blood just geysered out of him, all over her. His knees were buckling; she was instantly sick. It's only then we slit the boy's throat, to put him out of his misery.'

Evil stood, still smiling, as his boss related his exploits.

'If it hadn't been for all the blood pouring down her front, I might have enjoyed Edwina myself, then. But I just didn't feel like it any longer. Decided enough was enough. Asked Evil to use the blade on her. He was disappointed, weren't you? Still had plans for her. Wanted to douse her cunt hair in lighter fluid and start burning her down there, he later told me, our director of pain. But I don't like the smell of burning flesh. Makes me indisposed. Nice story, eh?' he inquired.

Teddy Caliban said nothing.

'I assure you,' the Man From Caracas concluded, 'that Evil has a fertile imagination. I'm sure he could come up with something highly original for you if you mess things up.'

'I won't, I won't,' Teddy said quickly. They parted.

The Man drove off, while Caliban and Evil walked toward the Alfa parked a hundred meters further, close to the Mall's principal building. As Teddy prepared himself to move into the driver's seat, Evil's hand on his shoulder stopped him.

'I'll drive,' the massive thug said.

'Why? It's my car . . .'

The hand moved down and Evil swiftly took one of Caliban's fingers, bent it backwards and broke it.

Teddy Caliban sharply bit into his tongue, but despite the sudden pain, refused to make a sound.

'Just a token warning, Caliban,' Evil said.

'You didn't have to,' Caliban rasped.

'Fear, Caliban,' Evil said. 'It's only business. Remember, fear.'

*

The phone in her handbag, on the floor by the bed, rang.

He was inside her.

They ignored it.

He moved within her with all the grace he could muster, while his fingers roamed the outside envelope of Anne's body like an army on the march, seeking out weak, sensitive spots, soothing the lust, the raging demons. Her responses were immediate as they communicated exclusively with their nerve ends, surfing the waves of an invisible sea of pleasure, allowing themselves to be overcome by the flux, drowning happily until a further wave rushed them back again to the surface for another struggle, and then seeking the oblivion of the deep all over again, a cycle of eternal despair and gratification.

This was the second time and, as he had promised, it was better. It was good.

She chewed on his lips, almost gasping for breath, as he continued thrusting inside her, his cock brutally colliding with the walls of her womb, scraping with merciless aggression against the pliant, sponge-like texture of her boiling innards. He slipped both hands under her, raised her pelvis upward and adjusted his position, increasing the angle and the depth of his penetration. One of Anne's hands moved to his hair, tugged on his locks while her other hand moved down to their genitals, lazily slipping along the wet ridge where they were joined and descended to his balls, which she began gently kneading as he still moved in and out of her, squeezing gently, stopping every time just that micro-second before the pain, as if ready to milk his seed manually.

They were both bathing in a sea of sweat, and the crumpled sheets were bunched up at the end of the bed, twisted up with the frantic movements of their feet.

'God,' he said.

'Yes,' she whispered.

They came almost together.

Entangled, the acrid sheen of perspiration drying fast over their bodies, daylight filtering through the drawn curtains.

'I didn't ask you what you asked me, did I?' she said.

'What's that?' he responded.

'Why have you come to Miami Beach?'

'A change of scene.'

'No, that's not enough, tell me more,' she insisted.

'There was someone in London.'

'And?'

'Nothing. Just had to get away.'

He took a swig from the bottle of mineral water by the bedside. Passed it over to Anne.

'A woman?' she inquired.

'Yes.'

'Her name?'

'Lynda, with a Y.'

'And?'

'And that's all. We're not together anymore.'

'It's a long way to come to escape her.'

'I'm not escaping.'

'Fine.'

She turned on her side.

'Fuck me again,' she said.

'I don't known if I can,' Jacob replied.

'Try.'

A finger brushed against her cheek and the electricity between their two bodies surged and connected again. He made a move to straddle her.

'No,' she said. 'I want to be on top.'

Positioned herself above him, her small ripe breasts standing firmly at attention, tips swollen, her gash gaping obscenely open ready to impale itself on him, a blinding vision of her pink inside walls as she adjusted her stance and widened the angle between her legs.

'Yes, it's nice that way,' Jacob said. 'I like to watch it moving in and out of you.'

'Just like a porno movie?'

'Exactly.'

They fucked.

Until they dropped. Limbs cramped, throats dry, physical exhaustion sapping their energy, genitals screaming and raw.

'Christ, I'm hungry.'

'Me too. I'll get breakfast on room service.'

'Great idea.'

They showered together in the cramped cubicle, washing away the night's excesses, scraping away the secretions of lust from each other's body, emerging both scrubbed white and purified from the jets of hot water. They were towelling themselves dry when the doorbell rang.

'It's the food,' Jacob said, wrapping the fluffy oversize beach towel he had been using around his waist. 'I'll go and get it.'

The bellboy was young and, like most staff at the hotel, Hispanic. His hair was slicked back with excessive Brilliantine. He set the breakfast tray on the table next to the dishevelled bed and waited while Jacob searched his jacket pockets for spare change for the tip. Egg, bacon, muffins and maple syrup requested by her, slices of melon, fruit juice. The agreeable combination of smells rapidly moved straight from the plates to his nose. Jacob found a few green notes and turned back to the waiter. The young man was standing there with his eyes wide open in disbelief and a lewd smile on his lips watching Anne who had stretched out on the sofa. She was still totally nude. Her legs were parted, wide open, one foot high up on the sofa's edge. She was smiling back at the bellboy.

Jacob irritably handed the few dollars to the guy.

'You should be paying me for the free spectacle,' he muttered, escorting him past the door.

'Nice lady, señor,' the young man said. Was that a leer on his face?

Jacob angrily slammed the door on him and turned back into the room. Anne was now using the nail scissors he kept in the bathroom cabinet, and was busy trimming her pubic hair.

'Why didn't you put something on?' he asked her.

'Didn't feel like it,' she replied, absorbed by her delicate task, pulling on a few recalcitrant tufts.

'He saw you naked,' Jacob went on.

'I know,' was all she would say.

Jacob could feel the first pangs of jealousy already.

'Let's eat. I'm starving,' Anne said.

*

Tallahassee.

The waitress dreamt of Paris.

She'd never been there; she'd only seen a hundred or so movies or programmes on TV. But something inside her knew that one day, she'd go there. She could smell it already. The perfume of the Seine, the fragrance of wonderful spicy foods lingering in the Parisian air. The thin, low buildings, the landscape of grey rooftops she would look out on from her hotel window. She touched herself, thinking of the men she would meet there. How they would caress her in all the right places and make her come again and again like a river, like a torrent, not like the clumsy guys from around here who always left her so unfulfilled, used. Men here just had no poetry, the waitress believed. In Paris, she knew, she would fuck a poet. It would be different. Well, a girl had to dream, hadn't she?

*

'How did it happen?' the doctor at the hospital asked Teddy Caliban.

'Caught it in a door,' he replied, as the medic placed the bandage around his broken digit, before they set the cast around it.

'Strange, there's no mark there,' the doctor insisted.

'Just do your job,' Caliban insisted and looked on at the neon-lit hospital corridor where Evil stood waiting for him.

3.

You Make Me Nervous

'It's Sunday,' Anne said.

'What do you want to do?' asked Jacob.

'Dunno. Something special. Maybe take a trip somewhere, like normal people do.'

'Sounds good. Anyway, if it's okay with you, we can stay overnight wherever we go. There's no need to be back by Monday.'

The idea appealed to him. He was beginning to tire of Miami and the beach.

'Don't you have a job to go back to?' Anne asked.

'No. I'm a gentleman of leisure.'

'How come?'

'Sold a business when I left London. I've enough to last a few years, if I'm careful.'

'What did you do?'

'I ran and owned a small news-gathering agency. Specialising in business and economics. Never really enjoyed it, just somehow fell into it, almost by accident. Started off as a local arts correspondent, then did some holiday cover in that particular section of news and current affairs when a friend fell ill and I stayed on.'

'Journalist, hey?'

'Yes. Started the agency right when they began farming out lots of work to independents. Thought, Why not? It worked.'

'And Lynda?' she asked.

'Don't even ask,' Jacob replied.

She still wore nothing. Bread crumbs had gathered in her lap, sprinkled like grains in her dark pubic curls and across her pale thighs. As Jacob's gaze travelled again and again across the enticing vista of her uncovered body, he felt the old stirrings rise. That familiar and oh so dangerous combination of sheer lust and fragile sentimentality that overcame him with the women who counted. The real ones. The ones, he knew from the outset of any chance encounter, who could so easily hurt him—and probably would in the long run. There hadn't been that many. Half a dozen, he reckoned. But he never would have swapped the final excruciating pain for anything in the world. The epiphanies always justified the later sadness.

He softly hummed a tune: 'On the road again . . .'

'What's that?' Anne asked.

'Oh, just singing. Ignore me.'

'I will,' Anne answered, rising from the breakfast table and walked to the bathroom to gather her crumpled clothing from the night before. She brought the body stocking to her face.

'Full of sweat,' she said. Sniffed the material again. 'Cunt,' she added. 'We'll have to go to my place to get fresh clothes.'

'Sure,' Jacob said.

She slipped the white body stocking back on as he watched her with unconcealed fascination. She stepped into the skirt and, turning her back on him, walked into the bathroom where she closed the door.

Anne emerged a few minutes later, dark red lipstick like an explosion of fierce colour across her features, highlighting the morning green of her eyes. She had combed her silken auburn hair back across her shoulders.

Looking at her, Jacob now dressed in black jeans and white short-sleeved shirt, said: 'I want to make love to you again.'

'Later,' she smiled.

'Is that a promise?'

'Indeed,' she said. 'So where shall we go?'

'I've been staying in Miami all these months,' Jacob remarked, 'and somehow I've never visited the Everglades. Have you?'

'No, I haven't,' she answered. 'It's a great idea. Yes. Let's go there. I've never seen a crocodile. My parents were ever so cruel to me when I was a child, they never took me to the zoo.'

Jacob walked over to the telephone.

'Let me arrange a car hire with the front desk. It'll only take a few minutes. The clerk's a friend. Won't even require any paperwork. The rental company has a desk down there and use a section of the hotel car park.'

'We'll drive by my place on the way. I'm in North Beach,' she said.

*

Out there in Radio Land, the morning DJ began his first shift. On the other side of the glass partition, the two engineers, looking like mirror images, both wearing their baseball cotton caps backwards, sat at the mixing console, each sipping Diet Pepsi straight from the can. The digits on the electronic time display moved, and the first engineer pushed the live button and gave the DJ the thumbs up signal.

'Morning all,' the disc jockey said into his microphone. 'I know it, you know it, this is Pirate Radio and you are listening to me, the Mark of God. None other, the guy with no name, or any sensible one at any rate. Just call me Mark of God. I'll answer your calls, if you do that. You bet. It's a brand new morning. Inside here, it's fucking dark, we don't want to know what the weather is like outside, do we? Just the darkness and me. What a programme, hey?, listeners? So let's start the day with our usual intravenous injection of rock and roll. The fix we can't do without. Put your arms around me, says the man who sings the song. This one's called *Shake*; it's by the Vulgar Boatmen. Happens to be one of my all-time faves. But then those are the only ones I would play for you all, aren't they? Sure. And don't forget my first traffic warning for today: If you sell your soul at the crossroads, be advised not to sell it cheap. End of the first lesson. On with the music.'

The Mark slipped his headphones off as the music began and initiated its endless journey through the electronic waves of Radio Land.

The guitar chords waltzed along faster than the speed of sound from the Canadian border all the way to the Rio Grande, across deserts and fields, cities and highways, the beat echoing against the varied landscapes, in and out of the ether, skipping across the mountain tops and the plains, making a beeline for the heart of madness.

'Tasty,' the DJ said to himself. 'Very tasty.'

And the music played on.

Racing with stealth under the curiosity of radars, rushing from the illegal radio station studio's subterranean bunker into bright daylight, connecting directly with the synapses of all those in the outside world who were plugged in or, alternately, switched on. All innocent onlookers. Characters in an unfolding melodrama.

The music reigned.

*

'I wonder what you must have looked like as a little girl,' Jacob said, as they parked outside Anne's white stucco two-storey apartment block.

'Rather cute, as a matter of fact,' she replied. 'Freckles, pigtails, your average small suburban red-haired kid, the sort of child the taller girls always picked on at the local grammar school when they wanted to bully someone.'

'Oh,' he remarked, as they emerged from the portico, 'you have a swimming-pool.'

'Never used it,' she said. 'The water's not very clean, and you should see some of my fellow neighbours. Not the kind you'd enjoy swimming with.'

They reached her door.

There was a note pinned to the door. On the back of a torn envelope. It read:

Anne,
Call me.
Urgently.
Teddy

'Who's Teddy?' Jacob asked.

'None of your business, Jacob,' Anne replied.

It felt like the first time she had actually said his name. So odd, he realised. Even in bed, entangled in the wildest of clinches and their embedded bodies contorted in the most pornographic of geometrical figures, she hadn't even whispered his name. Not even then.

She opened the door to the apartment.

They walked in.

There was something anonymous about the place. Boring rental furniture. Dull-coloured walls and peeling ceiling. A few half-empty suitcases sitting in a corner, a reflection of Anne's transient nature. Books and magazines liberally scattered all over the front room. Beyond the other door, the bedroom, an unmade bed, more detritus of clothes and magazines. The kitchen corner was neat and clean, seemingly rarely used. This wasn't a place where you lived, Jacob thought, it was a place you passed through. On your way to other things, better things.

'I'm not apologising for the mess,' Anne said, slipping out of her skirt, and leaving it where it dropped halfway between the door and the bedroom on the brown marble-like tiles.

'You don't have to,' he replied.

'I won't be long,' Anne said, moving toward the bedroom. 'Half an hour. No more. Read something while you're waiting,' she suggested. And closed the door.

Jacob found a chair and brushed last week's Sunday edition of the *Miami Herald* off it. Looked around him. The place she lived in. The room which contained all her secrets, the awful intimacy of this woman he still knew nothing about.

He picked up a paperback. Anne Tyler. He'd read it. Another book. A bodice-ripper romance. Examined the cover. Yes, the woman in passionate embrace with the bronzed and rippling-muscled pirate (or was he an Arab prince?) did look a bit like Anne. Why shouldn't her story be true?

He leafed through the book, listening for her sounds on the other side of the door. Read a few random paragraphs. But he couldn't concentrate on the text. Or any text. Being here with all her possessions around him was unsettling.

He rose from the chair. Picked a green silk blouse from the floor and arranged it over the jacket strewn across the only other chair in the room. There was another item of clothing under the blouse. A pair of black knickers. Lacy. Flower-patterned. Almost rolled into a ball. Jacob leaned over and took them in his hand. Unfolded them. Traced a fleeting pattern across the flimsy material with one casual finger. Looked towards the door of the bedroom and brought the knickers up to his face. Unfurled the material so that the crotch line met his nose. Closed his eyes momentarily and inhaled the strong taste of Anne's dried secretions. Held his breath. Heard her moving on the other side of the door.

'God, oh God, what am I doing?' he said to himself and reluctantly withdrew the soiled underwear from his face. Feeling awkward and hot, he put the knickers away, on the chair, under the blouse.

'Are you okay?' she called.

'Yes. Yes, I am,' he blurted out, dry-throated.

'Just got to cut my nails and put some make-up on,' Anne shouted. 'Another ten or fifteen minutes.'

'That's fine,' he replied. 'Take your time.'

Encouraged by her prolonged absence, Jacob looked into the handbag she had left by the door. A man's brown leather wallet. Fifty dollars or so in cash. Assorted business cards; mostly of local businessmen. Clients? Credit cards in the name of Anne K Ryan. He would have to ask her what the K stood for, he decided. Scraps of paper with various addresses and phone numbers. Mostly in England. He recognised the code for Cambridge on quite a few numbers. A dialling code he knew well. He delved deeper into the bag and scooped out the rest of its contents. The cellphone. It had rung insistently during the night, he recalled. He now noticed it was switched off. Sundry pills and tablets. Her passport. He eagerly leafed through the document.

The K stood for Katherine.

She was thirty. Her birthday had been just a couple of weeks back. It also stated she was married. Who? An entry visa from New York's Newark airport. Valid six months. Had just another few weeks to go. Tourist visa only. She was soon to become illegal. Maybe she needed help?

'Won't be long now,' she shouted out.

Hurriedly, Jacob dropped everything back into the handbag and carefully replaced it where she had initially left it and sat down in the chair again, picking up the paper's colour supplement.

When she emerged, she was wearing a short, tight white tee-shirt outlining the dark hardness of her nipples and revealing the flat surface of her stomach and the whirlpool of her belly button, cut-off shorts reclaimed from an old pair of jeans and string sandals whose intricate laces circled halfway up to her knees.

'Cool, hey?' she asked.

'You look just great,' he reacted.

She looked so young, now. Even had threaded a white ribbon through the silken red waterfall of her hair.

'Let's go, then,' she said.

'You're not calling Teddy back?' he asked impulsively.

'No,' she said coldly, and made for the door, picking her handbag up on the way.

*

Evil ordered him: 'Try again.'

Teddy Caliban dialled Anne's number. They were sitting in his midtown office. Outside, the noonday sun was settling over the sleepy buildings. The beaches were full of families and tourists. The hurricane season would be upon them soon, Teddy reflected, and the unwelcome hordes would thin out.

After a suitable interval, he put down the receiver.

'She's switched off. Her battery's dead or she's not taking calls,' he said.

'I don't believe this,' Evil said.

'It's Sunday,' Teddy protested.

'The day of rest, I know,' Evil answered. 'Fuck it.'

Teddy poured another round of drinks.

'Any good tapes?' Evil said, pointing at the TV and the video cabinet.

'Sex?' Teddy Caliban asked.

'Of course,' said Evil. 'Do I look as if I'm into Shakespeare or *Masterpiece Theatre*?' he chuckled.

Teddy shot him a dark look.

'With lots of anal,' Evil insisted.

'Most of them feature some,' Teddy said, looking through the two piles of cassettes inside the cabinet. 'I don't think I've got an all-anal, though.'

'Maybe with an English redhead getting a good back door screw,' Evil added.

'Are you already fantasising some future scenario?' Teddy inquired.

'No. Just thought you'd put her through her paces before you used her on legitimate business,' Evil said.

'And filmed the proceedings?'

'I would,' said Evil, burying himself in the plump leather chair as Teddy finally selected a video for the thug's edification.

*

The short drive north went like a dream. There were barely any other cars heading up the highway, at this time of day. Most would have left much earlier. The constant music on the radio punctuated their idle thoughts with a persistent, sensual beat. Neither was in the mood for much conversation. Day-dreaming away, sitting in the front seats of the black rental coupé, lost in private universes, quietly pleased by the nearby presence of the other. Stolen visions of the whiteness of her uncovered thighs, of the regular patterns of the dark hairs on his forearms.

The road unrolled ahead of him like a shroud as he drove on, all his senses alert to the warmth of her nearby body reaching him in waves, the memories of the way she felt, the light caress of her lips against his, her tongue inside his mouth, her fingers roaming around his private parts, unwillingly comparing her touch with those who had come before, the girls in France, the ones from Poland, the coltish Americans, the tall heartbreaking blondes, the shorter ball-busting ones, every one different, every body different, each face unique, all the images of beauty and despair blending inside his head until he had to mentally disconnect from the overwhelming weight and presence of the past before he felt like screaming in protest at the rude intrusion. And concentrated on the road.

Anne fought the maelstrom of images. Her father dying. Having to put him in the ground. The library of her past burning down. The men. The loneliness. Was this one any different? Would he end up betraying her? Hurting her? Like a movie unrolling on a screen made of flesh. The chapel in Cambridge. The white dress she didn't deserve to wear. The early days of poverty. The seduction of older men, their quiet, insolent assurance. Their financial ease and the way they could shamelessly hire hotel rooms by the day when they wanted to screw her. The Trusthouse Forte one by Heathrow, in the shadow of the M4, the curtains drawn, how he had taken her so exquisitely, opening up a hundred new visions of pleasure she had seldom believed existed before, how somehow even his cock was different from those she had glimpsed, been fucked with before. The colour, the thickness, the shape, the texture of its soft mushroomed head, entering her with the ease of a dagger after all the hesitations, no he didn't use condoms, didn't it feel better this way? Oh yes, oh yes, she had said as he invaded her, changing her forever. She opened her eyes, interrupting the movie. The Florida landscape raced on by.

'Look,' she said.

'What?' Jacob asked.

'That sign there. Lake Woolrich. With that kitsch picture of rustic old-time cabins and fishermen. Another mile further down the road. Let's go there.'

'Okay,' he said, weaving the car into the right hand lane.

'I'm sure there will be somewhere nice to eat by the Lake. I want to eat by a lake,' she said.

'Who can resist a woman's whim?' he remarked, slowing down as he approached the highway's exit. The trees on either side of the flat road were growing thicker.

*

As the action on the television screen hotted up, Evil unzipped his flies and pulled his penis out.

'Feel free,' he said to Teddy Caliban.

'Thanks but no thanks,' Teddy replied, consciously avoiding looking over at the thug's member. He knew he didn't want to know.

'Your loss,' Evil said, masturbating away.

'You broke my bloody finger, remember, makes it awkward,' Teddy added.

'Use the other hand,' suggested Evil.

'I'm not ambidextrous,' Teddy said. 'I can only use the one hand, the one you happen to have injured.'

Evil began moaning softly as his climax approached.

Teddy rose. This, he could miss.

'I'll be in the other room, reading the paper,' he announced.

'Suit yourself,' Evil said.

*

They ate at a cajun joint far away from its Louisiana roots. Spicy boiled crawfish. Two overflowing plates of the pungent deep red shellfish. Eating with their fingers, juice clumsily spraying over their no longer white tops. He cooled his throat with home-made lemonade, she with rose wine.

'Have you ever been to New Orleans?' Jacob asked Anne.

'No. Miami's the only place I've ever really been to in the States. Just spent a few days in New York when I arrived. Hated it. Not my kind of town.'

'You'd love New Orleans. Just the feel of it, the food, the atmosphere. Weather's sticky, though,' he said.

'Take me,' Anne said.

'Really?'

'Yeah, one day you can take me.'

'You're kidding?'

'I'm not. If we're still together, you can take me there in a few weeks. I've got an important job coming up in Miami. I want to take a vacation afterwards. So, when that's done, if you want, we can go.'

'I'd love to,' Jacob said.

Still together?

The joint's owner walked up to their table to clear the plates full of empty shells away.

'Tourists?' he asked. He was bald and his pate was burnished by years of sun.

'Yes,' Anne said.

'We don't see many tourists around here any more,' the lakeside bar's owner told them. 'People these days prefer the Amusement Parks. Specially if they have kids.'

'I see on the menu you sell cotton candy?' Anne asked.

'Indeed we do, missy. I'll bring some along'

Anne purred as the old man shuffled away.

'Great. Just great,' she said.

She decided afterwards she wanted to swim. The old man recommended they follow the lake's shore for another quarter of an hour, where they would find a small creek with a tiny beach.

'The water's real nice there, all clear, no industrial contamination' he said. 'You kids will be able to skinny dip to your heart's content.'

'Oh, yes,' Anne said.

Once they reached the creek, she shed her clothing with alacrity. Jacob retained his underpants as he tentatively neared the water. He'd never liked it cold.

'Oh, you spoilsport,' Anne screamed as she noticed.

Ran toward him and summarily slid his pants down to his ankles. Took his hand in hers and pulled him over to the lake.

'Christ,' Jacob exclaimed. 'It's freezing!'

'Yes, it is,' Anne said, letting go of him and wading deeper into the green waters.

And plunged in, her red hair trailing behind her like a net, a splash of colour against the calm surface of the lake until it was dragged further down with her and disappeared.

She emerged, a minute later, like Venus from her perennial half-shell, water pearling down the white walls of her body, drops cascading over the sharply erect tips of her breasts, running across her flattened thatch.

'It's wonderful,' she shouted at him, as he still stood barely ankle-deep in the lake, just a few yards away from the protection of the small beach.

Laughing her head off, Anne plunged once more into the lake and swam toward him. As she reached him, running out of water, she rose slowly, squatting one moment on her haunches, her head facing his crotch.

'Oh, you poor thing,' she giggled maniacally. 'You're all shrivelled up.'

And took him into her mouth.

Later on, the sky darkening ominously above them, they searched for a motel for the night. They had to retrace their way back to the highway, and drive for almost an hour until the neon sign of a Best Western finally beckoned.

The room was identikit cheapo-cheapo Americana and thoroughly depressing. But all they required was a roof and a bed.

'I think I'm falling in love with her,' Jacob reflected. 'I just can't, I mustn't.' He knew how vulnerable he still was.

However, he made love to Anne that night with a delicacy that surprised even him, riding the waves of her rising pleasure and synchronising his touches and movements outside and inside of her with accurate precision, conjugating the vocabulary of her desire with all the right responses.

They clung together like orphans in the mad tornado of sex, bonded by the roaring twister, egging each other onward to even more savage thrusts and moans, abandoning all modesty and semblance of civilisation.

Out of breath, wet, his whole body an antenna capturing the young woman's naked emotions, Jacob adjusted his position, pulling Anne into place, raising her legs above his shoulders as he kept on digging deep into her and slipped a hand under her rump. Explored for the crease and found her other aperture. And brutally slipped his finger in, breaching the ring of tense muscle with his swiftness.

'JEEZUS . . .'she screamed.

Jacob stopped.

'Did I hurt you?' he asked.

'No . . . no,' Anne panted. 'It's good, it's good, put it in deeper. Go.'

Afterwards, they fell asleep, slumped against each other, with all the heaviness of innocence.

Jacob awoke halfway through the night. Probably the noise of the cars buzzing by on the nearby Highway. He turned over. Anne was quietly sobbing in her sleep.

4.

Summary Cannibals

The waitress came down from Tallahassee by Greyhound bus. She had a few remaining vacation days left, and she sure as hell wasn't planning to spend them on her own, inside the four close walls of that grey apartment she loathed so much. She knew she would never find a poet in Tallahassee. She was also aware that her own biological clock was ticking loudly. She wanted a baby. A blonde baby. It had to be a little girl. With blue eyes. Whose silken hair she could spend hours braiding into intricate, decorative patterns, with tiny coloured plastic beads at the extremities. She'd seen women do that on a travelogue on TV about Jamaica and its beaches.

She stuffed a change of underwear into an overnight bag, together with her toiletries, selected her shortest skirt, the blue cotton one with the white polka dots and wriggled herself into the red, ruffled tube top, then slipped on her leather sandals with the silver buckles.

The plane to the big city would only take an hour or so, she knew, but with the bus, she'd save at least sixty bucks. Which could go a long way, her gut feeling told her.

On the drive down, a couple of rude home boys—she thought she remembered them from high school days, or maybe not, they all did look much the same to her—kept on bothering her. Jokes, banter, but all too quickly the familiar lewd propositions, all part of a serving girl's burden, she realised. As the bus raced along, she had to keep pulling the tight skirt down to her knees for fear of showing her white panties to the guys. She blanked out their intrusion and imagined herself pushing a pram up and down Parisian streets. She found it difficult to picture this very precisely. Realised as an afterthought to the daydream that she couldn't even speak French. Of course, poets never did earn much money, she reckoned, so she would have to go to work. But she was confident that the diners in Paris would be busy and in need of her services. All she would have to do would be to memorise the names of the dishes and a few standard pleasantries, she guessed. Corned beef hash, juice and muffins must be much of the same in every country. That wouldn't change. Of course, over there, they'd drink red wine with their meals.

The amorphous dreams inside her head came to an end as the bus approached the outskirts of Miami. Determined to ignore them, she hadn't even noticed that the black guys had already disembarked at the previous stop. She walked down to the narrow washroom at the rear of the coach and applied her make up with care. Powder, eye-liner, blusher, lipstick. Used the tweezers on a couple of recalcitrant eyebrows. Yesterday, she'd had her hair done at Lucy's Parlour and her dark hair shone with health. Yes, she thought to herself, this will do very nicely. Looked further into the patchy mirror, downward. The tits were a bit heavy, but still firm; the waistline could be thinner, but what could you do working all hours of the day with all that food around, and the smells of fat and cooking? You could put weight on just damn inhaling. Her thighs worried her, they were a bit lumpy. A few months ago, they were selling this exerciser for the stomach and thighs on the Shopping Channel and she'd impulsively sent off for one. Every morning before work, and at night before bed, she would spend a quarter of an hour bending and pulling, but it didn't seem to have made much difference so far.

Still, the men back at the Bordersnakes Café liked her; all the male customers did. They were always inviting her out, plying her with drinks, didn't mind screwing her when she allowed them to, when the itch was too strong and she had to accept second best, mostly out of boredom. They appreciated the way she looked, how she took care of her body. But she knew they were, one and all, simple men. Maybe a real poet would want more. Give something back. She'd once stolen a few skin mags from Joe Bob Wootton's mobile home after he'd boozily convinced her to spend the whole night there and quickly fallen asleep, spread eagled over her, without even finding the energy to come inside her. Too much liquor. At least he hadn't been sick all over her while screwing; that had happened once to her friend Marie. She'd looked closely at the pictures of the women in the magazines, taken mental notes and, yesterday, in preparation for her Miami adventure, Sandra the waitress had, blushing deeply as she did the deed, carefully trimmed the shape of the hair around her pussy. Like the impossibly glamorous girls in the skin magazines. She knew that poets wouldn't like their women too hairy.

She left the toilet. Two other women standing right outside gave her dirty looks as she came out. They would have spent as long inside if they'd gotten there first, she knew, and breezed past them.

She returned to her seat. The tall Miami skyline was already visible in the distance. Sandra felt a dizzy knot in her stomach.

Maybe he'd fuck her on the top floor of a skyscraper?

It would be like heaven, she knew. She smiled. The old man along the aisle smiled back. Sandra squirmed in her seat as the bus began to slow down.

*

As Jacob swung the car into the rental space beneath the hotel, Anne's right hand alighted gently on his wrist. Her touch was warm.

'It was really nice, Jakey, thanks ever so much. I had a wonderful time. I really did,' she said.

'Me too,' he replied. 'But don't call me Jakey. Jake, maybe. Not Jakey. Makes me sound like a kid.'

She smiled back at him, mischief etched on her pink lips.

He pulled the key from the ignition.

'So,' he said as they both sat silently in the penumbra, 'this must be the moment of truth.'

'Hey?' she questioned him.

'When I have to ask if I'll see you again?'

Her smile turned into a gentle laugh.

'Of course, Jake,' she answered.

'I am a child, Anne, I'm greedy, I'm impatient, when?' he asked.

'Soon, very soon,' she said. 'There's this one job and then we can find the time, a lot of time, I promise.'

They left the car and took the elevator to the lobby.

The marble decor was flooded in fierce daylight. The clerk at the reception desk barely gave them a second glance. Jacob just stood there, dazzled by the brightness, waiting for her to make a move towards the door and Ocean Drive. She didn't.

Anne looked up to him.

Her ruffled red hair burnt like a sheer fire in the eyes of the sun.

Jacob swallowed once. Fear, again, lurking down in his stomach. I'm not in love with her, I'm not falling in love because this way unhappiness lies, he whispered to himself.

'A last drink?' Anne suggested.

'A drink?' he repeated.

'In your room.'

'Now?'

'Now. Or, if you prefer, a last fuck.'

He nervously looked around him, but apart from the clerk busy counting credit card slips at the desk, there was no one around.

'I'd rather call it making love.'

'Is there a difference?' Anne asked him, already swivelling back towards the elevator.

'I hope so,' he remarked, and followed her. 'Yes,' he said, 'I'd like that very much.'

The elevator doors opened as Anne pressed firmly on the lobby level button.

'It's hot in here,' Anne said as the elevator moved up through the building.

'Yes,' Jacob agreed. 'We can take a nice long shower together to cool down.'

'I'd prefer a bath,' Anne answered.

Jacob mopped her sweating brow. 'It's quite a large bathtub. We'll both fit, you'll see.'

'Good.'

*

It was already afternoon by the time Anne returned to her apartment. She'd insisted on taking a cab. She knew that if she'd allowed Jakey to drive her back, they would have just ended back in bed again. He was nice.

The red flashing light on the telephone indicated an avalanche of messages.

They were all from Teddy.

Urgent. Demanding. Angry. Pleading. Puzzled.

Fuck you, Anne thought.

Knowing she would probably have to again very soon, which made her flesh shiver.

She pulled her clothes off, showered, raided the refrigerator for the end of the orange juice and a few pieces of cheese, slipped an old tee-shirt on and wandered across the two small rooms picking up discarded underwear and stuff, feeling the gentle breeze of the conditioning waft between her bare thighs. It made her randy, this insidious caress of the air against her genitals and her naked rump. Finally, she decided she couldn't put it off any longer and sprawled out on the rickety couch and dialled Teddy's number.

Another man picked up the phone.

A deep bass voice.

'Yeah?'

'Teddy, please.'

'Who is this?'

She ignored the question. Something in his tone bothered her.

'Teddy, please,' she repeated.

'Who the fuck are you?' the dark voice demanded.

'Anne Ryan,' she finally said.

'Ah,' the guy said. 'We've been waiting to hear from you. You must have been a busy lady.'

'Can I speak to Teddy,' she insisted.

'Where the hell have you been, Anne?' Teddy asked. 'I tried your place. Nobody knew.'

'I went away. Wanted a bit of sun.'

'I needed you here,' he insisted. 'What were you up to?'

'Well, I'm sorry, Teddy, but you don't own me. Our relationship is a business one, whether it's the sex or the job. It doesn't give you any other rights to my life. And who is that other guy, anyway?'

'My business associate. He wants to meet you. Things are all set up. You have to leave in the morning. If you'd been in touch with us any later, the whole damn thing would have had to be called off.'

'You mean, it's all on? As we agreed?'

'Yes. Get your sorry ass over here right now.'

'I need to freshen up, Teddy,' Anne said. 'Let's make it tonight.'

'No. Now. Right now.'

She knew there was no point pleading otherwise.

'I'll slip something on and I'll be around.'

The other man came on the phone again, must have been listening on another set, 'Come as you are. I'm sure it would be fun,' he said.

'Not as much as you think, you dirty bastard,' Anne answered before slamming the phone down.

If she had known what he looked like, she wouldn't have used the parting shot. He was monstrous. Overgrown, pug ugly, like a tree trunk clumsily growing out of an elegant silk suit, at odds with every element surrounding him. His bald pate was severely scarred. Anne found him genuinely frightening as he gave her the once over at Teddy Caliban's penthouse apartment.

'I'm Evil,' he introduced himself.

'I'm sure you are,' she mumbled.

'He's part of the deal,' Teddy added. 'What he says goes, Anne. Don't forget that. Mr Evil means business.' He held his arm limply against his side.

'Yeah, business,' said Evil, waving them to the table.

His back was even more massive than his front, Anne observed. A veritable wardrobe.

'You've never been a courier before, have you?' Evil asked.

'No.'

'Good. That's what Mr Caliban told us. We like people who are new to it. They look more innocent, more normal.'

'I was told it wasn't drugs,' Anne interjected.

'That's correct,' the big man said.

'Are you sure?' Anne protested. 'Really?'

'What do you want, woman, an official letter on embossed headed note paper endorsed by a lawyer?' Teddy snickered.

'Well, I would like to know what I'm carrying; it would be nice to know,' Anne insisted.

'We find it better for couriers to stay in ignorance. Better security that way,' Evil said.

'Okay,' Anne finally agreed. 'So, tell me what needs doing?'

Teddy poured three glasses of bourbon. She hated the stuff. She gulped it down all the same, conscious of the burning gaze of Evil running up and down her body.

'Listen carefully, Anne, this is the way it's been planned. This is the gospel according to your good friend Teddy Caliban.' He passed an envelope over to her across the table. 'Tomorrow morning, you take the early flight to Caracas, ticket and a thousand dollars in cash are in there. If they ask you why you're travelling to Venezuela, you say it's tourism, a bit of shopping, you've heard the stores there have nicer things than Miami. Remember: always act like a tourist. You take a cab from the airport. You have a room booked at the Tamanaco Intercontinental. Go straight there. You stay two nights. During the day, do some shopping, buy a few dresses, some shoes, some wood carvings in the Indian market, whatever takes your fancy. Don't make friends. Stay at all time on your own. Use the cash. Do not use your own credit cards. The room has been prepaid through a travel agent, so you'll only have to take care of the supplements, drinks and such. The flight back is on Thursday afternoon. You be on it. And go straight to your apartment. We will contact you there. Absolutely do not try and communicate with me here, whether when in Caracas or after you've returned. We'll be watching you to ensure there's no one on your tail. When the time is ripe, we'll meet up and pick up our merchandise.'

'And I'll be paid when you get the stuff?' Anne enquired.

'Yes. Twenty five thousand, as agreed. Is it all clear?'

'Absolutely.'

'Good,' Teddy Caliban said.

'The seafood's good in Caracas,' Evil added. 'Just stay in the city centre, have some nice meals, spend the cash. Keep away from others, keep your damn pants on. We can't afford for anything to go wrong, understood?'

'Yes,' she sheepishly acquiesced.

Teddy poured another round of drinks, a satisfied look spreading across his face. As the two men on either side of her gulped down the bourbon, she set her own glass aside.

'I'd rather not,' Anne said. 'Haven't eaten since breakfast and my stomach is pretty empty; the booze won't agree with me much.'

Teddy, pleased by the fact that the official part of the encounter was now over, solicitously asked: 'Are you hungry? You should have said. I'll call for a takeaway, Chinese, Indian, Mexican? What do you fancy?'

'I'd rather go, Teddy,' Anne protested. 'I've got to get ready, pack...'

'Oh, come on, Anne, it's been a few days, you could stay a few more hours. We could celebrate the deal. I still have some of that great coke.'

He looked up at Evil.

'And my business associate was about to leave, weren't you, Evil?'

'I'm too tired, really have to clean up, Teddy,' Anne said. 'You didn't give me a chance over the phone, you know.'

'As a matter of fact, Mr Caliban,' Evil slowly said, extending his hand across the table and placing it on Teddy's undamaged hand, 'I wasn't thinking of leaving at all.'

Both Anne and Caliban looked up at the man in dismay.

'We're in this business together,' Evil added. 'So why shouldn't we all celebrate together, hey?'

His other hand moved to Anne's bare shoulder. The skin on his fingertips was rough. She shuddered imperceptibly.

'No way,' she exclaimed. 'I'm not sleeping with either of you, let alone the two of you together. No way. You pigs. And if I hear another word, I'm backing out.'

She stood up angrily.

Teddy tried to placate her.

'I was only thinking of you and me, honey. It wasn't my idea...'

Evil stood up in turn.

'Afterwards. When you get back from Caracas, then we'll celebrate properly with the little English lady, won't we, Teddy?'

Anne, feeling the onset of panic, began making her way to the door.

'Evil, let's talk about this later,' Caliban said to the thug. 'Let Anne go now. We'll talk.'

Evil smiled. 'Well, she'd better not forget the envelope.'

Anne blushed and came back to the table to pick up the plane ticket and the cash.

Caliban was still sitting there, fuming. Red-headed little slut, he could guess from the colours in her face she'd spent screwing the weekend away with some other man, or men. He'd teach her a lesson, when the time came. A real lesson.

Evil moved up to Anne.

'I'll see you out to the elevator,' he said.

As they waited for the lift to arrive from the lower floors of the apartment block, the thick-set man placed his palm against her butt and whispered in her ear.

'If anything goes wrong, Anne, I shall stick my fist inside your cunt and rip you apart from the inside.' She remained silent. 'And I shall greatly enjoy doing it, you know. I hurt people, you see, and I'm good at my job. So don't mess things up.'

The elevator arrived. She felt she had been waiting for a century or more.

'See you in a few days, Anne, one way or the other I know it's going to be fun. I just hope it's good for you too.'

The doors closed and she was alone at last.

She felt sick. Bile rising all the way up her throat.

She was beginning to regret the whole thing.

Oh shit. And shit again. London suddenly felt so faraway.

*

'I'm going out,' Evil said. 'Need some fresh air. It's too stuffy in here.'

Teddy nodded silently. They hadn't spoken a word to each other since the English woman had left, an hour earlier. The bottle of bourbon was long since emptied.

'Do you think I need my coat?' Evil asked. 'Not sure if there's a storm about to break or not. Looks that way,' he peered past the verandah.

Teddy glanced round at the windows.

'Just in case, take it,' he muttered.

Evil left the apartment leaving him alone. At last. Not that there was anything he could do. He picked up the phone and dialled Anne's number. The damn answer machine intercepted the call. Yes, that's what he wanted to do, now he was rid of the bloody thug. Hell, why did the Venezuelans dispatch him over? They knew they could trust Teddy Caliban.

Eduardo Golightly y Robertson Caliban was not a complicated man.

He just had problems with women.

He required no psychotherapist to explain it. He could live with the problem.

Very early in his sentimental career, back when he was a teenager, and still an unimpressive wayward nerd, too many WASP would-be prom queens had messed him up, stood him up, let him down for others, for jocks, and the grudge inside him had festered like a dark flower of anger.

Even now that he had enough money and all the social graces to play the man-woman game with a modicum of manners, there remained a core of anger inside Teddy.

Making love to women was like making war. Something inside him sought vengeance even as he enjoyed the feel of their skin and the sweet taste of their kisses. So he had to push harder inside them, until they hurt. He had to make the thrusts ever more savage, and if the woman, often perversely, came to enjoy his brutality, Teddy would then lose all interest in her and quickly let her go. He wanted to see the pain in their eyes, the marks, the scratches on their flesh. Sometimes, he could almost come with his eyes closed, imagining images of savage devastation of torn female flesh, of pain.

In truth, he found most women deeply boring. Like all men, he was looking for something else, something different. He even eschewed pretty ones; too shallow, too loud.

He found it easier to screw hookers. If he paid over the odds, they ignored the pain he inflicted on them. There was this agency in Coral Gables he used a lot. Reliable. Discreet. Most of their girls were unlike your average prostitute. Had more class. And innocence. Most of them were just housewives doing it out of boredom, seeking extra kicks, or part-time actresses or models in search of that extra cash to bridge gaps between real jobs. They worked harder at the sex, were less transparently uninvolved. This is where he'd come across Anne, the red-headed English woman.

The first time with her had been different. He'd needed an escort, a girl who'd look good and bright, and wouldn't embarrass him at the sit-down dinner at the Fontainebleau following the Motor Parts Suppliers' of Dade County Convention. He'd loved the idea she'd be British. A great touch, that was.

She'd been waiting for him at the hotel bar and behaved impeccably throughout the evening. Just a touch remote, but a good conversationalist with his suppliers, witty but not too much, pretty but not aggressively so. She had shown no irritation when some of the men pawed her while dancing. She seemed good at her job.

He'd offered her an extra five hundred to stay the night with him. She had agreed. He'd drunk too much, and could barely keep himself hard. She was small but had a great body. She didn't say much and it was all over in a few minutes. He asked her to stay longer, ready for more serious action when his energies returned, but she said she had this modelling gig in the morning.

He booked her again a week later.

Found out more about her. That she was game for a South American run, seemingly needed the money real bad. That she liked a nose full of the white Peruvian powder, but then all the whores did. But when she'd stripped and he'd entered her quickly, the damn woman was just too passive and once again he'd come too fast. There was the faint suggestion of a smile on her face as she lay there under him, silent—not even a moan or a fake sigh—as his come trickled weakly into her, as if she was telling him she was in control, that he would never own her totally.

Elusive, slippery, that's what Anne was, Teddy knew.

And the more she eluded him, the more he wanted her badly. He didn't just want to fuck her pale body, he wanted to hear her scream, beg, seek forgiveness, cry her pretty eyes out as he ravaged her, acknowledge his brute strength. Jesus, he almost frightened himself, the way he wanted to do bad things to this woman. She was just asking for it. Bitch!

*

Anne selected her clothes for the Caracas trip. The phone kept ringing every quarter an hour or so. Either Teddy or Jakey, she knew. She ignored all the calls. Neither of them left messages on the machine.

She didn't have enough clean underwear and the washing machine in the basement was out of order. She'd have to buy some new stuff when she got to South America.

Didn't need that much, anyway, she'd only be staying in Caracas a couple of days.

She walked over to the fridge and picked a can of beer.

Remembered how her husband back in England always hated when she drank beer, said he could smell it on her breath.

Well, that was yesterday, wasn't it, and she gulped the cold, refreshing liquid down.

She switched the radio on, surfed quickly through the wave bands, seeking anything but Cuban or mariachi rhythms. Alighted on some unknown station right at the end of the dial.

'...It's always *The Wrong Time, The Wrong Place* innit?' said a distant DJ, out there in Radio Land.

Anne smiled.

The music exploded from the small transistor radio, washed across her untidy room, swirled around her tired but satisfied body and moved out of the apartment, threading its way into the Miami dusk. Anne closed her eyes. Relaxing at last.

But every time the darkness took over, the memories returned. The shards of her previous life.

'Damn,' she muttered to herself, as the piercing chords of an electric guitar in full rock 'n' roll flow invisibly caressed the nape of her neck and she felt herself shivering as the melody captured her from head to toe.

No more memories.

This is why she was here. In Miami. No longer in London.

Running from yesterday.

'Yes,' the voice on the radio said, as the tune faded away, 'it's me, Mark of God, your unreliable host today. All the music you can handle, music for every day of your life, music as a soundtrack, music as a way of life, yeah! You've just heard Marshall Crenshaw and *Twenty-Five-Forty-One*. Our man in the weather centre is still predicting dark storms, so cover up out there, y'all. And if rain makes you think of Europe, what do you say if we have some music from those watery climes? Here's one from the Pogues, folks. And if today's Tuesday ...'

'No, not *Tuesday Morning*,' Anne blurted out. 'No.'

'The song's *Tuesday Morning* folks, so sing along and think of rain ...' the DJ continued.

Anne ragefully threw the radio to the floor and compulsively continued her packing.

*

Jacob couldn't sleep. He kept on tossing and turning.

The thin white sheet lay all crumpled up at the bottom of the bed.

Every so often, he'd look out for the LCD display on the alarm device and notice that barely ten minutes or even less had elapsed since his last glance. The night went on forever.

He was bone tired, following the weekend with Anne, but it didn't help. Sleep just wouldn't come. Storm clouds seemed to be gathering over the sea and Jacob struggled with the situation. Things were going too fast, he realised. It had the momentum of a car crash; you knew the vehicle was out of control, and your mind worked in slow motion, telling you to do something, anything, but your arms wouldn't respond, and the car careened further into an uncontrollable spin, and you braced yourself for the inevitable impact, idly wondering whether you would even survive it.

The glass of water on the bedside table was empty. Jacob rose to fill it again.

Decided on the spur of the moment not to go back to bed but to take a walk. Slipped on his jeans and a thick grey sweatshirt. Hunted under the settee for his battered brown loafers, and picked his wallet from the jacket hanging on the kitchen chair.

Walking directionless, wrestling with his unusual thoughts, Jacob was caught out by the storm an hour later. He had almost reached the causeway and took refuge in the nearest sheltered place, a bar called the Nighthawks Café near the coach station.

Cigarette smoke floated down from the ceiling like a bank of low clouds.

Jacob got himself a coffee from the counter and looked around for a table to sit down. The place was crowded. Refugees from the outside storm like him, regular vagrants, overflow from the coach station waiting for early morning transportation.

Few tables had space, or at any rate with anyone he'd wish to share it with. Jacob had never known how to communicate with tramps or drunks. Something in him rebelled when confronted too closely by them. Guilt or fear of becoming one of them? He was standing by the serving counter, nursing the hot coffee cup when he noticed a couple rising at the back of the room, leaving a solitary customer at the table they'd occupied.

Jacob zigzagged his way towards the free space.

Without even looking at whoever was still sitting there, Jacob asked them: 'Do you mind if I sit?'

It was a woman. She looked up at him.

'Sure, honey.'

'Thanks.' He sat down. She was chewing on a doughnut, her other hand holding on for dear life to a small overnight bag she'd placed by the side of the chair.

He took a sip of the coffee. Tasteless but hot.

'You're not from here, are you?' the woman asked.

He smiled back. She was quite pretty, in a plain way, probably late twenties. Too much lipstick. Too many rings on her fingers.

'Yes,' he agreed.

'I know,' she ventured. 'Australian?'

'No. English,' Jacob answered.

'Oh,' she said, visibly disappointed by her mistake. She extended her hand. 'My name's Sandra,' she revealed.

'I'm Jacob. You can call me Jake,' he told her.

She took another bite of the doughnut.

'So what are you doing here in Florida?' she asked.

'Oh, you know, this and that. Bumming around, a long holiday of sorts.'

'Really?'

'It's warmer than home, so it's a good place to be, I suppose.'

Outside the rain kept on pelting down. They continued their conversation. Sandra was insatiably curious. Jacob felt comfortable with her, somehow. Oddly enough, he and Anne never did talk that much. The flesh had been stronger than the word. Coffee followed coffee.

She was a waitress in Tallahassee and had come down to see the bright lights of Miami Beach. She lived so close but had never been before. She'd spent the day walking around the Art Deco district like a tourist, and had come back here to get her bag, before the storm broke, to look for a hotel room for a few nights.

'I'm sure they have some free rooms at mine. It's not too expensive,' he told her.

'Wow!' she reacted. 'Really?'

Jacob indulgently smiled back at her. She was so genuine. Almost too naive for her age.

Underneath the transparent plastic mac, her chest was almost bursting out of the restraining confine of an impossibly tight red blouse.

'So how long have you been here already?' she inquired.

'Too long, I suppose,' Jacob replied.

She was about to comment when they were distracted by the raised voices of an older couple at a table across the room. The woman, swearing loudly, had spilt the contents of her glass all over her lap and appeared to be blaming her companion.

'Night life, hey?' Jacob said.

'Yeah,' Sandra sighed. And continued her questioning. 'Have you ever been to Paris, Jacob? I hear it's very close to London, isn't it?' she asked him.

'Yes. Often,' he replied.

'Tell me,' she asked.

The night was drawing on and, now, Jacob felt all the tiredness surge over him like a mighty wave. The smoke in the bar was getting to him; the girl was nice but was beginning to get on his nerves. He needed the rest. He glanced at the windows. The rain outside had abated.

'Listen, Sandra,' he told her. 'I have to go, you know. Have to catch up with my beauty sleep. I've got a trip coming up soon, I think. Maybe New Orleans. With a friend. I really have to go back to my hotel. Sorry.'

He laid out a few bills on the table top for the extra coffees, and stood up.

'Jacob?'

'Yes?'

'Your hotel ... you mentioned they might have rooms. Do you think I could walk along with you?'

'I suppose so,' Jacob said and she followed him silently from the Nighthawks Café to the Governor Hotel, cruising steadily through the Miami late night, avoiding puddles and sleeping drunks. All the while, Jacob's mind raced through crazy scenarios. Lynda. Anne. Sandra. How he could not invite her up when they reached the hotel, without offending her, hurting her feelings? But when they did, she resolutely approached the night porter's desk and booked herself a room for two days.

'See you tomorrow, maybe,' Jacob said as they parted on her floor.

'Yeah,' Sandra said.

Jacob began climbing the stairs to the next floor. She called him.

'Jacob?'

'Yes?'

'Have you ever written poems?' she asked.

He paused.

'No, I never have,' he answered.

But they both knew he was lying.

And though Jacob was all too aware he once had penned maudlin lines, he also knew he would never write poems again.

5.

Living On Stolen Time

The courtesy coach ran through the landscape. Following the initial white highway, the road from the airport to Caracas city centre was now a litter of shanty towns and patched-up market stalls hawking pock-marked fruit and ersatz Inca—or was it Mayan?—wooden hand-carvings. Anne had been shunted to the back of the vehicle, lodged uneasily between a mountain of shuddering Samsonite cases and the incessant chatter of a group of returning silk-suited businessmen.

She peered out of the window.

Watched the dark-skinned kids, the mangy dogs, the dirt and other parading images of Third World poverty unfolding outside.

Ahead, the skyscraper skyline that beckoned was much the same as that of any big American city, but here—still ten miles away—the teeming humanity frightened her. Through the thick glass of the dusty window, she could smell the desperation, the sense of hopelessness that pervaded every person and object beside the road.

This was what poverty was really all about, she realised.

This was one of the reasons she was here. To make enough money to banish the spectre of want forever.

Somehow, the spectacle outside justified it all. The tensions in her late marriage, her damaging ambition, even the fact that she had sold her body several times already. It was only a means to an end. The look of absolute indifference in the face of that old woman over there, standing with her feet in the gutter at the intersection where the bus slowed down for a moment, that look was justification enough, Anne reckoned. Not me, she knew. She could take the occasional humiliation, the men and their grubby hands and dirty nails scratching inside her, the way they only wanted her body. The risks, this smuggling caper. At the end of the day, it would all be worthwhile. I'm not going to end up like them. No way.

She swivelled forward in her seat, banishing the road and the dirt from her field of vision.

She was wearing her power suit. First time she'd worn it since London.

A grey wool ensemble with discreet white checks, the skirt falling well below her knees, split on the side so that she could show off her well-shaped legs whenever she wished to.

The only touch of colour was a green silk scarf casually draped around her neck, in perfect contrast to the sharp auburn reflections of her hair and the porcelain white of her skin.

One of the male passengers had been watching her.

'First time in Venezuela, Miss?' he asked.

'Yes,' she nodded.

'You'll like it here,' he said.

'I hope so,' Anne answered. The man was sweating heavily. The bus had no air-conditioning.

'You are very beautiful,' he continued. 'Have you come to work in one of our clubs?'

'No.'

'Come, come,' the businessman said, smiling. 'There is nothing to be ashamed of. Only the most beautiful women work in the clubs of Caracas.'

He thought she must be a dancer, or a stripper.

'No,' Anne replied. 'I'm just a tourist. A few days shopping, you know.'

'I see,' he said. 'I would be honoured to show you around, if you allowed me.'

'Aren't you married?' Anne inquired, looking down at ring on his left hand.

He followed her glance, shrugged.

'Ah, you know, it's not important. This is South America.'

'I'm sorry,' she continued. 'But I have come to see a friend. I will not be on my own.'

The man sighed theatrically.

'This must indeed be a very lucky man,' he said.

'I suppose so,' Anne replied. The man gave her a half-hearted smile, turned back to his travelling companions and reverted to Spanish. No doubt liberally commenting on her and her body parts, she reckoned. Bastards.

She looked out of the window again. The shanty town was thinning as they approached the concrete walls of Caracas.

*

'The British woman has landed. She is on her way to the hotel. There were no problems with immigration.'

'Good,' the Man From Caracas said, as he put the phone down. A gentle morning breeze caressed the tallest branches of the surrounding trees. From his vantage point on the house's outside deck he could see the whole valley unfold below him. A view he would never tire of. He hated cities. If only he could live here forever. Among the rustling of the leaves and the silent sounds of chirping birds and insects.

He reluctantly walked back inside and summoned the twins.

They were staying in the old slave quarters at the other end of the plantation, and it took them twenty minutes to reach the main building.

'She's in the country,' the Man said.

Both the Frenchmen nodded.

He could never tell them apart. Tall, gaunt, pale-skinned, the two brothers always wore the same grey anthracite double-breasted suits. The cloth hung lifeless against their bodies, and they never were seen in public with jackets unbuttoned. It was even rumoured they slept in their suits. Plain white shirts and black silk ties completed the ensemble. Evil had recruited them a few years back and they had proven quite reliable. Always got the job done. Quietly. Safely. Like undertakers.

The Man From Caracas walked to the wall safe and punched in the combination.

He pulled a small maroon velvet sack from the safe and emptied it on to the glass coffee table.

The jewels poured out.

'Aren't they beautiful?' the Man asked his two henchmen.

Both remained silent.

The six small diamonds shone in lazy splendour, catching every moving sun ray that drifted over the forest, trapping their fire and energy, feeding on the brilliance of the daylight.

The Man held each diamond against the light in turn, savouring their purity and sheer incandescence.

'I really hate to let them go,' he remarked.

But he knew he had to. The small jewels represented much of his available cash. Since the US Feds had turned the screws on the Grand Cayman private banks, the money laundering system had been all fucked up and, right now, this represented the best way of moving drug funds.

He lovingly fingered the small diamonds one last time, mentally imagining a woman's body adorned with them: like a Borgia-like feast, a dark-haired, tall Indian woman spread out on a table, surrounded by fruit and a parade of exotic leaves, each diamond set into her naked, stretched body, one in each eye-socket, another stitched to the tip of her tongue, two others like hoods over her dark areolae and the final one embedded under her clit hood. He felt the saliva rise in his mouth at the thought of his tongue roaming over the woman's body, moving from warm flesh to each diamond in turn and extracting it from its orb with his tongue or his teeth, tearing out the sacrificial woman's tongue, severing her nipples with one sharp bite, swallowing the bud of her clitoris like a soft oyster, until all the fiery diamonds were safely nesting in the hollow of his cheeks, tasting of blood, warm like fire, each an exquisite and forbidden corpse.

His thoughts were interrupted by the movement of the twins as they picked up the velvet bag and dropped each diamond back inside.

'Probably tomorrow night,' the first one said.

'Better to do it the evening before she departs,' the other one concluded. 'No need to have the stuff hanging round her hotel room too long.'

'Right,' said the Man From Caracas, then added, as the two men prepared to leave the room, 'And give the bitch a salutary shock. Don't want her getting ideas.'

'As you wish,' one of the identical Frenchmen said.

*

It was already afternoon by the time Jacob woke up. This time, he'd slept too well and most of the day had gone by. The bitter, pasty taste of yesterday's coffees stuck at the back of his throat. He needed a shower and a sugar fix.

And a shave. It felt like sandpaper taking root all over his face.

Later, as he dried his hair, he noticed the piece of paper that had been slipped under his door. It was from Sandra. She wrote that she really grooved on Miami Beach, had spent the whole morning falling in love with the place and had decided that she wished to live here, for good. Someone had mentioned a possible job in a bar further up toward North Beach. If he wanted, maybe they could meet up there around six, maybe have a drink, a meal. No obligation, like, but it would be nice.

Jacob tried Anne's number. Still the answer machine. She had said it would be a few days.

Today, he didn't wish to be alone.

Felt confused. His feelings all mixed-up. The past colliding in overdrive with whatever the future with Anne might hold in store. A bit scared, also.

The company would do him good, he felt.

The Underground Dive was situated on a small road that connected the mid-reaches of Collins Avenue and the mainland, just a stone's throw away from a couple of the big tourist hotels. It was a topless joint (bottomless after eight) but right now was Happy Hour.

'You get two drinks for your five bucks,' the bouncer at the door said.

It was dark inside. A tall, thin stripper was going through the motions on the raised stage, undulating against the central pole. There were just a few men sitting around on low chairs around her domain, slowly nursing their drinks, their eyes fixed on the way the dim spotlights highlighted her skin as she moved to the rhythm of the music.

Jacob had barely sat himself down when another stripper, wrapped in a loose bath-robe, approached him with the offer of a private lap dance at the back.

He declined.

'I still haven't had a drink,' he pointed out. She moved away into the shadows.

The girl on stage theatrically shed her bra and shimmied toward her sparse audience. One man slipped a dollar bill into her garter but none of the others were as generous.

'What'll you have?' a waitress brushed against his shoulder. She was topless, quite voluptuous, shiny metal-like pasties covering her nipples, wearing a short ruffled skirt that went no further than mid-thigh, and dark stockings held up by the taut line of red suspenders. She had a better body than the stripper displaying herself on the stage, Jacob thought.

'Coke. No ice,' he asked.

'Oh, it's you, you did come,' the waitress said. It was Sandra.

'Hello,' Jacob said. 'I see you've got the job.'

'Yeah. But I'm on the day shift. It's only topless. I can live with that. I'd never do the other. You have to retain some dignity, don't you? I'll bring your drink along. I finish in half an hour. We can talk then,' Sandra said, moving back towards the bar.

The final song in the stripper's set was coming to an end, and the thin girl on the stage hastily unhooked her bottom, to reveal on the last beat a thin G-string that still obscured her genitals. In the brief interval between her set and the next girl's, half the men sitting in front of the stage made for the exit.

'Licensing regulations, you know,' Sandra said bringing Jacob his drink, 'they have to keep something on until it gets dark.'

'Makes for a lot of disappointed customers,' Jacob remarked.

'Not really,' Sandra said, placing the cold glass on a paper mat in front of him, 'the girls good give service at the back.'

Jacob looked up. The girl who had just exited the stage had just propositioned two of the remaining male customers and they rose to follow her past a discreet door at the back of the bar.

'See,' Sandra said.

Jacob nodded. The new girl on stage was squatting on her haunches, her mound just a few feet away from him. She sported a navel ring.

'It doesn't bother me,' Sandra later said, as they sat on stools at the bar, ignoring the strippers and the growing crowd of punters. Her shift was over and she was fully dressed again, in the same outfit she had been wearing yesterday.

'It was nice of you to come, Jacob,' she said, slowly sipping her dry Martini. 'It's a great town. I know I'm going to like it here. But you're the only person I know. I hope we can be friends. I know we can.'

Her hand moved across the wood of the bar, reached his fingers. He retreated.

'I like you, Sandra,' he said. 'But there is someone else, you see.'

He could read the disappointment in her eyes, even in the penumbra.

He continued: 'But I would like it if we could still be friends. I really would.'

'Who is she?' Sandra asked.

'She's also English. I only met her the other day, but I know it's something special. So I don't want to spoil it.'

'Makes sense,' Sandra said.

'Yes,' Jacob continued, 'I can't take any risks. The last time I was with someone who meant a lot to me, it went bad. Really bad. It all collapsed. People were badly hurt. I can't afford another mess, Sandra.'

She extended her hand towards him again. This time, he allowed the contact.

'Tell me,' she asked.

'You don't want to know.'

'I do. Get it off your mind, Jacob. It'll help.'

'It's a silly story, really. So ordinary. There's nothing noble or tragic about it at all . . .'

'Tell me,' she insisted gently.

On the stage, one of the women was stripping to a tune he recognised by the group James. Couldn't remember it's title, though.

'We met. She was married. We were crazy. Took no precautions. Sometimes, you don't think of things like that. Being together is all you desire. It consumes you, eats you up inside. We didn't know, but she became pregnant. She must have been late, and I reckon she still wasn't certain. Couldn't tell her husband, he'd know it wasn't his. He was a maniac for contraception. So she said nothing to either of us. Let matters drag out. Ignored the pain in her gut. Of all days, she collapsed at her own birthday party. Of course, I couldn't be there. It was an ectopic pregnancy. The foetus was blocked inside one of her fallopian tubes and just kept on growing till the tube literally burst. They did their best, but it was too late. She died.'

'Oh dear,' Sandra said.

'By the time I found out, she had already been buried. Christ, it was so unfair . . .'

Jacob gulped the rest of his glass down with one thirsty sip.

Sandra's eyes kept on asking.

'Yes,' he nodded. 'I suppose that's why I'm here. Getting away from it all. Trying to forget, not very well, that in a way I'm the one who killed her . . .'

'No, you didn't,' Sandra pointed out. 'It was an accident.'

'I know,' he acknowledged, 'but it doesn't help.'

'What was her name?' Sandra asked.

'Lynda. With a Y.'

'Oh.'

'Do you think it's silly for me to point out how to spell her name properly?' Jacob asked her.

'No. Not at all,' Sandra replied. 'It seems . . . right.'

Her hand gripped his. The bar was becoming crowded. It was now the bottomless hour.

'Friends,' she said. 'Just friends.'

'That would be nice,' Jacob said, relieved. Then, 'Let's go and have a bite somewhere. I feel like eating now.'

'Me too,' she confirmed, rising from the stool.

*

The men entered the room in the dead of night. They had a master key. They were familiar with the hotel from prior operations.

The grey suits they wore blended with the pale half light that leaked through the half-open shutters. Anne kept the windows closed to blank out the clamour from the street far below that just went on all night: car hooters, the shriek of brakes, snatches of melodies from travelling radios, the loud voices and laughs of the Latino men and women. She had been kept awake most of the previous night.

They moved with stealth past her bed, ignoring her, toward the bathroom door.

The first Frenchman turned the handle. Which squeaked.

The second one quickly glanced back at Anne's form, spread out under the bed covers.

The noise migrated lazily past her brain. Made no real contact. She turned round, pulling the blanket with her. She was now facing the bathroom side of the room.

The first intruder slipped into the bathroom, leaving his twin to keep guard outside the door.

He closed the door behind him and switched the light over the wall cabinet on. He wasn't particularly bothered if the woman did wake up. He needed the light. As his eyes adapted to the sudden glare, he noted the geography of the small room, the space between the sink and the tub, the angle of the shower rail, the white towels scattered haphazardly across the sink and floor. Women were always untidy. At least this one hadn't left undies or stockings hanging around.

The toothpaste tube stood by the sink, between a can of hair spray and a bottle of contact lens solution. Good, a large tube. That would make things easier.

He placed one of the large white hotel towels on the corner of the bath tub, sat down on it and pulled the bag of diamonds from his jacket pocket. Carefully, he unfolded a blue handkerchief from his other pocket over the tiled floor in front of the sink and emptied the velvet sack. The six diamonds floated out on to the blue cotton.

The Frenchman held his breath a second or two, then searched for his wallet where he kept a small pack of razor blades and a pair of metal tweezers. Then, taking hold of the toothpaste, he set to work.

It was precision work, and he was good at it. Slow, meticulous and tidy. Incision, insertion, empty-handed retreat, and again.

It was hot in the bathroom, and sweat began moving from his forehead to the stiff collar of his shirt.

He interrupted the operation and picked up the glass by the sink and poured himself a drink of water. Kept the tap running to cool the water down. Drank some then, as an afterthought, splashed the remaining water over his face and poured himself another glass.

On the other side of the bathroom door, his twin brother smiled as he heard the faint noises of water behind him and fixed on the bunched-up shape of the woman on the nearby bed.

In her sleep Anne was, as usual, struggling with memories. The ones that never went away.

She was lazing in a lukewarm bath in a hotel near Heathrow airport, idly daydreaming, while the white stocky shape of her lover moved by the sink, in the periphery of her vision, shaving slowly, his nose just an inch away from the bathroom mirror. The tip of her breasts floated motionless on the surface of the water as she looked back at her body. She said something, she didn't know what, and the man turned round towards her. And suddenly he had her husband's face. Like a dagger in her heart. She couldn't move. The shock somehow paralysed her and she lay there motionless as the bath water ebbed away down the plug hole, gradually revealing what had been submerged: the sex-ravaged state of her body, the bites, the scratches, the bruises, the ugly, geometric shapes of deep red flush spreading like leprosy across the softness of her skin. The water gurgled as it ebbed away and, above her, the shower-head began to leak, heavy, cold drops raining down like a metronome on her forehead. Drip, gurgle, drip, gurgle, the water went.

Anne opened her eyes.

The sound of the water was outside the dream. It was here.

A band of light shone through the perimeter of the bathroom door.

There was someone in there.

And, as she realised this, she also noticed the grey shape standing at attention in front of the door.

'Who . . .' she tried to say.

'Keep quiet, my dear, sshhh . . .' the shadow said with a strong French accent.

'But . . .'

'You don't see us, do you, Miss Ryan?'

'How do you know my name?' she asked.

'Because we're in this together, and neither of us can leave before what we have come to do is accomplished.'

'I see,' Anne said.

'Is she awake?' another French-accented voice said, back in the bathroom.

'She is,' the first man said.

'It's almost done. I won't be long now,' the other said.

'Good,' the grey shape said.

Anne's eyes were getting accustomed to the surrounding darkness, but the man's face was still bathed in anonymous shadows. Only his eyes gleamed in the uneasy penumbra.

She didn't quite know what to say. So, this was the connection. Teddy's people. She had to repress a faint smile; this was all to melodramatic, straight from the pages of some pulp story. She pulled the bed cover up to her chin, just her head and flowing hair remaining visible to the guy. Anne suddenly became conscious of her vulnerability.

Inside the bathroom she could hear the second Frenchman moving around, replacing things, then he switched the light off and opened the door.

His silhouette in the dark room was even greyer than his acolyte's.

'Damn,' he remarked. 'I can't see anything.'

'Switch the light on,' the second man ordered Anne, pointing to the switch above the bed.

She slipped an arm out from under the blanket and clicked.

The two men were identical twins.

They both stared at her.

'So you're Miss Ryan,' said Frenchman One.

'Our new courier,' Frenchman Two continued.

'Yes,' she nodded. They were scary.

'I'm sure your Miami people have told you about their rules. Well, let us tell you about ours.'

'Listen,' the other one said.

'You don't know us, see. You wouldn't recognise us in a crowd, would you?'

'No,' Anne nervously agreed, her fingers gripping the edges of the bed cover tight against her body.

'Good.'

'For you, we don't exist, do we?'

'No,' Anne kept acquiescing.

'Because if you do, Miss Ryan . . .'

'You're in deep shit . . .'

'Very deep faeces indeed, my dear.'

'I understand, I do,' Anne replied, wishing they would now just
go away.

'That's easy to say . . .'

'Much too easy . . .'

'See, we have to know you mean it . . .'

'I do, I do,' Anne continued.

'See,' the second one went on, 'we have to make you understand
how truly serious we are.'

The two brothers looked at each other, exchanged glances.

'Redhead, hey? Do you think she's a real one?'

'Easy to find out,' the other one said and moved to the hotel bed
where Anne was cowering.

He lowered his hand towards Anne, took hold of her fingers and
separated them from the bed cover and sharply pulled the material
away from her.

She was wearing a short white silk night dress. She had been
sleeping on her stomach and the nightie had slipped up, baring her
left thigh and buttock.

'Nice,' the first man said.

'But it doesn't answer our question, does it?' the other Frenchman pointed out.

'Turn round, Miss Ryan. On your back.'

Anne opened her mouth to protest, but as she did so the one on
the left took a gun out his jacket side pocket. She choked her protest
and clumsily rolled over on to her back, straightening the night gown
with one hand so that it unfurled all the way down to mid-thigh.

The Frenchman with the gun approached the bed. Lowered the
weapon to her eye level.

'This is a 9mm Glock, Miss Ryan,' he said, waving the gun in
front of her nose.

'A thing of beauty,' his brother said, as the matt metal angles
caught the light.

'You can't improve on a Glock . . .'

'It's an instrument of truth.'

He lowered the gun, caressing her throat with the barrel, continued the downward path of the weapon along the opening cleavage
of her bare upper-chest. When the revolver reached the borderline
of the silk fabric, he dragged it over the thin obstacle, allowing it to
travel over the small rise of her breast.

Anne caught her breath.

The Glock journeyed on down her prone body, beyond the lower
slope of her chest, over her stomach, imperceptibly grazing across

her crotch, until it reached skin again beyond the final frontier of the night gown.

She briefly believed this was going to be the extent of it, as the weapon paused as it made contact with her knees.

'We require an answer, Miss Ryan.'

'Open your legs.'

The gun's pressure against her knees increased. She reluctantly allowed it space between. The Glock immediately took control of the space.

'There, there ...'

The revolver began its ascent between her legs. Soon it reached the tenuous barrier of the silk night gown and slid underneath, pulling the thin fabric upwards, away from her body. The Frenchman raised the gun higher, drawing the folds of the night dress with it and unfurled the garment from Anne's lower half. The fabric was now bunched up across her breasts.

The two men feasted on the brazen spectacle of her fiery pubes.

'She is,' one said.

'Indeed,' added the other. 'Good thing we didn't take bets on it.'

'Lovely colour, Miss Ryan. Goes very well with your skin. Did you know my brother here has never had a redhead.'

'That's true,' Frenchman Two said. 'Never.'

'I've always told him he was missing an important experience.'

The one with the gun lowered the gun toward her bare stomach.

'Open your legs more,' he ordered her.

The metal made her shiver. She spread her legs wider.

'Wider.'

The Glock pressed against her stomach, until she had adopted a satisfactory angle.

The two men moved to a better vantage point, literally looking into her.

'Isn't it pretty?'

'Very.'

'It's a symphony of colours.'

'But what lies beyond the rainbow, eh, brother?'

He brought the 9mm Glock down to her sex lips and gently applied pressure against them with the nozzle of the gun. Stretched as she was, she knew she was already half open and could offer little resistance as the metal moved an inch or so inside her.

'Very pink,' one of the men said. She couldn't even tell them apart any longer. Her belly was on fire, her brow fevered. Christ, she wanted to pee badly and the coolness of the metal against her stretched labia only served to make things worse. The man holding the weapon finally pulled the Glock out, brought it to his own lips, and sucked the nozzle clean.

'Delightful,' he finally said. 'The flavour of a redhead.'

'A night to remember, I think,' the second Frenchman said, pulling the razor blade he had used earlier from his top pocket where he had wrapped it in the blue handkerchief.

'Jesus. Please,' Anne begged, terrified by the sinister turn of events.

'Don't you worry, Miss Ryan. I just want a little memento of our night together. Something to remember you by.'

He kneeled by the bed and pulled a tuft of her pubic hair upwards.

'You've got a bit too much there,' he said. 'You surely won't miss some, will you?' he remarked.

And snipped off the orange curls.

Which he then placed inside the handkerchief.

The other Frenchman replaced the blanket over her body, banishing her nudity to the darkness beneath, as his brother rose and they retreated back together to the hotel door.

As soon as she heard their steps retreat down the corridor, Anne jumped out of bed and made a beeline for the bathroom where she was violently sick.

*

Later, in a state of cold rage, Anne ransacked the bathroom to find out what they had been up to. If, after this ordeal, she was expected to carry drugs for the damn bastards, she just knew she couldn't go through with it. In her present, turbulent mind, she would have poured even the best quality cocaine down the drain in an instant.

It took her an hour to even think of the toothpaste tube, as her mind momentarily emerged from the red fog.

After she had squeezed the paste out, she could still feel the small bumps inside the plastic container. How had he got the stuff into the tube? There was no visible join. She slit the container open with her nail scissors.

She was no expert in jewels, but even she knew these diamonds were worth an absolute bomb.

Fuck-you money, she reflected.

And returned to bed, leaving the diamonds among her scattered toiletries on the side of the bathroom sink.

She slept badly.

The bad dreams returned on cue like familiar friends. But this time, the 9mm Glock was a new partner in the nocturnal adventures. Now her husband shot himself through the mouth with it, before connecting the hosepipe to the Vauxhall's exhaust in the well-insulated garage of their newly-acquired south London semi-detached house. She knew, even in her dream, that the sequence of events made no sense, but it happened anyway. Another variation was the anonymous letter denouncing her affair, which her husband received in the mail, was now written in French. He couldn't read French, neither could she, so why? It's only a nightmare, Ma, and anyway it's mine. Fleeting images of her lover cutting his toenails while taking a bath, and then methodically using a blunt razor blade to slit his wrists wide open, red rivers flowing from his body into the bath water and she, waking in the hotel room, to find him cold and drowned in the lake of his veins and trying in a panic to think of a story to tell the police, no, the dead man in the bath is not my husband, I don't even know him. My husband has already killed himself once. And her boss interrogating her later, blaming her for having sold world rights to the affair to the wrong foreign publisher. Familiar sights: the spires of Cambridge, the wedding chapel, the Brighton sea front, but every image just a degree off, the colour not quite right, one detail out of a thousand subtly different, like a parallel world concealed behind the real one, a world she can never reach, always a moment away, the world she might once have been happy in, but that she was banished from in punishment for her cold heart.

The images fly round in circles, faces of people, faces of men, the contrasting bodies of men, their long, thick cocks digging savagely inside her, their thin lips chewing her tongue, their fierce fingers drilling additional holes all across her body. The hurt in their eyes. Like a mirror reflecting the fire in her hair.

In her sleep, Anne moaned ceaselessly, wrestling with the demons. Her hands pulled at the shoulder strap of the silk night gown and tore it away. The morning finally came, abundant sweat dry and pungent under her arms. She washed rapidly, gathered her belongings and packed. She had bought no souvenirs. Just before leaving the hotel room, she scooped up the six diamonds and swallowed them.

6.

That Man-Woman Thing

She rang Jacob as soon as she had passed through customs at Miami Airport. Found a phone on the circular concourse opposite one of the snack bar concessions. Pizza smells assaulted her senses as she dialled his hotel number. The operator put her through to his room.

'Hi, it's me, Anne,' she said.

'Welcome back,' he answered. 'How was your trip?'

'Ghastly.'

'Oh, I'm sorry.'

'It's not your fault,' Anne pointed out.

'At any rate, it's nice to have you back in town. Lunch?' he suggested. 'I've missed you, you know.'

'I'm still at the airport, Jakey. Something has come up.'

'Something wrong?'

'Not really.'

'So?'

'So . . . things have changed.'

A knot formed itself in the pit of his stomach as he anticipated the worst.

Why did women change their mind about things so easily, so arbitrarily?

'Are you still there?' Anne enquired as the brouhaha of the airport rose to a crescendo behind her voice.

'Yes. I'm here,' Jacob said.

'Listen,' she continued, 'the other day, you suggested we might go away . . .'

'To New Orleans, yes, it . . .'

'I want to go now,' she interrupted him. 'Today.'

'Fine with me,' Jacob replied, overcome by relief. Surprised, also. 'There's nothing keeping me here in Miami. Tell you what: you're on, Anne.'

'I can't promise much, Jakey. You'll have to trust me. Accept me for what I am. But don't ask too much of me,' Anne requested, other travellers brushing past her, manoeuvring their luggage carts.

'I understand,' Jacob said. He shifted from one leg to the other. He was barefoot.

'There's a problem, though,' Anne continued, feeding extra coins into the airport phone to keep the line open. 'I need my clothes. They're back at the apartment building, and I can't go there. Someone might be on the look out for me. I'll explain later. They don't know you, Jakey. I need a real favour. I'll send a cab to your hotel with my key and you'll have to go and retrieve my belongings. Do you mind?'

'Sure,' he said.

'Then we can join up here, and hit the road.'

'Do we plan to return to Miami eventually?' Jacob asked her.

'No,' Anne replied decisively.

'So I'll have to pack my own things too. And I'll need to buy some sort of cheap car. You're not usually allowed to drop rental cars out of state.'

'I can give you some money for the car later, in a few days,' Anne suggested.

'That's okay,' Jacob said. 'I'd been meaning to get one for some time. I can afford it.'

'That's great, Jakey. You don't know what this means to me. It's going to be so good, you'll see.'

'Yes,' he agreed.

'I'll go and find a cab and give the driver the key to my place. You should get it at your hotel in under an hour.'

'I'll be waiting,' he said. 'Gathering up your stuff and mine, emptying the bank account, finding a car, it's going to take me several hours, Anne. Hopefully, I can get to the airport by mid-afternoon. Where can I find you?'

Anne paused for a moment. She didn't want to remain visible in such a public place, although she didn't think Teddy Caliban and the other thug were keeping a watch on the airport.

'I know,' she said. 'The airport hotel. The lobby is on the actual concourse. On the top floor, there's a restaurant. I'll go and have a meal first. I'm starving, didn't have any breakfast. I'll be at the bar afterwards. You can't miss it. And, Jakey?'

'Yes?'

'Try and pack all my clothes. I haven't got much, brought so little over from London in the first place. It's all in the cupboard in the bedroom and the nest of draws near the phone. And get my CDs, I'd hate to leave them behind.'

The Miami airport hotel.

She'd been there once before, on the first job the escort agency had assigned her. A South American doctor, in transit to Panama. He'd been polite but rough. She still remembered the dark, painful bruises his prying fingers had left on the back of her thighs as he forced her legs upward to increase the angle of penetration.

'See you soon,' Jacob said.

'Yes,' Anne replied, hanging up the phone and melting away among the airport crowds.

*

Anne was right. Teddy and Evil had not thought of watching the airport. Having been warned of her departure from Caracas in the morning, they were parked in Caliban's white Alfa Romeo outside Anne's apartment block, waiting for her imminent arrival.

Following precise instructions from the Man, the plan was for Teddy to call Anne out to a nearby bar the moment she stepped through the door, while Evil quietly retrieved the merchandise from her luggage. She had been given the impression there was to be a short cooling-down period before the exchange. This way she wouldn't have time to think of alternatives or get up to any other funny business. Teddy was looking forward to seeing the British woman again, without Evil around to queer his pitch. She would be paid out of his share; the cash being transferred directly into his bank account after Evil had confirmed safe arrival of the small cargo. This would give him a perfect opportunity to arrange a lengthy assignment with her to both settle up and catch up for lost time.

Teddy's gaze followed every passing pair of female legs, silently savouring the shape of each rounded backside as they sashayed by, mentally comparing their geometry with Anne's pale arse, remembering the small mole that stared out just under the lower curve of her right half-cheek. He could already feel the beginning of an erection blooming inside his slacks as he pictured himself taking the young woman from behind, his large hands spreading her generously apart. Another woman walked by, crossing the empty road in front of the car.

The day was cloudy.

'Fuck this,' said Evil, growing impatient.

'She won't be long now,' Teddy Caliban remarked, shaking off his daydream. He switched the car radio on. Bouncy Cuban rhythms danced through the car. Evil grunted. This wasn't his kind of music. Teddy shrugged and, turning the dial, surfed the airwaves. The predictable cacophony of static, snatches of music and voices high and low ensued. Finally, Evil waved his hand at Teddy and said: 'There. That station. Sounds good.'

Teddy sneered.

'I didn't think of you as a heavy metal freak.'

'It's not heavy metal music,' Evil replied very seriously, almost offended by Teddy's lack of specific musical knowledge. 'It's death metal. Very different.'

The power chords zigzagged up and down through the sports car, while the two men kept on assiduously watching the apartment building's entrance porch.

The war dance finally came to a reverb charged ending, and a DJ's voice replaced the music.

'Yes. That was our daily dose of Viking burial requiem, a special request, one-time only to you from me in Radio Land. Makes you want to go out and rape and pillage this fair land, doesn't it? Seriously though, when it comes to orgasming guitars, give me Television's *Marquee Moon* any day. And why not? We'll play that later, folks. But first, a message for all our friends in the muggy South: take care, there's bad shit coming, so keep those asbestos umbrellas wide open . . . Mark my word, this is the Mark's public health message for today . . .'

'What the fuck is this?' groaned Evil, switching the radio off. 'I can't stand all that hippy drivel.'

A cab drew up by the apartment block and a middle-aged white guy in black trousers and tan shirt emerged, holding a couple of brown suitcases. He gestured to the cab driver who switched off his engine and began his wait, while the man entered the building.

Teddy and Evil resumed their surveillance in silence.

'Gum?' Teddy suggested.

'You must be joking,' Evil said. 'It rots your teeth.'

Storm clouds gathered ahead, towards the beach. Midday came and went. A couple of senior citizens left the building, walk unsteady and slow, followed by a mangy dog.

Ten minutes later, the guy who'd gone in earlier came out. The two cases now appeared much heavier as he gestured to his cab driver to open the boot of his vehicle.

'Who's he?' Evil asked.

'A daytime thief?' Teddy suggested.

'Can't be anything of value in those apartments. This is not a classy area,' Evil concluded. Then, as an afterthought: 'Write down the cab number. Just in case.'

Teddy did.

The cab moved off.

When darkness came in late afternoon, they were still parked there, growing increasingly irritable with each other, bored, worried, hungry.

'I don't think she's coming,' said Evil.

'Surely not,' Teddy said. 'We made it bloody clear to the bitch not to stray. Didn't we?'

'This I'm going to enjoy,' Evil remarked calmly.

'Let's wait another half hour, please,' Teddy asked.

'She's not coming, I'm telling you,' Evil replied.

Teddy's gut was conveying the same message to him. The two senior citizens and the dog returned.

By the time Teddy and Evil finally gave up the ghost, Jacob had met up with Anne at the airport and they were already halfway to Naples, heading for Sarasota in a ten-year-old red BMW 316i.

*

'We drive through the night,' she'd said. 'Can you manage it?'

'I think so. I caught up with my beauty sleep while you were away.'

'Good.'

'Anyway, if I tire a bit, you can take over.'

'I can't. I've never learned to drive.'

'I see you're an old-fashioned woman at heart,' he joked.

'You don't know me at all, Jacob,' was all she said as they ate up the night road.

'We should be able to get to Fort Lauderdale by morning,' he said, as she slumped back in the seat. Her stomach was aching. Either the diamonds or the spinach and crab dip from the restaurant above the airport. She'd have to ask Jacob to stop at the next service station. She wasn't looking forward to it. It sure was going to be messy.

The silence between them lengthened as the car roared onwards through the darkness.

She wanted some music, but didn't wish to start a conversation with Jacob now. She knew a request for the radio to be turned on would inevitably lead to a discussion of their respective musical tastes. She didn't feel ready for this right now. She turned to look at him. He was deep into his own thoughts, eyes fixed on the road as he drove. She didn't really know him, she realised, observing the sharpness of his profile, the angle of his nose. She was no longer sure whether she really wanted to know him, to find out more about him. No longer even knew whether she would allow a man access to her body ever again. She closed her eyes and remembered the 9mm Glock. Shivered.

'Are you okay?' he asked.

'Yes,' Anne replied. 'I'm just tired. I need to sleep.' She closed her eyes again and welcomed the night.

'Sweet dreams,' Jacob said.

*

The Man From Caracas was furious.

'Find her,' he instructed Evil.

'What about the guy?' Evil asked. 'She's with someone. Couldn't have planned it on her own.'

'You'll know what to do with him. But it's her I want,' he added. 'And the merchandise, of course.'

'Understood,' Evil said.

'I want her alive. Very much alive.'

'Caliban?'

'Do you think he's involved?'

'No. He wouldn't be that stupid.'

'But he is stupid, isn't he?'

'Out of his depth, I suppose.'

'I leave him to your appreciation. He might be of some help in tracing her. See what you can do.'

'Fine.'

'And Evil . . .'

'Yes, Boss?'

'I want the British woman. Get her back to Miami. I'll fly over. You can play your little games with her, but I want her alive. I will teach the whore that you don't mess with me. She wants the diamonds, I will show her how best to display them. I'll have every one of them sewn on to her body with thick thread and needle while she screams her guts out, you'll see. One diamond sewn to the tip of her tongue, one each to her nipples where they will sit like on a throne of blood, a gently decorative one to her navel, like all the bitch models do, and the final two I shall sew myself inside her pussy, on to her clit and in the crack of her arse. See if she likes herself decked out pretty with all those shiny pieces attached to her pale skin like pieces of coal, stinging like the fires of hell. Then, when she has become accustomed to the pain, I shall cut every diamond away from her body with a pair of sharp scissors, taking back what is mine, each one still attached to her flesh, set against the small white and pink bed of her detached skin. The pain will be so bad she will faint. Later, we'll get her back to the plantation where she can be used as a plaything by the men, and when they are tired of her, we can mate her with the dogs and the horses until her heart gives up for good. I will make a lesson of her.'

'That would be good, Boss,' Evil said, relishing the obscene tale of the man's desired revenge. 'I shall find her.'

'I know you will, Evil,' the Man said.

Evil walked back into the room where Teddy Caliban had been waiting nervously.

'So, what does he say?' Teddy asked frantically.

'No surprises. He wants her back, and the diamonds.'

'And me?'

'You're to help. Otherwise you're history.'

Teddy slumped down on the sofa.

Evil sat beside him. The sofa groaned under his weight and Teddy sank lower.

'So,' Evil continued, 'we visit Miss Ryan's place next.'

It was child's play breaking into Anne's apartment, but the state of the place only confirmed to them she had fled the nest.

'You're sure you've never seen that guy before?'

'Positive,' Teddy said.

'It must have been him who cleared her stuff out. Have you still got that cab's number?'

It took a handful of calls to identify the cab's company and a few green bills to convince the dispatcher to check his logs. The guy had gone back to a hotel further up the beach. The only customer to have checked out yesterday was an English guy called Jacob Jones. The receptionist's description identified him clearly.

'And you don't know where he was going?' Teddy insisted.

'No,' the clerk answered. 'No idea.'

Evil leaned menacingly over the desk.

'Mr Jones, hey? Are all your customers Smiths and Jones'?'

'I swear, it was his real name,' the clerk said, convinced they were cops or something. 'I actually saw his passport. It was his real name.'

'I see,' Evil said. 'Did you ever see him with any women?'

'As a matter of fact,' the clerk hastily said, 'there were two women with him just recently. Another Brit, a small thing with long red hair and Sandra.'

'Sandra?'

'He introduced her to the hotel. She's still staying here.'

'Is she?'

'Yes.'

'What's her room number?'

'Oh, she's not in now. She's a working girl, waitresses at the Underground Dive.'

'I know the place,' said Teddy, with the first smile of the day spreading over his face.

A phone call to the strip club's manager confirmed she was in and that her shift ended later that afternoon. She was pointed out to them when they arrived. But prudence dictated they not confront here there and then, and the two men sat themselves by the stage and spent the next few hours watching the three daytime strippers succeed each other with a growing lack of enthusiasm and artistry. The women soon learned to ignore them as they refused to tip for every suggestive gyration or partial unveiling, but that was fine with them. They both agreed that the waitress was much more appetising than the girls on wanton display, which made the coming interrogation somewhat more interesting. As the bar cyclically emptied and they were often the only spectators, one of the strippers even reached the point where she refused to unveil her breasts for lack of dollars being tucked into her garter or thrown on to the stage. It was just one of those cheap afternoons. Evil and Teddy drank silently, patiently counting the time away, both mentally trying to think of what the connection might be between the buxom waitress standing daydreaming at the bar, the damn Brit and the absent Anne.

*

They had reached the outskirts of Fort Lauderdale and Jacob's eyes were hurting. He'd never enjoyed driving at night and was badly out of practice. He could feel the onset of a bad migraine. The flickering roadside neon sign of an identikit motel flashed on 'vacant', and he slowed down before turning off the highway on to the approach road.

Anne was sleeping in the other front seat, the seat belt crisscrossing across her chest. She'd been dozing fitfully since their last stop for fuel, when she'd spent an unconscionable amount of time in the bathroom and had given him a dirty look that said, 'Don't ask' when she returned to the BMW.

As he eased the car between the geometrical white lines of a parking bay, Anne opened her eyes sleepily. Looked around her.

'Why are we stopping?' she asked him.

'We're past Fort Lauderdale already, Anne. We've made good time,' he replied. 'I just can't drive any longer. I need to rest. There's a motel. We can take a room. Get some sleep, freshen up and we can get going again in the evening.'

'What time is it?'

He pointed at the digital clock in the dashboard.

'Five-thirty in the morning,' he answered.

'A shower would be good,' Anne said, straightening up in her seat and rubbing her eyes. She pulled up her handbag from the car's floor, opened it and handed Jacob a hundred dollar bill.

'What's this?' he asked.

'Pay cash when you get the room, Jacob. Don't use credit cards. Not yet. Please.'

'You'll have to tell me what this is all about, Anne.'

'In a few days. Not now. Go and find us a room.'

The teenage clerk asked him whether he wanted a smoking or a non-smoking room and Jacob realised he didn't even know if Anne smoked. No, probably not. He would have known from her breath.

'Jesus, what an ugly room!' Anne remarked as she switched the light on.

'Standard Best Western Inn,' Jacob remarked. 'Anyway, we won't be here long. We'll find something better when we reach New Orleans.'

Anne headed straight for the bathroom with her bag. Jacob slipped his shoes off. His socks felt clammy. He heard the hiss of the shower and knocked gently on the door.

'Yes?' her distant voice asked.

'Can I join you?'

'No, thanks. I feel too dirty. Got to wash the last few days away. I'll be out soon.'

When she emerged, Anne was wearing a long white cotton night gown that reached all the way down to her feet, leaving only her feet and arms exposed. She flopped down on the bed, her still wet hair cascading like an explosion over the green bed cover. Jacob gave her a quiet smile.

'I'll clean up now,' he said, and headed in turn for the bathroom. Her cans and bottles were scattered over the thin shelf above the sink. Moisturisers. Mousses. Shampoo. Conditioner. Contact lens solution. Hand cream. Cleanser liquid. Jacob inhaled deeply as he moved under the shower head and switched the water on. The whole bathroom still smelled of her. An apricot-like fragrance. A smell, he knew, he would never forget. He was good on perfumes. Lynda used Cabochon. Honey and crushed flowers. The lukewarm but fierce stream splashed over him as Anne's smell invisibly entered his blood stream forever. He looked down. He had a hard-on.

The bedroom was in darkness when he left the bathroom. She was curled up under the blanket on the right side of the bed, her face turned towards the window. Jacob, nude, slipped under the cover and moved toward her. He made contact with the fabric of her gown and sensed her warmth through the thick material. By now his erection had subsided. He cradled against her, his whole body adopting her mould, spoon against spoon. Anne remained motionless, but he could hear from the rhythm of her breath she was not yet asleep. He moved a hand toward her, allowed his fingers to brush her damp hair, lingered downward to the nape of her neck. Kissed her there.

'No, Jacob,' she said quietly. He didn't move his lips away.

'I'm sleeping,' she told him.

'You're not.'

'I am, you know,' she replied, purring gently as his tongue kept on licking the exposed flesh of her neck until it came in contact with the fabric of her nightgown and retreated.

'Later,' he said.

'Tomorrow,' she agreed.

'You mean today . . . This is already the morning.'

'So it is,' Anne said lazily, moving just an inch away from him.

'I'm tired too,' Jacob admitted. 'Anyway, we have all the time in the world.'

'I hope so,' Anne said and they both fell asleep, while outside the new day's sun made an unsteady ascent over the horizon of the motel's neon sign and the straight line of the awakening highway.

*

'Undress,' Evil ordered.

He knew it was always best to instil fear from the outset, make them vulnerable.

They had picked Sandra up as she left the strip joint and had brought her back to Caliban's apartment. There was nowhere for her to run, and the knife in Evil's hands was a convincing argument. Teddy had insisted they cover her eyes for the drive to his place. Evil didn't give a damn whether the woman knew where she was being taken or not. She had guts, Evil had to admit. She hadn't screamed or attempted anything silly. Or bombarded them with hysterical questions or pleas.

The two men watched as she reluctantly climbed out of her tight skirt and pulled the colourful tee-shirt above her head.

'The rest. Now,' Teddy asked her.

She shed her underwear.

'Tasty,' Evil remarked.

Teddy pulled a chair up and motioned for the waitress to sit down. She lowered herself down, keeping her knees held tightly together, trying to salvage whatever dignity she could from the situation.

'Apart,' Teddy Caliban insisted, pointing to her legs.

She refused to spread. Evil moved up to her, took hold of a bunch of her hair in his clenched fist and gave it a violent wrench. Tears came to Sandra's eyes and she slowly opened her legs.

Satisfied, the two men pushed the chair forward and sat themselves down in front of her on the black leather sofa, which gave them a vantage point on her crotch. Sandra wiped an involuntary tear away from her eye.

'What do you want?' she finally said plaintively.

'Information,' Evil said. 'That's all.'

'I don't understand,' Sandra said.

'The British guy. Jacob Jones. Who is he?'

'Jacob. He's . . . I don't know. Just a friend. He was kind to me,' she told them.

'Did you fuck him?' Teddy interjected.

'No. He had someone else,' she replied.

'Who?'

'I don't know,' she said. 'I think she was British, too. But I don't even know her name.'

'We have business with the two of them,' Evil explained, lighting a long Cuban cigar, drawing the smoke in with a deep breath, causing the tip to burn bright red. He moved the lit end of the cigar towards one of her nipples and held it there, while terror invaded the woman's eyes as she sat paralysed on the hard chair.

'Where are they?' Evil continued, waving the cigar across her bare breast. Teddy Caliban watched in fascination, almost hoping the woman wouldn't answer and Evil would have a reason to take his sadistic interrogation one step further.

'I . . . I don't know. I haven't a clue,' Sandra pleaded. 'I've never even met the woman. Only saw Jacob for a few days. He was just a tourist, you know.'

Evil moved the cigar tip an inch forward; she could feel its heat radiating towards her already.

'I swear to God I don't know where they are, I really don't,' the captive waitress almost shouted.

The cigar returned to Evil's lips as he allowed himself a benevolent smile.

'We believe you. It's Sandra, isn't it? But it's important we find them. They have something that belongs to us. Think. In your conversations with the guy Jacob, did he ever mention any plans? Projects?' The cigar menacingly moved back towards her.

She was sweating badly.

'Thirsty? Do you want a glass of water?' Evil inquired.

She nodded.

'Teddy, get Sandra a cool drink, she's feeling hot.'

Teddy rushed to the kitchen, afraid of missing anything.

Evil was mopping the woman's brow with a tissue when Teddy returned, while still waving the cigar a couple of inches away from her eyes. She looked as if she was about to burst out in tears.

'Think, Sandra,' Evil said brusquely.

'I am, I am . . .' she answered.

'Harder,' he said.

The red, incandescent tip of the cigar was drawing cabalistic patterns in the air in the orbit of her body.

Her eyes lit up.

'Yes,' she almost screamed.

'What?' Teddy Caliban shouted.

'New Orleans. That's it, New Orleans. He said he was thinking of going there soon, very soon. New Orleans, New Orleans,' she frantically said.

'Good girl,' Evil said. 'When was this?'

'Just a few days ago,' Sandra said with great relief, as she watched the cigar retreat before Evil extinguished it against the glass of the nearby coffee table's top.

'Very good,' said Evil. Then to Teddy 'We have good contacts there. Should be easy to track them down.'

Sandra looked up at the two men, her fear now fading as she realised she had somehow betrayed Jacob, wondering if they could be this nasty to her how bad they were likely to be with him? It was an awful thought.

'Please, it's all I know. Let me go now,' she begged them.

Teddy Caliban shot Evil a significant glance.

'Yes, Sandra, it's all over,' Teddy said. 'So surely now, we should celebrate, can't we? Be good friends.'

He rose from the leather sofa. Evil smiled benignly.

Teddy poured them each a glass of bourbon from the well-furnished bar. Handed Sandra hers. She drank it in one gulp. She'd needed it badly. She knew what was coming. She supposed it would dull the feelings and the indignity.

Teddy took his shirt off, placed his hands on her shoulders and motioned her up from the chair.

He walked her to the side of the sofa and with a gentle shove had her bend over. Evil was sitting quietly, still sipping his drink slowly, savouring the pungent burn of the alcohol against the back of his throat. She heard Teddy unbuckle his belt behind her and slide his trousers down to the floor. His hands kneaded her arse with greedy ardour. Slid the belt in front of her and tightened it against her breasts. Teddy Caliban spat into his right hand, distributed the wetness around the tip of his surging penis and roughly entered her.

'Yes,' he moaned. 'Yes.' And pumped into Sandra, every forward movement of his pelvis pushing her whole body closer to the sitting Evil as her balance on the edge of the sofa shifted its centre of gravity.

She felt no pleasure from his repeated thrusts inside her. Like so many of the men she had known, he had no art, was too metronomic, monotonous even. As he fucked her assiduously, Teddy enjoyed the spectacle of his hands roaming over the vast expanse of her rump, the way the pendulous shapes of her breasts hanged loose and swung freely on Evil's side of the sofa. The pleasure rose within him. He picked a small ice cube from the now empty glass of bourbon he had set aside earlier and inserted it inside her anus and dug it in with his finger. Sandra shuddered. Felt the fire inside her quickly melt away.

Teddy's movements accelerated.

'Hey, Evil?' he shouted to the other man.

'What?' Evil asked.

'This feels good. Why don't you partake. We're partners, aren't we?'

'Why not?' Evil said, shifting in the seat as he raised his backside and pulled the zip of his trousers open. He extracted his cock from his undergarments and turned towards Sandra's face. He was limp, but big. He moved his member closer to her and forced her lips open. Still soft, he filled her mouth totally and she gagged repeatedly as Teddy's thrusts into her increased in strength and the forward momentum impaled her further on to Evil's growing cock.

Her mouth was beginning to ache as she sucked away and she was about to close her eyes to distance herself from the dull pain when she noticed Evil's hand moving towards the jacket he had left draped on the other side of the black leather sofa. His eyes drilled into her, demanding her silence as he pulled a knife from the jacket. The one he had threatened her with outside the Underground Dive.

Teddy's movements inside her were becoming more and more frantic. It barely took a second. Evil raised himself, his thick trunk planted inside her, pulling her head upwards as he shifted. The knife danced above her eyes in a swift circular movement and cleanly slit Teddy Caliban's throat to the very bone. He came in a shuddering motion inside her, pouring his warm wetness around her innards, then died. The blood from his gaping wound jetted fiercely on to her body, pearling down the side of her breasts over the dark leather and the floor and he collapsed down on to her arched back.

Evil pulled his quickly detumescing cock out of her mouth.

Sandra was shaking, or was it Teddy's final nervous spasm.

She finally closed her eyes.

Minutes passed. The weight on her grew heavier.

She then realised that Teddy was still buried inside her.

She opened her eyes. Evil was still sitting there, nursing his drink, watching her.

'Get him off me,' she shouted at him.

'You're right, Sandra,' Evil said. 'Before rigor mortis sets in . . .'
He sniggered, rose and brutally pulled Teddy's body off the waitress. The blood was still pouring in torrents from the dead man's severed neck.

Sandra straightened herself. She was a mess. The darkening blood was draped all over her, reminding her of the image of Sissy Spacek in *Carrie*, while Teddy's come kept on dripping out of her.

'You need a shower, girl,' Evil remarked. 'Then you and I are going for a long drive.'

'Where's the bathroom?' she asked him.

7.

Tender City That Beats So Raw

The Man From Caracas knew he was a dirty old man. But when you have the cash and the power, you also control the fear and you don't give a damn about what other people might think.

He was also an educated man. In his time, he had read most of the Marquis de Sade's books. In French, back when he had studied comparative literature at the Sorbonne. Those had been good days. He'd been younger, of course. But even then he'd jerked off like crazy when reading all the dirty bits in the Sade books, and there were a lot of choice pieces, carefully lodged at regular intervals between the dubious pseudo-philosophical discourses.

There was no harm in being a sadist, he reckoned. At least he knew the word's etymology. He remembered how, at the weekends, when there were no lectures to attend, he would post himself at the table of a café on the corner of the Boulevard St Michel and the Boulevard St Germain and spy on the all the young women passing by in all their finery and insolence. They were all so appetising, the girls of Paris. He took a particular fancy to the American ones, leggy, naive, easy prey. Maryann, yes, Maryann, he reflected. With her long straight hair the colour of straw. Who blushed so often and would allow him to touch her everywhere, but would freak out if he made contact with her budding sixteen-year old breasts. He never found out why, how she had acquired this strange phobia. At any rate, she would let him do anything to her and he had soon taught her some tricks her pimply high school boyfriends would never have dreamed of. Positions, variations, perversions. It must be Europe, she must have thought, they do things differently here. She always lay there

like a plank, insensitive to all his extreme attentions. Never reacted.
Even when he could read the pain on her face. Like an object. Willing
to suffer all the despoiling and the degradations. Accepting her new
education from this good-looking South American who reminded her
of Desi Arnaz on *I Love Lucy*. Maryann had been an interesting experiment.

Would Anne Ryan be similarly passive, the Man From Caracas
wondered?

The loss of the diamonds was annoying, but he could live with
it, he knew. It was only a month's drug business profit. In a way, he
hoped that when Evil found her, she would no longer have the gems.
It would make the torture more interesting. She would not be able
to plead for mercy offering the return of the diamonds in exchange.

Evil would find her.

He was good at that. Loyal, a one-track mind, a gentle brute.

Just a question of time.

In the meantime, he could sit back, be patient and begin some
wonderful scenarios for the British woman. He no longer enjoyed
hurting calculating whores for whom every blow or scar had a mon-
etary equivalent, or indulging his sick fantasies with the dispensable
Indian girls from the mountains. Come to think of it, he'd never handled an English girl. Even back in Paris. They'd always been American, German or French.

He'd have to come up with something original. She had overcome her fear and proven she had the guts to steal from his organisation. He owed her something different for that, some ingenuity.
He would have to prove to her he was more than just a common
garden variety dirty old man and sadist.

He had cut, he had torn, he had burned. He'd had others kill on
his behalf. What would be right for Miss Ryan?

A redhead, he remembered Evil or Caliban mentioning.

He imagined a palette of sharp colours. How nicely blood might
blend with her natural tones. Orange hairs, the likely deep pink coral
shades of her innards and the fiery red of blood leaking across her
crotch, as her vagina was sewn shut. Interesting. He'd read about it
from some true crime case in America. He'd have to keep her alive,
though. Probably insert some tube for her to pass urine through and
not burst her bladder or something inside.

The Man From Caracas smiled. Give him time, he reckoned, and
he could devise some more elaborate experiments. Something sur-
gical, maybe. He'd always been morbidly fascinated by the experiments he'd read Nazi doctors had practiced in the camps. Some new

opening, perhaps. In her throat. So that the twins might fuck both her mouth and there simultaneously?

The smile broadened as he indulged his sickness.

'I'm waiting, Anne Ryan, I'm waiting,' he said aloud to the empty room.

*

Having ordered Sandra to the bathroom to clean herself up, Evil had shoved Teddy Caliban's body on to the floor. Listening to the water splash, he had moved swiftly to the bedroom and pulled sheets and blankets from the unmade bed and proceeded to roll the dead man up in them.

Sandra came back out.

Still nude, but the blood all washed away. She seemed dazed.

'Dress,' he told her. She did so.

'I'm sorry I put my cock inside your mouth, Sandra,' Evil told her. 'It was only a way to distract his attention and move nearer to cut the son of a bitch.'

Sandra had seen a couple of men die before. Some of the bars she had worked in had been rough and there were often fights. One drunk had sunk the edges of a broken beer bottle several inches deep into another's skull. An off-duty cop who had inadvertently come across his wife, or girlfriend, with another man had emptied an automatic into the other's gut. She'd get over this killing too, she knew, in time. But like people who lose a hand or limb and still experience it present ages later, she could still feel the dead guy's stiffness inside her, and it made her nauseous.

'I'm sorry,' Evil said again.

Sandra looked up at the massive shape of the bald-headed thug. His tiny eyes seemed to be pleading with her.

'It's okay, I suppose,' she responded.

'Good,' he replied. 'So you do forgive me?'

'I forgive you,' Sandra said. What else could she tell him?

'I owe you,' he said.

'So will you let me go?' she asked. 'No one will ever hear anything about what happened, I swear to God.'

'I can't,' he said. 'I need you. You know what the British guy looks like. We'll go to New Orleans. You'll have to identify him for me. I'm positive the woman we're looking for is with him.'

She knew she had no choice in the matter.

'I promise I will look after you,' Evil continued. 'I'm just doing a job. I have no quarrel with you. I like you very much, in fact. But we'll have different beds wherever we have to stay. I won't touch you. Promise.'

'Fine.'

'Good. I'm told New Orleans is a nice place.'

'So have I. I read in a magazine they have a lot of writers and poets there.'

Nothing was going to change Sandra's dreams. Tallahassee was a place of the past. She was determined never to return. Maybe Louisiana would be a better bet than Florida, she supposed. She snapped out of her daydream as Evil asked her to help him pull Teddy Caliban's wrapped body to the apartment's front door.

Sandra looked back. The blood from the dead man was darkening as it dried all over the black leather sofa and the floor.

'Shouldn't we clean up?' she suggested.

'No need,' Evil said. 'Nobody cares about the guy. No one's going to miss him. Let it be.'

They used Caliban's Alfa to drive one hour to the swamps where Evil consigned the body to the alligators that would thrive in the murky waters. Emotionless, Sandra watched the big man dump the parcel of rolled-up sheets and hastily retreat back to the car. As the dark shape slowly sank below the surface, she felt a faint stab in her gut, as if Teddy's penis remained lodged inside her and was dully pumping away. She attempted to banish the unwelcome sensation by thinking of all the poets in New Orleans.

'Let's go,' Evil said, driving off in haste, 'we have to find the road to Fort Lauderdale. Are there any maps in there?' pointing to the glove compartment.

Sandra couldn't find any.

'We'll buy maps at the first service station,' he suggested.

The night swallowed them as the moon disappeared behind a thick bank of clouds.

*

Leaving Florida behind them in the wake of their car, Anne and Jacob sped up the coastal highway that ran parallel to the Georgia and Alabama State Lines on their way to the Crescent City.

Jacob hadn't heard Anne rise from the bed. She had been fully dressed and ready to depart from the depressing and drab motel room by the time he woke.

'We have to go,' she said. 'I want to get to New Orleans sometime tomorrow.'

'Why such a hurry? Won't you tell me what it's all about?'

'When we get there. Maybe.'

Around two in the morning, that dead hour of the night when even the ghosts stay away, the monotonous patterns of trees on both sides of the road racing by, the flat light of the quarter moon like a shroud over the landscape, her smell, ever-present, strong, suggestive, close to him.

The tiredness was getting to him. His eyes hurt. His arms felt stiff from all the driving, his body tense.

He inhaled her perfume.

The fragrance made a beeline for his gut. Keeping an eye on the road, he quickly glanced at Anne sitting beside him. She had snapped out of another long doze, and watched the highway ahead, eyes wide open, silent.

'I want you,' Jacob said.

'I know,' she answered. 'I can feel it.'

Her right hand moved toward him, settled on his knee. The warmth rose like a wave through his body.

'It's like a need,' he added. 'Urgent, primal. How many days has it been since we last made love, Anne? Feels like an eternity. And this longing just keeps on growing inside me, invading my senses until I feel like screaming or throwing myself at you.'

'I know,' she said. 'I know the feeling.'

'I need you really badly,' Jacob admitted, a lump forming in his throat. Fear? Desire?

Her hand gripped his knee. 'Yes,' she said.

'Yes?'

'It's been over a week. Let's do it.'

'When?'

'Now.'

'I'll look out for a lay-by,' Jacob said. 'There must be somewhere safe. And quiet.'

They drove on for a few more miles.

In the glare of the BMW's lights, a sign for a beach resort stood out. Ten miles only.

'By the sea?' Jacob suggested.

'Yes,' she agreed. 'Yes.'

They turned off the coastal highway and plunged into the deepening darkness. Past a small, sleeping town, on to smaller roads, almost dirt tracks, seemingly leading nowhere, following the distinctive scent of the nearby ocean.

Engine off. Silence. The water shimmered by the edge of the cove, feeble waves lapping against the shore. It felt like another world, watching the Gulf of Mexico fade into the heart of the night.

'Here?'

'Here,' she confirmed.

'Do you know what?'

'No.'

'I've never done it in a car.'

'No need. We'll go outside. It'll be so much more comfortable,' Anne said.

'Are you sure? You won't be . . . we won't be cold?'

'Of course not.'

She finally withdrew her hand from his knee and opened her door.

'Take your shoes and socks off,' Anne shouted over to him as she walked out on to the small beach. 'The sand is wonderfully warm.'

He followed her out.

His eyes grew accustomed to the penumbra. Shards of moonlight danced gently on the sea surface. Anne undressed. There are moments you never forget. They carve their memories deeply inside you. For Jacob, this was one of them.

Her body, like a landscape, stretching, in softer shades of white across the darker hues of the sand, the colours of the night sky above falling over the calm expanse of her skin, her flesh, like a sacrament, filtered through the dying glare of the car's headlamps. Her body in sweet repose, an altar for his unfaltering adoration, from thin pale neck to burning cunt to ticklish toes, a subtle geography of his all-conquering desire interrupted here and there by scattered, minor imperfections: random moles, discolourations of the skin, the enticing canvas of freckles, minute birth-marks. Her body, indelibly etched alive like a frozen computer screensaver on the backdrop of his unforgiving memory. Naked. Sacred. Her breasts gentle hills, her rump a daunting elevation, the gash of her vaginal lips a byway into unforetold treasures. Her mouth a subliminal echo of her fading, moaning, hard-breathing voice. Her straight silken hair a battle-ground for his fingers and hardy explorations, her eyes opaque, questioning, child-like, deep pools of remoteness. He moved within her, fingers scraping the fine sand, sweeping it up under his nails before massaging the grains against her warm skin, Her fingers wandering too, pressing against his weak spots, teasing his balls, stretching herself wider and seizing his stem to force it deeper into her, her other hand extending itself under him and entering him too. His lips adhered to hers, breath circulating between their bodies in a circular motion, as they in turn ran out of breath and were refreshed by the other's exhalation and gasped in sheer desperation, sucking the air from the most remote part of their lungs before succumbing at last and separating reluctantly for a quick, soothing brace of night air which they greedily devoured with all the impatience of a deep sea diver breaking the surface after an eternity below the waves. He sank again, deeper towards her centre. His brain was totally disconnected from the external world, listening to inaudible music in a foreign language. If the tide had come in now and caught them, they would have drowned unaware, possibly to awaken somewhere else, in a world beyond the world. They thrashed wildly, feeling as if they were actually floating on a cushion of clouds, oblivious of the sea breeze rising slowly and dancing electron-like around their joined bodies. Rolled across the beach bed as the pleasure shot across their disjointed limbs and pulled them even tighter together, sand sliding in and out of their outer and inner crevices, adding real pain to the existing friction between their genitals, tearing at the thin outer layer of their sex skins.

'It hurts, doesn't it?'

'Yes, but it's good. Don't stop.'

They knew they were going to be red, itching like bloody hell as the skin turned to dry scabs, scorched for days after this, but continued their frenzied coupling nonetheless.

'Now, now. PLEASE.'

'Yes. Yes.'

'JEEZUS . . . yes . . .'

The red fog submerged them.

Later the Gulf water was cold when they dipped in to wash their exertions away.

'Shit, it's burning me,' Anne screamed, with the hint of a laugh in her voice, as she squatted down in the sea to clean herself.

'It's the salt water,' Jacob said. 'All that sand must have torn away the top layer of skin . . . Ouch . . . !' he screeched, echoing her, as the cool water reached his lower stomach. 'Me too!'

'I don't think I've ever felt so sore down there,' Anne remarked. 'God, there's sand everywhere. It's even inside me . . . '

'We'll have to find a room around here,' Jacob suggested, unenthusiastic about rejoining the main road right now.

'No,' Anne replied, still splashing water around her crotch area. 'We clean up as best we can here, then we get on our way to New Orleans. We'll catch up with the hygiene there.'

'If you insist,' Jacob said.

'I've got some cream in my bag,' she said, pointing back at their car. 'It'll sooth the chafing.'

'I suppose it will have to do,' he concluded, wading out of the water and toward his crumpled clothes.

But even with the dull, burning pain radiating up from his cock, he somehow knew it would never be as good again. Jacob sighed.

*

The group had convened a stone's throw away from Corpus Christi, Texas. The tourist season was over and this family-owned bed and breakfast inn had agreed to allow them the run of the place for a couple of weeks. They were masquerading as a writing group on their annual get-together. They'd agreed a flat rate per person for the fortnight and arrived throughout the Sunday from sundry ports of call. There were twelve of them. They varied wildly in ages, appearances and backgrounds, and none had ever met before. The connection had been on the Internet where they had somehow discovered their common interest. Their obsession.

They were all generally soft-spoken, well-mannered, seemingly affluent, and the couple who ran the bed and breakfast felt quite reassured by their eminently acceptable appearance as the writers arrived at their establishment in turn. The kitchen was well-stocked, both with fresh and frozen food, they had prepared a list of the liquor stored under the downstairs bar and the group had been quite willing to lodge a substantial deposit a few weeks earlier. The owners were travelling to Vancouver to visit close relatives and this group booking was a godsend, filling the inn when normally they would have had to close it.

All their visitors appeared so trustworthy. The owners drove off to the airport, satisfied, convinced the place was in good hands. And so what if the group finished off all the liquor. They'd already paid for it, twice over. They were damn welcome to it. At this time of year, there wasn't much in the way of attractions at the resort. Anyway, they had said that afternoons and evenings they would be work-shopping manuscripts, whatever that was.

Each member of the group repaired to the room they had been allocated, on the simple first-come, first-room available basis they had previously agreed on. Men. Women. Young. Middle-aged. A finely-tuned cross-section of society. A couple of students. Business-men. Housewives. Secretaries. Industrialists from widely differing sectors. Accountants. Doctors. A television executive. A sales representative for an academic publisher—the nearest they came to the actual act of writing. A plumber. An Air Force cadet. A statistician. A lounge room piano-player.

Kirk, who worked in television and had previously been designated spokesman, said: 'We'll eat at eight. Something light; then we begin to plan. As we agreed before, the first experiment will be on Tuesday. Okay with everyone?'

They all nodded their approval, and separated. Some of them had travelled great distances to get there and badly needed the rest. Physical well-being was paramount for the project.

Five of them met up in the pool room an hour before meal time. Either they couldn't sleep or were just not tired.

'Nice to meet you all.'

'At last.'

'Likewise.'

'Never thought we'd finally make it here, all of us.'

'Well, we have,' said Kirk, pouring himself a glass of orange juice.

'I'm really excited,' said one of the women.

'So am I,' said one of the accountants.

'Look,' said Kirk, pointing at the pseudo-antique wall clock. 'It's seven. He's on the radio.'

'Switch it on.'

'Let's listen.'

'Know what?' the older woman remarked, as Kirk walked over to turn on the large boom box he'd brought along to Texas. 'His voice on the radio sure makes me horny.' She smiled mischievously.

The other woman present nodded approvingly.

The two men sitting at the table avoided each other's eyes, as if ashamed to admit the disc jockey had a similar effect on them too.

'He's The Man,' Kirk said, plugging in the radio. It was already tuned to the right frequency and duelling acoustic guitars attacking a Dylan song burst from the large speakers. The younger woman tapped her feet to the heavy beat.

' ... *Maggie's Farm* by Chris and Carla from the Walkabouts. Unplugged but heavy,' said the DJ, his familiar dark tones bringing all the listeners in the pool room into his confidence. 'This is the devil's hour out there, folks, but this is the Mark, the Mark of God, speaking to you through the darkness. One more song, and I'll be opening the lines for our daily dose of dialogue from nowhere. Let's stay in Seattle. Here's Mark Lanegan and *Sunrise*. You know him from Screaming Trees, but I'm sure you'll agree that this is in another league altogether, guys.'

The younger woman lowered herself to the floor and sat on the carpet, crossed her legs in a yoga-like position, closed her eyes and allowed the music to invade her. The others watched her.

'It is a nice song,' the accountant quietly said to the others, even though it wasn't his kind of music. The tune was short and soon faded away.

'Tasty, tasty,' said the Mark in his studio faraway in Radio Land. No one had a clue where he broadcast from. Or what he looked like. 'Talking time. Truth time. Let's hear it from you. Tonight's for the regulars, the gang, the faithful, the true disciples, so I won't insult you by spoon-feeding you the number. You know it. You know it's good to call. Come on. Reckoning time is nearing. Speak to the Mark...'

Kirk dialled the familiar 1-800 number on his cellular phone.

'Hi, this is the Mark of God. Who's this?'

'It's us,' Kirk confided. 'The group.'

'Nice to hear from you, TV man. So tell me, do you have news for me?' the DJ asked.

'Yes. We're going for it...'

'The big one?' the Mark inquired.

'Yes. We've all decided to risk it. We're together for the first time, all of us,' Kirk confided.

'Beware,' the DJ warned. 'But I wish you good fuck as you set your controls for the heart of the night. Truly. Hardy travellers, all. See you maybe on the other side?'

'Will you?' Kirk hastily ventured.

'Just enough time for another song, before I take my next call from a disciple,' the DJ interrupted him and cued in a new piece of music.

The rest of the group were trooping into the room. Kirk switched the radio off.

'Surely,' he assured those present. 'The time could never be more right for it, can it?'

They all acquiesced.

This was the reason they had come to Port Aransas.

*

New Orleans beckoned, ever approaching; he could feel the spirit, the drunken energy, the knot of fear all grow nearer as the the car rolled its way along the two-lane blacktop highway, leaving Florida behind. He had phoned ahead the night before from some other anonymous roadside motel and found them a room at a medium-priced hotel on Burgundy Street. The woman at reception, taking his booking, had informed him that the rooms were in separate buildings in the garden at the back, that used to form the old slave quarters. Historical, she had said.

Anne had, again, dozed most of the way.

Jacob still had too many questions to ask her.

They were speeding past Tulane University, approaching the city, when she opened her eyes, yawned lazily and turned her face toward him.

'Nearly there?'

'Yes. Half an hour or so.'

'Good.'

'Anne?'

'Yes.'

'Why won't you tell me about England? More about yourself.'

'What do you want to know?'

'Everything. What you were like as a child, what school was like, growing up, life? I want to know all of you.'

'No, you don't. It's the other men in my life, in my past that you really want to know about. You guys are all the same.'

'Not only. Just you.'

'There's nothing to tell you, Jakey. I'm simply not an interesting person.'

'Oh, come on.'

'No. Really ... I was a young girl, naive, stupid, full of fantasies. I was a student, dazzled by the images of art, envious, poor. I had dreams. I had aspirations. Then, somehow, I became a wife, a working housewife, and lost my ambition, forgot that there was something else out there ...'

'You were married?'

'Yeah. Then I succumbed to lust and lost everything. So I came to America, land of dreams and riches and all that, you know?'

'I see,' was all Jacob could respond, right then.

'Satisfied?' she questioned him. 'There, you see, you know all about me.'

'Somehow, it's not enough, Anne. I've hurt people too. And now I'm here with you and I'm hooked on you. Badly. And I don't want to harm you or be harmed by you. I see your face, your body under mine when we make love, and my heart is already so jumbled up, not knowing what to do next. I want more of you, so much more, but it's difficult to express. You're good for me, you're bad for me. You're danger ...'

'Like it said in that book, I'm damaged, Jakey ...'

'We both are. That's what makes this so important, can't you see?'

'All I can see is that you'd better learn how to unhook yourself when the time comes, Jakey.'

Highways merged and they soon plunged into the city that never sleeps. He lost himself momentarily in the Financial District before turning on to Canal, and finding the gateway into the Vieux Carré. As they slowly inched their way through the narrow streets, Anne was awe-struck by the unending parade of metal whirlpools of the carved iron balconies, the shuttered windows, the glimpses of hidden voluptuous courtyards, the ceramic squares on the corner of each street displaying each one's name in both French and Spanish.

'It's beautiful. I'm going to love it here,' she exclaimed.

The hotel was picturesque in the extreme, the living quarters a series of cottages scattered among the grounds, rickety two-storied buildings with winding wooden stairs lodged haphazardly between a succession of overgrown palm trees, tired flower beds and circular paddling pools.

The air-conditioning in their room was on the blink, but the bed was vast. Anne threw herself on it with glee and bounced up and down a few times, as Jacob set their luggage down against the red brick wall. The room smelt musty, reminded him somehow of sex and a fleeting thought crossed his mind about the couple who had made sex there last and he tried to imagine in which position they had copulated and what the woman's moans had sounded like. Anne's movements caught his attention and he snapped out of it.

'I'm hungry as hell,' he said. 'All the driving.'

'Fine with me,' Anne answered.

'Don't you want to shower, freshen up?'

'No, we'll do that later. Let's go eat.'

They were both in the mood for seafood and the old man on duty at the front desk recommended a place by the river they could reach on foot. This was a place for walking, give your motor car a rest, he informed them. In the French Quarter mostly everything was within walking distance.

They made a detour through Bourbon Street, wading their way through the drunken crowds and their plastic glasses of beer, the echo of all sorts of different music blaring out from the open-windowed bars: jazz, Dixie, rock, rhythm and blues, the little black kids tap-dancing to the sounds, the doormen for the strip joints and the beckoning smells of spiced food from the myriad restaurants.

They emerged on Canal and turned left to the river, past the looming steel skeleton of the giant casino that was under construction.

They ate at Lemoyne's Landing, in the shadow of the old 1812 wall, gorged themselves on bowls of gumbo and huge platters of boiled crayfish, watching the orderly arrival and retreat of the Algiers Ferry nearby, which bridged the heavy Mississippi river. Stray pigeons swarmed busily outside the restaurant. Evening came with streaks of pink dripping through the sky. They walked back to the hotel by Jackson Square, following the bend of the river, past the moorings of the old steamboats and paddle wheel vessels now restricted to tourist runs to the bayous. Humid warmth pervaded the encroaching night and as they cut across Chartres to reach their hotel, Jacob could feel his shirt sticking to his back.

She climbed the wooden stairs to their floor ahead of him and his eyes couldn't keep away from the soothing sway of her arse against the thin material of her jeans.

She twisted the key in the lock.

'Let's fuck,' she said.

Their parts still hurt from previous excesses, but it made little difference to that night's intensity. Sometimes the sheer strength of despair can overcome physical pain.

Anne unzipped his trousers.

Jacob dug his fingers into her.

As the lovemaking progressed, Anne's movements became more convulsive and her nails scratched him badly as they raked across his back and buttocks and she beckoned him even further into her, almost seeking pain, disappointed that he wasn't rough enough with her. He came quickly, spurred on by her greedy needs, realising he was leaving her in an unsatisfied state.

Sleep soon captured him into its safe harbour as the distant sounds of Bourbon Street faded on the borders of his consciousness.

*

The next morning, while Anne was showering, Jacob hastily went through her things. He knew all the clothes, CDs and trinkets in the case, he had packed them himself. He concentrated on the small bag she had been carrying when he had picked her up at Miami airport. A couple of lightweight skirts, silk blouses, used underwear. In the side pocket, he came across the discarded stockings all bunched up into the bottom corner of the bag. He was about to abandon his search, when he impulsively buried his fingers into the shiny nylon ball and felt the hardness at its centre. He pulled the stockings out, undid the knot holding them together and the six small but perfect diamonds dropped into his palm.

He caught his breath. The water in the bathroom was still pouring noisily down over her, splashing against the tiled floor. Anne was humming loudly, he could recognise the Tom Petty song, above the sounds of the shower.

More likely unanswered questions.

He quickly replaced the diamonds in their nylon hiding-place and stuffed the stockings back into the bag. Then found the discarded airline ticket at the bottom of the bag. Her itinerary. Caracas. South America. She had told him she had been on a modelling assignment in Baton Rouge.

Somehow, none of this really surprised him. He already knew there was something dangerous about Anne. Was this why he was falling so heavily for her? Maybe.

Or the fact that all too often she kept on reminding him of Lynda. Different face, height, hair colour, but a similar deep pit of mercy in their eyes, a word here, a word there, an intonation, a movement, a spasm while they made love.

The perfect Jacob trap.

Anne emerged from the bathroom, the large white towel wrapped around her, her hair wet and dripping on to the bedroom's wooden floor, with a wide smile on her face.

'Let's be tourists,' she suggested. 'I've always wanted to have my breakfast at the Café du Monde.'

'Why not?' Jacob said.

He knew this would be the wrong time to question her about his discovery and her whereabouts the previous week.

'What do you want me to wear?' she asked him. 'What would I look good in?'

'It's quite warm outside,' he said. 'Something light and colourful, I suppose.'

'I know exactly what,' she said, dropping the towel as she swivelled round, unveiling the wonderful shapeliness of her arse in all its unnatural pallor, and bending over to rummage through the case that held all her clothes.

The sheer sight of her like this turned his mind to mush and deeply perverse thoughts of pornographic sex.

'Damn it, I'm starving,' Anne remarked as she emptied half the case on to the bed, searching for the right garments and combination of colours.

Jacob stuck to his customary black trousers and tee-shirt. Black made him look a bit slimmer.

A jazz trio played Dixie tunes outside the Café du Monde while the mostly Asian waitresses swarmed around the terrace taking and serving orders of coffee, juice and *beignets*. The powdered sugar from the *beignets* fell everywhere, momentarily staining their clothes, fingers and cheeks.

'This is delicious,' he said.

'Yes,' she agreed, munching on the doughy bun, its sugar invading the oval borders of her lips, making her look like a happy clown. 'This beats any old English breakfast, doesn't it?'

He nodded, enjoying the moment and its essential innocence and uncomplicated joy.

They watched the hippies drift over across Decatur from Jackson Square and sit on the steps that led to the river. Japanese tourists manically snapped away at each other and at the spectacle of the pierced and tattooed youngsters congregating with the hobos and their trolleys full of plastic bags. The horse-drawn carriages touted for business. Nearby, funnels hooted over the Mississippi.

Jacob enjoyed the look of wonder sparkling in Anne's eyes.

'This is New Orleans,' he said.

'Yes. I like it. I like it very much,' she answered.

'Great town, eh? Is it your first time here?' The guy at the next table asked them.

He was tall, smartly dressed in an anthracite grey suit with a white open-necked shirt. Deeply tanned, probably in his mid forties, wore a sharply etched beard with flecks of grey although his slicked back hair was jet black. The woman sitting with him looked on indulgently, as pale as he was tanned, her whiteness highlighted by her dark purple lipstick.

'Yes,' Anne answered him. 'We're from England.'

'How interesting,' the man said. 'Planning to be here long?'

'Maybe,' Anne replied. 'We're at loose ends. Just going with the flow, I suppose.'

'O'Neal d'Ath,' the man said, extending his hand to shake hands with Jacob who up until now had remained silent, and then Anne. 'This is Rebecca, my companion.'

The woman just nodded in their direction and continued sipping her coffee.

They introduced each other to the couple.

D'Ath and Rebecca were natives of New Orleans, their families had settled here almost two centuries ago. They had inherited their money.

'You might say we're in the same boat as you, people of leisure,' d'Ath joked.

Extra coffees were ordered and their conversation rambled on, principally between d'Ath and Anne. Rebecca never said anything, just smiled, shrugged her shoulders or nodded. Jacob was not very good at small talk whenever he was not in a one-to-one situation. He was better at silences, he knew. Words were important. He often felt that using them indiscriminately was just a waste.

He realised that, apart from Anne and Sandra, he hadn't really had a real conversation with anyone since he'd come to America. And never missed it.

The New Orleans couple lived in the Garden District and d'Ath effusively sang its praises.

'You must see the District. It's like a world away from the Quarter. I know ... Rebecca?'

'Yes?' her voice was amazingly hoarse.

'We must show Anne and Jakey around. Wouldn't that be nice?'

'Yes,' she approved laconically.

'We wouldn't want to impose,' Jacob said.

'Not at all ...' d'Ath answered.

'We'd love to,' Anne volunteered.

'That's a deal, then,' he said. 'Most tourists here just have no culture. You two are so different, I knew that straight away, just looking at you sitting here earlier.'

He moved his hand across to Anne and fleetingly touched her wrist. Jacob watched his long, manicured fingers linger on her skin.

'We're having friends around tonight for a small dinner party. Some theatre people, musicians. Why don't you join us?'

'Oh, really.' Jacob protested.

'It would be lovely, wouldn't it, Jakey?' Anne answered.

The man's hand retreated and he wrote his address down on a page he tore out of his diary. They agreed on six o'clock, while it was still light, so that they might admire the surrounding magnolia gardens.

Later, back in their hotel room Anne and Jacob, dressing for the evening, had their first row.

'Aren't you at least curious, Jakey?'

'No, I'm not. And anyway, please don't call me Jakey in front of other people. It sounds as if I were a child. There's something creepy about them. If you ask me, all he wants is to get into your knickers, for all I know.'

'So what? Is there any better form of flattery? Anyway, didn't you see the way Rebecca was eying you throughout. She likes you.'

'Oh, come on, Anne.'

'We'll go there, enjoy ourselves. Who knows?'

'Who knows what, Anne? I thought we came here to spend time together?'

'You shouldn't be so possessive, Jakey. It's ugly.'

'I'm sorry. It's just the way I am.'

'Well, I don't like it.'

'Oh, fuck you, then . . .'

'Charming.'

Standing in the hotel lobby, waiting for the cab to arrive.

'Have you ever been to South America, Anne?'

'No. Why are you asking?'

'I don't know. Just a thought.'

'Well, let me tell you, it's a place I have no wish to go to.'

The cab drew up on Burgundy.

8.

Turning My Yearning To A Blaze

The house clearly spoke of old money. Shielded behind a wall of dark trees on a side street in the Garden District, it looked like a smaller version of all those pre-Civil War mansions they had seen in countless movies. There were already half a dozen cars on the circular drive. All were expensive sports models, waxed shining clean, unlike Jake and Anne's dusty red BMW that hadn't seen a car-wash since Miami.

They parked on the gravel road, ahead of the other cars.

The door to the house was open. A tall grey-suited black security guard stood to one side and waved them in. Anne took hold of Jacob's hand as they moved into the sumptuous hall. An oversize crystal chandelier loomed above them, facing a majestic staircase winding up the floors above. D'Ath stood halfway down and greeted them loudly: 'Ah, my wonderful British guests have arrived!'

He was wearing a smart tuxedo.

Jacob in his casual cream jacket, colourful short-sleeved shirt and usual trousers, felt quite underdressed for the occasion. Anne had put on her short white dress. The one she had worn at the Miami night club where they had met. Underneath he knew, she wore flesh-shade stockings, held up by a delicate, thin white silk garter belt.

'Welcome, welcome to my house,' O'Neal d'Ath called. 'Do come this way. All our other guests are already here.' He kissed Anne's hands when she reached him. They ascended the polished marble stairs behind him. Through a window they caught a glimpse of a large garden full of magnolias in full bloom.

They emerged into a large room where the guests were lounging about on a series of leather divans circling a grand piano. With a sigh of relief, Jacob noted that few of them were as formally dressed as d'Ath. Some men had even discarded their jackets and rolled up their shirtsleeves. The women, on the other hand, were scattered around the room, dressed in all their finery. Diaphanous evening dresses, elegant black lounge suits, silky, shimmering outfits. Rebecca rose to greet them as Anne and Jacob approached in d'Ath's wake. Her raven hair was pulled back tightly, emphasising the deathly pallor of her face and the night darkness of her lipstick. She wore incredibly tight black velvet trousers, moulding her legs, seemingly spray-painted on like a second skin. Jacob couldn't help himself noticing how the thin material even sloped forward to follow the outward curve of her mons, the thin ridge of her slit clearly delineated against the velvet. He looked up. Her equally black silk shirt was quite opaque, her sharp dark nipples aggressively stretching its fabric.

With a smile on his face, d'Ath presented them to his companion. Rebecca leaned forward and kissed Jacob straight on the mouth. Then did likewise to Anne. D'Ath called the others up and effected introductions. Within a few minutes, neither Jacob or Anne could remember any of their names.

The lemonade was cool and refreshing. They all wanted to know about England. About the London scene. About them. Anne mixed with ease, moving among the men, swapping banter and unrevealing information. Jacob was similarly unforthcoming about his past, visibly proving a bit of a disappointment to d'Ath and Rebecca's guests. He could clearly see that Anne and he were the stars of the show. That the others had been summoned here to meet them. But what show? Why them? The unease inside him grew.

Small groups formed, dissolved, reformed around the room, centred on the two hosts and Anne and Jacob as the meaningless conversations ambled along. Outside the window, a fragrant New Orleans night was falling.

Jacob found himself isolated with Rebecca and two other women discussing some English writers he hadn't even read. He looked round. Anne was at the other end of the room, sitting on one of the plush divans with d'Ath and another, older man. She caught his glance, smiled back at him, a look of mischief on her face, somehow reminding him how she had earlier mentioned that Rebecca fancied him. He blushed. Something he rarely did. Rebecca's revealing attire was difficult to ignore. He turned back toward his two interlocutors.

' . . . Byatt's no prude, though,' the other woman said. 'That scene in the movie of *Angels and Insects* where Patsy Kensit is caught in *flagrante delicto* with her brother. I swear I wetted myself. She'd had her pubic hair dyed blond and the guy was still partly erect. Really thick one. They must have forgotten to have edited that bit out. I was amazed.'

'You're right,' Jacob said. 'I also saw the movie. But I haven't read the book, I'm afraid.'

'Must have been a hot set,' the woman said.

'To make you wet, my dear,' Rebecca said, 'takes a lot. I sure will have to catch the film.' She laughed gently, raising her left arm to smooth back her hair, her hand brushing against Jacob's in the process. The other woman shrugged and moved away to join another conversation. Rebecca's eyes looked straight into Jacob's. What did she want, he wondered? She knew he was with Anne. He averted her gaze and looked beyond her at some of the guests on the cushion-bedecked sofa against the wall, by the window. A faint breeze animated the shimmering curtains.

There were two men and a woman on the sofa. The woman's breasts were out of her blouse and the man on her left was quietly massaging them, manipulating the tips to hardness, while the other's hand was buried under the woman's skirt, visibly fingering her crotch.

He hastily glanced away and found Rebecca's eyes again. They looked all the way inside him, the smile on her lips as knowing as ever. He felt a sense of panic overcome him. Looked away. Searching for Anne.

She was still in the other corner. Her and d'Ath. Still in deep conversation. His hands were slowly stroking her cheeks, seemingly with her approval. Jacob felt rooted to the ground as he watched the other man touch Anne.

'It's all right,' Rebecca said, her hand settling on his waist.

Jacob turned his head slightly. To their right, by the grand piano, sprawled on the ground over one of the expensive Afghan carpets, another man, trousers rolled down to his ankles was entering one of the women, the many layers of whose evening dress had been bunched up around her waist, revealing her bare behind, while in front of her another man kissed her quite passionately, his hands fondling her breasts.

Jacob peered across the room again.

D'Ath's hands were moving inside Anne's dress. She stood there, passive, accepting his exploration. She sensed Jacob's gaze and the look in her eyes said, 'So what?'

'Our little party,' Rebecca said, moving closer to Jacob. He could feel the rock hard tip of her nipples against his shirt. He shivered.

The woman's hand moved down the front of his trousers and began unzipping him. He knew he was already hard.

'With your English guests as the main course?' he ventured.

'Quite.'

'You've got quite a nerve, you know?' he said. She pulled his penis out.

'Why?' Rebecca protested. 'If we see something we like, why shouldn't we help ourselves? Selfishness is an art. Don't worry, we're not planning to share you. We invited some friends along to make the atmosphere more comfortable for the two of you. They're content with each other.'

'How reassuring.'

Most of the room's occupants were now paired off in various combinations. Rebecca followed his look.

'Isn't it nice?' admiring the bodies in assorted states of undress and copulation.

'I suppose that's one way of putting it,' Jacob said. Her mouth engulfed him, the dark lipstick smearing itself all across his stem. He looked over one last time.

Anne and d'Ath were talking. Her nails were dug into his now uncovered chest, her dress was gaping open on the side. He nodded. They walked to a nearby door that led to another room. She wanted privacy. Jacob felt a small sense of relief. At least he wouldn't have to watch another man actually fucking her.

Rebecca's warmth began radiating through him and he closed his eyes. My first damn orgy, he thought.

*

The Man From Caracas listened to Evil's report over the telephone. New Orleans. He knew the place. There were some good private clubs there, where money could buy you anything you wanted. Dark little places off Bourbon. He briefly thought of flying there to be present at the kill, so to speak. But reason dictated he stay and wait for the outcome. Evil would know how to find the Brits. He was reliable. Maybe lacked imagination. But New Orleans was a small place. He would quickly catch a sniff of them. He was bound to. And then the Man would get his merchandise back. And the redhead.

Hand in pocket, he touched himself.

The scenario that would welcome her was still developing inside his head.

If they pulled all her front teeth out, say, she would give damn good head. But it would have to be done surgically, carefully, he reckoned. Under anaesthetic. Didn't want the pain to overcome her too early in the proceedings. Her ordeal must be prolonged as much as it could be managed. He knew how much he would enjoy the terror in her face before they gave her the gas and it dawned on her that she would awake toothless forever. And how he would explain in lingering detail how his men would stretch her for days on end, an assembly line of impalers until she was wide enough to accommodate the horse. Surely she would shit in her pants at the thought. If he allowed her to wear any. Which he doubted. It would make an interesting spectacle.

'Yes, Evil,' he said, as his henchman completed his report and detailed his plans. 'Just get on with it.'

*

Evil put the phone down. His boss actually sounded rather pleased by the turn of events.

He had just arrived in New Orleans and, with difficulty—some software convention beginning in a few days—found a room at the big Sheraton on Canal Street. Sandra sat on the side of the bed, watching his massive back. She had never stayed in such a beautiful hotel and the luxury that surrounded them just took her breath away.

There was only one bed in the room. She knew he had asked for two; she had been standing by him at the reception desk. But this was the only room for two still available in the whole hotel.

In the elevator, he had told her that she could feel safe, that he wouldn't take advantage of the situation. It was a very large bed, she saw, big enough for the two of them, even with his sheer bulk.

'What now?' she asked him, as he shoved his small overnight bag into a corner with his foot.

'We take things easy,' Evil said. 'Relax a bit. Eat. I'm really famished. Then we'll walk around a bit. There are some places, some people I have to see to put the word out about the woman and her boyfriend.'

'Surely, the odds are against you,' Sandra remarked.

'Don't count on it, babe,' Evil answered. 'If I know the woman, she's bound to surface somewhere I have contacts. I'm quietly confident.'

'What will you do when you find them?' she asked.

'My boss wants her badly. So I shall deliver her to him in one piece; don't worry, I won't harm her. Only a little if she proves difficult and requires a sharp shock warning...'

'What about him, Jacob?'

'He's not needed. He's disposable,' he said.

Sandra felt a twinge in her heart. Jacob had been the nearest to a poet she had ever met. She resolved to help him escape if she could. But how?

'Let's go out,' Evil suggested. 'Food, things to do.'

'Can I clean up first?' Sandra asked.

'Sure.'

She rose from the bed and walked to the bathroom.

'But leave the door open,' he added, taking her place on the bed where he could watch her.

The bright bathroom was a cavern of pleasures. She'd never seen one so clean. It was almost a pity to wash here and disturb its sheen. The taps were gold-coloured, the towels abundant, white, thick and fluffy. The complimentary soap came in gleaming brown plastic containers. There was an enormous hair-dryer plugged into the wall by the sink and a dozen or so miniature bottles of shampoo, conditioner and creams of all sorts. She could literally live here, Sandra thought.

She splashed water over her face and towelled herself dry. Broke open the transparent wrapper of the free toothbrush and brushed her teeth thoroughly. They had been on the road for a few days and she felt filthy everywhere. She could see Evil watching her over there. He smiled back at her.

She moved sideways and pulled her skirt and knickers down. Here, he could no longer see her. She sat herself on the toilet and peed.

Evil avidly listened to the nearby sound of her innards emptying.

'I need new clothes,' she said, returning to the hotel bedroom. 'You've brought me here and I have nothing to wear. All this,' she said, pointing to her crumpled clothing, 'is dirty. Needs to be cleaned.'

'Don't worry,' Evil answered. 'I'll help you shop. No problem.'

He treated her to oysters and jambalaya at the Pearl. It was still mid-afternoon but the all the restaurants were full and the town alive with vibrant energy. Sandra had never seen a place like this. It was all so different. Noisy. Exciting. There were some clothing shops on Chartres Street.

'Don't worry about the cost,' he said.

She bought a couple of new outfits that looked and felt good. He settled the expensive purchases without a single comment, pulling a rolled wad of green notes from his pocket. He was loaded, she saw.

'I still need underwear,' she told him. 'You know what's it like, a girl can't wear the same thing all the time.'

He nodded. They walked back to Canal where she had spotted

a large Woolworth. While she made her choice among the rows of lacy bras and knickers, Evil shyly turned his back, gazing at the racks of trainers.

'Is that it?'

'Yes,' Sandra said. 'But I'd like to go back to the hotel now, and change first, before we walk about any further. I've been wearing this for too long. Feel unclean. It won't take me long, promise.' They were just a couple of blocks from the Sheraton; Evil agreed.

She pulled the new clothes out of the shopping bags and prepared to go to the bathroom to change.

'No,' Evil stopped her.

'What?'

'Would you mind if I watched you dress?' Evil asked. 'I would like it very much.'

Sandra was primarily taken aback by his request. Then she shrugged her shoulders. He had, after all, seem most of her already. Her top at the club, all the rest and more at Teddy Caliban's apartment. Hell, she'd even given him a blow job. What the damn, anything to keep him happy. He was a killer, she remembered. So, one more guy would see her nude. Doesn't make much of a difference, she supposed.

'Okay,' she agreed.

She slipped out of the dirty clothes. Turned back and asked him to unhook her brassiere and then bent over to slide the soiled knickers down. She straightened up and allowed Evil to view her whole body.

He stood there, motionless, drinking the sight of her in with the hungry look of a child painted all across his rough-hewn features. Her heavy, voluptuous breasts spilling out, puckered dark brown nipples almost square, strong waist and thighs framing the abundant curls of her pubic delta. Lines on her neck, thin stretch marks zigzagging along the side of her rump, stains, burns on her hands and forearms. The body of a waitress.

She let him watch, scrutinise her nakedness.

'I'm not that young any more,' she said. 'The dancing girls, the kids at the club had thinner bodies, tighter muscles and butts.'

'I know,' Evil said. 'But you're more real. That's the way I like women.'

Sandra thought she understood. Younger women would ignore men like him. They thought ugliness was a sin.

She held out the underwear she had bought earlier.

'What do you want me to wear now,' she asked him. 'Which colour? Black or white?'

Black became tonight's intimate colour. She suspected that was what he would choose. She then allowed him to select among the dresses. He went for the most sober one. A flowing, knee-length thin dark blue dress with pleats.

They left the Sheraton and were soon swallowed up by the French Quarter crowds.

*

'I thought we were together.'

'We are, Jakey.'

'So what was that all about?'

They were back at the inn on Burgundy, undressing for bed. She had emerged from the room without d'Ath a couple of hours later. Jacob had been waiting for her, by now fully dressed again, with Rebecca asleep, her head in his lap, surrounded by the smell of sex that permeated the room. Most of the other couples had by then disappeared, Just a few remained, all asleep, cuddled together, nude, man against man, woman against woman, on one of the deep leather divans.

They had walked out of the house, hailed a cab and been driven back to the Quarter without saying a word to each other.

She threw she white dress she had discarded into a corner of the bedroom and turned to him.

'That was about the fact I can do whatever the fuck I want to do, Jakey.'

'To fuck anybody, you mean?'

'You don't own me.'

'I know,' he said, dejected.

'Look,' she added, 'we can still be together. I like you, you're good for me, really. But sometimes, I want to try different things.'

'Different men?'

'There was something about him. I don't know what. A form of darkness. It attracted me. I wanted to know what it would be like.'

'So you did?'

'Yes. Anyway, I didn't see you rejecting Rebecca's advances, did I?'

'So, what was it like?'

'I thought you'd never ask, Jakey.'

'I did. You know us men, we want to find out all the details, that's the way we are.'

'It was frightening, but it was good. He's very experienced, masterful. From his first touch, I knew I would allow him to do anything to me, really.'

'What do you mean?'

'He didn't bother about much foreplay. Just fingered me a bit to see how wet I'd get. Then he ordered me to get on all fours and took me in the arse . . .'

'Christ!'

'His cock was very long. It felt like a hard snake worming its way down into the pit of my stomach. At first it really hurt, but I quickly got used to it, as he pumped away. He stayed so hard all the time. After the initial pain subsided, you know, feeling returned to my sphincter muscles and I even managed to tighten them around him and squeeze him until he came inside my gut. I'm sure I screamed when he did. But he didn't withdraw afterwards and somehow remained bone hard and was soon thrusting again, reaching even deeper until he was assaulting my inside walls with such fury I felt I was going to faint. I just don't know how long he stayed inside me, I lost all sense of time.'

'I'm not sure I want to know, Anne.'

'Oh, come on. Haven't you ever done it that way to a woman, too?'

'Yes.'

'The one in London?'

'Lynda, yes.'

'So, don't tell me it doesn't feel good.'

'It can,' he agreed.

'What about you and Rebecca?'

'It was okay.'

'No. Tell me more. Everything.'

'Her cunt is shaven . . .'

'Would you like me like that, Jakey?'

'I don't know.'

'Go on.'

'She's very demanding. Kept on asking me to slap her as we were fucking, to hurt her. It was difficult, with all the others around in the room. I felt very self-conscious. I was thinking about you, also . . .'

'Did you think of me while you were screwing her?'

'Yes,' he admitted. But didn't tell her he was also picturing the image of Lynda's face and body at the same time.

'I know,' Anne said. Her eyes clouded over. 'There was this other man in London. I fell in lust with him. We had an affair. One of those mad flings that begins casually but soon skids completely out of con-

trol. I'd go back to my husband late at night. Lies. Pretexts. While
the affair went on, I would of course occasionally have to make love
to my husband, to keep up the pretence of married life, the duties.
And, every time we did, I would picture my lover, imagine it was
him. And soon I no longer even felt guilty that I was fucking one
man and imagining he was other. That's the way things are, I suppose.'

'What happened?'

'Bad things happened.' She unhooked the bra and her small
breasts poured out of the constricting material. 'Enough about the
past.'

'If you say so.'

He unbuttoned his shirt and undid his belt.

'Jakey?'

'Yes?'

'I'm sorry. Sometimes the lust becomes too great. I won't go with
him again, I promise.'

'That's okay.'

'Thanks, Jakey.' She leaned over towards him, kissed him on the
cheek. 'Come on,' she said, pulling on his trousers and lowering her
mouth in the direction of his penis.

'Wait . . .' he said.

'What?'

'I have to wash,' Jacob said. 'Haven't had a chance since . . .'

'Since Rebecca?' she asked, pulling his cock out the pants. 'God,
it looks good,' she said. Moved nearer. 'It still smells of her. How
exciting. Damn it, I'm a tramp, aren't I?' And began licking his penis
clean.

Both were soon fully undressed. Noisy voices from a distant bar
reached them through the half-opened window. The room surrounding them felt remarkably small after the spaciousness of that evening's Garden District mansion. She extended her arm to the side of
the bed and switched the light off.

'Jakey?'

'Yes,' he tiredly said.

'I want to ask you something?'

'What?'

'Fuck me like O'Neal did.'

'I don't know if I have the strength.'

'I'm sure you have. I want you to,' her hand raked through his
hair and she nibbled his ear, her tongue digging inside the ear, some-

thing she knew excited him wildly. 'His come his still inside me. I want you to push it in even deeper.'

'You're disgusting, Anne . . .'

'I know. But you like it, don't you?'

'How can I resist?'

'You're thicker than him, you know. I hope it doesn't hurt too much, that it fits.'

She turned on to her stomach, raised her rear and Jacob squatted into position above her.

'I know about the diamonds,' he said in the darkness.

'I reckoned you'd find out sooner or later.'

His hands moved down to her rump, fingers sliding down the thin valley separating her arse cheeks.

'I stole them from someone who'd done me harm. That's why I had to leave Miami,' she said. 'We'll find someone who can give us good money for them. What with hotels and restaurants, your cash will soon run out and it's time I helped.'

'It's dangerous,' he said, lubricating the tip of his penis as he lowered himself down on her.

'They haven't a clue where I might be,' Anne said.

He pierced her.

*

It had been a boring evening, hiking from bar to bar, with Evil often disappearing into back rooms for lengthy conversations with shady types. She'd spent most of her life in bars and diners and even though the New Orleans scene was livelier, it wasn't Sandra's idea of an enjoyable night out wearing brand new clothes.

After the first four watering joints, she switched to fruit juice. The beer had started to make her feel giddy and a tad nauseous. Maybe it was the heat.

Evil finally decided he had passed the word along enough for their first evening here and they returned to the bright lights of the Sheraton. Sandra was so tired she thought nothing of stripping unceremoniously in front of him before slipping between the welcoming bed covers. She realised she should have bought a nightgown at Woolworth's. There was always tomorrow. Within minutes, she was sound asleep.

The mirage of Sandra's naked body was carved inside Evil's mind. He emigrated to the bathroom, treasuring the unveiled mental image of the woman sleeping soundly on the other side of the door and jerked off rapidly to let the pressure off in his brain and body. Then he took a shit. Waited quarter of an hour sitting on the toilet after he'd flushed to allow the smell to evaporate. He didn't want it to move back with him to the bedroom.

Finally, he got into bed with great delicacy, taking care not to disturb her and settled at opposite poles from her, as far as he could be without falling off the side. He was naked, too. He was not in the habit of wearing pyjamas, although tonight he felt he should, to shield Sandra from his massive nudity. Sleep was difficult to come.

His mouth was dry, as he listened to the steady sound of her breathing across from him.

More images assaulted him. How Teddy Caliban had humiliated her by getting her to sit spread eagled on the chair and Evil had been hypnotised by the dark line of her slit behind the thick curls as she did so. The look on her face as that bastard Caliban entered her from behind. Served him right. Should have cut him slower, made him suffer more, Evil reckoned with regret.

Sheltered between the mattress and his body, his erection unfolded again. He touched himself, to relieve the need, inhaling Sandra's faint scent. The bed groaned under him.

In her sleep, Sandra moved round, now facing him. One breast had rolled loose from the bed cover. Somehow sensing his warmth on the far side of the hotel bed, she inched nearer to him. Evil heard her move ever so closer and lay quite motionless.

In Sandra's dream, poets and drunkards mingled and the events of the last few days blurred together in the wrong order, the lack of logic of the sequences unfolding and extraneous characters from her past or even nowhere blending in to the storyline quite effortlessly until nothing made sense any more. The black kids on the Greyhound, the blood pouring down on her in Miami, turning round to see the face of the dead man impaling her and recognising Jacob the Englishman, buying switchblades at Woolworth, and a woman with flaming red hair but no face laughing at her like crazy while returning her omelette and hash browns because they were too salty.

She tossed and turned several times until she reached the warmth. Her hand draped itself across Evil's hulking body. The dreams faded slowly. Her movements had pulled the blanket away from the top of her body and the coolness of the silent air conditioning seeped through her consciousness. She instinctively brushed her arm down to pull the blanket back and her hand made contact with Evil's hard jutting penis. She was already hovering on the borderlines of sleep. She awoke. Opened her eyes. Saw where her hand was.

'I'm sorry,' she said. She could see his eyes shine dully in the room's penumbra.

'No, I'm sorry,' he blurted out. 'It's me.'

'No, really,' she said. 'I didn't realise I'd moved across so far.'

'It's difficult,' Evil explained. 'Being so close . . . You're such a beautiful woman, you see and . . .'

'No, I'm not. I'm very ordinary,' she said.

He reached out for her face, as if to silence her lips.

'No,' Evil whispered tenderly. 'It's just that . . . it's you that I want to kiss.'

His hand lovingly moved from her lips to the tip of one her exposed breasts and teasingly circled it.

Sandra rolled back against him and took his cock in her hand. He was big, but she'd known worse. She moved her lips against his and kissed him. At first, he was shy and wouldn't allow her tongue entrance. But she pressed again and he opened his mouth, and their breaths mingled. He tasted surprisingly sweet. Some men had absolutely foul breath, and those were usually the ones who insisted on burying their tongues in her throat. She wrapped herself around the big man's bulk. He was soft all across. Her free hand caressed his bare scalp and she felt a tremor rush across the thick cock she held in her other hand. Sandra raised herself above him and opened her legs wide to straddle him.

Then lowered herself on to him.

*

In his studio, the disc jockey was pensive. He had another hour before his next shift on air. There was nobody anchoring right now. Just two hours of non-stop music. He needed the rest. The world outside was a burden. The crazies seemed to be in control. When people rang through, he could feel all the anguish and the pain that surrounded them. And it hurt.

He wanted to help, but he was no longer sure if he could make a difference.

Once he had believed in the saving nature of the music.

But even that seemed contaminated these days.

You just couldn't be sure.

Sure, out there, they needed guidance, but did they really listen to him as he spun his wisdom and his records? Did they actually believe in his existence. Was he more than a disembodied voice waltzing along the country's airwaves punctuating the suffering and the fleeting joys of the lost?

But then, when the red on-air light went on, he threw himself wildly into the job and gave of himself like a latter-day saint, body and soul, with no holding back. Transmitting into the wilderness, he could feel alive again, immortal. The nagging doubts receded and certainty was absolute and every word he shouted into the microphone was another word, another sentence thrown into the face of God. By the Mark, the Mark of God.

Truly, yeah.

*

They were lazing in bed, still exhausted by the previous day's excesses, when the phone rang around late morning, interrupting their respective silences.

'Who can it be?' Jacob said. 'No one knows we're staying here.'

'Probably O'Neal . . .' Anne ventured.

'But you told me . . .'

'I told you I wouldn't sleep with him again, and I won't. But he's going to help me find someone to buy the diamonds.'

'You didn't tell him about them, did you?' Jacob protested.

'No, of course not. Just told him I had some jewellery I wished to sell. Nothing more.'

The phone rang again, its red light flashing.

Anne picked it up.

'Hi . . . Yes, very well . . . No, we're still in bed . . . Rebecca sends her love, Jakey . . .' He made a silly face at her in response while she went on speaking to d'Ath. 'Corner of Barracks and Bourbon, yes, we'll be there . . . Hum . . . Hum . . . Fine. See you there.' She put the phone down.

'Well?' Jacob asked.

'There's a man he wants me to meet. He says I can trust him. Tonight around ten o'clock in some private club.'

'Am I invited, too?' Jacob queried, a look of annoyance over his face.

'Of course, you are, Jakey. Apparently, it's a place Rebecca performs at some times. She'll be there tonight, O'Neal says.

'She never mentioned anything about it to me,' Jacob remarked. 'What sort of performance, I wonder?'

'From the looks of her, I'm sure it will be educational,' Anne said. 'I wonder if that's why she's shaven?'

'You've got a one-track mind, Anne Ryan,' he said, holding her tight against him. Life was returning to his body.

They spent the rest of the day pretending to be tourists, taking a paddle boat tour to the river's bayous, but returned disappointed at not having seen any crocodiles. They even visited the local Hard

Rock Café at nearby Jackson Square, where Anne enjoyed the best cup of tea she'd had since arriving in America.

From outside, the club looked like any other French Quarter house, with its plant-festooned wrought iron balcony and wooden shutters. Barracks Street was plunged in darkness and there seemed to be no light filtering through the building's windows. Jacob rang the bell and a peephole opened.

'We're meeting Mr d'Ath,' Jacob said. 'He invited us.'

They were asked to wait and a minute later the door opened. A matronly woman took them down a dark corridor to the back of the house which led into a cavernous, high-ceilinged room full of cigarette smoke. It looked much like any other bar, with a small stage at the back and a zinc counter on which a barman was laying out drinks. Chairs were scattered across the room.

'We're here,' O'Neal d'Ath cried out, waving at Jacob and Anne. 'Come on over.'

D'Ath was casually dressed, black shirt and jeans and brightly-coloured waistcoat. Rebecca was sipping a beer from the bottle, her whole body swathed in a heavy bath-robe which reached down to her feet. Jacob guessed she was wearing very little underneath.

The customers' conversation was like a low hum around the bar, reluctantly filling the room's space by default. This was not the usual mood of a group of casual drinkers, Anne recognised. They were waiting for something, smothering their impatience with mindless talk.

'This is a very private club,' d'Ath told them. 'There are only a couple such in town. Very exclusive. The guy who owns it will help you with your stuff, Anne. He's always on the look out for nice jewellery. Collects it. He'll join us later when Rebecca goes on. The shows we put on here are rather particular. No one is a professional, so in a way that doesn't make things completely illegal, I suppose. Just people enjoying themselves. Sometimes things get a bit extreme, but we're broad-minded, aren't we?' he winked at Rebecca.

He filled Anne's wine glass up for the third time. Jacob could feel Anne's rising excitement. Shady, possibly deviant activities seemed to turn her on. The white wine didn't help, either. He knew he was not going to enjoy this evening.

*

In Corpus Christi, the first experiment had failed, Naturally, they were disappointed, but somehow they hadn't expected instant success in their endeavour.

'Our minds are too focused on the act, on our ultimate aim,' one of the businessmen rationalised. 'Maybe we need a catalyst, someone who can channel all the energy in the sheer pursuit of pleasure, and expand it to a higher level.'

The others nodded.

9.

An Unquiet Soul

The lights dimmed and a loud voice from a concealed speaker said:

'And now . . . Rebecca.'

She rose from her chair, throwing back the heavy garment she had been swathed in. What she wore underneath—or what little she wore—was spectacular. She was quite naked apart from an intricately designed network of thin black leather straps and bands crisscrossing her whole body. The flexible leather trestle cut into her bare flesh, wrapping itself around her like strings across a parcel. The bands surrounded her breasts and genitals, obscenely tightening the flesh so that it protruded unnaturally, her white globes forced up, down and forward like square pieces of cold meat and her shaven sex jutted out like a fruit ripe for picking.

The whole effect was enhanced by the fact she had coloured her nipples and the edges of her labia with the same dark purple lipstick that adorned her lips.

She moved slowly toward the small stage, swinging her hips in the secure knowledge that every set of eyes in the room was fixed on her.

Anne gripped Jacob's hand.

'God, she's got guts,' she whispered.

They were unprepared for what might happen next. Surely, Rebecca wasn't about to do a strip act; she was already more than naked. Anyway, she wasn't that kind of woman.

The MC's voice on the speaker echoed again: 'And for our pleasure and edification, here comes Sarah.'

No one applauded.

A blonde woman rose from a nearby table where she had been sitting on a man's lap. Her hair was cut extremely short and she appeared almost boyish. She wore a long white cotton print dress and a studded dog collar around her neck. She hesitantly made her way past the tables and reached the edge of the stage where a spotlight came to life and caught her in its glare.

Rebecca beckoned her up.

A second spotlight came on, bathing the two women on the small stage in searing white light. Sarah seemed incredibly young. Barely out of her teens, although the sunken look in her eyes witnessed the fact she had lost any innocence she might have once possessed. The closely-cropped hair, pale make-up and clumsy posture were designed to foster the impression of youth.

'She has displeased her master,' d'Ath told Anne as his hand moved to fondle her breast. She gently pushed his hand away. 'You'll find this interesting. It's a ritual of punishment. Rebecca's our best whip mistress.'

Rebecca, at least a foot taller than the other woman, fastened a small chain to Sarah's dog collar and led her to the back of the narrow stage, the hot oval spotlights following their movement. A metal pole embedded into the wall extended six foot forward and Rebecca had to reach high to connect the chain to the ring on its extremity. Thus bound to the contraption, Sarah was forced to stand on tip-toe to prevent the dog collar biting into her neck. Rebecca languorously circled her victim, her white skin glistening in the light, and ordered Sarah to stand in a cross-like position, arms extended on her sides, and legs wide open, still uncomfortably tethered to the pole by her neck. Sweat was already pouring down the young woman's face.

The whole room was silent.

Rebecca momentarily left her victim centre-stage as she moved to the wing to retrieve a bag.

She returned with a fierce-looking flick-knife and proceeded to systematically cut Sarah's cotton dress away, piece by piece, unveiling the blonde woman's body in the process. She was not wearing any underwear. She was heavily tattooed, intricate patterns of flowers and Oriental dragons snaking their way across her shoulders and circling her legs. One of the carved monsters' tongue extended to the tip of one of her sunken breasts, as if biting it. Her pierced navel emerged as the heart of a black rose and Jacob found himself fascinated by the spectacle below. At first, he thought she was also shaven, but squinting revealed the existence of a thin curling forest of near-albino white pubic hair, through which her pink slit—

stretched open by her position—was pornographically visible like a line of blood. Extending up from the slit was the trunk of a tattooed black cross, its crossbar heading the almost invisible pubic thatch. The effect was fascinating and Jacob knew he was turned on. Rebecca spinned the woman round so that the audience might enjoy a different view. There was a shocking single tattoo crudely drawn across her back: an anatomically-precise sketch of a heavily-lipped vagina over which the word SLAVE had been inscribed.

Jacob gulped. Looked round at Anne. She was transfixed by the spectacle. D'Ath's roaming hand was now on her knee. She ignored him.

Having displayed her prey, Rebecca called out to the hirsute man in the audience who had sent Sarah forward.

'How many lashes for the bitch?'

'Fifty,' the man shouted back.

'That's really a lot,' d'Ath whispered to his guests. 'She's going to hurt badly.'

'Why?' Jacob asked.

'You know,' d'Ath said. 'Sometimes, the pleasure is worth the pain.'

Rebecca had pulled a whip from the bag and began the punishment. No inch of Sarah's painted body went untouched as Rebecca circled her with the whip and lashed out at regular intervals. The first five blows to her midriff and backside saw the slight blonde woman shudder. The following one bit into her shoulders and the back of her legs. By the twelfth, Rebecca began drawing blood. Fifteen. The mistress of punishment now deliberately aimed at Sarah's breasts and genital area. Twenty-three. Thin lines of blood seeped agonizingly slow from the cut flesh, blending colours with the distorted images of the tattoos. Thirty. Every new lash brought a fierce, brief scream from Sarah's lips. Thirty-two. A particularly cruel blow which caught the side of her neck and the young woman stumbled briefly, losing her balance, her weight solely supported by the dog collar and the chain. Rebecca straightened her out. And attacked again. By now, Sarah was crying, but still not a word of protest passed her lips. In their seats, Anne and Jacob cringed. He knew he shouldn't, but he was desperately hard. Anne's face was flushed as she kept on watching the atrocious spectacle.

D'Ath was counting the blows with relish.

On the forty-first lash, Sarah could no longer overcome the pain and lost control. Urine spurted uncontrollably in a graceful arc, missing Rebecca's crotch by inches. But the young woman somehow remained conscious until the final blow, and Rebecca finally unhooked her and she stumbled down on to her knees, thin pearls of blood like razor cuts across the white expanse of her flesh.

Rebecca proudly stood tall and faced the audience, a thin layer of sweat bathing her whole body and the shining leather straps criss-crossing her.

'Who will pay my price?' she asked loudly.

'She will,' said Sarah's master, pointing to the blonde woman's prone body.

'So be it,' Rebecca said.

'This is her favourite part,' d'Ath said, nudging against Anne. 'Enjoyed it so far?'

'Yes,' Anne gasped, brought back to reality from her trance.

On stage, Rebecca was fixing a monstrous strap-on dildo to her own elaborate leather harness.

'Is she . . .' Anne asked.

'Yes,' said d'Ath.

'But it will tear the woman apart,' Anne protested.

'That's the idea,' d'Ath said approvingly. 'But the punishment must be paid for.'

Rebecca manhandled Sarah into a suitable position and thrust herself into her. The bleeding woman made no sound. Already the audience seemed disinterested.

Jacob had to look away, but Anne, fascinated, kept on watching. Soon, the spectacle came to an end as Rebecca brutally withdrew from Sarah's body. The blood was everywhere, drying against both women's bodies. Rebecca unhooked the implement and cast it aside. The spotlights were switched off.

'Interesting, hey?' said d'Ath.

'Yes,' said Anne.

'Let's go to the back. You have to meet Stan. To talk about your jewellery. Come.'

'I'm coming, too,' said Jacob.

'Fine.'

Rebecca had already showered and was dressing into more con-ventional attire when they entered the dressing-room. There was no sign of Sarah, who had been quickly spirited away by her companion following the public performance. For reasons of safety, Anne had brought only one of the diamonds along with her. Stan, a nondescript middle-aged man with sandy hair and a gold stud in one ear closely examined it, as Jacob, O'Neal and Rebecca milled around them.

'Looks valuable,' Rebecca remarked, slicking her hair back.

'Where did you get if from?' d'Ath asked, but Anne ignored his question.

Finally, Stan pronounced that the diamond certainly appeared genuine, but that it was out of his league. He was at a loss as to where Anne could profitably dispose of it.

'Wrong kind of town,' he concluded, handing it back to Anne. 'This is serious money. LA, New York. Vegas, maybe. Not here.'

O'Neal and Rebecca eagerly invited them back to their mansion, but Anne and Jacob declined and were dropped off at the Burgundy Street inn. The night had gone on long enough.

*

'I have people to see,' Evil said.

Sandra had just had breakfast in bed and was brushing the crumbs away. The strong aroma of the coffee still lingered around the bedroom. He slipped on his grey jacket and handed her a hundred dollar bill.

'We can have lunch together,' he suggested. 'You can do some more shopping.'

'Yes,' she replied. 'I still need some things.'

He walked to the door, turned back.

'Are you okay?' he asked her. 'About last night?'

'Sure,' Sandra replied.

'I didn't hurt you?' he inquired.

'Just a little,' she admitted. 'But I'm fine now.'

'I'm too big for normal women,' Evil said, with a touch of sadness in his voice.

'It'll be fine,' Sandra reassured him, eager for Evil to leave. She needed the quiet, the solitude, to begin thinking again.

She knew he was allowing her a way out. While he was out on his errands she could well leave the hotel and town. But she also knew she no longer wished to do so. He was a thug, she realised, but he also seemed a good man. And those were hard to find. Maybe fate had brought them together. And Jacob.

Evil trusted her. She resolved not to disappoint him. Yet.

She picked up the phone and ordered another full breakfast from room service. She had an ogre's appetite today.

*

'I tell you, Jakey, I was wet. Soaking. I just don't know why I found it so exciting.'

'I agree. There was something fascinating about it. Sick, also.'

'Jesus. What are we turning into?'

'I don't know. It's worrying.'

'There were moments when I wished it was me on that damn stage . . .'

'Playing which part?'

'Either.'

'Christ!'

'She had power up there, flaunting her private parts with such an utter lack of shame. I was jealous. Maybe part of me is rotten to the core but, you see, I'd like to know what it feels to be up there, on parade on a stage, starkers, taunting an audience. Although I don't think I'd have the nerve.'

'How do you know that?'

'Because . . . Listen, Jakey, in Miami there were days when I was so short of cash I thought of accepting some skin modelling job that came my way, but I couldn't stand the thought. Or stripping, even.'

'How did you manage?'

'Don't think badly of me, Jakey. I turned a few tricks . . .'

'Oh, Anne . . .'

'The agency said they had safe, reliable customers. There were only four or five . . .'

'You're not even sure of the number . . .'

'Please. In a one-to-one situation, you just accept it's only sex, a trading of bodies, you even try and enjoy it a bit.'

'Stripping would have been a healthier option.'

'I'm the wrong height. Wrong body size. Do you really believe men would pay money to see me writhe nude, rather than screw me?'

'I would have spent a small fortune in buying lap dances from you, for sure . . .'

'You pig, Jakey.'

'Can we change the subject?'

'Yes.'

'Hotel life and travelling don't come cheap, Anne. My cash will last another week. I've got funds back in England, but it's something of an emergency fund, for when I go back.'

'Were you really thinking of going back?'

'I suppose so. I never thought America would last forever. Long enough for the ghosts to fade away.'

'I'll sell the diamonds. Somehow.'

'How?'

'O'Neal said he'd put me on to some other contacts.'

'When was this?'

'While he was driving us back here. You were at the back with Rebecca.'

'I don't trust him.'

'Do we have a choice?'

'Yes,' Jacob said. 'When he arranges the next appointment, I'll go on my own and see if I can agree a sale for the diamonds.'

'One at a time, Jakey. I'm afraid of drawing too much attention if we tried to sell them all together.'

'You're right.'

'And if all else fails, I can always find a job stripping in one those Bourbon Street burlesque joints . . .'

'Very droll.'

'Matter of fact, you could join me. Loads of places also advertise nude men. We could do a double act. Maybe even fuck on stage? The ultimate live show. Good money there, I'm sure . . .'

'I'm too paunchy,' Jacob remarked. 'I'd likely be banished from the stage to behind the 25 cents shutters of a cheap peep show.'

'I'd pay more,' Anne said.

'What, to see my hairy backside wibble wobble in the full throes of ecstasy? I don't think the crowds would find the prospect very appetising.'

'You fool. Come here and hold me tight.'

She was sitting childlike, cross-legged on the bed, wearing one of his extra large tee-shirts.

'You feel so warm.'

'I know. Only my feet are cold, let's get under the covers.'

'Anne?'

'Yes?'

'Tonight, I just want to hold you. Nothing more. Just to feel you so close, here, with me.'

She looked down.

He smiled.

'Just a normal, healthy reaction to your proximity,' he said. 'Proves that I don't need a whip or blood to develop a hard on.'

He inhaled deeply. Apricot.

*

O'Neal had arranged an appointment with a jeweller at the far end of Magazine Street. A close friend of his family, he had assured them.

As they had agreed, Jacob went alone, taking an old-fashioned bus from the corner of Canal Street. Anne said she planned to stay in that afternoon and relax, read a paperback or magazines.

The place was more like an antiques emporium, with a window full of wooden rickety furniture and a parade of chalk-faced Pierrot and Columbine dolls lined up on series of shelves. There was no jewellery in sight and Jacob hesitated before pushing the store door open to the sound of metal chimes.

'Forty,' the white-haired store owner said, following a lengthy examination of the diamond he had brought along.

'Is that all, forty dollars?' Jacob protested.

'Forty thousand, Mr Jacob. Forty thousand dollars,' the man answered calmly. 'I realise the piece is worth somewhat more, but Mr d'Ath tells me you are seeking a quick sale with no questions asked and that adds a negative premium to the transaction, I fear.'

Jacob was aghast.

And Anne had another five back at their hotel.

Who in hell had she stolen them from?

'I presume you'll be wanting cash?'

'Yes, I suppose so . . .'

'It will only take an hour. A phone call to my banker and he will arrange a courier. We can wait here. I will close the store and we can take drinks at the back while we're waiting,' the man suggested.

'Could I give a call myself. I have a partner. Just to get approval, you understand?'

'Of course.'

Jacob rang the inn on Burgundy Street and asked to be put through to their room. There was no answer. She couldn't be asleep; he knew how loud the telephone was. Maybe she'd gone out to get something else to read. To the Bookstar store on Decatur, or the second-hand shop they'd spotted on Dauphine.

He agreed the deal and waited for the money to arrive.

*

The moment Jakey had left for the appointment, Anne had contacted O'Neal. She explained that she was in bad need of cash and had to raise some fast. Refused point blank his offer to help out, and told him that Jacob must not know.

'I was thinking, maybe, a few shifts at one of those nude girls joints on Bourbon? Where all you have to do is dance. No funny business.'

'Although they all advertise 'bottomless',' O'Neal said. 'The law obliges you to keep a G-string on. It's a bit of a con.'

'Even better,' Anne said. 'I'm sure I can do that.'

'I'd come,' he assured her.

'Just for a couple of afternoons, say?'

'When Jacob wouldn't suspect?'

'Exactly,' she said. 'There's so many of them. Could you suggest any club in particular? You know the Quarter so well.'

'Well, there's the Foemina, near the intersection with Toulouse. Classy. Clean. I know someone who works there.'

'Could you recommend me? Give me an introduction?'

'Of course. His name is Milo. He sometimes supplies working girls for our special sessions. Those pay well.'

'I don't think I'm quite ready for that sort of stuff, O'Neal . . . '

'One day maybe, hey?'

'I don't know . . .'

'I'll call him. Let him know you're coming along.'

'Thanks.'

Milo was waiting for her, seated behind his desk in the manager's office, a younger man than she had expected, wearing a neatly-pressed pin-striped shirt and regimental tie. His hair was combed forward to conceal hints of baldness.

'Why?' he asked her.

'Money,' Anne replied.

'No. I know your type. You're in it for the thrills, aren't you? You want to know what it would be like out there. Am I right?'

'Yes,' she conceded.

'Knew another like you a few years back in New York, also happened to a Brit, a tall lanky blonde. She was bloody dangerous. First time on stage, didn't know what to do and ended up breaking every fucking rule, fingers inserted everywhere. Almost got the place closed down.'

'I'll behave,' Anne said.

'Show me your body,' Milo said.

Anne had expected this and was wearing the stockings and the black lace suspender belt. She bent down and pulled the flowing lightweight dress up to her waist. Did a few turns.

'Good,' approved Milo. 'Pull your pants down,' he ordered.

'O'Neal said it wasn't really bottomless on stage,' she protested.

'I know. But I want to see. Red pussy gives me a kick.'

Anne exposed herself.

'Appetising,' Milo said. 'You're a bit short, though. You'll have to wear very high heels; makes the dancing difficult. Anyway, everything has to come off for the one-to-one sessions at the back. The wider you open up for the punters, the better the tips. Don't worry, you don't have to put out. That's the line we don't cross.'

'I see,' Anne said.

'You can pull them up,' Milo said. 'I've seen enough. I'll give you a test to see how you perform. You'll have to borrow an outfit from one of the girls, they won't mind.'

He rose from his chair.

'Come, you can stay at the bar and watch the others for an hour or so. It'll give you an idea of the routines and what the guys like. Then you can try it out for yourself. You might prove interesting. You're different.'

She followed him through a warren of corridors to the club's performance area.

'Say, you could wear glasses for your act,' he suggested. 'They'd look good on you. Makes you look even more educated. And sluttish. Men like to fuck teachers, reminds them of school days.' They reached the bar and he instructed the barman to serve her a drink.

On the stage, an opulent Latina was undulating against the central pole. The audience was sparse. It was still mid-afternoon.

*

The thick roll of notes bulging from his wallet, Jacob had returned to their Burgundy hideaway. Anne was still out. No one at reception could recall when she had left. The shifts had changed mid-afternoon. There was no message.

He checked her toiletries pouch; the remaining diamonds were still hidden there. He looked through the cupboard where she had hung her clothes, to try and determine what she might be wearing but his knowledge of her garments was too patchy. The morning *Picayune* was still open on the bed at the sports pages.

All he could do was wait.

Where in hell could she have gone to? He guessed O'Neal and Rebecca's. He didn't know their phone number. Anne had it.

He would give her another hour. Then he would cab over to the Garden District to find her.

*

That morning Evil had spoken to the Man From Caracas. His intuition had been proved right. The two Brits were still in New Orleans somewhere. The rumour on the street was that some foreign woman was trying to sell a very expensive diamond. The prey was getting nearer, but Evil still hadn't tracked down anyone who had actually encountered Anne Ryan or the guy with her. Maybe he should spend more time on the trail. But he treasured his lunch with Sandra. Watching her eat was a treat in itself, as she voraciously attacked all the exotic food they served. They hadn't done it again since that first evening at the Sheraton, but Evil was hoping she would be willing to again tonight.

There were too many bars in this town, he reckoned. Too many bar men and bouncers to speak to.

He emerged from Toulouse Street on to Bourbon. The street was filling fast as happy hour approached. The brightly flashing lights of the Foemina Club caught his attention as they highlighted a gallery of faded photographs of voluptuous women in the window. Most of the women pictured must be grandmothers by now, he estimated and it would be their granddaughters actually strutting their stuff inside.

A sad brunette in one of the old photographs reminded him of Sandra and he recalled how she'd kept her eyes closed throughout their time together that night, only opening them again after he had finally discharged with a mighty groan of relief. Then she'd rushed to the bathroom to clean herself up, even though he'd told her she was safe, he'd had a vasectomy some time back.

He needed a drink, anyway. Evil walked into the club. Declined use of the cloakroom. Nodded his approval of the $6 minimum consumption and sat himself at the bar, with his back to the two stages, only one of which was currently in use and ordered a Dos Equis.

The beer was most welcome. He could feel the sweat spreading under his armpits, staining his grey coat. Damn humidity!

'You here for the convention?' the bar attendant casually asked him.

'No. Just a tourist,' Evil replied.

'Having a good time?'

'Yeah ... You've got a nice place, here, friendly sort of town.'

'We like it,' the barman said.

'I was wondering ...' Evil remarked.

'Yeah?'

'Do you get a lot of Brits around here?'

'Sure. We get all sorts. Brits, krauts, Australians, they're really into the spirit of things, especially around Mardi Gras time. They come from all over the place ...'

'Served any Brits here over the last few days?' Evil interrupted him.

'Nope,' he answered. 'But there's that new girl having a try out over there. I think she's English.' He pointed in the dancer's direction.

Evil turned his head round.

The woman on the stage was clumsily undulating her sweetly-shaped white backside, missing half the beats of the music she was supposed to be dancing to. A green sequined string was caught in the crack of her arse as she shook her assets one way and then the other.

'Looks like amateur night,' said Evil with a smirk.

The bored barman had already moved away and was busy serving another customer sporting a convention badge on his lapel.

Evil swivelled across his stool to watch the stage.

The stripper had now turned round and was facing the sparse audience. Her hands roamed over her smallish breasts, teasing the nipples, as she shifted her weight from one leg to another to catch the rhythm of the music. Her face was still partly in darkness as she slithered backward in a awkward simulacrum of sensuality. A black guy sitting at the very edge of the stage beckoned her over, waving a greenback. She hesitantly moved forward, leaned down closer to him and he slipped the bill inside her G-string's loose elastic as she squatted inelegantly on her high heels. She rose and her face was caught in the full glare of the stage's ceiling lights.

The pale features.

The long red hair.

Evil choked on his cold beer.

It was Anne Ryan.

He looked again as she shimmied away from the stage's edge to continue her workmanlike dance number.

The heels made her look taller, but it was her. There was no doubt in his mind about it. Bingo!

What what she doing performing in this cheap joint?

Never mind, he'd find out in good time.

Evil set his glass down on the bar and took a seat by the stage, next to the black guy who had tipped her. This was working out perfectly. He watched her go through her pole routine with more enthusiasm with talent. The black guy applauded loudly. He must have a thing for petite redheads, Evil guessed. Taking this as a cue, the young woman ventured forward again, possibly hoping for another tip before the song ended. She looked down and met Evil's eyes and comic grin.

'Shit,' Anne muttered. 'It's him.' And instantly remembered his name. Evil. Panic invaded her. She glanced beyond him at the room. Where was Teddy? There was no sign of him, though. She looked round, missing yet another beat. Milo was standing there, shrugging at her incompetence.

Evil began to rise.

Without waiting for the music to end, Anne rushed frantically to the back of the stage and threw herself down the corridor that led to the dressing-room. The next performer, a mulatto girl called Victoria who had loaned her the stripping outfit, was standing in the doorway and she brutally shoved her aside.

'Hey, girl, take it easy now,' Victoria protested, but continued to make her way to the stage where she was now expected for the next act of the club's burlesque assembly line.

As Anne ran from the stage, Evil quickly put his bulk into gear and ran in her direction, only to find Milo obstructing his passage.

'You stop right here, man,' the club's assistant manager said.

Evil tried to force his way past him and a struggle ensued. Noticing the fight, several men in the audience quickly rose and beat a hasty retreat from the club. This was not a place they wished to be found in should the cops have to intervene.

Milo was surprisingly agile for someone so much smaller than Evil. A slippery customer who escaped Evil's initial holds and even managed to kick him violently in the shins. Brute force quickly prevailed, though and Evil soon brushed Milo away, having summarily broken his collar bone in the process. But by the time he found the dressing room, Anne had already had time to seize her dress and locate the back exit. She emerged into the dusk wearing the sequined G-string and nothing else. A couple of black kids who were drinking hooch in the alley whooped and hollered as she ran by them, pulling the dress down over her head and rushed out into the thick crowds walking up and down Bourbon Street.

When Evil reached the alley, the kids pointed him in the wrong direction.

'She went that way, man.'

Anne's heart beat wildly as she ran towards Barracks through the labyrinth of drunkards and sightseers weaving their way from bar to bar. She suddenly realised she was shoe-less, when she trod on a small piece of glass. The pain knifed its way through her body, changing the adrenaline to sheer fire.

She stopped, found a gap in the crowd and sat herself down on the kerb to pull the piece of glass out of her foot. She was bleeding. She tried to steady her nerves. People were giving her strange looks; her dress was wide open on the side, she had forgotten to zip it up in her flight from Teddy Caliban's acolyte. She looked back several times in the direction she had come from, as she hurriedly adjusted her dress. But there was no sign of him. There were so many people milling around that it was easy to lose one's self. She allowed herself a sigh of relief.

She rose and continued down Bourbon. She had left her handbag at the Foemina Club. She didn't have a cent on her. Burgundy Street was in the other direction. She couldn't go back yet. Maybe they were waiting for her there. Evil and Teddy. She wanted to phone Jakey. To warn him. But maybe it was already too late.

New Orleans' gaudy night surrounded her completely. She was lost in this alien city. She felt like crying.

An hour later, she walked into a crowded bar on the corner of Barracks and Decatur, opposite the now-closed market where only this morning she and Jacob had shopped for garlic-flavoured pistachio nuts. There were several men at the bar. She waited until a seat became free between two of them and slotted herself in. The guy on her right barely glanced at her. The younger one on her left could at least manage a smile. Here we go, she thought.

She ordered a stiff drink.

'Hi,' she said to the man. 'I'm Anne. I'm from England. Listen, I need a favour. My handbag was stolen on Bourbon Street. I need a quarter or whatever the phone requires.'

'It's a rough town,' the guy said and dug into his pocket for a handful of coins which he gave her.

'Thanks ever so much,' Anne said.

'They have a phone over there,' he pointed her in the right direction.

There was no answer from their room. The hotel said Jakey had been out since late afternoon. His car was no longer in the inn's car park. Did she wish to leave a message? No. Anne felt cold fear pouring over her. The Miami thugs. A wave of despair flowed across her despairing mind.

She returned to the bar. The young guy was still there.

'Any luck?' he asked her.

'No,' she blankly said.

What now? She couldn't even afford the drink she'd ordered and consumed and already she thirsted for another to blank the terror from her mind.

'Can I offer you another drink?' the young man offered.

Oh well.

'Thanks, that's really kind of you,' Anne replied, forcing a tired smile on to her lips.

'I've never been to England,' he said. 'I hear it's quite beautiful.'

'Yes,' she said, nursing the vodka she'd asked for. Without orange it tasted fierce.

'Is it your first time in America?' he continued.

Here we go, she thought.

'Listen,' she said to him. 'Let's cut the small talk.' He looked at her uncomprehendingly. 'Do you have a car?'

'Yes. I do,' he replied.

'I'll make you an offer. Drive me as far away from here as you can manage and I'll do anything.'

'Anything?'

'Yes.'

He agreed.

'You're on, babe. When?'

'Now. Right now.'

'Let's go, then.'

The real estate sales associate fortunately had little imagination and several hundred kilometres only cost her a couple of blow jobs and a perfunctory screw. What the hell, Anne reckoned, another man won't make any difference at this stage of my life. What her husband didn't know wouldn't hurt him, would it? He couldn't kill himself again, could he?

10.

Frail My Heart Apart

D'Ath and Rebecca didn't arrive home until dawn. Jacob had spent the night outside the large Garden District house waiting in his car, the creeping cold slowly chilling his bones. He'd rung the bell several times, even though all the lights were off. Just in case. But there had been no answer.

He tried to stay awake, spying on the empty mansion, waiting for the couple and Anne to return from some orgy or other. He was certain she was with them. There was that crazy look in her eyes when she spoke of lust. Of sex. She just couldn't stay away, could she? He knew it was time to cut her adrift, let her float away into his past. The relationship made no sense any longer. This was not the way to forget Lynda, whoring and chasing excess along those mythical American highways. Romantic gestures were not what they used to be. He was way past teenager stage, surely. But then he if he lost Anne now, what remained? Losing one great object of lust was bad enough, but two was pure negligence.

Sure, he could forgive her, a wonderful gesture. But then Jacob also guessed Anne wouldn't even crave forgiveness. She was following her own sordid and carefully mapped-out road to some form of private hell. He was just a passenger along for the ride. A mere hitchhiker caught up in her turbulence, in the hypnotic wake of her white skin, cabalistic freckles and silken flame hair.

Which left him absolutely nowhere.

The colours of the sky shifted outside as cloud formations aligned themselves for the coming of dawn.

He was partly dozing when he heard the car's wheels crunch on the gravel drive. A metal blue Range Rover was drawing up along-side him.

Rebecca alighted. Noticed him sitting inside the parked vehicle.

'It's Jacob,' she said aloud to d'Ath who was still in the driver's seat.

Jacob opened his window.

'We were wondering who it could be,' she said to him.

D'Ath waved at him as he moved to the Range Rover's back door and opened it.

Two small children. No more than four or five years old climbed out, helped to the ground by d'Ath.

'How nice to see you, Jacob. By the way, you've never seen our twins, have you?' Rebecca said.

There was no one left inside their car.

The children looked at him with curiosity.

'This is Jacob. He's a good friend,' d'Ath explained to them, as he walked with them to the front door.

'Come along,' Rebecca suggested. 'Let's go inside. It will be warmer. Have you been waiting for us long? It's dreadfully early . . . Hasn't Anne come along with you?'

'No. She couldn't,' Jacob answered following them to the kitchen. 'Are they your children?' he asked.

'Of course,' she said. 'They'd been staying up in Baton Rouge with their grandparents for the past week. We'd missed them so much, hadn't we, O'Neal?'

'Awfully,' he confirmed. 'But their kindergarten term begins to-morrow so we had to bring them back.'

The last time they'd seen Anne was when they had dropped her and Jacob at their Burgundy Street lodgings the other evening. Though, d'Ath revealed, she had called him on the phone, wanting some information about a club on Bourbon. Hadn't said why.

'I'm sure she will be back soon,' Rebecca told him, pouring cof-fee. 'Probably met some people and went on a bar crawl. You know how New Orleans is. You shouldn't worry, Jacob. She's probably sleeping it off already in your hotel room.'

He rang through. She wasn't.

'How did it go with that diamond of hers,' d'Ath inquired, chang-ing the conversation.

'Fine. Absolutely fine,' said Jacob. 'He gave me a very good price.'

'Anne will be delighted when she finds out,' d'Ath said.

'I suppose so,' Jacob replied. Then, 'What was the name of the club she asked you about?'

He was standing outside the Foemina half an hour later. It was closed. The refuse lorries were picking up the debris of the previous night's drinking and the plastic-booted municipal workers hosing the sidewalk clean of beer and vomit. The early sun rising above blended the smells of beer and puke as it reached the pavements. The stench was nauseating.

*

Evil was furious with himself. He just hadn't been fast enough. The surprise of discovering Anne Ryan baring her butt on that stage had slowed his thought processes. He should have grabbed her the moment he recognised it was her clumsily shaking those small tits at the club.

A try out the barman had said, he remembered.

Needed cash, maybe? Didn't want to trade the diamonds for fear of raising the organisation's attention?

Stripping was probably easier than whoring. Especially in a town like this with its hundreds of bars and joints. Anybody could find a job entertaining drunks. They didn't know the difference between crap corner and a quality strut.

Later today, Evil knew that he would have to do the grand tour of the burlesques, although he felt confident that the Ryan bitch was already miles away. Had to make sure, though.

On the bed, Sandra was reading a Harlequin bodice-ripper.

He had to let her know he would be out all day. Not back until late at night. He hadn't told her about the near thing on Bourbon. No need to worry her.

But what about the English guy? Maybe he was still around. She might have ditched him in her haste to leave town.

'Sandra?'

She set the book down.

'Yes, love?'

She'd never called him that before, he knew. A warm glow spread across his scalp.

'Tell me about the guy, Jacob? Everything you can remember, what he looks like, how he dresses?'

'Why?'

'Remember, that's why we're here. I'm paid to find that woman of his.'

*

Yes, they remembered Anne at the Foemina, sure they did. Because of her Milo had bloody well landed in hospital. And Victoria had bruises the size of Oklahoma on her shoulder and thigh. Not very appetising for the customers, was it?

They explained how this brute of a man had rushed at her and fought with the day shift manager.

'But what was she doing here?' Jacob asked.

'I don't know,' the bouncer said. 'I'm only here today because Milo is out of commission. Wasn't here yesterday. She was some friend of Milo's, I think.'

It was an explanation, but it made no sense.

Jacob drifted off.

Evil walked on by on the opposite pavement, shielded from him by a bunch of rowdy conventioneers, unaware of his presence. Sandra just wasn't that good at describing people.

Both spent the next seven hours searching for Anne, tramping around the Quarter, never quite meeting, tracing the spidery pattern of a hesitation waltz across its busy, narrow streets. Oyster bars. Clubs. Designer boutiques. Thrift shops full of glad rags. Restaurants. Tourist gift shops. Ice cream parlours. Juke joints. Sex shops. Antique stores. Praline manufacturers. The Voodoo Museum. Picture frame shops. Straight bars and gay bars. The Orgy Room. All-hours grocery stores. Doll shops.

There were redheads in abundance. But every single one had the wrong face, the wrong shape, the wrong name. The two men even had drinks in the same bars twice during their peregrinations, less than half an hour apart. Jacob was paying for his coke, no ice, when Anne rang the inn on Burgundy and left the message. It would be hours before he found it.

His feet were killing him. He hadn't walked this much in ages.

He didn't even know any longer where he was going, in which direction he was more likely to find her. Left, right, here, there. Just had no clue. Remembered his first month of mourning for Lynda, revisiting all the places they had visited in London, the Soho Square park bench, the hotel bar, the pub where they met at lunch time, the coffee bar across the road, the mystery book shop where she bought all her reading. Turned in his tracks and headed down toward Jackson Square to the Café du Monde, where just a few days before Anne and he had enjoyed their first New Orleans breakfast. Yes, a sickly sweet doughnut buried in powdered sugar would do him just fine.

Every table under the canopy seemed occupied. He stood there, deflated, searching for a free chair.

'Jacob!'

A woman's voice.

Not Anne's. She always called him Jakey anyway. American.

He looked at the centre table where she was. Didn't recognise her at first. She waved at him.

Christ, the waitress from the Miami Greyhound station. What was her name? Sandra. Yes, Sandra.

'Jacob, I've found you,' she said, indicating the empty chair next to her.

'Hi. This sure is a coincidence,' he said.

'Maybe,' she replied with an odd smile on her face.

'Never thought I'd see you here,' he told her. Thinking he'd never thought he'd even see her again.

'Well, you did say you were planning to visit the Big Easy,' Sandra said as casually as she could manage. 'I had some time on my hand and thought why not?'

'Why not, indeed?'

'It's a great place, isn't it?' she said.

A short oriental waitress came to get his order. Sandra asked for an extra serving of doughnuts.

'Been here long?' he asked her.

'Just a couple of days . . . You?'

'The same.'

'Back in Miami . . . you mentioned you had a girlfriend. Is she with you?'

'No. I think she's left. Here. Me. It's a bit complicated to explain.'

Her heart lifted at the news. Maybe now Evil would ignore him. Let him go. With that sad face, that land of darkness under his eyes, Sandra thought, he should be a poet.

Her hand ventured across the sugar-covered table top.

'Jacob?'

He looked up from his coffee. The tip of her finger reached his arm. His warmth. What should she say now?

'It's you that I want to kiss,' she said.

He betrayed no emotion.

'That's nice,' he said, his eyes, his heart still distant.

'Sleep with me, Jacob.'

Sandra was about to add, 'Make me a baby,' but the old German couple at at nearby table were now listening to their conversation.

'You don't want me, Sandra,' Jacob replied.

'I do.'

'You don't even know me,' he added.

'I know enough,' she said. 'Anyway, what's knowing you got to do with it. It would just be sex. I'm sure you'd be kind and tender. You're that kind of man.'

'You don't know me,' he repeated.

The German couple moved away, profoundly embarrassed by their eavesdropping.

'Don't you find me at least a bit attractive?'

'Of course I do. But . . .'

'But what?'

Dusk was nearing, strands of pink separating the late afternoon crowds, the brouhaha of the Crescent City was increasing by the minute as its night people came out to play.

'It's just the wrong time, the wrong place, Sandra, you know . . .'

'Will it ever be the right time and place, Jacob?' she gripped his arm. 'I'm not asking for that much, am I?'

'Just a fuck, you mean?'

'That makes it sound ugly,' Sandra remarked. 'Just one night together.'

'I don't know . . .'

'Please.'

Would the touch of another skin make him forget the pale flesh of the lost?

'No woman has ever asked me the way you have, Sandra,' he said.

'So take me.'

There were forks in the road, he knew, but since you could never go back on your tracks, it didn't really matter which one you took on your journey onwards. You'd never discover what you had missed on the road not taken.

'Where are you staying?' he finally asked Sandra.

'Not there,' she said. 'I'd rather go to your place. It will be more comfortable.'

She wanted to hold his hand as they walked back through the heart of the Quarter, but crowds going in the opposite direction kept on briefly separating them. They crossed the human tidal wave flowing through Bourbon Street and the night opened up.

'What a cute place!' Sandra remarked as they bypassed the inn's reception area and took the side door leading to the garden and the bungalows. He already had his room key. As he guided her past the ice-machine to the wooden stairs, she asked:

'Kiss me. Touch me.'

'Upstairs. Soon.'

He saw the red message light flashing on the telephone as he switched the light on.

His heart jumped a beat. Anne? D'Ath?

'Listen, Sandra, I seem to have a message downstairs. Use the bathroom if you wish, I won't be long.'

'Can't it wait?' she protested mildly.

'It could be something important. Business, you know,' he explained.

'Be back soon, then.'

Jacob made his way back to reception, hoping against hope.

MR JONES, ROOM 24

VERMILION HOTEL. PORT ARANSAS, NEAR CORPUS CHRISTI. TEXAS. COME QUICKLY. DON'T CALL. MISS YOU.

ANNE

Sweet relief.

Back in the room.

'It *was* important, Sandra. Very,' he explained to her. 'She hasn't left me. She's in trouble. I have to go to her.'

'But...'

'Now...I'm really sorry. You're a sweet person. I'm sure it would have been good, but it's just not possible any longer. You must understand.'

He was already stuffing assorted clothing he'd pulled out of the recessed closet into a case. She saw the dresses, the lace woman's underwear.

'Yes,' she said with resignation.

'She means a lot to me,' he pleaded.

'But do you really know her?' Sandra asked.

'All too well, I fear,' he answered.

'Her name's Anne, isn't it?'

It didn't strike him as a strange question right then. He'd probably mentioned her name to Sandra back in Miami.

'Yes,'

'Where are you off to meet her?'

'A place called Corpus Christi. It's in Texas.'

He swept through the bathroom, collecting the rest of his stuff.

He settled his bill with hundred dollar bills.

'Can I drop you off somewhere?' he asked her. 'I've got a car. It's in the parking lot.'

'The Sheraton on Canal Street,' she replied.

'No problem. I know where it is.' He picked up his change from the night porter.

'I feel guilty,' he said as they reached the towering skyscraper and she opened her door.

'Don't.'

'Do you need any money, maybe?'

'No.'

He was already revving the engine, eager for Texas.

'Wait,' Sandra said, walking round the front of the car to the driver's side. Then leaned over—his window was open—and gave him a kiss on the left cheek. Jacob smiled and drove off.

'Where have you been all this time?' Evil complained as she entered their room.

'Out and about,' Sandra said. 'How was your day?'

'Rotten. Those two Brits seem to have disappeared off the face of the Earth.'

'Too bad.'

'Tomorrow I'll begin checking the hotels. They must be staying somewhere close. I'll start with the cheaper ones. Don't worry, I will find them. It's only a matter of time.'

*

'What happened?' Jacob asked her. He was exhausted, had been driving for hours along endless highways to get here, the landscape barely punctuated by the passage of seedy motels and semi-abandoned gas stations.

They were sitting in a corner of the bed and breakfast's pool room. Other guests lounged about, huddled on the opposite side of the room.

'This guy recognised me,' Anne explained. 'A thug from Miami. I just don't know how they found out I was staying in New Orleans. But it couldn't have been coincidence. They're after me, Jakey. Because of the diamonds. They're really bad people.'

'I sold the first one,' he told her. 'A lot of money.'

'I managed to give him the slip. I was scared. Still am. Didn't want to go back to Burgundy; I feared they might have hurt you and were there waiting for me.'

'No. I didn't come across them . . .'

'Hitched the first lift I could. Took me all the way to Texas. All I had were the clothes on my back.'

She was wearing a man's flannel shirt and baggy jeans he couldn't recognise.

'I was penniless. Wandering outside on the promenade with nowhere to go. Kirk saw me, came across and offered me shelter. They're all very nice people, Jakey.'

Kirk must be the tall one over there throwing them regular glances. The jeans must be his. Was she sleeping with him?

'I'm here now,' Jacob said softly.

'Thanks.'

'I need to rest, I really do,' he finally said, too weary for any more conversation. Whatever the situation was, he had no choice but to accept it. He'd had no sleep for days.

'I'll arrange something,' Anne said, and walked over to the others to confer.

The room was spartan compared to previous American hotels. He had no clue whether she had been living in it; all her belongings were still in the BMW's boot. In his present state, he didn't wish to ask.

He stripped down to his tee-shirt and slipped between the covers.

'The car keys are in my pocket. You can get your stuff, I brought it all along,' he told her, as she lay down alongside him.

'There's no rush,' she whispered, her fingers wandering gently through his tangled hair. He fell asleep.

'I'll keep you company,' she softly said and cuddled up to him. But for her, sleep never came, only the fear, the faces, the memories. Like a nightmare of guilt that could never end.

*

Sandra dropped her shopping bag on the bed. She'd bought herself sandals and some fancy French perfume.

Evil's sudden blow to her face came as a total surprise.

The pain registered sharply, as her right cheek caught fire. She stumbled.

'Why?' she plaintively asked him. His face was quite impassive.

'Because you have lied to me, Sandra,' he answered. 'And as much as I like you, I can't allow myself to forget the business I'm in. The catching people business.'

'I don't understand,' she said.

'You were seen leaving a hotel on Burgundy Street with Jones, the British guy, the other night. Don't deny it, please. I don't want to have to hurt you more.'

'I...I...'

'He checked out. The night porter saw the two of you. He left in a hurry. Paid in cash. When I asked him to describe the woman, I was convinced it would be the redhead. But there was no mistaking the way he recalled the dress you wore, the one I bought you on Chartres Street, and the way you look. I couldn't believe it at first. Sandra, I need the truth.'

'Yes. It was me . . .'

'Do you ache for him so much?'

'No. It's not like that. He doesn't even want me. I just like him. It's all one way traffic,' she said. 'I swear.'

He believed her.

'How . . . ?'

'It was pure accident that we met again,' she told him. 'At first, I don't think he even recognised me.'

'Where are they now?' he demanded.

The burning in her cheek was subsiding. It had only been a bad slap. Could have been much worse. She'd seen him with Caliban. She braced herself for another blow and said: 'I know where they are. When he left the hotel, he was going to meet her. But I can't tell you, Evil. You can hurt me all you want, but I beg you to give him forty-eight hours grace before you set off after him. Jacob's a good man. He has nothing to do with your business. He's a poet, even if he doesn't know it himself for sure. Spare him, I beg you. It's the girl's fault. You said so yourself the other day. Catch her but let him go.'

'Why?' the hulking thug questioned her.

'Because somewhere inside you there's still some human decency.'

'You're crazy, woman.'

'Forty-eight hours.'

'I must be crazy,' he said. 'Not a minute more. Then you tell me where they are hiding.'

'I swear,' she said with a huge sigh of relief. She didn't think he would even consider her desperate proposal. 'But you'll spare Jacob?'

'As long as he doesn't interfere,' Evil added. 'She's the one I want.'

'Thanks. Really.'

She undid the buttons of her blouse, pulled the floral skirt she was wearing down by its elastic waistband and shed her underwear. She stood naked facing him.

He remained motionless, his massive bulk obscuring the rest of the room behind him.

'This is me,' she said.

'You are beautiful, Sandra,' he replied, the light from the ceiling fixture reflecting on his bald scalp.

'Forty-eight hours,' Sandra reminded him. 'Do to me what you will.'

*

They had all gathered after breakfast around the long wooden kitchen table. Anne, Jacob and all the members of the group. Outside, it was raining and the wind raged.

Anne had no longer been in the bed when he awoke, but was now wearing her own clothes again.

'You're going to think we're all mad, Jacob,' said Kirk, visibly acting as a spokesman for the others.

Jacob sat silently, at this stage giving the motley bunch the benefit of the doubt. They were all watching him, anxious for his reaction. Anne had warned him: 'They want to talk to you'. His life was moving forward in overdrive since Lynda's death, since Miami at any rate, and he felt that now nothing could surprise him. Some of the women were attractive, but they all had that strange expression. A steely gaze that belied fanaticism or something even more disturbing. The skinny bottle-blonde, Julianne, was mechanically twiddling her hair—her roots were showing—clad in a thin bath-robe that gaped open to reveal her sunken breasts. None of the others seemed to notice. He did.

'I have an open mind,' he answered.

'We've all assembled here for a purpose and we wish to ask Anne and you to assist us in our endeavour. Fate has carried you to us, has made you a part of the equation ...'

'What do you want us for, then?' Jacob asked.

'We come from all four corners of the country, but all of us have one thing in common. For over a year now we have been listening to a disc jockey on the radio. He calls himself the Mark of God. He broadcasts from an illegal station, a pirate radio. I know, it makes no sense, no pirate station could transmit all across the continent. It would require relays, covert arrangements with the federal broadcasting authorities. I work in television, I realise that. But he does, we have all heard him, whether in Los Angeles, Cedar Rapids, St Paul, San Diego, Eugene, Sarasota, Portland, Houston, Boulder, Rhode Island, Brooklyn, Charlotte, Scottsdale or Carlsbad. The places where we live ...'

'He speaks to us,' Julianne continued. 'We can phone him on-air, even though he often speaks in riddles. The other thing we have in common is that we are seekers. We all believe there is something else out there, that there's more to life than living ...'

'Sounds like New Age crap, hey?' said Joshua, a balding middle-aged insurance executive from Des Moines. 'Happiness on the instalment plan, a joy supreme on the never-never. But happiness is just what we are lacking. There's a hole inside each of us. I have enough money, a loving wife, two healthy kids, security, all that shit. But still my life is incomplete . . .'

'Most of us have tried all the distractions the world has to offer,' said Toby, who looked like a student barely out of his teens. 'Affairs, excess, drugs, religion, drink, travel. But it always reaches a point when you realise you're running after the wrong solution, that there is perhaps no solution . . .'

'Maybe, you're perhaps asking for too much?' Jacob interrupted them.

Anne had moved to his side. 'Listen to them, Jakey,' she said under her breath.

'Don't you?' Kirk queried.

'It's not the same thing,' Jacob replied. 'I'm always asking for the unattainable. But I'm conscious of the fact. That's the difference.'

'And if you got what you wanted, Jacob,' Joshua asked, 'would it be enough, would nirvana be yours?'

'I don't know,' he said. 'Somehow I never have. The goal posts move. Situations degrade. Happiness turns to shit . . .'

'Exactly,' Rhonda, a teacher from the East Coast pointed out.

The coastal winds battered Port Aransas, faint tremors coursing through the hotel walls.

'So, what can you do about it?' Jacob asked them. 'That's how life is. There's no choice, we accept our lot. We battle on through, do our best, even if it's not good enough. Boring, I know, but what are the damn alternatives? You just seize your meagre allocation of joy, your share of tenderness when it passes by, try and make it last as long as you can. Entropy wins in the end, though.'

'Alternatives?' Julianne laughed.

'We listen to the radio,' Peder from St Paul added.

They were crazy, Jacob briefly decided.

'And the disc jockey tells us there is a world beyond the world,' said Kirk. 'Where things are different.'

Yes, thought Anne, a world where lust had never assaulted her the way it had and where she was a quiet, simple suburban housewife, with a husband who returned home every day on the stroke of seven, a mortgage, dinner parties, and the cool breezes of English summers.

Oh yes, Jacob reflected mockingly, a world where he would be visiting Miami on some business or other and met this pretty tourist from home, and they fucked like rabbits and returned to London together to be happy ever after, with a growing brood of screaming kids, just like in a story book.

'What other world?' Jacob queried.

'The land beyond,' Rhonda replied.

'Beyond death,' said Joshua.

'Which we are planning to reach,' Kirk informed him.

'How? By the 38 bus? Scheduled or charter flight?' Jacob asked.

'You're a sceptic,' Julianne said.

'Did you expect me to be otherwise?'

'Anne said she was willing to assist us,' Kirk pointed out. 'And she insists you be her partner.'

She took hold of his hand and gripped it. Her touch was so warm and soothing. Her pale green eyes pleaded.

'I want to try, Jacob. Please,' she told him.

'Try what?'

'We've been planning our expedition for months,' Kirk said. And went on to explain their wonderfully bizarre plan.

It was all too unbelievable. Like some X-rated science fiction story.

The group believed that the sexual energy released through a series of strong common orgasms would breach the borderline. A chain of little deaths leading to the big one. If they could coordinate the release of their pleasure, it could just work. They all would embrace the moment of oblivion with welcome minds. Apparently, their first attempt had failed. For lack of the right catalyst, a proper conductor. They knew both Anne and Jacob were still closely linked to the dead and could form the bridge they all needed. All they were asking was that the British couple join their next attempt.

'That's the worst justification for group sex I've ever heard,' Jacob joked, but he knew Anne had committed them. At least, it was him she wanted to be involved with, and not Kirk or one of the others. Small mercies and all that.

But it still made little sense to him.

Tonight would be the night.

Later that afternoon, alone with Anne at last, Jacob complained.

'There's no harm in it, Jakey,' she pointed out. 'We'll be doing it together. If all else fails, it'll just be another nice fuck. It doesn't cost us. We've both done worse.'

'Speak for yourself, Anne,' Jacob said, irritated by her compliant attitude.

'And, who knows? Maybe there's something in it. If we get to the other side, we might see all those people from the past, our personal ghosts. We can at last say sorry to them. Obtain the forgiveness we all crave so badly. Exorcise them. Give it a chance, Jakey, please.'

'One way or the other, Anne,' he said, 'when it's done with, we start afresh, okay? We have the money, and the remaining five diamonds. We go north. Lose ourselves. It's a big country. The Miami guys will give up.'

'I was told Vancouver was nice?'

'Rains a lot,' he said.

'We're Londoners. Surely we can get used to that.'

'Let's rest, then. We're putting on a show tonight, aren't we?'

'That's the spirit, Jakey.'

*

Evil was a gentle lover, for all his bulk and violent instincts. Attentive to her comfort, mindful of the comparative fragility of her body. Awkward also, almost childish in his clumsy impatience. Inexperienced in both the giving and taking of pleasure. Sandra had to guide his large hands along the erotic topography of her body, to the weak spots, over the right areas other than her sex. Never had she had to teach a man so much of the language of lovemaking. In a way, she was touched by his relative innocence. The way he tried to conceal the ugly scars on on his back and abdomen from her when he undressed, and shuddered uncontrollably whenever she drew her tongue across the scars before she straddled him. She enjoyed his eager, 'How good was it for you?' questions after every new bout and the glee painted all across his rotund face whenever he managed to get hard again, thanks to her steady ministrations. He had a good heart, she supposed.

Day followed night followed day, as New Orleans outside ignored them.

She ached everywhere, inside all the way to the gut from his abnormal size, outside from the prolonged weight of his body on her.

'It's been forty-eight hours, Evil,' she said.

'I know,' he told her.

'Jacob and Anne are in Texas. Some place near Corpus Christi.'

She hoped they might have moved on by now.

*

They had cleared all the furniture from the small hotel's rectangular dining room. The only light came from tall, fragrant candles set along the perimeter of the room. Anne and Jacob entered. All the others were already there, waiting.

'Conversation is superfluous,' Kirk said. 'Just concentrate on your sensations. The rest will come naturally.'

They all shed their clothes and paired off.

White bodies embraced. Touch. Lips. Fingers. Tongues. The mapping of the flesh began, like a sacred ritual. Limb against limb. Old against young. Like moths to a flame, they came together in the writhing and the secretions.

The storm outside still screamed blue murder, bombarding the Texas coast from high like a squadron of fighter jets from hell, all their missiles locked on to the shoreline.

Julianne and one of the men were locked together just a few inches away and Jacob, still sucking greedily on Anne's hardening breasts, two fingers already inside her, had his eyes locked on the vision of the woman's stretched-open pudenda, as her partner prepared to mount her. Jacob looked away.

Anne moaned loudly, responding to his efforts. Another woman—was it the student from San Diego?—echoed her.

A sea of sighs floated across the room, as the movements became more frantic and the couples unconsciously aligned the rhythm of their thrusts on each other.

Under him, Anne's body was melting in his hands, adhering to his skin like a familiar shroud. She raised her pelvis to meet him.

'I want you inside me,' she said.

He adjusted his angle and advanced.

The fire. The blinding and shocking obscenity of the fit, the jig-saw puzzle of their bodies finally complete. Jacob held his breath. Anne exhaled.

'Yes. Yes.'

Her muscles tightened around him, capturing him in the safety of her soul. He moved. She responded. Again. The lava-flow beginning to move in the heart of his balls. All around the room, the pleasure levels rose, ever faster.

Panting savagely nearby, Julianne dropped her hand on his backside and began fingering him while the speed of his descent into Anne increased. The man in the pairing to their right extended his hand and brushed against Anne's nipples. All the copulating couples were now touching in some way or other, a living daisy chain spanning the width of the dimly-lit hotel room.

Anne and Jacob were almost unaware of the others now, selfishly intent on their hurrying free-fall into their own private abyss, running standstill for the flesh, mouths mated like Siamese twins, gasping, sharing the last few molecules of air irrigating their bodies before the coming explosion dispersed it.

His cock felt as if it was stretching inhumanly, further and further inside her body, hard as iron, worming its way straight through to her heart. I am in love with this woman, he knew. For the good times and the bad times. Until the sundering came. The flow swelled inside him. Her nails dug into the raw skin of his back.

The storm that gripped Port Aransas roared like a mighty herd of mythical beasts around them. Not that they heard it. The only sound inside their heads was the chant of desire unbound, the loud hunger of need. The wetness poured from her. In his mind, he could track the slow ascent of his come through the narrow conduit at the very centre of his cock. The river rose. Anne ran out of breath. Gasped. Her body, shining from the abundant sweat which seeped from every pore and him, shuddered, and her movement against him accelerated, quickly achieving an epileptic urgency.

The surge flowing through her reached him. He retreated one last time, and savagely plunged into her, stabbing her with all the strength he could summon. And let go. His juice spilled inside her, like a dam bursting. She screamed. He groaned with all the energy of despair, trying to summon her name on his parched lips.

They came. Together. Their lungs hungry for air. Their brain cells in total disarray. Their bodies barely held together by the electricity they had just generated.

The room around them no longer existed. Or the world outside. Texas. America.

Cunt and cock joined, they floated in the ocean of oblivion. Abdicated even their humanity. Souls bobbing in the darkness. Maybe this was death, after all. Their inner eyes following the same movie flickering in the distance. The masked usher helped them cross the river that separated them from the screen. The film rolled at the wrong speed. Images jumped. Lynda on the hospital bed, surgeons cutting through into her bloody stomach; Christopher connecting the Vauxhall's hose pipe and closing the garage. Both of them walking hand in hand in a field, behind them the land of death littered with forest-covered mountains. The face of a child. The one who never was. The one both Anne and Jacob knew they had killed.

So, death was no more than just another nightmare.

They opened their eyes, the tide inside them slowly ebbing. Her green eyes peered silently into his dark pupils. He looked back into her. Air returned to their lungs. Both knew this was not the time to speak. They deliberately closed their eyes again. And fell asleep still inside each other, the juices of their passion still bathing their genitals, seeping out slowly on to the battleground.

11.

Love Like A Spasm

I n sleep the ghosts. In light the emptiness.
Anne stirred, her mouth dry, a feeling of lethargy cushioning her
whole body. Warmth behind her. Jakey. Sensations returning, rising from the drowsy depths of her slumber. A tinge, pleasant, undeveloped in her vagina. He was still inside her, embedded softly, his body cradled against hers, his breath breezing on the back of her neck, heavy, regular, almost a snore.

She couldn't move. If she shifted, she would dislodge him and she did not wish to. It was a nice feeling, a connection that was no longer sexual.

She allowed the quietness to sweep over her, abandoning herself to her perception of the small currents of pleasure slowly rising through her insides, as her walls acknowledged the intrusion. Created a modicum of friction through an imperceptible adjustment of her position against him, ever so cleverly digging her bum closer on to the impaling member.

He grunted in his sleep. But remained immobile.

'Jakey?' she whispered.

Still no reaction.

She repeated his name several times.

'Hmmm?' His head moved an inch and his mouth buried itself in her hair.

'Can't you feel it?' Anne said. 'You've been inside me all night. Isn't it wonderful?

'Hmm . . .' he lazily acquiesced.

'Stay . . . PLEASE.' She could sense him about to move. Her muscles tensed, tightened, trying to hold him in. 'Kiss me,' she asked him. She turned her face. His dry lips brushed against her cheek.

'You're warm,' he said.

'Am I?'

His cock grew thicker inside her. She charted its rise as the blood rushed thrillingly back to her erogenous parts. Soon, he filled her again and began moving slowly, navigating her wetness with all the delicacy he could summon.

Neither of them wanted this early morning lovemaking to be brutal or hasty.

'Love me,' Anne said.

'I think I already do.'

He wrapped his hands around her and held her breasts, as his stomach repeatedly slid up and against her rear. Her mind drifted off as Anne willingly succumbed to the hot flush coursing through her body.

'CHRIST!' she heard Jacob shout, snapping her out of the lazy, selfish mood she was wallowing in.

'What is it?' she asked.

He pulled out of her.

'What?'

'The others,' he said. 'They're not here.'

For the first time today she truly opened her eyes. The room was quite empty. The candles had all burned out and disappeared into a bed of dry white wax. Clothing was scattered willy nilly across the large room. But there was no sign of any of the members of the group.

A cold feeling gripped her stomach.

'Maybe they all returned to their rooms?' she ventured.

'And left us here, on our own?'

'Discretion and all that?'

'No,' Jacob said. 'There's something very wrong. I can feel it.'

He was still lying close to her on the rug. They separated and he got to his feet. An eerie silence pervaded the whole room.

He walked to the door and moved into the hotel lobby. Conscious of his nudity, Jacob checked the front door. It was still locked. From the inside. The key just dangled there.

'Anyone around?' he shouted out loud.

There was no immediate response. Anne had emerged from the room and had slipped on a white T-shirt.

'No one?' she queried.

'Not down here.' Jacob replied.

She looked into the large kitchen where, just the day before, they had all greeted Jacob on his arrival from New Orleans. It was empty. She checked the top of the stove for recent activity. Cold.

Jacob climbed the stairs. Anne followed.

None of the bedroom doors were closed. And every single one was uninhabited. 'This is crazy,' thought Jacob hurrying from room to room with similar results.

Anne had lingered behind and came out into the corridor from the second or third bedroom they had checked.

'Their clothes and belongings are still all there,' she said.

'Are you sure?'

'Absolutely. This one was Kirk's. It's quite unchanged from the other day.'

He joined her as she entered the room again. There was only one bed. Albeit a double-sized one. More questions. Now Anne was on her knees, pulling a large suitcase out from the bottom of the closet where shirts and jackets hung forlornly. She opened the case and pulled out a gun.

'What's this?' Jacob asked.

'Kirk's handgun,' Anne said. 'He showed it to me. Told me how it had once saved his life when some carjackers had a go at him in South Central LA.'

'So?'

'So, there is no way he would have gone anywhere without it. He just wouldn't.'

'They must be somewhere. It must be some sort of joke,' Jacob protested.

'Jakey? When we screwed yesterday, what happened to you?'

'I must have passed out . . . Or gone to sleep as soon as I came. It's been a rather tiring week, if you haven't noticed.'

'I didn't fall asleep. I know that, Jakey. I passed out, too. Don't you find that unusual?'

'The whole bloody orgy was unusual,' he pointed out.

But tried to recall the final moments of that wonderful fuck. How the electric pleasure attacked his whole soul and his consciousness had blanked out. No, surely not.

'They've reached the other side,' Anne calmly stated.

'It's not possible.'

'Do you have a better explanation?'

'No.'

'That's what they were seeking. They knew what they were doing.'

'So you really think every one of them is now gambolling in pleasant fields on the other side of death? That they managed to fuck themselves to death, through death?'

'They must have. It was a very serious endeavour for each of them.'

'I still find it difficult to believe.'

'I know.'

They retreated to the kitchen and fixed themselves some food and coffee. Jacob had slipped on a pair of jeans, but Anne still wandered around bottomless, which did his libido no good at all. There was something wonderfully, obscenely sexy about her like this, the white bum and dark red tufts, the shifting swing of her hips as she walked to and from the cooker. Did she even know what it did to him? He sighed.

'Feels funny,' he said.

'What does?'

'Us having breakfast like this. Biting into this toast while you have milk and cereals on the other side of a wooden table. So domestic.'

'I suppose so.'

'Can I ask you something?' he ventured.

'I won't lie. So don't ask questions if you fear the answers,' Anne said.

'The people here ... who were here. You said Kirk invited you in ...'

'I told you already. I was wandering aimlessly on the promenade, by the sea front. Had no place to go. Left my handbag in New Orleans when the thug started running after me, so had no money, well just a twenty dollar bill from the driver who dropped me here ...'

'That was kind of him,' Jacob remarked.

'Well, not really. I had to earn it ...'

'Oh, no, Anne ...'

'Nothing comes free. It was a long drive,' she said.

'Shit. And Kirk?'

'Did I sleep with him?'

'Yes.'

'Not really ...'

'What do you mean, not really. Yes or no.'

'The first night he stayed in Julianne's room. But they asked me to join their second rehearsal for the expedition—that's what they called it—and yes, Kirk was my partner. But it wasn't very good. I was too uneasy and they suggested I call a partner who was better used to me.'

'Me? Is that why you called me here?'

'Not only that, Jakey. You also had the diamonds.'

'I don't believe you, Anne. You sell your body for just a few quid to anyone who does you a good turn, you . . .'

'I told you once, Jakey, you don't own me.'

'But I thought you liked me? I really did.'

'I do,' she replied.

'So?'

'I have a cold heart, Jacob,' she emphasised his name. 'I do bad things. It's just the way I am. It's too late for me to change. You have to accept me that way. Otherwise, it would be better if we parted ways.'

He fell into a lengthy silence.

He felt like crying. But grown men are taught not to.

*

The coastal storm was too strong for Evil to keep on driving through the night. There were no other cars on the road. For Sandra, it was a strange part of the country, a landscape so different from the Tallahassee suburbs where she had been brought up. Felt like being between nowhere and nowhere.

The neon lights of the motel beckoned to them and they pulled up.

Evil fell into conversation with the night clerk. Yes, a couple had stopped there—when was it?—a couple of nights ago, the guy clearly remembered. The woman was definitely a Brit, but he didn't think the guy was, had a local accent.

Evil asked for the same room.

'I smell her still,' he said, wandering through the anonymous motel bedroom, sniffing away at the air.

Sandra did likewise, but no odour caught her attention.

Evil pulled the bed cover off the bed and buried his nose in the pillows and sheets.

'Apricot,' he declared, with a broad grin on his face. 'That's what the bitch smells of. I remember now.'

'I can't smell anything,' Sandra said.

'You've spent too long in greasy diners,' he told her. Then, speaking to himself, 'We're getting nearer, Miss Anne Ryan. Soon, very soon.'

But, later, when she visited the bathroom, she felt she could just about catch a whiff of fruit in the air. It bothered her all night long, as Evil slept soundly at her side. By morning, she could smell the British woman's scent everywhere. It gave her a bad headache. Jacob, she could smell nowhere.

*

Purgatory time in Radio Land. That time of night when the DJ knew that no one was listening. Who'd bother at such an ungodly hour? When he could play many of his old favourites twice in a row if he wished to, or even a whole album by the same group or artist.

The red light over his console came on.

'Hello night birds, this is the Mark, your jolly old Mark of God speaking to you from the twilight zone, where all your fears come alive, the mermaids sing and the beat goes on. And on. And on. This is Gary Heffern singing *God Your Hello*. Listen to the words; they're only words but every one counts. Listen . . . '

The music faded up. Mournful, leaping from the transmitter into the sweet ether, spreading wings across the continent, skimming over deserts, lapping coastlines, tiptoeing between highways and interstates, dancing like a firefly, gonzo rock 'n' roll patterns through forests, lakes and plains, controls aimed at the heart of the darkness beyond.

He inserted another CD into the player. Terry Allen's *Juarez*, a C&W operetta of love, booze and knives on the Mexican border, he was particularly partial to when his mood ran to blue. He programmed every single track. The broadcast was now on automatic pilot.

His disciples were gone and still, he didn't know the truth. They had left him behind. Made the passage, leaving him in the dark. Were they gone forever or maybe nearer to him now? He could only guess. But life went on: he spun the discs and people still played the game of life. Not very well. His mental antennae were stretched out. Distant vibrations reached him: bad things about to happen, pain and a shocking melancholic journey unfolding with all the inevitability of a road crash. He should be communicating with them. Warn them somehow. But the lassitude was becoming infectious. He knew this time he would say nothing. Let the drama unfold in all its sordid detail: small-time passions, easy options, puppets all.

On the other side of the thick glass, a relief engineer was reading the sports pages of yesterday's newspaper. The Mark rolled his seat back from the console and rose. He opened the drawer where he usually kept medication, biscuits, chocolate and aspirin and pulled out the gleaming gun he'd kept there for weeks.

A Beretta. Illegal.

He pulled his promotional sweatshirt over his head and undid his trousers. Soon he was standing naked at his broadcasting console. The engineer still hadn't lifted his nose from his reading.

He sat down again, waited for the record to come to an end. Not long now.

As the final chords played themselves out, he lowered the microphone to his mouth.

'That was Terry Allen. This is the Mark. This is the sound of farewell . . .'

He placed the gun's nozzle inside his mouth and pulled the trigger. The bullet sped through the top of his mouth, shattering his teeth, gathered momentum, impacted against bone and raced through the soft tissue of his brain before exiting through the back of his head. What was left of his face slumped over the microphone, causing feedback.

He was now in the land of the dead.

The engineer finally raised his head.

*

Jacob was angry with Anne. Normal conversation seemed useless. Her answers had a logic he couldn't accept. Damn it, he knew he loved this woman. How many more was he going to love and lose, or have betray him. Time was running out. Maybe Anne was the final one, his last chance. So he had to hang on. Accept the bad with the good, balance the pain with the joy.

'Sometimes, I don't understand you,' he said.

She took her empty plate to the sink. His eyes followed the dance of her arse cheeks as she moved and leaned over to wash the dirty utensils. The darker line of her cunt opening was clearly visible through the protruding hairs.

He angrily swept the breadcrumbs and table mats to the ground and called her.

'Come here, Anne.'

She looked round, recognised the need in his eyes and approached.

He took her by the waist and pulled her up on to the breakfast table.

'Here?'

'Yes.'

She slid herself backward and stretched out so that only the lower half of her legs was hanging over the edge. Jacob unzipped and straddled her.

'Just like a James M Cain story?'

'Why not?'

He wanted to hurt her. He felt like tearing her apart with his vengeful cock, scratching the pale skin of her stomach and drawing blood. But he couldn't and the geometry of affection soon overcame him again. He knew she'd let him. Her eyes said, 'Dig inside me, crucify me, punish me, make my tears pour' and her passive limbs welcomed his violence, almost sought it. Once in her, though, his attack crumbled and her rapid wetness turned the assault into a more gentle conjugation of mutually satisfying movements. That was his problem, he just cared too much. Sexual anger too easily gave way to feelings. One day maybe, he would become accustomed to the art of the blind, unfeeling fuck. But this was not the day.

Later.

'Friends again?' Anne asked.

'Haven't we always been?'

'Thanks, Jakey.'

They were tidying up what had been the orgy room, gathering the clothing of all the missing people. Anne was tidy by nature. She carefully folded each garment in turn before placing them into three separate piles. One for the skirts and dresses, another for the trousers and shirts, the third mixed both male and female underwear.

'How meticulous,' Jacob remarked.

'The man I lived with back in London always kidded me about my sense of order and organisation.'

'I'm not surprised.'

'When I married him,' Anne revealed, 'I worked as a copy editor for a special interest magazine. Some people would find it boring, but I enjoyed the work, the maniacal precision required in checking facts, proof-reading the same copy over and over. He wanted me to leave the job, stay home, start a family, but I was happy in my job. Of course, I had aspirations . . .'

'You've never talked about your past . . .'

'Because there wasn't much to say. Or I had nothing to say. In my heart, I always wanted to be a writer, but whenever I attempted to start a story, I found I could invent stories, but I had no message to convey. Everything turned out derivative . . .'

'A writer . . . I hope I don't end up as a character in a future story . . .'

'Don't worry, I don't think there will be future stories, Jakey. I gave up on it a long time ago.'

'Why?'

'Difficult to explain . . . Seeking ideas, I began to watch people more intently. I tried to second guess what lay behind their faces, what their lives were all about. What they were thinking, why they looked, dressed the way they did. And I quickly realised that I didn't give a damn about the women. I'd never had many girl friends when I was younger. No, it was the men who began to fascinate me. There were so many out there. And soon every one of them seemed more interesting than my career-orientated carbon copy husband at home. I watched them, on the train, in the street, in pubs. I began wondering what they would look like unclothed, how much hair they would have on their chests, how big their cocks might be, how it would be feel to be touched by some of them. Kissed—I began sucking mints several times a day, to keep my breath fresh, you see, in case. Screwed. I surprised myself by the boldness of my thoughts . . . '

Anne fell silent.

'What happened?' Jacob asked.

'At first nothing more than guilty reflections. Had to go to Wales for business one day. Was introduced at a reception to this man who worked, fairly high up, in local government. Shared too many drinks with him. We flirted, I suppose. Before the evening ended, he whispered his hotel room number to me. I didn't go, but I was up all night speculating. All the ifs and buts. He was dark and good-looking, different. Nothing happened that night but something inside me knew I was capable of lust, of betrayal . . .'

'And?'

'The next time, I went over the edge. There was a man. We did become lovers. At first I had no guilt about what was happening. It was wonderful. The sex was like something new, as if I'd never had sex before, done it right. But those things don't last, do they?'

'What about your husband?'

'He's dead.'

'How?'

'Nothing,' Anne replied. 'Life.'

Jacob knew it would be better not to probe further. The hurt was still there, floating quietly under the thin surface of things, ready to burst through on the slightest pretext. He was well aware of hurt. He was a past champion of the discipline.

But, having completed her domestic chores, Anne continued:

'I no longer look at men that way, Jakey. I have lost that curiosity. But now they see me. As if the experience has somehow changed me and I now appear different to them. They glance my way and they see a woman who has known lust and they greedily demand their share of it. I can't give them my soul, so I lend them my body. It's a fair trade. It doesn't commit me. Just empty experiences, because none of them ever manages to fill my need. Oh, I'm talking nonsense ... Don't you feel that way, sometimes, that you always want more? I don't mean money or possessions. Like there's a hole inside you and you have to fill it. Even if it means degrading yourself even further or badly hurting others in the process ...?'

'Yes, Anne, there are times you hurt. I can vouch for that.'

'Because you're too sentimental, Jakey. We're both too old to be romantics.'

She stood.

'Time to get out of here,' she said.

'I agree,' he replied. 'Too many ghosts littering the place. We'd better move on.'

'Listen, Jakey. I feel comfortable with you. Safe. If you can put up with me, accept what I am, then fine. We can stick together. If you'd rather split, that's fine with me, too. We can share the cash you got in New Orleans. You wouldn't be out of pocket with what I've cost you so far ...'

'Trying to pay me off, Anne?' he joked. 'It'll cost you a lot more than that to get rid of me.'

'Great,' she said. 'So where do we go?'

'South, we're talking Mexico; north, California, or beyond.'

'Las Vegas is north, isn't it?'

'Yes.'

'That should be the best place to dispose of the other five diamonds.'

'I reckon so.'

'We'd have a believable motive to start off loading them without calling attention to ourselves. Anyway, I hear that in Mexico the water invariably gives you the runs. Not my cup of tea. I reserve my right to judge when the time is right to sell the diamonds, though.'

'And then?'

'Then we'd have enough fuck-you money to do whatever pleases us. Caribbean. Asia. Maybe Europe. The world's our oyster. Fuck-them money. No more worries.'

'It's your money, Anne.'

'While we're together, it's as much yours, Jakey.'

'That's the nearest I've had to a proposal,' he smiled at her.

'Indeed,' she confirmed.

'Vegas,' he said.

'There's not much to pack. Most of our stuff is still in the car. Let's just clean up first and then be on our way.'

'Deal,' he agreed.

*

They bought a map at the first gas station they came across and chose the best route to Las Vegas, carefully avoiding major cities and main roads past Lubbock.

There were passes through the Rockies well south of Albuquerque. At this time of year, there would be no snow, they guessed.

'Ever been to Vegas?'

'No, but I've seen the movies.'

The desert stretched forever. Punctuated by a lunar landscape of yellow fields, telegraph poles, and the central uninterrupted line of the blacktop unfurling under their wheels. Once you've seen a John Ford vista of orange, crumbling hills and mesas, you've seen them all. Come back, Thelma and Louise, all is forgiven. As Anne couldn't drive, the onus was on Jacob to stay awake. The sheer monotony of the drive didn't help, nor the poverty of their small talk. How did she manage to fall asleep so much, abandoning him to the thrill of the road too often?

To keep himself awake, he timed the distance between roadhouses and fuel stops, never fully filled the tank to make the pit stops more frequent. Got into the habit of buying a few dollar's worth of beef jerky at each new roadside store, which he chewed on as he drove on.

'That looks disgusting, Jakey. It really does,' she remarked.

'Not at all. It's quite nice, in fact. Like beef chewing gum.'

'Yechh . . .'

But the chewing kept his senses alive as they plunged deeper and deeper into the surrounding mountains and Anne damn well conveniently fell asleep again.

One night found them in yet another Best Western motel close to Tucson, but the coffee bar was closed and they were recommended to a roadhouse down the highway. It turned out to be a giant barn of a place, with a bar the length of a football pitch, burgers the size of Mount Everest and every variety of beer under the sun. Most of the men wore ten gallon hats and looked like they could shit bricks with their eyes wide open. A fiddle band set up on one of the two stages, and most of the couples deserted their tables to assemble on the dance floor. The line dancing was exquisite to watch. Even the ugliest dancers had grace and elegance as they moved to the plaintive C&W tunes, sliding across the floor in unison, hand in hand, with the fluidity of pouring water.

'Wouldn't you like to able to dance like that, Jakey?'

'They never taught those steps to me at school, I'm afraid '

After the band's set, the majority of the couples returned to the seating area. Whoever was in charge of the music put on an R&B tune. Anne shot out of her seat.

'This, we can do, Jakey. Come.'

He followed her with great reluctance to the vast dance floor. They were obviously strangers here, looked and dressed the wrong way. Apart from the fact he was not keen on dancing right now, he didn't wish to attract any undue attention. The moment Anne started moving her compact body to the rhythm of the song's loud brass section, his intentions were well defeated. It was as if all the tensions of the days since he had first seen her dance in the Miami club were being jettisoned as she threw herself into the music. He kept her company in the most minimalist fashion, knowing all the time that the eyes of every single man—and no doubt, many of the accompanied ones too—were locked on her.

She twisted, turned, swung herself around with abandon, her shirt unbuttoned enough to reveal she was wearing no bra, her tight arse stretching the fabric of her white jeans, with no visible panty line. He knew this was the case; she'd complained the day before that she was sweating too much on the BMW's leather seats. Eyes closed, she moved sensuously like a young feline, exuding sex from every pore, lost in her trance of forgetting, free at last of the weight of things, living only for the sway of the sound around her head.

The song came to an end, but another soul number followed quickly.

'I'm too tired. From the driving,' he complained. 'Let's go and sit down and finish our drinks,' Jacob suggested.

'No. You go. I'll join you later. One more dance.'

He edged back to their table and she remained, alone, an almost solitary dancer on the floor, caught in the desire of all the men avidly watching her as every languorous movement of her body stoked the still concealed fires of their desire.

An enigmatic smile spread across her lips as she undulated and writhed, as if in the throes of love. A smile that reflected the release of all the tensions that had been coiled up inside her, but read so differently to the guys in her audience. Sweat was forming under her arms and below the nape of her neck, sticking to her thin shirt, spreading fast like a Rorschach test across her back.

The music finally ended and she returned to Jacob.

'That was so good,' Anne said, gulping down her beer.

'You were very provocative, out there,' he remarked.

'I didn't mean to,' she replied. 'I just felt so ... free.'

A tall guy had detached himself from a group at the bar and came across to them.

'That was quite a dance, little lady,' he said admiringly.

'Well, thank you,' she replied.

'Never seen you here before?' he remarked.

'Just passing through,' Jacob said.

'Yes,' Anne nodded.

'My friends and I were thinking, maybe you'd like to join us for a few more beers? Are you folks from Australia?'

'That's kind of you,' Anne said, 'But we have to leave early in the morning, and I think we've already drunk a bit too much. The beer here's quite powerful.'

'Australia, yes,' Jacob added. If the Miami guys were on their trail, which he thought highly unlikely, that would certainly confuse them.

Disappointed, the tall guy walked back to the bar and his group of friends. They cast mean looks in their direction

'I think it would be safer if we left straight away, Jakey,' suggested Anne. 'I've a feeling I wouldn't much enjoy gang rape Arizona-style or you in a wheelchair.'

'Right,' he agreed.

'A girl can't even enjoy a dance on her own without men getting ideas,' she said.

'I seem to remember that's where I came in,' Jacob remarked.

Past the roadhouse door, they made a run for their car. As they drove off, they noticed the group of men standing on the steps of the building, watching them.

They were not followed.

Another day followed of flat desert landscapes as far as their eyes could see, punctuated by a million and one differently-shaped cacti. They looped around Phoenix and Scottsdale and were soon on their final lap.

The heat was increasing unpleasantly and the car's air-conditioning ground to a standstill. Jacob drove shirt-less. Anne unbuttoned hers. They hadn't passed another car for hours in either direction. Didn't know when the next gas station would be. Jacob kept a couple of spare cans of petrol in the back, so he was not unduly worried.

'Jakey, please, you've got to stop. I can't wait any longer. I have to pee.'

He slowed down and parked in the midday sun.

'There's nowhere to go,' Anne complained as she opened her door.

'What do you mean?'

'There's no shelter. That huge cactus over there's too far. I'm not going to walk all that way.'

'Anne, there's no one around.'

She moved a few yards on to the powdery desert soil and lowered her trousers and squatted down, with her back to him. Jacob watched and listened. It took her ages until the flow trickled to an end. She rose and began pulling the trousers up.

'Wait,' Jacob asked.

Walked over to her, past her and then turned to face her. Anne's features were slightly flushed from both the heat and the relief of the long-awaited pee, her shirt gaped open, her freckled breasts half visible, her sex was exposed as her trousers were still crumpled around her knees. He knelt before her and brushed his hand across the wet lips of her sex.

'Let me dry you,' he said.

And moved his tongue to her crease to lick her clean.

'Jesus,' she moaned.

His tongue continued an inward journey.

'Jakey?'

'Hmm?'

'There's that blanket from the Vermilion place in the boot. Go and get it.'

High noon desert fuck. There's always a first time.

*

Dusk approached as they emerged from the long afternoon of the desert, the sky above darkening by the minute.

One instant, there was open space, the next a symphony of light exploded above the close horizon. Las Vegas. Like a jewel in the desert. There is usually a wonderful exhilaration entering a new city for the first time, an anticipation of things to come, of pleasures to be. But as the neon lights spread across their dashboard, both Anne and Jacob felt truly dazed by the unfolding spectacle. Forget the movies, this was the real thing.

12.

The Deep Mystery Of Bodies

Evil and Sandra reached Port Aransas two days after the freak storm that had buffeted the coastal resort. Repair crews and square-built utility men in blue dungarees swarmed over the small town. The Vermilion building had been spared. Barely a few tiles seemed to be missing from its roof, while the neighbouring houses were all missing gutters, outside pipes, picket fences or some other sign of devastation: uprooted trees breaking through windows, curtains torn and spread like shrouds over dirty lawns.

There was no answer at the door. The bed and breakfast appeared to be empty. Maybe the storm had scared the occupants away?

Evil discreetly interrogated some neighbours. There were so many insurance assessors around, his questioning came as no surprise to them. It appeared the owners had left on vacation following the end of the tourist season, but one woman did remember that a group had hired the place outright for a week or so. Had seen some of them shopping at 7 Eleven. They must still be there.

'No,' Evil answered. 'There's no answer.'

He waited for night to fall and expertly broke into the building through the back garden while Sandra waited for him in the rental car.

There was no sign of the two Brits. Or the others.

There were suitcases in some of the rooms and tidy piles of clothing at the foot of some of the beds but no other evidence of the guests or of his quarry.

He swore.

The trail seemed to have gone cold on him.

All that time being held back in New Orleans.

'Sandra, Sandra, it's all your fault,' he mumbled under his breath as he returned to the parked car under cover of darkness.

'Well?' she asked.

'They're well gone,' he said.

'Any ideas?'

'Damn no.'

They drove off, in search of somewhere to stay. The air inside the car felt stale.

'Have you been smoking?' Evil asked Sandra.

'No. You know I don't smoke. Why?'

'I don't know,' he muttered, looking our for the lights of a hotel as they distanced themselves from the coastline.

She could feel the anger seething inside him.

'I've got to think,' he said distractedly.

'What?'

'Think hard what I would do if I were in their shoes. Where would I head to? What brought them here, anyway? This is not an end place, just a stop along the way. Where from here? What do you think?'

She had no idea. Wouldn't have told him even she had.

'Not Mexico. She likes her comforts too much, that Anne Ryan. She must still have the diamonds. Too difficult to launder them south of the border, I reckon . . .'

'What diamonds?' Sandra asked.

He ignored her.

'It's either Los Angeles or Las Vegas. Must be. That's where they're running to, our two Brits. Makes sense.'

'My parents took me to Vegas when I was twelve,' Sandra remarked. 'It's so bright and colourful there. First time I ever left Tallahassee.'

They found a Holiday Inn on the outskirts of Corpus Christi with plenty of rooms to spare. By now, Sandra had a heavy suitcase full of new clothes. Evil didn't even offer to carry it from the car to the hotel's reception area. She pulled it along until a black porter came to her assistance. Evil registered them in.

'Welcome to Corpus Christi, Mr and Mrs Simon.'

Sandra beamed at the female clerk, standing there in her crisp uniform as she smiled at them.

'Can you see the phone is connected. I have important calls to make.'

'Certainly, Sir.'

Evil dutifully reported back to the Man From Caracas. But he wasn't there; had gone to the city for a business appointment. One of the French twins took his message. He could never tell them apart, neither in the flesh nor on the telephone.

'Hungry?'

'Yes, Evil. It would be nice to eat.' She hoped a meal together might sooth his anger.

He dialled room service and ordered a couple of club sandwiches and beer.

'I shouldn't have listened to you,' he told her later. 'We should have come here earlier. They'd still be around. Because of you, I'm doing my job badly. It's wrong, Sandra. What is that guy to you, anyway?'

'Nothing,' she protested.

He'd drunk both bottles of beer and not touched his food. He looked at her.

'I want you,' he said.

He entered her without any form of foreplay. She was dry. It really hurt. He thrust into her with calm rage, stretching her abominably. Very quickly his orgasm surged and as he came, his large hands circled her neck and slowly began pressing against her throat. As his come spurted into her, she tried to catch her breath but the pressure of his thumbs was increasing and she gasped, almost choked.

'Stop . . . It hurts . . . Don't do that . . .' she pleaded.

He stopped applying the pressure against her throat and withdrew quickly from her.

'You make me so angry, Sandra. Why do I want to almost strangle you? This is turning into a damn mess. I want you so badly, but part of me wants to harm you because you're interfering with my job. I'm a professional. I can't allow you to disturb things,' he blurted out rapidly.

She did not answer, rubbed the skin protecting her throat, it felt so raw.

'I'm sorry, Sandra. I'm sorry,' Evil said. 'I didn't want it to be like this.'

Sandra now realised that Jacob would never be safe from him.

*

In their vast room at the Imperial Palace Hotel, Anne and Jacob were making love, twenty storeys above the casino floor and its infernal din of slot machines running in greedy overdrive.

Her body was tense as he moved smoothly in and out of her,

trying to tease out more of a response. He could sense the frustration rising inside her. Vegas was disappointing. Boring. They'd decided to wait a week or so before venturing out to find a buyer for the diamonds. They had to get a better feel of the place first. To avoid complications. But there was so little to do. Walk up and down The Strip, eat steak and lobster meals at ridiculously cheap prices, even have complimentary champagne breakfasts in the morning, wander across the myriad casinos distinguished only by their baroque architecture and design, and that was it. There was little else to do and Jacob in particular was not the gambling type. They had no taste for the big shows. Boring. Money was everywhere they went, soaking the atmosphere in a debilitating cloak of cheap greed. And nights were even worse. Watching the parade of lights from their window, the crowds of mostly blue-collar gamblers circulating from gambling den to gallery, holding their plastic cups of tokens, the flashing sign of a 24 hour wedding chapel. It wasn't a place for them.

'Harder, Jakey, harder,' she urged him on.

As if she wanted him to harm her. He hastened his pace.

'Yes, that's better.'

'I don't want to hurt you,' he said.

'Hurt me. That's what I want.'

'You've got the wrong guy then. The worst I can do is talk dirty, if you so desire,' he whispered in her ear as he forced her legs on to his shoulders to increase his penetration.

'Oh, yes, Jakey, that's good.'

A deep flush was spreading across the top of her body.

With one hand under him, she cupped his balls and squeezed them until she felt the pain reduce his sensitivity to the friction of the chafing genitals. She released her hold and moved further under his crotch and he felt a finger swiftly dive inside his rear, stimulating his gland to extremes.

'My throat, Jakey. Take my throat.'

He moved his hand to her neck and, invited by her urgency, slowly began squeezing her throat.

'Yes, yes,' Anne moaned. 'Harder still.'

'It's dangerous,' he said, reducing the pressure.

'No,' she insisted. 'Continue. I want to feel what's like to be strangled as I come. They say it's heaven, the nearest you can get to death ...'

Jacob's thumb held tight against her carotid, but his touch remained light. He knew there were limits to what he could do in the throes of passion. And borderlines he would not cross. It appeared

Anne had no such qualms. The rage within was racing her to the very edge of love, everything had to be experienced, and always proved insufficient in dampening the insatiable core of her need. There was always something more, something further.

With one final deep thrust, Jacob allowed himself to come. She wasn't there yet. He saw the anger shine in her eyes, as she continued to grip him wildly and rub her crotch against his retreating member.

Later, as they dressed, Anne asked:

'Do you mind if I indulge in a bit of gambling in one of the casinos, Jakey? It'd be interesting to see what it feels like. We'll do it at Caesar's Palace. Those Roman guards and vestal virgins are just too much. It'll be fun.'

He didn't think it would be, but the spectacle of them gambling some serious money might make it easier to find an outlet for the diamonds. One of the hotels, maybe? They'd think Anne and he wanted the cash to gamble further.

*

'This is bad, Evil,' the Man From Caracas said down the telephone to his distant henchman. 'Very bad.'

'I know,' Evil conceded.

'How did it happen?' the Man asked.

'I just wasn't fast enough. It was my fault,' Evil said. He didn't want to mention Sandra. She should not be part of the equation.

'Do you require help? Should I send the twins over?'

'That won't be necessary,' Evil replied. 'Maybe later when I have an idea where the fuck they've gone. Maybe then.'

'I have to trust you, Evil,' the Man said.

'You always have done in the past, Boss. I will find her. This has become personal.'

'Don't spoil her for me too much, Evil,' the Man From Caracas said. 'I've been making all these wonderful plans for little Miss Ryan. Very imaginative. Very creative.'

'I'm sure you have.'

'So I wouldn't want to be disappointed, would I?'

'You won't be.'

'Good.'

'I've contacted our best men in all the main cities on the West Coast. We have ears open all over the place. Their descriptions have been circulated and all our people are on the look-out for the diamonds, should they be offered. Those two Brits can't stay invisible forever. The net is just waiting for them. It's just a question of time. I'll call,' Evil concluded.

Sandra had been sitting on the bed, listening to his side of the conversation.

Evil explained. Anne Ryan. The diamonds and their purpose. The betrayal and theft. The organisation. His role.

Nothing surprised her.

'And when you catch her? What happens then?'

'If she comes with the diamonds, I dispatch her to Caracas. The Boss will see to her there. I wouldn't like to be her. She'll die, of course. But it's what happens before, what he does to her, it'll be really bad. I've seen him angry and with women he's at his worst. If she plays silly buggers and doesn't tell me what she's done with the merchandise, I'll have to make her talk. Either way, it won't be pretty.'

'Do you have to?' Sandra asked.

'Yes. I've done it before,' Evil said calmly.

Sandra sighed. 'So what now?'

'We wait.'

*

Once Anne's gambling began, it only took eight days to lose the cash they had left from the sale of the first diamond. It consumed her. There was little Jacob could do. It was her money, after all. As he watched, helpless, it was like a life study in addiction as she hastened down the slippery path, from slot machines to blackjack, to whatever card game could help her lose even faster. She wasn't good at it and she knew it. It was just a faster way to oblivion and all her senses cried out for it.

Their coupling had now become desultory, a tired and casual mating to disperse the memories of yet another dark day. She increasingly sought the pain in their automatic nightly embraces and he wanted no part of it. He was willing to fuck her body, not her mind.

'That's it,' she said one morning as he was shaving in the bathroom.

'What?'

'The money's gone.'

'Already?' It didn't surprise him. 'So what we do now? My credit cards are extended to their limit.'

'And mine are no longer valid,' she said.

'I'm not even sure whether I have enough to settle the hotel bill,' Jacob said.

'That bad?'

'Yes, Anne ... Isn't that what you wanted?'

After cleaning it, he replaced the razor in the toiletries bag. The diamonds were concealed in a pot of face cream next to it.

'There is a guy at this small casino at the far end of the Strip who said he might be interested in buying one of them. But he needs to keep it for a few days, to have it checked, he says and I don't think I can trust him,' Anne said.

'Whatever, we'll have to find a cheaper place to stay.'

'How?'

'We'll have to get some work.'

'Doing what?'

'Think of something ... Vegas is a service industry, there must be loads of casual jobs going.'

'Yeah ... you know all those free newspapers you can pick up on the Strip? Maybe I can find a modelling job.' She walked over to the bathroom mirror, displaced him and fluffed her hair up.

'I shudder to think what sort of modelling assignments those papers can offer,' he said. 'I don't think they shoot romance novel covers in Las Vegas ...'

'There must be something,' Anne continued.

Within a few days Jacob had found a cabbing assignment. The money was poor, but the tips were good. Vegas was a place where punters tipped big, didn't want to be thought of as cheap. Half of the runs involved taking tourists and conventioneers to and from the airport. He had to improve his small talk, though. They moved out of the Imperial Palace to a shabby apartment block on the edge of the desert, where they managed to rent an already-furnished two room apartment on a weekly basis.

Anne signed up with an agency who found her frequent modelling assignments. She told Jacob most of the jobs were for mail-order catalogue work. He didn't believe her. She wouldn't groom herself so meticulously before every job, powdering all over her body, teasing her hair with conditioning mousse the way she did if it were only for a session involving boring chain store-standard clothes or work with children, as she sometimes pretended.

She couldn't be stripping in one of the hundred clubs that sprouted everywhere over Vegas. She wasn't tall enough, and there was too much competition from would-be showgirls in that area. What he didn't know couldn't harm him, he reckoned and they needed the money. They had agreed to leave Vegas at the earliest possible opportunity.

In fact her first job was as a nude model for a photography class. She doubted if many of the men present even had film in their cameras as they circled her, clicking away, like noisy birds of prey. At the end of the first one hour session, two of the photographers approached her and offered her double the fee she was earning before agency deduction to remain another hour and do a more private session with them.

'Only modelling. No funny business?'

'Of course. Something more intimate.'

She asked for the money up front. They didn't mind.

It was still modelling. She remained nude and they kept their clothes on as promised. But the poses they required were now more intimate. She had to touch herself, spread her legs apart so that the lens could capture the moistness of her cunt.

'Wider now, darling.'

'Take your nipple between your finger, that's it, yes, nice.'

'Throw your head back.'

'Let your hair fall over your face.'

'Bend over,' the photographer was on the floor behind her, sliding under her, photographing her apertures.

'Gee, you're wet, aren't you?'

She was. Couldn't control the rise of the excitement inside her.

'It would be nice if we had some props,' the second man said.

'Maybe next time, I can bring some,' the other amateur photographer suggested.

'Fine with me,' Anne said.

Easy money.

They brought her some of the photos they had shot. They surprised her. She didn't expect herself to look the way she did in them. Bigger. Redder. Raw. Obscenely intimate.

Following the second private session, the two men suggested that next time they could arrange for another model to share the hour with Anne. She would still be paid the same amount. The idea intrigued her. The bodies of other women interested her. She remembered occasionally leafing through skin magazines at the railway station she commuted to in London, and wondering how women could display so much and yet still retain such an innocent composure. It would be interesting.

But it wasn't a woman who joined her after the main group departed. It was a young mulatto guy.

'This is Hector,' the photographer introduced them. Anne hesitated. Tightened the thin bath-robe around her nudity.

'This is not what I expected,' she told them. 'I'm quite happy to model for you, but there are limits to what I will do,' she assured them.

'I'm gay, lady,' Hector said.

'We only want photographs, darling. Some nice poses. That's all. The two of you only have to simulate stuff,' she was told.

'We've got a commission,' they explained.

'Who sees these photos? Where do they go?' Anne asked.

'We download them on the Internet. It's a living.'

Hector began to undress. Anne watched him shed his clothes. He was a beautiful animal. She'd never screwed a black man. His cock was already fully erect.

'Okay, let's go to work. Darling, take your gown off and stand by his side.'

Click.

'Now, move together, pretend you're kissing.'

His flesh was wonderfully soft and warm. His cock pressed hard against her stomach. He was at least a foot taller than her and lowered his head to adopt the required position.

'Darling, make it look convincing. Put your arms around him, his waist.'

Click.

'Now, Hector, you lie down on the floor there, on your back. Yes, like that. Darling, come on over and hold his cock in your hand and pretend you're about to lick it, think it's hot, think of ice cream . . .'

The mulatto retained his hardness, she could almost feel his pulse through the cock as she gripped it and adopted the pose.

Click.

'Put your mouth nearer.'

Click.

'Tongue out. Closer.'

She faltered slightly as she leaned forward and the tip of her tongue actually brushed against Hector's ramrod of a cock.

Click. Click.

'That was nice . . . Now, let's get a few snaps in the doggie position . . . Darling, get on all fours. Open your legs a bit more. Come on, stretch those bum cheeks apart. That's it. Hector, you position yourself there and hold your cock nice and straight as if you're about to push that nice big thing inside her. Yes . . . Nice . . .'

Click. Click.

She could feel her juices racing forward. The thought briefly occurred to her that it would be nice if he did fill her with that thing of his. But the photographers were already ordering them into different configurations.

'A sixty-nine now. As if you're eating each other. Darling, you lie on your back and let Hector straddle you.'

Click.

How did his cock remain iron hard so long? It dangled barely an inch from her lips and his heavy dark balls brushed against her chin as he lowered his mouth towards the opening of her vagina, as each photographer knelt at either end to catch the combination of mouths and genitals in glorious gynaecological close-up.

Click. Click. Click.

'Lady, you're in heat or something,' Hector remarked, holding his position. 'You smell mighty strong down there . . .'

Anne blushed to her roots.

The session earned her a hundred bucks. By the time she returned to the apartment, she'd already squandered most of it on the higher stakes slot machines. Only took five minutes, even though she'd doubled her stake first time round.

The woman at the agency called her in and demanded their cut from the private sessions, which she had found out about. Anne was now badly in debt to them and had no choice but to accept escort duties.

'I won't go all the way,' she told the woman.

'Won't get you many tips, Anne,' the woman pointed out. 'There's a lot of competition out there for good pussy.'

'Blow jobs. No more.'

'Your problem, girl. Just bring me that money by the end of the week.'

'I will.'

'And when you report for work tomorrow, wear something sexier. Tell you what, with those small boobs of yours, no need to wear a bra, hey?'

Anne knew she was on the wrong slope again, but she told herself that she didn't really have any choice. Just surviving. The tricks in Miami hadn't been that bad. Until Teddy Caliban. It wasn't even her whole body, just her mouth. She would have to buy a supply of mint candy.

Half the punters she met in the bars of the smaller hotels and casinos the agency people were sending her to, summarily dismissed her when they discovered she didn't offer full service. Others were too drunk and lazy by the time they found out, that a hand job or her mouth provided sufficient relief. This went on for a week. Mediocre tips, though and awkward excuses to Jakey, when she didn't get back to the apartment until after his last shift. Then an Air Force sergeant physically threatened her when she refused to put out and chased her screaming from his room at the Mirage, drawing the unwelcome attention of the hotel detective. She'd have to steer clear of the Mirage for a few weeks, which was bad news, as it was one of the richest hotels on the Strip. Big tippers.

She did college kids in car parks. At least there was no need for her to undress for the occasion. Businessmen in town for trade shows stuck to their cars—probably had wives or girl friends back in their rooms. A film grip from Boston couldn't keep talking all the time she was sucking him off. Held her head down so she was reluctantly obliged to swallow his come. Strangely bitter. Liked her enough to arrange a date with a friend for later that evening. Negotiated in advance a generous payment if she agreed to provide them both with blow jobs.

'And that's all?' she checked.

'Absolutely, babe,' he assured her.

They met in his room at the Paddlewheel. The other guy was a rough-looking Italian, who introduced himself as Tony.

'A redhead, whoa!' Tony exclaimed, surveying her lecherously.

'You're still sure you won't put out, babe?' The grip inquired. 'We could make it worth your while.'

'No,' Anne said calmly. 'Shall we go the bar downstairs?'

She didn't want to stay any longer in the room alone with them. She'd do them downstairs in the car park after they'd had a few drinks.

The two men chose to go to another bar a mile down the Strip. Fine with her. The walk and the cool night air would do her good.

They bought fine champagne and proved fun company with malicious tales about the movies they'd worked on, full of tell-all stories of unexpected celebrity actors.

'I have to go and powder my nose,' Anne excused herself, the champagne already filling her bladder.

'Don't be long, babe.'

'We'll be waiting.' Tony said.

While she was away, they must have spiked her drink. Her head soon began to spin and she became a spectator at her own show, as they blamed her indisposition on the heat and drink and quickly settled their check.

'The lady's not used to good champagne,' Tony told the concerned waitress. 'We'll get her out into the fresh air. She'll soon come to.'

She was supported by both their arms as they swept her to her feet and dragged her to the exit. She was fully conscious of what was happening, but her muscles felt totally paralysed and the words painfully coming out of her mouth came out jumbled and useless.

Tony held her up, as his friend moved forward to call a cab.

He wrapped one of her arms around his shoulder and began fondling her roughly.

'I've always wanted me a bite of red pussy,' he said. 'Bitch, this is going to be the night of your life. Just you wait . . .'

The cab drew up.

Jacob was lost in thought as the two men supporting the drunken woman squeezed into the back of his vehicle.

'Where to?' he asked.

'The Paddlewheel on Convention Centre Road,' he was told.

'And make it fast, man, we've got ourselves a hot piece of ass here, don't want it to go cold,' sniggered the other guy.

Jacob shot a quick glance at his rear mirror. In the darkness, he could see one of the men inching his hand under the apparently unconscious woman's skirt. The other had opened his trouser front and pulling the woman by her long hair settled her face on his crotch.

'Suck on this, bitch. It's only an hors d'oeuvre . . .'

Jacob switched back to the traffic. He'd been warned about scenes like this and instructed to ignore them. That sort of town.

The woman moaned quietly as her mouth was breached.

He heard her say, 'No' and his heart skipped a beat.

Looked into the rear mirror again, his eyes getting accustomed to the darkness behind. The voice, the hair, yes, that skirt.

Shit!

He pumped the gas and the cab brutally surged forward.

'Calm down, man,' a voice from behind said. 'We're not in that much of a hurry . . .'

Weaving across lanes, Jacob looked out for the first opportunity to draw up to the kerb. Preferably somewhere dark, away from the gaudy neon lights that dominated most of the Strip. The opportunity arose and he came to a sudden halt with a screech of brakes.

He rushed out of the cab and pulled the back door open.

'What the hell?' There was surprise over the faces of the men. Anne slowly raised her face from the man's now detumescing penis, recognised Jacob standing outside. Tears began to flow from her eyes.

'Out! Now!' Jacob screamed, pulling on one of the men's sleeve.

'But . . .'

'Now. You, by the other door. And leave the woman there. You bastards.'

'Man, this is none of your business. The girl's with us. None of your concern. She's just a cheap whore, anyway . . .'

Jacob's leg shot forward and his foot hit the Boston film grip in the balls. He fell to the ground, writhing in agony. Tony had made his way around the cab and readied to throw himself at Jacob, when he saw the gun in the cab driver's hand.

'Okay, okay, now. It was just a bit of a fun. You can have her,' Tony said, putting his hands in the air to avoid any confusion. 'I'm told she doesn't even give a good blow job . . .'

Jacob waved the Beretta menacingly. Tony pulled his friend up from the ground and began dragging him away.

'Jakey . . .'

Anne was sprawled across the back seat where the two men had left her, clothing in disarray.

'Anne, Anne, what mess have you got yourself into, now?' he moved to hold her.

'I'm sick . . . They put . . . something . . . in my drink,' she slowly said.

'Christ!'

'Get me to a hospital, please, Jakey.'

*

The telephone rang. Sandra picked it up. Evil had been on the toilet for ten minutes already, reading the day's newspaper.

'Yes?'

'Who's that?'

'It's Sandra.'

'Who the hell are you?'

'I'm with Evil,' she said.

'Get me Evil.'

'Yes.'

'Pronto.'

He was already there, took the phone from her.

'It's Archie. The Brits are in Vegas.'

'Las Vegas?'

'Yes. An off-duty cop, a mate of mine, reported them at the hospital yesterday night. She was in some sort of trouble. They had to pump her out. She's okay now. He's got an address.'

'Suicide attempt?'

'Not sure, but I don't think so. Drugs maybe. And the guy is with her. Jacob Jones. He signed her in. Same address.'

'Thanks, we owe you.'

Evil slapped the phone down and picked it up again.

'Operator, get me the airport and book two seats on the first available flight to Las Vegas. I'll settle when I reach the airport. Any possible route. Doesn't matter if we have to change planes on the way. Whatever is fastest, and have my room bill ready, I'll be down in a few minutes. Thanks.'

He looked at Sandra triumphantly.

'We're on the road again, kid,' he said, beaming. 'And this time she's not getting away.'

Her bag was already packed. As he'd ordered.

13.

In The Movies, They Don't Show The Pain

The plane touched down with a dull thud. They had both carried their luggage on board to avoid delays on arrival. There had been a two and a half hour wait at Dallas/Fort Worth for the connection. Evil had bought her a bunch of women's magazines, but Sandra could not concentrate on them. The big adventure was unfolding and nearing its end and she was worried about the outcome. Somehow, she was no longer dreaming of blonde babies; the journey here had inoculated her against the thought of happy everafters. The job at the diner in Tallahassee was gone. They had no doubt long since replaced her. Evil had come back with a box of cigars as well as the glossy publications.

'What are those?' Sandra had asked him. 'You don't smoke.'

'Thought I'd treat myself,' he had said. And put the small box away inside his hold-all.

The plane slowly taxied towards the ramp and finally came to a halt. Evil was quickly out of his seat and urging her along the central aisle. They disembarked, moved along the tubular pathway and entered the airport terminal. There were people playing slot machines even here. The monorail smoothly transported them to the main building. Giant palm trees adorned the airport's central concourse. Sandra's eyes looked around in amazement as she tried to keep up with Evil's rapid pace.

They reached the cab rank and Evil ordered the driver to take them straight to the address he had been given by his acolyte. Jacob's cab happened to be two cars away, as he waited for arriving travellers, but they weren't to know that.

Evil remained ominously silent throughout the short journey into

town and down the Strip to a more down-trodden area on the edge
of the desert, beyond the lights and moving colours of the bright City.
They pulled up by a two-storeyed whitewashed building.

'I know this place,' the driver said, as Evil searched for change
in his pockets.

'How come?' Evil queried.

'It's just that one of the other drivers lives in one of the apartments here. Strange guy. English. Doesn't speak too much with us
others. But he's okay. Just a quiet one. We don't get many limeys
working the cabs . . .'

Evil reflected silently. Then asked: 'Do you think your colleague
might be in right now?'

'No. He was at the airport, too. Saw him there when I picked you
up. On the same shift as me, won't finish until ten tonight.'

'Really?' Evil remarked. He turned to Sandra who was dragging
her case out of the car.

'Listen,' he said to her quietly. 'I don't want you here. It might
be ugly. Why don't you go straight to the hotel and I'll join you later?
It's a credit card booking. Tell them they can get my imprint when I
get in.'

Then to the cab driver: 'I just thought, it might be difficult to get
another ride from here after my business is done. Why don't you
take my lady friend to the Imperial Palace, on the Strip.' He slipped
the driver an extra ten dollar bill and carried Sandra's case back to
the cab. Sandra slid herself on to the back seat.

The cab drove off, leaving him on the sidewalk with his hold-all.
He looked up at the flaky walls of the poorly up kept building. Apartment D. That would be upstairs.

*

Anne had stayed in since she'd returned from the hospital.
They'd washed the junk out of her and only kept her in overnight;
there had been no permanent damage.

Even though Jakey never actually said so, she knew he was happier with her not going out on further modelling assignments. She
realised how much of a fool she'd been. It wasn't money, though,
that made her do it. No, there was something rotten deep inside her
core. Everything she had, she'd managed to spoil. He hadn't asked
much about that evening. Very little, in fact. As if he didn't want to
know the truth about how the damn lust and her sexual curiosity
turned her into such an irresponsible slut.

She was going to lose him, too. She had to get to grips with her
life. Do something about it now.

For the last few hours she had been trying to write a letter. To her mother, whom she hadn't seen for months. After the funeral at which both sets of parents had gazed so reproachfully at her—she'd always had that feeling that her own parents actually preferred her dull husband to their own daughter; he was more reliable, less of a wild card—she'd told them she was going away on a trip. Her mother hadn't even asked where or for how long.

The letter-writing was not going well. A sad mixture of rambling excuses and derivative self-justification. She seemed to be crossing out one word for every two words she managed to set down. Too much copy editing. The magazine contributors were always complaining about her generous use of the blue pencil. When she heard the the knock at the door, she welcomed the interruption.

Probably Christian Scientists, Seventh Day Adventists, Jehovah's Witnesses or whoever else was on a mission to purge the wrong end of town today.

A welcome distraction.

She was certainly in the mood for a right argument.

She opened the door.

'Christ!'

'So we meet again, Miss Ryan,' Evil said.

'You . . .'

'You didn't think you'd get away, did you?'

'How did you . . .'

'I'll invite myself in, shall I?'

His foot was in the door, not that she'd even had the time to think of slamming it back in his face.

He brushed past her into the room, closing the door behind him, clicking the latch and attaching the chain the landlords had thoughtfully provided.

Anne stood as if she had been nailed to the floor. Her brain danced the light fandango, desperately exploring options, possibilities. But every new thought was a dead end.

'Where is Teddy? Teddy Caliban?' she asked him.

'Dead, Anne. I can call you Anne, can't I? I feel I know you so well already.'

'Dead? Why?' was all she could say.

'He had to pay for your foolishness,' Evil said.

'But it had nothing to do with him,' Anne protested, thinking all along: Why the hell she was trying to protect the bastard?

'We assumed that was the case. But he shouldn't have let it happen nonetheless. He shouldn't have let *you* happen, should he?'

Evil smiled and it chilled her to the bone.

'I didn't plan to steal them, you know,' Anne protested. 'It just happened . . .'

'Makes no difference,' he said. He walked over to close the window, surveyed the apartment. 'The diamonds belonged to our organisation. And we don't enjoy being made fools of by a little tramp like you.'

'I . . .'

'It's too late for excuses,' he interrupted. 'The other guy, Jones. Was he in it with you?'

'No. He's just a friend. Helping me out.'

'Good. So it won't be necessary to dispose of him . . .'

'What about me?'

'You, Anne, are on a straight road to hell.'

He pulled the chair she had been sitting on to write the letter away from the table. She froze. Evil was built like a wardrobe. She knew there was no way she could resist him in this confined space. His bulk dominated the room. The scars on his cheek and bald scalp read like fateful prophecies.

'The only choice you have is at what speed you want to race down that road, Anne Ryan,' he said, pulling off his jacket and throwing it on the back of the chair. Without it, white shirt tight against his chest, he appeared even more massive. A sharp ache shot through her stomach.

He indicated the chair.

She sat down.

'Now we talk.'

'Yes,' she nodded.

He towered over her. She pulled her bath-robe closer; she had taken a shower earlier and was only wearing a thin pair of cotton Marks & Spencer knickers underneath. Normally she didn't bother about underwear in the flat, but her period had begun yesterday.

'Where are they?' he asked her.

'I don't have them any longer,' she lied.

'Don't you?'

'No. I threw the toothpaste tube away back In Caracas. I was too scared to take them through customs. That's why I ran away after I got back.'

'You disappoint me, Anne. We're not fools, you know.'

'But it's true,' she insisted.

'You lie to me,' he said. 'Just like a cheap South Beach whore. I thought you were different, Anne.'

He moved menacingly closer to her.

'Stand up,' he ordered.

She silently shook her head.

'NOW!' he shouted.

She stood.

'Open your robe.'

Anne obeyed.

'Small but perfectly formed,' Evil said, watching her. 'I'm sure it annoys you when they say that,' he chuckled.

'Pull those underpants down.'

She had to bend to do so.

'A genuine redhead . . . The twins told me about it . . .'

Anne shuddered at the memory of the two Frenchmen. He noticed her discomfort.

'Oh yes, the twins are looking forward to seeing you again. Our boss has promised they can have you for a week or so, before he finishes you off. Or what's left of you . . .'

She could feel the cold surround her unveiled body and invade it. Her stomach was hurting, her bladder felt as if it were going to burst. Picking up the knickers from the floor, she realised she was leaking slightly. Blushed deeply.

'Give me those.'

She handed him the small white garment. He crumbled the knickers with his fist.

'Sit down again.'

She held her legs closed tight as she settled on the chair, the gown gaping open at the front. Evil approached. She shivered uncontrollably.

'Open your mouth.'

He stuffed the underpants in her mouth.

'Don't want to alert the neighbours, do we?' Evil said.

She couldn't talk now. Felt the cotton absorb all the saliva in her mouth, and dry despair take hold of her throat.

'You need to be taught a lesson, Anne Ryan.'

He walked over to the bag he had been holding when he had presented himself at her door. Opened it and pulled something out. His back obscured her vision. He turned back to her.

'You've caused me much grief. I have a reputation, and you've tarnished it with your silly capers. In Miami, in New Orleans. So this is going to be personal, you see. Something that might remind you of me on a long term basis.'

He approached the chair and pulled the robe over her shoulders and down to her waist.

'Then I shall ask you again where the diamonds are, Anne. All you have to do is nod, say, twice. But only if you're finally going to be telling me the truth. We know you still had them back in New Orleans. So further lies are useless, see.'

She looked past him at the closed window, as if trying to escape his spell. The day was slowly draining to an end.

'This is to prove once and for all we are very serious and must not be messed with, Anne Ryan.'

He walked to the back of the chair, pulled from his pocket the switchblade he had used so expertly on Teddy Caliban, flicked the blade open and, with his other hand, cupped Anne's right breast. He rubbed the nipple almost distractedly, waking its erectile tissue and feeling it grow and lengthen under his finger. He then approached the blade. The hand teasing her breast retreated and moved to her shoulder, firmly holding her down against the seat of the chair. Anne squirmed as she helplessly watched the shining blade move closer to the flesh of her breast.

With one swift slash, Evil cut into the underside of her soft tissue.

Anne screamed with all the might her lungs could summon, but the sound drowned silently in her throat. Her body convulsed briefly and the chair shook under her, but the pressure of Evil's hand on her shoulder saved her from falling over as the excruciating pain moved through every single nerve in her body.

She was short of breath. In agony. Evil, confident the initial burst of pain had drained, let go of her and walked round the chair to face her again. Tears were welling around her eyes.

His hand moved to her chin and forced her face upwards so she could see him.

Through the haze clouding her vision, Anne watched him raise the bloodied and still shining blade and lick it clean with his advancing tongue. 'Now you will never forget me, Anne,' he said. 'And neither will I.'

She just sat there, still shaking, as the pain assaulted her senses in unending waves.

Evil came closer, his face now inches from the deep cut flowering on the underside of her right bosom.

'I don't think you're going to want a career in stripping now, Anne,' he said. 'Very messy.'

He paused a moment.

'All that blood,' he continued. 'Don't want you getting infected, do we?'

He took a cigar from the box he had earlier pulled from the hold-all, and struck a match. Drew a few times on the cigar. Watched its tip redden.

'We have to cauterise you. The Man In Caracas wants you healthy for his little games.'

And stubbed the cigar's smouldering end down on the bloody wound. The flesh sizzled. Anne screamed again. Surely no, it couldn't get worse. Like razor blades cutting her heart, her guts, shredding her brain into filaments of sheer agony, slice by slice. Her bowels opened. Her eyes closed.

'So, where are the diamonds?' Evil asked.

She didn't respond.

She had fainted.

*

As the cab driver made his way back towards the heart of Vegas and approached the Strip, Sandra asked him: 'The English driver you mentioned. What's his name?'

'Jake, I think,' he answered.

'Can you raise him on the radio?'

'Not really,' the cabby explained, edging his way into the traffic and threading the car into the right lane. 'I can call HQ and leave a message. But I can't talk to him directly. That's the way the system works. I think the company believes all us drivers would be chatting all the time and clogging the air, if it wasn't designed that way, I reckon. Talking about sports, no doubt . . .' he added. 'And you know what? I think they're right.'

He laughed gently.

Sandra smiled along with him.

They were passing the Mirage's volcano just as it was erupting. Sandra had seen it on TV. Normally, she would have been fascinated. But she had other matters on her mind.

'I need a favour,' she said. 'Badly.'

'Tell me, lady,' he said.

'I need to contact the English guy, Jake. Can you send a message for him through your switchboard?'

'That's a mighty unusual request . . .'

Sandra dug into her handbag, grabbing all the money she had there.

'I'll pay you,' she said.

'No. It won't cost, lady. No problem.'

'Thanks.'

'I've come across a lot of weird things on this job, in this town. Lady, join the club . . . You don't even know the guy . . .'

'I have a thing about Brits,' she explained feebly.

'I'm a Polack,' the driver said. 'That means I have no chance,' he chuckled.

'Go figure.'

They were approaching the Imperial Palace.

'So what's the message you want to give Jake?'

'Tell him to meet Sandra at the Imperial Palace. You must say it is very urgent. Please.'

The cab drew up in the hotel and casino's forecourt.

'I'll call through the second I leave,' the cab driver assured her.

'Promise?'

'I swear.'

Sandra alighted. A porter raced across to get her case. The cab took off. Sandra registered and sent the luggage up to her room. She would wait downstairs. The reception area was already part of the casino. Too many people around. She decided outside was better. Moved to the busy forecourt where coaches were unloading tourists by the dozen and the bellboys busied themselves frantically loading luggage on to their carts. She crossed over to the traffic island that separated the hotel from the Strip, sat by the wall and began her vigil. Here, she could see all the cars come and go. Waiting for Jacob.

He was between fares when the call came through.

Asked for the message to be repeated.

What was Sandra doing here?

Miami. New Orleans. Now Vegas. Was she following him? How?

He changed direction at the first intersection and ten minutes later he arrived at the familiar Chinese-style hotel with its imitation pagoda front. He saw Sandra sitting at the edge of the fore-court, a forlorn figure among the surrounding frenzy.

'What are you doing here?'

'Oh, Jacob, thank God . . .' He looked different from their previous brief encounters. Drawn, tired.

'What is it?'

'Evil is at your place . . .'

'Who's Evil?'

'A gangster.'

'What?'

'He means your friend Anne harm. He's very dangerous . . .'

'How long has he been there?'

'About half an hour.'

'Jesus.'

He rushed back to the cab. Sandra ran after him.

'I'm coming with you.'

*

Evil had ransacked the apartment without finding the diamonds. Anne was still unconscious, slumped in a pool of excrement and blood on the chair, head back, obscenely exposed, spread-eagled, though the spectacle was far from erotic.

'Where the fuck could she have hidden them?' he wondered aloud.

He looked around at the woman. Why did she have to let go like she did? Now he'd have to clean her up before he could take her with him and begin the journey back to Caracas. He didn't relish the task.

He'd need help. Fortunately, the organization had enough contacts here in Nevada. It would only take a few phone calls. He scanned the lounge and then the bedroom for a telephone. But couldn't find one. Damn!

The thought suddenly occurred to him: what would he do with Sandra now? Would she still want him after she'd witnessed what he had done? Would she come to Caracas? Stay with him? He hoped so.

He filled a saucepan with cold water at the sink and poured over Anne Ryan's face. She moved. He slapped her face hard. Her eyes opened.

With consciousness, the pain raced back. Anne shuddered. Gasped for air. Choked, forgetting the gag he had stuffed her with. He extracted the cotton underpants from her mouth. Her tongue was numb. Parts of her body were literally on fire, others she could no longer feel.

She focused on Evil, standing menacingly at her side.

'Now, Anne, I can do worse, you know. You can't imagine how much a woman's body can take in way of punishment. Do yourself a favour. Where are the diamonds?'

She realised with shame she was sitting in her own shit and menstrual discharge.

Her brain somehow switched back on again as the adrenaline began racing through her veins, and she remembered where she was. And why. Her heart dropped.

'So?' Evil reiterated.

Downstairs in the street, Jacob insisted that Sandra stay in the cab.

'You'll be okay, Jacob?' She queried.

He showed her the handgun he was carrying.

'Is he armed?' he asked her.

'I don't think so,' she answered. 'But he has a knife . . . Be careful, I've seen him use it.'

Jacob quietly climbed the stairs, his ears straining for sounds from the apartment. He could hear the man's voice. Not Anne. He brought the key to the lock.

Inside, they both heard the lock click and they turned their eyes to the door.

Jacob opened it. Saw the chain and broke it with his shoulder.

The spectacle was sickening. Anne was sprawled on a chair, blood across her front, ravaged, a monstrous shaven-headed man in shirtsleeves leaning over her, brandishing the smoking tip of a large cigar just an inch from her eyes.

Evil straightened. 'Ah,' he said, 'the boyfriend.'

Jacob was rooted to the spot, hypnotised by the dreadful sight of Anne's ordeal. The smell reached him.

'Oh, Jesus!' he exclaimed.

Evil moved a foot or so toward him, away from his victim. Her eyes focused on Jacob, filled brimful with hurt and pleading. Her throat was so dry she couldn't even speak out his name.

The thug dropped the cigar and pulled the switchblade from his pocket.

'I said I might spare you,' Evil said. 'But sometimes promises are difficult to keep . . .'

Jacob raised the Beretta and aimed at the big man.

Evil sneered when he saw the gun in the Englishman's hand.

'I don't think you're the shooting type,' he said, taking another step forward.

'Try me, you bastard . . .'

'The diamonds are in the bathroom, in the face cream . . .' Anne called out.

Her voice distracted Evil.

Jacob pressed the trigger.

Evil was right, Jacob had never shot a man before. But this was easy. The gun's kickback surprised him and he had to take a step back.

And watched the red flower bloom in the centre of the thug's gut and saw him stumble down to the floor.

A profound sense of relief came over Jacob as he stood silently, still cradling the gun in his two hands, the way he had seen marksmen hold pistols in documentaries and films.

Sandra burst through the door behind him.

'I heard the shot,' she panted. And witnessed both casualties.

She ignored Anne, on the chair, and knelt by Evil's body and checked his pulse. By now the blood was over his front, turning his whole shirt from white to red.

'He's still alive,' she said.

*

Jacob picked Anne up from the chair and carried her to the bathroom. She felt so light. As if her soul had flown away, halving her body-weight in the process. She held on to his shoulders.

He wet a flannel with warm water and began cleaning her up.

'I'll be all right,' she said. 'Looks worse than it is.'

He pulled the bloodied robe away from her battered body and started wiping the caked blood off her front. When the worst of the blood had been cleaned away, he saw for the first time the deep cut the thug had inflicted on her breast.

He couldn't stop himself and had to turn round to the sink and be violently sick.

'It could have been worse,' Anne said weakly, not quite believing what she was saying.

'I hope the bastard dies,' Jacob said.

Sandra was in the front room, bandaging torn strips of sheets around Evil's girth, desperately trying to stop the life-blood from draining out of him. He was still breathing, albeit with difficulty and was conscious again. He whispered a phone number to her. Asked her to call it. Someone would come with help.

'Turn round. I'll do your back,' Jacob said to Anne.

'I can do it, please, Jakey,' she said.

'You're in no state,' he pointed out, and began scraping the shit and other secretions from the lower part of her body.

'You're kind to me, Jakey,' Anne said.

'Just be quiet. Save your energy,' he told her and continued the cleansing. When all else was done, he finally washed the dried tears away from her face. Her lips were dry and parched, a constellation of sores.

'He gagged me,' she explained.

'We don't know who else is aware of our presence here,' Jacob explained. 'We'll have to leave town.'

'Yes,' she agreed.

Fifteen minutes later, they were heading into the Nevada desert, having gathered all their belongings into the BMW's trunk. Sandra had gone off to phone a doctor, she had said. Evil lay semi-comatose where he had collapsed. As they had left the apartment, Jacob could not summon the will-power to shoot the thug again and finish him off. He knew he should, but even after what he'd done to Anne, something inside him rebelled at the thought.

Close to the Hoover Dam, Jacob and Anne looked wearily over the road map.

'California's the obvious place.'

'Yes, too obvious.'

'We could go further north. Head for Canada?'

'Canada sounds nice. With our passports, we would be legal there. That could help,' she pointed out.

'Might be easier to cash the diamonds,' he ventured. 'Less of an American connection.'

'No, Jakey. We've got to get rid of the diamonds. They can only bring us bad-luck.'

'It's all we have, Anne. However tainted they are, it's our ticket to freedom.'

'If you say so,' she reluctantly agreed.

'I know people in Vancouver,' Jacob said. 'Someone I once worked with.'

'It'll be cold . . .'

'So what? I've had my share of sun for this year. It might feel more like home.'

The car hit a bump in the road.

'Ouch . . .' Anne cried.

'Still hurting?' Jacob asked.

'Yes, but not as much. The pain killers you got at the gas station are beginning to help. It's going to take a few days. It's just the rubbing against the shirt . . .'

'We'll stop somewhere. You can wear one of my shirts. I will get one from the suitcase. They're larger, will fit looser on you.'

'Maybe. I don't know which pain is worse, from the cut or from the burn,' she said. 'I can't even tell them apart.'

They agreed to drive through the night, to put as much distance tonight between Las Vegas and themselves.

Round midnight, they stopped at a small roadside diner where they convinced the owner to pack them some extra sandwiches to go and purchase a few bottles of water and soda. They set their provisions down on the car's back seat. Their faces met.

'Thanks, Jakey. I would have died there without you.'

'We're together, Anne. Remember that.'

He leaned closer.

'It's you that I want to kiss,' he said, doing so tenderly. He could remember the expression from somewhere, but couldn't pinpoint where. Strange how life is full of holes.

The car raced up the white line of the blue asphalt flat top.

*

The men came and spirited Evil away from the apartment block. Sandra accompanied them. They found a doctor who was willing to keep his mouth shut, the bullet was extracted from Evil's gut and a bed arranged in a private clinic ten miles out in the desert.

The medic pointed out to her that Evil had the strength of an ox. Most other men wouldn't have survived a bullet there and the heavy blood loss. He would be okay. Just needed his rest. Time to muster his energies again.

No questions were asked.

Sandra commuted daily from her room at the Imperial Palace to the clinic where she spent the day at Evil's bedside.

'He wasn't due back until after ten,' Evil remarked on the first day he was allowed solid food again. 'And he had a gun. Too much of a coincidence.'

Sandra looked on silently.

Evil continued his monologue: 'But he should have killed me. Leaving me alive was not professional. He will pay. Sooner or later.'

Sandra opened her mouth to say something.

'No, Sandra,' Evil said. 'This time, he's gone too far. I can't allow the guy to get away with this. I know you like the guy, but he's crossed the line.'

He cleaned the mashed potatoes clean from his plate.

'I hate this stuff,' he said.

He passed the empty plate over to Sandra and wiped his lips.

'I know they still have the diamonds,' he pointed out.

'And you have me,' Sandra said, bending over the bed to place a peck on his large, smooth forehead.

She could play the waiting game, too.

14.

Waltzing Naked In The Eyes Of God

Seattle Winter.
'The money I had cabled through from London, it's almost gone,' Jacob said, scanning the bank statement.

They were sitting in the small kitchen of the condo they were renting in Bellevue, on the other side of Lake Washington. Dark trees sheltered the apartment from the sky, and the whole place appeared to be permanently plunged in relative darkness.

Jacob had found a part-time job at one of the large software companies down the road in Redmond, translating technical manuals into French. It was all jargon, never even occupied his mind. Anne stayed home. Silent. Writing letters she never posted. Watching soaps and game shows on the TV. They had agreed not to try and find a deal for the diamonds for another month. By then, maybe their trail would have grown cold and hopefully their pursuers might have forgotten them.

They were becoming an old couple already. Despite the mad silences and the lack of conversation. Acquiring silly little habits. She always laid out the table before they ate. He always cleared it and washed up while she made the coffee. Read the Sunday papers together, each with their own favourite supplements in turn. The way the small things of everyday life slot into their allotted positions and never change, without either of the participants even noticing. They slept in the same bed, but sex was rare and lacked urgency. The commingling of underwear in the same washing machine. Anne was still badly depressed. Obsessed by the horror of the Vegas events. Even though the deep scar was not visible under the thick tops she now wore, she remained acutely conscious of it, refusing to let Jacob see her when she bathed or at night or let him touch her breasts when they did fumble under the bed covers, seeking heat from each other more than anything else. The wound was healing, the thick scabs had dropped away to reveal the new rawness of the skin but the scar was carved deep in her thoughts. Once a week they fell into the habit of driving off into Seattle over the bridge and the high water for a coffee in Pioneer Square or a movie in Capitol Hill. Sometimes, she would spend the whole evening without saying a word to him. Intimate strangers.

Jacob waited. Hoping against hope her mood might change as the ghost of Nevada faded in their memories past.

The more Anne retreated into her privacy, the more he ached for her, loved her with a despair that surprised even him, a hardened survivor of earlier wars. The fact that he could not possess all of her, was incapable of penetrating her heart, was like a slow form of torture and every time he watched her only served to compound the hurt and the ache, the yearning that consumed him.

He wanted more. Living together was insufficient, he wanted the availability of her once radiant face, her pale body and fiery hair, and temporary loan of her cold heart. He wanted it all, the intensity of their first fucks, the raging desire of his jealousy; he longed for an Anne who hadn't suffered the way she had, who was free of this American nightmare; Anne as she had been back in London before he'd known her. The woman he probably had passed a dozen times in the street, on Charing Cross Road, the underground, who might well have sat in cinemas watching the same movie as him, listened to the same concerts in smoke-filled clubs, eaten with her back to him in the same restaurants, the Ganges or the Water Margin. Anne before she knew him. He wanted the impossible. Longing for less was just not on.

'You never talk about your life back in England.'

'I've told you before, it's not a subject I wish to discuss.'

'I know. I was just curious, I'm always curious.'

'Why?'

'I was beginning to think that maybe we might return to London. Together. It might be interesting. Seeing it all with new eyes, as changed people...'

'We have unfinished business here in America, Jakey.'

'No, we haven't, Anne. What is holding us back? There's nothing. Just sordid things. The past that brought us here, the diamonds, the wanderlust, badly-digested memories of American road movies. Illusions...'

'I'm not ready to go back.'

'When will you be?'

'Don't rush me, Jakey. I can't stand being rushed.'

'Rush you? You've been vegetating in this room for months now. You never do anything. You're just feeling sorry for yourself, Anne. Come on, snap out of it. I don't wish to sound cruel, but much of this you have brought upon yourself...'

'Have I? Do you think I wanted to have my breasts slashed and burned? I'm not that much of a masochist...'

'That's not what I meant, and you know it.'

'Well, that's certainly the way it sounded to me.'

'You're only twisting my words.'

'Oh, fuck you, Jakey...'

'The perfect answer to everything, hey?'

'What do want me to do? Tell me. Be honest,' she finally said, exasperated.

He was tired. He just wanted the row to be over. The silence to return as it was before, uncomfortable but tolerable. He was afraid of pushing her over the edge. Of saying one word too many, that she could seize on and misinterpret.

'I don't know,' he replied.

'See.' As a gesture of conciliation, she rose and began clearing the cereal box, milk carton, plates and cutlery from the breakfast table.

'No. I'll do it,' he protested.

'It's okay,' she said. 'You're right. We stay cooped up in here, getting on each other's nerves. We should go out more, maybe?'

'It costs.'

'Perhaps I could get a job. I'm getting bored all day, waiting for you to come back.'

'What sort of job were you thinking of?'

'Something casual,' she said. 'We haven't got green cards, Limits the options. Someplace where there's no paperwork and not too many questions asked. Waitressing? In a bar or a restaurant. They've so many coffee houses around the University District. There must be some vacancies going, surely.'

'Perhaps.'

'Are you sure?'

'Yes. It'll be a good thing to do...'

She coughed. The drizzle and cold weather was reaching through the wooden walls of the condo apartment and for weeks now she hadn't been able to shake off a bad cold.

'Anyway,' she said. 'Why go back to London? We've got enough rain here . . .' She smiled.

Jacob's heart warmed. It had been days since he had seen her smile at him that way. Like a child. His wounded romance cover girl. He'd found a couple of paperbacks back at the Elliott Bay bookstore where she was quite recognisable on the front cover, in chaste embraces with macho long-haired hunks or Regency beaus. He'd brought them back to Bellevue. She told him stories about the sessions. They'd laughed together at the silliness of it all. Brought out a bottle of wine. Got drunk. They'd even made love that evening. She'd kept her top on, though. It had been weeks, he came too quickly and felt guilty about it for days.

*

Evil had moved out of the clinic in the desert after completing a full recovery. He and Sandra moved in to the New West Motel, at the airport end of town. The place was functional, cheaper and less gaudy than the Imperial Palace. At least there was no casino and hordes of bothersome visitors from New Jersey and elsewhere to crowd them. Through his local contacts he acquired a gun. Should have had one first time, he reckoned. A Sig Saur. Good weapon. Reliable. Not too heavy.

While they waited for news of the fugitives, they did all the tourist things. Paraded up and down the Strip at night, gambling small amounts in the main hotels. Gaped at the white bears in the Mirage galleries, went to shows, visited the Hoover Dam and the desert where strange flowers still bloomed in the baking heat. This is what it must be like being married, Sandra thought.

He didn't ask her any questions about the events surrounding the shooting. She didn't have a ready explanation to explain her betrayal, had he done so. Days shifted by effortlessly.

Sandra knew he was good to her, and for now that was enough. She couldn't ask for more, she reckoned. He touched her with care, mindful of her pleasure, holding back, almost sentimental when he sensed degrees of joy animating her body as he lay on top of her, trying to minimise his sheer weight.

'My aim is true,' he said.

'Yes?'

'When all this is over,' Evil told her, he wanted her to return to Caracas with him. Well not quite, he had this small compound on the plantation a few hours away. 'We can be together. The weather's always pleasant. The fruits are tropical and invariably sweet. I've worked twenty years for the organisation. I'll cut down. So that I can spend more time with you. You'll see, it will be good.'

His big rough features melted into those of a lovelorn teenager when he said these things, almost making her forget how ruthless and bad he could be.

'Will you come?' he asked her.

'What would you do if I didn't?' she inquired.

A dark cloud shielded his small tight set eyes and he flinched.

'What is it?' she solicitously queried.

He touched his stomach where Jacob's bullet had entered his body.

'Nothing,' he replied. 'There's just a twinge, sometimes . . . '

But the only pain in his gut was the knowledge that she now knew too much.

'You poor thing,' Sandra said.

'Don't worry. It never lasts long.'

*

The Man From Caracas was annoyed at the delay on the American front, but life and business went on.

New couriers were found for the Miami run. Who proved more reliable. The shipments resumed. Anne Ryan's consignment was just a drop in the ocean. The success rate was high. Encouraged, they began smuggling the drugs themselves on occasions. Recruited Cubans back in Florida. They always wanted the money and knew to keep their mouth shut.

Only two consignments were lost in three months.

A sniffer dog became suspicious of one of the men while he passed through passport control at Miami International and the guy panicked, began to run, bringing more attention to himself.

The customs people X-rayed him and then fed him an overdose of laxatives. They didn't have to wait long.

The other operational failure was more unfortunate. This woman, Gloria, was actually engaged to one of the accountants at headquarters. She had to swallow the stuff which had been carefully wrapped inside condoms, so she could carry the drugs through in her stomach. She also happened to be five months pregnant. Made things look quite realistic. That's why the couple had agreed, the baby was going to be an extra expense. Poor cow. She had almost gagged a few times while she was ingesting the condoms. It was sometimes painful. Her teeth must have grazed or cut one of them. She navigated her way through the airport successfully, but once at the hotel where she was due to deliver the goods, one of the condoms must have broken. The chambermaid who found her said it wasn't a pretty sight. Naturally, there was no way they could claim the body and get the drugs back. Chalk that one down to the law of percentages, the Man reckoned.

Why did women always get the wrong ideas? They almost lost another shipment a few days later. The misadventure occurred with some high society chick the twins were keen on balling. Probably another who wanted to do the run for kicks rather than the cash. The Man had been slightly suspicious. Wrong kind of courier. He instructed the twins to fly to Florida ahead of her and watch her closely from the moment she left the airport.

He never found out whether she intentionally tried to give them the slip, or if she strayed from the carefully agreed plan by accident, making a detour by one of the fashion malls before the hotel where her room had been booked. The twins intercepted her as she entered the shopping precinct.

She was still alive when they cut her open to retrieve the goods. Not for long. They brought the photographs of her body back to the Man. Most interesting, he thought.

And his idle thoughts returned to the elusive Miss Ryan. Wondered whether, if the slicing was done surgically, he could then have her sewn up again before he had more fun?

*

Anne knew that agreeing to find work in Seattle was a bad decision. There were men. There would be temptations. She knew the dark core was still present inside her. But if it made Jakey happy.

She took the bus into town, emerging from the bus tunnel by Third and Smith Tower, within easy distance of Pioneer Square and all its coffee bars and other joints.

This was a young town, she discovered. The first ten bars she tried had no vacancies, not even part-time. A job was advertised at an oyster bar, but she had no experience opening the bloody things. Even the dingier places had no need of her. A couple of owners or managers actually remarked that she was too old for the job, too many students were already available. They could take their pick.

She was wearing her long blue skirt and a thick white cardigan, but the cold was chilling her bones. She had to get herself a winter coat. There was still a few more months of this weather to endure. She visited Nordstroms, but the prices were just too much. She just couldn't afford any of the coats she fancied. She ambled on, surrounded by the Seattle hills, her mood darkening with the rapid passing of the day.

The lobby lights of the Hilton on Sixth shed a warm glow on the pavement outside.

Anne walked in and headed straight for the bar.

She'd take the nine o'clock bus back to Bellevue. Had a couple of hours to kill and no way was she staying outside.

She soon caught the attention of a solitary man, drinking on her own, as she was, looking aimless. And available.

'You staying here?' he asked.

'No. Just having a drink.'

She turned round. He looked youngish, clean, okay.

'Let me get you another ...'

'This bar's really boring,' she said. 'I'll take you up on the offer if we can go somewhere else.'

'Sure.'

She slid off her stool. The guy was over six feet tall, loomed over her.

'Let me pay for this,' he said.

'Thanks.'

She managed a fine meal at the Inn at the Market, a hundred dollars and several drinks out of him. She warned him early on: 'I don't kiss, I won't undress but a blow-job is not out of the question,' thus putting the transaction on a business-like footing.

He actually declined the blow-job when they reached his room for the one-for-the-road final drink. Probably had a wife and two and a half kids back in St Paul, and was terrified at the idea of possibly catching something contagious from her. A hand job would do. A bit expensive, he felt, but he could put the meal and drinks on expenses.

The last bus had gone by the time Anne reached the terminal. The taxi ride home over the lake made a sizable dent into her earnings. Jacob was sound asleep. She'd think of some valid excuse in the morning.

The next day, she returned to Seattle and bought the dark blue coat.

Her nose was running. She'd been perusing the English papers at the newsstand by Pike Place Market and crossed the street, stopping to extricate the tissues from her pocket, and looked up at the fading photographs of strippers past in the window of the corner porno joint. She grinned. She was positive the place back in Bourbon Street had displayed exactly the same photographs, yes, the slightly plump piece of beefcake there. Standard issue advertising crumpet ...

'Hey, lady, what's so funny?'

The bouncer was calling out at her.

'Nothing.' She noisily wiped her nose.

'Looking for work, lady?'

'Yes. But not your kind.'

'Who said on stage?' he said. 'You're not the type, anyway. Too short, for one. Good hair, though.'

'Thanks for the compliments,' she called back, readying to move on.

'Hold it, lady. There is a job going.'

'Doing what?'

'We need a cashier for the day shift. Interested?'

'Maybe.'

She started the next day. The cabin was warm. The job undemanding. Most of the place's business was done at night, so things were never very busy during her hours of duty. She had told Jacob she had found a job at a cinema. Well, it was, in addition to the stripping and the private cabins. The films played on a continuous loop. Five dollars for four movies. Not that anyone remained inside that long. They had usually managed to jerk off long before the end of their first feature.

From time to time, Anne would venture into the dark screening room. She was fascinated. She didn't realise people could do such things, that certain women could accommodate so many alien intrusions. Much of it seemed almost physically impossible. And she thought she had been lustful? Compared to much of what she could see here, she was strictly small fry. A dabbling amateur in matters of sex.

It was repellent, but every day she still managed to find the time to view more. Witness new variations, further couplings on the flickering screen, improbable gymnastics, awesome cocktails of limbs and secretions.

'Hey, red, don't you want our cash?'

She snapped out of her reverie and saw the three greasy-haired bikers waiting on the other side of the glass. They appeared to be drunk.

She took the bills and handed them some change, and pressed the entry buzzer.

One of the men tapped on the window as he passed.

'Are you red beneath too?'

'Fuck you.'

'Oh, a right angry little limey. Maybe we should fuck you instead. Why don't you come out of your box and join the show inside?'

She ignored them and they trouped by, entering the club, leering at her.

They came out an hour later, even drunker, shadowed by the bouncer on duty, complaining the girls on stage were too old and ugly and none of them had red hair.

Anne was finishing her shift. She had a bad migraine. Decided to take a short walk before catching the bus to Bellevue, and began walking up Pine Street, unaware that the three bikers were following her.

'Hi little red!'

They surprised her as she reached the Egyptian Theatre. Surrounded her. There was no one around. She was helpless. They dragged her into the alley that bordered the theatre.

'Fuck us, hey, bitch . . . What you need is a proper lesson in manners. Think you're better than us? Well, the colonies are going to fuck you . . .'

The tallest of the trio unzipped his leather pants and pulled out a fat cock.

'Suck on this, red.'

The biker behind her brutally tripped her and pushed her head forward to impale her mouth on the other's penis. Anne calmly began to move her tongue around the intruder, feeling the tip of the cook unfurl from the foreskin as it grew inside her.

'Good, good,' the man said, enjoying the sensation. 'She's done this before.'

The third man was at the entrance of the alley, as a look-out. The one behind her pulled her coat and skirt up.

'Let's see if she is really a red 'un?' he roared with laughter, pulling her knickers down to her ankles. 'Oh, yeah, she really is!'

He stuck a sharp finger into her vagina. All she could think as she continued sucking on the big one's cock was whether his nails were dirty.

'And she's wet . . . She's enjoying this, the bitch . . . Fuck, that's not wet, that's a river . . .' He twisted the finger inside her and inserted a second digit.

Anne knew. She couldn't help it.

'Didn't I tell you all these Brit chicks are all sluts beneath their prim and proper looks?' he said to the other. 'We sure are going to have us some fun tonight.'

The biker behind entered her with a sharp shove, unwittingly forcing her mouth down even further on to the cock that filled her mouth. The heaving penis scraped against the back of her throat.

They both came quickly and called the third one over for his share. The tall one held Anne by the hair as the look-out walked over, pulling her painfully upwards. She could feel his come slither down her thighs.

'No,' the third biker said. 'Why should I get sloppy seconds? It's not fair. Tell you what, though, let's take the bitch home. We can play some more private games. It's getting too cold here, don't even know if I can keep my pecker up . . .'

'Good idea, compadre,' one of the others said.

'You can't . . .' Anne protested, conscious of the incongruous sight her knickers twisted around her booted ankles presented.

The unseen fist impacted with her stomach. She crumpled and passed out.

*

He'd checked the cinema. No one even knew of her. Jacob returned to their condo. Maybe there would be a message. There wasn't. And waited. Didn't know what to think. Why would she leave him now? The diamonds were still safe in the bathroom. It made no sense. None at all.

Anne returned two days later.

She rang the bell. The bikers had abandoned her handbag with the keys in the Egyptian's alley.

Jacob opened the door.

She was a sight for sore eyes.

'You!'

'I've been bad, Jakey. And no, it wasn't the Miami people this time,' she added, cutting his first question short.

He walked her in. She was uneasy on her feet. Her new blue coat was filthy. She clutched it around her as if her life depended on it.

'I walked from Boeing Fields, took me all night,' she said, sitting down. 'I'm so tired.'

'You should have taken a cab. I would have paid.'

'I just couldn't think straight. I was in a daze. It was my fault, Jakey, entirely . . .'

'You can tell me later,' he said.

'No. Now,' she insisted.

Her hair was in disarray, as if it hadn't been washed for weeks, a wide purple bruise stained her forehead, and there were cuts around her mouth. Jacob poured her some hot water from the kettle.

'Later.'

'No, you must know, Jakey . . .'

'You don't have to tell me anything,' he said.

She carefully sipped the water from the mug. Then set it down, empty, on the table. Stood up. Opened her coat.

Anne was naked underneath. Her body was full of bruises. Only the mutilated breast seemed to have been spared. The inside of her thigh was badly cut. But his eyes focused on her crotch. He stayed silent, couldn't look away, hypnotised by the spectacle.

Her pubic hair had been totally shaven away and the swollen lips of her unprotected sex protruded almost unnaturally. Never had he seen her more naked. The reason for the swelling was apparent. A small silver ring had been inserted, joining the two labia.

Jacob gulped.

Where her orange curls had been, the words SLUT had been roughly written with blurry blue ink.

Anne turned round.

'I know it's bad, Jakey. I can't see. Need a mirror. What did they do, there?' she asked him.

She bent over. Her anus was torn and blistered.

Jacob could feel the bile rising up to his throat.

Surrounding her anal entrance, the same clumsy blue lettering spelt out CUM HOLE.

'Shit!' he mumbled.

Rushed to the sink and brought back the kettle, a sink towel and a bar of soap and frantically tried to wash the words away.

'It won't go away, Jakey. They tattooed me. It's permanent.'

'Jesus,' he sobbed. 'Anne . . .'

'It's my fault,' she said. 'It always is.'

'Which bastards did this to you?'

'It doesn't matter,' she said. 'I just attract trouble. Maybe it's God's way of giving me a message.'

'Come on. You don't even believe in God and all that . . .'

'Listen,' she sat down and wrapped the coat back around her despoiled body. 'It still hurts like hell. Down there. Everywhere. I really need some pain killers.'

'We'll drive to the nearest hospital,' he said. 'You've got be seen to.'

'No, Jakey. I can't let anyone but you see me like this. Anyway, if there are doctors or nurses, they'll want to know how it happened. The police would get involved. Like being in a freak show. We can't run that risk. Just find me something to help the pain go. Please.'

He was in bed with her later that day, tossing and turning, gadfly images of what had happened to her screening in overdrive through his head when she woke.

She moved closer to him. Cradled against him.

'How are you feeling?' he asked her in the darkness. He could feel her seeking his warmth.

'A bit better. We'll have to try and get some stronger pain killers tomorrow,' she remarked.

'My poor love,' he said.

'Maybe morphine would help,' she suggested.

He didn't know where he would get morphine legally, but that was beside the point.

He would.

Anything Anne wanted.

One hour further into the night.

'Are you asleep?'

'No. I'm finding it difficult. What about you? Is the pain still as bad?'

'Getting used to it,' she said. 'I suppose you can get used to anything in the long run.'

'That's what they say.'

'I knew my nudist days were over after Vegas,' she said. 'Now I can kiss bikini thongs goodbye, can't I?'

Somehow they did manage to fall asleep.

*

'That's a very interesting diamond, Mr ... Smith,' the jeweller at the small shop in Kirkland said. 'A very nice piece, indeed. Would you mind telling me where you obtained it?'

'I was told you would ask no questions.'

'Is that so?'

'Yes.'

A moment's silence ensued as they stared at each other.

'Thirty thou.'

'Deal.'

'Cash, no doubt?'

'Of course.'

'Tomorrow?'

'No, as I explained over the phone, today ...'

'It's a very large sum. I never keep that much here.'

'Call the bank. Ask them to send it over. I'll wait.'

'Such a nice piece,' the jeweller said, picking up the telephone. 'Isn't it?'

The hospital intern sold him the morphine for a thousand dollars. Jacob had no idea whether he was being swindled or not. And it didn't matter. If this is what it took to assuage her pain, then so be it.

15.

To Be Only Given As Much As The Heart Can Endure

The heart of the night.

Somewhere in America.

'... Dispose of your junkyard religion and listen to the Mark. Yes, once again for your pleasure, none other than the Mark of God. Long time here holding this crown, sending you music in a foreign language. Oh, indeed. Listen to me all you travellers of the sweet airwaves, we must make good again, capture the night back and liberate the dreams. Oh yeah. Listen to the song, listen to the words of wisdom, the sound of one drummer reaching out. This is the Mark. This is Ron Sexsmith with *There's a Rhythm*.'

The quiet melody began.

'Sweet sounds ... Welcome back to the nightmare, folks. I'm at the wheel for the long drive. Hear me roar US of A. All you lost, all you toilers in the mines of anguish, I bring you relief. Tunes that will sooth the tortured souls you carry. The next one's for the best of you, the next one's for the lovers everywhere, the bodies simmering in the fire, gasping for air, the innocents of the flesh. I am the Mark. This is the music of REM and *Electrolite*.'

The duty engineer prepared the next tape as the REM tune unrolled and travelled swiftly up the launching ramp of the transmitter into the wilderness.

A good thing they had taped all the disc jockey's previous programmes. They would just go on repeating them until the right replacement came around the bend.

The October 19th show would unspool next.

Wasn't that the one when the Mark went on about angels, improvising a mighty rant? At least the music never dated. In that respect, the man had certainly had taste. For a certificated crazy.

*

You learn from experience. Now Jacob always carried the gun he'd picked up in Port Aransas and had used in Vegas on the Miami thug. There was no point in taking needless risks.

With the cash, they'd moved into Seattle proper. Found a small house on a three month rental beyond the University District. Afterwards, they were thinking of looking for somewhere to live on one of the many islands scattered across Puget Sound. You could only reach them with the ferry. It would be quiet and peaceful, they hoped.

Anne was getting better, although she was heavily dependent on the morphine. Apart from the obscene tattoos, there had been no permanent damage. The body was a resilient machine. The bruises and aches had long faded. Her hair was growing and beginning to obscure the first inscription. She decided to keep the ring. At first, he didn't know why she did so, but he found it oddly sexy, decadent, sometimes giving him a hard-on when he thought of it. They no longer made love. She said she wasn't ready yet. They still argued a lot. About small things. About nothing.

Mostly when he tried to convince her to cut down on the drug, now that the pain was no more than a memory. She denied this. And he knew the real pain was mental, as she tortured herself, blamed her errant nature for everything that had happened.

Spring made a tentative appearance after the snow had melted in the nearby hills and the continuous barrage of rain took a break.

Her favourite restaurant served fish and seafood with a grand view that overlooked Elliott Bay. It was actually her idea to have an evening out. They'd been real homebodies of late. As they tucked in to their food, Anne revealed that it was her birthday.

'I didn't know,' Jacob said. 'You'd never told me. If only I'd known, I would have bought you something...'

'What would you have bought me, pray?'

'That's not fair,' he answered. 'You haven't given me time to think, or shop... How old are you?'

'I didn't think gentlemen were allowed to ask that,' she smiled.

'Who said I was a gentleman?'

'I'm thirty, Jakey. Today.'

'A milestone.'

'Make love to me tonight.'

'I thought you'd never ask,' he beamed.

'The ring turns you on, doesn't it, Jakey?'

'It does. It's rather perverse, considering.'

'Time passes. We have to forget how I came to get it. I like it, too. Feel like such a wanton woman . . . All those men walking outside, the couples at the other tables, the waiters, how could they imagine the way I am under this dress . . . Christ, I am a slut.'

'No. You're just Anne, my dear dear Anne,' he said soothingly, taking her hand briefly in his until the *maitre d'* arrived with the new bottle of wine.

They had left the car parked in a small lot by the Alaskan Way Viaduct at the bottom of the steps from Pike Place Market.

It all happened so quickly. The way things do, leaving you no time to think.

They were at the bottom of the steps, a hundred yards from the car when they were caught in the blinding headlights of a vehicle coming from the direction of the Aquarium. As Jacob put his hand up to his eyes to cut out the glare, he caught a brief glimpse of the passengers in the front seat. Sandra and the Miami thug.

'Run!'

He reached for Anne's hand.

'What?'

The other car, an Audi, had passed them but the driver had hit on the brakes violently and come to a screeching halt a short distance away. They had been recognised.

'It's the guy from Vegas. In the car.'

'No,' Anne screamed.

They ran desperately for the BMW, the heavy undigested food in their stomach slowing them down.

He was fumbling in his pocket for the keys as he heard the other car make its U-turn and come toward them. The central locking clicked open and Jacob and Anne wrenched open their doors and dived in. Ignition. As he pulled away from the dark lot, the pursuing car was a mere thirty yards or so away.

He began racing straight ahead of him, still incapable of coming up with any sort of plan or specific direction to take. They both rushed by the Bay Pavilion. Jacob realised he didn't even have his lights on as the shadows of the overhead viaduct fell on them as they continued their parallel course.

The car behind was still the same distance away.

Jacob put his foot down on the gas. Anne sat motionless on the other seat, watching with fear the road ahead disappear under their wheels.

In films, Jacob reflected, car chases were more decisive, or spectacular. He couldn't go any faster, the revs were already in the red zone and the steering wheel shuddered under his grip. Even at his top speed, he could make no impression on the other car. They were evenly matched.

His mind snapped back into gear, now that the flow of adrenaline was ebbing. If he stayed on this road, they would soon reach the old harbour. He reached a decision.

'Anne,' he shouted out to her over the roar of the engine.

'What, Jakey?'

'I just can't outrun them. No way.'

'What then?'

'I'll make for the port area. It will be deserted at this time of night. We'll have to take a stand.'

'But...'

'I've got the gun. The moment the bastard approaches, I'll just shoot. It worked the first time. I'll empty the whole barrel into him if I have to, I swear.'

'Are you sure?'

'We don't have any choice.'

Hell, this whole car chase was quite ridiculous, Jacob thought. Where was the police when you needed them?

He raced on and soon the gloom of the old port cushioned the two speeding cars, as Jacob suddenly left the road and drove on to the harbour tarmac.

Evil followed.

Another two hundred yards and they would be at the water's edge. Jacob slammed his foot on the brake pedal, while fumbling for the gun in the inside jacket of his pocket.

'Here we go. Anne? When I get out, stay in the car, on the floor. You'll be safer there.'

The car slid to a halt. He couldn't have calculated it better; the water was close by. He opened the door, rolled out on to the cold ground and raised the gun. The other car had also stopped.

An ominous silence descended on the area. Jacob heard a car door open and slam, as he tried to focus his vision, slowly getting accustomed to the darkness.

Suddenly he saw a moving shape distance itself from the pursuing car. He levelled the weapon and aimed in its direction. The shape became clearer. He pressed the trigger. The noise was deafening. And followed immediately by a series of further gunshots.

The other man was also armed.

Jacob's heart sank.

And he had missed with his first shot.

The odds were worsening.

Jacob squinted, searching for his opponent again in the deep curtain of shadows.

He briefly thought he saw the paler shape divide, like a ghost, into two. He pressed the trigger and the weapon roared again.

Expecting an instant response, Jacob crouched down by the BMW's back wheels. There was no immediate reaction from the direction of the other car.

A minute passed by.

Then another.

The silence had become as deafening as the earlier gunshots.

Jacob realised he was holding his breath and inhaled deeply. He knew he hadn't found his target. He had been shooting totally blind. The other was playing games with him.

'Jacob!'

A woman's voice was calling his name over there.

Sandra.

'Jacob, don't shoot, it's me, I'm alone, you're okay,' she shouted. He kept his gun aimed in her direction.

Waited.

Finally, she detached herself from the night's darkness and approached. She was alone.

'Sandra?'

There was blood over her outstretched hands, as if she was coming to him with an offering.

'Where is he?' Jacob asked.

'Dead,' she calmly said.

'Did I hit him?'

'No. I'd taken his knife. He wasn't expecting me. After he took his first shot at you, I knew I had to do something, end this whole nightmare. So I did.'

'Are you sure he's dead?'

'Yes. Evil is dead. I checked.'

Jacob rose from his defensive crouch.

'Anne . . . Do you hear that. He's dead. We're safe. You can come out now . . .'

But, inside the BMW, she made no movement.

He opened the door on the driver's side, dreading what he would find.

She was still in the same position he had left her, but her eyes were closed.

'Anne!'

He ran round the front of the car to open her door, ignoring Sandra's presence. Opened it. There was blood spreading across her lower back.

'Shit!'

'What is it?' Sandra asked him.

'She's been hit. His first burst of bullets must have gone straight through the car and caught her. No . . .'

She was still breathing.

With all the care he could summon, Jacob pulled Anne out of the car and lay her on the back seat. She opened her eyes.

'You're going to be okay, Anne. Just hold on. You'll see.'

He placed his jacket over her front, as she was beginning to shiver.

'Sandra, can you drive?'

'Yes, but it's been some time.'

'Take the wheel. Just find us a hospital.'

Sandra moved into the driver's seat as Jacob crowded himself into the back with Anne's head on his lap. Her breathing was alarmingly intermittent. Sandra drove off.

There was a wry smile piercing the pain on Anne's lips.

'I think the bullet's in my vagina,' she said. 'I can feel it there. Poetic justice, I suppose.'

'Don't talk, Anne,' Jacob said. 'You'll tire yourself unnecessarily. Please.'

'It's no good, Jakey. It's no good. This whole mess is coming to an end for me. Gives you a chance to get out in one piece . . .'

'Don't say that.'

'I was already damaged when I came to America . . . Didn't stand a chance . . . Lust made me do it . . . Jakey, Jakey, I'm sorry I hurt you so much . . . I couldn't help it . . . The demons were there inside . . . My own demons . . .'

He could feel her drift away as he held her.

'PLEASE!' he cried.

Her eyes were clouding, their pale green depths enshrouded by the incoming waves. Her lips parted.

'You . . . were too good . . . Jacob.'

They were still nowhere in sight of a hospital as Anne died.

*

Sandra and Jacob returned to the apartment with Anne's body.

'How did he know we were in Seattle?'

'You sold one of the diamonds. The news spread fast. They're everywhere, you know.'

'I see.'

'He was bound to find her. Him or another,'

'I realise. Thanks for your help, Sandra. Without you, I might be lying there too, I suppose. And you saved me in in Las Vegas, too. What are you going to do now? Are you going to be safe?'

'Yes, I think so. They don't know about me. Evil never told them much. Reckoned it was his own private business, as long as it didn't interfere with the job at hand.'

'Evil?'

'That was his name.'

The weight of the day's events suddenly felt like a terrible burden on his shoulders. He no longer had any curiosity about how Sandra had met Evil or why she had followed him so far. All he knew was that Anne was dead. And he remained. Alone again. A bloody curse.

'What will you do now?' Sandra asked him.

'I don't know,' he reflected. 'Probably return to England. There's nothing keeping me here any longer. London's as good a place as any to rejoin the living dead.'

Sandra knew he was not going to ask her to join him.

Somehow, she'd always known it would be that way, all along the road, from one coast to another. She, also, had been following a dream that didn't exist.

'We'll have to dispose of her body,' Sandra said.

Jacob flinched.

'Wherever she's found, there will be questions. That you won't be able to answer, Jacob,' she continued. 'Even if you left the country, they'd trace you.'

She was right.

'Fine,' he said. 'But I would like some time alone with her, Sandra, please.'

'You loved her?' she asked him.

'Too much,' he replied.

She lowered her eyes. 'I'll be in the other room.'

'Thanks.'

She was no longer bleeding.

Her skin was paler than it ever had been, but her long silken hair kept its shine as he spread it across the pillow on both sides of her head.

He slowly undressed her, taking care not to tear any of the clothes as he peeled them from her body. He washed all the blood away with a damp flannel and admired the splendour of her outstretched nudity. Her curls had grown back thicker, obscuring the dissonance of the tattooed inscription. The pink outer reaches of her gash shone quietly under the naked light bulb they had been meaning to cover with a lamp shade for weeks, the silver ring binding the labia now a delicate adornment.

He contemplated her charms with solemnity.

Her stolen beauty.

Repaired to the bathroom and extracted the diamonds from their bed of face cream. Picked up her lipstick tube.

Painted her nipple and the stump bright scarlet, so they now matched.

Placed the diamonds on her unveiled flesh, as if entranced in some pagan ritual. One on each eye lid. One in the gentle crevice of her navel.

The final one he inserted delicately at the entrance to her vagina, below her clitoral hood, above the bridge of the ring.

Each diamond fiercely caught the reflections of the strong light bulb, spreading fire and ice across her inert body, a lattice of crazy fire flies in slow motion enveloping her like a shroud.

Then, he undressed and lay down by her side.

Maybe he slept, maybe he didn't. The morning forced its way through the customary rain clouds. The cold day raced by. Then dusk came, and Sandra was knocking on the door. He opened his eyes. It felt like only minutes since he had joined Anne on the bed.

He looked back at her.

The diamonds no longer shone with such fierce aggression. As if Anne's body had absorbed some of their inner strength.

'Yes,' he answered.

'It's getting late, Jacob,' she called out. 'We have to do it tonight.'

'Must we?' he asked.

'Yes, Jacob.'

He opened the door and came out into the kitchen. He was nude. Sandra said nothing. Watched him move, the sharp angle of his buttocks, the sculpted shape and colour of his cock. Sighed softly.

Jacob realised he hadn't dressed.

'I'm sorry, Sandra,' he said, moving back in the direction of the bedroom. 'I didn't realise. So many things on my mind . . . '

He turned. His balls swung gently against his thighs as he did so.

'It's fine,' she said, mentally storing away the images of this man's body she would never get to touch.

Back in the bedroom, Jacob dressed hastily and retrieved the diamonds from Anne's body. The lipstick on her sinking breasts he left untouched. He knew that's how she would have liked it. He was about to call Sandra in when he paused.

This was just too savage. Getting rid of her body as if she were unwanted refuse. He needed something of her. To keep. To help not forget her.

He put his mouth to her cold dry lips.

'You'd understand,' he whispered.

He found the nail scissors in the toiletry kit and made a careful incision in her labia and pulled the silver ring away. There was no blood where he had cut, just a meagre stream of pale, transparent liquid. Jacob unhesitatingly lowered his mouth to her cunt and sucked the cut dry.

The ring fit perfectly around his small finger.

'I'm ready,' he called Sandra.

They rolled Anne's ever so light body in the sheets and, under cover of darkness, carried her to the car.

Two hours later, they consigned her to the shimmering depths of Puget Sound.

*

Kirk and the other members of the group were naked and helpless on the other side of death.

'So this it?' one of them said, with a tinge of disappointment.

'It's beautiful,' Julianne pointed out.

'But where are all the lost?' the accountant plaintively said, who secretly pined for a woman now ten years dead he just couldn't erase from his goddamn memory.

'They must be in that country beyond the mountain chain,' Kirk said.

'So, we still have further to travel?' another asked.

'They're waiting over there, you'll see. Keep the faith.'

And the expedition set off again.

*

'Have a good flight, Jacob,' Sandra said as she dropped him at Sea Tac International. There was a flight to London in two hours. He was booked on it.

'And you have a good life, Sandra,' Jacob said.

'I will,' she replied confidently.

Before leaving Seattle, he had insisted she take the remaining four diamonds.

'I have no need for them any longer,' he told her. 'Anyway, with my luck, they'd stop me at customs and find them.'

As she protested, he had said: 'You deserve them. Here . . . '

He had asked her not to turn the engine off.

'I just hate partings at airports or railway stations,' he smiled at her. 'Just go, now.'

She steered slowly into the departing traffic.

'See you,' he called out at her, turning his back on the road and made his way into the registration hall.

*

'Hello. My name is Sandra, Evil gave me your name and number.'

'Where the hell is he?' the Man From Caracas roared down the line. 'He hasn't been in touch for days. He's a bad boy . . . '

'He's dead,' Sandra told him.

'Is he?'

'Yes.'

'And who the hell are you?'

'Sandra. I was Anne Ryan's accomplice.'

'Were you? And where is that bitch?'

'She's dead, too.'

'Is this a joke?' he asked.

'No. Two of the diamonds have gone. I have the others. I wish to return them.'

'Do you really?' he queried her.

'Yes.'

'You know I do not have a forgiving nature?'

'I expect you don't,' Sandra said resignedly.

'That I will have to punish you for the sins of your partner in crime?'

'I know.'

'Will you beg for forgiveness, Sandra?'

'If you ask me to.'

'Do you have red hair, too. Like your friend?'

'No. I'm a blonde. Well, not truly. It comes from a bottle.'

'Where are you?'

'I'm in room 302 at the Stouffer Madison Hotel in Seattle.'

'Wait there,' the Man From Caracas said. 'It won't take long.'

'I will,' Sandra replied and put the phone down.

The Man From Caracas summoned the French twins.

It looked as if he wouldn't have to change his lovingly-devised plans too much, after all. He walked over to the window. He could see the stables in the distance.

In her hotel room, Sandra ordered the most expensive item on room service. Sadly, she knew there were no poets in South America.

On Tenderness Express

For Dolores

"For in tremendous extremities,
human souls are like drowning men; well enough
they know they are in peril, well enough
they know the causes of that peril,
nonetheless, the sea is the sea, and these
drowning men do drown."

Herman Melville

DRAGGING AROUND THE CHAINS OF LOVE

1.

Martin

I am a liar.

An unconvincing narrator. A most unreliable witness.

So feel free to believe or not whatever I say. You may judge me for all I care, decree that I am guilty of this or that, or blameless, or indifferent.

Your call.

As for me, I don't give a fuck.

*

So, how did it all begin?

Barely a year ago.

In London.

A suite of offices in Holborn in a massive building of grey stone. Traffic gridlocked outside the bay windows of the suite, the sheer greyness of a British autumn morning already leaking into the soul and bodies of all of us. Joan, my assistant cum secretary cum decorative addition to the IKEA decor of the offices I was renting was away ill, yet again suffering from migraine. I was bored, idly surfing the Internet on my laptop, joining chat rooms left right and centre, spreading doubt and equivocation as I adopted a new persona on each occasion, swapping cybergender, teasing, provoking, offering myself, playing coy, alternately knowing or falsely innocent. As good a way to waste time as any other.

I was forty-four.

At forty-four, F. Scott Fitzgerald of St Louis, Minnesota, had already drunk himself to death. No such luck for me. I couldn't even stand the taste of alcohol and if anything was going to kill me in the long term, it was the subtle blend of caffeine and sugar in the Coke or Pepsi which I drank by the gallon. An ambiguous death wish if ever there was one. How could death by cola ever be romantic?

I had money in the bank and no will to live.

Sitting there, morose, waiting for the past to catch up.

Counting the pulses of the cursor on the computer screen, as it metronomically awaited my further orders to set sail for another forum.

Or the welcome interruption of a telephone call.

But all I had for company was the pain deep inside.

Until the knock on the door.

Business. The best possible distraction.

He was tall and beefy and boringly dressed in a brown double-breasted suit, hair trimmed regulation office length, early signs of baldness already visible, mid-thirties I reckoned. Corporate type. Small squinting eyes, thin colourless eyebrows, grey socks peering between trouser turn ups and sensible City shoes. Wife having an affair was my first guess. I handed him my card 'Martin Jackson, Private Investigations. Nothing Gained. Just the facts in exchange for your treasured cash. Nothing too Sordid, please'. He flinched. Just another geezer with no sense of humour.

I asked him to sit down.

A police siren faded in and out from the busy street outside. He coughed.

He took out a cigarette. Remembered distractedly to offer me the pack. I declined.

'You come highly recommended,' he said.

'That's nice to know,' I answered, not in the least bothered who had given him my name. By hook or by crook, I do my jobs and then draw a final line under them when they are completed. 'So . . . ?'

He squirmed in his chair, throwing me insecure glances across the desk.

'Naturally, anything you say is in utter confidence,' I tried to reassure him. 'Even if we agree not to pursue the matter further.'

He nodded.

Then raised his receding chin an inch or so and spat it out.

'It's my wife.'

Bingo.

It usually is.

The look on my own face remained impassive. The few friends I used to have always said I should play poker. Hadn't done since my teens when matchsticks were the only stakes.

'Your wife?' Sympathetically.

'Yes.'

'And?'

It was the usual story, with some variations. There are no new stories.

Couple marry. Probably too young. Go through poor but happy days together, hand in hand, hearts oblivious of deeper realities. Careers begin (his, at least). Money worries. The inevitable cooling down of ardour. Neglect. Wanderlust. Pressures accumulate. A fraught house move and mortgage complications. She feels he is now taking her for granted. He can feel her becoming distant. Both increasingly working late, only greeting each other quietly as they undress for bed at night. Their lovemaking is dull and predictable. One day, her face looks different, there is a shiny otherness present; she is dreamier than ever. Strangely distant. Indifferent. He suspects another man but dares not ask. Then, one day, a letter arrives in his in-tray at work. Accusing her, denouncing her extramarital activities. He can stand it no longer and confronts her. At first, in tears, she denies it but soon breaks down and admits to the affair. Promises him she will end it immediately. Blames him partly for his unthinkable blindness all these past months. He swears he will forgive her. They will start again. Spend more time together. It all ends in tears, in each other's arms at three in the morning. Feeling closer together than ever, or at any rate, since their initial coming together as students in Cambridge and the no frills wedding in the college chapel. So, it's all decided, the marriage will endure. Her affair will deliberately be forgotten. Erased in his memory. But two days later she doesn't return in the evening from work. He assumes she's missed her customary 6.27 commuter train. He goes to the station to meet the next one. He'd returned earlier to prepare dinner himself. A simple vegetable salad. He's vegetarian. She isn't on the following train. Or the one after. He haunts the station until the final train comes and goes, rushing between the station and their new house to check on telephone messages. There are none. The following day he phones her job and discovers she had taken the previous day off. Another day goes by and he forces himself to go to work, his heart seizing every time the phone rings. But it never is his wife. He assumes the worst. That she might have gone back to her lover and will never return to him. During their initial row, in a spirit of appeasement, he had carefully refrained from asking the man's identity. He now bitterly regrets this. He hasn't a clue who her lover might be. Never had a clue while it was going on; doesn't have a clue now.

It's been nearly three weeks now. He's past the heartbreak. Just worried. Not a word from her, she hasn't even returned home to retrieve her clothes, her books and other personal things. So unlike her. He hasn't changed the locks, assuming she would have come visit during the daytime while he was at work to retrieve her belongings. No one has heard from her at her publishing office. They're angry. None of this makes sense to him.

So, now, he's sitting in my office, the latest in a long line of unhappy husbands. Pale demeanour, sorry eyes, shaving cuts dotting his square chin. Isn't my job great!

'Have you been in touch with the police?' I asked my hapless visitor.

He hadn't. Still felt she would somehow return to the harbour of his arms; after all, they had made up, or so he felt. He had forgiven her, and it would be too embarrassing to place the whole matter in the public domain. So his brother, an architect in South London, had suggested using a detective. Just to find out the truth. And if she had left him for good for the other man, at least there would be confirmation. A sense of closure.

'Yes, closure is very important,' I said.

He nodded.

For once, we were on the same wave-length.

'So,' he finally asked. 'Can you take the ...' he hesitated to use the word 'case'; too many bad films and books had depreciated the word. 'Are you willing to look into this?'

I agreed to. A job is a job after all.

I explained the leads I would pursue, the time involved, the effort, the likely cost. Cheque or cash would be fine, I preferred not to take credit cards.

He passed over the envelope he had brought along, containing an assortment of photographs of his wife taken over past years (one taken in sand dunes outside of Scarborough on the Yorkshire coast, another with her tousled hair windswept in front of the Beaubourg Centre in Paris on an autumn day the previous year, he pointed out), addresses: where she worked, the friends he knew she had. I asked further questions, desultory queries about her life before him, parents, university, likes and dislikes. I studiously noted down the answers on my pad, feigning interest and attention.

'I'll do my best,' I reassured him as I led him to the door. He left.

I made an immediate beeline for the toilet and was violently sick.

*

Two hours later, I felt no better. The nausea still treated my whole body as occupied territory, and as much as I tried to exert some will power, there was not even a hint of a resistance army regrouping, ready to fight the drop dead feeling that appeared to have won the war within. I still wanted to vomit, but there was just bile lurking inside me and that only made things worse. I locked up and walked the hundred yards to the first of the legion of sandwich shops in the nearby area. Egg, cress and mayonnaise on white bread. Yes, once inside me that sort of lethal formula should do the trick. Help me be sick again as the vile mixture curdled in my throat and stomach. But somehow the food settled and all I was left with was a feeling of utter emptiness.

On my desk, the brown envelope Christopher Streetfield had left lay unopened. I toyed with it, tracing its shape, weighing it in the palm of my hand, holding it to the light. Photographs, a list of names and numbers. What was left of a man's life after the fall of the bomb of lust . . .

A sorry landscape.

Inside my head, it felt like a pressure cooker.

I desperately needed something to happen.

It did.

At this stage in a *noir* book or movie, a husky-voiced long-haired blonde knocks on the door and asks the private eye to search for her missing friend or relative, with ambiguous hints of payment in bodily kind thrown in.

She didn't even knock. She walked straight in.

Her hair was auburn, though, and cut short.

And it was her younger sister she sought. A little sister, with ironic shades of Chandler! I was sure I'd read the book already. But it hadn't involved John Le Carré the first time around.

She'd found me, of all places, in the Yellow Pages. I didn't even know I was there. Kept on being rude over the phone to tele-salesmen trying to convince me of its display virtues. Strange how fate plays little tricks on you.

Her name was Nola Poshard. French grandparents, and I suspected some far back miscegenation in the family, a hint of darkness in her skin and eyes, some exotic, venomous flower, predatory, cold-hearted but siren-like attractive. Nola.

The sister's name was Louise.

Nola had come into possession of a major book collection. A past lover of Nola's had left it to her some years previously, to assuage his guilt or hers over previous indiscretions or heartbreak. She had kept the bulky collection, of mostly modern firsts, in storage for ages, having no particular interest in its contents or what the books had represented for her erstwhile lover. I got the impression he might even have killed himself over her, but the hard expression on her face when she related the collection's history prevented me from inquiring further.

Eventually, she had decided the cumbersome collection needed valuing and had been amazed by the final figure the rare book dealer had quoted her. He had also recommended that, should she wish to realise its maximum value, it would be preferable to sell in separate lots, or at any rate some of the best pieces individually. One item in particular had intrigued him. A seemingly one-of-a-kind curio. A book he'd actually heard of but which he had always suspected was apocryphal. Not actually a book, as she explained, but an advance uncorrected bound proof.

Le Carré, having completed his new novel, *The Night Manager*, had his secretary send his publishers the diskette. This was eagerly welcomed and passed on to the production department so that advance proofs might be printed for major buyers, reviewers and other publicity and marketing purposes. On receipt of these, several copies were biked to the author's Hampstead house where it was soon discovered, to utter dismay, that the diskette in question had been that of the first draft and not his final version of the novel. Further, the initial draft actually named many of the real names of persons and companies involved in the Arms for Iraq controversy which had partly inspired the novelist. All the proofs were summarily destroyed and the process repeated with the correct diskette. Though not end of story, as Le Carré's publishers were then already in the process of takeover talks with a smaller, more aggressive house. Maybe someone in production or dispatch or any department threatened by future cuts had managed to secrete a copy of the proof's first stage before they had all been pulped? Allegedly, according to the dealer, one copy had once surfaced at an auction in Texas, but this was unconfirmed.

Seeing the volume amongst the cardboard boxes temporarily housing Nola Poshard's inherited collection, he had remembered the tale and distractedly checked the final chapter of the book (both the first and the second proofs sported the same cover). And, there it was, a different ending to the one he remembered. It was difficult to actually ascribe a value to this one-off, but he was confident that it would fetch a premium price amongst American collectors due to its unique nature and the curious publishing history that surrounded it.

'So,' I asked Nola Poshard. 'What happened to the book then?'

'The proof,' she corrected me.

'What happened to the proof?'

'The little slut stole it,' she said.

'Tell me about her, your younger sister.'

'What do you want to know?'

'Basically everything,' I answered. 'If I am to find her, those sort of details do come in handy . . .'

Louise wasn't actually her sister, but a half-sister. A fish-out-of-water blonde in a family whose antecedents stretched back to early Cajun days in New Orleans, and where fiery hair and darker skin were the norm. I was thankfully spared centuries of family history, and given the bare bones. From the tone of Nola's voice, Louise certainly sounded like the black sheep of the family, but then I had the feeling Nola was herself no stranger to black thoughts or actions and this was a bad case of pot and kettle. But a potential client is a client and you just keep your trap shut if you wish to stay in the private eye business.

I completed my note-taking and began my usual spiel about expenses, costs and this and that and confidentiality and ethics, But Nola quickly interrupted me.

'Yeah, I know all that, Mr Jackson. So spare me the details. I can afford you and the time it takes to track down the little bitch. All I want to know is whether you can take the case on or not.'

'I can,' I answered.

'And right now?' she queried me, her gaze landing on Streetfield's brown envelope on my desk. 'Do you have any other cases on at present?'

'No. I'm quite free to take your assignment, Ms Poshard,' I replied with great assurance. 'Nothing else in progress.'

'Good,' a thin smile crossed her scarlet lips. 'Because I want you to devote one hundred percent of your time in finding Louise, and the book of course. You should have no distractions.'

'In all fairness,' I pointed out, 'the cost of the operation could well mount up to much more than the value of the book, you know.'

'I'm aware of that, Mr Jackson, but that's beside the point.'

'If you say so, Ms Poshard,' I noted.

'I do.'

'And when I catch up with Louise, do you want me to get the Le Carré proof back for you? Or just advise you of its whereabouts and hers?'

'Find her first. I will then decide on the next step to be taken,' she said.

Something gave me the feeling that she didn't give a damn for the book, however rare it might happen to be. It was her little half-sister Louise she wanted back. And badly.

We got down to business. I had a long list of questions. I opened my notebook again.

Nola Poshard didn't have all the answers and it was agreed I would visit her house the following day for the photographs and documents and extra information I required to tackle the case properly. I also wanted to see Louise's erstwhile room there. How often people left simple clues behind when they did a disappearing trick. Although not seemingly Mrs Streetfield ... My new employer paid the upfront money in crisp bank notes, that still smelled of the deep corruption of a bank vault as opposed to the shabby filth of the corner cash dispenser.

I watched her as she rose and made her way to the door. A classic backside and legs to kill for. Stockings for sure.

'Until tomorrow, Mr Jackson,' she said, peering briefly over her shoulders.

'I will have made some enquiries already by the time we see each other,' I assured her, my eyes still fixed on the horizon of her pantyline, daydreaming of the tanned flesh and its treasures barely concealed by the taut material of her black skirt.

'That would be nice,' Nola Poshard murmured as she walked out the door. Echoing my thoughts exactly.

*

Once again I was on my own. With the muted, almost distant sounds of the Holborn afternoon traffic for company. The Streetfield envelope and its contents sat silently on the desk as if in a spotlight. The knot in my throat tightened. I took the brown package and buried it inside the left drawer. Next to my passport, post office savings book and last will and testament. Forced my mind to travel back to the swishing noise the stockinged thighs of Nola Poshard made as she sashayed out of the office earlier, her smell all animal, radiating lust with natural allure. Yes, she was damn attractive, that I knew. But there was also danger there. Essence of femme fatale. Just like in a book.

. That's how it all began.

Two cases. Two women.

The second and final part of the story of my fall.

2.

Cornelia

There were few things Cornelia cared about.

The dance, the music and her books.

She knew she didn't fit in, hadn't emerged from the same mould as other women.

Or men.

But basically, she didn't give a damn.

She was self-sufficient, had no starry ambitions, lived for the moment and knew that if worse came to worse she would always somehow survive.

Because she had the moves. And she had the looks.

There again, her looks didn't conform with fashion or boring standards of beauty, but they were distinctive and she knew from past experience that they worked; she could turn on the charm at will. Bed most men or women she set her eyes on.

And, within limits, she also enjoyed sex.

Although, whenever she found leisure time enough to reflect on the matter, she also found the occupation highly overrated. Entertaining, yes, but the pleasures it provided her were as much mental as they were sensual and body-related.

Cornelia had no heart.

She couldn't blame the fact on a poor childhood or traumas of the past or any other plausible excuse. She'd been born into a relaxed middle-class environment, her parents had never divorced (despite a parade of explosive rows over the years which she often witnessed with much puzzlement but little anguish), she'd never lacked for anything, so she reckoned she just must have been born that way.

She couldn't understand this thing called 'love'.

It just escaped her.

And neither could she stand the sight of pets.

So, by the age of twenty-five she had accumulated a baker's dozen of past lovers in her smooth passage through teenage years and early adulthood, none of them having ever graduated to live-in status for more than a couple of weeks; been the object of three requests for marriage and been on the wrong side of two failed suicide attempts which both men blamed on her cold, indifferent heart; had enjoyed a brilliant academic career and attained a supreme form of confidence that convinced her she would continue sailing through life with much ease, but needed some sort of hobby to keep the boredom at bay.

On the rare occasion she confided with her mother about her lack of empathy with other members of the species and the fact that few subjects managed to grip her attention long enough to exercise her imagination, her mother was reminded of a charming anecdote which, although rather funny at the time, now contained the paradox of Cornelia's life in a nutshell. As a child, Cornelia would always tire of new toys and dolls within hours and would sit around moping on the carpet, and when asked what the matter was—she had only begun to speak a few weeks before—answered that she was boring; what she had tried to say was that she was bored.

She was capable of demonstrations of affection, so that could pass muster, she reckoned. So, it was just a matter of pretending. In both high school and then Yale, she involved herself heavily in student theatrics; she had the perfect looks and distance to play most ingenues in the repertoire, and scientifically used this training in her trajectory through the world of men and lust and other distractions.

When the time came for her to choose a subject for her thesis, she was at a loss for ideas. Most of the angles academia suggested did not attract her in the slightest. To everyone's surprise, not least her somewhat shocked and bemused tutors, she opted for sociology and an in-depth study of the sex business in the Boston area, suggested by some copy-editing she had done for student publications and then a small magazine devoted to literary erotica started by two budding ex-student entrepreneurs she had worked with on the student journals.

For a whole year, she immersed herself in the seamy side of Massachusetts life, frequenting topless bars, interviewing strippers and local whores, gaining access to hidden away brothels which catered for both the student and business population of the area. Her subject was frowned upon by the university and there were threats to withdraw her research grant and not a little controversy on the campus. But she was clearly fascinated by the subject and one of the most gifted students in her year, and a little pressure she covertly exerted through a journalist she had somewhat conveniently bedded soon saw the academic authorities come to their senses and accept her work.

She was granted a PhD with honours.

Her approach to her subject had proven impeccably detached, intellectually rigorous and defused any sordid aspects her trawl through the the world of sex as a commercial transaction might have raised.

So Cornelia was now Cornelia PhD.

And at a dead end.

The conquest of academia had effortlessly been accomplished and the concept of further challenges to overcome held little attraction. Of course, she knew she now had to make a living. Her parents were willing to help out for a short period if necessary, but Cornelia knew she had to survive on her own, with no obligations to others holding her back.

At this stage, she knew only one thing: she had no wish to ever become an academic and follow the career path she had borrowed until now. The people and atmosphere just bored her.

She found a junior editorial position with a minor New York publishing house and moved to the West Village where she found a small apartment she could barely afford. After just three months, life bored her again and, further, she was flat broke. Because by now she had an expensive habit. Not drugs; she'd tried some, they did nothing for her. Books. She'd always found, from childhood onward, that reading was the best cure for boredom and had quickly begun accumulating a collection of her favourite books. At Yale, in the countless used books emporiums that still littered the Boston suburbs, she had come across countless first editions of books she had particularly enjoyed and began collecting certain authors, genres or illustrators. The walls of her studio were carpeted with wooden shelves groaning under the weight of her books, every one carefully shielded in protective plastic covers which she would finger with the nearest she would ever come to love. Her books became her life. She moved from the publishing house to a magazine company who were willing to pay her an extra five thousand dollars per year, even if the job mainly consisted in penning more literate blurbs to accompany the fuzzy photographs of celebrities in various states of undress supplied by the paparazzi of the world or snatched from video screens and movies the actors would have wished to erase once and forever from their filmography.

But as her book collecting progressed—by now, Cornelia had moved from provincial used bookstores and thrift shops to the Strand's rare book room and dealer's catalogues—so did the prices she was having to pay for her discoveries.

A genuine first edition of John Irving's *A Son of the Circus* came her way and she sadly found she couldn't afford it. Her pride precluded assistance from her parents or reliance on a loan. Cornelia realised she had to find new ways to make money. She convinced the dealer in Bethesda to hold the volume for her for a week until she had puzzled out her financial predicament.

A chance encounter outside the St Mark's Bookshop the following day offered an unexpected solution.

'Hey, Cornelia,' a woman's voice shouted out.

Cornelia looked up and recognised a woman she had interviewed two years before in Boston, when she was researching her thesis. She couldn't recall her name. They had a drink together and one hour later Cornelia auditioned for a bar in Alphabet City which was short of strippers. She knew she had a body and looks men lusted for. She was no prude. It just sounded like easy money to supplement her publishing wages.

In retrospect, she knew her audition must have proven somewhat amateurish. She'd tried to recall all the bump and grind moves she had observed in such a detached manner previously, but found she couldn't attain the same level of vulgarity. She would have to find her own moves, her own style. She knew she was too stiff and could see from the puzzled look on his face that the joint's booker (or was he the owner?) couldn't quite make her out. She stood butt-naked in front of him, the bar was empty, her grey CK underwear crumpled on the ground where she had thrown it in the throes of her stumbling dance. She moved up to him. Unzipped him and sucked him off. The whole procedure only took a few wordless minutes. He came inside her mouth. She detached herself from the bar-owner's cock, took a few steps back, grasped a glass from the counter and spat out his come.

'When can I start?' Cornelia asked.

One week later, the John Irving first was on her shelf.

Four weeks later, she left her publishing job. She could earn as much money doing six shifts a week stripping. She found another, better quality club, where the men tipped better and made less demands, which allowed her to concentrate on her dancing and develop her particular style. As befits a Yale PhD, Cornelia felt she could make her own rules, and made it a rule to restrict her sex work to dance alone; no shower work, mud or fat wrestling or private sessions behind closed doors. And she charged twice as much as the other women for a lap dance, which only served to make her more desirable to the men who could afford her.

It was just work, she reasoned. Her body was a commodity and she was not selling it, just supplying it on loan. It allowed her more leisure time to read, see movies, relax. Initially, the new life was good.

But book collecting is just another vice. It feeds on itself and never stops. Every new book acquired breeds interest or need in another, often more elusive as well as expensive.

The prices dealers or catalogues were quoting began to soar.

Cornelia ruled out prostitution, or running like a mad cow between too many clubs and bars in search of the extra necessary greenbacks, as a step too far, and began making enquiries into ways of making quick money when the right book came onto the market.

She had the looks and the intelligence, and her questions in the dressing rooms and dark bars soon found the right ear.

There was a phone call, followed by a meeting she had to attend blindfolded.

The man in the darkness facing her had asked her if she knew how to handle a gun.

She had. Her father had taught her and she had been on the university shooting team, it had been a momentary challenge.

A proposal was made to her.

Someone out there recognised her quirky talents and thought she was made of the right stuff.

No harm would come to her if she said no.

And the money was excellent.

She was given a week to come to a decision.

It only took Cornelia forty-eight hours to make her mind up.

It was just another transaction. She needed the money; someone needed a job done.

She wasn't even nervous about this new and decisive turn in her life. She knew her affection for other people bordered on the non-existent and that she didn't suffer from guilt. Neither was she religious or sentimental. Or even squeamish (apart from snakes or eels or other such slithering beasts).

So, it was agreed.

There would be telephone calls and there would be occasional jobs.

The assignments would be infrequent and she was given latitude to turn any down so it wouldn't be counted against her. A few months down the line, she asked for the arrangements to be changed, so that she would just make contact and indicate her willingness to take on a job. That is, each time a new book came on the market which she could ill afford to purchase from the proceeds of her dancing.

He—or was it they?—at any rate, it was always the same voice at the other end of the phone line, readily agreed to this.

Thus did Cornelia Irish's new life begin.

Exotic dancer, as some still described her chosen profession, book collector and killer.

*

She would always remember the first book she killed for. It became a prized item on her shelves. A symbol of her independence from the nine to five grind. Two thousand dollars it had cost her. A copy of the much sought-after Doubleday edition of J. G. Ballard's *The Atrocity Exhibition*. Most of the initial print-run had been pulped and publication cancelled. Few volumes had survived and he was an author she liked, even though this particular book was her least favourite. Too linear; Cornelia loved the art of the story where a tale went from A to B. She'd always been somewhat systematic in her approach to life, always taking new steps in her stride, climbing every mountain or molehill in turn, one at a time, with downright obstinacy in her refusal to panic, whatever the circumstances.

The doorman cum bouncer at her club had put her in touch with the Organisation. They had arranged for her to pick up the gun in the cabin of a peep show close to Forty-second Street before the onset of Disneyfication. An East German small calibre. The hit was a name called Vargas, a South American businessman. A pencil-thin guy in his thirties. She'd met up with him at the bar of the Royalton on East Forty-fourth Street. He thought she was a high-priced whore and Cornelia did nothing to change his opinion. It had been a few months since she'd last had sex with a man and this one was not unattractive. One on one in his hotel room, she felt, was a safer option and, after all, she needed a fuck, and sending him on his way with a satisfied libido would do no harm. He was still dozing in bed as she put the cushion over his head and pulled the trigger. The gun had a silencer. No mess, clean kill. She felt quite proud of herself. She had already dressed and was out of the room five minutes later, having carefully cleaned all the surfaces she remembered having touched while Vargas fingered and caressed her. Extra precaution: she even took the soggy condom from the bin and disposed of it a few blocks away. She wasn't sure whether police scientists could get a DNA trace from her own secretions on the outside of the latex, but there was no point taking unnecessary risks.

So easy.

And she bought the Ballard book and had cash to spare.

There were two more hits in the following six months. The Egyptian businessman also wanted to bed her, but that night Cornelia wasn't in the mood and anyway the guy had greasy fingers and made her shiver every time he touched her. She excused herself and visited the bathroom. Took the gun from her purse and unlocked the safety. When she emerged from the bathroom, the short, fat guy was already half undressed, standing there by the elaborate four-poster bed of the Broadway luxury hotel, his bulging stomach straining against a white vest that barely reached his navel, his cock still soft, and still wearing grey socks held up by suspenders. The sight of the socks and the suspenders was even more ridiculous than his cock still at half-mast and his broad smile as he saw her move closer to him.

'I thought you had gone in there to undress, my dear,' he said. Then noticed the gun in her hand, aimed at his heart.

But Cornelia had the advantage of surprise. Overweight men in a state of undress and still wearing socks don't tend to react very fast.

She quickly raised the gun and shot him through his forehead. Out of the corner of her eye, she caught sight of some bone and brain matter and a corolla of blood whistling through the air in slow motion behind him, like fireworks against the room's cream-coloured walls. The unholy mess landed on the bed before the Arab's body finally hit the floor. Back in the corridor, she was about to call the elevator when she heard steps around the corner and raced to the stairs to avoid being seen.

That night, she replayed the hit a hundred times in her dreams and was surprised the sight of the man's head exploding hadn't shocked her somehow. Seen too much violence on TV, she reckoned.

The man's death earned her a signed copy of Patricia Highsmith's early lesbian novel *The Price of Water*, which she had published under the name of Claire Morgan. Cornelia found the book profoundly disappointing once she got round to reading it a few days later.

No matter.

Nothing's perfect.

The next assignment that came up proved messier. She had to

travel to Chicago and felt uncomfortable functioning in a different environment to her New York patch. It was a weekend job with Columbus Day added on. A woman on a dirty week-end with a Wall Street banker lover at the Drake Hotel. Establishing some sort of contact with her was a tough one. She couldn't use her seductive wiles and allure this time. She trailed the woman a whole day and managed to get a room next to the adulterous couple and, as she had been taught back at school, listened to their muted sounds of coupling by cupping her ear against the bottom of a glass which she held against the thin wall separating the hotel rooms. She felt a right fool. In the morning, after observing the clandestine couple sharing breakfast, Cornelia got her opportunity as the man and the woman separated and her target went on a shopping spree. It was touch and go but Cornelia didn't think she would get another chance. The woman was changing in a small cabin on the mezzanine floor of a Victoria's Secret branch on North Michigan. Cornelia knew it was too crowded to use the gun she had been provided with. Clad only in her underwear to avoid suspicion, she stepped from her own alcove toward the exiguous cabin where the other woman was changing. Fortunately, the other woman was short and slight so Cornelia had a height advantage. The whole operation was wordless. Before the target could protest at her intrusion, Cornelia had swished the scalpel straight across the woman's throat. The blood squirted everywhere. Over the floor, over Cornelia's white skin and garments, over the pile of discarded lingerie the woman had accumulated during the course of her shopping. But it had been the right method and no sound disturbed the changing area as Cornelia lowered the still spasming body to the floor. She quickly rushed back to her own alcove and slipped her suit on over the blood that still ran down her long limbs and slowly made her way to the street, trying not to attract attention.

Back at the hotel, she had to burn all the stained clothing, after cleaning herself in the shower. Then she took a cab to the airport after settling her bill. Cash, of course.

The mysterious intimate apparel murder even made the next day's newspapers. There was no suspect. The women in the store only had eyes for the lingerie, not for the other customers, particularly if other women's shapes proved slimmer or younger. Cornelia felt no need to keep the cuttings, though.

She suspected it was the cuckolded husband who had ordered the hit, but reckoned it wasn't for her to reason why. It was just a job, a means to an end. And the fee for the kill acquired her a set of early Modern Library firsts.

It was after the Chicago job that she asked the Organisation to change her status. From now onwards, she would only take a job on her own terms and time. She was surprised they accepted. She already had enough money in the bank for another six months with normal expenditure. She even cut the number of sets at the two clubs where she worked and steered clear of evening slots, where the customers were rowdier and keener to date her or have her more than just dance. The owners protested, but Cornelia gave them no choice. She knew by now she could easily find a job stripping in any joint in Manhattan. Told them she was resuming her studies, needed more time. They reluctantly agreed. After all, the wonderful Cornelia already had so many regulars who only came to watch her dance, and attracted a better class of customer, they reasoned.

*

She settled into a satisfactory routine. A few hours dancing a week, which paid for the rent, utilities and groceries, and the added income from her extra-curricular activities accounting for the luxuries: books and clothes.

Then there was Holly. Holly Fox.

Met in a bar, and her first real sex with another woman since early fumblings and stolen kisses in a school dormitory in her teens.

The night with Holly at the Gramercy Park apartment was one Cornelia would remember for a very long time. She had somehow never thought it would be so tender and enjoyable, and frenzied in its quiet acceptance of another kind of love. Cornelia danced for her. Holly had never been to a striptease show and had been completely taken by surprise when Cornelia had revealed her profession. So, all part and parcel of the rites of seduction, Cornelia had obliged with a particularly sensual private show.

In all honesty, Cornelia had never thought of herself as a lesbian, but now realised she was indeed bisexual, and was amazed that not everyone was. Being with a woman was good, different, although if pressed she would admit to the fact she would never be able to totally give up cock, even if the owners of the cocks seldom tickled her heart well enough to even contemplate a more permanent relationship than a one or two night stand. She liked to be filled. By something warm. And she enjoyed sucking cock. Relished the spongy texture, the heartbeat her tongue could always perceive under a cock's thin skin.

But Holly was nice and, for the first time in ages, Cornelia felt a need to spend more time with a person. She knew that Holly could be both lover and friend; she could laugh with her, and fuck. The combination just felt so natural.

Which didn't stop her from mixing the powder with a night drink; and in the morning Holly was dead beside her.

At least she knew the woman's death had occurred painlessly, as she lay in her bed in the wake of a satisfying come, with hope and pleasure in her heart.

As a result, the first edition mint condition dust jacket of Malcolm Lowry's *Under the Volcano* became a bit of a sentimental favourite of Cornelia's, amongst all the books in her growing library.

From then on, Cornelia decided not to mix business with pleasure. It could only complicate things, make them messier. If she had to use her body to get close to a target, so be it, but only in the last resort. The killings had by necessity to remain impersonal, anonymous.

There was a guy in Brooklyn Heights. He fell through a window. Like a brick. Ernest Hemingway.

An Italian guy in Alphabet City. She'd been warned of his drugtaking. Doctoring the junk was child's play. Larry Clark's book of photographs of kids in Tulsa. Chillingly appropriate, she thought, but a mere coincidence. First she found the book, then she got the assignment.

But she preferred using guns. It was cleaner, more clinical, although she always had pangs of disappointment after every job when she had to dispose of the weapon she had used. But those were the rules. And they made sense.

She met a man. Maybe all the killings had melted her heart, rendered her vulnerable, but she tried to make it last longer. Going against ingrained habits. Gregory, his name was. Greg. It was nice while it lasted and she even thought of disconnecting from the Organisation. Dreams of tender domesticity and picket fences briefly clouded her thinking. But she had lied to him. A lot. When he discovered she stripped, he left.

Never again would she become close to anyone, she decided, and returned to her treadmill.

She hated the next job, in California. Disposing of an obnoxious porn filmmaker. In order to get close to him, she had to masquerade as an actress and got herself fucked every other way before she could retreat to the privacy of the house and retrieve her gun. Parading nude on the set, she had had no way to conceal it and was forced to go through with the whole disgusting charade. There were two studs present and she took great pleasure in executing them too. No way could they live and later boast how they had DP'ed this gorgeous New York stripper. She finished all three off with crotch shots before destroying the film which stored every minute of her infamy. F. Scott Fitzgerald's *Tender is the Night*. A very expensive acquisition, costing her more than she had wanted to pay.

The episode left a very bitter taste in her mouth for months and it wasn't until nearly half a year later that Cornelia allowed herself to be tempted by another book.

The job proved easy. Brooklyn. Faking a suicide. If the target had been cumbersome, she feared beforehand she might actually have to give up the whole contract killing caper. But by the time the Fredric Brown set proudly sat on her shelves in the Greenwich Village apartment she still lived in, she had put the past behind her and reconciled herself with the way things went.

The next kill was on her home patch of the Village, a British guy who seemed to know what was coming and offered no resistance. Because she had been given lines for him, she knew the job had been ordered by another woman. Whose name had to be the last word he heard. He took the bullet with a look of relief. It was following this easy assignment that Cornelia got herself the tattoo, in memory of the Sig Sauer she had used.

It appealed to her irony.

A small present to herself.

For keeps. Forever.

And, damn, it felt sexy.

3.

Martin

The deep of night accepts no lies. In dreams, the truth.

A persistent migraine, unrelieved by dissolving a couple of aspirins in a glass of fizzing Pepsi Cola, had forced an early night on me. As I fell asleep, I was already wrestling with daydreams and a kaleidoscope of images out of control rushing through the crowded turnpike of my mind, as I tossed and turned like an epileptic under the duvet, begging for closure, for the past to magically fade away if only temporarily.

The persistent, monotonous drip-drip of the rain outside the window punctuated my swirling thoughts of random events, women, places and sordid past cases.

Finally, all the ambient noises merged into utter silence: the rain falling on my leafy, suburban street, a floorboard in the corridor that sometimes creaked, the hot water flowing through the old central heating pipes, all the secret sounds of a house in darkness, magnified somehow in my highly-trained imagination. All became quiet, absolutely still.

I was dressed again, eating under-spiced food in an Athens taverna, bouzouki muzak punctuating the air, half-reading a book while stealing glances at a lone woman eating at another table and trying to guess her nationality. Her eyes meeting mine. Complicity. Loneliness. Jump cut to me fucking her in a hotel room (mine? hers?) and my gaze captured by a small, square plastic clothes label incongruously stuck to the very centre of her right butt as I sweatily thrust in and out of her cunt, oblivious to the obscenities she is spouting about how this lover of hers in Istanbul the week before lent her to a friend and watched them doing it. Hard inside her, my rhythm metronomic, insistently ploughing her stretched mid-western pussy, trying anxiously to decipher the writing on the label without losing my sexual concentration. She must have known she was on the pull tonight, I guessed: had slipped on brand new panties, not that I had given the flimsy garment any damn notice when undressing her in lustful frenzy. Cut. I was a child again, boiling inside at the sheer injustice of the world, lodged uncomfortably under my teacher's desk at primary school as punishment for something or other, red in the face at the thought of what the other school kids must be thinking, saying about me. Running around the playground time and again, my knees bruised, my chest on fire, imagining that I'm the Czech champion Emil Zatopek. Years later, swimming in a broad, dirty river, my heart full of the folk music of Joan Baez and Bob Dylan I've just discovered and thinking obsessively of Christel, the German exchange language student with whom I am platonically sharing a tent in nearby Fontainebleau forest this night. Christel who is four years older than me, already a woman, insisted I turn my back when I visited her in her garret flat amongst the Paris rooftops near the Gare d'Austerlitz, and she washed herself in the basin in the middle of the room. But I peeped. Of course. Christel whom I followed some months later to the Vallée de Chevreuse, seeking her at the youth hostel, but she didn't appear and, my heart asunder, I walked miles and miles seeking her on every farm or isolated café where she might be working before forlornly hitching back to Paris as night drew near. Flash forward to who knows when in the sad parade that was my life. A New York hotel room where I am thrusting in and out of the wrong woman and taking out my anger on her, my hands closing on her wrists and leaving dark marks, my teeth biting into her neck as I thrust violently in and out of her, it's not her fault, it's just that she's not the woman I want to be here, the one I crave for is back in London or is it Frankfurt, being ploughed doggie-style by her husband or some other fucking stranger. So I continue to batter the insides of the one I am with, from Finland she is but no longer lives there, I can feel my cock fully extended scraping against her innermost recesses, and she moans and she moans and I feel like screaming and telling her not you, not you. Out of the corner of my eye, I watch a small cockroach slide down the hotel room wall and move into my suitcase. I smile but I keep on fucking the woman. In New Orleans too, many years later, I saw a cockroach dance a slow tango on a wall. It was also a hotel room, there was also a woman with me in that room. I don't recall the sex we had, all I remember was that the air-conditioning was wonky and we had to change rooms twice.

Slow fade. Teenagers in a circle on the carpeted floor of a Kensington mansion, playing a game of truth, and one guy whispers boastfully that he has had Catherine, small, adorable buck-toothed Catherine, and my heart sinks and I want to die as my whole sixteen-year old world collapses around me like planets colliding in the silent void of space. Flashback. My mother in a hospital bed, her face and body now but the shroud of a skeleton, eaten away inside by the cancer from the damn cigarettes, and me, not finding the right words to say, unable to conjure tears (they always come later) or any sign of emotion. The blankness of me. The inability to express pain on the outside. The coldness of me. The killer inside. Oh oh oh the memories are now on the rampage, like flaming battalions of marching ants ravaging my brain and there is so little I can do to stop their inexorable advance. I am asleep and I am awake and I am aware that I am the prisoner of a dream, of a film that unfolds and I can't reach the stop button on the damn VCR. And an insidious voice that comes from nowhere and everywhere keeps on flashing forward to the next section in the story, the one part I have no wish to experience again. Ever again. Eyes, a body, a voice, a woman who just melts my heart with the sheer shadow of a smile, a mole on her left breast or is it a birthmark, a tooth out of alignment, a small scar on her right cheek. No, I try to shout out loud, you are not welcome in this dream. You do not belong there. I probably twist my body convulsively around the bed and will her to not advance further into the dream. This is my dream. Mine only. So fuck off. Stay out of it. Stop torturing me. And somehow it works. For a moment at least. I will her away and the dream becomes the night and my heart stops and I die and it's a field of green that stretches beyond the horizon and I'm standing in the forest, looking out into the clearing. Everyone is dressed in black which makes no damn sense as it is pitch black, night, deep and devouring and black on black is just another contradiction, and what the hell I'm dead but I'm still here and I'm standing, my heart shattered into a thousand small pieces, like elements in an impossible jigsaw. I start walking. The ground beneath my black-socked feet is soft but dry. I am out of the forest. The others have now gone. I feel lost. I am lost. I turn my head around in all directions, looking for familiar bearings. There are none. The darkness is ever present. I close my eyes to listen to the night. I am blind, I am asleep, I am dead, I am deaf. Then a morsel of light appears, indistinct, distant, flickering on the screen rising under my eye-lids. I stop walking. I float among the darkness. So this is it, I catch myself thinking. The famous white light. The white pinhole slowly begins to expand. It is circular. Deep as a tunnel where the exit is still miles away. I relax. I have accepted the inevitable and am about to renounce all control over my body and senses when a voice, soft, vulnerable, just says 'hello', like on picking up the telephone. The voice. Her voice. It's above me, around me, behind me, ahead of me, inside me. Sounds like a long drawn out 'hello'. Hellooooo. Teasing almost, overflowing with quiet emotion, and I find myself torn between two directions, the white light that beckons and a woman who reminds me of things unfinished, of a closure that never really happened. The light grows stronger and I yearn for its blessed release, but all the time the words she says are being carved into my flesh with all the pain a kitchen knife cutting across skin can inflict and she is saying over and over and over again that this is just too easy, ain't it, that I can't get away like this, dying is too good for me. Dying is no solution. In the deepest recesses of sleep, I try to fight back the siren tones of her words because I know now that if I don't do something about it, fast, real fast, soon it will be more than her voice, it will be her face there in the darkness, her eyes, her pale naked body, and once again, unending loop of pain, I will have no choice, I will run towards her to beg for forgiveness, abandoning forever the embrace of the white light that would help me forget, that would cauterise my memory. I try to say something but my throat is sealed. I struggle to form words but my tongue is no longer there to help. I have to say something to her or I am lost. But already the light ahead of me is fading and the contours of her face are beginning to take shape. In all her heart-wrenching beauty. My silent scream is loud enough to wake the dead. Her face fades. And again I am asleep and again I am alive and again I am a world of insufferable pain.

*

I awoke from the nightmare, and all around me it still felt like hell. The mess of the bedroom, the smell and dampness of my own body baking between the dirty sheets and the winter duvet, the flashing red light of the radio alarm I hadn't reset since the day the electricity had been cut off at the mains while the engineer had installed the new digital box that now allowed the whole building to view a fantabulous forty-nine channels. Flying across the wide screen of my mind were all the memories that just wouldn't go away and kept on relentlessly crisscrossing my neurones like imps dancing at Halloween with large wooden brooms stuck up their arses. I checked my watch, my status symbol and obscenely expensive Tag Heuer. It was late enough. Time to get up and go to work.

*

It was the sort of leafy, quiet street where the cheapest house would have cost the average punter a lifetime of salary cheques as well as the total proceeds minus pimp commission for selling both his mother and younger sister into slavery. A metal gate protected the courtyard from the rest of the riffraff that roamed this neighbourhood between Swiss Cottage and Regent's Park. I announced myself through the intercom and the gate opened and I made my way through of flock of polished BMWs and Volvos to the front door of the house. Nola Poshard was waiting for me here.

'Good morning to you, Mr Jackson.'

'Ms Poshard.'

'Did you sleep well?' she asked me.

No point in lying.

'Actually, no,' I answered.

She didn't bother to ask me why.

Not that I would have told her.

A man has to have his privacy.

'So ...' she broke the awkward silence and led me to a large room that looked back on a surprisingly large garden considering the part of town we were in. 'What is it you need now, to begin your investigation in earnest?'

I looked around the room. Modern furniture. Chrome and dark wood and unsettling geometry. Philippe Starck maybe. Tasteful prints in glass frames scattered across the walls. Watercolours, sketches. From where I was couldn't quite distinguish the subject of most of them. Maybe I did need new glasses. But nowhere could I see books. For someone who was intent on retrieving a rare book, Nola Poshard didn't appear particularly sold on displaying the manifold joys of literature.

I took my place on one of the leather couches.

She was wearing black leggings—no, too thin; stockings or tights I decided—and an outsize green sweatshirt that ended midway down her thighs. She knew she had great legs. You don't, or at any rate shouldn't, wear leggings otherwise.

'I haven't much to go on, you know,' I finally told her.

'I realise that. What can I do to help? I really want her found.'

'And the Le Carré book?'

'Of course.'

She took a cigarette from a pack open on a close-by antique desk. Damn, I hated women who smoked. Spoilt the kissing. Not that I even thought I had the slightest chance to ever lock lips with Nola Poshard, femme fatale and ice queen of this parish.

'Tell me everything about her, warts and all' I suggested. 'I need to get some mental picture.'

'You've seen her photos I left with you, haven't you? And I told you everything yesterday anyway.'

'Yes,' I said. 'But it's not enough. It's not just what Louise looks like. Tell me a bit about what makes her tick, her past, her habits, good and bad, the sort of men she likes, the perfumes she wears, the way she dresses, her taste in booze or drugs, her favourite clothes ... All the things that make her Louise.'

'Gee, Mr Jackson, I don't know where to begin.'

'Call me Martin,' I said.

'I'd rather not,' she answered. 'Let's keep this on a purely professional level, can we?'

'OK,' I nodded. 'So tell me about Louise.'

*

How do you condense a person's life into words? Nola gave me the chronology, the details of family betrayals and outside episodes of lust, guilt and happenstance that had caused Louise's arrival and a deep-seated sense of envy between the two sisters. But it felt like another world, a sordid veneer of facts, things that had happened to others, and I felt no connection. The story, as she monotonously intoned it as she sat close to me, was just a confection of words. On their own, they made a sort of bizarre sense. Together, I couldn't grasp them and their implications. Was I in the wrong job? The hem of Nola's shirt kept on moving up as she spoke, the occasional flurry of her hands as she sought to emphasise a point of history pulling the thin material a little further up her thighs. My gaze rested on her knees, and the pale outline of a scar on the left knee—a childhood fall?—captured my attention. She spoke of Louise's perversity, how she flirted with older men from an early age, tested her sexual powers on them with wicked insolence, but it was the sort of tale I had heard a thousand times before. I knew there was no point in trying to understand the sexuality of younger women, it just made no sense and had to be accepted wholesale with all the other wonders and contradictions of the world. Some men had the key, I'd never had. But beyond the bare bones of Nola's diatribe against her younger half-sister, I could now sense what was missing here: emotions. A sense of a real person, with flesh, bones and feelings.

I interrupted the monologue.

'OK,' I said.

'OK what?' Nola queried.

'OK,' I repeated. 'I think that's all I require for now.' A thought occurred to me. 'Could I see her room?'

'Her room? There's nothing there. Don't think I haven't searched it thoroughly.'

'I'm sure you have,' I told her. 'But I would still like to see it, you know, spend some time there. Detecting is a bit of an impressionist patch,' I explained to Nola, 'not just information: little touches, intuition, details both important and casual. You just never know what is going to provide a lead, a direction. People always betray themselves in the small details. What they least expect often betrays them.'

'I see,' she acknowledged.

'Please,' I insisted. 'And I'd like to spend time alone there.'

'Fine,' she finally agreed. 'If that's you want. You're the investigator.'

'And you're the client, Ms Poshard.'

*

A young girl's room. Who has since become a woman. In this room? In this bed? With a man, a boy her own age or an older one? Pastel shades, soft furniture. A bedspread with flower motifs, matching pillows. Dolls and old teddies still piled up in one corner. Fading stationery on a wicker desk, with Hello Teddy motifs. Inside the drawer: hardening sticks of spearmint gum, yellowing photos of school friends, parents, even Nola still vampish ten years or so earlier in a garden by a pool about to jump, a broad grin addressed to the camera. Polaroids of a dog. Pencils in need of sharpening. Dust. Eraser debris. I closed the wicker drawer; never thought I'd find a diary still there. 'Dear Diary, I'm about to steal the book to spite that damn sister of mine and god knows what else and I am running away. I'll be staying at 218bis rue Saint Denis in Paris where I expect the detective she hires to find me, but only after I've fucked every man there under forty.' I smelled the room, hunting the distant fragrance of Louise's childhood, her loves, pains and fears. With the dust came a mixture of scents, dead flowers, green notes, a sharp acidy tang, soap fading against soft skin, anger, sadness. Briefly I thought I recognised one of the strands: Anaïs Anaïs maybe, but then it was gone. I moved to the bed. The sheets were immaculate, the bed had been changed since Louise's hasty departure and clean linen substituted. Never mind, I was no expert in reading cum or secretion stains or sufficiently Sherlock Holmes-like in coming up with mighty deductions from the differing pubic hairs still scattered across a tired set of sheets. I slipped a hand between the mattress and the bed's frame. Nothing. Too obvious.

An old Compaq sat on the dressing table. I switched it on, lingered pensively while it booted up and explored the computer's memory. There was nothing there, all files had been erased as far as I could see. I unscrewed the back of the machine and pulled the hard drive out. I knew a company in Wandsworth who could do wonders extricating information from seemingly censored corners.

The scent of her soap was, naturally, stronger in the small en-suite bathroom, even though the cleaners (or Louise, prior to her departure) had thoroughly cleared it of cosmetics, leftover soap bars and even towels. I nosed around, my mind clutching at straws. The cabinet still held some unsuspicious run-of-the-mill medicine: soluble Disprin tablets, shocking pink Ibuprofen pills, Migraleve tablets, a toothpaste dispenser, tubes of lip salve, spare toothbrushes. The fixtures were standard, the shower curtain plastic and opaque. I had an idea and stepped over to the toilet and lifted the top of the porcelain cistern. Bingo. Lodged behind the plastic float was a wodge of plastic. I pulled it out. Ah, the influence of bad movies!

It wasn't a gun, or the hoped-for diary full of gushing revelations, but a bundle of postcards. All from foreign cities, addressed to Louise care of a PO box at what appeared to be a nearby post office, and each in the same distinctive, cursive handwriting.

I disposed of the plastic wrapping in the bin and slipped the handful of cards into my jacket pocket.

The text revealed little.

Endearments. Fantasies. Feelings. 'I miss you'. 'I want you'. 'Wish you were here'. 'If only'. 'A city without you.'

A man of few words.

Amsterdam. New York. New Orleans. Seattle. An interesting mix. The family, I recalled, had its roots in Louisiana.

I turned my back on Louise's room and made my way down the stairs. Nola still sat where I had left her, deep in thought, draped over the heavy leather sofa. The level of her hem was now approaching indecency, not that discovering whether she was wearing tights or stockings would make any difference to my libido.

'I'm done,' I told her.

'See yourself out, then, Mr Jackson.'

She barely looked up at me.

'I will report back as soon as I have any worthwhile information, Ms Poshard.'

'I do hope so,' she said.

'Trust me, I'm a detective,' I said as I walked towards the front door and Regent's Park.

The femme fatale of the parish didn't even smile.

Cold-hearted, I decided.

*

And there was the problem in a nutshell. Cold-hearted women turned me on, and right now, in the taxi threading its way through the midday rush hour along Wigmore Street, I had an appetite for sex.

This is where the mean street crusader in most stories picks up the phone, and after a a quick browse through his little black book suggests a chat over drinks about past times to some old flame, or some pliant assistant who's absolutely besotted with him. I had neither mobile phone nor secretary and the last woman who'd taken me to her bed was highly unlikely to repeat the invitation. In fact, I was desperately trying not to think of her. She'd fucking broken my heart and more.

I tapped on the partition and alerted the cab driver.

'Change of direction, mate. Can you take me to Waterloo?'

He turned into Baker Street and the traffic we encountered became even thicker.

*

Darkness comes earlier at this time of year and even though it was barely three in the afternoon, the lateness of the season and the heavy grey skies combined in a false dusk as we reached the railway station's zone of concrete bunkers.

I had the driver drop me off in the shadow of the Millennium Wheel and made the rest of the journey to the railway arches by foot. The entrance to the Kubla Khan was in a slight recess, and the sign advertising the presence of the health club was discreet in the extreme and most passers-by would not even notice it.

I paid my ten pounds entrance fee and signed myself in. Mike Smith. This was an establishment which was big with the worldwide family of Smith. The attendant didn't even look up at my face. Well-trained in the art of discretion.

I was handed two medium size white towels and a locker key attached to a thick rubber band, and shown the way to the changing room.

Sitting on the wooden bench surrounded by a gallery of upright lockers, I undressed. A black guy was doing likewise in another corner of the small room. He nodded silently at me as he pulled his boxers off to reveal a somewhat awesome penis which appeared to be already semi erect. Or at least I hoped it was. He smiled as my gaze locked on his cock. 'You like?' he asked.

'Nice,' I said. I had no wish to offend him. The rest of his body was particularly fit; toned muscles rippling along his back as he bent over to slip the rubber band holding his locker key around his ankle. So that's what the rubber band was for.

I slipped my T-shirt off, then my socks. I was sorely conscious of the fact that inside my final piece of underwear I was still quite small and limp.

'First time here, eh?' the black guy called out.

'Yeah.'

'Nice place. You'll like it. Very relaxed,' he said.

I pulled my briefs down past my ankles. Threw the garment and rest of my clothes inside the locker and stood, naked, to turn the key in the lock.

He was watching me do this while tieing one of his own towels around his midriff. I did likewise. I began stretching the key's thick rubber band across my foot and towards my ankle.

'You top or bottom?' the black guy said.

'Switch,' I answered, and then added, 'but sometimes prefer to be bottom.'

'In that case, you'd better put the band around your wrist, man,' he said. 'It's a code. If you're looking for action, if you know what I mean.'

I straightened up and inserted my left hand through the rubber band's girth.

The black guy laughed and left the changing room. I adjusted the towel around me. I had to push my stomach out to keep it fixed around my waist. I walked out into the corridor leading to the facilities.

*

The shower area was in semi darkness and empty right now, which gave me courage as I dropped my towel to a bench and thoroughly cleaned myself after getting the balance between hot and cold water right following some halting experimentation. Other men came and went as I washed. Few of them even bothered to cover themselves with towels. They came in all shapes and sizes. Quite a few orientals, some younger men with skinhead cuts and tattoos. Finally, I left the shower, dried myself and ventured further into the innards of the health club. The first sauna room was rather crowded but I found myself a place on the edge of one of the wooden benches. The man next to me was openly playing with himself. It was so dark in there that, beyond him, I could barely see the white outline of the other bodies present. But soon the heat got to me and I was gasping for breath. It had been years since I'd been to a sauna, and I had forgotten how the air was so thin and the heat attacked you all the way down your throat. I closed my eyes, hoping to surmount the feeling of oppression, but failed abysmally. The burn inside was moving down towards my lungs. I rose to my feet and made my way to the door. As I did, a hand in the darkness brushed against my cock and muttered something unintelligible.

Outside again, I caught my breath, relaxed. Then realised I'd left my towel in the overheated cabin. The other one I'd been given was in the locker. I reckoned I didn't need it yet and delved further into the darkness of the Kubla Khan. A second sauna cabin on my left appeared even more crowded and smaller than the first. Through the glass window all one could see was a jumble of bodies, and much movement. I passed. Down the corridor I could see a brighter-lit window. The steam room. Approaching, I noted a phalanx of bodies dotted around the periphery of the humid, misty room.

What the hell, I thought, let's see how low I can go. It didn't matter anyway. Kay was gone from my life forever and I knew I had to take the punishment in some form or other.

Naked, I entered the steam room.

Within a minute or two of seating myself at the edge of one of the benches, the man next to me began caressing my cock. I said nothing. Allowed him to continue. Soon, I was hard as he handled me with due care and attention, caressing my shaft within his clenched fingers, delicately slipping a finger across my glans. Amidst the whiteness of the steam room, I turned my head to see who he was. Just another man, middle-aged, a trifle overweight, with early signs of baldness. As he wanked me with his left hand, his right one played with his own cock which jutted out from the fold of his lower stomach and the curly bush of his pubic hair, thick, uncut, the mushroom head a darker hue of purple than mine. He was looking straight ahead of him, into the cloud of steam that floated there, as if I didn't even exist and his hand was manipulating a toy, an object. I felt no excitement as he handled me, his busy hands ignorant of the rhythm my pleasure required. This went on for another minute in absolute silence. Then, there was a grunt and through a clearing in the steam I saw another white body kneeling on the stone floor just a couple of metres away from me, and as my vision improved I realised the man was sucking another off, his head bobbing up and down in the lap of, I thought, the black guy who had greeted me in the changing room. The sound had come from the throat of the coloured man being pleasured. Had he just come in the other's mouth? The steam surrounded them again.

I moved my right hand in the direction of the lap of the man jerking me off and, hearing no objection, took hold of his penis, brushing his own hand away. Felt rubbery, not quite what I'd expected. Clumsily, I fingered his humid foreskin, then his shaft, trying to remember the way I liked women to touch me there.

'Suck me,' he soon whispered in my ear, leaning towards me, his hand deserting my cock and lingering across the small of my back as my manual attempts at playing with him floundered.

I didn't even hesitate. I knew from the moment I had entered the health club that I would go with the flow, to the bitter end of this. My hand moved away from his cock and I rose from the wooden bench, placed myself on my knees on the slippery surface of the floor and drew my face level with his crotch. The middle-aged stranger adjusted his position by opening his legs wider. I moved my head forward.

He held his cock aloft.

I opened my mouth and took him whole.

I sucked him with eyes closed. I could feel the texture of his skin, the difference between glans, stretched foreskin and the rougher surface of the shaft as my tongue explored him slowly. From time to time, he would thrust his crotch forward, the cock digging deep into the back of my throat and I had to react quickly and modify my angle of suction to avoid choking. Actually, I reflected, it wasn't that unpleasant. But neither was it pleasurable. This I knew both instinctively and because my own cock had detumesced and shrunk. I applied myself to the fellation, wondering when he would come and whether I would have to swallow it. He stayed hard, and warm, inside my mouth and as my tongue slithered up and down the shaft, I thought I could feel the beating of his heart as I moved along the darker veins that crisscrossed his cock.

Right then, there was movement behind me and I felt a touch on the nape of my neck, a kiss. From another stranger. Then a hand cupped my buttocks, and a finger was drawn down the crack of my arse. My mouth intimately attached to the cock of the sitting man, I was unable to react to this new contact and didn't break the heavy silence of the steam room. A wet finger dug itself, nail and all, past my anal sphincter and broke into me. I tried to relax my muscles, to allow it passage.

I had just adjusted to this penetration when the man I was sucking pushed my head away and rose and, without a further word, still erect, walked out of the steam room. The man who was skewering my rear behind me bade me to rise and his body rubbed itself against me. His finger abandoned my anus and I could feel the hardness of his member press against my buttocks. For a few moments, we both stood there while he rubbed against me, his body felt all greased up. I tried to turn my head to see who he was, but with a hand, he indicated I should stay still. Finally, I heard him say 'I have a condom; come upstairs with me.'

I did.

There was a row of cabins of different sizes under a low, dark ceiling. Each had a plastic mattress. He held me by my cock, like a dog on a leash as we walked up the narrow metal stairs to the private cabins. He selected one of the more spacious ones and led me inside.

'Do you want privacy?' he asked.

'I'm not bothered,' I answered quietly.

He left the swing door to the cabin open. As he pushed me to my knees onto the cold mattress, I saw the shadows of other men grouping themselves by the door to our cabin, to watch.

My partner, a skinny guy with a smooth chest and a long thin cock, presented his penis to my mouth and I accepted it. It was easy after the first time. I sucked him with a semblance of vigour until he was rock hard. I could hear his breath grow more shallow as I did so. Out of the corner of my eye, I noticed he had a blurred tattoo on his left arm and saw that some of the men outside the cabin watching me sucking him were playing with themselves.

'Now,' he said.

He positioned me on the mattress, applied some cream to my opening and placed his cock at its point of entry. One thrust and he was inside me. I was surprised it didn't even hurt. And then the stranger fucked me. I didn't even know whether he was wearing a condom or not. Once again, I felt no pleasure, wondered what all the fuss was about, what kicks other men got out of being buggered, forced, but I also knew I was being too analytical about this. He moved rapidly inside me. Just felt like taking a shit in reverse really. Being stuffed, dilated further with every one of his thrusts. One of the men by the open swing door approached and presented his cock to my mouth, as I was being shaken by the forward movements of the man fucking me. I shook my head to decline but he wouldn't take no for an answer and his penis soon breached my lips. One more, or less I figured. Now I was being truly fucked. But a few perfunctory licks of my tongue against his pee hole and he withdrew with a jerk and I felt his come splash against my chin and upper chest. And I felt a warm sensation inside my arse as the first stranger also came.

A minute or so later, I was already on my own on the mattress, my two transitory partners gone, the spectators departed for other spectacles and the ejaculate dripping out of me and down my legs.

In a way, it had been too easy.

Like so many other things, was this all there was to it? I wondered as I washed away all the traces of my usage in the shower downstairs.

By the time I hit the street outside, a sea of commuters was marching from all directions into the maw of Waterloo Station as dusk settled over the London grey.

4.

Martin

The computer screen flickered blue as I settled my backside into the leather comfort of my designer armchair. Joan had called in. Chicken pox. She'd be away for a few weeks. Hoped I'd cope on my own.

I'd manage. Batman without his Robin.

Who needs a sidekick anyway?

I connected with the various search engines and systematically explored all the key areas of the case: the Poshard family, book collecting and recent auctions, the cities that appeared to be at the epicentre of the affair.

Hundreds of bytes of information flowed across the screen and I began the necessary process of elimination.

Martin Jackson, Internet Detective! Made me sound like the valiant hero of a pre-war pulp magazine. See him surf, see him crash, see him find the woman (and preferably the missing book)!

The phone rang. It was Christopher Streetfield, wanting to know what progress I had made in locating his missing wife. I pacified him.

'Not much to go on, Mr Streetfield,' I said. 'But there are one or two avenues I'm looking into. Some possibilities. I will get back to you as soon as I have something positive. I just don't believe in making uneccessary promises or raising my clients' hopes in vain.'

'I fully understand,' he agreed.

He was off to Norway the next day for his work, and provided me with his coordinates there.

'I'll keep my mobile charged up, so you can contact me any time while there,' he added, with a touch of gentle desperation.

'OK.'

I put the phone down. I felt no guilt about lying to him so blatantly. Since the moment I had accepted the assignment I had had no intention whatsoever of investigating his wife's disappearance. How could he not read it all over my face? Are all cuckolds so blind?

I returned to the web.

It was like reading tea leaves. So much junk, so much detail, but you had to narrow in, focus on some small clues here and there and try and make sense of it all. The previous year, a crooked telecom executive had sold me various codes and I was now able to hack in to a number of databases with full access to a welter of financial and personal records. It had been a perfect investment, and half of my successful cases since had unravelled across my screen, the pieces of who had done what to who or stolen this from that or checked into the wrong hotel with the wrong partner had unfolded ever so easily amongst the lingering tracks of credit card transactions. What a detective needed these days was a keyboard, not a gun.

First, there was a piece of information here that appeared of interest, then another there, then yet more items amongst the undigested, unedited load of information floating out in cyberspace, hidden like nuggets of gold between the flotsam and the useless shit that crowded the information highway. One thing led to to another and then again further down the pixel road; as my fingers danced an elaborate waltz over the keyboard, I avoided the dead-ends, the branches in the road that looked as if they would lead nowhere, and began making some vague sense of the whole farrago, translating intuitions into hard fact. It was at least three hours until I looked up from the screen again. Yes, certainly some interesting leads. Names that connected to the Poshard family that somehow shouldn't; curious connections; unexplained oddities in various recent book auctions. I blinked, rubbed my eyes. Walked over to the small fridge I kept in the far corner of the office. In a *noir* novel, I would have kept my booze there, the traditional bottle of whisky or bourbon, or maybe a gun in the ice compartment. Instead, I broke off a chunk of Brie cheese and gulped it down, followed by a sip from the cola bottle I kept at the foot of my desk. I returned to the computer screen, connected it to the printer, loaded it up with paper, scrolled along the relevant lines and clicked. For the real work, the hours of peering at words and data, I still needed old-fashioned sheets of paper.

Soon, I'd downloaded all I needed from the day's trawl.

Time for the leg work to begin, I reckoned. Never my favourite part of sleuthing.

A few telephone calls for flight and hotel bookings and I was ready. I sat there, pensive, thinking ahead, still trying somehow to erase the past beating at the doors of my brain. I ignored an incoming call, as I was certain it was Christopher Streetfield, again chasing me about the damn case of the missing wife. Who did he think I was, Perry Mason?

He didn't leave a message, but I recognised his number as it scrolled along the thin LED line.

Damn him, why couldn't he try and forget about her?

I must have sat there for at least another couple of hours, thinking of nothing in particular, unable to void my mind completely. Pangs of hunger brought me back to reality.

I put the print-outs into a folder and placed this inside my Samsonite case. As an afterthought, maybe a case of professional integrity, I also gathered the Streetfield papers, still unread in their manila envelope, from the drawer I'd banished them to and dropped them in. After all, the fool had actually paid me some cash to do his impossible job.

*

Alongside the train, the motorway into Amsterdam was jam-packed with cars, slowly sputtering along in the early evening gloom. A good thing I'd remembered that the train from Schipol was both faster and cheaper. Soon, I was making my way through the bowels of the Central Station, an anonymous middle-aged man dressed in black, quietly invisible between the backpackers, the housewives from the provinces and an assortment of luggage-laden tourists that preceded the rush hour commuter traffic out of the city. The cold beat a way through to my very bones as I crossed the first canal and the wind assaulted me at full-frontal strength.

I quickened my step and made for Leidseplein.

The first appointment I'd set up was for the following morning so I had the evening free. I set up the laptop in my hotel bedroom and checked my e-mails, then took a warm shower and changed into a warmer shirt. All I was planning was a meal, maybe an Indonesian—I hadn't been to Amsterdam for years—then an early night. Possibly pick up a hardcore mag or two, you could find them all over town, and wank myself to sleep.

It was the way the young woman in the hotel bar looked me straight in the eyes as I walked out of the lift that caught my attention.

She seemed lost, her soft blue eyes begging for attention with quiet despair. She wore a black trouser suit and a grey chenille sweater and her hair was short, brown with gentle blonde streaks.

First impression was that she was just a teenager, but as I held her gaze I quickly realised she was much older. There was a dignity in her stance that touched me. If she was on the make, her face distinctly said that this wasn't the sort of thing she was accustomed to.

Instead of moving through the lobby and out onto the street, I stepped over to the hotel bar. I was in no rush to face the bitter cold outside.

Her eyes followed my path.

'Hello,' I said.

'Hello,' she answered. She had a strong accent. But it wasn't Dutch, I knew.

'I'm Martin. Are you alone?'

'Yes.'

'Can I join you? Offer you a drink?'

'Sure,' she said. 'My name is Aida.'

'Where do you come from?' I asked her, easing myself into the chair next to hers.

'Lithuania,' she answered.

'Interesting. But your name makes you sound Egyptian,' I pointed out.

'I know. My mother liked the opera.'

'Verdi?'

'Yes.'

She ordered a glass of red wine while I stuck to mineral water.

'From Vilnius?' I inquired.

'You know?'

'Know of it. Never been there,' I told her.

'Most people think I'm Russian. It's all the same for them,' Aida said.

She had lovely cheekbones.

'So what are you doing in Holland?' I asked. 'You're a long way from home.'

'A man. Met a Dutch man,' she informed me, but her tone of voice sounded bruised.

'Where is he now?'

She studiously sipped her wine. Even sitting there, she appeared tall. Slim, small-chested and a touch nervous, it seemed to me.

'At home.'

'You still live with him? Married?'

'Yes. No,' Aida said.

'Care to clarify that?' I smiled.

'He's my ex. But I still live in his house.'

'I see.'

'I have a little boy. Two years old.'

'With him?'

'Yes. But since I had the baby, I just don't love him any more. We don't have sex any more. We live by the sea. It's a very small house; we have to share the bedroom.'

She lowered her eyes.

'So what brings you to Amsterdam today?'

'I'm not sure I should tell you,' she said, looking up at me again. Her eyes seemed to float between grey and blue.

'You don't have to,' I tried to reassure her. 'After all, I'm just a man talking to a woman he doesn't know in a hotel bar, and by tomorrow no doubt we will be strangers again.' I don't know why I suddenly said that. My problem is I've always been too fatalistic or seen too many movies and should have learned long ago that life is nothing like films.

'Wow!' Aida said.

'Sorry, that was a silly thing for me to say.'

'No, I liked,' Aida replied, the trace of a smile taking shape across her full lips.

'Good.' I smiled back, as sincerely as I could manage.

'Well, three days a week I work in the chocolate factory. But most of the money I earn goes towards paying the baby sitter and I want to get a place of my own for myself and the baby,' Aida said. 'So I was thinking of earning more money . . . ' Her words faded away and she looked down at her knees again.

'How?' I asked.

'I just cannot live with him any more. Since I told him I didn't want him, he frightens me. He's, what you call it, manic depressive and I'm afraid one day he might harm me and the baby.'

'Do you really think he would? His own child?'

'Last summer, I met a Swiss man on the Internet and went to live with him, in Bern, for a few weeks. He was very angry when I did that. But I tell him I cannot love him any more.'

'What happened to the Swiss guy?' I inquired.

She finished her wine and carefully set the glass down on the bar.

'It was a mistake. He just wasn't right for me . . .'

'How?'

'It's only when you live with someone you really find out about all their habits. At first, he was nice, it made a change, but soon he began to irritate me, small things, always a maniac about timekeeping, orderliness, those sort of things.'

I ordered Aida another glass of wine with a nod of the head towards the hotel barman.

'Sexually? Was it OK?' I asked.

'It was different, but not enough to make me stay,' she replied, holding my gaze.

'So you came back to your Dutch boyfriend?'

'Yes . . . I had nowhere else to go.'

'Lithuania? Family?'

'Marcel wouldn't let me take the baby away.'

'So, do you do this often?' I asked Aida.

'Do what?' she was visibly puzzled by my question.

'Meet men in hotel bars?'

She blushed deeply.

Blurted it out, and it was obviously the truth.

'It's the first time,' she said.

'Really?' I insisted.

'Yes. I walked round the red light district this afternoon, watching the women in their windows, wondering whether I could ever do that. I was thinking of talking to one, asking what I should do, but I got frightened. Just couldn't find the courage to appear in a window under a bright light exposing myself as they do and selling my body to any man who would want me. I just wouldn't be able to cope with older ones, the ugly ones . . . Silly, no?'

'Not at all. It would be a momentous decision to take,' I said.

'Have you ever been with a prostitute?' Aida asked.

'Yes,' I admitted. 'I was nineteen.'

'Nineteen would be good,' Aida said. 'I wouldn't mind too much.'

'It was too fast, too mechanical. There was no tenderness. Just a financial transaction,' I told her. 'How old are you, Aida?'

'I was twenty-eight two weeks ago,' she answered.

'I like you Aida,' I said. 'But I wouldn't pay you money. I decided I would never do that again, since that first time.'

'I guessed so.' She shifted her legs, her body still facing me alongside the bar.

'There must be other ways to earn money,' I ventured.

'Yes,' Aida said. 'But not enough. My Dutch is not good enough. Maybe as receptionist in a hotel . . .'

'Hmm, yes, your conversational English is quite good.'

'But unless there was somewhere to stay, an apartment that came with the job, and the little boy, Nidas, was old enough to go to school, it wouldn't be enough to stay independent.'

'You've thought about it a lot, I see.'

'Yes. Before you arrived, I was sitting here thinking of solutions. Maybe I should put an ad in a newspaper, offering myself as a mistress to an older man, who could give me a place. I could give him sex.'

'It's a bit drastic solution-wise,' I pointed out. 'I'm sure there must be better opportunities.'

She looked up at me and in the penumbra of the bar, the tip of her nose shone and her vulnerability assaulted me with all the strength of an emotional whirlpool. Instinctively, I took her hand and mine.

'Your hand is so warm,' she remarked.

'I know.'

There was a moment's silence while our thoughts swirled around the bar in a hesitation dance that only we two could see. For a minute or so I wrestled with my conscience, or what was left of it, as I pondered whether I should pay her after all. Something about her attracted me. A lot. It was only money, after all. I had it. She wanted it. I wanted sex. And she was no common street whore; just a clumsy, touching amateur. By tomorrow night I would already be out of Amsterdam. What the hell? My resolve was changing. But Aida beat me to it.

'I like you too,' she said. 'You are . . . different from other men, I think.'

We went to my room.

*

She had been wearing a padded bra and her breasts were slighter than I had guessed. I found them adorable. A dark beauty spot stared at me from the underside of her left nipple, a perfect touch of imperfection that tugged at my heart, as I licked and sucked on her teat like a new-born child and listened to her gentle moans. She lay on the bed, passive, naked to the waist down after we had kissed for an eternity, standing in the narrow corridor that led from the door to the actual bedroom, tongue assaulting tongue as if our lives depended on it. With every new assault of my lips on her open mouth, I could feel her shudder. Either out of nervousness or lust, but her reaction encouraged me to delve further down her throat, to grip her tongue in my suction or drill my own tongue even further down. She responded sweetly, a hand brushing across my unruly hair as I embraced her, our bodies pressing against each other, every heartbeat amplified through the material of our clothes, every degree of heat created by our desire bathing us in its glow. Lips still attached, I had allowed my fingers to roam under her chenille sweater and had, after a couple of clumsy attempts, managed to unclasp her bra and loosen its hold. Then I had detached myself from her and straightened her arms above her head and tugged the sweater off and gently pulled her along to the bed and helped her position herself over the silky cover and resumed our urgent mouth contact.

'OK?' I whispered, catching my breath between kisses, two of my fingers kneading a nipple into hardness.

'Yes,' Aida said. 'Very.'

'Good.'

'No man has ever kissed me like you do,' she continued, a gentle smile spreading across her features and her eyes bluer than ever.

A perfect invitation to continue.

My head lowered itself towards her face, and my free hand slid under the waistband of her black trousers, fingers soon stumbling against the bush of her crotch. Hot, humid, hungry. I breathed deeply as her reaction coursed from her genitals all through her body and her lips fluttered as they rubbed against mine.

I detached myself from Aida and knelt by the foot of the bed and unbuttoned her trousers. Pulling them off, she raised her rump to assist my undressing her. She was wearing pristine white knickers and when I rolled her around, I saw they were thongs and a lone small pink pimple adorned her left bum cheek. I couldn't resist licking it, kissing her flaws with all the affection I could muster. She undid my shirt and we resumed our feverish but unhurried embrace. She remained silent. So did I. Words were no longer required.

I had resisted the temptation too long as I partook of Aida's sweet full lips at lazy leisure, but I finally slipped the final white garment off her long, slim body and uncovered her cunt. Her thin curls had recently been trimmed into a tidy triangle (in preparation for tonight's much-thought-of accession to whoredom?). I buried my face in it, my nose digging deep into the hair and skin, eager for the scent of her intimacy. There was barely the trace of a smell, which initially surprised me. I withdrew my face and looked into her ultimate privacy. Her labia protruded slightly from the her pubic thatch, a dark pink gash in the core of her inner darkness. I put out a finger and parted her. Immediately I felt her abundant wetness and my digit sunk in deep into the heat of her small furnace. Inside, Aida was on fire. I moved my lips closer again and traced her gash with my tongue, tasting her unique mustiness. Quickly her labia filled and I plunged my tongue into her depths and began to suck on the loose folds of her flesh. Lower down the cunt opening, thick ridges of puckered, soft, darker skin surged outward like the roll of a small hill. I soon located her clitoris and sucked it out of its bud and chewed away. Tremors ran through her body from top to bottom and I spread her legs open around my head and invaded her with my fingers. She was a quiet one, neither a shouter or a moaner, but then again she couldn't disguise the pleasure I was providing her with, and each time I came up for air she let her breath out momentarily, as if asking me not to stop.

One time, she actually whispered 'Stop teasing me, please.'

Finally, she began shaking uncontrollably and came.

I kissed Aida. Her eyes shone. I had left the bedroom light on throughout.

I moved away from her and stood up and rid myself of the rest of my clothes and lowered myself beside her. Squashed myself against her on the exiguous single bed, enjoying all the joyful heat radiating from her naked flesh. She soon slithered away from me, reversed her position and unhesitatingly took my cock into her mouth and began hungrily lapping at it. Unlike many women, she did not take the shaft in her hand to minimise its length, but gripped my buttocks and impaled her mouth on me, taking all of my penis deep inside her without choking. She worked fast on it, gobbling it up and down with wonderful, childlike relish, even though I was not totally hard yet. Too many thoughts crowded my mind, fighting a complete erection, of others, of Kay, of times before, of the way women whose faces or names I could not recall had fellated me before. But few had done so with such enjoyable abandon, I knew.

Finally, I knew it was time, and I extricated myself from her avid lips and positioned myself above her and prepared to enter her.

'Haven't you got a condom?' she asked.

'No, Aida,' I replied. 'I somehow hadn't prepared for this encounter, you know.'

'It's OK, I have one in my handbag,' she said.

She got up and walked over to the bag she had left on the coat hanger by the door and returned quickly. Her naked body in motion looked so enticing and I felt myself attaining full hardness. Small hanging breasts, solid rump, thin legs and a graceful movement of the hips as she moved from and back to the bed, her skin so pale and white and already dripping with sweat.

'You have a lovely cock,' Aida said, as she unrolled the condom. 'I've never had a man with a, what you call it, circul ... circom ...'

'Circumcised,' I helped her out, wondering what the word was in Lithuanian.

'Circumcised cock ... It looks so ... cute,' she said. She began rolling the thin latex across my glans. 'What does it feel like to be like that?' she asked.

'I'm not sure I can answer that question,' I told her. 'I've never had a chance to compare, you know.'

She giggled and completed her task.

'I like it doggy-style,' she said. 'Please.'

She turned round and I finally entered her with a single thrust.

The first fuck with Aida was good and we unbelievingly came together. The combined view of her white arse shuddering while my cock buried itself inside her was heavenly, pornographic. I watched with hypnotic concentration as the darker ring of her anus sometimes dilated slightly as my cock dug deeper into her and, just before I lost all control, actually slipped a finger inside her there where it fitted effortlessly in.

'Taip!' she cried out. Her only words during our lovemaking.

Later, between the sheets, relaxing, quietly recording every minute of the fuck at the back of my mind, enjoying her soft presence next to me, absorbing her smell and warmth, it felt so comfortable. She felt the same.

'Do you believe in reincarnation?' Aida asked.

'Actually, no,' I replied. I was not one for mumbo jumbo or new age claptrap. 'Why?'

'It felt as if we knew each other already, you know, some time before. It was so easy, so natural,' she said.

'I don't think so,' I objected gently.

Hinting she's been with a lot of men before.

This is how I discovered I was only the fifth man she had had sex with. It didn't feel that way. She had a great natural talent for fucking, it seemed to me.

Aida's story: the first was a Belgian who was on holiday in Lithuania; they'd become friendly but no more and had begun to correspond and some months later he had out of the blue invited her to go on a Christmas holiday with her. They had met up in London where she'd given up her virginity to him in a small Bloomsbury hotel, and the next day they had taken a charter flight to a Thailand beach where they had alternated sunbathing and fucking for a whole fortnight. She now said she hadn't particularly enjoyed it or him, but had felt obliged as he had paid so much money to fly her there and pay for the holiday. Had apparently given up his job and savings to organise the trip. Never again, she decided on her return, would she feel obliged to have sex with a man because he was entertaining her or spending money on her. Six months later in Vilnius, there had been a one-night stand with a Pole. She had been very drunk and he had been very rough was all she said. (Later, in the morning, I discovered he had forced her to have anal sex and she was deeply ashamed to admit she had enjoyed a particularly strong come as result.) The following summer she had saved up enough to travel in Europe, and met up with the Belgian man in Holland but had somehow ended up sleeping with a friend of his, a Dutch man. She never returned to Lithuania when he asked her to live with him. She'd become pregnant and had a termination. The dreams that ensued had been awful and the second time she had found herself pregnant, she was determined to have the child. But by then, the relationship with her Dutch lover, a boat builder, was already deteriorating.

The little boy was born and she stopped sleeping with Marcel, even though they still had to share the same bed. While nursing the baby, she found out how to surf the Internet on his computer and discovered the chat rooms. Thus the Swiss episode. They met for a night at the Krasnapolsky Hotel off the Dam when he came to Amsterdam. He invited her to Switzerland with the baby. She went. He insisted she shave her genitals and also wanted anal sex. She quickly realised he was not right and returned to Holland with her tail between her legs and begged her Dutch ex's forgiveness. Which he granted, after all they still had the little boy in common. Which brought me up to date.

It was midnight on my watch. I had become hard again. We fucked. Missionary position this time, so I could see her wide blue eyes implore me with a thousand silent words as I moved in and out of her and wiped stray hairs away from her hot forehead. That look just killed me, I knew. One I would find it hard to ever forget. Damn her. Why couldn't she come with her eyes closed as most do. She came, I didn't. Grew soft again. She had said nothing when I thrust myself inside her with no protection. She rang home on her mobile, informing whoever that she was not returning that night. We fell asleep.

Morning came and I was aching all over. She still slept peacefully. I moved the cover away from her body and parted her legs. She still dripped my seed between her thick lower lips and I buried my tongue in her cunt and woke her with repeated assaults of lust. Her eyes still shone like beacons.

I shaved as she lazed around. Had to tell her I had a series of meetings that morning. We crossed the canal for breakfast in a café. She had a croissant with thin slices of cheese and ham and a mug of hot chocolate. I watched her eat. Sex gave her a wonderful glow. She had a train back to her village on every half hour so was in no hurry. She was not expected at the chocolate factory today anyway. There was a small record shop opening right then, shutters being pulled aside, across the narrow street from the café. She shyly asked if we had time to look inside. We had.

Aida had atrocious taste in music by my standards. I bought her the new Metallica double-CD and one of operatic arias she had heard of on a commercial for margarine which had featured a catchy tune from Delibes' Lakme. She was delighted. I gave her my business card and noted her address and mobile number. I walked her to Central Station where we parted quietly. To my relief, she was not into emotional good-byes. Neither was I and I was glad to be spared further words. My vocabulary and mood was just not up to it this morning. It reminded me of so many other early mornings or late night separations and trains to marital beds that still wrenched my insides into sharp, jagged pieces.

*

Hank Van der Meer was waiting for me between the philosophy and anthropology sections of the Athenaeum bookshop. A gangly man with a shock of red, curly hair and John Lennon glasses who could only have been an academic or a book dealer. He was both.

He took me to a drugs bar nearby where he ordered an absinthe, while I stuck to my usual soft drink.

I introduced myself as a journalist preparing an article on the more clandestine aspects of book collecting, suggesting he had been recommended to me at a London auction house by someone whose name I wasn't allowed to mention. Actually, his name often appeared on my web searches when it came to rare books whose provenance was often shaded in irregularities. In civilian life, Van der Meer taught the history of book publishing at a special book trade school here in Amsterdam.

Without specifically identifying the Le Carré book, I described the circumstances surrounding its origin and asked him what would be the best way to either acquire or dispose of such a choice item.

It was like pushing a button or clicking on the computer's 'search' button and I frantically tried to keep up with the rapid pace of Van der Meer's pontifications, jotting down all the names on my legal pad. Many I had come across before during the course of my initial search, but I noted them anyway. But there were also new names and places. He ordered another drink and became more con-spiratorial, and showered me with tales of bibliophilia galore. Scams, crooks, forgeries, desperate collectors, shady book scouts and run-ners, legendary operators.

I asked him about likely purchasers of the book, if it came on the market. This set the Dutch academic thinking. Actually, he couldn't see the book appealing to more than a handful of private collectors. Now, university libraries, that was another thing alto-gether. The item I described was a curiosity, after all. An anomaly. And most genuine collectors specialised in specific authors, publish-ers or subjects. There were a few mavericks he could think of in Texas and California. Then there was some woman in New York, Cornelis something or other, who was always on the look-out for extraordi-nary items in the field of modern firsts, but she was a bit of a mystery in the trade. Was never seen at auctions and only worked through a handful of dealers. A bit of a legend, really.

I wrote all this down, like a real journalist, paid for the drinks, thanked him.

My next meeting was soon upon me. A more dubious under-world contact who had the lowdown on smuggling rare items across borders. We met outside the American Discount Centre on Kalver-straat. As arranged, I carried a copy of the *Financial Times* under my arms. He acknowledged my presence and I followed him down the street. He preferred to talk while we walked, spurned my suggestion we sit for a coffee or a drink. He seemed to look at me with much suspicion and was taken aback that all I wanted to talk about was books. He provided some information, but I wasn't making much progress truly. Some of the same names kept on popping up in the conversation. A rich collector in Texas whose name he didn't know and was into both stolen paintings as well as rare books. I asked him about Cornelis and a deep frown crossed his forehead. 'You mean Cornelia?' he asked.

'Maybe,' I answered.

'If I were you I would steer clear,' he suggested. 'That woman is trouble.'

But, when pressed, he had never met her. It was all just hearsay. Some broad in New York with a serious reputation, who was heavily into book collecting. He agreed to make a phone call and arranged for me to meet up with another source that afternoon. I thanked him.

I had a couple of hours to spare before the next meeting and walked briskly among the Amsterdam traffic, along canals and tram lines. All the time, I could still smell Aida and the touch of her lips all over me. By now, she must be back in her village, playing with her baby. I hoped she didn't get round to putting that ad in the newspaper and sell herself cheaply to some man with money who would only use her. 'Willing to be a Mistress'? 'Will fuck for apartment and roof over my head. Anal optional.'? 'Hot Russian girl seeks Sugar Daddy'?

The following meeting came to nothing. The small bald man in his Gestapo-like leather coat and clumpy shoes had a poor grasp of English and knew nothing about the unscrupulous side of the book world. I tried the Poshard name out on him and drew a blank.

I had open reservations on a series of flights back to London and decided to catch the first one. As contingency, the hotel room was booked for a further night, but I hadn't expected to sleep over another night. At the reception desk, they couldn't find my key. Suggested I maybe go to the room, as the maid might still be up there.

The door wasn't locked. Expecting a Surinam matron busily airing out the bed sheets and no doubt sniffing disapprovingly all the excesses of the night before, I innocently walked in. Trust a British detective to not know the rules of the game. As I stepped into the room and closed the door, there was a soft, muted shuffle of feet behind me and I felt a massive blow to the back of my head.

It all went dark.

5.

Cornelia

It had been some months now since Cornelia's last contract and she was getting restless.

There had been empty, sleepless nights. With no passing man or woman to appease the boredom of loneliness. She knew there was something missing in her life. Her heart was untouched, guiltless in the face of all the horrors she had witnessed and the murders she had committed.

There were days when she lost herself in her dance, content to swim along to the rhythm and flow of the music, impervious to the envious gaze of men touching themselves in the darkness or fantasising wildly at the sight of her unclad body. She was of late spending a small fortune on CD's and spent hours putting together new compilations of songs which she changed every week to strip to. But the pleasure of the mindless declination of music and body movements never supplied her with more than temporary release.

Her heart was still as cold as stone. Cornelia knew this would never change. It was the way she was made and she had no time for regrets. There had been hurt on the rare occasions when she had allowed herself to experience feelings, whether as a child or as fully grown woman, and she felt no need to repeat the bad experiences. She had to make do with what was left. Her books, the wonder of a melody that could reach down deep inside her, a pleasant meal, the smells of Manhattan on a spring day, the satisfaction of a kill cleanly executed, the feel of the wind on her cheek as she raced up Broadway towards the Strand early on a Monday morning to peruse new arrivals with a nice twinge of expectation. But small pleasures were not enough to appease the hole inside that seemed to be growing at an exponential rate.

Someone had once remarked to her that there was just too much beauty in the world, but Cornelia was blind to it. And the fact just made her damn angry.

It also worried her, as the state of boredom settled intangibly over her life, that she missed the thrill of the chase and kill.

The blood lust.

So, for the first time ever, there being no new book she was in desperate need of, and with her checking account still in relatively healthy shape, Cornelia phoned her contact number and made herself available for an assignment.

There was always work for a trained assasin.

It was just a question of waiting, now.

She took a deep breath as she replaced the receiver, realising she had taken a brand new step in a whole different direction. She knew it had been a mistake within minutes, but her pride prevented her from calling back and cancelling her request.

She took a cold shower.

She had been stupid.

What next?

A notch by her tattoo for every new kill? In ink or by scar?

Stupid, stupid girl!

*

'Getting a liking for it, are you now my dear?'

She knew there was no point pretending. The voice at the other end of the line knew more about her than she did herself. She had long suspected he, or they, even kept an occasional watch on her. Caution was understandable. But she feigned surprise.

'What do you mean?'

'You still haven't read the books you acquired last time around. And you're sitting on a tidy pile of cash. You could even give up the dancing for, say, a year and live on your savings.'

'So?' Cornelia retorted.

'So, I have a job for you,' was all he said, not rising to her bait.

'Good.'

'But you will have to be patient. The target is not yet in the country, but we have solid evidence she will be arriving soon.'

'A woman?'

'Yes. You've never objected in the past. Female solidarity and all that!' There was a dark streak of irony in his voice.

'It's not a problem. Never has been,' Cornelia answered.

'Fine.'

'I'll be on standby, then.'

'Excellent. Usual fee?'

'No problem.'

'Good girl. And, tell you what . . .'

'Yes?' Cornelia queried.

'Maybe you could vary your stage moves. Devise something a little different while you're waiting for the call. I think your boredom is showing in your set; you've become a little mechanical, my dear.'

So, he came to watch her, it appeared. Cornelia shivered. She was about to ask him more, but the phone went dead as her interlocutor hung up.

Receiver still cradled between shoulder and ear, Cornelia wondered about him. Which face in the audience was he? Which goggle-eyed anonymous spectator? Did he wear glasses? Did she excite him sexually? She had a posse of regulars; some came, some went, it was difficult to keep track of them all in the blurry darkness that surrounded the stages on which she performed, and anyway she never did give much thought to the men who lapped up her every indecent move. She smiled: maybe he had even liked the tattoo. She put the phone down. Her heart suddenly felt lighter.

She helped herself to an apple from the refrigerator and, greedily munching through it, began to sort out her latest pile of CD's. So he felt she needed to put some variety in her act, did he? So be it. She would need a new set of songs then. Special tunes indeed.

It took her the whole afternoon to make her mind up. Switching and changing endlessly between the tunes that had recently caught her fancy. Not all could be danced to, she knew, as she assayed tentative steps barefoot on the thick rug of her front room to the new songs. Back and forth she moved from the improvised dance floor to the compact Aiwa hi-fi, recording, erasing and recording again until she was satisfied by her new sequence.

It began with Bruce Springsteen's 'Lift Me Up', a tune she had first heard over the closing credits of the John Sayles movie *Limbo*, and which was the only decent thing on the soundtrack CD. It was a melody that just chilled her to the bone, Springsteen at his most melancholy falsetto with a surging wall of synthesised strings rising behind the plaintive call for love and help. This she would dance to with her eyes shut. The song demanded it. She stripped down to her underwear and practised her moves, tentative at first but soon growing in assurance until every chord paralleled a flexing sinew.

She followed this with the Walkabouts' 'Crime Story'.

And for her finale, after much experimentation, Cornelia at last settled on another haunting melody, also from a movie soundtrack, a short Scott Walker song from *Pola X*, which she had to replay in a loop so it would be long enough to dance to.

New moves he wanted, new moves he would get.

So what if the music was a touch plaintive? The clubs always complained about her left-of-field choices. Asked her for more cheerful, upbeat tunes. As if the paying customers cared as long as they caught sight of her tits and pussy. But she always told them she came as package, the music and her. No negotiations.

What did they expect her to dance to? 'Big Spender' or 'Gentlemen Prefer Blondes'? Damn it, a girl had to retain some sort of integrity if she was displaying her wide open cunt to any punter willing to part with as little as five dollars for a watered-down beer.

*

'What the fuck was that exhibition all about?' Ade was crimson with rage as he faced Cornelia in the makeshift dressing room she shared with the other girls on duty today.

'OK, so it was a bit more raunchy than usual,' she replied, wiping the sweat from her body with the green flannel towel she always brought along in her bag. None of the other workers here used green towels. Gave her a feeling of safer hygiene. She hated the place's antediluvian shower stalls and always avoided using them. She'd wait until she returned to the apartment before taking a cleansing bubble bath to wash away the sin and sweat. 'Aren't you always begging me to be more upbeat?'

'Upbeat? Raunchier?' Ade sputtered. 'Couldn't you see what you were up to, Cornelia? It just wasn't like you . . . Fingers everywhere, those bends . . . You'll have the place closed down. You don't realise.'

'Come on . . .' she tried to counter his protests. 'I've seen some of the other girls get up to much worse.'

'Not here you haven't, Cornelia. We offer exotic dancing, titillation, not hardcore pornography, gal. There are definitely limits. Even here.'

'Don't go overboard, Ade.'

'What got into you, anyway?' he asked.

'Let's say there was a good friend in the audience, and I wanted to give a show to remember. OK?'

He downed his glass of vermouth.

'I didn't notice anyone special out there. Seemed the usual crowd. Although some of them seemed to be going somewhat red in the face.'

'So,' Cornelia volunteered, 'They will all make return visits . . . '

'I have no doubt about that, Cornelia. But I'm afraid that if you pull that stunt again, you're out of here on your fanny. I know you have friends in . . . how shall I put it, interesting places, but I'll have no choice. I'm not about to endanger our license.'

Cornelia threw her towel on the bench and slipped her T-shirt on. Ade stared at her nudity. There were two types of women, he knew, those who began the process of dressing with knickers and those who started with the brassière. He had never drawn any ontological conclusions from this choice but always suspected those who covered their top first, leaving their cunt and ass in full view must be hotter than hot in bed. Which left Cornelia, who never wore a bra in civilian life. He'd always wondered about her sex life.

As she dressed, she asked him:

'But did you like the music, Ade?'

He shrugged, turned his back on her to leave the dressing room.

'The music stank . . . But you were sensational. You were too good for them or any spy from the Giuliani clean-up brigade.'

'Thanks, Ade,' she shouted back at him over the sound of the honky tonk music to which the next dancer, a plump black girl with her share of silicon, was stripping to on stage.

'But,' he reminded her, 'Tonight's was a one-off performance. Comprende?'

'Spoilsport,' she mumbled and slipped on her jeans.

'I heard that,' he shouted back at her.

She gathered her stage clothes and make-up and stuffed the lot into a tote bag. Moments later, she walked out onto Madison. It was approaching midnight, the evening wind had died away and the air was unusually cool and clear. She walked down in the direction of the West Village. She needed to clear her head and thoughts and forsook her usual cab. On Sixth she reached the large Barnes and Noble down by Twenty-third Street. It was still open and she walked in. There was not enough time until closing to explore the new fiction section and she lingered by the magazines.

She leafed aimlessly through a handful of women's magazines, then moved on to the health and cookery rack. Across from it a lanky teenager in baggy jeans and black leather jacket looked up at her and put down the magazine he had been reading, a furtive look on his face. A skin mag, Cornelia noticed out of the corner of her eye.

She smiled at him.

Didn't they say in all the lifestyle magazines that book superstores were the new pick-up places for young professionals?

'Hi,' she greeted the stranger.

Looked him up and down. No pimples. Clean shaven at least. He would do. Right now, the load felt heavy and she didn't want to spend the night alone.

'Hello,' he tentatively replied.

'The place is closing in a few minutes,' she pointed out.

'I know,' he stuttered.

She went up to him.

'I'm Corrie,' she said.

'Jay.'

'So, Jay, do you have any plans?'

'Not really,' he answered, shuffling his feet.

'Listen,' she said to him. 'I won't beat about the bush: I'm damn lonely and want company tonight. And seeing you standing here at this time of night, I assume you're lonely too.'

He reluctantly nodded in agreement.

'Care to be lonely together?' She ventured a hand towards him.

A burly security guard by the store's main door announced closing time, distracting his attention.

For an instant, Cornelia panicked. It occurred to her she hadn't yet had her post-dance bath, and a thin cake of sweat no doubt still enveloped the geography of her skin. Further, she had totally forgotten to wash her fingers, and she remembered acutely how, during the course of the new set, she had aggressively fingered herself in the heat of the action. And that she had been wet, at the thought of the owner of the voice at the other end of the line being in the audience.

She abhorred vulgarity. Surely, making a pass at this young man was the height of irresponsibility? Why not push her fingers under his nose and ask him to sniff. 'Here, this is me, this is my cunt, this is the unsheer fragrance of my despair! Smell, smell me, damn you!'

She fell back to earth.

The young guy, surely he couldn't be older than twenty or so, shot her another nervous glance.

Then, 'Maybe not,' he said. 'It's a bit too ... sudden, you know what I mean ...'

But still he didn't move.

What was it with him? Cornelia thought. Maybe my boobs aren't voluptuous enough, my hair isn't teased, I don't dress like a stripper should? Thinks I'm just another student with a head full of complexes, too much trouble to handle. Or he's too good for me? Or I'm too good for him? Bet he'd get hard soon if I only told him I'm shaven below. They all love that. Men.

She seethed.

But she kept her calm.

'A romantic, I see,' she joked.

The boy blushed and made for the store door.

Cornelia walked home, taking a shortcut through Washington Square.

She just didn't understand. She had offered her body and he'd wanted her heart too. The affectional greed of men would never cease to surprise her.

She spent the night with a good thriller and rock music blaring out at maximum volume on her headphones. And a long soak in her bath tub, contemplating the deformed image of her crotch through the vacillating green water. The tattoo stared at her and she contemplated making it disappear by growing her pubic thatch back. But decided against it.

*

She returned to her own innocuous dance routine, to Ade's great relief. The guys in the audience had become a tad restless on some days; maybe her legend had grown by word of mouth since her notorious session and they now expected more. She even added a big band tune to her tape and took a tip from Anita, the Italian girl from Milan who taught her how to do a headstand with her legs indecently wide apart but just out of the punters' view. The stunt drew a few extra tips, but was hell on her wrists.

She found several new work outfits at Religious Sex on St. Mark's Place. One in shiny black leather, evoking tantalising echoes of S&M. Another was of wonderful see-through silk and even came with matching stockings and garter belts. She also experimented on a couple of occasions with cans of liquid latex which she sprayed on to herself in the changing room like a second skin and later gradually peeled off as her set progressed. But it proved too painful and also lacked elegance when a whole area would sometimes tear at an inopportune moment or in the wrong place. It also made her itch afterwards and a striptease artist with visible pimples and sores would just not do, she knew.

Cornelia waited for the call but it was unusually slow in coming.

She killed time as best she could.

She even timed a whole day to fit in five movies in quick succession, dashing between the floors and screens of the Union Square multiplex. By the end, she couldn't even remember a single incident from the first late morning film.

And the pager she carried in her purse stayed silent.

She even contemplated getting round to read all of Proust or making a start on the books by Tolstoy or Dostoevsky she had always relegated to later times.

The weather invisibly warmed and she switched from jeans to a light flannel dress she always wore around Easter time. Gee, another ritual. Was she becoming an old spinster with a sackful of habits? Better keep a sense of humour about it all, she reckoned.

One of the few girls from the club with whom she had a tentative friendship came down with the flu and asked her if she could help out by taking over her slots at another joint up East Side. Cornelia agreed. It was a club she had never danced at. Had a dodgy reputation. At any rate, it was only for three days. When the management insisted she conform and follow her set by offering lap and table dances, she didn't resist. A rough crowd, and she grew tired of all the roving hands she had to smack down every time they tried it on. Which only seemed to encourage the guys further. The one working girl, the strange one, the pretentious one who thought she was better than all the others and refused to put out. There was a queue for her when she vacated the stage.

So she lap danced.

So she table danced, their bad breath swirling across her bare flesh as she undulated, the stale smell of tobacco assaulting her senses.

'Come on . . .'

'Wider, babe . . .'

'A nice present if you join me in the john . . .'

'Don't be so precious, it's only a hand . . .'

'An eenie-weenie finger . . .'

'That's what I call a pussy, girl. Would love to fist you . . .'

'Just a blow job, swear it won't hurt . . .'

'Tell me, do you like it up the ass, sweetie? You'd love it . . .'

She was tired, pissed, her calf muscles hurt. This was her last day here and the final lap dance. The guy was just a cipher, some anonymous executive in a grey three-piece suit. Not a talker, at least. He sat on the chair while Cornelia paraded in front of him, dancing, flexing her extremities, opening herself for his perusal. Cupping her slight tits and teasing her resolutely unaroused nipples for his delectation. Watching him mentally drool. A damp back room at the club.

She watched the seconds slowly tick away on the clock on the wall. One minute to go. He'd only paid for five. Time to assume her final position in the rigmarole. She retreated from him, took a step back, turned so that the man was now gazing at her back, the regal whiteness of her backside. Walked back towards the seated man, her hips still swaying gently to the sound of the music in the club on the other side of the wall. Reaching him, Cornelia squatted down and sat herself on his knees. He was hard. Of course. It was too much not to expect. She resumed her swaying, slowly grinding her arse against his lap. Glanced at the clock. Only a few seconds to go. Wouldn't have time to come. Some did, she always knew when, felt the heat through the layers of their garments and the sudden softening of the cock, or the electric pulse that coursed through their body as she rubbed against them. She could hear him breathe. Peppermint gum. Suddenly she felt his hands roughly circle her and grab her breasts.

'No hands,' she screamed over the loudness of the music.

'Oh . . .' he meekly protested, but didn't take his hands away, painfully kneading her nipples.

'You know the fucking rules . . .' she told him, and deliberately peed all over his lap. Damn, he had it coming! They all did and he was paying the price. And stepped off him and out of the private room.

'JESUS!' he cried out as Cornelia disappeared. The circular stain of her urine fast spreading across the greyness of his trousers.

She knew he wouldn't have the guts to lodge a protest. And wondered mischievously how he would explain the stain to his wife. He'd been wearing a wedding ring. Most of the private customers did.

*

Cornelia was washing her smalls in the bathroom sink when the call came.

'Sorry it's been so long, my dear.'

'It has,' she said. 'Problems?'

'Circumstances,' he said.

'I see.'

She felt like asking him whether he had attended 'the' performance, but resolved not to bring the subject of her dancing up unless he did so first.

'The target arrives in the country tomorrow. On the way to New Orleans.'

'The famed Big Easy,' Cornelia said. 'I've always wanted to go there.'

'Now's your chance, my dear,' he answered. 'You'll have to make the hit locally. The target has a plane connection in Chicago, but I would never advise working in airports. Too dangerous, a recipe for all sorts of disasters.'

'I understand.'

'Local arrangements will be made for you.'

'Good.'

This meant she wouldn't have to travel carrying obvious weapons. They would be made available to her on arrival in New Orleans. The Organisation's planning had never let her down. So far.

That evening, she picked up the customary dossier. The woman was indeed pretty. The details provided about her were few, but Cornelia also knew that the less she knew the better. Tomorrow's flight to New Orleans made a connection in Chicago and would arrive early evening. Arrangements had been made for her cover in the form of a short-term contract with a local club. There was no need to stretch credibility, after all.

She added a bunch of dance tapes and a couple of flimsy work outfits to the luggage she had already prepared that afternoon.

Like every night before an assignment, Cornelia slept badly. She moved and stirred but it wasn't her habitual sense of heightened expectancy. She was aware it was not a case of nerves either, no, it was something else. After all the waiting, there was a deep sense of lassitude within her. A tiredness she had never felt before.

Maybe her life had reached a crossroads.

And changes would have to be made.

But where? And how?

*

As the plane banked over Lake Pontchartrain in its downward approach to the airport, Cornelia in her window seat barely noted the landscape beneath, lost in a daydream of roads not taken and a twisted labyrinth of memory.

She had by now convinced herself this would be the last job she accepted. A final hit for the road, so to speak. A clean cut elimination to keep her record unblemished. Maybe she would travel. Warmer climes, beaches, somewhere her heart might benefit from the sun and lose its natural coldness. Make her more human. Normal. Maybe one day it could be the white picket fences. But deep inside, she knew she was just fooling herself.

The fasten seat belts announcement shook her out of her reverie.

She brought her seat upright before the attendant could chide her for not doing. The aircraft landed with an imperceptible bump and, for yet another time, she memorised her dossier. The address of the club, the small hotel she would be staying at a few blocks from the notorious Bourbon Street, the telephone numbers she had to rely on—one for a suitable weapon, another in case of emergency, and yet another for legal advice if all else failed.

The overhead light was switched off and, in unison, half the passengers rose from their seats and began gathering their bags from the overhead compartments. Cornelia lingered in her seat. She had no wish to wrestle her way out of the plane and knew she would overtake most of the hurrying passengers on the concourse; she had longer legs.

The heat and the humidity hit her full in the face as she exited the airport building. She took a deep breath of air. Yes, she was going to like the place, she could feel it in her bones.

She caught a cab to the city and banished all her confused thoughts to the depths of her memory. This was now Louisiana time. Cornelia switched to work mode.

Here I come, Miss Poshard. Your angel of death.

6.

Martin

I opened my eyes.
I was no longer in the room.
Amsterdam, stranded.

I was a captive of my own nightmares, full of the floating grace of women's bodies. Kay's pallid languor, Aida's darker, more sensual, supple limbs flaying, mouths, shifting configurations of wide-open lips shaped for an obscene blessing of my cock. Moles, beauty stains roaming at liberty over the geography of their skins. A nipple there. Kay, Aida, Catherine, Lisa, Jasmine, Evelyn, Montana, whose? As soon as I focused on one curve or an orifice, the view changed and the landscape merged into a tangle of crumpled sheets.

In the epicentre of the darkness where I hung, a body without a body, there were eyes. Brown, pleading; pale blue, begging; green, inviting like a tropical lagoon; grey, hard and resentful.

I closed my eyes, beckoning the darkness back.

A bright light shone against my retina. And again the spectacle of naked bodies, long legs that went on forever, a midnight choir of sheer unadulterated desire.

And the blood.

And the silence.

And the shocking vision of Kay in a bed of blood, her eyes hanging on to consciousness, drowning in anger, in surprise, and the scalpel flying through the air and ravaging the virgin snow of her uncovered skin. Like a silent movie, every gesture in exaggerated slow motion as if it wasn't real, just a stylised version of life. And death.

I recognised the dream that had been pursuing me for weeks now and I realised there was just no running away. I was in an Amsterdam hotel room and lay unconscious, immobilised in the hand-cuffs of my torment. And here I was to linger forever, my own version of hell, the lower circle of my infamy, the punishment for my past betrayals. I cried. Without making a sound, or shedding a real tear. Ever the liar.

On and on and on and on.

Finally, I emerged from my purgatory and my first thought as I broke out of the zone of darkness was: what possibly had I done wrong? The cases I took on were never dangerous: missing wives, sisters or books. Which seldom called for violence.

I shook my head and got to my knees. The bedside lamp was on. I was now alone in the room. My aggressor hadn't stuck around. I looked at my watch. It was still there; the most expensive item on me, so that ruled out an opportunist thief, I reckoned. I'd only been under for ten minutes at most, it seemed. I looked back. The door to the room was now closed. I saw the key on the bed and my emptied Samsonite and all its contents strewn across the thin carpet.

I washed my face with cold water and finally regained all my senses. Swept my fingers across the back of my head: the bump was already fading. I'd live. Maybe have a bad headache later.

I tidied up the contents of my case. At first, there didn't appear to be anything missing. My notes on the Poshard case were still in the inside pocket of the jacket I had been wearing all day and the intruder hadn't thought of frisking me after I'd fallen down. Possibly worried that the noise might attract someone to the room he had flown the coop, almost straight-away. But it didn't make sense. If I'd come across an opportunist thief, he would have taken my laptop, my passport, my wallet or the Tag Heuer. But they had all been spared.

Then I realised the manila envelope with Christopher Street-field's notes and the photographs of his wife was missing.

A shiver ran down my spine.

No, it didn't make the slightest sense.

It was the wrong case.

Or a warning that I was stepping on the wrong toes.

But whose?

Naturally, at the hotel desk they knew nothing, hadn't noticed anyone suspicious inquiring about me. I made no fuss and settled my bill and took a cab to Schipol airport where I caught the first available flight back to Stansted.

Strong gusts of wind swirling down from the coast were assault-ing the airport runways and the flight was delayed for an hour. I rang Aida.

Her voice was wonderfully chirpy.

'Aida here.'

'Hi, it's me.'

'It's so nice to hear from you.'

'You got back safely?'

'Yes. I got caught in the rain while I biked back to the cottage, but it was a nice feeling. But my ex was very unhappy I stayed out all night, you know. He knew from my shiny eyes. I can't hide what I've been doing. Sex. He got very angry. Sometimes he scares me. I really have to find somewhere to live on my own, well, with my little boy.'

'I'm sorry about that. Listen, Aida, I'm at Schipol. Just wanted to say how much I enjoyed yesterday night. I felt comfortable with you. It was nice. Really.'

'Me too.'

'I have some travelling to do, but I'd like to see you again. I don't know when. One day.'

'Yes,' she said, with no hint of emotion.

'You'd like that too?'

'Yes. I'll never forget the way you kiss. You're a treasure,' the young Lithuanian woman said, aiming an arrow straight at my heart.

'Really?'

'Yes, the treasure in my collection.'

'Your collection? Makes it sound as if I'm just another cock in your zoo of men . . .'

'No,' Aida said. 'I told you, you're my fifth.'

I still didn't know whether I should believe her. But I wanted to.

'I'm flattered to be listed as a treasure, then. Highly flattered.'

There was an announcement on the departure lounge tannoy.

'I have to go, Aida. I'll stay in touch.'

'Yes.'

*

The taxi driver took the Midtown Tunnel route in from Kennedy and it was New York.

Again.

Manhattan. That island of lost souls. So many times before, my search for missing spouses had brought me here. As if such a small island, however jampacked with bodies, could ever be a perfect hiding place, a refuge for hearts on the run, a sanctuary from a past that hurt too much. Maybe the anonymity of its deep canyons lined with skyscrapers, its frantic pace and cacophony of languages and cheap trainer shops on every damn corner?

Before leaving London, I'd called Streetfield and told him I had a lead on his wife and had to go to New York to follow it up. He seemed to accept the news with no surprise, as if nothing would ever catch him wrong-footed again. He sounded low, about to give up on her forever, I felt. Which suited me, of course. Didn't even enquire what sort of extra costs my trip to the US would provoke. I didn't ask him for new photos to replace the ones stolen in Amsterdam. I had no need for them.

I lowered the cab window to escape the unbearable fumes as the car plunged into the tunnel after the inevitable traffic jam leading up to it.

My hotel was off Washington Square and I quickly unloaded my case, connected the laptop to the awkward slot under the telephone set, checked for e-mails and slumped down on the bed for a few hours to fight the insidious effect of the jet-lag. I never can sleep on planes.

The doze was dream-free for a change.

My New York contact man had no name; he preferred it that way. In my mind, and in my occasional notes, he was just John Doe. The name he'd once suggested when I insisted on some form of identification in our communications.

We met for a meal at Veselka, a Ukrainian restaurant on Second Avenue. I provided him with the names I'd so far harvested in my quest for the younger Poshard sister, and asked for the skinny on crooked book dealers, here and across America. I also mentioned Cornelia.

Doe's eyes clouded over.

'Yes, I know Cornelia,' he answered, sipping on his cup of borscht.

'What's the connection?'

'I'm not sure,' I answered.

'She's bad news. Freelance, but trouble by all accounts. But you might be barking down the wrong avenue. She's not a gal who gets involved with missing people. Quite the contrary. Better known making people disappear. Permanently. Or so the rumour goes.'

'Actually, her name cropped up with regards to the rare book connection.'

'Doesn't make sense to me,' John Doe said.

'Forget Cornelia, then. What else can you tell me?'

A Polish waitress with sultry lips brought my dish of pierogi.

'The Poshard girl has been in town. A few weeks ago. But no one knows where she is now. Might already have left.'

'How do you know that?' I asked him.

'Reliable sources.'

Apparently, she had stayed at the Algonquin Hotel. Had seldom left her room. There was a man with her, though. Much older than her, middle-aged, upper-class, could have been her father, someone from the hotel had said. But Doe couldn't get a more precise description of the man who'd been with Louise.

At least, this gave me something to go on from here.

We finished our coffees. Silence settled between us.

'And the sister, Nola, arrived in town this morning,' John Doe then said.

Curiouser and curiouser.

Something inside was ringing alarm bells and telling me that the damn rare book was just an excuse, that Nola Poshard had little interest in retrieving it. Hmmm.

'Where is she staying?' I asked.

'Also at the Algonquin. The Poshard family always stay there, it appears.'

'That's on Forty-fourth Street, isn't it?'

'Yes, east of Times Square and Fifth.'

'Maybe I should visit.'

'Perhaps you should.' There was the hint of a smile drawn across his gaunt features.

*

McNelson Sheldon inspired little confidence and I could imagine the shiver of disgust coursing through the spines of all the books he handled as they passed between his hands. A repulsive little sod. We'd met in the Rare Book room at the Strand, on Broadway. It was now mid-afternoon and I felt I was on a wild goose chase.

But Sheldon had actually heard of the book. It wasn't apocryphal. Apparently, one copy had been auctioned in Texas a few months before, long before its disappearance from the Poshard collection, so there must more than one of these unauthorized proofs in existence. The slimy dealer passed his tongue over his dry lips and informed me that the book had gone for over ten thousand bucks.

'A quite unique item,' he added. 'So many rich collectors in Texas with more money than acumen, I reckon.'

I asked him about Cornelia.

'A bright one, she is,' he smiled broadly. 'She doesn't only collect. She also reads the books. Interesting criteria. Very idiosyncratic.' She was a good customer of his. I asked how I could get in touch with her.

'The Le Carré proof is just not her type of book,' Sheldon insisted. 'Not at all.'

'I'd still like to talk to her,' I added.

'Elusive lady,' he pointed out. 'She always makes the contact, not me.'

I managed to extract her PO box number at Cooper Station from him. That was all he could give me.

Why did I feel I needed a thorough shower after I'd parted with the pockmarked dealer?

I settled down at my Washington Square Place hotel, now ready for a proper night's sleep. Out of habit I booted up the laptop. I had mail. It was my Wandsworth computer magician to whom I'd passed on the Poshard sister's stolen hard drive. It appears it had been deliberately wiped clean barely a week ago. I checked my diary. The day before Nola Poshard came to me with the case. However, he had managed to retrieve a single document file whose ghost somehow hadn't deserted the computer's cavernous memory and had been sent as an attachment to an e-mail to Louise Poshard on the very day I assumed her sister had tried to eliminate any evidence. He was sending it along, as a text file. It was big at over 20k, but anything Nola had tried to hide from me must have some significance.

I clicked to open the salvaged file. At first, it wouldn't work so I had to reconfigurate things a little. A task that always made me nervous. Finally, the screen on my laptop filled with words. A story. A life.

First came a note, a letter:

My sweet Louise,
Thanks for New York. It was everything I expected and more. We agreed not to talk further about our situation, but all I can do is feel revulsion about the hold Nola has over you. I am a writer. I write. For what it's worth, I felt strangely compelled to write down our story. I hope you recognise it, that I have not been too melodramatic. One day I hope you understand why I have written about us this way.
Will I ever see you again? After that house in New Orleans. A tender kiss and a desperate hug.

There was no name or signature.

Fiction? Reality?
That night in New York I could find no answers in my mind after reading Louise's tale.

THE SILENCE THAT STANDS
BETWEEN THE WORDS

7.

A Hotel Room Fuck (or The Story of Louise)

How they first met is unimportant.
Or, at any rate, another story altogether.
A different one.

Actually, it was in an Internet chat room.

Here, they both arrive at Kennedy Airport on different flights from Europe, barely one hour and two terminals apart. Initially the flight she had suggested taking was bound for Newark and cheaper, but he had been unable to coordinate his own travel arrangements to match hers.

After retrieving his case from the luggage delivery area and verifying her flight details, he kills time wandering through the busy, rundown hallways and alleyways of the building cluttered with passengers in various forms of transit. Idly wandering what she might actually look like. Checks out the stroke magazines in the Hudson News concession. There's a new one he's never come across before, called *Barely Legal*. He nervously glances aside as he leafs through it. Time passes slowly. A double cheeseburger and fries and a large coke take up another ten minutes.

He finally makes his way toward the terminal where the Virgin Airways flights disembark, dragging his own case behind him on its dodgy wheels. A screen announces the arrival of her plane. She must now be queuing at passport control. He finds a seat to the right of the luggage pick-up area from which vantage point he will see all the passengers emerging through the corridor from immigration. He holds his breath one moment. Suddenly, the whole thing doesn't sound so wise after all. What if, what if?

The Gatwick flight crowd streams through the corridor. So many

of them, the plane must have been quite full. Saunter down the short
flight of stairs towards the luggage carousels.

She is among the last to emerge. A dozen times already he has
convinced himself she isn't on the plane. Had been playing a game
with him all the time. Had missed the flight by barely a minute or
so back in Europe. Had been discovered by her Masters and held
back in captivity. Had come to her senses and realised this whole
New York thing was quite pointless after all.

Finally, a slip of a girl with luminous features makes her way
past the security guard posted at the top the short flight of stairs and
tiptoes her way down, concertina'd almost by two burly six-footed
businessmen in charcoal-coloured suits and matching attaché-cases.
Her dark blue skirt is short, swirls around her knees. Her T-shirt is
white, its thin material clinging to her skin. Even from where he sits
he can see the outline of her nipples through it, or is it the rings?

Jesus, she is so young!

But he knew that already, didn't he?

As she reaches the bottom of the stairs and her involuntary escorts scatter in different directions, she looks around the luggage
enclosure, seeking him.

Her eyes alight on him. The sketch of a smile spreads across her
lips.

He stands up. Smiles back at her.

His heart skips a beat or two or three.

She stands there motionless, as the arriving crowds mill all
around her, a statue of perfection at the centre of the hurly-burly of
the airport.

She slips her rucksack from her shoulders. He moves toward her,
feeling all around him freeze, like a slow motion scene in a movie
with the soft rock soundtrack missing and replaced by a cacophony
of disruptive languages in a cocktail of voices.

Inches apart.

The heat from her body reaches toward him, a hint of spearmint
on her breath.

'Hello, Louise.'

'Hi there.'

She leans over, kisses him on the right cheek.

He briefly imagines she's telling herself he's so much older than
she thought, fatter, less than handsome.

'For a moment, I thought you weren't coming,' he says, as behind
her the luggage begins to accumulate on the conveyor belt.

'I said I would come,' she answers. 'Why should I not?'

'I'm just rather insecure,' he says.

'I'm a lot of things,' she smiles. 'But not that.'

'So, no regrets?' he asks her.

'Not yet,' she tells him. 'You asked me to come. Here I am.'

'Good,' is all he can summon as an answer. Then, 'What does your case look like? We'll look out for it.'

'I haven't one,' she says, pointing at the rucksack at her feet. 'This is all I've brought. Some change of underwear. For my first time in New York I thought it would be nice to buy some new clothes while I'm here.'

He smiles. 'We can buy them together. That would be nice.'

'Sure.'

'They must have been surprised when you checked in back in London, no? Travelling so light?'

'I just said I was a student.'

'I see,' he says.

She bends to retrieve her rucksack.

'Shall we?' she asks.

'Yes.' He picks up his case. 'Let's go and find a cab.'

The driver must be from Haiti, he reckons. His radio is tuned to a station full of static, reggae and rap and French patois.

She sits close to him on the back seat. He tries to recognise the perfume she is wearing.

JFK Boulevard. Van Wyck Expressway. Jamaica. Queens. Past La Guardia and the mortal remains of some long past exhibition by a dirty lake. The car is held up for fifteen minutes on the approach to the Midtown Tunnel. The driver puts a hand through the partition, requesting toll money. He still has a pocketful of coins from his last trip to America. He'd been promoting his latest book, a study of contemporary French literature. The joys of a five-city East Coast tour.

In the darkness of the tunnel, she places her hand on his. Since meeting up at the airport, they have barely spoken. Mostly about the weather; here, back in London, in the south of France where he now lives. How their respective flights had gone. Had she managed to sleep, and how he had spent the time reading. The in-flight movies and meals. Small talk at its most banal.

They finally drive out of the tunnel into the canyons of Manhattan and he breathes a sigh of relief. In the hotel room, he knows, he will be more eloquent, less shy and tongue-tied.

The traffic in the cross streets slows them down further as they navigate the traffic lights up to midtown.

They finally reach the hotel he has booked them into. Not the usual one where most staff in reception know him already, but one close by. He pays the cab driver. A porter rushes forward to assist with the luggage. There is only his case propped in the cab boot against a worn spare tyre. She carries her rucksack by its strap, and straightens her blue skirt as she steps out of the yellow vehicle.

He catches the porter's glance. Feels suddenly like a guilty, dirty old man, with this young girl at his side. Twenty-five years age difference. I am a cliché, he thinks. Damn it, he's not going to feel guilt now, is he?

At reception they make a big fuss of him. Ten years since he has stayed here last, according to the computer.

The elevator. The long corridor festooned with Andy Warhol prints. He inserts the electronic card key into the slot, the door flashes green and opens.

'Welcome to New York, Louise,' he says as a wave of infinite tenderness washes over his heart.

*

There is little for him to unpack as she uses the bathroom to freshen up from the journey. He listens to the water splash behind the door as he hangs his shirts and jackets in the cupboard. It's only mid-afternoon.

She emerges. Smiling sweetly. Now she looks even younger. Wonderfully slim, her loose dark hair falling over her shoulders, reaching midway down her back. Her waist looks as if he could hold it within his two outstretched hands. Her breasts jut against the thin material of her white cotton T-shirt, and his eyes can't avert themselves from the hypnotic shapes that strain the alignment of the whiteness. He guesses the strap of a bra over her shoulders but the cups must be soft and barely disguise the ever-aroused state of their contents.

'Are you hungry?' he asks her.

'Not really,' she answers. 'I snacked on the plane. But it wasn't very nice, I must say.'

'It never is,' he remarks. 'Because of the time difference with Europe, I always find it better to have a meal when I get here, as late as possible. Puts one's body clock on New York time. Otherwise, we'll end up waking in the middle of the night and we'll feel even more tired.'

'If you want,' Louise says. 'Is it what they call jet-lag?'

He nods. Gazes at her.

Her eyes are pale brown, a delicate colour variation he would give heaven and hell to be able to define. The knot in his stomach grows ever more painful with every passing minute. Eventually, he knows, he will have to get to grips fully with this crazy situation he has somehow engineered.

'Shall we go out? Maybe down to the Village. Have a walk. I'll show you around. Maybe see some shops for you. Have a bite to eat.'

'Whatever.'

It's spring. The sun is out. Everything feels unreal.

They walk. It feels like miles, but neither of them are tired. They browse. He can't help visiting a few bookstores. She gets a top at Urban Outfitters, but will not let him pay. He introduces her to a Belgian chocolate bar that's not available in Europe. They have an early dinner, around seven, in a Thai restaurant on Third Avenue, near the corner of St Mark's Place. Night falls. They are about to catch a cab back to their hotel when a pea-coloured chenille sweater catches her attention in the dimly-lit window of a thrift store. This time, he insists on paying. As they exit the shop, she pulls her purchase out of its paper bag and slips it on.

'It's suddenly grown colder, hasn't it?' she remarks.

'Yes,' he agrees.

There is sea of yellow cabs cruising down the Avenue, all with their lights on. He extends his arm to hail one. The driver is from the Ukraine, and insists on practising his English on them when he discovers that he hails from England. He has relatives in Swindon, and is surprised to learn he has never actually come across them. He answers that he now lives in France. Louise remains silent about her London origins.

There is a new porter on duty at the hotel door. To avoid judgment on their apparent age difference or the risk of being told he cannot bring young ladies into the hotel—a thought that has dominated his mind throughout the cab ride up from the East Village—he exaggeratedly holds his card key aloft as they walk into the hotel. Possibly guessing his embarrassment, Louise hold his hand in hers, whether to compound his self-consciousness or reassure him, he is uncertain.

Green light.

The door opens.

The room is not overly large, the sparse furniture purports to be antique, a Picasso face is spread across the left wall, the narrow double bed—by no stretch of the imagination anywhere near king-size—dominates the landscape that is going to be theirs for the next four days. Heavy brocade curtains are drawn. It's a quiet room; he is not sure whether the window gives on to Fifth Avenue or not.

She drops her rucksack to the floor, kicks off her flat shoes and approaches the bed. Tests its firmness with her hand and then sits on its edge as he watches her. She pulls the new sweater over her head. Looks him in the eyes.

He remains silent.

Attempting to put off the inevitable, maybe?

'So?' he finally ventures, 'am I what you expected?'

The wrong age, the wrong middle-age spread, the wrong short-sighted eyes, the wrong kind of clothes, the wrong size cock, the wrong man?

'I don't know,' she replies. 'You tell me.'

Then, as an afterthought, 'but I do like your voice.'

'Is it the voice of a Master, or the voice of a slave?' he asks her.

'Do you really want me to answer that question now?' Louise says.

'You're right. I don't. Maybe you can tell me at the end of the week.'

'Exactly. I've agreed to come here with you, but I can only be myself, you know that already . . .'

'Yes,' he quickly interrupts her. 'And as we talked before, back then, I respect your nature, I shall not attempt to change it. You are what you are, I accept that fully.'

'Good. I'm not seeking to be rescued . . .'

'I understand . . .'

'I am yours for this week we shall spend together in this room. Totally. Do to me what you will. Use me. Beat me. Humiliate me. My only pleasure is in giving myself. For you, I will be no different than I have been for others, with others. My holes are yours. All I am is a body, with holes made to be filled, used . . .'

Hearing her say it like this hurt even more than when she had initially written it.

But he tried to show no sign of the torment spiralling across his heart.

'I understand,' he repeated.

As she rises to her feet, she utters the last words he will hear from her until the following morning, 'I know there will be tenderness, but please, oh please, do not fall in love with me.' Thereafter, there were sounds. In abundance. But no more words. Only moans, sighs, cries, the whole orchestral palette of sex.

She approaches him. Closer than they have ever been.

Her lips move toward his.

They kiss.

She tastes of Middle-Eastern tea.

He takes her into his arms. Holds her tight as their kiss continues. Tongue. Teeth. Breath held back. His hands now linger all over her, feeling her softness, exploring her warmth, he feels her eager responsiveness as tremors of lust race through his body. He takes a step back, interrupting their feverish embrace. Recalls all she has revealed of her subservient nature.

'Undress,' he orders her.

Her eyes look up towards the light fixture.

'One item at a time,' he continues. 'I want to examine your body.'

She lowers her eyes and proceeds to pull the white T-shirt off, twisting its folds over her head, mussing her long brown hair which falls back down on her shoulders. Her skin is porcelain white. His heart tightens as sudden memories of another woman with the same pale skin flood back through his mind. Small flowery patterns crisscross the flimsy flesh-coloured bra she is wearing. It has no underwiring. Her small, pert breasts clearly don't require any. Her hands move to her back and she unhooks the bra and her chest is fully revealed. There is a dark mole an inch or so below her left nipple. Discreet dots of pigmentation are scattered across the approach to her modest cleavage, too pale even to merit the epithet of freckles.

The golden rings hang from her nipples, catching a fleeting reflection of the light from the hotel room's ceiling fixture and its three low-wattage bulbs. They are thin, half the diameter of a wedding ring. She watches his eyes alight on them. She straightens her back, offering her ringed breasts to him. He extends a hand, touches the metal adornments. They feel light. Carefully he twists one of the rings and observes the way the darker, puckered flesh of her nipple follows the movement of the ring between his fingers. Her gaze is unflinching. He twists further, and with a finger of his other hand begins to manipulate the other ring in similar fashion. He watches as the pierced nipples harden and lengthen imperceptibly as he continues to manipulate the gold rings and her nipples. He pulls on one of them and he sees her flinch. But she says nothing.

Finally, he lets go and allows his now-free hands to roam over her shoulders, caress her back. His plunges his fingers into her loose hair, pulls her head back and kisses her again, his tongue delving as deep as he can manage toward her throat. He can feel the rhythmic beat of her heart.

Her sharp nails begin to scratch his own back.

He keeps his eyes open as he kisses her. Notices the faint pale pink scar on her upper lip. Almost shaped like the letter N. Remembers its origin: Nola and the male friend also called N were drunk and had heated a paper clip in the flame of a lighter until it glowed red and tried to brand her with their joint initial.

He pushes Louise gently away.

'Suck me,' he tells her.

Nude to the waist down, like a fragile doll in her blue, now billowing skirt, she lowers herself to her knees, face in alignment with his crotch, and unclips his belt, unbuttons the top of his trousers and pulls them down to his knees. He is already partly hard and his cock is straining against his dark grey boxer shorts, an obscene bump of maleness.

She inserts a finger under the elastic and releases the cock.

He realises momentarily that he probably smells down there: the eight hours flight and sweat, the long afternoon walk, the sweat, the heat. He should have washed first.

Her mouth approaches. Her tongue licks his shaft, slowly, tantalisingly; a hand cups his heavy, dark balls and her lips close in on the glans as she takes him into her mouth. The heat is wonderful. She allows him all the way in, his tip bumping against the back of her throat. She doesn't gag as she impales her mouth over him. No woman has taken him in so far without choking. She has, he knows, been mercilessly trained by previous users under dire threat of punishment or violence. His cock grows inside her mouth.

Her tongue surrounds his hardness, dancing lightly around his captured stem, teasing, licking, caressing. Her lips hold him in a soft but firm vice, slip sliding over his engorged flesh, welcoming his invasion, wordlessly inviting him to thrust ever deeper into her.

His eyes wander across the horizon of the room. The Picasso head is watching them as the young girl studiously keeps on sucking his middle-aged cock.

At this rate, he knows, he won't last much longer. He does not wish to come so soon, inside her mouth. He retreats, withdraws from her mouth. She looks up at him, puzzled, thinking maybe she hasn't performed well enough and is due for punishment.

He attempts a smile of kindness to reassure her.

'Undress,' he asks her. 'Take the rest off now.'

She obeys.

Stands up and unzips the blue skirt. It slips to the hotel room carpet. The shape of her body is the nearest he has come to witnessing perfection, outside of doubtlessly doctored photographs in magazines. At the age of twenty neither gravity nor the ravages of time have yet taken hold and begun their seditious work.

Her knickers are modest, thick white cotton, practical, sexless.

She bends over slightly to pull them down.

He knows what to expect. From what she has written.

He also knows it's the first thing that initially attracted him to her, and convinced him he had to see her one day. A prurient curiosity that betrays the filth in him.

The bunched-up piece of white underwear now lies in a small heap on the carpet. She straightens up. His eyes move up her smooth legs. Slowly. Almost hesitantly.

It's as he knew it would be.

His turn to move to his knees and bring his face to her genital area.

Quite hairless, both above and around her cunt. Like the crotch of a doll or a pre-pubescent girl.

Not a wisp of hair, not even a darker shadow of hairs past. The same milky white shade that characterises her whole body.

And the rings.

Gold.

Each one a thin band, like a cheap wedding ring.

Eight of them.

Four hanging from each labia, in perfect alignment, pulling both outer lips out of the central gash, the darker, redder skin like meaty folds on a butcher's stall, raw, almost bloody, as if the necessary piercings had only been done recently.

He gasps.

Incongruously wonders whether there is enough metal here to set off airport alarms.

Each set of labial rings are held together by a thin contraption of stainless steel, like a nurse's large safety pin with three branches. The middle one is threaded through all the rings while the two outer ones squeeze the pin tight and the whole is kept closed by a minuscule padlock.

He advances his fingers, gingerly touches the chastity device protecting her entrance, and his hand feels the intense heat emanating from the invisible depths of her cunt.

The rings effectively seal her tight. There is not even space to insert a finger. As she had warned him. Even at period time, she is unable to use a tampon and has to rely on sanitary towels.

'It's awesome,' he whispers in the now hushed silence of the room. 'It's . . . beautiful.' And barbaric, he thinks, but he is so turned on.

He can't take his eyes off her locked cunt.

She remains quite silent.

Observing him.

Judging him?

This older man, with his thinning hair, his cock jutting out as if on military parade, his love handles, the sombre bags under his eyes, his trousers bunched up around his ankles.

He finally takes off the rest of his clothes and asks Louise to lay down on the bed, on her back, and indicates she should open her legs wide.

He kneels, forces the angle between her thighs even wider and examines her like a doctor, mentally storing every detail of her adornments, her mutilation, as he gazes at the brazen display of the wonder of her jewelled portals.

He moves his face against her cunt, feels her inner warmth vibrate toward his cheeks, tries to slip his tongue between the minute gaps between the rings, but there is no access. She is utterly sealed.

Louise extends a hand, musses his air, sensing his obvious frustration.

He is on his knees at the foot of the bed, his head at the apex of her thighs, inhaling deeply, trying to seize the ineffable smell of her.

The sheer hardness of his cock weighs against his stomach.

He thinks of investing her mouth again, but Louise shifts on her side and repositions herself on all fours on the bed, her rump raised toward him. A perfect, pale sphere, punctured by the darker heart of her anus; both her hands move back to either side and stretch her globes apart, inviting him. He wets his cock and thrusts himself into her arse in one swift movement. His head punctures the tight sphincter and his whole cock is quickly embedded inside her. She shifts to accommodate him better.

He digs inside her and for the next ten minutes, an eternity, he fucks her arse watching the skin around her aperture distend with every in and out movement of his thick cock. He moans. She moans. He sweats. The perspiration drops from his forehead to his chin and then onto her back, where it pools slowly, a small transparent pond of humidity vibrating intensely to the accompaniment of every tremor that crosses her body as he tries to force himself ever deeper into her bowels. His lips are dry. She bites hers, out of pleasure or pain. His heart beats a light fantastic. Picasso is on the wall. They are bathed in the clandestine sounds of the hotel. Their fuck is an island of motion cut off from the rest of the world. He holds back as long as he can manage. Below the dark piston of his cock and its mechanical assault of her innards, the rings shine, wetness from above and inside her bathing them in an unmistakable sheen of lust. His frenzied eyes mirror his soul, flitting from arsehole to ring-bedecked cunt, and his hardness just refuses to fade away.

Her sounds of sex are silent. Gentle cries, repressed gasps, deep breaths. She adjusts the position of her body to accommodate his movements, to accept him even deeper, her sphincter muscles tightening rhythmically around him before releasing his penis again, then tightening again capturing every renewed attack. His tip is deep inside her bowels. Where it burns. And feels good.

Finally, he can hold out no longer. Louise's whole body is just made for sex, a finely-honed machine for the benefit of his pleasure. He comes. He roars. Her name. A profanity. Feels his come burst out of him and bathing her insides, like a river of sin, a torrent out of control. He rests his hands on the bed, bent over her, the beat of his breath returning to normality. Silence. At last, he feels his hardness begin to recede and pulls back, withdrawing his still pulsating cock from her. It emerges, bathed in come and inner juices. Her hole is shockingly dilated, red raw at the edges, like a small dark bottomless crevice. Never has he witnessed a sight so pornographic and, at the same time, so shockingly beautiful. The temporary scar his raging cock has left on her.

But he also knows she did not come.

They lie down together, moist body against pale body.

'Tired?' he asks her.

He pulls the covers over their bare bodies.

She nods, her eyes half-closed.

'It's the jet-lag catching up,' he says. It's only ten at night in Manhattan.

He wakes at two in the morning, still 9pm European time, with a hard on, his mind and body in tumult. She is on her side, her back to him. He pulls her sleeping body toward him and the contact of her flesh only accentuates his desire. He pushes a finger into her arsehole. She is still dripping, leaking his earlier come. He slips his cock into her and begins fucking her again. It takes him ages to orgasm as he rages against her with every movement, angrily seeking release. At one stage, he surprises himself and finds his hands beginning to tighten around her thin neck as his thrusts take a vengeful rhythm. He quickly releases the pressure of his fingers there. He doesn't know whether she is awake or still sleeping. But her whole body accepts him.

He awakes again; there is a thin sliver of light peering through the heavy curtains. Early morning. This time Louise is no longer sleeping, busy sucking on his cock with greedy appetite. Her eyes stay closed, he sees, as she does this.

When he is fully erect, she squats above him, stretches her rump cheeks open and plants herself on his cock, once again taking him deep into her arse. When he finally comes, the feeling is so strong, he thinks he is going to pass out.

'So, do I please you?' she asks, her first words since the previous evening.

'Yes, Louise, you do,' he answers.

Q & A

'So who is Nola?'

'She's my half-sister.'

'How old were you?'

'Sixteen.'

'Tell me about it, her and you. How it happened.'

'I was born in a well-off, heavily Catholic family. We weren't rich, but life was easy and I was spoilt as a child. My sister is somewhat older than me. I've always believed she was very unhappy about my arrival at such a late stage. The family had been in flux with remarriages on both sides. But there was money.'

'How did she become aware of your submissive tendencies?'

'I think that she somehow always knew.'

'And she exploited it? You must hate her.'

'No, I don't. I love her, feel very close to her.'

'When did she first take advantage of this knowledge?'

'I was a good pupil at school, but I excelled in sports. I particularly enjoyed gymnastics, I was told I had talent. For my sixteenth birthday, I asked for private lessons in one of the City's better clubs. My parents agreed to it, and I was signed in for lessons two evenings a week and following school on Wednesday afternoons. Nola insisted on accompanying me, as a chaperone of sorts. I remember her often mocking me when I was younger, because of my lack of feminine opulence. 'The Plank' when I was thirteen, later 'No Bum' when I reached fourteen. My body developed late.'

'Your half-sister seduced you?'

'Not quite. She was very pleasant to me during the course of the early lessons. She watched my training and soon recognised my innate talent and the suppleness of my body. Initially, I attended the lessons wearing shorts and a T-shirt, but soon the teacher asked me to wear a dancer's leotard so that she might able to supervise and see how all my muscles worked. She taught me a lot, often correcting my stance or the use of the wrong muscles with a small wooden cane. Nola befriended her and was soon assigned to holding the cane.'

'She beat you?'

'Lesson after lesson, the instructions became more and more difficult to follow and she would strike me harder, with the assent of the instructor. I always felt they were in total collusion. Surprisingly, I began to look forward to her striking me, even though it was sometimes painful. To this day, I still hanker to submit to her; she was so beautiful. So tall and her hair so dark and red. And her severity struck an unusually responsive chord inside me as I took instruction. I think I had basically been submissive in spirit ever since my early childhood.'

'How come?'

'Even as a child, I recall never wishing to be a princess when we played games with my sisters or friends. I preferred to imagine myself as a servant.'

'How did the relationship progress to you becoming, so to speak, her slave?'

'After the course of lessons came to an end. I continued my gymnastics training, this time solely under Nola's supervision. Soon, she began to realise, I think, that I was sometimes making deliberate mistakes, and she began striking me for no reason at all, and noted that I did not object. One day, for the first time, she struck me badly with her long, thin cane before our session even began. Told me it was to encourage me. She had guessed my masochist nature. That day, following our work-out, I deliberately followed her into the shower and confessed how attractive I found her and that I was in love with her. She surprised me by replying that she had lusted after me ever since I had been younger, and her earlier taunts had just been indications of her disguised desire for me. We kissed.'

'And?'

'She warned me of her dominant character and that, in any form of relationship, I would have to submit to her will. I readily agreed. She made love to me there and then under the shower. It was heavenly. She knew every spot to touch, as if by magic.'

'Had you been with boys before?'

'Somehow, I had never been attracted to men much. I'd kissed one or two boys, even allowed one to fondle my breasts under my shirt, but I hadn't ventured further.'

'You were still only sixteen?'

'Yes. From the next day onward, I began following Nola's instructions. I wanted only to please her. She said I should no longer wear jeans and dress like a tomboy. I must always wear dresses or skirts, no pantyhose, only stockings. Every day after school, I would go to her room and wait for her to return from her own lessons or the bookshop where she sometimes worked on a part-time basis. She would often leave instructions for me on small pieces of paper on the kitchen table. This was a time when our parents were often away travelling and we had to fend for ourselves. I had to follow these most precisely. One day, she left an apron for me to wear, alongside the note. I was to become her servant.'

'What was the sex like?'

'In bed, she was brutal and authoritarian. She enjoyed ordering me around, loved to humiliate me, sometimes inflicted much pain. But I enjoyed it more than I had enjoyed anything in my life before.'

'I don't want to sound like a dime store psychiatrist, but had you previously felt unloved, unwanted at home?'

'Not at all. It's just the way I am. I don't think anything will ever change my nature.'

'How did things develop, then with Nola?'

'After three months of living like this, rushing to her room every day straight from school, all feverish, anxious for more of her harsh love and punishment, desperately trying to get away from college work over the week-ends to spend more time with her, I just decided to leave school altogether and put myself completely at Nola's service.'

'Did your parents suspects anything?'

'This was the time when they moved to Belgium. Nola said she was old enough to look after me. After all, we'd been on our own for long periods of time already. We weren't kids any longer. So we were both given a generous allowance.'

'So, you lived alone with Nola from then on?'

'I was her maid during the day and her toy at night. She became even harder on me now, would not accept a word of disobedience, insisted on only the highest standards of house work, cleaning and cooking. Whenever I failed, or forgot an instruction, the beating was most severe. The worse it became, the happier I was.'

'Tell me how.'

'For Valentine's Day, she bought a whip and a pair of handcuffs for me. The whip was to be used on me, of course. Thereafter, most days she handcuffed me before leaving for her work. Thus constricted, she said I would have more time to think of her all day. Naturally, my work around the house suffered badly. Which gave her even more opportunities to use the whip on me. But sex with her after every whipping was better than ever. I could wish for no other fate. Very soon, she began to use the whip on my body for no other reason than arousing me further sexually. Now she no longer even needed a reason to beat me, mark me.'

'And you enjoyed this?'

'I was deliriously happy. This was what I was born to be. Later, she would take me to the West End and Soho on special shopping trips to a basement store that specialised in fetish and S&M apparel. She bought increasingly sophisticated devices and clothing for me. She would make me wear elaborate black leather outfits that made me look like a whore at a sadomasochists' convention. She had me play with toys in front of the assistants in the store as she exercised her power. Would have me gagged, plugged, displayed. Force me to wear underwear she had deliberately dirtied before. Back at her home, I had to serve her completely, in every detail. It soon became my task to lick her clean after she had been to the toilet. She loved me and I loved her. I thought this bliss would last forever.'

*

Mid-morning in the Manhattan hotel room. He calls out for bagels from Mom's Bagel's two streets away. For him, a garlic bialy with Nova Scotia lox and cream cheese, and a plain bagel with cream cheese and jelly for her.

They devour the food in bed, close to each other. He feels comfortable with her, their bare bodies touch as they shift, neither draws back from the contact. He loves the fact that, like him, she is a creature of silence, doesn't find it necessary to make small talk and fill every precious moment of silence with needless words. A thin dollop of red jelly drops on to her left breast. He bends over and licks her clean, his furtive tongue nibbling on her ring, stretching the tender skin beneath. A warm feeling suffuses his abdomen. Blood already coursing back towards his tired cock.

Aware he is probably in no condition to perform again yet, he draws back and takes the kiss to her lips.

She smiles.

They have opened the curtains. Sunlight floods the room, the bed, their uncovered bodies.

He tells her about the last time he stayed here. For two nights in a row a couple in the room next door had practised particularly noisy sex, the sounds of which could just not be avoided through the thin wall, keeping him awake and arousing his own lust. The woman had been especially vocal, every thrust inside her provoking further moans, gasps or profane vocabulary in her lexicon of pleasure. The man, on the other hand, appeared to copulate in silence, leaving all vocal accompaniment up to his partner, but must have had incredible staying power as the sounds of their frantic lovemaking reverberated through to his room for almost two hours. On and on the sounds of nearby sex continued and he had begun to wonder what this shrill, enthusiastic woman might actually look like. The following night, the carnival occurred again in the adjoining room. On the third day, as he was leaving his room for his morning appointments, he finally caught a glimpse of a woman closing the door to the next room. To his disappointment and amazement—by now, he had visions in his mind of Greek goddesses or hardcore stars of the pornographic screen—she was a stocky, matronly Chinese woman in an old-fashioned fur coat draped across her shoulders, wearing sensible shoes and with a chignon in her hair. Anything but his dreams.

Louise laughs at his story.

'Well, I don't think we bothered the neighbours much,' she remarks. 'We're both wordless fornicators, I noticed.'

He smiles back at her. Preferring not to tell her his other story of a hotel room fuck. In Paris, window opening on to a sea of Latin Quarter roofs. Where the sounds of the adjoining room had in fact been more muted but still caught his attention. Aroused, he had taken a glass from the bathroom and stuck it against the separating wall, cupped his ear against it and listened to the couple frolicking a few inches away, and masturbated to the sound of their fucking.

Finally, they get up.

In the light of day, he finds her more beautiful than ever. And younger. Less than half his age.

'Who gets to use the bathroom first?' he asks her.

'You go,' she answers. 'I feel wonderfully lazy this morning.'

He shaves. Christ, does he look tired! The new razor blade revives his skin. He washes the foam away and cleans his teeth. He tests the heat of the water bursting from out of the shower head, finds the right balance of hot and cold and steps into the shower. He is soaping his cock, washing away their combined juices, when he hears her knock on the bathroom door.

'Yes?'

'Can I come in?' she asks him.

'Of course,' he replies. There is no need for false modesty now.

She tiptoes in, walks across the damp tiles and sits herself on the toilet bowl. Facing him, legs wide apart, she proceeds to pee as he stands under the pouring water just a few feet away. He notices the eight rings hanging loosely from her labia as the thick stream of urine jets out of her, and realises the safety pin and the padlock are no longer in place. His first glance at the pinkness inside her cunt as her leaves separate, gape, to make way for the release of her warm stream.

She looks up at him, with a wry smile on her lips.

His eyes interrogate her silently.

'You never asked,' she says, as the last drops of pee keep on dribbling out of her. 'A real Master always does, he orders.'

'I didn't realise . . .' he mumbles.

'I was allowed to bring the padlock key with me,' she confirms.

'I see,' is all he can feebly say. Feeling as if he has failed the first test.

'Can I join you under the shower?' Louise asks.

'Of course,' he says.

Her body shines under the pounding water. They embrace. Kiss. Separate. Their hair soaking wet now. United by the cleansing spurts of hot water. They soap each other with all the delicacy they can muster. Kiss again. They step out of the shower. He turns to switch the water off and when he turns again to face her, she delicately takes his cock in her wet fingers.

'There was still some soap,' she says.

She squeezes it. Hard.

He takes her hand away.

'Stay like that,' he says.

She remains immobile, water still dripping down the expanse of her body. He takes hold of a towel and dries her, enveloping her body in its softness. He glides his finger through her hair.

'Oh, Louise,' he says.

'Yes?' she asks.

'I want to make love to you properly now,' he answers.

He bends and picks her up in his arms. She is so light, he notices; and they make their way from steamy bathroom to the bed in the hotel room now blinded with light.

He pulls a curtain half-closed. There is still enough light for him to see all of her.

He installs her on the bed. She remains inert. Her opening gapes, as if alive, breathing like an invitation to pleasure. He delicately spreadeagles her limbs in a semblance of crucifixion across the crumpled sheets and buries his face in her cunt. He opens her up at long last and spies the infinite nacreous shades of her inner walls. Parting her, rings to each side, he plunges his tongue inside her and a tremor flashes through her whole body. She still tastes of soap but her juices are soon abundantly flowing, pungent, aromatic, overflowing, bathing his chin as he labours away now, playing with her engorged clit. He has reached his destination, her portals of paradise. The velvet pearl pulses strongly against the tip of his tongue. Louise moans. Widens the angle of her legs further in acceptance of his adoration. His face retreats. He looks up at her. Her face and the whole area leading to her breasts are flushed a deep hue of pink. Her eyes are closed.

He inserts a finger, then two, inside her cunt. She is like a furnace inside. He moves his other free hand towards her rear and sticks a finger inside her arsehole, where she is still gooey from their earlier exertions. Louise gasps as both her holes are invaded.

Through the incandescent body heat, he feels the pulse of her heart beat against his probing fingers. He bends, withdraws the digits and takes her now protuberant clit between his teeth and nibbles away at it. He feels her close to coming, for the first time since they have been together. His mouth takes leave of her copiously flowing juices and he climbs over her and inserts his cock inside her.

A wordless sound passes her lips.

Tenderness sweeps across his heart as he begins moving inside her. The fit is exquisite. The gold rings on either side of her cunt lips slide effortlessly against his shaft, enhancing the sensations without overpowering them. As he thrusts in and out of her, the thought occurs to him that if he were her Master he would have her pierced yet again, a ring or a stud in her clitoris, just to enhance the friction against his glans as it labours and retreats against her opening time and again. Yes, a nice thought. And a big if.

He closes his eyes in turn and surrenders to their first moment of love.

Q & A

'How did things begin to change in your relationship?'

'She liked to show me off to others. Demonstrate the extent of her power over me.'

'Men? Women?'

'She would invite friends to our house and play at humiliating me in front of them.'

'How?'

'By having me wear the outfits she had bought for me. Playing games she knew I was bound to lose and then punishing me for my mistakes. I would have to strip in front of her guests and have my rear caned or whipped. If there were other women, she would make me lick her sex in their presence, sometimes had me lie on the floor while they peed over me. I would have to serve food naked but for a dog collar and was forbidden to react while they pinched me, touched my intimate parts, sometimes tried to trip me to cause further punishment.'

'But were there men?'

'Initially, only one. A close friend of hers. His name was N. He's a lawyer from the city.'

'Was he her lover?'

'No, Nola hates men, sexually. But she was close to N. She liked exposing me to him, making me bend over so that he could peer inside me, even touch, which she knew I hated. The more ill at ease I was in these situations, the more it excited her and the crueller she became with him as witness to my degradation.'

'What sort of things would she do for him?'

'She liked to demonstrate my absolute obedience. One day, I was made to lie on my back on the floor as she inserted a series of ever-larger objects inside my vagina which I had to hold wide open for them. First a dildo, then a bottle, then a cucumber. All the time, I could see the bump inside his trousers swell as she teased him and said wouldn't he like it to be him in that nice virgin cunt.'

'You were still a virgin?'

'Technically, yes. I hadn't yet been penetrated by a man. By Nola and objects only.'

'How did it happen, the first time?'

'With N. One morning, Nola summoned me and instructed me that I should take a taxi to his apartment and do every single thing he would ask me to do. When I protested, she whipped me badly. Said I did not understand what true love was. I argued that I did. But she owed N some debt, and he wanted me and that was that. Anyway, she told me, it would be good for my training, I had to be broken in. I went to him. Hated every moment. Later, there were other men she loaned me to.'

'Did she ever want to watch you being fucked by them?'

'No. If she was there, she would move to another room.'

'But did she ever ask you about what happened with the men?'

'Curiously, no. Although I was avid to tell her all, to demonstrate the extent of my affection for her by describing the pain they had inflicted on me, how they had used me, violated all my holes, made me choke on their filthy penises and forced me to swallow their ejaculate, played with me, beat me too. I wanted to tell her, Nola, I have accepted all this for your sake. But she never asked. And if there were marks, cuts, bruises on my body, she would whip me in response, as if it were all my fault.'

'Sounds very much like one-way traffic to me.'

'She said that the coming of my seventeenth birthday would mark a significant point in our relationship. That I had satisfied her so far and she would show me her gratitude on this occasion.'

'What did she do?'

'We drove to Hastings on a Saturday morning. I thought she would be getting me new outfits at the Soho fetish shop, but this was not the case. It was a large building in the suburbs of the resort, a doctor she knew well. I would come across him again at the special parties. He used electrolysis to depilate my pubic area. I'm told it will never grow back again. Then, he pierced my breasts and fitted the rings I still have now. I was in heaven. I was Nola's slave, in both body and spirit.'

'What are those special parties you mentioned?'

'They occurred later. I will tell you.'

'OK.'

*

Their second full day in Manhattan. The spring weather is clement. They walk. Catch cabs. Shop. Snack. Battery Park. The Cloisters. Central Park, watching the squirrels hop along the scarce vegetation.

They talk.

'Are you happy?' he asks her. 'It's such fun showing you this city, all these places I have known and liked for years. I try and imagine what it feels for you to see them for the first time.'

'It's nice,' she answers. 'But you're too soft with me. I don't deserve this, you know. If I were in your place, I would be crueller, much harder. Somehow I think you're too sensitive. Almost like a girl . . .'

His face clouds over.

'If you were in charge and I was a girl, would you fuck me?' he quietly inquires.

'I would,' Louise says. 'I would stretch you, hurt you until you plead for mercy, but I wouldn't give you any. I have been taught well. Switching is no problem.'

'I see.'

'Would you prove your devotion to me by letting me treat you like that?' Louise asks him as they cross toward the Plaza Hotel.

He doesn't hesitate.

'I would,' he replies.

'OK,' she says.

They catch a cab which takes them to a dark side street near the Port Authority Terminal. In a sex shop manned by Pakistani assistants they buy a strap-on dildo. Flesh coloured, veined, awesomely realistic and life-size. And handcuffs. So that he doesn't change his mind, she says.

He is in no hurry to return to their hotel room.

He reminds her she wanted to go to Macy's.

She wanders indifferently through the designer label departments.

'I want to buy you something nice,' he insists.

'Why?' she queries. 'How do you want me to dress? Like a whore or a princess?'

'As a young woman.'

She agrees to stockings, a silk cream-coloured see-through blouse and a flowing skirt in rainbow colours.

They arrive back at the hotel mid-afternoon. The room has been made, and the smells of sex have faded.

'Undress,' she orders him, herself stripping from the waist downwards and fitting the strap-on around her waist. He notices she has reattached the safety pin and the padlock.

He silently sheds his clothes, takes a step towards the bathroom, planning to wash the sweat away from his body.

'Don't,' she forbids him. 'I want you dirty, I want to smell your vileness as I fuck you.'

He knows he shouldn't protest; his face reddens as his arse crack feels all clammy, and his feet sticky.

'On your knees. NOW!'

He gets down on all fours.

'Raise your head.'

He does. His eyes are parallel with her labial rings, he notices she is seeping there. She is excited. She thrusts the artificial cock toward his mouth.

'Suck me,' she intimates.

The rubbery material fills his mouth, the taste is unpleasant. She only lets him suck the dildo for a minute or two then withdraws it and places herself behind him. All she wanted was for him to wet it.

She places the strap-on head against his anus and begins pushing it in.

It enters him with surprising ease. Initially, there is little pain and he is almost disappointed.

The feeling doesn't last and soon he is biting his lips to repress heartfelt sounds of anguish as Louise goes to war on him. Viciously twisting the implement of torture within his gut as she endlessly adjusts her stance to increase its depth, the angle of attack and the unremitting pressure on his protesting bowels. He knows she is enjoying this. But he reasons, beyond the valley of pain, that she deserves at least this; that this is his own particular way of experiencing some of the humiliation that has been lavished on her by so many others. He communes with her as she keeps on fucking his arse, until the skin inside and outside of the hole is raw and mutilated from the friction. His heart beats wildly, bile pools at the back of his throat, he has difficulty breathing. There is no longer any pleasure in the act for him.

Then, as suddenly as she entered him, she pulls it out in one swift movement and he momentarily feels as his whole insides are being suctioned out.

He collapses, stomach first, onto the floor.

'There,' she says. 'I think you would make a better slave than Master. Very docile. You take your suffering in silence; that's a a a good sign,' she remarks.

For a moment, the germ of an idea settles in his mind. An image of the two of them as slaves, collared together, made to perform for the benefit of others.

At last, he rises, as his breath returns. Louise now sits on the bed, watching him. The strap now detached from her, her hands shielding her jewelled pubes.

'I hurt you, didn't I?' she asks, watching him rub his hole with the back of his hand. There is some blood.

'You did,' he says.

'Then I must be punished,' she says. 'That is the way.'

As he washes the traces of the fuck away some minutes later, he realises she is now testing him. It's scary: could he ever become her Master? Keep her?

He dresses.

The crease of his boxer shorts rubs painfully against his bruised flesh as he walks back into the room. Louise is watching a game show on the TV set.

'I'm taking you out,' he tells her, switching the programme off.

'Where to?'

'Never you mind.'

Somehow he always knew it would come to this.

She understands.

Asks: 'How should I dress?'

'Like a whore. Wear that blouse and no bra, and stockings. And your shortest skirt. No underwear.'

She nods.

Night falls as their cab rushes down Fifth toward SoHo. He instructs her. At all times, she will sit with her legs open; there is to be no false modesty. She is his property for tonight and the following day and he will broach no disobedience. She will only talk when spoken to. She indicates her assent to his terms.

'You will take no pleasure from what is done to you, because I won't either . . .'

'A Master would take pleasure in displaying me,' she interrupts him.

He slaps her cheek, as punishment for her uncalled verbal response.

'Quiet, now.'

Her cheek reddens from the blow. She lowers her eyes. The driver looks inquiringly into his rear mirror at the older man and the young woman. Even though the light outside is dimming, he clearly saw her nipples through the shimmering blouse as she entered his cab, and he tries to get a better look.

A jazz club. Grimy walls, cigarette smoke, dissonant melodies running like waves across the ceiling over the sparse audience. He has her drink vodka and orange, although he knows she dislikes the concoction. Men at the bar glance in their direction. Her skirt is hitched up to mid-thigh. He fingers her under the table. She squirms.

Her rings are wet with her secretions.

He informs her of the fact. Presents a finger to her.

'Lick me clean.'

She does, just as the waitress approaches their table inquiring after another round.

'Touching,' the waitress mumbles, visibly disapproving and mistaking Louise's appetite for a gesture of love.

'Isn't it?' he responds with a wry smile.

The tension is palpable, as he summons his courage.

She senses it and remains damningly silent and expressionless.

Finally.

'Anything?'

'Yes,' Louise replies. 'Anything, it is my nature to be a slave.'

He rises from his seat as the band on stage finish their set in a flourish of drum rolls and reverb, takes hold of her hand and they make their way to the toilets. He briefly holds his breath and then enters the men's, followed by her. There is a harsh smell of antiseptic lingering in the air, the ceiling is low, the surroundings claustrophobic. There is no one there. Just a yellowing row of urinals, a creaking fan circling like a low-flying aircraft close to the peeling, concrete ceiling, a sink with a dripping tap, a dirty towel, and behind a wooden door painted jet-black the lone toilet seat. He opens the cubicle and orders Louise to sit. He pulls her blue skirt up to her waist, unveiling her rings, and opens the buttons of her blouse so that her breasts are also on display.

'Like that. Yes.'

She doesn't answer.

'The first man to come in,' he says.

She nods silently.

They wait. Each passing second extends to eternity.

Finally the door swings open and a tall black guy walks in, hands already unzipping his flies. He heads towards the urinal, his back to Louise in the cubicle.

'Hi.'

He recognises the guy, who played bass in the band, a lanky man in denim.

'Hi, man. How ya doin'?'

'Listen. I have something for you . . .'

The musician starts peeing.

'Nah, man, I have my own supplier. Thanks anyway.'

'It's not drugs.'

The black guy shrugs.

'Yeah? What, then?'

'I have a woman here. She'll suck you dry for free. Interested?'

The man looks over his shoulder at him, weighing the seriousness of the offer.

Notices the open cubicle and Louise sitting there, splayed open, all her gold rings on display.

He catches his breath.

'What's in it for you?' he asks, turning round and zipping his jeans up. His eyes are now fixed on the obscene spectacle of the young woman, her white flesh like a beacon in the sordid surroundings. 'Wow,' he whispers to himself.

'I watch. That's all.'

'You serious?'

'Absolutely.'

'I'd always heard you limeys got your kicks in weird fashion,' he says, a grin spreading over his dark features.

He approaches the cubicle and its immobile prisoner. He unzips and pulls out his cock. It's long, thick, uncut. Offers it to her, hesitantly as if all this is about to disappear in a puff of smoke and is but a crazy mirage, a drug-fuelled dream. Louise bends her face forward to take the cock.

'Sweet gal,' says the musician as her lips first graze his stem, before she takes him all in. 'Will she swallow?' he asks.

'Yes,' he answers.

And watches the spectacle.

Black against white.

Black inside white.

To the bitter end.

After it is over, he allows her to adjust her apparel and cups his hands together to allow her to drink the tap water and wash her mouth.

Relief floods over him that no other man entered the bathroom while the three of them were there. He's not sure he could have controlled the situation any further.

Still, she says nothing.

They finish their drinks and listen to the first quarter of an hour of the band's second set. He hails a cab and they return to the hotel.

This is the first night in Manhattan they do not make love.

Q & A

'Did things happen that you particularly disliked?'

'Many. What I still found most difficult was when she invited friends around to demonstrate her power over me and my subservience, and took great pleasure humiliating me in their presence. The sex I didn't mind. But I did feel shame. More so, when we left the house to go to parties and she had me walk out onto the street wearing accessories and clothing which were so explicit as to provide little doubt as to my status as her personal slave. A dog collar, a skimpy maid's outfit, sometimes even a thin metal chain that connected to the handcuffs she made me wear for the short walk to the car park.'

'You were afraid that people might recognise you?'

'Not really, I did not like the fact that my slavery might be recognised by others.'

'I'm not sure I understand. You are proud of what you are.'

'I know. The worst time was when she invited a girl I thought had previously been my best friend when I was still at school along for tea to the house one evening. I hadn't seen her for nearly a year. I had to wear the maid's outfit with the apron and serve them in silence as my erstwhile friend's smile nauseated me. When asked if the tea and biscuits I had baked were to her liking, my friend, no doubt previously prompted by Nola, expressed reservations and I was told the only recourse was for me to be flogged in her presence. Which Nola did with unusual ferocity. I was made to bend across a chair a few inches away from where my friend sat, my dress was pulled up above my waist and my knickers pulled down to my knees, and I still remember every blow against my bare skin even now. When Nola had completed the punishment, she actually invited my friend to beat me likewise. Which she agreed to do, the damn traitor. I couldn't sit for days after that beating. I'm sure they had both planned this for ages.'

'You were going to tell me about the parties?'

'There were two sorts. Once or twice a month, Nola would have friends, mostly other women, sometimes couples for drinks in the evening. I would be made to serve. I recall now that this was already some time after the death of our parents in a car crash. We had both been left the whole estate but as I was still under-age, Nola had control of all the money. Very often I would have to provide evidence of my servility and accept a flogging or the caress of the whip. The guests would seldom become involved. This was more a demonstration of Nola's power over me. At most, I would have to display my body for their after-drinks recreation, allow them to touch, twist my breast rings, provide evidence of my absolute docility and obedience.'

'What sort of people were these friends of Nola's?'

'Professional, middle-class, middle-aged, the women were lesbian or bisexual but she would never loan me to them. Their fun with me was restricted to the games with me on that particular evening.'

'The other parties?'

'They were more extreme. Infrequent also. I think I only attended five. Usually took place on Saturday nights and ran through the night. Never at the Regent's Park house Nola and I now shared, usually at plush residences somewhere outside London or in major provincial cities. I never knew where exactly we were, as I was blindfolded by Nola as we neared the locations.'

'Sounds frightening.'

'It was. Nola said I now had to prove that I was fully trained as a sub and these parties would be my final test. I was eager to prove her confidence in me was well-placed, and swore I would do everything I was told. It wasn't easy, but then I had little choice.'

'What sort of people attended these parties?'

'People like Nola. Genuine, experienced Masters. They were here to show off their slaves, male as well as female. We all wore collars and were forbidden to talk to each other as we were cuffed together awaiting our fate for the evening. Whatever happened to any of us, we were made to watch, and looking away would result in further punishment.'

'What happened to you?'

'Even now, I can't talk about many of the things that were done to me, or I was made to do to others.'

'What can you reveal?'

'Often the Masters would play games, make bets on us, pick cards for the humiliations that would be inflicted on us. A party night would seldom pass by without my not having been used in all holes by all the Masters present, male as well as female. On my first such party, my anal virginity was auctioned. I was blindfolded and made to kneel and suck every cock in the room, including the male slaves who were present. Unbeknown to me, the first one who managed to make me gag and retch would be designated to be the first to bugger me. I had successfully sucked three of the men and swallowed without heaving when I felt another place himself in front of my mouth and heard sniggers around the room. I knew something was wrong right there and then. A voice behind me remarked that I might require some help, and my hair was brutally pulled back and my head pushed forward onto the expectant cock. He was so heavily hung that the pressure applied to the back of my head forced me to swallow him and he was shoved all the way into my throat. I couldn't breathe. My lips were stretched to their fullest around its thickness and no air could pass from my lungs to my mouth. I couldn't help being sick all over him right there and then. It had been a set-up. He was one of the young slaves and his penis had elephantine proportions. At the next party, I was told he measured twelve inches or more.'

'Jesus!'

'I had no choice. After being made to clean up the mess I had caused, I was installed at the centre of the room as all watched and the young boy sodomised me. It hurt badly. I bled for days. I even fainted halfway through and had to be revived with smelling salts.

They had no pity on me. When it was over and I stumbled back to the far wall, where the other slaves were grouped, I noticed Nola had not remained in the room for the dubious ceremony. One of the other girls, she was a tall, red-haired beauty with ever so pale skin, whispered to me that she had gone through the same ordeal. They always chose the pimply young slave boy with the enormous cock for a female slave's first experience of sodomy. Something about stretching us for further use. A Master saw her talking to me, chided her and announced this was one transgression too far. Could she not manage to keep her mouth closed long enough? Next time, she would be the one to be punished. She went paler than pale and tried to prevent her tears from flowing. I saw that she was terrorised. In the meantime, the young boy who had hurt me so much was now still the centre of attraction and being made to suck his own Master to hardness before he was made to kneel on all fours himself and his Master buggered him in turn.'

'How could you accept such things, Louise?'

'Because Nola ordered me to and I was in love with her.'

'The things we do for love . . .'

'I missed the next party. My anus was still bleeding days later and Nola had to take me to the doctor in Harley Street to have two stitches put in to repair me. The doctor just smiled when he examined me, as if he knew exactly which cock had done the damage. Nicely dilated, was all he commented upon, just right for the rest of us now.'

'He was an accomplice?'

'Yes, a founding member of their circle. When I had healed sufficiently, he was the first to take me in the arse at an ensuing party.'

'While you were being used by others at these parties, what did Nola do?'

'She liked to whip and torture the other Masters' female slaves. I once had to watch her fist another girl who appeared to be even younger than me. She had never, until then, done that to me. The poor kid screamed so much they had to gag her, but Nola's cruelty knew no bounds and she kept on twisting her hand and pounding the kid's innards to jelly.'

'You must have been scared by that.'

'Yes, but not so much as the day I had to watch the tall redhaired girl being punished. She had accumulated too many faults, according to her Master, and had to be made an example of. And all of us other slaves present were warned that if we even looked away one single second, a similar fate would befall us. It was awful.'

'What did they do to her?'

'She fought against them but she didn't stand a chance. It took four Masters to hold her down, while another brought in a huge dog...'

'No...'

'They placed her in the right position, kicked her legs apart and had the dog fuck her. Even now, I still have nightmares thinking of what I saw. Its paws scratched deep lines of blood across her back as it squatted over her and did the deed.'

'God!'

'That very moment, I swore I'd commit suicide if I ever allowed something like that to happen to me.'

'I can imagine.'

'Later, as the others played with the rest of us slaves, I saw her sobbing against the wall. They had connected her collar to the dog's leash and she sat there motionless while the animal greedily lapped up his own come which was still oozing out of her. I never saw her again. She was never brought to the other parties I attended, even though her erstwhile Master was present. Now, he had another woman.

'What can I say, Louise? And you were still only seventeen?'

'After that night, I think Nola began to sense my unease about the sexual escalation in the relationship. A couple of days later, she stuck a Polaroid next to my bedside table. She had taken it when the red-haired girl was being violated by the dog. This was clearly a warning to me not to doubt her resolve and dare any form of disobedience to her will. But we only attended two more special Saturday night parties during the course of the following six months, and nothing more untoward than sex and whippings occurred, as if the group knew they had crossed a dangerous borderline. At the final party Nola took me to, I could somehow feel her distancing herself from me already, but I did not wish to acknowledge that a page was about to be turned. That night, the tall pimply young slave boy with the uncommon endowment came up for punishment and I was fitted with a strap-on and made to fuck him. I had never realised before I could switch from sub to becoming a most ferocious, vengeful dom. I plundered him with a vengeance. He also bled abundantly and I eventually had to be pulled off him by Nola. She had of course used a strap-on on me on many occasions, but we had never switched; she was not into penetration.'

'You said things were changing?'

'For some time, Nola had hinted that the present she was planning for my eighteenth birthday would be unforgettable. Two months prior to the event, she took me again to the doctor in Harley Street and my lips were pierced and the eight rings installed. I was told it would take some weeks to heal. Nola seldom used me in the weeks between my labial piercings, and often only returned home late with no word of explanation.'

'So what did she actually gift you with for your eighteenth birthday?'

'There was not even a greetings card in the morning. I slaved away in the kitchen all day and she came home around seven. She asked me to follow her to the bathroom, ordered me to undress, examined my rings and the now-fully healed piercings. I was told to close my eyes and felt her fit something across the rings. It was a special kind of safety pin which fits through both sets of four rings and closes with a miniature padlock, totally sealing the entrance to my vagina. There was a kind of beauty to it, this chastity device whose usefulness I couldn't quite understand. Later she explained to me that she had tired of me, wished to install a new friend in the house. By fitting me with the padlock she would still control me from a distance. I was to leave her house the following day! I was dumbstruck. I cried for hours.'

*

They spend their final day in Manhattan as normal lovers might.

They linger in bed, have breakfast sent up, touch, kiss, caress, talk about the weather.

He plans their day. They will lunch at a small Japanese sushi bar on the corner of Thirteenth and Sixth. She tells him she has never eaten raw fish before.

'You'll see,' he reassures her, 'it's nice.'

They catch a movie at the Angelika, trawl Tower Records for the obscure country and western CDs still missing from his extensive collection, explore the quaint streets of Alphabet City and end up with a final meal in a cajun joint close to the Flatiron Building. Oysters, gumbo and whatever entrée catches her fancy.

'Fattening me up, eh?' Louise remarks.

'Exactly, you're all bones and rings, my dear . . .'

He's not sure if she appreciates the joke.

'I'm off to shave.'

'OK.'

When he returns from the bathroom, her face is flushed. Her eyes shift when he looks at her, she appears guilty.

'What is it?' he asks.

'I've been bad.'

'How?'

'While you were washing, I touched myself.'

'So?'

'You didn't use me last night. I needed relief.'

'It's not a problem, Louise.'

'It's wrong for a slave to seek her own pleasure without the consent of her Master. You must punish me.'

His heart sinks.

So this is the way it is.

He handcuffs her to the bed post and arranges her nude body in the shape of an X across the soft green bed cover. She is not wearing the safety pin. As he widens the angle of her legs, her cunt gapes.

He hangs the 'Do Not Disturb' sign outside the door and leaves her in the room, captive, laid out like an offering, though not for the maid!

He loiters around reception until he finds a suitable man. A German tourist, wealthy-looking but with no taste in clothes. At first, the man does not take him seriously, but he insists. They share a coffee in the breakfast room. He explains. They do the deal. He gives the German the card key to their room.

He has no wish to watch.

'You have two hours,' he says. 'Be out of the room by then. She is handcuffed. I have the keys with me. She will not speak, or cry, or scream.'

'And I . . . ?' asks the German, begging for confirmation of his dreams.

'She is totally yours. Anything you want.'

They are two of the slowest hours of his life. He walks four blocks north, then five blocks south. Peruses every window without even noticing their varied content.

When he finally returns, Louise is still handcuffed to the bedpost, the taste of another man still leaking from her, dotting her stomach, her face, her breasts.

She smiles at him.

His slave.

That night, he sleeps badly, his mind in tumult.

Sunrise comes early, with a blanket of low clouds waltzing over the top of the highest skyscrapers.

He tells her about the dream.

In it, he has failed abysmally at becoming a Master and the only alternative is to become a slave himself. To stay with Louise, he sends a begging letter to Nola offering himself in exchange for further time with her. His pitiful demeanour makes her laugh but, as a game, she accepts.

Initially, she puts him on a diet, having no need of an overweight slave. Then, when he becomes suitable she shaves his pubic hair and brands him, a large N carved into his buttocks. He is allowed to sleep in the same room as Nola and Louise, but on the floor, at the foot of their bed where he is forced to listen to their lovemaking and Louise's severe beatings. He is beaten too, made to wear an apron and serve their food; if ever he is caught with an erection he is whipped until he bleeds. But he is happy now, just living under the same roof as his companion of slavery. Eventually, he is allowed to attend the special parties where his role is to suck all the men to hardness before they fuck Louise, then to lick them clean after they have withdrawn from her orifices. In turn, she is to prepare the men who bugger him. He is no longer allowed to touch her, only to watch the increasing stations of her degradation. But the punishments get worse and worse, as he finds it impossible to repress his excitement as his cock invariably reacts shamelessly every time another man penetrates her.

Finally, the circle of Masters decrees the ultimate punishment at the next party he is to be brought to. Which is when he awoke.

'A companion in slavery,' Louise remarks. 'Yes, I think that would be quite appropriate for you . . .'

'Would it?'

'But it's all a dream, you know, Nola hates men, she would never want you as her slave. If you had a wife to offer in exchange for time with me, maybe then she might entertain your proposal. Dream on.'

'I will,' he says.

Q & A

'What did you do when Nola threw you out?'

'I pleaded, made a fool of myself, threw myself at her feet. Even begged to be retained if only as a servant, so that I might look after her and her new, young mistress.'

'Did you meet her, this new girl?'

'Yes, some months later. Tall, blonde, everything I wasn't. New. Virgin territory for Nola's cruel whims.'

'But she didn't allow you to stay on?'

'No. I was desperate. I thought she would never have me back. I had given up my studies without obtaining any diplomas or qualifications, how could I find a job, somewhere to live? Nola controlled my trust fund. During the two years I had spent with Nola I had deliberately lost the few friends I had before our encounter, I had nothing, I never even had any more normal clothes to wear. Nola had once mentioned, almost as a joke, a couple who had on two occasions visited her soirées and been witness to my servility and asked where they could find a similar maid. Maybe I could go and place myself in their service. The idea didn't appeal to me. Become a servant to people I had already privately served as a slave. But I had no other alternative. Nola phoned them and a deal was agreed.'

'And that's where you are now?'

'I've now worked here two years almost. They leave for work—they are both senior managers for a large insurance company in a nearby town—early in the morning and my duties are to keep the house clean, wash, iron, dust, prepare the food. I am not allowed any mail or telephone calls. I play on the Internet. Watch TV. They are hard on me. The woman has custody of the padlock key, but she is capricious and often declines to set the rings free, particularly when I'm having my periods. It amuses her. Most of the time, I am just their servant, but sometimes they remember my nature and my past, usually when they have drunk heavily. He fucks me, she watches, has me lick her. Christmas last, I was seemingly too enthusiastic while he used me extensively and the next day, out of jealousy, she beat me badly.'

'Do you still hear from Nola?'

'Not often. She keeps in touch, though.'

'Do you still love her?'

'Yes, as much as ever.'

'Will she ever have you back?'

'I live in that hope, but I realise how unlikely it is. I'm realistic.'

'Are you happy?'

'Yes, in my own way. But living with my owners is boring. The house is in the middle of nowhere. The only contact I have with other human beings is when they take me on holiday with them. Spain in the summer; a house in the mountains in France at Easter. In Spain, I am allowed to wear shorts and bikinis. The padlock is taken off and I am allowed to be naughty. I fuck boys, with rubber protection of course. They don't mind as long as I'm not late back at their villa to cook the meals.'

'Can you see your life remaining the same for years to come, Louise? A leading question, I know.'

'I'm only twenty. I am a sub . . . But I don't wish to work for the

Masters again. After New York, I might try somewhere else. It was whispered about at the parties sometimes, between subs, between our being used. It's a house. A sort of brothel. A house of punishment, for adepts of dominance and submission. In New Orleans. I might ... I don't know ... N once said I would be a pearl among inmates there. I've often dreamed of New Orleans. My grandfather came from there.'

'But N's the man who tried to brand you.'

'I know, but I think he would prove a good Master for me.... He's attuned to my nature.'

'It's your life.'

'It is.'

'And I'm no knight in shining armour, Louise. I have no mission in life to change your nature. You touch me, though. I feel much tenderness for you.'

'Do you think you could be my new Master, then?'

'I'm not sure. Willing to give it my best shot ...'

'If you were a true dom, you would know already. I don't think you are somehow.'

'I'm sadly aware of the fact. But I still want to see you again. Badly. Please, Louise.'

His plea is an act of desperation.

'Maybe. Let me think.'

*

He packs.

He had asked the day before whether they should purchase a case for the clothes they had bought together, but she had declined. She came with nothing and insists she should return to her owners similarly. It would be suspicious other-wise and, unlike Nola's, she does not appreciate their beatings. He realises he has never even asked her what alibi, what lie she had used to justify her trip.

He watches as she stuffs the barely-worn chenille jumper, the rainbow skirt, the cream see-through blouse, the stockings and sundry knick-knacks into the hotel room's wicker waste basket. He's packed the cuffs and the strap-on in his own case, although he's thinking of disposing them in a wash-room at the airport. It would be too embarrassing to be searched at customs.

They take the lift in heavy silence. He settles the bill with his credit card and the doorman hails a cab.

'Newark.'

It's early morning, ahead of the commuter traffic. The journey takes barely half an hour. Throughout, he holds her hand in his.

Way down his throat, there are a million words he wishes to say, but they break up like flotsam against the rampart of his lips. He knows he hasn't the eloquence to change her life. Or his.

Her flight is a whole hour earlier than his.

Her thin, fragile silhouette disappears down the neon-lit corridor that leads to her departure lounge. He has checked: her plane is on time. They haven't even said goodbye. Before the bend, she turns, smiles and blows him a kiss.

He knows he will never see her again. The e-mails will continue for a short time, then they will slow down and a day will come when she just disappears, the property of a new Master, who will forbid all contact with her former life. And his mind will imagine the worst. Violation. Torture. Death. Because the life she has chosen is a one-way street.

And his heart doesn't own the right passport.

8.

Martin

I clicked on 'Save'. Then 'Save As'. Typed in 'Nola'. I had no printer with me, so the tale would have to stay inside the bowels of the laptop for the time being.

A veil of sadness descended upon me as I sat in the darkness, my eyes illuminated by the blue glow of the screen. I knew of Internet affairs of course. But somehow, the true nature of Louise and her unnamed, older lover resonated deep inside me and I felt for him, and for her dearly.

Now, I knew why Nola was so intent on finding her half-sister again. And the book had damn all to do with it.

Even though the hour was somewhat late, I rang Nola's hotel. It was time to talk, I'd decided. But she'd already checked out. It was child's play to follow her trail. She'd ordered a limousine airport service. The driver had dropped her at the United terminal at Kennedy. A quick browse through the schedules showed no direct flight to New Orleans, but a convenient connection in Raleigh-Durham.

At last, some of the pieces were beginning to fit.

But I was far from pleased to have been taken for a fool by Nola.

Actually, I was fuming. Maybe I would have to find Louise before she did.

9.

Martin

The drunken revellers swarmed up and down Bourbon Street balancing their plastic cups of beer with alcoholic agility. On the wrought-iron balconies of the hotels and bars, even drunker punters looked down on the crowds below and offered gaudy beads to women who were sufficiently inebriated or liberated to flash their tits or more to the sound of much applause. In the early morning, there would be rivers of beer in the gutter which the city workers would hose away together with the massed detritus of the night before, an unholy mix of beads, crushed plastic, vomit and worse.

I moved away from the throng and met my local contact outside the Café du Monde. Two old black musicians were camped on the sidewalk and entertained the customers with old-fashioned jazz tunes, while tourists snapped away to their heart's content and kids gripped their animal-shaped balloons.

It appeared that Nola had settled in to the Dauphine Orleans Hotel, a stone's throw from Bourbon. And she was asking the same questions I was. Seeking Louise in the madness of the Vieux Carré, barely two weeks from Mardi Gras, when all hell would no doubt break loose across the city. She was not alone and he hadn't been able to identify her male companion, a tall grey-haired man of European appearance. The room was registered in her name only.

But there was no trace of her younger sister.

I thanked my contact for the meagre scrap of information and handed him a hundred dollar bill. He was an ex-policeman, still plugged in to the local zeitgeist and eager to help.

'Is there much of an S&M scene?' I asked Neil.

'This is the Big Easy,' he answered. 'Every scene you can think of and more is present, and generously available.'

I smiled. Persisted.

'We'd be talking of something very illegal. Not just a run of the mill brothel, with a smidgen of corporal punishment, a show to entertain the clients. Real stuff, pain, serious stuff?'

'I can think of a few establishments. But they are very private. Have to be,' he said. 'But they're out of my reach. The protection is much higher up. Couldn't help you gain access.'

'Names will do. And whereabouts. I'd take it from there.'

He scribbled a few lines on one of the paper serviettes and slid it over to me.

'Can't help you if anything goes wrong, though,' Neil added. 'These places are way beyond my scope. I'd be careful, if I were you, Jackson. And do keep my name out of it, please. I'd appreciate that.'

I nodded my understanding.

Around Jackson Square the portrait artists and palm readers were packing up their stalls and young goths lazed around on the steps of the church, all pale skin and heavy kohl make-up, like vampires awaiting the fall of night.

I treated myself to an oyster po'boy at the Napoleon House and lost myself in the wake of the crowds of increasingly noisy tourists and sidewalk tap dancers, my steps punctuated by the conflicting cross-rhythms of the bands in the open-door bars on each side of the street. Blues fighting country wrestling with rock duelling with dixie, a whole symphony of loud syncopation in full, heavy flow.

I'd investigate the S&M joints the following day.

Back in my room at the unfashionable hotel on Burgundy Street, I called up Nola. Felt like confronting her. She, and her male companion, were not in. I didn't bother to leave a message. It would have been rude anyway.

*

The following morning, to keep him off my back while I concentrated on the Poshard sisters case, I mailed Christopher Streetfield. I didn't promise any results in the ongoing search for his wife, just wanted to keep him on the hook. I was certain that whoever had jumped me in Amsterdam had nothing to do with his job; the file must have been stolen by mistake. There was no other explanation. Who else would want the photographs of Kay and the addresses and telephone numbers of her few girlfriends from university days? It must be a coincidence and I couldn't allow my mind to linger over it.

I cased the clubs Neil had told me about in the morning. The

Magnetic Fields just felt wrong somehow; as I watched its doors from the window of a nearby bar where I was nestling an espresso, I caught sight of a couple of cleaners about to enter it and quickly approached them. Pretexted I was interested in joining and just wanted to see what the inside looked like. They hesitated but a few greenbacks soon changed their mind and I was allowed a quick peep. There was something awfully vulgar about the place, lush carpets on floors and strung across walls, deep leather seats. This was no place of danger or transgression, more like a swingers' club for tired executives. It was just a pumped-up strip club from all appearances.

I mentally crossed it off my list. Surely Louise had better taste, or more of a death wish.

The Moby Lounge was a different kettle of fish altogether. From the outside, it just looked like another French Quarter villa with a leafy garden behind its gates obscuring the view of the house beyond. It was at the wrong end of Bourbon, well beyond the noise and the gay zone, almost at Ramparts level. It screamed discretion. More than just another gentleman's club where things might sometimes get out of hand. Could this be the house Louise had alluded to, unless her lover had fictionalised their encounter and its attendant dialogue?

I resolved to return here that night, when the place opened.

But I still had a whole day to waste and no wish to do the obligatory bayou and crocodile tour on the Creole Queen riverboat, let alone visit the Aquarium of the Americas.

Around lunch hour I stationed myself close to the Dauphine Orleans. Sure enough, I soon caught Nola Poshard and her tall escort leaving the hotel. She looked stunning, her legs flowing forever under the thin material of her red taffeta skirt. I followed them a few blocks and saw them take a seat for lunch at Tujague's on Decatur. Perfect. I knew the place from a previous visit to the Crescent City and there was no way they'd be out of here for at least 90 minutes. I rushed back to their hotel.

Gaining access to their room was child's play. Chambermaids are always leaving their carts unattended in hotel corridors and, as I expected, a set of pass-keys was handily hanging from a door on the next floor up while the maid went in search of the extra hand towels I requested. I carefully slipped a single key off the ring and walked up the service stairs to Nola Poshard's floor.

They had not been sleeping together and both double beds showed signs of having been slept in. This was no surprise. I quickly rifled through drawers and luggage but failed to find anything interesting or at any rate relevant. Damn. Nola's selection of underwear certainly had its aesthetic charms, but anyone could have told me that from just looking at the way she walked and behaved. I was about to draw a line under this ill-thought venture into my current employer's privacy when, force of habit, I slipped a hand inside the jacket the tall guy had left draped over one of the chairs by the door to the bathroom.

What I found gave me a start.

The photographs of Christopher Streetfield's wife.

Definitely the very same that had disappeared in Amsterdam.

Curiouser and curiouser. And damn worrying. My mind in overdrive, I raced through every possible connection.

There were none that made sense.

Apart from one: Nola knew the truth—I was the connection.

A wind of panic blew through me.

I just couldn't see how they knew.

It was impossible.

My breath resumed its normal status.

I put the photographs back in the inside pocket of the jacket where I had found them. I had no need for them, so there was no need to advertise the fact I'd been in the room by retrieving them.

There was no one in the corridor. I crept out of the room and took the elevator down to the lobby, leaving the stolen pass-key in an ashtray.

I spent the afternoon putting every fact of the case, the two cases, under my mental microscope, puzzling through every step I had taken since that first day in London, the words I'd said, the people I'd seen, spoken to, fucked, been fucked by, squeezing every fact I could retrieve every which way, but still the whole picture just refused to settle into a simple, comprehensible pattern.

I must have dozed off briefly, my mind a total blank. As ever, it was an interlude of bad dreams, and ghosts. Ghosts? Who was I kidding but myself? One ghost.

When I snapped out of my lethargy, I immediately saw the envelope that had been slipped under my door.

It had been written by a woman. Elegant, cursive letters, with surprisingly square o's and a's. Educated.

It said we appeared to be searching for the same thing and suggested we join forces. Between 6 and 8 at the Firebird on Toulouse. I was to look for a small tattoo of a gun. There was no signature. Just the letter C.

*

From where I sat, just a few feet away from the stage where she danced, the stripper appeared strikingly tall and towering from the elevated position where she gyrated, if not particularly voluptuous, but what she lacked in breasts she more than made up in assurance and supple grace.

She had begun her set as I entered the anonymous club where a few men were quietly sipping their five dollar drinks and trying to avoid the eyes of the other punters for fear of recognition. A matronly waitress navigated between the sparse tables prompting the reorders.

I had unashamedly placed myself at the table nearest the stage and could count every speck of dust still lingering here and there on the shiny surface of the dance area.

The girl on stage had begun her moves to a slow, melancholy Bruce Springsteen song, bathed in the heart of a solitary red-weakening-to-pink electric spot which highlighted her body against the diffuse darkness of the club's recesses. Next to her, a shiny metal pole anchored the stage to the club's low ceiling.

She was already partly undressed. Just wore a black bikini ensemble which contrasted sharply with the deep white of her skin. No high heels or stockings or other accoutrements of the skin trade. Her movements were steady and measured as she milked every nuance of the drowsy melody, each curve of her body losing itself in the hypnosis of the music, espousing the languid rhythm. She didn't even look at the audience, her eyes distant and focused on the world inside her, no come-on, no invitations for further tips, as if totally indifferent to the sordid environment she navigated through as she danced. But she was sexy, I had to admit. Rather. As she turned and turned, her regal arse strained against the thin material of her bikini bottom and every minor tremor of her leg and thigh muscles seemed to lead back, to end in a tremulous movement in the very apex of her crotch. But still her face showed no emotion as she lost herself in the music.

The girl had class. She was a stripper not a teaser. Others would have begun their set shielded in a layer of gaudy, so-called sexy outer clothing and built the desire with every shedding of garment, promising more with every discarded item. This young woman was saying 'Here I am; this is what I am; I'm tall and skinny and white as porcelain and my tits are just an A or B cup but I have a great butt and you can pay and watch but can't touch and I enjoy what I do and live in a world that's much better than yours, so there'.

The music segued into an REM tune and, without ceremony, she undid the clasp of her top, allowed it to float to the floor and quickly revealed her breasts, all pale, pink, soft nipples, and her left hand gripped the metal pole and she gracefully propelled herself into a full-circle revolution with both feet just a few inches off the ground, came down again and resumed her gentle sway to the music. Her small breasts were firm, high, and didn't even move or shake during the rapid manoeuvre. Nice. Now, her body began flexing as she hastened the dance in unison with Michael Stipe's anguished accents, her strong pelvis now the very centre of her exertions.

I looked around at the other punters. Some spoke, others watched, but none seem to take any notice of the fact that this stripper was out of the ordinary. She leaned backwards, her crotch stretching against the fabric. Resumed her upwards position and then leaned forward, cupping her breasts in both hands and teasing the nipples. Standard moves from the manual but ones she managed to accomplish with a total absence of vulgarity or titillation. If she'd been wearing a garter or moved nearer to the edge of the stage, as others invariably did, I would have slipped her a few dollar bills with great pleasure, in appreciation of her skill and attitude, but she remained glued to the centre of the dance area, always within reach of the metal pole, swaying, dancing; I even thought I heard her humming along to the tune under her breath. A patina of breaking sweat now covered her upper body, emphasising the glitter she had conservatively sprinkled over herself earlier, every shiny eye capturing my imagination, lodged in the curve of her neck, dusted thinly over the valley of her breasts and then, daringly, almost as a line, an arrow from her navel to the still uncharted, unknown area shielded by her black bikini pants, like a promise of dark desire in her most private parts.

The song came to an end. The tape jumped and the third and final tune of her set began.

A small group of football fans wearing the Bordeaux colours of their team had entered the club and now sat to my right. Noisily ordered their drinks. Made a disparaging remark about the stripper's lack of frontal assets.

I turned my attention back to her.

The plaintive accents of an Aimée Mann song.

Once again with no sense of theatrics, the blonde on stage removed her final piece of clothing and I held my breath as her body reintegrated the private country of the music, and she began to sway, her long legs rooted to the ground, held ever so apart, like a fragile tree in the wind. The storm rose and the branches of her limbs embraced the motion, her head rolling a little as she wavered, fully exposed in the glare of the spotlight.

As the lingering song reached its chorus, the stripper slowly moved, for the very first time, to the edge of the stage, right in front of where I sat, her cunt level with my eyes. She was shaven, the darker, discreet line of her gash like a forgotten scar on the surface of her Barbie crotch. A nicely plump pudenda incongruously highlighted by the arrow of glitter. The blonde crouched. The top of her body shivered along to the strains of the rock 'n'roll beat of the song. I couldn't help my gaze following the downward move of her crotch as she squatted. Her cunt gaped open, revealing a scarlet darkness. Her hands caressed her upper body with deliberate slowness and then finally lowered themselves and momentarily shielded her cunt, just as my eyes had caught a glimpse of shiny moistness, like an infinitely thin spider web connecting her stretched-apart labia. I looked up into her eyes and took a direct hit. She was watching my reaction. Strong, brown eyes that seemed to delve deep into me. We were now caught in a grip of recognition. A contact. As if we were the only two people present here and the rest of the audience and the surroundings didn't even exist. Just the stripper, the music and me. It had become a private show.

Her hands drew away from her cunt lips, lingering ever so daringly over them as if she were actually going to open herself up completely and reveal her innards.

She drew herself up from her squatting position and straightened her body again. Her movements quickened as the finale approached and the drum and bass punctuated the acceleration of the song's rhythm. But still inches away from my eyes.

I pulled myself away from the enticing contemplation of her displayed cunt.

Close to her gash, on the border of her shaven pudenda, there was a small dark patch. I squinted and it came into focus.

A tattoo. Of a gun.

The music faded away as the blonde's dance turned motionless and the spotlight hiccuped away from her.

There was scattered applause, and in the penumbra I watched her bend to pick up her abandoned garments.

'A nice round of applause for this very special performance from our New York guest Cornelia!' some compere said over the scratchy sound system. 'Time to reorder, guys. In a few minutes, we have the popular Charmaine...'

*

We met outside the bar and walked two blocks in silence to a quiet Starbucks. Cornelia wore a simple white short-sleeved T-shirt and jeans. In the open air, I could see the natural features of her face were as untouched by superfluous make-up as they were on the stage. No one could have guessed she was a stripper now.

Just lipstick, a soft, warm shade of red against the unnatural pallor of her skin. This was a woman who didn't spend much leisure time in the sun.

She set her bulging shoulder bag down on the floor by the table.

'So . . .' I said.

'We meet,' she said, in answer to my unformulated question.

'The gun tattoo came as a surprise, I must say.'

Cornelia smiled.

'A present to myself after my last job.'

'It's different, I admit.'

'Yes, so much less vulgar than a flower, a rose or whatever most gals would have there. Don't you think?'

'I've been hearing a bit about you over the last few weeks.'

'Have you? Not all bad, I hope?'

'I'm not sure. Sometimes second-hand rumours can prove confusing.'

She ordered an iced tea.

'I know you're seeking Louise Poshard,' Cornelia calmly stated.

'I guessed so.'

'So am I.'

'Really?'

'I even guess we have the same paymaster. They can be such a nuisance, can't they? They never trust anyone to do the job properly.'

'An interesting assumption.'

'And we both guess she might be in hiding at the Moby Lounge, don't we?'

'At this point, I should ask you how you've arrived at such a conclusion,' I said, enjoying this sparring game with Cornelia. 'But maybe I shouldn't insult your intelligence. Some of my contacts actually told me you can prove dangerous, so I shall carefully refrain from doubting you.'

I watched the quiet smile spread across her perfect lips.

'Dangerous? Little me? Well, I do wonder how?'

'You've a body and a way of dancing well capable of provoking a heart attack in the unprepared,' I ventured.

'You liked?' Cornelia asked.

'Very much,' I admitted.

'Good. It's nice to feel attractive. But I dislike mixing business and pleasure, Martin,' she added.

Where had I heard that before? Nola Poshard. What was this, a surfeit of femmes fatales?

'You're not my type anyway,' I lied.

She ignored this.

'I just thought it would be useful to meet. I think we can help each other.'

'Can we?'

'Tonight, you were maybe planning going to the Moby Lounge?'

'Correct.'

'You wouldn't gain entrance. I've checked. Very strictly members only, I fear.'

'I see. Can't say that surprises me, what with some of the likely goings on inside.'

'Strong stuff?'

'That's the story. S&M stuff.'

'Oh. That would explain why the people here couldn't get me admittance, even as a . . . working girl. Had no contacts.'

'I suspect the Moby Lounge entertainment is strictly in-house, not hired in,' I said.

Cornelia frowned.

And for just an instant it made her look vulnerable, her brown eyes clouding, her mind racing in overdrive, her gaze faraway. I almost saw the child Cornelia had once been.

Which, incongruously, redirected my own thoughts towards the now-so-distant Aida. And my heart gently skipped a beat. Where was she now? Back in the cramped Dutch coastline cottage, or on a train towards Amsterdam or at another bar in another hotel, waiting for the right man, about to take her hesitant step into whoredom? My material girl.

The thought passed quickly and I was back in New Orleans.

'There might be a way the two of us could gain access to the Moby Lounge. Easier as a couple,' Cornelia said.

'Tell me.'

'I know someone, back in New York, who could effect an introduction. But we'd have to assume a role, blend in with the scene,' she continued.

'I'd be game,' I told her. I already knew there was no way I could get in there on my own. I wouldn't fit. With this curious young woman it might well prove possible. But deep inside I also knew her agenda wasn't the same as mine.

She buried her hand inside her purse.

'Do you have any quarters?' she asked me.

I found a handful.

She rose from her chair, unbelievably slim and towering, the fabric of her thin, white T-shirt straining against the silhouette of her hard nipples, her tight jeans clinging to the moody curves of her arse. I sighed. She made her way to the washroom where our waiter had advised her the telephone was.

I sipped slowly on my espresso, my teeth a sieve between the syrupy streams of sugar I had drowned in the coffee and the bitter harshness of the concentrate.

Cornelia returned five minutes later.

'I think it'll work,' she said. 'I have to phone back in an hour for confirmation.'

I nodded silently.

'People who know people who know people, you know,' she said.

'Working in the sex industry has it perks, I see,' I said.

'It's only part-time,' Cornelia answered. 'A gal has to make a living, pay for the bare necessities.'

'You've been stripping long?' I asked her. I had never known strippers before, but nonetheless she didn't fit the preconceived mould. Not just the way she looked, danced, but the attitude, the voice. She was in category of her own.

She ignored my question.

'We have an hour or so to kill,' she said.

'I can think of worse things,' I feebly joked. But then I've never been your private eye who is also a knight of the mean streets and can crack a quip at the drop of a whiskey glass. Don't misunderstand me, I have a sense of humour alright, it just works with a time delay.

This naturally drew a blank look from Cornelia.

'Another coffee or two or three?' I suggested.

'Nah,' she said. 'I need some fresh air. Been cooped up indoors too long.'

We walked out of the Starbucks.

Onto Magazine Street, tourists ambling along, idling time away outside the antique-shop windows while musicians and puppeteers displayed their wares on every street corner.

We were wary of each other and the aimless walk through the Vieux Carré was full of silences. Something about the way she walked, her stance, reminded me somehow of Kay. As ever, the memories brought an anguished knot to the heart of my guts. Chin forward, whole body in languorous pursuit. Rather distinctive. She appeared more interested by the displays of the few used bookstores we came upon, or the prints in the photographic gallery. Jewellery and clothes didn't seem to interest her much.

She ignored point blank all my questions about her interest in Louise Poshard and I felt at a disadvantage. She appeared to know so much about me and why I was here in New Orleans, while she remained an enigmatic if savagely sensual enigma. I had been dealt the wrong pack of cards and even my old poker skills were of no use to me here.

An hour passed.

Full of question marks and a state of uneasiness and apprehension.

There was bank of telephones just past the lobby of the Bourbon Sonesta, to the right of the oyster bar. With a nod, Cornelia indicated I should wait for her amongst the disembarking tourists.

She stayed away almost fifteen minutes. Halfway through her absence, fearing she might have given me the slip, I peered around the corner at the wall of telephone alcoves and spied her speaking calmly on one of them and jotting down notes on a piece of paper.

'It's on,' she told me upon returning to the hustle and bustle of the crowded lobby.

'Great.'

'Tomorrow night,' she added. 'That's when the next party occurs. We've been recommended. Serious East Coast practitioners of the dark arts,' Cornelia smiled mischievously. 'Think you can pull it off?'

'I'm sure you will prove of invaluable assistance in the matter.'

'So who plays sub?' she asked me.

'Not sure I can picture myself on a leash,' I said.

'Yes, I suppose dom is easier to impersonate,' Cornelia replied. 'I'll play sub, then.'

'You're the artist. Shouldn't stretch you,' I jested.

'Just games, Mr. Jackson,' she said.

'Am I expected to play Master in full leather regalia?' I asked her.

'I don't think the Moby Lounge is into that. I'd suggest you just wear your usual all-black. Maybe add a tie, say? Will make you look more elegant, forceful, no?' Cornelia winked at me.

'And you?'

'I'll find what I need on Bourbon. Just a few touches to add to a work outfit.'

'Oh, yes,' I said. I'm sure she had a varied and most interesting *garde-robe*.

We made arrangements to meet in twenty-four hours or so. Cornelia declined my invitation to gumbo and oysters at the Red Fish Grill.

She faded into the street crowds, as much as someone so striking can ever fade. Their image stays in your mind. For a very long time indeed.

*

After my meal, I made another visit to her strip club. I was now keen to see her at work (or was it play?) again now that I knew her slightly better. OK, so I wanted to see her body again. Those small tits that just beckoned for the caress of a distracted finger, those long legs that went on forever, the ever so crooked front tooth that appeared whenever she half-opened her lips whilst dancing in a parody of lust, the strategically-placed tattoo, that cunt. But the other girls paraded one after the other as the evening grew old and no sign of Cornelia. I asked and was told she no longer worked there.

Back in my room, images of Cornelia taunted my imagination and I relieved myself by hand. Maybe it was tiredness or the grief I was still carrying, but the flesh on the screen of my imagination, the skin so white, so cold, all spun around, flesh like a whirlpool, pictures of Kay crying, of Aida's mole, all effortlessly merging with Cornelia's dance of desire.

I came.

And with it, the guilt.

In torrents.

10.

The Truth and Nothing but the Truth (or, Another Story)

H e sees her at a party at the Brighton Pavilion. A cocktail party sponsored by a Rupert Murdoch-owned publishing house. Chardonnay, orange juice, stale peanuts and crisps.

Her frizzy hair like a Medusa head, all wild blonde curls fighting a losing battle against the forces of tidiness. Her gawky walk, like a rare animal not quite used to her body's equilibrium, long tentative strides across the party floor, a glass and a plate balanced in her left hand as she moves from group to group, both confident and shy.

Who is she, he wonders.

He's in town for the day, has been invited to give a small talk to the Crime Writers' Association Conference about the realities of the private investigator's life in today's Britain. He's preceded by a retired customs officer who debunks smuggling, and is followed by a pathologist with a case full of gory slides, who will attract ten times the amount of questions. The audience carefully takes notes. They are mostly middle-aged women with blue rinses who think writing about crime is jolly entertaining.

Hello, he introduces himself.

Oh yes, she remembers him. She was in his audience, didn't he see her, at the back towards the right of the hotel function room? He hadn't. Maybe it was the spotlights shining in his eyes. He is sure she would have stood out. He apologises.

She is talking to a retired police inspector from Nottingham. He is not sure whether the boring man is also here as some sort of adviser or has actually turned to writing mystery books in the wake of his retirement. He gathers she works as a junior editor for a small, independent London publishing house. Has been asked to set up a new crime list and is cruising for authors and contacts.

He nods and mumbles and never really joins the conversation. The room is noisy. He notes her eyes are brown and her skin has a milky pallor against which her wild hair stands out in striking contrast. He's sure the colour is natural but the curls must be the result of a perm. But you don't ask about things like that in public, do you?

The party breaks up and the crowd disperses to return to the hotel where the talks are continuing. Someone asks him a question and she moves on. He loses track of her. Later, she is not in attendance.

It's the conference's last night.

He sees her again at the bar in the evening, she smiles a hello of recognition but is already too busy with other interlocutors and he can't draw her away.

He gives up and opts for an early night. Watches a softcore sex film on the pay channel. It's so tame he has difficulties achieving an erection.

He is up early for breakfast. Leaving the hotel's restaurant he notices her, hair still dishevelled in wondrous splendour, sitting in one of the armchairs in the reception area, dressed in a blue dress with small white polka dots. Her left bra strap is visible over the soft contour of her shoulder. Black.

People are queuing up to settle their bills.

He walks over to her, greets her.

Morning.

She looks up from reading a Sara Paretsky paperback.

Oh hello.

It was nice talking.

Yes, she agrees.

But they never did manage a proper conversation, did they?

So, back to London?

Yes, she nods, they exchange a meaningless glance and she closes the paperback shut.

For a brief moment, he feels shy like an eighteen-year old courting the belle of the ball.

Are you catching the 10.05?

No, I'm being picked up.

I see. Pity . . .

Yes, she agrees.

Someone calls over to him. He excuses himself; it's just someone wishing to exchange business cards. When he looks back, she is already gone.

On the train back to Waterloo, he reads the Sunday newspapers. But she is on his mind.

A strange awkward beauty emanated from her, there was the faint trace of a scar on her cheek and he wonders how she got it. Wore no make-up save for a deep pink shade of lipstick. She attracts him.

Two mornings later in his Holborn office, he pulls out the conference programme and looks up the membership list. Yes, there she is listed alongside the name of the company she works for. He obtains the telephone number from inland directory enquiries.

Remember me?

Oh yes, you were interesting.

Really? I'm pleased I made an impression.

He knows she is smiling.

I was wondering...?

Yes?

Maybe we could meet for a drink? Talk?

He feels the smile broaden. Maybe she was expecting him to call?

Yes. Why not?

We never did have a chance down in Brighton, did we?

That's true, she agrees.

The knot in his stomach loosens.

We can talk about crime, she continues.

Yes. It's a vast subject.

A lot to talk about.

Indeed.

He finds out her offices are in Goodge Street so they are fairly close to each other. Her lunch hours are somewhat busy for the rest of the week, she has this horror novel to copy-edit which has been delivered late and it's her only chance to catch up. Why not Friday evening. A pub off the Charing Cross Road. Six-fifteen?

He readily agrees to the time and place.

Two nights before, he is idling the evening away at his flat leafing through all the magazines he has somehow accumulated over the last few months and not yet read. One of them features a portfolio of nudes by the American photographer Gerard Malanga. A photograph, a woman nude in three-quarters view by a window, her face in darkness, her hair turned into a halo of light by the sun outside the window, catches his attention. The body shape he reckons could be hers. The black and white emphasises the nude woman's pallor and she has strong hips. Yes, it could well be her. This time, the erection comes easily.

She arrives on time and, not without difficulty they find a free table in the basement bar. The noise is deafening, all the Soho bright young things and office wannabes chattering away, screaming for attention at the outset of the week-end, and the jukebox itself drowned by their frantic conversations.

She wears a white blouse and jeans.

Have you ever been to America? he asks her. The photograph of the nude woman at the window has burned a deep hole in his libidinous mind. It's a chance in a million but he's not about to ask her if she has ever posed nude.

No, but I've always wanted to. But there's never been time, or the financial wherewithal. You?

Yes, often. I love it, find it so fascinating a place, you know.

I imagine it must be.

So, finished your copy-editing?

She has.

He asks her about the book.

The way she describes it, the novel sounds interesting, a tale full of sound, fury, incest and stranded birds on a northern shore. It's her first purchase as an editor and she has a strong belief in it. The author's previous two books for other publishers were commercial failures but she hopes this one, with her editorial input, will be a breakthrough (it won't: the reviews will prove decent but the sales abysmal, he will find out later).

She asks him how he became a private detective. Tells him he doesn't look the type.

He informs her he left his dirty trench coat, dark glasses and rolled-up copy of yesterday's *Times* back at the office with his secretary whose name is Velda.

The joke raises a laugh.

She has a few crooked teeth and this imperfection in her just blows him away.

The first half hour races by full of a hundred things unsaid. By now, every word they say to each other over the din can be heard clearly, in contrast to the opening minutes of the dialogue when so much had to be repeated over the background noise of the pub. Her eyes shine. The perfume she is wearing wafts towards him at irregular intervals, a smell he knows he will always associate with her thereafter. Green flowers, a touch of musk, a hint of perspiration and fresh soap.

They finally reach their first silence.

He gets another round of drinks.

So what did you wish to talk about? she asks him, snapping him out of a whirlpool of confused and contradictory thoughts.

I didn't realise we hadn't been talking, he smiles back at her.

You know what I mean.

Do I?

Unless you have a book project you want to pitch to me, and I don't flatter myself there were editors at the conference with a much bigger purse for the right project, I don't think you called me to discuss crime and its sundry implications, somehow.

You're right.

He knows it's time to come clean.

I just wanted to see you. Something about you, the way you talk, you walk, all those clichés. Damnit . . . I find you awfully attractive.

I thought so, she answers.

The response could have been worse. She could have laughed, walked off, slapped him, or just said no, you pitiful man.

I hadn't realised my lust was so obvious. Or have you taken classes in reading body language?

Actually, my company has published a book on the subject. But I haven't read it, I must confess. Terrible of me, no?

A glimmer of apprehension rises in his gut.

Her eyes look down deep inside him.

Estimating.

Weighing.

Judging him.

The sort of examination he sadly knows he can't sustain indefinitely.

He breaks the ice.

So where does that uncomfortable declaration leave us? Or me? he asks her.

The silence between them stretches over a few seconds and it feels like a whole century of indecision.

I'm married, you know, she finally says.

William Tell in drag deliberately missing the apple and going straight for his heart.

I didn't know.

The fool in him hadn't even bothered to look down at her hand. And the now obvious wedding ring.

I see, is all he can force himself to answer.

But I'm flattered by your attentions, she continues.

And flattery will get me nowhere, he suspects.

There are moments when you know silence is the worst option on offer. If he said nothing right now or just 'sorry' he realises they will part in a few minutes with platitudes and that would be that. He forces himself to say something, anything.

So . . . how long have you been married? he asks her.

Seven years, she replies.

You must have been young.

The year following university.

What does he do? He almost asks what the 'lucky man' does, but doesn't.

Journalist. Financial and business. For a press agency.

I see.

She lowers her eyes.

He takes me for granted, she volunteers.

He seizes the safety line and immediately changes the subject.

They spend another hour in the pub basement. Small talk. He admits he's not much of a drinker.

Are you in a hurry? he asks her.

Not really, she says. Don't have to be home until ten or even a bit later.

He suggests they eat.

She accepts.

After the meal, they retrieve his car from the underground car park below Bloomsbury Square and he drives her to Charing Cross station. He's willing to take her all the way to south London but she's happy to catch the train. Blocked in traffic in Trafalgar Square, his left hand rests on the hand brake. Silently, she moves her own hand over and gently touches his. He drops her on the Strand, outside the station.

He calls her at work the next day.

Another drink?

I don't mind.

They meet in the bar of a large West End hotel. It's quieter. They share a couch. He can feel the heat from her body. Is hypnotised by her hair. Tries to count every wild curl on her head.

It's difficult, she says, I like you too.

She allows him to caress her neck, distractedly twirl some of the loose curls hanging there against the milky white of her skin.

They part around eleven. He feels hollow and the look in her eyes speaks of quiet despair.

On Monday, he rings her.

I want you, he says.

I know, she calmly replies.

I want to sleep with you.

Another early evening bar in another anonymous hotel, leather furnishings, barman with slicked back hair, a background of soft whispers isolating them from the world around.

They exchange sexual histories and intimate confidences. Their glasses are now empty.

Come, he says.

They walk the half-mile to his office block.

He unlocks the suite.

In the darkness, they kiss.

Hands everywhere.

The infinitely soft cushion of her breasts, the imprint of her teeth scraping against his invading tongue, bodies grinding against each other.

Your hands are so warm, she remarks as he explores the landscape of her flesh.

She catches her breath before the renewed onslaught of his lips.

Soon they are both dishevelled, his shirt open, her fingers brushing the hairs on his chest, raking his front, her blouse open and her bra unclipped, the pink aureolae of her small breasts on fire from the savaging of his tongue and delicate teeth, her tights rolled down to her knees, the humidity from her sex staining the front of her white knickers.

They surface for air.

She glances at her watch. It's already past ten.

I really must go, she says.

What did you tell him you were doing? he asks.

She straightens her clothing.

He's on a later shift, she says. Won't be home until eleven at the earliest. He'll be so tired he'll just walk in and slump on the bed.

Good, he says. He would hate the idea of her husband fucking her tonight. She had earlier revealed that she prefers to be taken in a doggie position and the image tortures his mind. Will keep him awake all night.

He has to go to Manchester on a case the following day and when he finds the time to call her office he discovers she is in a meeting.

He doesn't leave a message. And then it's the week-end. Three days out of touch.

During which time he tries to imagine all the things she might be doing. Cooking, dusting their flat, shopping, seeing a movie, peeling potatoes, reading. But all that stays in his mind is her husband's cock ploughing her with vulgar vigour. Is she a moaner? A quiet one?

He receives her letter in Monday's first mail. Just as he is about to call her.

They have gone too far, she writes. It's wrong. All very wrong. Maybe they should stay apart. Maybe meet up in a few months, just as good friends, you know.

Damn, she has had second thoughts.

He writes her a letter in which he summons all his powers of persuasion. By the end of the week, she has not answered. He writes another. Two weeks pass by. All he can think of is her, and the Amazon-like grace of her lanky body. A letter a day. He surprises himself by finding new words, new things to say, every time he puts pen to paper.

Please, he says. Change your mind. Give me a chance. Give us a chance. Just once. She had, in conversation, revealed past occasional thoughts of adultery with other men she had come across, passes made which she had turned down. She has always been faithful. I am not just another man is what he is trying to say.

It's been ages since he has wanted a woman the way he wants her.

She phones.

Enough letters, she says. We have to talk.

The next evening. The bar of the same hotel. Usual time.

Yes, he says.

He's already sitting when she arrives, her customary gin and orange awaiting her on the small table. She appears distant.

He apologises for the bombardment of letters. Explains how strongly he feels for her, how he realises he is asking her too much, how if it never happens she will always wonder at the back her mind how it would have been, a self-serving and cowardly argument he recognises, how this, how that, and. . . .

I will, she suddenly says.

What? he says.

He doesn't understand.

I will sleep with you, she says.

The trapdoor under his stomach opens and he plunges in head-first.

They make arrangements.

Neither of them wishes to succumb to vulgarity, no office floor or flea-pit hotel for their affair. Not for their first time together, at any rate.

Somewhere discreet, they decide. Outside London.

They become lovers a fortnight later. It's a Tuesday morning. In an airport hotel, the distant rumbling of planes taking off or landing barely audible through the plate glass windows. He finally unveils her cunt and its forest of darker blonde curls is in harmony with the jungle of her hair. He sighs. Kisses her warmth, his tongue slowly parting her labia and tasting her for the first time. Strong, salty, intoxicating.

He retreats. She takes a step back and lies down on the bed. He approaches the intimate geography of her genitals, quietly opens her with all the delicacy his fingers can muster. Her insides are coral pink, ready to explode. He invades her with his mouth. She widens the angle of her legs. He is kneeling by the foot of the bed, still dressed, now installed between her thighs.

He nibbles, licks, pulls and chews her inner folds, searching for the nerve ends of her pleasure, and soon her heartbeat speeds up and tremors pass through her body, shaking his soul as the electricity moves imperceptibly from her redness through to his tongue.

Finally, she cries out.

I want you inside me. Now!

He quickly undresses and holding his cock in one hand to guide its entrance path, he enters her.

The threshold of adultery is so easy to cross.

She is not a moaner.

Neither is she totally silent.

With every few thrusts, she just whispers 'Jesus', 'Jesus,' as he pumps into her and the volcano of her loins radiates its implacable heat, their skin incandescent and wet, fingers digging into rumps, scratching, holding on to each other with the energy of despair.

They have become lovers.

The affair will last ninety days.

The lovemaking that first morning stretches well into the afternoon. They exhaust each other, always eager for more, avid for further sensations, as if throwing away one at a time the shackles of their previous lives in a frenzy of desire.

He takes a shower. Returns to the room. She is lying on the bed, obscenely spreadeagled on the cover, her cunt still gaping open from his assaults and leaking his come, raw, lips swollen from the blood rush and all the friction. He stands watching her beauty in such wonderful disarray. She opens her eyes, sees him and beckons. He moves nearer and she takes his cock in her mouth and soon revives him.

Finally spent, it's now mid-afternoon, they share a bath and he traces hieroglyphics on her wide back as she cups his balls with delicacy, exploring this body which has now become hers.

The early evening traffic on the M4 is unusually busy and she almost misses her 6.27 train from Charing Cross. She has told her husband she was away at a day seminar on publishing contracts in north London and can't afford to be late.

She is the first to call the following morning.

No regrets? he asks her.

None at all, she answers.

She is in fact surprised at how little guilt she feels. She never thought it would be so easy.

Again?

Yes.

When?

It's awkward for her to take too many days off from her job without arousing her husband's suspicion at the dwindling of her holiday entitlement. They meet for drinks halfway between their respective offices, find it difficult to keep their hands to themselves and make a frantic beeline for his office where they fuck still half-dressed on the floor.

They manage two meetings a week. She uses every excuse they can concoct for her evening absences from home: sales conferences, drinks with colleagues, meetings with authors from out of town.

They are consumed by each other, travelling on a runaway train of absolute lust and gratification.

Between the fucking, she is quiet, almost reticent to discuss the affair.

Yes, she says to him, the sex is great. Surely, that's enough?

For him, it no longer is. He is the one who has to return to an empty bed and think of her sleeping next to another man who still touches her, makes love to her, shares a life of small nothings, sees her face drowsy when she awakes in the morning, watches her dress, shave her legs, fart, sigh, live. He knows she is only giving him a small part of her and he wants it all.

Initially, he realises, it was lust, something about her that made him vibrate all other, but now he has tasted her, it has turned into something else and he fears telling her this. He's in love. And no longer wishes to share her.

They fuck like rabbits, abandoning all modesty or civilised manners.

She has her period. They fuck. He withdraws his cock from her innards, all coated with blood, dripping come and jam-like matter. He wipes his hand on his red cock and paints the white expanse of her flesh with their combined emissions, outlining her nipples with sharp red circles. The carpet remains stained for months.

He comes inside her once again. She slides away from him and takes his cock, still coated with her own secretions, into her greedy mouth and cleans him.

One evening, he just doesn't know how he has managed to retain his hardness for a fourth fuck in under three hours, and his orgasm courses through him like a bomb exploding, both sheer pain and ecstasy. She is on her knees on the hard office floor, her rump raised, the way she likes it with her husband or previous men, he knows, he collapses on her as he comes. She turns her head back.

Are you OK? she inquires.

Yes, he whispers. I love you.

She doesn't respond.

He disengages from her, withdraws his already limp cock from her gash and lowers his mouth and licks her raw cunt, his tongue sliding inside her and sucking out his own come. It tastes of her. Then he kisses her mouth. They exchange the fluids. She knows what he is doing and does not protest in the slightest.

The more they fuck, the sharper his desire for her becomes.

He turns down any job that might take him away from London if only for a day, in case it's an evening when she can free herself.

They manage a whole week-end together, thanks to a regional book fair in Nottingham. It's the first time they have spent a whole night together. Not that they sleep that much.

They have their first argument.

He binds her hands to a chair while they fool around. She is immobilised. He positions himself and enters her unexpectedly. She is already soaking wet and soon comes with a blissful scream. She confesses to other fantasies of bondage and submission. He refuses to untie her and fucks her mouth until she chokes and gasps for air.

They stay entwined for hours, the silence between them worth more than a thousand words.

She is on duty at the Frankfurt Book fair and he tags along, spending the nights in her room when she returns from the daily round of parties and receptions. He hates the German town and its invasive greyness and dead buildings and sky. He trawls the red light district during the day. On the second night there, they try anal sex for the first time. Something they've long discussed and fascinates them both. It just happens in the midst of an embrace, there is little resistance and he breaches the wall of her sphincter without undue pressure. Jesus, Jesus. She is wonderfully tight and the heat around his cock feels strangely different. He comes quickly. It felt good for him. There is vain feeling of triumph, and jealousy: something she has never done with her husband. She falls asleep soon after.

They return to London.

She has a holiday booked, arranged long before they met. With her husband.

He attempts to dissuade her from taking it, but she refuses. No way can she justify that.

He is annoyed.

She is annoyed he could even have asked and refuses to tell him where she and her husband are going.

Not New York, I hope? he queries.

No.

He is reassured. He has promised her he will take her there the next year.

She is only away for a week. His curiosity is intense.

He remembers her husband was brought up in Scarborough, on the Yorkshire coast. And that his mother was a bit of an alcoholic, according to her.

He locates the mother and calls her on the phone.

He pretends to be an old university friend of her son who is anxious to get in touch, and learns they are in Ibiza. The woman is garrulous and he conducts a long conversation with her, quizzing her about the marriage and the fact the couple have no children despite all their years together, a sore point over which Kay has always clammed up. She clearly is not enamoured of her daughter-in-law. He is confident the woman will have no memory of their telephone conversation within a few days. He introduced himself under false name anyway.

How was Ibiza? Sunny?

You bastard. How did you find out?

A private dick has his ways.

She just smiles mischievously.

Their routine is now well-established. She phones him every morning at 10.30 after they have both processed their mail. If she cannot free herself in the evening, they share a sandwich over her lunch break in a Soho Italian coffee house. If she can find an alibi, she comes straight to his office; they no longer require the pretext of a hotel bar to meet in before a fuck.

Arm in arm, still wet from their sexual exertions, a mountain of tenderness growing between them, they sit on the floor. It's a colder night, she is wearing his shirt.

So?

So what?

Well, it's nearly three months.

Already?

Happy?

Of course.

So say so . . .

I'm happy. Satisfied? What else do you want me to say. This juggling isn't easy, you know, one of these days he's going to become suspicious.

Leave him.

What?

You heard me. Leave him. I want you to live with me.

Gee, it's such a big step to take.

I know.

Throwing away seven years just like that.

Listen, Kay, you said the other day I was the best lover you had ever had . . .

Four other guys and a husband don't make me an expert, you know.

He smiles.

I want you, he says.

You have me, she answers, pointing to her body, she is still leaking.

I want all of you.

Can't you be satisfied with what you have, Martin?

I love you.

The next day, she is attending a sales conference in East-bourne and sharing a room with another female colleague so he is unable to join her. Followed by a week-end. A dinner party she is organising for some friends from her Cambridge college and some City friends of her husband's. Their next assignment is on Monday evening at his office.

Her Monday morning call is late.

When she phones, her voice is cold and remote.

Can we meet at lunch?

Sure. A pleasant extra. But still OK for tonight?

The pub off Charing Cross Road, she suggests.

She walks in on the hour, one of the rare punctual women he has ever known, he reckons.

Why does his heart feel so bad the moment he sees her?

She has had second thoughts, she tells him. She just doesn't want to hurt her husband. He is too dependent on her. The affair is going way too fast. They cannot go on like they have been.

You mean you want it to be over?

He is struck dumb by the pain that races through his soul.

I don't know, she says. Maybe we can stay apart for, say, three months? Not see each other. It will give us both time to reflect, to think about things.

That's a brush off, Kay. You know it, I know it.

No, Martin. Let's just see if we feel the same in three months?

I know I will.

She is annoyed.

Well, I won't know what I feel until then.

He loses all impulse to protest any further. He is aware nothing will sway her determination.

She rises from the seat. She hasn't even touched her drink.

Bye.

He feels sick.

Worthless.

Maybe he knew deep inside the affair could not last forever, but he never thought it would end this way, so suddenly, with no real sense of closure.

He stumbles back to his office in a daze.

In his mind he composes a final letter, a plea, a cry for help, a supplication for a love lost, a last-chance missive.

It takes him two hours to get it right or thereabouts. Lengthy, complex arguments, expressions of devotion, a mature adult acceptance of rejection, a wish to remain friends, shared joyful past memories and all that. In essence, he begs for just one more meeting, one last fuck, the mercy fuck he feels he deserves.

He prints the page out.

Rings her.

Hi.

Oh! You know I don't like you phoning me at work.

I know. I'm sorry.

Is your desk still close to the fax machine?

Yes.

I'm sending you a letter right now. Wanted you to read it immediately. The post wouldn't have reached you until tomorrow.

I see.

He feeds the sheet of paper into the fax machine and punches in the publishing house's number.

It's coming through, she said.

Can I wait while you read it?

I suppose so.

There is a long silence. He hears her coughing.

I see, she says.

I'm begging you, Kay. For the sake of all we had. Please, pretty please.

He can feel her hesitation.

All right, she finally says.

Thank you, he says. Tonight?

No, not tonight. I promised Chris I would be home early. Things we have to talk about.

Tomorrow then?

OK, she replies.

Relief washes over him. And he realises it's a Tuesday.

Usual place and time?

She agrees.

He then asks her if she could wear the clothes she wore for their first Heathrow hotel assignment. The swirling multi-coloured dress, the black bustier, the stockings and the low-heeled ankle-high boots.

The request doesn't surprise her. By now, she's well accustomed to his sentimental touches. But she reminds him that a final evening together is not going to change her decision.

I am sadly aware of that, he answers.

She hangs up.

By the end of the day, he is in the heart of the deepest blue funk. Filled with both sadness and unfathomable anger. He searches his mind for schemes, complicated methods that might lead to her returning to him, but also knows how futile they all are.

He can't think of life without her any more.

It hurts too much.

He's going mad.

Is she going to tell Chris about the affair and the last three months tonight and beg for his forgiveness, save her marriage?

He doubts it, she's too secretive for that, he feels. She will attempt to mend bridges, set the marriage back on the right track, but without giving herself away.

What if her husband found out? Surely, he would never accept it, would throw her out.

He frantically drafts an anonymous letter to the journalist, denouncing her. Can't send it to their flat. Too obvious. His work? Makes a few phone calls and discovers the address of the press agency.

What if he confronts her with it? She'd recognise the printer. For a brief moment, he thinks of cutting every single word or letter out of newspapers and magazines, but realises it would take ages and is just too corny really. Kay would guess he was the sender. She wouldn't forgive him or come back to him under any circumstances if she suspected him of such a vile and under-hand piece of action.

His despair deepens and takes on a darker tone.

If her husband was no longer on the scene, maybe?

A car accident?

Murder?

Could he actually murder a stranger anyway? Well, not quite a stranger, just her husband.

No, he'd become the first suspect.

And lose her a second time.

But the seed has been planted in his mind.

Above all, it's his jealousy for Chris that consumes him, burns all the way down to his guts. It's not that he can't live with the rejection but the fact she has chosen this other man against him. This bastard of a journalist who will continue to enjoy the favour of her eyes, the despoiling of her body, the cushion of her silken flesh, who will hear her say Jesus, Jesus when he accidentally hits a raw nerve when they fuck, who will peer at the squareness of her regal white arse as her intimate apertures beckon, the red rose flower of her cunt, the puckered brown crater of her anus.

The pornographic images drive him halfway to crazy.

No other man deserves her.

His Kay.

His wonderful Kay.

And the nightmare of his imagination rushes onward. He can picture it all: she returns to her husband but eventually gets bored with him again, but out of pride refuses to return to the safe harbour of of his arms and finds another man who pleases her lust, another cock to fuck her, to use her.

No. It's inconceivable. Mustn't happen.

There is a perverse, twisted logic to it. He knows he's not the first jealous man to come up with the equation, but it's no consolation.

If I can't have her, then no one should, he mutters, sinking into a heavy sleep.

It's a rare occasion when she is late but, today of all days, she is. The anxiety dances frantically around the pit of his stomach. He runs through possibilities: she has changed her mind and will after all deprive him of his last, mercy fuck, Chris has forbidden her to come, she can read his mind and knows what he is thinking of doing, something bad has happened to her. The rushing thoughts dance a light fantastic in his brain.

He knows her habit of always using the back stairs when she comes to see him, rather than the front entrance of the building and the lift. Discretion being the better part of valour and her phobia of being seen here by someone who might know her. He had an extra key to the side entrance cut for her two weeks into the affair. So no one will see her entering the building. The way she wanted it.

He hears her long, steady steps in the corridor outside his suite of offices. She knocks.

He takes a deep breath.

Opens the door and lets her in.

Hello.

Hi.

He attempts a peck on her cheek, a peace offering, but she turns her face away. Her eyes are cold, dark steel.

He looks her over.

As he requested, she is wearing the outfit he remembered so well.

She walks past him to the main office and sets her bag down.

He locks the door.

I came, she says.

Thank you, he answers.

I'm sorry it has to end this way, she tells him. But one day you'll agree it's better. Less acrimonious.

I never felt there was any acrimony, he protests.

There would have been, she continues. It was all going too fast, Martin. Getting too serious.

I'm truly sorry. I was just being honest with you about the strength of my feelings.

Yes. And that's what worries me.

Why? he asks her.

She doesn't answer him.

I told Chris all about us yesterday night. Well, that I had been having an affair. I didn't mention your name or who you are, that would have been pointless really.

And?

He was very hurt. But he had his suspicions, you know, all my absences and late evenings. He blames himself, feels he was too obsessed with his own career, neglected me. He was angry, too. Insisted that I tell him who you are.

So what will happen with the two of you?

I've apologised. It was a long night. Neither of us slept at all. He knows I am breaking up with you tonight and is waiting for me at home. I only have an hour or so, Martin. I've promised I will be on the 9.10 train.

He knows?

Just that I'm telling you it's over. He doesn't have to know more.

I understand.

She reaches for the lower button of her bustier.

Let's do it. For old time's sake. Her tone of voice is quite unsentimental and angers him deeply. She wants it to be a cold, passionless fuck.

She continues to undress.

He just stands there waiting and watching as every button is undone, every piece of clothing unzipped, stockings rolled down and her black lacy knickers lowered.

Her beauty overwhelms him.

She is naked.

She looks at him, humourless.

Your turn, she says.

It had often been a running joke between them how much he liked her fully undressed before he shed any of his own clothing. My voyeur, she used to call him.

He drowns in the vision of her nudity.

His heart shatters and flies to every corner of the zodiac.

How do you want me? she asks, still remote and business-like, clearly eager for the whole, now distasteful act of fornication to be over.

The condemned man's final wish? He tries to make a joke of it, but she is in no mood for it and remains impassive.

For a few brief seconds, the unacceptable side of his mind imagines her below him and his sharp cock digging deeper inside her than he has ever travelled, literally tearing her apart.

But this is not to be an act of vengeance or vindictiveness, he reminds himself.

On your knees, he orders her.

She turns her back to him and goes down to the carpeted floor.

The bottle of chloroform and the cloth are on his desk, out of her sight.

He places the piece of fabric over the bottle's opening and tips it over. The colourless liquid soon soaks in. He goes over to Kay and places the cloth against her face, smothering her nose and mouth. With his other hand, he holds her down. She doesn't struggle much and her energy quickly ebbs and she falls unconscious, her knees buckling, falling on her side. Her foot catches the edge of the desk and twists. Another bruise in prospect. He remembers how her milky skin marked so easily.

And how the strength of her orgasms would colour her whole front, flushing scarlet, from neck to cleavage. A tell-tale sign of extra-marital sex which sometimes took almost an hour to disappear and had to be taken into account together with her return train schedule from Charing Cross station.

The deed is done, and he knows that now there is no turning back.

No more sentimentality.

He has the medical and the true crime books that were given out to the delegates at the crime writers' conference. He has studied them well over the course of the last twenty-four hours. He pulls the large plastic sheets from their protective wrapping, and lines up the extra large black refuse liners.

Inside his desk drawer are the scalpels and saws.

He knows it's going to be messy.

Already in his mind he is rehearsing the disposal of the remains. He has it all very carefully planned out. A private detective can think laterally, guess how the opposition reasons.

What he is about to do is horrible, he is aware, but it's easier to make body parts disappear. A whole body has a bad tendency to reappear, whether buried, drowned or concealed. And is so much easier to identify.

But Martin knows he will see it through.

It takes him almost two days to cut up Kay's body and another week to scatter the bin liners all over the country, using a judicious combination of building sites, rivers, burial grounds, industrial ovens and sea.

Throughout the whole operation, he forbids himself to even

think. He goes through the sad motions like an automaton. The plan works. The hardest part is burning her clothes. In a moment of folly, he even hesitates, thinks of retaining something that will remind him of her, that will still harbour her smell, her lost intimacy, to cover the encroaching images of saw against bone, of scalpel slicing through sinews, of her million curls before he fed them to the flames. But he knows it would be wrong. And dangerous.

So, finally, it's over.

But, as he feared, he can't forget her, and the memories of their love and his infamy begin to grip his life in a cruel lock of self-loathing and disgust.

The nightmares begin. Invading every corner of his sleepless nights, eternal torture with shades of hell, a film loop he can't stop, unrolling on and on, every variation more painful than the one before, cutting, shredding what's left of his soul.

No one comes asking for her.

He concentrates on his job. Traps another adulterous couple in a Golders Green bed and breakfast and obtains the necessary compromising photograph. He finds a lost dog. Locates a hacker who's playing havoc with a chemical conglomerate's web site. Checks up on the truth and falsities of job applicants for a head hunter.

Life goes on.

He still thinks of Kay.

Every minute of every day, even when his mind is switched off. Sometimes he sheds tears. There is no one he can talk to. Every day is a day in hell.

His mind is wandering. There is a knock on the door.

The name of today's client is Christopher Streetfield.

And a true professional never turns a job down, does he?

11.

Martin

What was I expecting? A dark, wet dungeon? The Hollywood version of a brothel with candles smoking and corduroy drapes over the stone walls like flock paper in an Indian restaurant? The House of the Rising Sun (well, this was New Orleans after all), with dusky black maidens barely clothed in white chiffon catering to all the customers' perverse needs with a look of terror and sad acceptance in their eyes?

It was none of that.

It was deceptively normal.

A drawing-room with understated Southern elegance. Well-dressed people sitting in deep armchairs and upholstered leather couches and conversing just above the level of a whisper while sipping tea or coffee from exquisitely fine porcelain cups and saucers balanced on their knees.

Cornelia wore a striking little black dress, its cleavage invaded by the porcelain white of her skin, the velvety material waltzing barely an inch from her nipples, her stockinged legs on full display from mid-thigh down. And a leather collar with sharp silvery metal studs around her long neck. Almost a dog collar, but no dog had ever worn a choker with such poise and calm. The ensemble was completed by a pair of shiny, black low-heeled shoes.

Every man in the room where we sipped drinks in silence only had eyes for her. As her presumed Master, I was an object of dire envy. I wore the black silk suit I only wore for weddings and funerals, made to measure on the occasion of a trip to Bangkok some years back. My shirt, socks, shoes and newly-acquired tie were also black.

If not sinister, I reckoned the outfit at least made me seem a bit slimmer than I was.

Some of the other guys were dressed even more formally, tuxedos, dinner jackets and colourful waistcoats, the women alternately garbed in haute couture dresses or, like Cornelia, in understated, demure outfits. At any moment now, I expected someone to bring out the cigars and beckon the women out of the room so that the men present could get on with their smoking and business talk. It was like being parachuted forty years into the past.

So, was this where all the curious strands of the case were meant to unravel?

I had not been idle during the past day. I also owned long lists of phone contacts and I'd sent and received several handfuls of e-mails pursuing the details of Cornelia's identity. It was too dangerous to stay in ignorance. By now, I knew that we were not searching for Louise Poshard for the same reason. Cornelia was danger incarnate. She was not in the business of finding people for the sake of finding them. What I still couldn't puzzle out was why her elder sister would take on my services to find the errant Louise and order a hit on her separately? Or was it just a charade and had Kay's husband ordered my own execution? Still, I had taken a shine to Cornelia and the vibrations coming from her direction did not feel dangerous to me. Nor amorous, I feared. I think I amused her. Which was better than nothing, I supposed.

But I knew I would soon find out

Cornelia and I had been offered tea or coffee by a middle-aged matron who had opened the door to us and confirmed our alleged identity. We had been expected.

'I will lead you to the lounge,' she had said, the accent sounded Texan to me but I was no expert. Once in Omaha, Nebraska, every local had thought I hailed from Australia of all places, so I knew how foolish it was to rely on a person's voice to pinpoint their place of origin. 'We are expecting further guests before we can begin. I do hope you can bear with us,' addressing me and rudely ignoring Cornelia, acting subservient at my side, a most alluring appendage.

A young, seemingly unattached woman in a white cotton smock played an easy listening classical repertoire on the piano in the corner of the large room.

A large, balding man in a perfectly tailored white dinner jacket walked over to us, a thick Cuban cigar in his hand smouldering aromatically. He smiled silently at me and I nodded in recognition. He took this as my agreement to circle the seated Cornelia.

At ease in her role, she modestly lowered her eyes towards the carpeted floor. With his other hand, he slowly touched her, dragging a finger around the curve of her neck. His smile widened approvingly and his fingers moved to her chin. A movement of his wrist and she raised her head and now held his gaze. A finger traced the contour of her lips. Cornelia half-opened her mouth and the finger entered her, both a gentle violation and an assertion of his domination. She sat proudly, sustaining the examination with icy determination. He withdrew. Looked back toward me.

'Well trained?'

'Yes,' I replied.

'I would love to see her put through her paces,' he remarked, drawing on his cigar. 'A most attractive specimen.'

'Yes,' I confirmed.

'Maybe later,' he suggested. 'Let's see how the evening proceeds.' He retreated.

I was about to mumble something in response when a new set of arrivals were chaperoned into the room.

Familiar faces.

Nola Poshard and the man I assumed to be N.

Like me, he was mostly clad in black from head to toe, but Nola was a veritable picture of menace, her fiery hair catching every ray of light in the room in a halo, her eyes dark and animal, circled by kohl, and her lips the savage red of dark rubies. She wore a pale beige leather dress which perfectly emphasised her lithe frame. Her bare arms were weighed down by heavy silver bracelets and her shining nails were painted dark green. Woman as night predator.

She saw me immediately. If my presence here surprised her, she kept her composure well.

She made a deliberate beeline for us. N followed a pace behind her.

'Mr Jackson . . .'

'Ms Poshard . . .'

'Somehow, I didn't expect you'd get this far,' Nola Poshard said to me. 'Welcome to a house of pain.'

'I was given a job. I'm doing it,' I answered.

'Well done,' she said. 'But I've managed to track the little bitch down here through another source, so you may consider your services no longer required, Mr Jackson. My cheque will reach you when you return to London.'

She caught sight of Cornelia in the seat beside mine. Her eyes lit up with both curiosity and sudden envy.

Unless Nola was a better actress than I gave her credit for, it appeared Cornelia wasn't her other source. My initial pet theory was falling down in flames. So, who was Cornelia actually employed by? Was there another player lurking in the dark of this strange game?

'Who is your lovely companion?' Nola asked.

On cue, Cornelia lowered her eyes again.

'Her name is unimportant,' I said.

'How true,' Nola smiled, giving Cornelia a lustful once-over. 'But a very beautiful object nonetheless,' she added.

I winced. Visions of ritual needles piercing Cornelia's parts and the sound of fierce whips breaking the virgin surface of milky skin and drawing deeply-etched lines of blood in geometrical patterns of infamy.

'Most beautiful.' The basso profundo of N's voice interrupted my brief daydream, as he confirmed Nola's assessment with a deep, connoisseur-like, sense of appreciation.

'Oh, I haven't introduced you,' Nola said. 'This is N. A very good friend.'

'We've already met, I think,' I answered.

He raised a bushy eyebrow.

'Although not in ideal circumstances,' I added.

I was now sure he was the man who had searched the room in Amsterdam and attacked me. Something in his posture confirmed it. You just have to rely on instinct in this game.

The lights dimmed.

*

During the course of my research the previous day, I had heard a story about this place. It had taken place six years before when it wasn't called the Moby Lounge and functioned more as a very special kind of brothel. Catering for the more extreme and depraved tastes of the Louisiana elite and hedonists. It was thought these events had contributed to the momentary closure of the establishment and its later reopening as a more exclusive place of pleasure for a similarly selective dom/sub clientele.

The story had touched something inside me and I couldn't erase it from my memory, despite its total lack of connection with the case at hand.

A young British woman had somehow ended up on the extreme shores of the Bourbon Street market for sex. She was on the run, but no one knew from what. A failed marriage, the police, depression, self-loathing, it could have been anything. She was ready for anything in this mad dash for oblivion. Whoredom, drugs, alcohol, she embraced them all avidly.

But even in the depths of her degradation, the endless humiliations she readily submitted herself to in her frantic bid to abolish her past, she held on to her inner beauty somehow. A quiet pride among the dirt and the exploitation of her body and senses. Never did she even shed a tear, even in the worst moments of pain. Which only served as an extra incentive for her users, her torturers, to imagine worse ordeals for her mind and body.

Maybe behind the dead eyes dulled by the beatings and forced sex, there was still a core of hope that sustained her.

They sold tickets to watch her being used by the most savage studs and disproportionately-membered freaks. She bled, winced but never said a word. The cocks cruelly stretched both her apertures, sometimes more than one at a time as she lay spreadeagled on a dirty mattress on an improvised stage, her hands bound to her side to immobilise her. They ceremonially attached her to wheels and whipped her until she fainted. They auctioned her to the highest bidder and relished the spectacle of her choking against the men who violated her throat, and seeing their come spill from her parched lips. They filmed her being fucked. She never protested. She had no need for money. Just the room upstairs in which she was locked every night following the atrocious festivities. And food.

Somehow her degradation gave her a saintly air. Her eyes were fixed on some invisible, distant image or redemption somehow.

Which only encouraged her torturers even more.

It's terrible how imagination has no bounds.

With thin blades, they cut the skin between her two breasts and had her copulate with them as the anaemic fillet of blood dripped downwards and washed over the intricate connection of their cocks and her genitals.

They erected a wooden cross and bound the English blonde to it in a parody of crucifixion and used belts on her, and obscenely thrust foreign objects into her. They held her there for hours on end, keeping her conscious with judicious cups of water to her lips or sponged against her burning forehead. They snickered when she couldn't avoid urinating in their presence and the jet shamefully spurted in an arc from her cunt. One of her torturers caught the stream in a glass and had her drink it. She retched but somehow avoided being sick. They smiled broadly when she could no longer avoid defecating and her face lit up with shame. They finally untied her and she had lost control of her limbs and fell to the ground, slipping in her own excreta. They shouted at her that she was just a dirty slut as she lay on the ground, hosed her down with a jet of cold water, washing away the feces sticking to her white skin. She became feverish for days following this ordeal and they took fright and fed her with antibiotics.

But the blonde with the mass of curly hair got better.

So, the violations worsened even further. Tijuana heyday memories . . .

Although now, they injected her with a strong tranquilliser before to render docile. Just in case.

She reached the final circles of sexual hell. Her eyes absent, in a daze.

By now the young woman spent most of her days in a state of quiet stupor under the influence of the drugs they were injecting her with.

A Man, also a Brit, arrived in town searching for her.

A ghost from her past.

He managed to track her down and, with the help of another whore who worked there and had taken pity on the English girl, bluffed his way in.

He locked himself in a room with her after paying for her services. No one knew what either had said. But he became her angel of salvation. Before anyone realised, he had offered her release from her terrible ordeal and broken her neck. And then hanged himself from the ceiling of the room.

The scandal was hushed up and six months later the place had reopened under a new name.

I asked the man who related this story to me what the names of the man and woman had been, but he didn't know. Not that this revelation would have meant anything to me. They were just two more souls who had been transported by a wave of past failings and misery to the shores of Bourbon, washed up into a world without pity which had no time for the frailties of the business of living.

*

It all begins to unravel.

In slow motion.

As if in a dream.

In stop motion animation.

Or, like in quiz, all of the above.

Take your pick.

Events in the flickering light of a strobe light. Difficult to fathom, their significance at times obscure, out of reach. Like a puzzle in the process of being assembled but somehow in the wrong order, defying sense and logic.

But then, as you know well, I am the one who is telling you this story.

This is how it happened.

This is how it might have happened.

This is the way I wanted it to happen.

Tick where appropriate.

Remember: I am an unreliable narrator and you have to trust my fallible imagination if events unfurl at which I wasn't even present, where I was not in the same room, could only guess at the words said and unsaid.

So, trust me, I'm a private eye. I can see things you don't see.

The lights in the room dimmed and the runaway train I had been a passenger on this far finally reached its confused destination in its journey through the map of tenderness, the map of human emotions.

In silence, like velvet, a half-dozen women were ushered in. Some were partly nude, others utterly so, all wore tight leather collars around their neck, a symbol of their servitude. They were all young, generally slim, and kept their heads bowed as they were led in and required to stand at attention by the wall.

I recognised Louise immediately. As did Nola, whose breathing just a chair away from me sharpened in its intensity. N purred a cruel sigh of satisfaction.

There could be no doubt about it. Even more so than in the photos I had been provided with, she was like a smaller, kinder version of her sister. The same lips, a similar litheness of body, the way she held her head. The flip side of Nola's dark coin.

All she wore was a bustier, beneath the emblematic collar.

Her genital piercings and jewellery were well in evidence.

'She is beautiful,' Cornelia whispered in my ear, 'in her submissive way.'

I couldn't keep my eyes away from the row of gold rings littering the mound of her cunt.

The young women standing next to her, denied all clothing, also had a ring below, but an inch or so higher than her slit, attached it seems to either her clitoris or its fleshy hood, I couldn't see from where I was sitting. Her dark, elongated nipples were also pierced by rings.

A third girl, she seemed the youngest of the bunch, had been allowed a modest dress, but sported a thick ring dangling from her nose, pierced through her septum, like an animal or the sort of African woman you'd see photos of in *National Geographic* or documentaries. It was horrible, the worst possible humiliation I could imagine.

A nod, and a couple rise from their seats and approach the parade of girls and lead one away to the nearby door she had just made her way through.

Murmurs.

There is no time to confer with Cornelia.

Nola and N are moving towards the exposed Louise as other spectators of the Moby Lounge move from cluster to cluster of attendants, few words exchanged, hands testing flesh, on shoulders and knees, a finger there between a submissive's teeth, her quality being estimated like a piece of meat. Cattle. A skirt being raised ceremonially by an owner to show off his woman's white rump to the appreciation of another dom. I realise it's not only the young slaves who have been made available to others, but there is a free exchange market operating between the couples present. Take your pick.

Cornelia nudges my rib with her elbow and motions me to follow her as she matches her step with Nola and N. I hasten to catch them up.

Louise raises her eyes and a look of dismay races through her features as she recognises her sister and the cruel gaze of the older man who once tortured her.

'So there you are, my sweet,' Nola says, triumphantly, passing her fingers through her sister's lank hair.

Louise remains silent. Slaves are not allowed to speak, it appears. But the fear that chills her is visible to all.

'You have a room where you may be used?' N asks the young woman.

She bows her head dejectedly.

'Let's proceed then,' Nola says. 'I think serious punishment is called for after your untimely escapade.'

'We should like to join the celebration,' Cornelia says.

N tut-tuts.

'Mr Jackson, I am surprised, a slave with opinions? Bad form. Very.'

The five of us are now in the corridor.

Cornelia's face reddens. She realises she has taken a wrong step.

We exchange glances.

'She is sometimes unruly,' I excuse her.

'She should be taught a lesson,' Nola says.

'I shall do so,' I answer.

'Maybe I should?' N suggests.

'Yes,' Nola continues. 'What a good idea. N is a very experienced disciplinarian. He will know how to instil some sense of obedience into your girl, Mr Jackson.'

Cornelia bites her lip.

'You join my sister and I,' Nola says. 'Let N teach your girl some manners. I'm sure there is a room available for them.'

I look Cornelia in the eyes. She imperceptibly lowers her chin. I'm sure she can take care of herself. We part.

Doors. Squares of light in the penumbra of the Moby Lounge's labyrinth of private alcoves.

*

'So you thought you could just run away, could you, Louise?' Nola says.

A tear pearls down Louise's cheek.

Nola hands me a pair of handcuffs and asks me to secure her sister to a heavy metal bar fixed into the wall. I do so as delicately as I can. Still, the young woman remains silent.

*

'Kneel,' N orders.

Cornelia obeys.

'I want to fuck your mouth,' he says.

Cornelia advances her hands and skilfully zips open his trousers and pulls his cock out.

He is already hard.

He enters her humid warmth.

*

I stand watching the two sisters embrace. Mouth devouring mouth, Nola's nails digging sharply against Louise's back, drawing a crossword of thin blood. I imagine tongues lapping, coiling against each other in the dark crevice that joins them.

Nola detaches herself from Louise.

'Yes, I always did enjoy the taste of you,' she says.

She turns to me.

'You like her, don't you, Mr Jackson?'

I am undressed. I had initially protested but Nola had insisted I shed my clothes. My erection is visible. I can't deny that they both awaken my senses.

'Suck him,' she orders Louise.

There is a look of protest in the young woman's eyes.

'Go to her, Jackson.'

I approach the wall where she is chained.

*

Cornelia is bent over a chair, her black dress raised to her waist. N is now on his ninth stroke of the thin wooden cane he has been using on her ass. The lines on her rump crisscross in a jungle of pink vegetation. He is skilful. The pain spreads with the accuracy of an arrow but she will not mark. With every contact of the cane against the porcelain of her skin, Cornelia shudders.

Her hands are bound behind her back.

She feels helpless.

Finally N ceases.

'I do believe you are not a true sub, my dear,' N whispers softly in her ear, the stale air of his breath wafting across her face. 'Too much control. A real slave would have been in tears by now.'

'Fuck you,' Cornelia says.

N smiles.

Inserts the end of the wooden cane into her anus.

'Bastard,' she mutters.

N brings a Swiss army knife out of his pocket.

The sharp blade flicks open and he pulls it slowly across the raw skin of her backside. He reaches the lower hill of her cheeks and cuts her. Quickly, on both sides.

Cornelia moans.

This will leave marks, she knows. Will hurt like hell every time she sits. The cuts are not deep but their placement is strategically chosen for maximum pain, now and later.

Her teeth mash against each other.

N grasps the hem of the black dress bunched above her waist and cuts across it. The garment parts on either side. She is now more vulnerable than ever.

The knife lingers along her back while N ponders where to hurt her next.

*

'She says she prefers women to men,' Nola says. 'But she is quite skilful, isn't she, Mr Jackson?'

I refuse to answer.

Nola had pulled me away from Louise's mouth just as I was about to come. Fellatio interruptus.

I stood there, pale, hairy, evidently overweight, my cock now drooping. While Louise was sucking me with all the energy of despair, Nola had moved behind me and wrapped the belt of my own trousers around my neck. Yet another slave on a leash. Another fool for sex.

Louise, on the other hand, has clearly given up, her silence full of acceptance. She knows she has lost. If she was expecting a rescuing knight, I am obviously not he.

Nola is in her element. We cower before her strength, both pitifully naked, embarrassed by our nudity. She has not a single hair out of place in her crown of fire, and looks a few feet taller than she is as she looks over us. Her toys. Our domme. The mistress of ceremony.

The final act beckons.

'So, dear little sister,' she asks, 'where is the damn book?'

'I sold it, 'Louise says.

It's like a blow to my gut.

'There IS a book?' I exclaim.

Never have I misunderstood a case so much, I realise.

'You little bitch!' Nola's hands smash against Louise's cheek. She flinches. Nola continues her assault, frantically attacking her sister. Louise's hands are still immobilised and she can barely protect herself from the blows raining down on her. I try to interpose myself but Nola ragefully kicks me in the shins, and violently pulls on the belt which tightens around my neck. I strive for breath and fall to my knees. Nola kicks me again. Her heel catches one of my ribs. It cracks.

*

'Who are you, then?' N asks.

Cornelia remains mute.

The blade plays a lingering tango across the nape of her neck as N applies further pressure to the long piece of wood encroaching her innards. He adds a finger and then another, stretching her sphincter muscle to impossible limits.

'Hmm,' N remarks as she still refuses to answer him. 'The gal has guts. So how can I untie that pretty tongue of yours, eh?'

He pulls his fingers out. Distractedly passes them under his nose, enjoying her smell. The wrong end of the cane digs painfully against her depths. Her insides are turning to jelly. More pressure, she knows, and the likely results will prove both more abundant and fragrant. Her face blushes deeply at the thought. Sexual use, she can live with but this sort of prolonged humiliation is deeply excruciating.

Suddenly, he spanks her ass violently with the open palm of his hand. It stings like hell. The wooden cane is dislodged by the impact. Cornelia winces. She can feel the skin of her back cheeks burn. She must be red as hell.

'Oh dear,' N remarks. 'Haven't we ever marked those sweet rear features of yours?'

She pointedly refuses to provide him with the satisfaction of an answer, however obscene.

He slips a hand under her front, cups her slight breasts and twists a nipple.

'But there are still some undeniable beauties at the opposite pole, I guess,' he smirks. 'Shall we explore?'

He pulls the sundered black dress from under her.

'Let's have you the other way up, my dear.'

He rises from the chair and allows Cornelia to roll naked down to the floor. Her shoulder makes uncomfortable contact with the thin carpet. Another bruise. He bends down to reposition her.

*

'A fuck to remember,' Nola says.

I am on my back. My hands are bound behind my neck, serving as a cushion of sorts.

Louise has manually raised another erection out of me.

Nola has Louise squat over me.

The sight of her fragile body, the marks, the cuts, the servile flesh, the golden rings that catch odd reflections of light, all bring a twist to my heart but I have no control over my cock which looms, hard as rock, to meet her.

Nola holds her by the shoulders and guides her down.

Her labia part, the rings slide against the taut skin of my cock and Louise impales herself on me.

She is very dry. The friction is both intense and painful.

Nola now manoeuvres herself directly behind Louise, also squatting over me, her backside in the crook of my hand, and orchestrates the jerky movements of our fornicating rhythm.

'Who did you sell the book to, Louise?'

Down, her lips open like a flower's jaw and engulf me.

'A dealer in Las Vegas?'

Up, she moves along my shaft, inner secretions coating me in her wake.

'What did you do with the money?'

Down, her ringed mouth of fire devours me.

I see her feeble smile.

'Spent it on a good cause.'

Up, her cunt vacuums me up, pulling the thin envelope of skin clothing my penis into her avid maw.

'You little bitch, you.'

Down, my glans scrapes against her cervix, as she grinds herself against me. I feel as if I'm still growing inside Louise, ready to batter a way into her very womb, reaching new, dangerous depths.

'In that case, sweet sister, you no longer mean anything to me. Maybe it's time to finally part ways ...'

Louise closes her eyes.

And yet, I know, she once thought she had loved her.

But it was not for me to say and I just lie there, still fucking her, being fucked by her, and Nola behind pulling those invisible strings.

I also close my eyes. In sheer despair at the turn of events. Would I ever understand how women thought, how hearts turned and swirled? I try to abandon myself to the moment, my whole being reduced to a thrusting cock. In the distance, my orgasm is rising in ever diminishing circles through the layers of my consciousness. I abdicate all control.

Soon, the wave of pleasure is in massive overdrive, a juggernaut speeding down the sharp hill of my senses and about to smash against the shore.

I open my eyes.

The ever-vulgar voyeur in me wants to see my fuck partner's face as I come.

Louise's remain closed, a patina of perspiration coats her forehead.

Up.

Down.

A rivulet of sweat rolls down the valley of her breasts.

Up. Down.

Her lips part.

My eyes focus on Nola, who is moving, close behind the rutting Louise. In her hands, a pink pill. She holds Louise's lips open and feeds her.

Her hands are circling Louise's neck.

Up.

Down.

*

N kneels by Cornelia.

'Pretty decoration,' he says, catching sight of her tattoo. Her shoulder is in pain. Her backside burns and the cuts beneath her buttocks itch uncontrollably. She is on her side. 'Nice cunt,' N adds with appreciation.

Cornelia's mouth is dry.

She hates this man with a vengeance.

'Ever been fucked with a knife, my dear? Truly fucked?' he asks her.

Maybe he wishes to position her better for the next torture, but he decides to loosen her bound hands. Cornelia knows this will be her only chance. The moment her hands are free, and before he can pull them forward and immobilise her again, she swings her left elbow against his body with all the energy she can summon. N flinches and falls back a step or two, Cornelia is on her feet, her dancer's legs unfurling.

She is first to the knife he had dropped on impact.

Without a word, she wields the blade against his throat.

'Ever been fucked by a knife?' she asks the slumping body of the man, as his eyes glaze and the blood spurts from the deep opening.

He is dead within a minute.

*

Two rooms.

Bodies. Entwined. White. Blood.

Nola stands by us as we dance the dance of death. I know what is happening. But there is nothing I can do. My body responds to the calls of lust like an automaton.

Still, we fuck.

I want to call out, but my throat is dry.

We fornicate like animals under Nola's cruel, amused glance.

Up and down Louise slides alongside my cock but I feel her strength slowly ebbing away as the poison takes effect.

Her face now reflects the pain in her chest, in her bowels. Her lovemaking movements are now just basic instincts. Her lips part further. Her face reddens. Her whole body shivers and finally triggers my pent-up orgasm. I come. Her eyes finally close. Her dying muscles clench wildly in their ultimate spasm and throttle my cock in a vice. The pain is unbearable. I lose consciousness.

12.

Martin

The road unfurled like a slow ribbon ahead of us. Cornelia and I alternated at the wheel of the rental Pontiac. One drove, the other slept, affording us a chance to nurse our bruises and pain as we raced along the highways of the South towards Nevada, crossing the monotonous Texas heartlands. We estimated Nola was three hours ahead of us, four or five at the most. She must be doing all the driving and would soon be tiring, we felt.

I assumed N was no longer a problem. When we had hastily changed into new clothes in my hotel room, I had spied the blood across Cornelia's front and knew it wasn't hers. She had kicked in the door to the room where I still lay attached to Louise's dead body. She had revived me and the moment I had opened my eyes, the pain in my genitals hit me. Jeez . . . just the thought of peeing felt like the ninth circle of hell, let alone the prospect of my next, and awfully distant, erection.

'You're lucky I got there before rigor mortis set in,' Cornelia remarked with a rare of display of bad taste and black humour. 'I would have had to cut you apart.'

'It's not funny,' I protested.

Cornelia's black dress was precariously held together at the neck by a safety pin.

'It's my fault,' she said. 'I shouldn't have left the Glock in my bag. Just felt a handbag would be searched or that a submissive would look unconvincing with a bag.'

'A fucking waste.'

My verbal requiem for Louise Poshard.

'Any idea where Nola has swept off too?'

'Las Vegas, I guess,' I replied.

'How come?' Cornelia queried.

'Louise sold the book to a dealer there, it appears,' I said.

'What book?' Cornelia asked me.

'The Le Carré proof. You didn't know about it?' I asked.

She didn't. I had to explain how the case began. Cornelia's eyes shone strangely as I related the whole story to her. She seemed fascinated. How strange: we both seemed only to be aware of separate elements in the puzzle, and had no clue about the whole picture. Rephrase that: I had no clue.

I cleaned up in the bathroom as Cornelia changed into a pair of my jeans and a blue shirt I was happy to spare. Bathed my genitals in tepid water to ease the nagging pain of Louise's last embrace, wondering whether bruises would show up on a penis.

Cornelia looked good in my clothes, but then she was the sort of woman who would look a treat in or out of anything.

'So, the end of the road?' I remarked.

I had found Louise. The fact that my employer had chosen to kill her ended my involvement in the case, I reckoned, however distasteful the whole farrago had become. All I knew was that I was not about to put in a claim for the final half of my fee. Some would even say I had been an accessory to the murder, though I only felt guilty of cowardice. But then that was nothing new for me. Anyway, the generous advance on expenses covered it already. I still assumed somehow that Cornelia had been hired to cover all possibilities, should my investigation have failed. I was wrong.

'I still have to complete my job,' she said. 'It's far from over. I want that cunt Nola.'

She worked the phone.

Nola had rented a car within an hour of leaving the Moby Lounge. With arrangements to drop it off in Vegas a few days later.

Cornelia asked me if I wanted to tag along. Perversely, I agreed. Nola had to pay for her treatment of Louise. I would be glad to see her get her comeuppance.

'I think there are direct flights from Moisan. We can catch one and be there before her. She has a long drive ahead of her,' I suggested.

'No,' Cornelia replied. 'My Glock won't get past airport security.' She waved the sleek, shiny gun at me, then buried it in her rucksack.

She had a point.

It was a very silent journey. Whenever I had questions for Cornelia, she offered no answers or pretended to be asleep. Several times, she had me relate the story of the book again. It appeared to fascinate her.

Telegraph poles.

Roadside shacks.

Gas stations with fly-infested bars where Cornelia always attracted lusty glances whenever we stocked up on water and potato chips.

More telegraph poles punctuating the flat horizon of fields as far as the eye could see.

Shabby motels advertising their wares and nightly rates in garish pink and mauve neon art deco letters.

We shared a room with two separate beds at the Magnolia Inn somewhere in East Texas. Each of us slumped down onto our respective bed and slept fully-clothed. I was so tired I never even dreamt. But I knew the nightmares would come rushing back at the first opportunity. Now that I was responsible for the deaths of two women.

On the road again and still no conversation to speak of.

Two hours out of Las Vegas and I was sitting in the noisy lounge of a small casino built in the middle of nowhere, an incongruous fabrication dropped into a John Ford desert landscape, for those who couldn't hold out any longer and had to gamble as if their life depended on it, before even reaching the mecca of the Strip. Cornelia was on the phone. A Vegas contact had hacked into the hotel network and located Nola Poshard at the Mirage.

Back in New Orleans, Nola had never heard Cornelia speak, so the ploy was worth trying.

The book would act as a bait.

It was Sunday mid-morning. Nola had booked in barely an hour ago so we assumed, rightly, she had so far been unable to contact the dealer who had acquired the rare proof.

Cornelia pretended to now be its owner and to have heard of Nola's interest in retrieving the item. And to be amenable to worthwhile suggestions.

Hook, line and sinker.

*

The meeting, Cornelia insisted, had to take place somewhere private, as they both knew of the book's strictly illegal nature. Nola readily agreed. Three pm at the km. 95 crossroads, one hour west of the Hoover Dam.

We had scouted the location earlier as we drove in. It was isolated. You could see for miles around for cars coming and any sign of life, or danger.

We ate. There was a steely determination in Cornelia's eyes. She devoured the jumbo steak meal with studied indifference, wincing every time she moved in her seat. At the motel, early that morning, I had witnessed the deep cuts beneath her buttocks as she showered. She had layered the cuts with gauze, but it shifted with every movement of her legs and the cuts rubbed against the fabric of the jeans.

We drove off.

'I presume you don't have a gun?' Cornelia inquired.

'I'm British. We're not allowed,' I answered.

'Figures.'

'Sorry.'

'You stay in the car, then, if Nola arrives on her own. I'll deal with things my own way. No need for you to get involved further.'

I had more than an inkling of her intentions.

Revenge?

I was still unclear about Cornelia's motivations. What had Nola done to her? Sure, the woman had slaughtered her own sister. But Cornelia had not been present and I knew that ice coursed through her veins and one more death meant nothing to her. Death was her business.

'What if she doesn't come to the rendezvous alone?' I asked.

'Then we'll modify the plan accordingly, shan't we?' Cornelia said. I was far from happy about the 'we'.

*

The dark Chevy Coupe inched down the road, shimmering in the heat haze. Its approach to the crossroads took forever. The sun shone in full splendour, high above us. Inside our car, I was wet, sweating like a pig. Cornelia had insisted we keep the engine switched off so there was no air-conditioning. She had changed into a thin T-shirt, but her forehead remained resolutely dry. Why is it women don't perspire as we do? She cradled the Glock in her lap.

Nola's car came to a halt on the right-hand side of the road, straddling the crossroads. She appeared to be alone inside the coat-dusted vehicle.

Cornelia opened her door and slithered out of her seat, the gun lodged out of view between her body and the back of her jeans. She crossed the dirt road by which we had parked and came to a halt, a few strides from Nola's Chevrolet. There was deathly silence. Nola finally came in view, her slim silhouette approaching Cornelia.

'You?'

'Yes,' Cornelia confirmed. Nola was outside of my line of sight and I couldn't see the expression on her face.

'So . . . the book?'

'There is no book, Miss Poshard. Only me.'

'What the hell do you mean?'

Nola took a step backwards.

Cornelia stood rooted to the same spot, the sun beating fiercely down on her blonde hair and shoulders.

'Louise sold the book.'

'I know that. She told me. In New Orleans.'

Nola was attempting to bluff it out. She had guts.

She caught sight of me sitting in the car.

'You're with him?' she asked Cornelia, nodding in my direction.

'So it appears.'

'He works for me,' Nola shot back. 'Jackson,' she called out, 'you helped me find Louise. There is no need for you to remain involved. Let it be.'

Getting no reaction from me, she faced Cornelia again.

'Who are you?' she asked.

'Just a book collector,' Cornelia answered.

'Stop bullshitting me, woman!'

Nola was seriously losing her cool now.

'It's ironic, isn't it?' Cornelia said with a gentle, understated smile, 'You seek a book. I'd love to get my hands on the book in question. And Louise sold the book to pay for my services.'

Cornelia shifted her legs slightly apart and pulled the gun from her belt.

'You're crazy,' Nola said, retreating, but she had no place to run. She quickly glanced across at me, her eyes expressing a thousand words. But all I could remember was the look of triumph spread across her features as she had choked her own sister.

'Posthumous retribution,' Cornelia said and raised the gun.

The first bullet slammed into Nola's forehead, the back of her head exploding in a flurry of fiery flowers of blood, bone and brain matter.

That initial bullet probably killed her, but Cornelia pulled the trigger another three times. They all punctured Nola as she fell to the ground.

I held my breath as Cornelia calmly walked back towards our Pontiac. What if the next bullet had my name on it? But she lowered the weapon as she neared me.

'When all is said and done,' Cornelia remarked, 'never mock the virtues of professionalism.'

'That's it then?' I queried, the bile rising at the back of my throat out of relief, fear and disgust.

'Yes.'

Cornelia moved into her seat.

'Time to go home,' she said.

*

We returned the car to the Avis depot at Las Vegas airport. We had thoroughly wiped it of prints beforehand. The Glock had been dumped in the desert, miles from the deadly crossroads. Cornelia was thorough.

Again we shared a room at one of airport hotels and both showered all the dirt and the sweat away in silence, Cornelia moving naked, in all innocence and splendour, between bedroom and bathroom, unworried about my presence. Never, I knew, would I see so much of a woman's intimacy and never even touch her.

Sitting in the departure lounge, waiting for our respective flights to New York and London, Cornelia opened up for the first time.

'It's been a mess,' she admitted, slowly sipping from a tall glass of iced tea.

'You're telling me. So, any plans?' I asked her.

'Yes. Time for a sabbatical. A leave of absence from the killing business. I'm tired.'

'So am I,' I said. 'Very.'

They called our flights.

Cornelia surprised me with a peck on the cheek.

'Goodbye, Martin.'

'The first time you've actually said my name,' I pointed out.

'Really?'

Cornelia smiled, turned away from me and took her customary long strides down the concourse.

*

Last night, the nightmares returned.

The carnival of female bodies, skin like silk, danced across my night, with the softness of cream, lips, breasts, wondrous curves in all the shapes of heaven, my heart floating across the loneliness, and somewhere, beyond reach, a strange feeling called hope.

Love.

Its tyranny.

The reason we live, and invariably fail.

The reason I killed Kay.

Lust, its contagion.

The reason I remain alive and face every new day with fear.

The reason I allowed Louise's obscene death.

Visions of beautiful bodies destroyed forever, flesh turning to maggots and dust and their pleading eyes in the surrounding darkness screaming at me, every sound a dagger cutting me open, shredding my own flesh into slivers of free fall agony. Essence of self-loathing. Then the screen tears and I awaken, alone at three in the morning in an empty bed in a North London flat, with just the memories. That will never leave me. Another day beckons, things to do, the business of living to keep my mind occupied until sleep comes again and, with it, the procession of horrors, the fruits of my betrayal.

I remain.

And my debt to the dead remains.

So, I shall get up and shave in the morning. Comb my hair and pull tufts of greying strands from the brush. Clean my glasses. Dress in combinations of blue, black and grey. Take the Northern Line to Tottenham Court Road and walk down New Oxford Street to my office in Holborn. Where I shall sit at my desk and accept cases. Industrial espionage, adultery, missing dogs and cats, petty theft. The loneliness tears at me.

It's my first day back following the Poshard case.

There's a message from Joan. She returns to work tomorrow. Hopes I'm well. Anything interesting been happening?

I process the snail mail and the e-mails. A few invoices, one or two possible jobs and tons of publicity leaflets and letters asking me to invest the money I don't have in every possible combination of trusts, shares, government bonds and other get-rich-quick schemes. By midday, the administration has moved from in-tray to out-tray.

There are seventeen messages on the ansaphone.

I click and listen.

Mostly enquiries. Nervous voices who don't know what a private detective might sound like. Some have left numbers. Others will call back. One stationery salesman and a double-glazing cold call. And, three days ago—I was still driving across Texas with Cornelia— Christopher Streetfield, his voice a whisper, asking how I'm getting on, any sign of Kay? Anywhere?

I phone him back at the press agency where he works. To admit defeat and suggest a refund. What else?

A woman picks up the phone on his direct line. Asks me who I am.

A friend, I say.

Streetfield committed suicide, she is so sorry to inform me. His wife had left him, you see. Hanged himself. Left an explanatory note.

I put the phone down.

My third murder.

But life goes on. With the right mental training you learn to take anything in your stride.

I find the mobile number Aida left me in Amsterdam.

Maybe she hasn't yet found Mr ight or Mr Rich or Mr Pimp? I could ask her to fly to London. Bring her child along. Sort of adopt them both. Something in her touches me. Her green eyes, her shy smile, the hurt buried within. I can't offer her much, I know, but maybe we can make a go of it. For a time, anyway. I know I'm more Mr Wrong than Mr Right. Don't know how I will adapt to a woman with a child fathered by another man. I'm too old for her, quite unprepared to start a new family. But I know I'd be convenient for her, provide her and her son with a roof above their heads, some security, maybe a passport. Eastern European women are practical by necessity. And one day she would inevitably meet someone younger or wealthier and leave.

I'm a realist: I know Aida is wrong. Too young. Too this. Too that. That her leaving me is inevitable. But, for now, she's all I have.

That's fine with me.

It would be nice to wake in the morning with the warm softness of Aida's body next to me. While it lasts. She might not banish the nightmares, but maybe her presence will deaden their implacable roar.

Unless they catch up with me and that knock on the door in the morning when I least expect it will be grey men with badges and questions about Kay.

And when they question me, I will not be evasive or a coward any longer.

I will at last confess to the murder of the only woman I have ever loved.

In the meantime, I continue living in a world full of women. I tap out the dialling-code for Holland.

Maxim Jakubowski

was born in Barnet but brought up in Paris. He followed a career in publishing by opening the Murder One bookshop in London in 1988. He writes, edits and publishes in many areas of genre fiction, including SF and fantasy, mystery and erotica. He edited the best-selling *Mammoth Book of Erotica* and its follow-up, *The Mammoth Book of International Erotica*. As publisher, he has been responsible for various cult imprints, including *Black Box Thrillers*, *Blue Murder* and *Eros Plus*. He has also published over thirty books of his own, including *The Great Movies Live*, *London Noir*, the *New Crimes* series, *Royal Crimes*, *Murders for the Fireside*, *No Alibi*, *Fresh Blood* (with Mike Ripley) and *The Mammoth Book of Pulp Fiction*.

He is an official advisor to several international film festivals, writes for a variety of publications, including *The Observer*, *The Big Issue*, and *The Guardian*, and reviews crime in a monthly column in *Time Out*. He is also contributing editor to *Mystery Scene* and a winner of the Anthony Award.

Life in the World of Women, his controversial collection of romantic pornography, was highly-praised in many quarters and led to comparisons with Kerouac and Miller. For some time he has been promising a novel featuring women, guns and blood. This is it.

www.ingramcontent.com/pod-product-compliance
Lightning Source LLC
Chambersburg PA
CBHW020244030726
47499CB00001B/46